THE EPIC FORGOTTEN

THE GIRL IN THE RAIN

FIRST CRUSADE

Ryan,

I hope you enjoy
this endeavor as much
as all others you
undertake!

All the best!

THE GIRL IN THE RAIN

J. CHRISTOPHER WICKHAM

*This story – as a whole - is dedicated to all
those who lent their voices to it
over the past two decades.*

*If you look hard enough, you
might just find yours…*

"Ideally, a book would have no order to it, and the reader would have to discover his own."

~Mark Twain

The Professor and His Twenty-Six Ghosts

The rain is tapping like heavy fingers...

... against thin panes of glass, and the master of this house has again become servant to an unwelcome guest. The windows haven't rattled this way in some time, and the room has remained just as silent in its exile, awaiting a night just like this one. I sit rigidly still at my desk, entranced by the thin water snakes that dance and undulate on the window, and realize that I have awaited this night as well.

I'd locked these doors months before, hoping that I wouldn't have to set foot in this room for a very long time. That was the last time I'd seen the storm or my other late-night visitor, yet I could still smell both beneath the scent of musty books, aged cedar and pipe tobacco. It lingers in this room like the voices that still echo here, some belonging to a man who'd once been alive, and the rest belong to others who've never drawn breath.

My name is Dr. James Campbell, keeper of the twenty-six ghosts, and I write this as I sit at my desk in a room that was once my study but is now a shrine to the dead and to those who only lived in dreams and dark places.

All around me, I feel the cold, carbon eyes staring from their individual 8 x 11 paper prisons. They knew that their keeper would return to liberate them one day, just the way they'd liberated their former owner, John Chapel. He was free of them all, and they'd been orphaned – delusions without a madman – left to a man who doesn't want them and doesn't believe in them. If I had my way, if I knew how, I would send them right back into the rain where John found them.

There hadn't been any rain since the day they buried my friend, and the only drops I've seen since have been drops of brandy, trying to forget about him and this awful room. That was four months ago; four months of no rain, four months of undisturbed sleep, and four months that the doors to this prison have been locked. A frantic phone call three hours before and a darkened, rumbling sky led me down that long hallway again, though.

I'm not sure which is more persistent – the rain or the widow who won't let me forget those things – and both announced their coming within seconds of one other. A ringing telephone threw my nightly routine into chaos, and as soon as the call ended, a sky-rending crack made me start and drop the receiver. There's something she wants from me, and at least she'd been somewhat clear about her intentions; the rain just continues to batter angrily at those panes of glass and howls.

I stare out at it, searching for the outline of one of those strange faces John insisted was there, and I find one staring back at me. I know that it's her, though, and not one of his phantoms – not his "girl in the rain"- because I can see the expression in her face. Even through two panes of glass – the window and the windshield of the black sedan – and the veil of water, I can see her anguish.

She's here again because she believes that I know what happened to her husband, and that I just didn't look hard enough, or that I just need one more piece of evidence for everything to fall into place. I wish that were true, but I'm no closer to an answer this night than I was on the first, and regardless of what she's turned up, I doubt that it will do much to change the final outcome of the story.

There were still only ideas and theories as numerous and varied as the pages of notes and journal pages piled up on my desk in the study where I'd left them months before. I've already spent far too many nights in this room, with these faces, dissecting John's story and struggling to understand what happened to him. I realize that I've been too harsh on the rain, which is only my jailor, and this room which has been my cell, the true "irons" about my ankles and my neck is the story itself.

I thought I was finally free of those heavy bonds, but I can feel the slack being drawn up again, twisted in the fingers of a widow and a storm just as relentless, making it difficult to breathe. I pull at the collar of my oxford, loosing another button as I watch her finally draw courage enough to step from the car, and I realize that no matter what I tell her, she will not listen. I understand that this crusade had begun anew.

~ Journal of James Campbell

THE GIRL IN THE RAIN

*"The great mass of men lead lives of quiet desperation,
and go to the grave with the song still in them."*

~Thoreau

Chapter *1*

Gwenn Chapel hesitated by her black sedan, staring up at the house through water-drenched lids. She was trying to prepare herself for the next leg of her journey, and though she'd just driven three-hundred miles that afternoon, it seemed a more daunting task to walk those final thirty steps to Dr. Campbell's front door.

She hated the rain, more now than ever before, and it felt like a thousand icy fingers clawing at her face and exposed legs. Her only choices were to either retreat back to the safety of her car, or brave that long trek to the door and hope Campbell let her in. There was always that possibility, given their last exchange over the phone, and she knew that her journey might very well end with her pounding on his door as the rain slowly drowned her.

Pulling her thin wool coat tighter, she pressed forward with unsure footing, legs wobbling like a newborn calf's, face turned towards the ground. She didn't dare look up at the water, for fear of what she might see there, and likewise, she didn't dare look back at the car that offered her refuge or she would surely retreat.

Halfway to the door, her courage and legs gave out simultaneously, and she sprawled upon the pavement with an anguished cry that was muffled by the falling water. Trembling white knuckles and slender, outstretched fingers met the hard ground, sacrificing a bit of flesh, but they were strong enough to break her fall.

Through a veil of Auburn-red hair, a heavy downpour, and two thick panes of glass, she saw the eyes upon her. He'd witnessed the entire affair beneath the motion light, exposing her struggle and her humility.

Pride forced strength back into her slender arms and legs, and she made the long climb back up as the rain whispered in her ear, telling her to stay down. Gwenn Chapel would never listen to that voice or abandon her husband's crusade as the man in the window had.

She didn't drown on the porch after all, the door swinging open after the first knock. The man greeted her in his usual fashion; a faint, uncomfortable smile, brief eye contact, and the customary glance downward at her legs. Campbell wasn't the sort to be so intrusive, he was just a man who paid attention to details, and reduced things to their most basic components. In this case, thanks to her husband, those components were her legs and eyes.

She hoped that he'd forgotten John's descriptiveness, and was simply noticing the bloody scrape on her left knee.

"I-I'm sorry...I lost my footing..."

He met her gaze again and managed an oddly-warm reply, "It seems that those I've had at my door recently, Mrs. Chapel, have all *lost their footing*."

A smile peeked through the auburn-red hair plastered to her face. She pushed it out of the way with the back of her hand, revealing a face that looked like that of a frightened child, not one belonging to a woman in her mid-thirties.

"You weren't out there long I hope?" He asked innocently.

"About ten minutes."

"I wanted to tidy up the place, you called last minute..."

"It's okay, I saw you watching from the window..."

His face turned red.

"I wouldn't let me in either, given the circumstances. I just thought...this new information would help us figure out what happened to him."

She produced the rain-spattered notebook she'd been clutching in her right hand. His eyes were called back again from her legs to the collection in her hand, and they seemed to glimmer when he saw the new pages tucked neatly inside, bound with rubber bands.

He tried to gently take the book but her fingers clung tightly. The notes she carried would either be a Rosetta stone, unlocking the cryptic pages already in Campbell's possession, or would only shroud the truth further in darkness - and that's what scared her the most.

With a trembling hand, she finally released the pages to him, as he invited her inside. He seemed not to care that she was dripping on an expensive-looking Turkish rug as he took her coat. His eyes were fixed on the notebook as he hung her coat on the rack beside the door, and he began thumbing through the pages as she unzipped her leather boots.

Her host was as engrossed in the pages as she was in the tastes of his decorator, and she complimented the perfect blending of dark maple accents, antique brass fixtures, and pieces that looked like they belonged in a museum. A banister spiraled up winding steps to her right, ascending to a balcony that overlooked the foyer, and then disappeared into the shadows above.

Campbell waited patiently for her to finish her small talk about his taste in décor, and then indicated the double doors beyond. Moving to the study and motioning for her to follow along the dimly-lit hall, her eyes moved from the Victorian wallpaper to his antique covering, and she tried guessing the age of both.

She knew that he was well into his sixties, but those years had been kind to James Campbell, and most guessed that he was a decade younger. His bones revealed the truth that his skin tried to hide, however, and she noticed that not all of the groaning and creaking came from the beautiful, old wood floors.

"Oh my," she whispered when they entered the room.

A fireplace cast a warm, orange glow over the comfortable-looking chairs, the many shelves of books and the antique desk against the wall. From the mantle, the chime of an old clock echoed through the dozen or so picture frames there, filled with memories as warm as the fire below. In one corner was a divan upholstered in the same pattern as the Turkish rug in the entranceway, and it was the centerpiece of a room designed to inspire serenity and a relaxed state for those who entered.

It was the choice in wallpaper on the far wall that disrupted that serenity.

Dozens of her husband's handwritten pages were tacked up there, covered with just as many sticky notes and thumb tacks of varying colors. Passages were highlighted, circled and connected by intersecting red and black lines, making the wall look like a giant Cincinnati roadmap. Most disturbing, though, were the many pairs of cold, graphite eyes staring back at her.

She still saw those faces in nightmares, despite telling John to take them down from the walls of his workshop behind the house, and they startled her no less now than they did the day she'd first discovered them. She never knew exactly where they'd been exiled to, but Campbell's study was the perfect place for them. The room had been transformed into a shrine to the dead as well as to those who'd never lived.

"It's…" He looked for the words to explain the room and its present condition, but she didn't need an explanation or apology.

"I thought *I* was the only one who lost this much sleep," she said, gazing up at the bizarre map on the wall behind the desk. "He really *did* tell you *everything*."

"Almost everything," he indicated the notes in his hand. "Where did you get these?"

She turned to meet his gaze with sparkling amber eyes, the firelight really making them shimmer the way John had described them. He'd said that they reminded him of a beam of sunlight shining through a whiskey bottle.

"Merrill Lake," she replied in a reverent whisper the same way her husband had whenever he spoke about the place.

It was hallowed ground to them, John especially, and a place that still held many secrets. Some had gone to get away from the world there, others to find rebirth, and a few to find something else. He'd never known exactly what happened there the night John Chapel last spoke of it, telling him, with an unsettling urgency in his tone, that he had to return there.

Now he had John's account of those events in his very hands, possibly the key to completing that broken map on his wall, but as eager as he was to read it, he had to turn his attention to other matters first.

He set the letters on a small side table beside his leather chair and offered the other to Gwenn as he grabbed a blackened iron rod that was leaning against the hearth. A sudden chill had settled over the room that bit at him through his double layer of sweaters.

As he prodded at the fire that had been slowly dying since his evening drink he reassured her, "It's okay, I'm not sleeping either and I could use the company. I was just getting used to him being here to talk to…and that chair has sat empty many nights."

"He sat in *this* chair?" she whispered.

"One in the same," he said, replacing the poker and creaking across the room towards his desk.

From a bar service adjacent to the far wall, he retrieved a bottle of brandy and a towel, handing them to her as he gave a nod at her leg.

"I don't think I'll need this; it's not that bad," she said.

18

"Might want to hold onto it just the same," he said in a queer tone.

She set the bottle on the small table beside her chair then scooted back, getting comfortable, and stretched her fingers out over the wide leather arms. Resting her head against the high back, she looked very much at home in her husband's old chair, and caressed the arms lovingly, but he doubted it was because of the quality of the leather.

"Is that your *famous* brandy John used to rave about?"

"Oh no, if you'd like the *good* stuff I can fetch it for you. I brought that bottle for your knee. The other stuff would be properly served in a warm glass, and is much better for chasing away miserable nights like this one."

She waved away his offer. "I'm fine for the time being. When he would come home after visits with you, I could smell it on him, and the smell on the towel just now...it reminded me of him."

Her nostrils flared, trying to pick up his scent, but she couldn't find it beneath the smell of damp air, musty books, aged cedar and pipe tobacco.

"He spent many nights here when he should've been home with you." It sounded like an apology.

"He didn't find much comfort at home or much of anywhere else besides this room and this chair. I couldn't help him, Doctor Campbell, and he knew that..."

"Jim," he corrected her.

"Jim," she repeated, as if it was funny that he had a real first name. "You were the one he turned to. He thought you could save him - save *both* of us – that's why I came here as soon as I found the letters."

The thin smile completely shriveled into a sullen frown then as he sat heavily back into his chair, scooping the letters back up.

"I don't know that what's in here will bring us any closer to the answers we're looking for, Gwenn. I hope you're not putting too much faith in these pages."

"I don't have faith in much these days, Jim, and what I did read didn't make much sense. That's why I brought them to you."

He let out a long sigh and took his reading glasses from the pocket of his tweed, fixing them on the bridge of his nose.

19

Unfolding the letters, he began to glance over them again, and then lowered them, pausing for verification. "You're sure you want to do this *tonight*?"

She nodded eagerly. "It was all I could do to not pull off to the side of the road and read every page on the way here."

"Gwenn, I'm as eager to see what's on these pages and will do my very best to incorporate that information into what we already know about your husband's case..."

She didn't want to hear what came next. Her hands were clasped as if begging or in some kind of prayer, knuckles turning white, and she squeezed her eyes closed just as tightly against his words.

"...but John's *unique situation* makes it difficult to consider any primary source material as valid."

"By *unique situation* you mean *crazy*?" she said, leveling a set of smoldering amber eyes at him.

"Even *with* this new information - be*cause* of this information - it could make it that much more difficult to sort out that confusing mess behind you."

"But you haven't even read--"

"Gwenn, I can't even give *these* pages a serious look until I've made some sense of the others," he said, indicating the strange montage on the far wall. "There are still too many unknowns, too many loose ends, and those need to be brought to a close before we begin asking new questions."

Gwenn furled her brow at him, "So you didn't even have all the information, and yet, you were able to diagnose my husband with a mental illness?"

"I'm a *history professor*, not a *shrink*, but he insisted that I take a look at his journal anyway and help him make sense of it. The things he was writing about...well...I didn't need a psychology degree to know that he needed a different sort of help."

"Did you even bother checking the things he asked you to?"

"I used every resource available - despite it going against what I believed in. The place he talked about and the people he communicated with *never existed* - not on any map or in any recorded document."

"You looked in a few history books and you didn't see any proof there so you flipped through his journal, found a few

20

passages about a *troubled childhood* and told him that was explanation enough for what was happening to him?"

"I *wanted* to believe in him, I really did, and out of respect for him and for our friendship I listened to him and weighed all the facts. In the end there just wasn't enough proof, and all signs pointed to the diagnosis that neither of you wanted to hear."

"*Dissociative Identity Disorder*? You and I both know that didn't even *begin* to describe what he was experiencing! People don't just begin speaking and writing in *dead languages*, Jim!"

"They also don't speak to the *dead* in the rain," he said, glaring at her over the rim of his glasses. "There are twenty-six faces up there on that wall – twenty-six faces that *he* created in his *own mind* to hide behind, Gwenn."

"Hide from *what*?"

Campbell held up the rain-spattered journal she'd handed him at the door. She frowned at it and shifted uncomfortably in her seat, almost the same way her predecessor had when he'd mentioned very particular pages of that journal. There were things there which neither of them had wanted to revisit, but things, nonetheless, that needed to be brought to light.

"He almost had me convinced that there was something more to all of this, and that what he was experiencing couldn't be explained through the known sciences. I almost overlooked *her*..."

She'd seen the charcoal drawing of the girl he was referring to, hanging on the back wall amidst those other twenty-five eerie likenesses. He'd watched her as she studied his exhibit, followed her eyes as they moved over each face, and there was no mistaking her expression when they came to rest on the carbon face of the beautiful woman. There was a blue sticky note affixed to the corner that read *Number 26*, but she knew, all too well, the name that was attached to that face.

Melinda Malowski: the name that was written on that wall of pages no less than three hundred times.

She scowled and dug her fingers into the arms of the chair, as though looking for a hand to grab at for comfort. "This isn't about *her* and you know it! You even told John--"

"You're right," he said, flipping the journal open as she watched nervously. "I thought she was at the heart of John's affliction, but as it turns out, there's *someone else* isn't there?"

21

The fire was recovering nicely and chasing away the chill of the room, yet she gave a little shudder and pulled a plaid felt blanket from the back of the chair to drape over her legs.

"That was *thirty years* ago," she protested. "My husband came to terms with what happened that day at the park a long time ago. Even Melinda's mother forgave him--"

"It doesn't mean that he forgave *himself*," he interjected. "In fact, I think he created this other place and everyone in it for the sole purpose of finding that forgiveness."

"You're wrong about my husband, Jim," she said with a smug expression. "*He* wasn't the one that was *hiding* behind something. I think you're afraid of the truth and you still refuse to see it for what it was."

"When there seem to be no answers, and things have become too much for us to bear, we hide within ourselves, as John did, or behind *faith*, and ignore the truth. What are *you* hiding from, Mrs. Chapel?"

"I have nothing to hide," she said with indignation. "I'm here to find answers, Jim, so that I can finally get a decent night's rest and go on with my life. If *faith* was enough for me and I could find some comfort there, I wouldn't be here talking to you."

He glanced down at the letters he'd left on the side table again, giving her a condescending smile. "But what answers are you looking for, Gwenn? Are you sure you didn't skim through these pages searching for an answer to that most nagging of questions? Settle up the *old debt*?"

The souring of her expression said that she was well aware of the debt he was referring to, while the crease of her brow and her downturned lip said that she didn't care for his inference. Leaning forward so that he would not mistake the seriousness in her face or miss a word over the crackling of the fire, she did some hissing and popping of her own.

"Dr. Campbell, I'm not here to settle some sophomoric pissing match with my old best friend. John and I had our share of problems and our marriage was far from perfect, but it was *me* that he ended up marrying, not *her*. It wasn't *Melinda Malowski* that took him from me...it was something else."

"Okay," he said, his voice lowering to almost a whisper. "If you're *serious* about this, then I need you to be completely honest – with me and with yourself – and hold nothing back."

She nodded slowly as she seemed to grasp exactly what was going to take place over the next few hours. They were going to have to revisit some very difficult things and it would most likely be one of the longest, most difficult nights since she'd received the call telling her that he wasn't coming home. Again, outstretched fingers searched for hands that weren't there, preparing herself for what came next.

He creaked back over towards the bar service, leaving her to gather her thoughts. Returning a moment later, he handed her a warm glass filled halfway with a liquid that was the same hue as her eyes as it caught the firelight.

"I don't care for brandy, Dr. Campbell."

"John said the same thing," he said with a chuckle. "You'll want it before this discussion is over."

She took a sip of the strong brandy, making a sour face as she did, letting out a long, sterile breath, and asked, "Where do you want to begin?"

"Thirty years ago. Page one. Tell me about the day he was so reluctant to talk about; tell me about the afternoon of February the twelfth…and the boys that were lost that day."

Chapter 2

Dawson Malowski's funeral was unlike anything John Chapel had ever seen. At the age of seven-and-a-half, he'd only been to one funeral before - his great grandmother's - and that was an experience in itself.

He'd never seen so many people crying in one room at one time, and more disturbing, he'd never seen a person so still and eerily quiet. His dad told him that he didn't have to go, but as a young man, he said that it was his choice whether he wanted to pay his final respects. He was being a young man again instead of a little boy, and he'd wished that he hadn't gone.

Everything about that day seemed more exaggerated and out-of-proportion than it had been for his grandmother's funeral. A boy of two got much more "respects" than his grandmother, and his mother told him that was because nobody ever expected a child to die.

There was lots of crying, way more than he had heard before, and it was a different kind of crying. It was soft, in stifled moderation, and with a gentle somberness before, but at this one it was agonizing, loud and uncontrollable. Both of Dawson's parents had broken down several times and his mother even collapsed once on the floor and another time on a couch. John had never seen such a thing; never witnessed such overpowering sadness as that.

He sat several rows back, behind the noisy family, again, out of "respects". From that distance, he could barely see the small casket at the front of the room, especially hidden within the colored canopy of flowers. It seemed funny to him that such a little person needed such a big place and so many flowers surrounding him. It took attention away from the fancy box and the boy inside, but then maybe that was the idea.

Sitting quietly in a neat row on the very front couch, all dressed in crisp black, were Dawson's siblings and his best friends; Dean, Steve and Melinda. The boys wore matching suits and Melinda was black head to toe. She had black, shiny shoes, black nylon leggings, and a black dress with matching sheer lace at the bottom and at the shoulders. In her hair were two dark ribbons holding up her curled ponytails. He hardly recognized them, and as they looked at him when he walked past earlier, they didn't seem to recognize him either.

Her small face was probably the saddest and he hated to see that as much as the boy in the box. Those eyes of hers had always sparkled at him and were a mixture of beautiful blue, like pictures he'd seen of the Mediterranean Sea. Now they were a reflection of her black attire, making her look hollow and empty inside.

Two days before, she was chasing him around Rain Tree park, laughing and giggling like girls of six tend to do. Her brothers, Dean and Steve, were playing football with the other boys there, and though they weren't giggling and carrying on, they were still having fun being boys. John had played ball with them many times, and it had only been "roster cuts" that benched him and left him at the mercy of their sister and her silly games.

The boys in the park took their football seriously, and just like real football, they had "playoff" games as the weather turned colder. Playoff games were a very serious thing, and they couldn't afford to have smaller, lesser-skilled boys – like John – playing and fouling up their chances. Only the biggest, fastest and seasoned players were allowed to play late into the winter for those games, and John didn't take it personally; he wanted Steve and Dean's team to win.

He didn't hate playing chase with their sister or her friend, Gwenn Lawson, either, but he pretended to because he didn't want to ruin his chances for the next season's team. It was better being tackled by a pretty girl than being knocked flat on your back by a boy three years and six inches taller than you anyway, and Melinda Malowski was probably the most beautiful girl he'd ever seen in all his seven-and-a-half years.

She had beautiful, golden ringlets of hair spilling down to the middle of her back, and thick, pink lips filled with perfectly straight teeth that were always smiling at him or hovering close to him as she spoke to him in whispers.

Melinda rarely talked to anyone without leaning in close to whisper in your ear, as if everything she had to say was of utmost importance and top secret. Gwenn found it obnoxious and had no compunctions about talking loudly and saying whatever was on her mind.

Gwenn, by comparison, was not a beautiful little girl. She looked more like a boy, with her shorter, reddish-brown hair, freckles, and unflattering outfits her mother dressed her in. She was proud of the fact that she could do everything a boy could do – sometimes even better.

John liked spending time with her too, because she did neat things like climbing trees at the river's edge or teaching him how to catch frogs and skip stones. Melinda didn't like doing any of those things, and she would nearly burst into tears if she got a speck of dirt on her hands or on her dress. Gwenn used this to her advantage, and as a way of trying to get John away from Melinda, luring him to the water's edge and getting dirty with him.

Even at that young age, the pair seemed to be fighting for his attention constantly. They would race up to the park after school, trying to beat the other one there, in the hopes that they would get to John first. If Melinda showed up last, she would watch the pair of them down by the river doing something gross, and if Gwenn showed late, she would watch them walking in the woods or by the fountain doing something equally gross.

Gwenn knew that girls her age weren't supposed to like boys or do those things, but Melinda would always take it to the next level – where she couldn't go – just to win. That would never change about either of them; Melinda would try to win at all costs in that eternal competition between them.

Melinda beat her to the park the day the awful thing happened, and had him over by the fountain, giggling and laughing. Gwenn saw them but she didn't tell Melinda's mother where they were. She was a good friend, the both of them knew, and she never would've told on them, even to get one over on Melinda.

John saw Gwenn sitting closer to the front with her mother, dressed in a girl's outfit for probably the first time in her life. She wore a similar black dress, ribbons in her auburn hair, and he was pretty sure that she'd even been wearing lip gloss when he'd passed her earlier. He liked Gwenn a lot, and that's why he felt awful for her for covering for him and Melinda both.

They should've been watching him that day, instead of leaving the responsibility entirely with poor Gwenny, and if they had been, he might not be up there in that fancy box. There were a lot of eyes that should've been watching that chilly February afternoon, but for some reason, all of them were on something else and no one knew why.

Dean and Steve were supposed to be most responsible, but they were too busy with their football – with it being "playoffs" and all. Next in line was Melinda, but she was too busy trying to get her daily dose of attention from the boy she had a crush on. That meant the responsibility fell to John, and since he was too occupied with what they were doing over by the fountain, that left Gwenny as the only set of eyes to watch Dawson.

It should've been the responsibility of the adults – that's what John's mom said – and Margaret Malowski shouldn't have yelled at any of them the way she did when she didn't even show up that day. John would never forget the way she was trying to catch her breath in between sobs so that she could yell and curse at them as she rocked her son's lifeless body, and no matter what anybody said otherwise, he would always feel partially at fault.

There wasn't a single adult that day at Rain Tree, and that had never happened before. Each of the parents took turns staying to watch the boys play football or the other kids running about, but that day, each of them thought someone else was supposed to be there. That's what the argument was about after Dawson was found and they all started showing up to see what the commotion was about. A mother held her son, and all around them, shouting voices could be heard passing blame of whose turn it was to be there.

John got up from his seat at the very back, escorted by his mother up the narrow aisle so they could pay "respects", and he noticed all of those faces watching him. Did they know where he was and what he was doing that day? Did someone make Gwenn talk?

He swallowed hard and turned his eyes back to the floor as they made their way to the front. Finally stopping at the casket, his mother squeezed his hand tightly, prompting him to look at the small metal box and the boy inside. Staring down at his expressionless face made him feel as cold as he'd felt wading through the icy water days before, when they'd first found him.

They heard Gwenn's bloodcurdling scream from across the park and immediately started running towards her. Melinda's shorter legs couldn't keep up and she almost fell as he was dragging her across the snowy field by the hand, and he had to

28

leave her behind to reach Gwenn fast. The other boys had no idea what was going on at first, and they thought it was more of their silly girl games, until John started yelling for Dean and his brother. They came next, and arrived in time to see John immersed up to his waist in icy river water.

"Where is he? Where is Dawson?!"

Melinda could only point silently, her throat almost completely closed off by fear.

"He's in the water?! You were supposed to be watching him damn it!!"

Dean rarely swore, and John had only heard him curse once before when he had gotten hurt badly in football. He threw off his thick vest and waded into the water to retrieve him from John, who was clutching him close to his chest.

He held Dawson's wobbly head up in his hands as Dean dropped to his knees beside him. "He doesn't look good, he's blue...he's not breathing!"

Gwenn stood by the icy water rubbing her arms for warmth, and he shouted back to her, "Gwenny, how long has he been in there?!"

She wouldn't even look at him. Dean repeated the question, louder, "Gwenny! Damn it! How long?!" There was the third time he'd heard him curse.

She jerked her head up and just shook it at him, still too terrified to move.

Dean pulled Dawson's jacket off and tossed it behind him, then put his face close to his to listen to breath that wouldn't come. "I don't know how to do this John! I don't know how to do it. Do you?"

He shook his head, and looked at the boys that had gathered behind them, "Does anyone know how to make him breathe? Where are the adults?"

One of the boys broke from the circle in a full run to find a grown up. Dean slapped at his brother's chest a couple of times and breathed into his mouth. He had only seen it done once on a T.V. show, but had never paid much attention. "What's that thing called that you do when someone chokes on food?"

John held up his hands, "I dunno Dean...I dunno that stuff!"

Dean said the bad word again and said something about him being older and supposing to know more than him. He lifted his little brother up several times in jerky motions, his head bobbing back and forth and a gurgling noise coming from his mouth. "This is supposed to get the stuff out of his throat...this is supposed to work! It's not working, why is it not working?"

As John watched Dean trying to make his brother breathe again and heard the girls squealing in the background, he turned in a circle looking for help from someone, from anyone. The boy who'd gone to find an adult seemed like he'd been gone for a long time and hadn't returned.

He noticed then, above the tree line, the old building that he'd seen dozens of times. It was always just part of the background and he'd seen it so many times that he'd never paid attention to the sign that gleamed in the darkness beyond the trees. He looked down at Dawson who wasn't responding and everyone around him seemed as frozen as he was. Someone had to do something.

He bent down and scooped him up, clutching the blue jacket tightly to him, and puffed at the other kids, "It's a hospital...there," he indicated with a nod towards the trees.

"Go!" Dean whispered. "You can make it!"

That was all the confirmation John needed, and he started at a dead run, carrying Dawson under the arms, towards the trees. His adrenaline was pumping and his blood was being chased through his veins by sheer terror. Branches whipped at his face and tore at his flesh, but he didn't feel it. The fear that had once frozen him in place now moved his legs for him and gave his small arms strength to do what he normally couldn't.

He broke from the edge of the woods and came into a clearing that was divided by a small, landscaped ditch. There was no pain in his ankle when it wrenched sideways as he made his way up the hill towards the hospital parking lot - it just gave out on him. He fell, twisting to one side to shield the unconscious boy from the ground. The wind knocked out of him, he tried to stand again and pick Dawson back up, wiping the water from his eyes that burned and blurred his vision.

The water was coming again as he stood peering into the metal box, and he wiped it away with the back of his hand, subconsciously touching the raised mark on his cheek with his fingertips. It would heal within a week and not leave a scar, but he would somehow always know it was there. His mother also dabbed at her cheek with a tissue as she said a quiet prayer, and then she led him away as he craned his neck to get one last look at the boy.

They passed the Malowskis once more, and his mother bent to whisper some kindness to Margaret, placing her free hand on her shoulder. She nodded and thanked her, but sounded as if she was speaking from the bottom of a well. Dennis barely noticed they were there, and he stared blankly ahead at a place somewhere among the arrangement of flowers. It was only the third time he'd ever seen Melinda's dad, and each time he looked progressively worse.

The last time had been at the edge of the parking lot at Beaumont hospital, where he'd stumbled with his son on the snowy hill. He was among the first of the adults to arrive, wearing khakis, a tee shirt, and muddy socks he'd run all the way to the park in. It was a far cry from the sharp suit, neatly-combed hair and polished shoes he'd been wearing the time before, instead of towering over them all, seeming like the biggest man at the park, he looked frail, small and bent at weird angles.

His glasses had fogged up and were hiding the full range of anguish and confusion in his eyes. It wasn't until he took them off to get a look at his son that John saw his eyes were red, beady and scrunched under by lots of wrinkled skin. Dennis was older than his wife, John knew that, but that day he looked to be about eighty. His mouth was drawn down in a permanent frown, and he saw an extra chin jiggle as he cried out his son's name repeatedly, trying to revive him.

He hadn't seen Dennis Malowski since that day, but his eyes were still red and weighed down by wrinkled, heavy folds. The permanent frown was still there, and his chin still jiggled as he mouthed unheard words to his son. He didn't even acknowledge John or his mother, and Marge spoke for the both of them. The boys were seated next to them and each nodded as he passed, but were afraid to speak to him, having witnessed the incident between John and their mother.

Once the funeral was over and they were safely out of her sight, they freely associated with him at the house, where the extended family had gathered to put together a dinner for everyone. The mood was a bit less somber, except those corners of the house where Dennis and Marge sat. Only the bravest among the family attempted to console or even speak to them, and that suited them just fine, because they preferred the solitude of those quiet corners as family milled about.

John was introduced to dozens of people who squeezed, kissed, or pinched his face. "That's how 'Polock' parties go" one of the older men explained to him after John had received his fifth face-pinching.

Melinda's grandmother was the only one who didn't squeeze or pinch him, and she was actually very kind to him. She sat and talked with him for a long time about all sorts of things, and when she had finished she told John, "You had best go find Melinda and be with her, she will need you in this tough time. She told me that the two of you were very good friends."

John nodded, not realizing until that very moment that she was probably one of his best friends, along with Dean and Gwenny.

"Very good friends take care of one another in times like this. When times are sad, and the world seems bleak, she will need someone like you John." She touched his face with a cupped hand and sent him upstairs.

He never forgot that kind old woman's words, and he felt like he had just been given the most important job in the world. She had left Melinda in his care, and it was his duty to look out for her as her best friend.

Even though he had never met the old woman prior to that day, he felt like she knew everything about him by what they had talked about. It was as if she could somehow see into his heart, and she was the only one at the house that day that had seen the same darkness in Melinda's eyes and not been too self-absorbed in their own grief to notice.

John headed upstairs, gripping the large railing in his small hand. Everything seemed so large where the Malowskis were concerned. Their house was huge and decorated with big paintings and big rugs, their cars were big and roomy, and the staircase that he was climbing was ridiculously over-decorated with Christmas lights still wrapped around the banister and picture frames following him all the way up.

At the top, he was standing at the end of a long, intimidating hallway full of doors. Each door was closed and he

32

could only guess at what was behind each of them. He knew that Melinda's was at the very end of the hall and looked out over the neighbor's pool to the west side. He walked slowly down the hall and felt the eyes of the dozens of other portraits follow and watch him as he approached her door. He rapped lightly on it and pushed it open.

She was sitting at her vanity at the opposite wall and was staring back at him in the mirror. Tears were still streaming down her face, and she was brushing out her pony tails, though the curls snapped back into place as soon as the brush passed through them, into the tight ringlets. He loved her curly hair and hoped that it would stay that way forever. John stood in the door awkwardly, staring down at his own shiny shoes.

"You can come in," she said plainly, as if she didn't care that he was there.

He stared at her in the mirror of the bureau, and watched as she brushed her hair methodically. The bureau was far too large for such a small girl, like everything else in the house, and there was an excess of hair ties, bows and jewelry scattered on the giant thing. Her legs dangled off of a large, plush velvet stool, and she wasn't even sitting all the way back in it. He imagined that she would grow into it someday, though he could never picture her growing older than six or any taller.

To her left was another over-sized piece of furniture in the way of a large four-poster bed. The posts were painted pristine white and there were sheer curtains tied back to each post that hung down from the top. A giant gathering of stuffed animals of every sort were piled high at the top of the bed, and still, there was enough room for three adults, yet it was all there for little Melinda.

"How are you…doing?" John blurted out nervously.

"I'm fine," she whispered.

John thought hard about his next words, he wasn't sure of what order he wanted to say them in. There were certain things that he wanted to tell her, but if he said them wrong, and out of order, that would be the end of it. He wanted to tell her that she was his best friend - more than Dean, or Gwenn, or anyone else – and he didn't know if she knew that. The kiss also still lingered in his mind and he'd wanted to ask her about it too, but it was most likely the last thing on her mind.

He would never forget it, although part of him felt selfish for even thinking about it at a time like this. It was their first special moment together, and it lasted all of eight seconds until that piercing scream echoed across the snow-covered treetops. Everything else from that day – which was only three days ago – was fogged over like an icy windshield except that moment. It was a small eternity packed into a few seconds, as his heart pounding in his ears, and her soft lips pressed against his.

"It wasn't *your* fault," he finally blurted out. "Dawson wasn't *your* fault, Mel."

She stopped brushing her hair and turned to look at him with her blank eyes. "I know. My mother said it was *your* fault."

John's face turned white. "*My* fault? I wasn't anywhere *near* him!"

She turned on her stool to look directly at him, "*She* said it was - *I* didn't. I told her that you were getting a drink with me at the fountain."

"You *didn't* tell her…"

John became frightened then at the prospect that she had shared their awkward, intimate moment with her mother. He'd wanted it brought up at some point to discuss it with her, but not like that.

"No, I told her we were getting a *drink*. That's what we were doing." She quickly changed the subject and he was almost glad, "She said you were the oldest and you should have been more responsible."

John turned from white to red then, and stammered, "More *responsible*? Dawson wasn't my responsibility; he was your *brother's*! Dean passed him off on us every time to play his stupid football! Where was *he*?!"

"That's just what she says. She says you were responsible for *all* of us." She hopped down from the vanity and stepped up onto the stool to sit beside him on the bed. "*I* don't believe that; it's just what *she* says. I heard my aunt talking to my other aunt, and she says my mother is just trying to find someone to blame to cover her own guilt…whatever that means."

She patted his hand and squeezed it tight. "It's not *our* fault John. You're my best friend, and I don't want you to ever think that I blame you, okay?"

34

He was glad that she at least brought that part up, because he didn't think he could tell her now that there was a lump in his throat and his eyes were burning. Rubbing her small hand with his thumb quietly, he noticed her neatly manicured and painted nails. Everything was so perfect about her, he thought, and too good for him.

His own nails were rough-hewn and bitten down. He lived in a small house with small things and his dress socks didn't even match - one was black one was dark blue. Looking in the mirror, he noticed how ragged he looked in comparison to her, and felt small next to her, despite being older.

"John, where did he go?" Melinda's asked in a queer tone. "Where did my baby brother go?"

John thought about it for a while, and remembered the conversation his grandmother had with him before her death. "Heaven, I suppose. That's where people go when they die. My grandma went there, and she's with God now," he explained, regurgitating the answer he'd been given.

Melinda frowned. "Is that where we go John...*all* of us?"

He nodded, "Sure we do, where else would we go?"

"My brother told me...Steven...that if we're not baptized before we die that we go somewhere else," she explained with an eerie authority.

He scrunched up his brows, a bit confused, "Melinda, your brother didn't go to *hell*! Children *don't* go to hell! Why would your brother tell you that?"

"He's scared that Dawson went there. Mom and dad never took him to get him baptized. None of us have been baptized, John. What if something happens to us?" She was getting worked up by the thought, the tears came again, and she squeezed his hands hard.

"Children go to Heaven Melinda - baptized or *not*! That's what my grandma told me and she knows *more* about church than your brothers do! She went for sixty years! She should know!" He reassured her.

"I don't want to go...I don't want to die! I don't want to go to a bad place!" She was whimpering in his shoulder, getting his white shirt wet with tears and snot.

John didn't know what to say to convince her that she wasn't going to die; after all, nothing had prevented that from

35

happening to Dawson, why couldn't it happen to any of them at any time?

She looked up at him with her big, red-rimmed pools of blue, her long lashes dripping with droplets of water. "John, please come get me…"

He wrinkled up his nose at the statement, not sure what she meant. "Come *get* you? Yes, I'll come and get you….where are you going?"

She sobbed, "Come up and get me…will you come up and get me if I die too? You're my best friend, please don't leave me there."

She wanted him to promise that he would just walk up to heaven and pick her up, like it was a place you could just drive to. Her young mind couldn't grasp concepts like Heaven, a soul, or mortality, and even he'd a hard time with it. She shouldn't have needed to understand something as complex as death at her age, and she was a scared little girl.

As opposed to attempting to explain it, though, he promised her, "If something happens to you, I will come and get you. I *will* come and be with you…no matter where you are." He kissed her forehead then and the rest of what they talked about, if anything, he couldn't remember.

Two months later, he would have to renege on his promise for he was moving away from the city to go live with his father. His mother had halfheartedly fought him at first, but eventually conceded and agreed that it might be too much for their son to handle seeing the people and places that would remind him of his traumatic experience.

When he arrived home one day after school, she'd packed his things for him and there were suitcases by the door. He panicked and screamed at his mother, telling her that he couldn't leave Melinda, and ran from the house as fast as he could.

It was the beginning of May and the heavy rains had come again. John ran through them so fast that he thought he could outrun those drops just as he thought he could outrun his fate. He ran four blocks to Melinda's house, and when Steve met him at the door and told him that she wasn't there, he ran another three to Rain-tree. She was there, sitting on the picnic table alone.

"What are you doing here?" He asked between gulps of air.

"My parents were fighting again, they fight all the time…what are you doing here in the rain?"

"My mom wants to send me away to my dad's!"

She stood back and screwed up one of her eyes at him, "Can't you come and visit? You're still going to come and see your mom right? I can come visit you when you do."

He shook his head, and stood with his hands on his hips still catching his breath, "No, the reason my mom wants me to go is because of *you and your mom*…she thinks it's bad for me to be around you and her!"

"What are you saying? Why would she do that? You can't not ever see me again - you're my *best* friend, did you tell her *that*?!" She was starting to panic too, and grabbed both of his hands tightly in hers. "What are you going to do? What are *we* going to do?"

"I don't know, Melinda…she won't listen to me. She thinks I'm messing up in school because of this, because of you and everything else. Maybe I can go for a little while and do really good in school and show her I'm better…then I can come back."

"No! You can't leave me alone John! I can't be here without you! My mom and dad fight all the time, Steve and Dean stay after school all the time so they don't have to come home and I'm all alone. She won't even let me play with Gwenny anymore. I don't have anyone but you!"

John looked up at the tall canopy far above them, watching the raindrops making their way through the thick network of leaves and branches. That canopy was supposed to be a sanctuary from the rain and make those beneath it feel safe, but that park didn't make either of them feel safe any longer. It had been their own special place, but with the death of her brother and now it becoming the stage upon which last goodbyes would be said, it was ruined forever.

He didn't have an answer to give her. He didn't have the words. He knew he'd made a promise to her, to be there for her and be her best friend, but he couldn't keep his promise and it was breaking his heart.

"No matter what, I'll come back for you - they can't keep us apart forever," was all that he could say as he watched that heavy rain force its way through the leaves above them.

She whimpered, "You'll be gone for a long time...you'll forget all about me."

John shook his head, "No! I'll never forget about you! I'll call you and write to you every day!"

His mother showed up then, and didn't look happy. She had been driving and walking in the rain, and she was drenched. He stood and had planned to run, taking a firm grip of Melinda's hand, but decided it would only make things worse. Instead, he said goodbye to her, holding her tightly until the moment he felt the strong hand at the back of his shirt collar. His eyes never left her even under a barrage of curses by his mother, until the car took him far away from her.

Transcript of recorded session with John F. Chapel
November 5th
Dr. James Campbell

Campbell: "That must have been very difficult for you."

John: "Yea I guess you could say it was the worst thing that ever happened to me at that point...and probably since. I did my best to convince my mom to let me stay, but she threatened something more serious if I didn't go with my dad."

Campbell: "*More serious?*"

John: "She mentioned professional mental help."

Campbell: "It was a pretty traumatic situation, you might have needed it."

John: "I think she would've dumped me off at a nut house just to be rid of me."

Campbell: "That's a pretty grim picture you're painting of your mother."

John: "You've never met my mother."

Campbell: "What about Melinda? What happened with her? Did they talk about getting her professional help?"

John: "She had the worst of it. Her parents were a mess, withdrawn, the house was so quiet and empty...and she was in the middle of it. They dumped a lot of it on her and that probably accounted for a lot of her problems later on. A bit of help might have done all of them some good."

Campbell: "I want to talk about her in a moment, but I want to address the incident in the park first. I think that could be the origin of your episodes."

John: "Why are we talking about this? I told you I didn't want to talk about him. I didn't have these episodes until much later."

Campbell: "You don't remember any bad dreams or missing time from your childhood?"

John: "No, this is all new. Why? What does that mean?"

Campbell: "People who suffer from multiple personality disorders experience complex "nightmares" and lapses in time like you told me that you've been experiencing lately."

John: "This isn't a *personality disorder*, this is something else. Why are we wasting our time with this crap?"

Campbell: "Humor me for a minute. Can you tell me about the dream? Can you describe this other man?"

John: "I don't know what there is to describe. It's like any other dream – mostly feelings and emotions. It's like I'm there, seeing through his eyes, but also watching him from somewhere else."

Campbell: "Tell me what he feels then."

John: "It's springtime, but the water's colder than I've ever felt, and I'm swimming but I don't know where or how I even got in the water. I can't see anything at first, and then there's this painful, blinding, white light, and the next thing I know, I'm lying beside a lake or a river somewhere. I'm wet and shivering."

Campbell: "So this boy…he *comes* from the water?"

John: "I don't know if he comes from the water itself, I just know that it's my first memory of him. Maybe he fell into the water…off a boat or something, I don't know."

Campbell: "It could be your subconscious trying to empathize with Dawson, seeing him beneath that icy water, helpless and frightened."

John: "I've had dreams about Dawson; this isn't the same thing."

Campbell: Your description also sounds like the experience of a newborn child: bright lights and confusion, and the wetness and shocking cold that a naked and vulnerable baby feels.

John: I suppose.

Campbell: A lot of split personalities are conceived at the moment a major tragedy occurs.

John: Conceived? That's an interesting word choice, Doc.

Campbell: Well, the way I see it, an alternate personality is "born" at some point - as real as any other person. What else do you remember about his surroundings?

John: Why is that important?

Campbell: If your subconscious created this personality, then it also created the world around him. Usually one is created before the other, in the studies I've read. I'm hoping you can give me some points of reference, something familiar that I can draw a connection to in your everyday life.

John: I can't tell you much about the lay of the land. Mostly trees – he's in a forest of some sort – and he's by a body of water. It's all I remember. Oh, there are tall reeds and sand too.

Campbell: He's alone?

John: At first, but then the girl comes, maybe a day later.

Campbell: And what did this girl look like?

John: What's with all the goofy questions? You have the drawings, doc. She looked pretty much like that, but a lot younger.

Campbell: They're very good sketches, but I'm sure they don't do her justice?

John: Well, physical features are harder to remember than feelings and impressions. She had a calming voice…very slight and graceful,…a gentle touch. I know she has blue eyes and her hair is blonde, beyond that, I'm at a loss.

Campbell: That's why I had you record these things in this journal, John, so that we don't miss any details. So by the rest of your description here, she was quite young at the time, maybe fifteen?

John: Not a fifteen from our time, but a fifteen from that time. More mature.

Campbell: This boy isn't much older is he?

John: Maybe a year or two at most.

Campbell: Would you say that it was the approximate age difference between you and Melinda when you met her again?

John: Look. This girl…I know she has a lot of the same features, she's not the same. I know what you're getting at, but there's just something about her that's…different.

Campbell: I don't think that we should rule this girl out as your subconscious interpretation of the one who broke your heart over and over again. This place you're describing sounds just like the place in this journal.

John: I really wish you hadn't gone poking your nose in those old pages. I would've torn them out if I'd been thinking.

Campbell: Well, it's a good thing you didn't – I think it's the only information that's given us any real headway. You haven't really given me anything else to go on.

John: I know what this sounds like, Jim, but you've got to listen to me. I don't know how I know that this is something different, or that this isn't Melinda, but it just is. I just…can't put my finger on it yet.

Campbell: Okay then, let's talk about her and this other place…

WANDERLUST

"Yet there's no rest or peace for me, imperious it drums,
The Wanderlust, and I must follow it."

~Robert W. Service

Chapter *3*

It was late spring, and the days were warm but the nights still held the memory of a winter recently deceased. In a thick grove of an unnamed forest was an unnamed man who spent his days sitting beside an unnamed lake thinking about a girl who, of course, was yet unnamed.

Every other creature in that forest had a name, and he remembered it, though he knew not how. In the trees were warblers and sparrows chirping, red and grey squirrels chattering, and at night, the bats screeched to find their way. He'd seen a fox or two as well as a handful of hares (which had been delicious) and even a pheasant (that had almost been delicious) beneath that canopy. In the small lake were trout and speckled salmon, among other species too numerous to list (not as delicious as the rabbit), and he seemed to spend the most time watching them from his stump beside the water.

For all those names he knew, he would have traded every last one of them for just one name: his own.

The man of the forest had been born much the way any other child was; confused, overwhelmed, wet and naked. Unlike most people, though, he'd been delivered onto a cold beach, a full-grown man, alone, and not given a name. He'd been left there without a stitch of memory or clothing, at the end of a bitter winter, without any idea how he would survive those first couple of days.

He remembered how he shivered uncontrollably and how his stomach ached from hunger so badly that it felt as though a dagger had been run through it. The forest had provided everything he'd needed, however, and he somehow managed. That wasn't altogether true; the forest and a mysterious benefactor had provided everything he'd needed.

In those first miserable days beside the freezing water, he was in and out of consciousness, suffered from delirium and was trapped in a body that was weak as a babe's. Each time he regained consciousness, he was staring at the same stand of trees and the same tall grasses swaying in the cold breeze, unable to move his head from where it rested in the sand, though not from lack of trying. Exhausted from his efforts and frustrated, he would close his eyes and drift off to sleep again.

It was either the fifth or sixth time (he'd lost count) his eyes fluttered open that he saw her. She was kneeling beside him, so that even with his blurred vision, he was able to make out her features.

She was a lithe, gentle creature with hair that trapped the very sun within its beautiful strands. Her wide, thin lips parted in a smile, and she whispered words to him that he didn't understand. It wasn't her hair, her lips or even the sound of her soothing voice that haunted him every night since she'd disappeared; it was her eyes.

They were exotic in shape and color, like two elongated almonds beset with small stars shimmering with blue light, like he'd seen in the night sky. That wasn't even what was most striking about them, though; it was the way they made him forget everything just by staring into them.

He forgot that he was shivering on the cold sand, forgot that every muscle throbbed, and that his stomach had begun consuming itself out of hunger. There was no memory of a place he'd called home, or anything in his possession that indicated that he belonged somewhere or to someone, but staring up those eyes, he felt such warmth and comfort that he felt like he was home and he did belong.

As quickly as she'd appeared, though, she was gone again, and that safe place among her eyes was gone as well. He was left shivering and more alone than before, realizing that she was out there somewhere and he couldn't reach her. The man in the forest owed his survival to her, for his will to live had been as faint as his pulse, but his will to see her again helped him overcome certain death. The things she'd left for him in the clearing didn't hurt his situation either.

He glanced over his shoulder towards the place he'd found her delicate footprints, and then back at the hatchet that he was turning over and over in his hands. The hatchet had probably been the most practical thing she'd brought for him, even more useful than the long shirt and breeches he was still wearing, and he was especially attached to it.

46

Every piece of lumber he used to construct his crude home with had been cut and trimmed with that hatchet. It had taken several days, and it still wasn't much more than a hut, but it was shelter and it was his.

He'd almost forgotten that dinner was cooking in his small shelter, and stood from his seat on the stump and went to check on it. Most of his cooking after dark was done inside the confines of his cramped home, so that none of the nearby residents could see the flickering of a fire in his secret place.

He knew there were others out there, more like the girl, but possibly less friendly. The gifts had been intended as more than tools for his survival, they were intended to be a warning, a sign that he was to stay hidden among the trees where it was safe. If that hadn't been her intention, then surely she would have come to fetch him by now. He often thought about those people and what they were like or if possibly one of them might know who he was, or where he'd come from.

It would be nice to know his own name or if he had family out there somewhere, maybe wondering what had become of him. But he continued to heed her unspoken warning and avoid those others, continuing to make his own living in the forest. Maybe that's what she had tried to tell him that day in the words he didn't understand, and just maybe she did know who he was and was trying to help hide him from others.

He could've been a criminal who'd done something awful and that was why she was hiding him and why no one that knew him had bothered to come looking for him. Maybe his family was ashamed of him and he'd been cast out of wherever it was that he once called home.

These things plagued him as he tore a small piece of rabbit meat from the spit and tasted it to see if it was ready. It was juicy, but still a bit too pink on the inside, so it would need a few more minutes over the fire. He frowned at the fire, seeing that it was in need of another log, and he fetched one from the small pile in the corner. The embers shot into the air, singing the rabbit, as the log settled and began to burn, and he sat hard on his bed to watch it cook.

It was about as much a "bed" as the four walls and pine branches were a "house", but again, it was something he'd made with his own hands and that hatchet. Sleeping on the ground, even for a young man his age, wasn't very pleasant, so with a little ingenuity, he'd constructed the small cot. The mattress was a deerskin stitched up with thread made from dried entrails and filled with feathers and dried leaves. This was supported between four solid posts he'd carved from a single tree, and cinched together with netting he'd woven from willow branches.

It was actually quite comfortable, and he'd spent several of the colder mornings beneath a pile of skins, trying to stay warm. Those skins had been taken with his trusty hatchet as well, and the meat from the two does and small black bear flayed by the same tool. The bear incident had actually been pretty harrowing, and if he'd had another soul to tell, it would've made for a great story.

He told the chattering squirrels the tale, and they seemed disinterested in listening to his adventures. How could they not laugh when he got to the part where he was interrupted taking his morning "constitutional" by the bear and was chased without pants back to the camp? How could they not cheer on his bravery as he faced the angry beast that was trying to take his smoked fish breakfast? He hated those squirrels; they just chattered all day long and weren't even worth eating.

The bear rug was his favorite, in any case, and before winter set in again, he would have to make some warmer clothing out of that skin. He checked the small shelf of his personal provisions, making a mental checklist of things he would have to stock up on before that winter came.

The single piece of brittle flint she'd left for him might not last him through the summer, and he would have to find more. His tinder and char stores were getting low also, as was his fish oil that was used for light – but that was of no concern, for he was out of linen as well. The girl had left him a single strip, and he'd used it up working long hours into the night, building the house.

He frowned at the lopsided shelf he'd built, frustrated by his dwindling stores. Despite the long process, the oil and tinder was replenishable, and he supposed that if he was going to be wearing bear skin winter apparel, that he could cut fresh strips from the shirt for his lamp.

Flopping back onto the bed with a long sigh, he laid his head back and closed his eyes to the sounds of the forest and the smell of the meat. He was tired of those sounds and he was tired of eating rabbit alone in his shack and telling his stories to squirrels.

The prospect of spending six more months alone in that place was depressing even for the mighty bear slayer of the forest. He'd trade every drop of fish pressings, every flake of char, his rabbit meat, and his furs just to see that girl again.

He renegotiated the silent barter from earlier in his head: he would also trade all of the names of the creatures he knew not for his own name, but for hers. As he tried remembering her face, the enchanting eyes he'd gotten lost in, and the strange words she'd said to him, his daydreaming delivered him into deep sleep.

Most often, he dreamt of things from the course of his day, like hunting a doe, swimming in the lake, or struggling to build a fire. On very rare occasions, though, he would have odd dreams like those from his first day beside the lake just as frightening and disorienting. On this particular evening, he had one that was both.

It began with him fishing with a forked spear, the way he used to do before he'd fashioned a suitable bow for hunting bigger game. A trout was wriggling on the end of his spear and he was sloshing ankle-deep in the shallows when the sky suddenly went dark and the lake was sprinkled with a light mist.

The sky flashed white with lighting and there was something besides burnt ozone in the air. He suddenly became terrified like the other denizens of the forest, and broke into a run towards his small shelter. He only made it as far as the shore when the sky let loose and the downpour fell on his head like a steel curtain.

The spear fell to the ground with the fish still impaled as his fingers went numb and his legs buckled. Sand and earth flew as the man fell facedown at the water's edge, already unconscious before his cheek scraped the rocky bank. Six feet away, the dying trout watched the man writhe as helplessly on the ground with his wide, staring eyes. His mouth seemed to mock his, opening and closing, no words coming, and the life-giving water fell and taunted them both as darkness overcame them simultaneously.

The fish went wherever it is that fish go when they expire, and the fisherman went elsewhere.

He found himself in another place where he felt even more displaced than the day he woke by the river, though much the same way. All around him the sound of water lapping at sand echoed from the trees, and his feet were touching something warmer and softer than before.

49

A horizon of reed-covered hills was broken up by a single figure, and he wondered if the trout had seen the woman before it died-the only other living thing around to bear witness to what he saw there in the rain.

She was sitting in the distance among the blowing reeds, her arms folded across her knees, and her golden curls acting as a curtain to tease him and hide features of her face. At first, he was sure it was the same girl who had visited him before, but as he approached, he noticed that she was as different from that girl as the sand of the beach was from that of his own in the grove. When she noticed him approaching, she turned and her lips parted in a smile, eyes twinkling at him.

The girl stood and brushed the sand from her backside and tried to keep her wild mane out of her face with one hand as she stood waiting for him with that smile. He stopped then, his legs no longer obeying his commands, and his breath caught when he saw her face.

She was young, probably the same age as the other girl, and her face still held the roundness of youth but womanhood was slowly creeping in. Her eyes were the deepest blue, and there was recognition in them as they smiled at him. Something was said and there was laughter, but it was lost to the wind and the lapping waves.

The wind kicked up and picked up a large patch of the sand to douse them with, both turning their heads to avoid a face-full. She laughed again and looked up into his eyes, draping her arms around his neck and pulling him close. He smelled her then, through the damp air and the water that had started to fall, and she smelled of violets and something else that he couldn't place. Her skin smelled of the beach, it was her hair that gave off that intoxicating scent.

It blew across his face like it had her own, and the curled ends tickled his nose. He parted her hair with both hands to get a good look at her face. The wind blew harder and the rain began to fall heavier, keeping a natural veil over her face. She looked to the sky and then at the line of the trees, whispering something and drawing back from him. He was only an arm's length from her, and as he stretched his hand out to pull her back to him, she was gone and the beach and trees all around him with her.

50

Like that, it ended with the intensity of a scream inside of his head, and it left him incapacitated for several minutes. He tried to shake the event from his head that night, and would every night after, but it was so vivid and haunting that it burrowed itself in his mind like a tick, impossible to shake. A feeling of loss and deep sorrow overcame him, and as he stared down at his shaking hands, he repeated the name that the wind had tried to steal from her lips - *John.*

Chapter *4*

John's eyes jerked open and he heard his own voice calling out the name, repeating it over and over again so that he might never forget it again. He'd known it that first day, but it had become lost in the barrage of nightmares and strange visions which followed. The girl returned to him to bring him one more gift, and though it wasn't quite how he'd hoped she would, he didn't take that visit for granted.

Sitting up from his bed, he finally knew what he had to do, and he began collecting what was left of his supplies. The girl had to be found, for she alone held the answers to all of those questions that were the cause of his restlessness. He didn't even know where to begin, but he had to leave that place or surely he would go mad. There was more out there for him than being the "bear slayer" and living in a shanty.

He left the rabbit to char over the dying fire - no longer thinking about food - and headed directly to the west, in search of his most dangerous prey. That's where he'd heard the voices from, carried on the wind through the trees, and he knew that's where he would find the girl.

Where she was, though, there were others, and he was at a disadvantage because he wouldn't know any of their faces, but they might know his. There could be friends or family among those faces, but there also could be those who meant him harm or who'd already tried to harm him, and failed to finish the job. In either case, he would be ready he thought, gripping his bow and patting the head of his hatchet tucked in his belt.

Breaking the edge of the forest, he came upon rolling hills of green grass, dotted by patches of wildflowers, and split by a dirt road. There were footprints, horse hooves and thin wheel tracks marking it, and the prospect of other faces waiting somewhere up that road inspired him to pick up his pace.

Ascending a large hill, he looked down upon a small collection of thatch-roofed homes (that looked like mansions compared to his) nestled in a lush valley of green. The road continued on far beyond the small village, probably to places even more impressive, but he was certain that he would find the girl there. So, he decided to descend the winding road and brave whatever waited for him there.

He waited for a red sun to go down and a black moon to rise as he waited, hunched down behind a low stone wall, watching the quiet place. Hearths began to glow and families chattered, sending orange light and their melodies from the small windows. He closed his eyes and listened to the sweet sounds of barking dogs, children crying and the high pitch of whispers and dinner table talk, basking in the warmth of light and sound.

The aroma of freshly-baked bread reminded him that he was hungry again, but he ignored his growling stomach, to watch the family through the window. There were five huddled around a plank board table, sopping up some kind of mixture with the warm bread. A dog growled from under the table, smelling the stranger no doubt, and received a kick from the father for its efforts, but rewarded by one of the children with a bite of his crust. When dinner was finished, the woman cleaned the crockery, and then retired with the rest to a spot in the corner where blankets were heaped on straw.

John watched them longingly, wondering if he'd grown up in a similar home with similar people. His own family might've lived in this very same community and could be huddled together somewhere not far from there. Hunger pangs were replaced by a sort of excited nausea at the prospect that he might discover more in that sleepy little place than anticipated.

He came upon another small farm with a barn and a larger home nestled at the far edge. The light still came from the window and the voice of a girl from inside made his heart race. He sat crouched down, just listening to the voice, trying to remember the other one that he'd heard only briefly before. A shadow emerged from the front door and headed towards the barn, and he held very still in the darkness so as not to be noticed.

It was the outline of a girl, but not the same outline that he remembered. She closed up the barn, and then returned to the house and the light was snuffed out moments after. Certain that it was safe to move from his place by the fence, he moved to pass between the house and the barn, and that's where he was discovered.

54

As he passed beneath the eaves, he noticed the small pair of eyes upon him before the voice called out, and he gave a start, "Are you here to take more of our grain from the barn?"

He whirled, ready for anything, but came face-to-face with a boy of about seven or eight with sandy blonde hair, standing with his hands behind his back. John smiled and knelt down to the boy, asking, "And what are you doing out of your bed so late at night, son?"

"My papa's at the pub again and he leaves my sister in charge, but when she goes off to sleep, I'm in charge. You didn't answer my question."

"No, I'm not here to take anything from your barn," he reassured him.

"Then what are you doing here?"

John squinted his eyes in the darkness at him, "What's that you're holding behind your back?"

The boy took a step back, eyeing him warily.

"Are you good with secrets?" When the man nodded, he confided in him and produced the wine skin from behind his back. "It's my papa's."

"What's in it?"

"Wine, of course," he replied indifferently.

"What are you doing drinking? How *old* are you?"

"I'm old enough - I said I was in charge. You still didn't tell me why you're here."

"Can *you* keep a secret?"

The boy nodded, taking a drink and scrunching up a brow at him.

"I'm looking for someone…a girl…about fifteen seasons, and with hair of gold."

He swished the drink in his mouth thoughtfully, resting one elbow across his arm, balancing the skin in his other hand. Jabbing the stem at him, he finally said, "Very pretty?"

"*Very* pretty," he nodded, grinning at the boy.

"That's Nicolette; George's daughter," he finally concluded, scratching at his small chin.

His blood grew hot in his veins at the mention of her name, and the good fortune that the boy knew who she was.

"Does she live nearby?"

"Yes sir," he pointed towards a cluster of homes on the opposite side of the road.

"Thank you!" He said, his voice crackling with energy, and shaking his small hand, then started towards the road.

The boy called after in a loud whisper, "But I wouldn't go there!"

"Why is that?" John asked, spinning on his heels.

"Because George is old and he's mean, and he'll probably give you a thrashing for taking up with his daughter."

John chuckled and knelt down to talk to him, "I do not intend to *take up* with her, thank you, but I do need to speak with her. It will take more than a thrashing from an old man to keep me away now."

"All the same, you can't see her," he said matter-of-factly.

"Why can't I see her?"

"Because she's not here," the boy replied simply. "She left with her father for Rouen yesterday and probably won't be back for a week - maybe longer."

"A week?" The energy drained quickly from his tone. "I don't know that I can wait that long...how do I get to Rouen?"

The boy giggled at him, which made him finally appear his appropriate age, "You have your heart pretty set on her? What do you want with George's daughter? There are *lots* of other girls in the village."

"I just need to see *her*...I have things to talk with her about. Do you know how to get to Rouen?"

He pointed again, "Follow that road until it forks to the west...or...east...I think. I've never been, and neither has my sister. My papa has been, but he's at the tavern with the other men. I suppose you could ask one of them how to get there."

John exhaled, frustrated, and rubbed his temples. He was only steps from the place she laid her head at night, but she was still just out of his reach. Walking into a tavern full of drunken men to ask the whereabouts of a young girl seemed like a worse idea than skulking around a stranger's farm in the middle of the night.

"*You've* never seen me before, have you?" He finally asked.

"No sir," he said, shaking his head. "There isn't a soul in Avandale I don't know-it isn't a very big place, you know?"

"Avandale? That's the name of this place?"

He nodded and asked, "What's your name?"

"John. I think."

"You don't sound sure," he said, chuckling. "My name is Pelleon."

John shook his hand, "It's a pleasure to meet you Pelleon. I suppose I should try to find my way to Rouen if I'm going to reach her."

"Well, you're not going to find her standing here with me. Are you headed to the tavern?"

"No, that might not be a good idea," John said with a sigh.

"So then, neither of us will have to worry about this exchange. I didn't see a man sneaking around our barn, and you didn't see a boy with a wine skin. Maybe you could come visit me again, though? My papa spends a lot of time in his cups and my sister doesn't particularly like me. Most of the adults don't say much to me around here."

John nodded, "I would like that, Pelleon."

After talking for a bit longer about the particulars of Avandale and Rouen, they bid each other a good evening and he took the long way around the road and the tavern so as not to attract attention.

He hadn't found her yet, but he'd added a name to the list of people who knew he existed, and that made him feel a bit less lonely. His first real conversation had been pleasant, and just interacting with another human was the best thing he'd experienced in a while. Though the boy hadn't recognized him, it had been valuable information: it meant that he was most-likely not from Avandale.

John wandered the long stretch of road for many days, searching for the girl from the lake. He'd headed west first, and encountered two more places like Avandale along the way. There were more friendly conversations, and his list of names grew, but none of those people had recognized him either.

The not-so-friendly folks weren't inclined to be as helpful, and some ignored him altogether, but they didn't seem to know him either. On the third day, he finally learned that Rouen was to the east and he had to turn around. Four days later, he finally reached the walls of the ancient French city, only to discover that

George of Avandale and his attractive daughter had left the night before.

He found himself sitting near that same spot beneath the eaves of the barn eight days later, sitting with Pelleon and sharing his skin. They sat up late, swapping stories, and Pelleon found John's adventures along the old Roman road quite humorous. He was just happy to hear that Nicolette returned safely and he knew her whereabouts finally.

"You don't have very good luck, do you?"

"I suppose I don't. How long has she been asleep?" He couldn't take his eyes from the small window that mocked him from across the way.

"Nicolette goes to bed about the same time as my sister. The girls wake about sunup and start their chores, so they don't stay up late like you and me," he explained, blowing rings of smoke.

"Don't you have to get up for chores?"

"No, do you?"

John had never thought about not having to wake up at a particular time as being an advantage of living as a hermit in the middle of a forest, but smiled at the thought, shaking his head.

"Why don't you have to get up for chores?"

Pelleon held out his foot explaining, "A sow stepped on my foot last season, when I was helping my papa, and I'm not big enough to do the heavy work anyway."

"Your foot looks fine," John said.

"Well, it's not! I've got a bad limp, so papa makes my sister do most of the chores, and that suits me fine," he said defensively, raising his voice a bit. "Why don't *you* have chores?"

"Never mind about *my* chores - I have plenty. You don't care for your family much, do you?"

"They're not my family - not my real family anyway - my mother passed three seasons ago from fever and I'm left with a lazy drunkard and a cruel wench who tries to tell me what to do," he spat out, quite irritated.

"You should be thankful that you have family, Pelleon, and someone to talk to. Some folks don't have any family - and they live all alone."

The boy cocked his head up at him thoughtfully then concluded, "Like you? That's why you're here, because you don't have anyone? You're better off, if you ask me."

"I don't remember my family, Pelleon, and I think the girl might have information about them, and about where I came from."

"I can't say as I remember much of my mother or where we came from either - I was only four when she died - but I don't spend too much thinking about it. My life is here now, staying up late and looking at the stars, sneaking my papa's skin and talking to whoever happens by."

"But you said your sister was a wench and you don't like it here?"

"We don't always have to like where we're at, I just said that it was the place I call home. It doesn't mean that this is the only life I'll ever know, and things will change as time passes; some of it by choice and the rest will be up to God. We have to make the most out of what we have - that's about the only thing I remember my mother telling me."

"Your mother sounded like a good woman, Pelleon, and you're a credit to her memory. Maybe there's something to what you're saying. This girl may not have the answers that I'm looking for, but that doesn't mean that I'm not supposed to find her for some other reason."

The sandy-haired boy gave his jack-o-lantern smile, "So you *are* going to take up with her?"

"We make what choices we can and leave the rest up to God, right?"

"So why are you standing here talking to me still?

"It's not that easy; I can't just go creeping into her house and risk waking up her father. What if I startle her and he wakes up?"

"You'll have a thrashing for sure," he said matter-of-factly. "But you had no problem sneaking right up to my door a week ago, or walking four days in the wrong direction looking for her. She's right there, across the road."

He couldn't argue with the boy's sound logic and so they concocted a plan that involved throwing stones through her open window. At least he would be a safe distance from the house if his small missiles missed their target.

59

Crouching beside a wagon across the road from her house, the pair of them took turns selecting the perfect stones for their mission. The smaller ones wouldn't clear the distance and the heavier ones echoed through the entire valley when they struck the house - at which point, John would frown at his attendant.

They became so caught up in their contest that he almost forgot the reason they'd started in the first place, until that reason suddenly filled the door frame. The silent chuckle that he'd been sharing with Pelleon was suddenly strangled from his vocal chords, as if a strong hand had found his throat.

He stared at her, frozen in place, as she stepped into the moonlight. Her hair was tangled and messy and her nightshirt was stained and dirty, but she was still more beautiful than he remembered. Even that morning he laid in her lap and stared up at her face, the sun, casting her hair and face in glorious bronze, had done her little justice.

She looked up and down the dirt road, hugging herself against the night air that played in her hair. Satisfied that whatever had disturbed her rest had passed, she turned to go back in, but a sharp hiss coming from the wagon caused her to hesitate. She scanned the darkness again and started heading towards the noise, her feet coming to a rest just on the other side of the wagon.

"Who's out here?" She whispered.

John hunched down and slowed his breathing, thinking his thunderous heartbeat was giving him away. She knelt down then to examine the underside of the cart, and her glimmering eyes shone at the two boys that had taken refuge there.

"Pelleon, is that you? Who is with you?"

John forced himself up, and dragged poor Pelleon with him, as he revealed himself. Her eyes went wide when she saw who it was, gasping, "You!?"

"Nicolette…?"

"How do you know my name? How did you find me? What are you doing here? You can't be here!"

"Please," he pleaded, putting up his hands, "I just need to speak with you."

"It's the middle of the night, I am not even dressed! Did he tell you my name? Did he tell you where to find me?" She demanded answers, flustered.

John jabbed a thumb at his cohort, "Pelleon told me where to find you, yes. Do not be upset please, I just need to speak to you. I've come a long way just to see you."

"Pelleon!" She said his name like a curse word.

"Please, Nicolette, I need you to tell me how you knew that I would be by the water that day? How did you know my name?"

"You came sneaking in here just to ask silly questions? I don't know who you are, I certainly don't know your name, and I just happened to find you that day because I do the wash - just like the rest of the girls in the village."

"His name is John," Pelleon interjected, grinning.

"I don't care what his name is! He needs to leave before someone finds him!"

"I'm not going anywhere until you tell me the truth! It's a big lake and I haven't even been to the other end of it, so how did you know where to look for me?"

"Are you *mad*? I don't know your name and I'd never seen your face prior to the day I found you. I happened to be there because that's where I like to go to wash and get away from the other gossiping women in this village. I didn't know you would be there, I assure you."

"So you had no idea that I would be there?"

"How would I have known that you'd be there?"

"We don't know one another? We'd never met prior to that day?"

"I assure you that we do not! Now go, I have nothing more to say to you, and if my father catches you and I out here in the road--"

"I'll get a *thrashing*?"

"Yes, a thrashing you'll *never* forget!" She stifled a smile, knowing that he'd obviously spoken with Pelleon thoroughly, for he was most afraid of her father.

"Then let him thrash me! I will suffer a thrashing if you will just answer my questions."

She shook her head and sighed at him. "You're not going to leave are you? Against my kind warnings, you will risk my father's temper? What do you *think* I know that can help you?"

"You said you'd never seen me before and that you didn't know my name, but I remember...*something*...from before. I remember you; it was you that called me by my name."

"I am very certain that we had never met prior, John, and I'd hoped to not see you after that day. I was only being charitable to a stranger who was in need because that is the Christian way."

"I owe you my gratitude then," he said.

"You can repay your gratitude by not bringing your trouble to this place, or to any of the people in it," she exhaled, very exhausted.

"What kind of trouble do you think I bring? I am no criminal. I am just a man looking for his home and for anyone who remembers a name. Certainly, there must be someone who can tell me where I come from."

"I am certain that there must be, John, but not in this place. There are fewer than one hundred people here, as I'm sure Pelleon has told you, and very few travel very far from here. If anyone knew your face, it would be my father or me, and I have never seen you. Perhaps you would have success in Rouen?"

"I've been to *Rouen* looking for you...I've come a long way, why will you not help me? You claim to be a good Christian, but your charity ends with leaving me a hatchet and some clothing?"

"You've obviously done well enough for yourself to survive haven't you?"

"Yes, but a man needs more than food in his belly and clothing on his back to survive. I've been living alone out there in that forest, with not a single face to call friend. If I don't perish of solitude out there, then surely I will from exposure once winter comes, and that will be upon your conscience - you should never have helped me in the first place."

She furled a brow, looking from the boy to the stranger, saying, "You cannot burden me with this, John; I did *more* than my part. Though I could not very well just leave you there to die, I also cannot do anything further. What if you are a criminal? What if you were cast out of another place? You said that you could not remember anything, so how are you so certain?"

"I don't remember, but I'm pretty sure I've done nothing wrong..."

"Well, I wouldn't worry about perishing to the elements, dragging that boy into this," she said, pointing, "was foolish and you've made things more difficult for yourself! He won't keep his silence in this matter, I hope you know, and men will be looking for you within the week, criminal or not!"

"He didn't want to involve either of us, and it was my idea to wake you! He's not a bad fellow!" Pelleon jabbed a finger from his left hand at her because his skin was hidden behind his back. "And I'm not going to breathe a word about him to anyone-you're *wrong* about that part!"

"*Good boys* don't go sneaking around people's homes or take up with strangers at all hours of the night, Pelleon. They should be in bed, where I've sent you many times before, and not bother themselves with things that aren't any of their concern!"

"That's right; you shouldn't concern yourself with *my* business then!" He replied smartly.

"Someone has to; the Lord knows your drunkard of a father won't! You are such an impossible and odd child…and are you drinking again?"

He finally produced the skin from behind his back and pointed it at her, "*You're* the impossible one! You help this poor man out of the goodness of your heart, but then tell him that he's not welcome here, and that you don't care what happens to him one way or the other. That's not very *Christian* of you at all!"

"What would *you* know about being a Christian? I've never seen you at service!"

"I don't need to go to service to know the difference between wrong and right, or to know that if you turn John away you may as well have left him for dead," he spat back at her.

"You *know* why he can't stay here! He would be in more danger here than whatever faces him out there in that forest," she exclaimed. "If you want to be his friend, then do so at your own peril and his. Someone will eventually see you, and then that will be the end of it!"

"I am sorry to have bothered you," John apologized. "I do not want to bring trouble to either of you or to this place, it was never my intention. I just needed to find you…I needed to see your face again…"

She turned her blushing face down to stare at her dirty toes so that he could not see how his words had affected her. "What is it that you want from me?"

63

He'd been fumbling with his words, trying to find exactly the right thing to say to keep her there, and if he couldn't win her over in that very moment, he knew that he would lose her.

"I think that it was God's providence that you found me that day, Nicolette. It could have been anyone else in this village, but it was you, and there must be a good reason for that."

He looked at her as though she was the most necessary thing in the world, and that, coupled with his words, softened her fear, though still not enough.

"John...I believe you, and I believe that God has some great purpose for you, but there is nothing here in this place for you."

The younger boy shook his head in disgust at his neighbor and turned to the defeated man, "John...we don't need her, I will go with you wherever you need to go. We will find someone that recognizes you...someone who can tell you the things you need to know."

He was close enough to touch her and felt that he'd almost reached her with his words, but she was still just as far away as she was eight days ago. She gave him a longing gaze as she turned away that belied her words.

She retreated hesitantly back across the road to her cozy little home, turning only once more before she closed the door, but he could not see her expression. Though Pelleon stood loyally at his side, he did not notice the boy there, but he could hear his words in his head, taunting him. He was reminded of how he'd failed in his part, and wondered when it might be that God was going to do the rest. He wouldn't have long to wait.

Chapter 5

Campbell closed his copy of the notebook and looked up at Gwenn with the same expression he used when finishing one of his lectures at the podium, right before he opened the floor to questions. She had also been a student of his many years before, and he recalled that she rarely joined the post-lecture forums.

It wasn't because she didn't understand the subject matter or that she didn't have questions, it was the simple fact that she was slow and deliberate in her digestion of the facts and in asking the right questions. Her essays always reflected her analytical approach as well as her command of the subject, so he never worried about her silence in his classrooms.

This time he wasn't certain if he'd lost her in the story, or if that analytical mind was busy at work, pulling apart the key facts and digesting them like usual. She just shifted within the chair, as if it had suddenly become the most uncomfortable place in the house, and looked anxiously from his expectant stare to the small recording device on the table.

"I'm sorry," he said, slipping the device back into his jacket pocket. "It wasn't my intention to upset you. Was hearing his voice too much?"

"No, it was actually very...therapeutic," she said, as tears welled in her eyes. "I haven't heard it in months...it was comforting."

He leaned forward and handed her a pristine handkerchief from the opposite breast pocket, which she gladly accepted, dabbing her eyes and marking it with black streaks.

"You were very thorough in your retelling, Jim, thank you," she finally said. "John never explained what he was seeing quite that way, and I was only able to pick out bits and pieces from him talking in his sleep and from what he wrote."

"I suspect you're not fluent in medieval French either?"

"No," she said, laughing nervously. "Neither was *he*. I was only able to pick out a few of the words from the journal from what I remembered of high school French."

"The medieval Norman language he was writing in these pages contains more Germanic roots than modern French, and is called *langue d'oil* – the *oil language*. I covered it briefly in my medieval history class and John had access to French law documents; the only place it can be found now."

"So he picked up a language from a couple of ancient law documents well enough to speak it fluently in his sleep? If that's your argument for his sudden command of a dead language, I'm not convinced."

"Of course that's not sufficient as far as explanations go," he said, adjusting his glasses on his nose. "But there are other variables we haven't explored."

"Variables? Like when you tried telling him that he was exhibiting autistic behavior?"

"I never said he was autistic," he corrected her. "I said that people exist who can absorb entire volumes of information simply by looking at them once, and not just autistic persons."

"Your eidetic memory theory?"

"Elizabeth Stromeyer was able to recall entire poems written in foreign languages and reproduce them years later."

"Stromeyer recalled dot patterns, she didn't absorb the languages; I studied her case and every other one that was remotely related to John's. What about what he wrote on the last page of the journal? The words he kept repeating in his sleep the week before he died?"

He knew the lines well, without even having to flip to the last page of the journal. They were the only words written on the page and he'd been over them a hundred times in his head.

Decipientem novit Hungarica
Sapientem custodit viginti sex praestrigiae in bibliotheca
Vidua tenet verba capella

"Gwenn, Latin is a tricky language to translate and can be interpreted a dozen--"

"*Vidua tenet verba capella*: *The widow carries the words of Chapel*? I don't know how much clearer that can be, Jim."

"This isn't a psychic premonition," he grumbled. "John was well aware of the inevitability of his situation, and he counted on you finishing this for him. He knew that you would come to *me* first."

"Fair enough, but what about the next part: *Sapientem custodit viginti sex praestrigiae? The wise man keepeth twenty-six ghosts in his library*? He's talking about *you*, Jim, and those…"

She gave a little shudder and pointed to the back wall over her shoulder, indicating the faces staring back at them with their charcoal eyes.

"The only thing puzzling about that passage is his word choice, given his supposed expertise in the language. *Praestrigiae* refers to *illusions* or *phantoms*, not particularly *ghosts;* he should've known the difference."

"Well, I don't know the difference," she protested, "and I studied Latin for medical terminology."

"So would you say that he was more proficient in the language?"

"He wrote entire pages in that journal and spoke fluently in his sleep, Jim, I would say that qualifies as more proficient."

"Yet he used the term *praestrigiae* to describe what he was seeing, and not *umbras,* which is literally *ghost*? *Praestrigiae* means a *hallucination* or *illusion*. Even the word *animas* - which means *soul* - would've sufficed, but he didn't use that either."

"Give him some credit; he was trying to recall what he was seeing through a haze of sleep and fitful night terrors."

"When he was functioning as a spirit medium?"

"He was speaking to *someone*," she insisted.

"Someone who didn't know the difference between two very *basic* words? He was channeling the uneducated?"

While John Chapel may not have been able to channel the spirits of the dead, his wife may very well have been channeling her anger into the fire that suddenly roared to life beside them. Her eyes smoldered at him in anger, brows becoming sharply-drawn lines, and the fireplace broiled with the same fury for a moment.

"What I would like to focus on is the passage I just read, not what language it's written in. It's something that kept getting John sidetracked as well, and missing the bigger picture."

"It's kind of hard to ignore and sweep under the rug, Jim."

"I don't disagree, but for now can we follow this through to its conclusion before addressing the more difficult questions?"

She nodded quietly.

"So do you understand how I associated this particular entry with the June fifteenth entry?"

"The June fifteenth entry? You mean the night he--"

"Yes, that's the one. On that wall behind you, I've color-coded the pages to indicate which I believe are linked and have unmistakable similarities. This first entry is marked with blue tabs, and labeled 'J-15' because I think it aligns almost flawlessly with the events of that night."

"The story you just told me and the night of June fifteenth are nothing alike, Jim, I was there, remember? I don't see how you can even draw the parallel," she said.

"Give me your summation of the entry I just read you, Gwenn. In your own words."

"Well...it's about a boy who is scared and alone, without a past, without a family or friends...and he braves leaving the safety of the home he carves out for himself with his own two hands to find this girl. He seeks her out because she's the only face that he believes he recognizes and thinks that she can give him the answers he so desperately needs. That's not at all close to the life my husband was leading on June fifteenth of that year."

"No? What kind of life did he have?"

"He had friends, he was somewhat popular, had a good family that loved him and put a roof over his head, and he certainly knew who he was and where he'd been."

"But is that his life, or the one that was forced upon him? Didn't he have *another* life that was taken from him? One that he was told to forget so he could be given a whole new identity? In fact, had the events of June fifteenth never occurred, would John Chapel have ever become the man he did?"

"No one knows for certain what kind of life he might've had if that night never happened, Jim. Maybe he would've had a better one, maybe be would still be alive and happy. Maybe he wouldn't have suffered nervous breakdowns because of...what she'd put him through."

"So now we're admitting that it was because of her that these episodes were brought on?"

"No, I'm saying that the stress she created opened him up for something else, and that she's only partly responsible. I still believe that there's something else to this. But had June fifteenth never happened, I believe that he would still be here."

"But what kind of life would he have had? A life without you? Without the people he touched and did so much good for? Do you think he would've been the same man without all of those things he endured which served to mold and change him?"

"I suppose not. Who's to say? Would he have been any worse off if he'd never made that trip? It's your contention that he was so miserable with the life he ended up with, so miserable with *me*, that he created another one in his head."

"Let's not stoop to self-deprecation just yet Gwenn. Let's focus on what you just said; about the trip he made."

"Well...he always called it *fate*, I suppose I did too. He decided to break with tradition for no good reason one Saturday night, and everything changed from there," she said with a sigh. "What of it?"

"So, a young man who had been quite content to stay within the confines of his safe little town, with the same old routine, suddenly decides to take a risk and break from that safety for no particular reason? And wouldn't you say that life for John Chapel, the life he really lived, started on that day? At *seventeen* years of age?"

He gave her a satisfied smile, knowing that he'd presented her with something almost indisputable, and watched her squirm in the chair again, fidgeting and fumbling for the right words. She started three different sentences, but let them die out after the second word, and finally nodded slowly.

"Okay, so I'll give you that. I can see some connection between the stories now, but there as many disparities between the two and still lots of questions."

"The *questions* are what began this, Gwenn," he said, staring at her over his thin-frames.

"I don't know what you mean."

"Simply put, I think the holes left in one story were the seeds for the other. From the unanswered questions and the unknowns, John began the second story, just like he was taught to do in my classroom."

"You're losing me..."

"When you want to write a thesis paper, Mrs. Chapel, where do you begin?"

"With a question," she replied with a smile. "So now his episodes and emotional breakdowns were his own special way of...writing a *thesis paper*?"

"You're oversimplifying, but yes. There were questions in that narration you just listened to, questions he desired so badly that he risked everything to find them. But where did those come from? They came from a decade of being separated from her, and built up over time, finally culminating on that June evening that ended...in quite a dramatic fashion, wouldn't you say?"

"You could say that," she said in a near-whisper.

"These same questions are found in this other story. There, we have a young man who suffers from an identity crisis, and has buried the truth so deeply within his subconscious that even he cannot access it himself. The only link to that identity is this girl, and the same applies to our John. "

"That's reaching, Doc."

"Is it? I saw a man sitting in that very chair dominated by guilt and regrets, and those two beasts can tear a person apart more than any other. He didn't see her again until he was *seventeen*, Gwenn, don't you think that it's a bit too coincidental? The story of this boy he writes about begins when he is the *same* age, and there's nothing before it, as if seventeen is when his life began."

"John had plenty of memories from when he was younger, and a life before that summer..."

"The life he knew was interrupted, and he spent a decade in a sort of...hibernation...until she returned. *She* is the key to his true identity and who he really is, but he couldn't call upon those memories that night either could he? Something stopped him just like it stopped the boy from the lake didn't it?"

"That night could have gone so much differently, and he could have changed how it went!"

"I have your husband's account of that night on tape, and I would like you to hear it. Then, if you decide that he's left anything out, by all means, indulge me..."

Chapter 6

In the spring of 1991, John Chapel graduated from high school and was looking forward to his first summer as a man. It was off to a promising start that first Saturday night in June, as he was cruising around town in his old 51' Ford coupe, radio cranked loud, warm breeze in his hair, doing his usual route. The "usual route" took him north of town where the pavement turned to gravel and dirt roads, then on a heading due west, deeper into "farm country", and finally back through the small downtown, just past the old drugstore where he used to spend his childhood reading comics.

First along that route was the old brick-colored ranch style home that belonged to Pete Brennan – the first and last guy he always picked up and dropped off. Pete was a giant of a guy and had been since he could remember, and one of the only kids he knew who had a beard by the time he was twelve. He couldn't remember the exact day that they became friends, but it was shortly after the birthday party he watched Pete singlehandedly clean the clocks of three bullies who'd been picking on him.

Not being a very big guy, John liked having Pete around, and that, right there, was the reason he always picked him up first. It was better than having a fully-loaded gun rack in the back window of your pickup truck (which happened to be one of Pete's aspirations), and nobody gave them trouble when he was in the car.

There were few things that the stone-faced, "Mr. Olympia-in-training" took interest in, and even fewer that would make him crack a smile. That short list included: guns, weight benches, war movies, and anything violent or exploding, but beneath his tough guy mystique, John knew that had a big heart and would've done anything for any of his friends. That's why he would probably miss him the most, of all his friends who were going away after the summer.

As the gravel roads turned into dirt, and they took that course westward towards their next stop, they discussed Pete's recent enlistment in the Army. For a guy like him, with a disposition like his, the military was a perfect fit. He was going to do a four-year stint and then it was the police academy for him, which had been a more serious aspiration than the gun rack thing. Brennan's father had nearly retired from the Detroit Police Department until he was killed in the line of duty, and that cemented his son's plans to follow in his footsteps.

It was a raw deal for Pete, but at least his dad was a good guy and he had lots of fond memories of him, unlike Chad Hunter's father. They always picked up Chad next, not just because he was on the way back into town, but because his house turned into a war zone after dark.

John had known him the longest of any of his friends, having met him only a month after moving to his dad's. Kirk Hunter, his father, grew up with John's father, and the pair used to run the neighborhood group of toughs back in the sixties. They used to wear leather jackets, put as much grease in their hair as in their hotrods, and were constantly in trouble with the law. At some point, his dad grew up and became a family man, but Chad's father just became an older roughneck, unable to let go of his wild youth.

His drinking became heavier, his temper quicker, and his police jacket thicker. Kirk alternated rehab and jail, and it seemed that if he wasn't in a bottle, he was in a cell most of the time. When he was home, he was a bitter, broken down man, who remembered days too fondly that he'd should've let go of, and took it out on his son. For that reason, Chad Hunter was a regular guest at the Chapel house, and they'd practically grown up together more like brothers than friends.

Hunter was a pretty good guy, considering his environment, but he had his own rebellious streak that he'd inherited from his father, and was no stranger to the local authorities. In his defense, however, they'd been keeping a close eye on him since he was old enough to ride a bike (or steal one) because of his father's reputation in that town. Chad might've turned out much differently if he'd been given a fair chance to begin with, but he played the cards he'd been dealt, and he always managed to have the winning hand.

Despite growing up in a household like that, Chad had managed to be one of the most popular kids at school, the quarterback of the varsity team, a state champ wrestler, and maintained high enough grades to get a scholarship to an art school on the west side of the state. He was tall, clear-eyed, and had a smile that could convince most girls to go out with him (at least once) and most of the guys to do something they shouldn't (at least once), and John was glad to have him on their side.

He came running down the driveway to meet them, dodging a thrown whiskey bottle and pulling on his leather jacket in one fluid maneuver. Pete already had the back door opened for him to hop into the car, just in case Hunter's dad decided to chase him all the way to the end of the drive. Before the door was even closed, John was throwing gravel with the back tires and they were speeding off towards civilization again.

The conversation was always predictable with him as well. His first comment was about the car and asking when the hell he was going to finish painting it, to which his response was always something pertaining to not having the money. Hunter had been the one who'd helped him restore the old thing, so he had a right to rag him about it. For the last three years, the three of them – John, his dad, and Chad – had spent long hours in the garage trying to bring the old heap to life like three mad scientists. Before that, it sat in a barn on his grandfather's property for thirty years, rusting and housing squirrel nests.

That car was the reason John never had more than ten dollars in his pocket for Saturday nights like this one. He'd taken a job with his uncle at his machine shop, working every night after school, just to finish the car. As part of his pay, he was able to use the equipment and he got a substantial discount on parts. There wasn't enough money for a professional paint-job, however, and eight cans of flat black primer had replaced the rosy rust color for the time being. The boys were still excited to show up at school with it that first day, and even though it looked like a dull, black tank, it was the coolest car in the lot.

The next comment out of Hunter's mouth was always directed at Pete's attire, which always consisted of straight leg jeans, motorcycle boots, and a black tee shirt stretched tightly over his chest and to showcase his big arms. Pete would look over his shoulder at him, raise a brow, and take a crack at his need to wear the stupid leather jacket despite it being nearly eighty degrees.

Hunter loved that jacket. It belonged to his dad when he was a younger street tough, and it was the one thing he prized. A few years back, the guys had been infatuated with old stories of

73

John and Hunter's dads riding around on motorcycles and roughing up guys in sweaters (just like the book they were reading in class) so they adopted an *Outsiders* motif. Each of them dressed in tee shirts and jeans, slicked their hair back, and donned leather jackets. John and Hunter's were the coolest, of course, because they were authentic "greaser" jackets.

They would listen to old fifties and sixties rock n' roll, watch old movies with Brando and James Dean, and raided the antique shop uptown for all of its related nostalgia and collectables. Thank goodness that fad passed (for most of them), because the local cops might've started giving them more attention than they were already getting. Hunter still held onto that jacket and those "glory days" of the "Outsiders", and made himself a target for the jokes, so John didn't feel bad for him once Pete opened up on him.

By the time they reached the first traffic light coming back into town, he usually had to intervene in their bickering and attempt to change the subject. It was no accident that their third stop was in front of the small duplex where Jeremy Connelly lived. If there was one good way to change the subject and make Hunter and Brennan call a temporary truce, it was by letting Connelly in the car.

The only one to ever break Hunter's detention record, yards carrying a ball record, and number of girls charmed into bed record was Jeremy Connelly. He also knew as much about guns as Pete, and could beat him at quoting cheesy action movie lines – which nobody ever thought was possible. By rights, they both should've each found a kindred spirit in Connelly, but for some reason, they both despised him. They would trade whispers back and forth about his more perfect hair and teeth, or how he couldn't bench as much as Pete and had most likely exaggerated the number of fights he'd won.

Their school had been his fourth in three years, and he'd supposedly been kicked out because he didn't like guys talking about his hair or his fight record. There was also some rumor about some scandal with a couple of the teacher's daughters as being the reason his transcripts were quickly processed to other school districts. John didn't doubt that, as he'd watched the way he was around women – of all ages – and even when he was caught red handed in the middle of something really bad, he would flash that smile and somehow get out of it.

He had become aptly named "The Con Man", a shortened version of his last name, and no one ever called him Jeremy. Con had a way of turning things around on you, and making you think a good situation was bad, a bad one good, and a very bad one was always your idea and never his. If not for him, he would say, Hunter wouldn't always be trying to think up bigger and better stunts to outdo him, and Pete wouldn't stay on top of his game with the movie quotes, trying to beat him. In a way, he was right, he kept the whole gang on their toes, and John couldn't imagine the group without him.

The only person they seemed to like less than Connelly was his cousin, Jackson Beck, or "J.B." for short. There was no particular reason why they should've liked him less; he was a clean cut kid with manners, good posture, and perfect grades. In fact, there wasn't a nicer guy at the school than J.B., but Josh, their last stop and resident comic book expert, always said he was a "Captain America trapped in the X-Men", whatever that meant.

John, Chad, and Connelly had spent more than their share of time in detention, but J.B. hadn't seen a single minute there his entire tenure at their school. In fact, he was always trying to keep the rest of the group out of detention, always pointing out the dangers and possible legalities of each bad idea Connelly or Hunter came up with. For that reason, J.B. was left out of the group when they decided to vandalize a fellow student's house, or when they wanted to go traipsing through cemeteries at midnight just for fun.

Pete and Hunter would stop gossiping and teaming up on Con, and immediately include him once his cousin got in the car. This, again, was no mistake or accident in John's route, and every seat was filled as part of a larger plan. He wanted the rest of the group to accept Connelly, and that could only be done by finding someone they liked even less. J.B. was a natural leader and very charismatic, so he needed to be kept off balance so he wouldn't be tempted to try to take control of the group from John – who was their unofficial leader.

It wasn't that he was the smartest, the best-looking, the toughest, or could even come up with the best Friday night plans, it was simply that he was the glue that held them all together. Without him, there was no group, and they rest would go their separate ways. In any other universe, where the laws of "cliques" and "natural selection" applied, that group would never be seen together in the same physical space. With John, they seemed to be able to bend the laws of physics and do things they wouldn't normally be able to individually.

He'd known how to utilize each of their specific talents and put them to the best use in any given situation, right down to planning the perfect pickup schedule that was genius in its execution. Only Connelly, who knew the art of manipulation and coercion, could see exactly what John had done, and he never made mention of it, but he respected him for it. He hadn't noticed that there was a pattern to everything John did, including their routine weekend route, until they made their last stop at Josh Allen's apartment one Saturday night.

Almost two years younger than the rest and six inches shorter, Josh stuck out like a sore thumb in the group. He dressed in clothing that was too baggy for his small frame, was awkward even sitting still, and nobody in that car knew why John Chapel kept a kid like that around. If there was a physical opposite of Hunter, Josh was it. His skin was pasty white, he wasn't at all physically imposing, and he pulled in fewer girls than Pete. He typically spoke too slowly to get a word in when the other guys were prattling on, and as a result, he would bring a comic rolled up in his back pocket to read for the trip into town.

It was his way of not being noticed, and John had already set the stage for him not to be noticed, by pitting the others against one another. Josh was just part of the backdrop, and that's the way John wanted it, to protect him. Connelly was great at reading people, and he had always known that there was another, quieter side to his friend John Chapel – possibly a side like Josh Allen exhibited freely but one that John kept hidden. He was into the comics, the artsy stuff and the goofy stuff Josh liked, so it was possible that there were days when John just liked to hang out with Josh and be himself.

He gave Josh a smile as he approached the car, hardly noticed by the others who were deeply engaged in another brainless discussion, and he wondered what secrets John had imparted with him that he hadn't with the rest. No doubt, a quiet kid like that who rarely talked to anybody was the best sort to tell your darkest secrets to. By rights, John wouldn't have trusted

Hunter, J.B. or even himself to tell those sorts of things to, and Pete, well, he just wasn't the right kind of guy to discuss serious matters of the heart with.

Connelly knew, through whispers in the group, that there was something troubling about his childhood that he never spoke of, and that intrigued him. He liked humbling Hunter with his bigger scores and scorecard, and giving Pete a run for him money on his movie quotes, but the fact that he might not be the only one with a rough past was a bit humbling in its own way. Since he'd become aware of the odd relationship between John and Josh, he'd been a lot friendlier to the youngest in the group, trying to discover what secret he'd entrusted him with.

In less than four hours, they would all find out.

After the last of the group piled into the back, John jammed on the accelerator and raced up the street towards their last stop. He'd driven that same stretch concrete, passed the same old places in town, and spent many Saturday nights with the same carload of friends, but there was something else mixed in with the kiss of that night air against his cheeks that he just couldn't place yet.

It was probably the welcome kiss of freedom and adulthood he tasted, becoming a man and leaving childish things behind, and as a young man, kisses of freedom were no longer innocent pecks, but something that probed its tongue in your mouth and made your insides catch fire.

Minutes later, they came roaring into the parking lot of the *Ice Cream Caboose*, which was already jam-packed with the usual cars and faces. Ever since they had been able to peddle their bikes around town, that place had been a popular hangout for the "cool kids", and they looked forward to the day that they could park cars of their own and sit on the hoods to hoot at the girls.

John remembered that first night they came tearing into the lot with the dull black tank-car and the younger kids on their bikes stared at them with envy. The excitement of being a "big shot" had worn off about the fifth visit, and the excitement of hooting at the same girls wore off not long after that. At least it did for him, Con and Hunter still looked like two dogs that were taken for an exciting car ride to get treats, their tongues hanging out and their heads hanging out the windows.

Before the car even came to a complete stop, those boys were popping the back doors open and halfway across the lot, focused on different groups of girls. JD always took his time surveying the crowd to single out the girl he wanted to talk to, and then coolly stepped from the car to make his approach. John quietly took his place on the warm hood with Josh and Pete leaned against the car crossing him arms, which were their usual positions.

The three of them weren't as eager to soak up the attention as the rest. Pete Brennan went along to hang out with the guys, and Josh could've cared less if he talked to a girl or not - he'd had a girlfriend on and off for some time, and he really wasn't as "slick" with the girls anyway. John usually sat on the hood, watching his three friends from afar, seeing which was making the most progress, and then would go to join them. He didn't seem very eager to leave the hood that night, though, and both Josh and Pete noticed that something was off about him.

Even when some of the girls tried to wave him over, running through his list of aliases: "Chappy", "Cap" and "Johnny", he gave them an unenthusiastic wave and remained on the hood. The first two were variations of his last name, and "Johnny" had stuck with him during their *Outsiders* phase, in which each of them adopted a name from the book.

"Pony Boy" chuckled beside him and turned to "Darry", saying, "Uh oh, J.B. is going to cry if they keep calling Johnny with *his* call sign."

"Yea," Pete snorted. "He'll be wearing that damned *Captain America* shirt again. How long did he wear it last time?"

"I think he had it on for a week straight," Josh grumbled. "I never should've told him that."

"Yea, it wasn't meant as a compliment," Pete snickered. "We know who the *Captain* is anyway – John will always be Cappy."

"Personally, I don't like the nicknames," John said.

"Don't like 'em?" Josh seemed surprised.

"Hunter and Con fought over who was 'Soda Pop' for months, remember?"

"Yea, and now we have Connelly's stupid *Regulator* crap!" Pete added.

"You're the one who insisted we go see the movie, Pete," John reminded him.

"At least nobody is wearing a cowboy hat," Josh laughed. "We got too carried away with the greaser stuff, and I'm glad that phase is over."

"It's over for *some* of us. Hunter will never get rid of that jacket or stop calling me Johnny."

"It's not a bad nickname," Pete reassured him. "It's pretty ambiguous."

"Yea, until Con starts shouting out 'let's do it for Johnny', and everyone remembers that line from the movie," John complained.

"It's still not as annoying as him doing the Regulator call," Pete reaffirmed. "I'm sure we'll get to hear that no fewer than fifteen times before we leave this parking lot."

"Which can't come soon enough," John snipped, hopping down from the hood, heading towards Connelly's group of people.

Pete and Josh shared a puzzled look and shrugged their shoulders, and watched him walk across the lot, where they tended never to go. He didn't stop to talk to Con or any of the girls surrounding him being entertained by his antics. Instead, he continued on to the front door of the ice cream parlor and bought a couple of sodas, then returned to the hood of the car to pass them out. Jeremy gave him an equally puzzled look, but continued talking to the girls.

John uncapped his soda and took a long drink from the ice cold bottle and made a comment about how he liked how cold the Ice Cream Caboose kept their drinks. Pete and Josh exchanged glances again, and it was the latter who finally addressed their friend's odd behavior.

"This is like our big night out, Johnny, and your first weekend that you guys are all free. I'm kind of surprised you're not out there putting on your usual show with one of the guys."

He glanced over his shoulder at his youngest friend and squinted his eyes, as if he'd just spoken a foreign language or his eyesight was going bad. With his pseudo-rockabilly haircut, his tee shirt and jeans ensemble, and that expression, it really made him look more like James Dean than ever. Hunter, of course, insisted that he looked the most like Dean, but in fact, the rest of them knew that Johnny could've almost played him in a movie. When his hair had been shorter, sure Hunter had it pegged, but since he'd grown it out, he had him beat hands down – and Chad was more of a Brando anyway.

"Yea, what's the problem, Cappy, you don't like chicks anymore?" Pete asked.

"What's wrong? It's like Josh said: this is our first big night of freedom, and yet, here we are at a fucking ice cream place, talking to the same old chicks, doing the same old bullshit!"

They were both kind of taken aback by his cursing and outburst, and Pete awkwardly tried to justify their Saturday evening plans. "Well yea, we're here *now*, Chappy, but this is where we always start. I'm sure one of the guys is coming up with a party or something for us to go to."

"Like the parties we always go to with the same old faces and the trio of idiots picking up the same chicks while we're sitting around talking amongst ourselves because we're bored to tears? One of *those* parties?"

Pete leaned back against the car, folding his arms, and bowing out of the conversation, knowing that what John was saying was how they all felt, and he couldn't argue with him.

"I have a journal sitting in the top drawer of my nightstand at home that has pages and pages of our 'adventures' from the past ten years – all good times, and I wouldn't trade those times for the world. But there are empty pages in there just waiting to be filled with more good memories, not the same old shit we've already done."

Josh wasn't sure where all of this was coming from. Maybe it was the fact that time was running out for them, and in a month or two, all of them would be scattered to the four winds. Or it could've been the same thing that he talked with him about the other day that was making him restless, and the secret they never talked about with anyone else. He'd thought that his friend was just venting and since forgotten about her, but how could he when he saw her name every morning that he opened his eyes. It was scrawled beneath the top bunk, and he was the only other person that knew it was there.

"So what do you want to do, John?" Josh asked quietly.

"My grandfather spent *his* first summer after school in France, fighting Nazis for three years and trying to get back to his girl in the states. My father spent *his* on the streets of Detroit, fighting alongside bikers and greasers against other bikers and

80

greasers and rode off into the sunset with my mom on the back of his bike. Me? I'm sitting in the parking lot and there isn't a Nazi or a greaser in sight!"

Pete scrunched up his brows, asking, "You want to…go start a fight somewhere?"

John let out a long sigh, hopping off the hood again, "No! It's not about the fighting!" He stomped off about ten feet from the car, whirled and jabbed his finger at them as he nearly shouted, "And you know what? I don't even mind nicknames – *Outsiders*, *Regulators* or otherwise – it's just that we've never done anything but whoop and holler them across the parking lot of a drugstore!"

He'd gotten the attention of his friends by then, and all of them turned to see what the yelling was about. J.B. and Hunter resumed their flirting, but Con excused himself and came over to see what was going on with the guys at the car.

"What's going on, Johnny?"

"Nothing, Con," he said, shaking his head, with his hands on his hips.

"Cap is sick of sitting here doing nothing with a bunch of nobodies, "Pete said.

"*Nobodies?*"

"Okay yea, Con, we're fed up with sitting here in this nothing town and watching you guys talk to the same recycled, nobody chicks."

"Those girls are hot, Johnny--"

"I don't care! Are there any of them here you *haven't* talked to yet? I mean, the only way you'll find *new* girls is by waiting until the under-aged ones become legal, and I don't plan on sitting here and waiting that long!"

"Shit, Johnny, what brought this on?"

"Just look around you Con; is this what you want to do with the rest of our last summer together?"

He did exactly that, turning a full circle, and when his gaze met John's, there was a look of understanding and awareness. "No, you're right; we can do better than this. Give me five minutes; I think I have just the thing."

Con walked back towards the group he was talking to minutes before, and then returned with a yellow flyer in his hand, waving it at them. He handed it to him without saying a word, and let him read it.

"Where did you get this?"

"Girl over there...she's the cousin or something of one of the girls I used to go out with and she's here from out of town. They're going to this thing. I think it might be cool. You need a change of scenery - I think we all do - so let's do it."

"What about Hunter and JB? Will they go for this?"

Con nodded, "If the other girls are going, there will be some familiar faces there to keep them entertained. But I'm with you, this place is getting stale, some new blood would be good for us."

At that point, Hunter and JB came walking over with a couple of girls in tow, to see what the private meeting was all about. When Connelly showed them the flyer, they seemed to not be as excited about it as the rest, and the girls were less-than-enthused because it meant serious competition. After several minutes of debate, taking an accounting of their money situation, and deciding that it was a gamble on all fronts, the only one who still wasn't on board was Hunter.

Going to a new place where his reputation wouldn't follow and spending money on an "unsure" thing seemed like a bad idea. Connelly had to his best salesman pitch, challenging his ego, his manhood and his sense of adventure to get him to consider getting back in the car. When that didn't work, they threatened to leave him by himself at the *Caboose*, and then he had no choice.

They still had to endure Con's obnoxious "Regulator call" as they set out, and Hunter's whining for the duration of the trip south on I-75, but the mood of the entire group shifted once they left the confines of their small town. The cabin of the old car was filled with something electric as they neared their destination and the promise of a new adventure in a new place. Even Hunter stopped bellyaching once they pulled into the giant parking lot of the old skate arena-turned-nightclub.

Chapter 7

The entire *Ice Cream Caboose* and all of its patrons wouldn't have filled a tenth of the lot they were trying to find a space in, and the boys were on sensory overload, trying to turn their heads fast enough to get a look at all the girls. They certainly put most of the girls from their hometown to shame, and the jaws of Hunter and JB suddenly fell slack.

"Holy shit!" was all Hunter could blurt out.

"Hey I *remember* this place!" John exclaimed. "I used to skate here when I was a kid!"

Jeremy was the first out of the car, "Me too - Just a few years ago!"

John laughed, "You skated a *few* years ago? I was like *seven* the last time I was here!"

"I'm telling you, this is the place to be," he reassured them. "Just wait 'til we get inside."

John led his group to the front door of the club and was immediately bombarded by loud music, perfume and beautiful people everywhere he looked. The lobby was packed full of people, and it wasn't even ten o'clock yet. They paid at the old ticket window to get through the second set of doors, where there were even more people.

"Holy shit!" the rest of them repeated Hunter's assessment of the place.

Inside, the room opened up into a large arena that had been the skating rink at one time, and was now a dance floor. Bodies were packed on the floor already, and guys took their places around the railing to watch the girls like wild dingoes looking for a wounded animal to take down. John went to the concession stand and bought a soda and Josh followed with him, leaving the others to stand gawking in the middle of the entryway.

John leaned against the wall near the concessions to do his own gawking. Con had been right; these people *were* good looking and everyone was dressed in expensive, designer outfits, had their hair perfect (he touched his to be sure it hadn't moved), and wore lots of jewelry.

Josh met up with him after he paid for his soda, "What do you think man? Is this the place to be? A lot classier than back home right?"

His oldest friend nodded and chewed on a piece of ice, "There's *class* alright - *too much* class. What the hell are *we* doing here man? They're gonna' sniff us out as a bunch of poor farm kids, we have no chance here. We shoulda' stayed home; the guys were right."

He had to almost yell over the loud dance music that was throbbing in their ears from the giant speakers all around the dance floor. "This was the right move, I'm telling you! We're in a better place, and things are going to *happen* here tonight."

Sipping his soda, he moved fearlessly towards the crowd, leaving John behind to marvel at his friend's sudden confidence. He had never been much more outgoing or social than Pete Brennan, but then again, maybe Josh had never been able to "stretch his legs" in that group. He chuckled to himself as he watched his protégé move through the crowd talking to girls. They were talking back to him like he was someone that belonged there.

Looking back towards the usual Con, Hunter, JB trio, he saw that they hadn't even formulated a plan for moving from their spot yet, and watching them squirm in the bigger "pond" they'd just been dumped into was truly enjoyable.

Pete was content to find a spot on the wall by John and watch as his friends prepared to crash and burn. He shared a big grin with his old friend as they watched Josh put the first points on the "scoreboard", fully engaged in a flirty conversation with an attractive, younger blonde. They noticed Hunter staring through the crowd at him, and watched his motivation go into overdrive. The second point on the board soon followed as he grabbed the attention of a tall and thin brunette.

They spied JB not long after, trying to put two points on the board, talking to two different girls at once. He was flashing them that irresistible smile and using his boyish good looks to their full capacity. John was almost sad that things had quickly resumed to normal, despite throwing them into a strange environment, and shook his head at them as he watched them from his wall. He was just glad for Josh and that the long shadow those three others cast wasn't falling over him for once, and he looked like he was actually having fun, no matter the score.

Never to be outdone, however, it was Connelly's fashion to always one-up the others in every situation. That night was no exception as he suddenly came barreling through the tightly-packed crowd towards the two of them. There was an expression on his face, like he had either won the lottery or seen a ghost - they weren't sure which - and he was on a mission of utmost importance.

"You guys have to come right now!" He demanded, tugging at John's shirt.

"I'm not done with my pop!" Pete bellyached.

"Okay your loss. John, you have to see this!" He said with urgency.

"What's going on?"

Connelly had him by the arm and was leading him back into the crowd before he'd even begun to explain himself, "I just found the two hottest girls you've ever seen in your life! They're just sitting alone over here and I told them I had a friend!"

On the other side of sweaty, undulating bodies Connelly pulled him to safety. He was fixing his hair and wiping other people's sweat from his arms as introductions were made, "Johnny, this is Gwenn and what was *your* name again?"

"Melinda," she introduced herself with a flirtatious wave.

"That's right, this is Melinda!" Connelly repeated in a voice that was muffled out by the sound of John Chapel's heart pounding erratically and the ice in his mouth being turned to dust as he clamped his jaw down like a vise.

On a normal day, in a normal crowd, anywhere else in the world, John would never have been able to single her out. However, they were in her city, and the girl sitting next to her was a dead giveaway with her auburn-red hair, light freckles and ruddy complexion. She grinned at him, and her amber eyes twinkled at him. It wasn't a smile of recognition; it was a flirty, come-hither smile that he had never seen the girl wear before. He looked from Gwenn to Melinda, and neither of them seemed to recognize him.

An eternity filled with muted voices, bile creeping up his throat, and tingling extremities followed as he could only stare at the both of them. He wondered if he had really woken up that morning or if he was still at home in his bed. "Surreal" didn't even begin to describe the moment, and "complete paralysis" would have been the most accurate term to describe John's reaction.

He finally regained his senses halfway through a polite string of questions: "...where are you from Johnny? What school do you go to?"

His hearing had returned but his voice was still lost somewhere amidst the bile. He continued to stare blankly and Connelly nudged him to remind him that she was talking to him, but all that he could do was take her in.

Her hair was parted in the middle, and spilled down over her shoulders, a hint of the tiny ringlets she once had still present. Her cheeks had formed perfect angles, completing a nice triangular shape to her face. The eyes that once seemed too big for her face finally were proportionate, but they were still as blue as the Mediterranean, and even more so because of the dark hues that she accentuated them with. Her lips were full and broad and her mouth was filled with the perfect, white teeth, which was a family trait. Her face was radiant and glowing, and made his legs want to give way.

She was wearing a revealing top with thin straps that crisscrossed over bronzed shoulders, and the rounded flesh that threatened to spill over in the front was something new. John had seen more than one pair of breasts in his day, some belonging to girlfriends and others airbrushed in garage calendars, but hers were more impressive than any photo touch-up could even come close to.

A bare, flattened tummy was exposed on the bottom half, a dark horizontal cross stretched across it where her belly button intersected with a thin crease of her flesh that was created from her leaning forward. She noticed it and seemed subconscious about it, so she leaned back to rest on her elbows and to eliminate the tiny fold, and threw her legs out in front of her.

She crossed her ankles and wiggled them back and forth in unison, so that his attention was drawn further down her long frame. The shorts she was wearing only covered the very tops of them, the rest were stretched out in full view for him to admire. He followed the legs down to the very bottom, where her toes were painted a pink pearl color and were strapped in with high-heeled sandals, and that ended his tour.

"He's not from around here." Connelly spoke for his friend who was still in a daze.

"Do you have a camera?" Melinda asked, playfully chewing her gum and leaning back on her elbows on the large, round ottoman.

"Huh?" John managed.

"If you have a *camera*, you can take a picture instead of standing there and looking me up and down for an hour."

John's face turned red, and he retreated back into the crowd, too embarrassed and nervous to say a word to her. He felt like his head was going to burst, or quite possibly his stomach might go first. Connelly excused his friend and then excused himself, then dove back into the crowd after him.

"Dude, what is *with* you? She is hot, but she's not *that* hot!" He called after John, who was making a beeline like a charging rhino to get through the sweaty bodies again. He pulled him off to the side, cutting a corner of the dance floor, and spun him around. "Johnny! What's wrong with you man, you look like you're going to throw up?"

"*You* go talk to them…on second thought, don't go talk to them; leave them alone. Maybe the red-head…wait, no…neither one." Then he pulled his arm free from his grip and kept moving, back towards the concession stand.

"Dude, what's wrong with *those* chicks? I know they're hot, and they've got money, but you can't let that get in your head. If we play this right, we never have to slum it back home again!"

"Nothing is *wrong* with them, nothing at all! They're hot, they're beautiful, and yes, they have money - lots of it! But neither of us is talking to them. Do you understand? Let's round up the guys and go back home and try to salvage the remainder of the night."

Connelly frowned at him and stepped closer, taking on his most serious expression, "Are you losing your cool bro? Are you wussing out on me? I need a wingman for these girls. You're a *Regulator* man, and Regulators don't bail on their wingmen! You're going back there with me, and we're gonna' talk to them. Which one do you want?"

"Connely, *Regulators* don't have *wingmen*! That's *two* different movies, and it doesn't make any damned sense! You can do it without me if you're really that stuck on those girls, and I'm not going back there to *pick one* I want like a *pair of shoes!*"

With that, he turned and walked right into the blonde that was standing right behind him, and he ended up nose-to-nose with her, staring into the sparkling Mediterranean.

"Well at least one of you has some manners. Hi, I'm Melinda, we met over there," she said, extending her hand.

He wanted to run away or at the very least, pull his shirt up over his face and coil up into a little ball on the floor, but he was trapped by an innocent-looking handshake. He finally took her hand and smiled, "My friends call me *Cap*," he croaked out.

She wrinkled one brow. "What kind of name is that?"

He laughed nervously, "Don't ask."

"Yea...so the whole thing where you got red-faced and stumbled back through the dance floor...was that an act so we would follow you or were you really embarrassed and shy?" She asked, pulling him away from the loud speakers, her fingers firmly on his. It gave him gooseflesh and the hairs rose on his neck, just feeling her skin against his.

"Because I thought that was cute," she continued. "Gwenn and I have had like twenty different guys try to come up and use slick lines, flash their jewelry and money for us, and that didn't work out so well for them. No one has tried undressing me with his eyes and then stumble away and not even tell me his name yet. Does that work on a *lot* of girls?"

He just continued to turn deeper red as he tried to untangle the tongue in his mouth.

"I'm sorry if I insulted you...I don't know what to say...you just look...well...really nice."

She continued to drag him outside of the deafening range of the speakers, leading him back towards the concessions area. "Buy me a pop and we'll sort it out."

Jeremy excused himself but neither of them heard him, "Well, I'm gonna' go keep Gwenn company then since you two need time to talk ok?"

Ten minutes later they were sitting at a table in the old cafeteria and talking the night away. He was sitting three feet away from the girl who had been both his best friend and the love of his young life, and she didn't even realize it. He didn't want to say a word to her, in the fear that she would recognize him just by his voice, despite it having changed over the years. As he listened to her, he tried to figure out a way to tell her the truth, and he would need to stall her until he could think of the right words.

"So, where's all your jewelry? And where's your jumpsuit? All the guys wear their walker wear these days, they must have been all out at the store when you got there huh?" She had her own little variety of humor and John liked hearing it.

He laughed and played along, "Yea, actually that guy over there took all of my walker wear out of the trunk of my tricked-out Mazda with the pimp lights on the bottom and the six foot fin on the back. Did you see that when you pulled in?"

"Yea I think I did! Was it the green neon or the purple neon?"

John replied straight-faced, "Mine actually has the black neon-you can't see it, but the pink fur-trimmed tires are hard to miss."

She laughed and crunched loudly on the ice leftover from her drink.

"Sexually frustrated?" he asked.

"I dunno why?" She looked up at him under dark lids and played with her straw as she chomped away.

"You're chewing your ice, that's either a life-long bad habit or it means you're frustrated in some way, usually sexually."

She winked at him and said, "I'll let you know some day. I don't know you well enough yet. I guess you're the authority - I watched you chewing on yours earlier. Where did you say you were from?"

He itched the back of his head and said, "I didn't...really. You were watching me earlier?"

She took another mouthful of ice. "Yea I saw you over here with your friend."

"We call him *Con* - short for Connelly - it's his last name. He likes to be called *Con-man*, but I still call him Jeremy, or just Con, it's...a stupid inside thing. Why were you watching me?"

"Oh, is that his *Top Gun* handle?"

"I'll tell you some day." He winked back at her and took a cupful of his own ice.

"I was watching you because I hate guys in gold chains and jumpsuits...I like boys in tight jeans and t-shirts. You and your friends at least know how to dress. So...*Cap*...what's that short for?"

John went quiet. He didn't want the night to end so quickly and for their conversation to go that way just yet. "It's not really either...a derivative I suppose...anyway, what school do you go to?"

"*Athens, Troy.* You?"

"Umm is that like Greek? Athens and Troy were two totally different cities..."

"Is that *like* History? You didn't answer the question - where do you go?"

"I don't *go* anymore, I graduated. Does that mean we can't talk now?"

"Ooh, an *older* man? How long ago? Are you in college now, or do you have a wife and kids?"

"Will it improve my chances if I'm forty-seven and have three kids?"

"It might." She winked at him again.

"I just graduated this year, I'm not *that* old."

"Where you graduate from? Anywhere I've heard of?"

"Probably not; it's this little hillbilly town place up north."

Her face soured, and he knew that she was beginning to place the facts together. There was a comfortable familiarity to him, that's why she initially followed him, but now the facts were starting to fall into place, and he could tell where her mind was going.

"You have a summer birthday?"

"Nope, I turned eighteen in February."

"Hmm....so what's your sign?"

He had to think on that one, luckily he knew astrology pretty well, and pretty much everyone in his family had a birthday in a different month of the year. "I'm a water sign..."

"Which?" Her blue eyes were piercing through him, as if peeling back the layers of the years on his face to see the little boy that she once knew.

"Pisces. Why? Are you a Zodiac nut?"

"Signs tell you a lot about a person, sometimes more than *they* tell you."

"You're out of ice; what now?" John changed the subject.

"We dance!" She slammed her empty cup down. "Or we can go get more ice?"

"We can get some to cool us off...afterwards," he said, dragging her back to the dance floor.

Within minutes, there was enough moisture on that floor to cool them down, and their glistening bodies pressed so tightly together that water flowed between them. It trickled down the back of her neck, spilling onto his arm that was draped across her back, and formed in the valley of her bosom that she brushed up against him, so that her scent would linger on his shirt long after they'd parted.

The entire time, their eyes were drinking one another in like their clothing drew in the vapor from their bodies. He wondered if it was the last time he would see her, and he could see that same fear in her eyes, as well as the flame of recognition trying to light. They were both trying to hold onto something that was elusive, like the words at the periphery of their tongues, trying to find those epiphanies. His mind was racing to find the right words so that he wouldn't lose her again, and hers, no doubt, was trying to place those haunting eyes of his..

They flirted and danced ever closer to the truth, but each time they were close to discovering each other, something stopped them. John would press his mouth close to her ear to say the words he was struggling with, but she would turn or twist just out of reach at the wrong moment. Melinda's own lips brushed his cheek, so close to his own, and someone would bump her and she retreated from her daring move. She never realized that he was trying to say anything in her ear, just as he never realized how close he was to kissing her.

When the music slowed and their world with it, he finally had the chance to tell her what he'd wanted, and he was no longer moving too quickly for her to kiss him. But they each seemed to have missed their moment, and fear made them hesitate. She didn't normally try to kiss boys she'd just met, and he realized the appropriate place to have the discussion he needed wasn't at an old roller rink. So, they both resigned themselves to just enjoying the rest of the evening and seeing what happened when that hour came when they had to part.

Neither wanted their moment taken from them, both secretly appreciating moments like this one, and knowing it could be taken in an instant. Inevitably, someone always ruins it though. The first time, it had been their mothers, and the second it was their friends.

"Get a room you guys!" Gwenn and Jeremy interrupted them, laughing as they danced past.

John laughed as he noted how much different she looked since last he had seen her. Poor little "Gwenny" had turned into "not-so-awkward-and-kind-of-hot Gwenn" since she had discovered makeup and tanning. The freckles faded and her hair color had toned down to a nice auburn-red. She and Jeremy had decided to make the most of being abandoned, and were dancing with one another, clowning it up.

A little sad that their private spot on the dance floor had been violated by their comedic friends, John stepped away and excused himself to grab some water. Connelly went with him, so that they could talk about the girls and so that they could talk about them. John listened to him prattle on about Gwenn and he nodded as if he was interested, but surveyed the room for the others.

Scanning the room, he saw Hunter and JB sitting at a table with three girls - not the same three girls from earlier – so he wasn't sure of who had the best final score. Not far from their table, Josh still sat with the same girl and was sitting on the same side of the booth with her - so things were going well for him obviously. Pete, of course, was waiting at his "post" by the front door already, planning their exit strategy. He was already checking his watch, and John glanced up at the giant clock on the wall.

It was twenty past midnight and almost closing time, and that meant two things; one, that two hours of time with Melinda had gone too quickly, and two, that Pete would be getting impatient and begin trying to round them up. Everyone looked happy though, and the night had gone better than he ever could have imagined. John reveled in the moment, and subconsciously glanced back at Melinda.

Her face shone like a star in the crowd behind them, and he could tell that she was happy by the beaming smile she flashed at him. He wanted so badly to tell her who he was, not hiding behind the familiar anonymity that had drawn her to him, but he didn't want to watch that star burn out just yet. Though he was uncertain how she might react, there was still a certainty that the entire mood of the evening would change. There would be a scene - whether good or bad - and he didn't want their reunion to involve a scene.

The whole dilemma was making him anxious and nervous. Only Josh, who knew the whole story, would have any kind of good advice for him, and he needed to get him away from the girl he was talking to just for a few minutes.

He and Con sipped at large cups of ice water talking about the girls as his stare was fixed on Josh, hoping that he would look up. The girls followed suit, drinking their ice water, staring at the two of them as they also chattered, giggling every few minutes. The blonde across the concession area had Josh's full attention and he was oblivious to his friends watching him.

"Did we hit the jackpot or what?" Connelly asked.

He'd been talking for some time, but John hadn't heard much of what he'd said preceding that ridiculous question. He wrinkled up his face at him and shook his head, then returned to his attempt at using sheer will to grab Josh's attention.

"What's your problem tonight? You wanted to come here, we score the two hottest girls in the whole place, and you act like someone died."

"I can talk about it right now, Con! We shouldn't have come…I shouldn't be here."

"So you weren't having the time of your life dancing with that girl out there? I've never, in all the years I've known you, seen you that thrilled about any girl! Now you're saying that you shouldn't have come? Is this about your little secret with Josh?"

"I can't lose her! I have to talk to her but I don't know how," he struggled to explain his situation in agitated fragments that only confused his friend more.

"Lose her? She's totally into you! Look at them falling over themselves talking about us!"

"You don't understand," John blurted out, slamming his cup down.

He needed to speak to Josh desperately, but he was intercepted by a firm hand on his arm. He was about to whirl on Jeremy and snap at him, but saw the girl with the woman's voice standing before him.

"All cooled off? Where you headed? They're playing the last song, come dance with me!"

She dragged him off to the floor and he had no choice but to follow her. To add insult to irony, Josh looked up as they brushed past the table and gave him a "thumbs up" only to receive a sour look in return.

They spent the last five minutes of the night together, though the last song was only just over four. When it ended, she stood swaying with him, humming the song that faded away. The overhead lights came on to remind them that their time was up, but Melinda kept her arms wrapped around him still, her head on his chest. She kept telling him how glad she was that he had come, that she had met him, and how it was one of the best nights she'd ever had. It only made it that much harder for him to tell her what he needed to, and what little bit of bravery he'd managed to build up during the song seeped out through his weak knees.

Most of the floor had cleared and people were filing out of the door before Gwenn and Connelly came to give them their second reminder. She tapped Melinda on the shoulder, "Come on love birds, we have to break this party up. Her mom doesn't like to wait, and she'll come in after us and make a scene!"

Melinda pulled herself away reluctantly, her fingers lingering on his shoulders and her impulsive notion to kiss him had returned. She stood very close to him still, looking up at him, trying to remember his face still. "Will I see you again? I know you're not from here...but will you come back?"

He wanted to tell her the truth right then, but he blurted, "You're so beautiful."

"Thank you?" She giggled at the compliment.

"I mean...I would like that," he said, though in his head the logistics of such a simple thing as a second meeting were seeming more impossible by the minute.

John's stomach lurched and tightened up like he was preparing for a car accident, scrambling through his options in his head. He could either let everything spill and hope for the best, or he could keep up the stranger act and start fresh with her, never telling her who he truly was. Perhaps she had forgotten about him; it had been over a decade and she'd never responded to a single call or letter he'd sent her. Maybe it was a second chance they'd been given and he wasn't supposed to tell her.

That would be deceitful though, and he would have to carry on the façade for longer than just one night. If things progressed and they became friends again, or something more, he would have to become an entirely different person and live a lie. As he scrambled with his thoughts, Pete pushed the arms of the giant clock ever forward with his roll call.

Pete began calling from the door, "Chad! Hunter! We're rolling....yea, right *now*! Where's JB? We're out of here. Yea, get her number let's go!"

He shot his large friend a warning stare from across the large hall, but there were too many faces in the way. Hunter and JB gathered by the door, and Pete moved down the list, "Josh! Finish it up!"

There was only one more on the list ahead of him, and Connelly was guaranteed to stall long enough that Pete would use every nickname he'd ever had, plus every variation of his Christian name. Then it would be his turn, and the truth would come out. All that he could think about was that day at Rain tree when he knew they were running out of time. He'd felt just as helpless now as he did then.

Pulling the yellow flyer from his back pocket, John spun around and handed it to her, "We have to go Melinda...Pete is impatient. Can I call you?"

She hesitated for a moment before snatching the paper from him. Moving behind him, she put the paper on his back and started to write. "I'm not giving this to you if you don't use it...I *hate* when people don't call. It's a *huge* peeve of mine."

"I promise I'll call you."

The authoritative baritone voice bellowed through the old rink, "Con! Connelly!"

Jeremy walked over by Gwenn to watch his worried friend secure a phone number and a second date. He called back to Pete across the thinning crowd, "Hold on a damned minute!"

"How you coming back there?" John called over his shoulder.

"I have three numbers...I don't know if I want to give you all seven. I think I need to get to know you better before I give you all the numbers." She was prolonging her time with him.

"Come on Mel, your mom's gonna' be mad if we don't hurry up," Gwenn urged her on.

The roll call kept coming. "Jeremy! We have to leave man! Johnny, you have the keys! We gotta' roll out now Cap, let's go!"

John was trying to coax Melinda into hurrying as she giggled playfully behind him, "Ooh he used your *handle* there Maverick, Haha!" She was writing slowly, "Should I make this out to *Captain Maverick?*"

"Just the number; I'll know who it's from," he said hurriedly, still trying to stare Brennan down.

His eyes were telling him to stop, and he knew where the naming went after he used Cap. They both noticed the large doorman trying to urge the others out into the entryway then, and knew that Pete would soon lose his patience.

"*Chaps*! Come on man! This guy is giving me the eye, we gotta' go!"

"Hold on a damned minute, I'm coming!" He shouted back.

Connelly started to make his way to the door to stall him so that John could say his goodbyes. Big Pete couldn't see the stare John was giving him through the large mass of bodies. Jeremy had made an effort, but didn't know that reaching the doorway with expedience was of paramount importance, so he couldn't really be blamed for what happened next.

"Chapel!!" The name echoed through the skate hall and seemed to bounce off every wall to assail the small girl behind him. John cringed and felt the pen stop moving.

"Oh my God!" came the whisper.

Melinda said it once but Gwenn kept repeating it, interspersed with "It's *him!*"

John turned slowly to face her, looking down. "I'm a *Cancer*...I'm sorry."

She held the paper out in front of her and it started to shake uncontrollably. She let it fall to the floor and never took her eyes off of his. It was half euphoric, half nauseating. She shook her head slowly at him, in disbelief. "I guess you won't need that paper, since you *won't* call"

She turned to walk away and he tried to stop her. "Mel I *tried* to--"

His mouth was slammed shut by a small, stinging hand across his chops, which rang as loudly as Pete's blunder through the halls. She jammed a small finger out at him "No more! I've heard enough lying tonight! You could've told me!"

She walked away from him and Gwenn walked with her but couldn't stop staring behind her. He bent over, picked up the paper and looked at it. There were only four numbers on it.

Josh ran over to see what was going on, "What the hell was her deal? What did you say?"

"It's what I *didn't* say..." he sighed, looking like he'd just had his soul ripped from his chest.

"What do you mean, John?"

"Melinda..." He choked out, crumpling the paper in his hand and letting it fall to the floor, watching her walk out of his life again.

ONE SUMMER, BESIDE A LAKE

"Every man loves two women; the one is the creation of his imagination And the other is not yet born."

~Khalil Ghibran

Chapter *8*

Campbell had gone to fix the pair of them a late snack and freshen up their drinks, and when he returned, he found his guest staring at the incoherent mess that covered the wall behind his desk. She had been studying one of the many drawings that were tacked there with pins and covered in colored notes. It was a sketch of a small lake, nestled among tall reeds and bent trees, with two unidentifiable shadows seated at the far edge. John had been quite an artist and was able to capture the feeling of a person or a place in his renderings quite well.

He'd looked at the scene many times himself, and allowed himself to become lost in its tranquility, trying to discern the figures that had their backs to him. She was obviously lost somewhere in that drawing, not noticing his return to the room, so he gently set the small tray on the edge of his desk to get her attention.

"Oh, sorry…I kind of zoned out there for a minute. I must be more tired than I thought," she said apologetically.

"His drawings have that effect on people I think. They almost look like real places and real people - it's hard not to get lost in them," he said, handing her glass back to her.

She stared at the ice cubes bobbing up and down in the brown liquid and smiled at him, "Are you trying to get me drunk, Jim?"

"I hardly think two drinks will get you drunk. I brought us something to eat and figured you would want something to wash it down. If you'd like a soda or something else, I can fix you anything you'd like?"

"No, the brandy is fine - it helps calm my nerves." She took a sip as she grabbed up a whole wheat cracker and a slice of Swiss, putting it eagerly into her mouth. "What is this place here? Is this where he met her?"

"I was hoping you could tell me," he said, munching on a cracker.

"How would I know? This is somewhere I've never seen…that only he saw."

"Is it? It doesn't look familiar to you at all?"

"Not really," she said, scrunching up her face. "Nowhere I've been anyway."

"Port Austin? Merrill Lake?"

She cocked her head, studying the drawing, and washed the cracker residue from her teeth with a drink of the brown stuff. There was a sour look on her face as she replied, "I haven't been in years, but I'm pretty sure this isn't Port Austin."

He sidled up beside her and studied the drawing, "You're probably right…the water, reeds, patches of sand, two figures seated nearby…it *couldn't* be Port Austin."

Gwenn picked up his sarcasm and argued further, "You see these trees here? The beach there has probably forty or fifty feet of sand, rocks and grass all around the water before you see a single tree. That much I remember. Merrill Lake has trees that hang out over the water like this drawing, but there's not really a beach to speak of."

"You're the authority Gwenn," he said, adjusting his glasses on his nose. "Then these two here have to be Nicolette and the other boy named John…but if you look closely…this girl's hair is worn straight, which was the fashion that Melinda was wearing it when they'd met again isn't it?"

"It's just a drawing. When he drew these, he couldn't tell one place from the other anyway."

Campbell smiled and returned to his seat, grabbing up two more crackers and squares of cheese. He sat and crossed his legs, grinning up at her as the cracker crumbs filled his beard. She stood with her arms folded, realizing that she had just given him ammunition.

"It doesn't mean that the place didn't exist! That's *not* what I was saying. I was just stating that John had trouble in the end sorting the two out. So what if he was overlapping his places and people in his drawings? He was doing the same thing in his daily life."

"Gwenn, your husband's notes and drawings of this other place were so convincing that I wanted to believe in them too, and Marshall invested his time and money in trying to find the place.

But you and I both know the finer details of his life so well that, if we look hard enough, we can find striking parallels can't we?"

"I'm not arguing the fact that there are similarities between the two stories where they took place, Jim, but this is *Port Austin* you're talking about: the *defining* moment of their relationship! Knowing John, I can't believe that he would miss any details whether in a drawing or written account. It's the one thing that he wouldn't have allowed to get jumbled up with the rest of that mess he had going on."

"And that's why you believe that this Nicolette existed? Because he wouldn't have allowed his memory of her to become...*diluted* in that way?"

"As much as I hate to admit it, I think his connection to her and to Port Austin was too strong."

"But you *do* believe that he was confused about the rest? You accept that his mind couldn't keep up with both places and that people he knew from his real life bled over into the other that he created?"

"I don't know. I just know that he didn't create this other girl from Melinda."

"Let's just keep comparing notes on what we know, Gwenn, and when we've finished with that, we'll determine what's what. Please continue on with the story and tell me what happened after that night of the fifteenth."

"John didn't tell you?"

"He didn't seem like he wanted to talk about it."

"I'm surprised. It was one of his all-time favorite stories."

"He didn't think it was pertinent to his case, so he tried to skip over it."

"You think it's pertinent?"

"It may be, or it might not be, I won't know until you share with me. If nothing else, it may be therapeutic for you to talk about the good days."

"Is *that* what *he* called them?"

"They weren't good days? Less complicated? Didn't you have your sights on someone else back then anyway?"

"I did, but that's only because the boy I liked was taken. I suppose they were simpler times."

Campbell smiled warmly at her, hoping it would coax the missing pieces from her. He did want to help her and thought it

103

would be good for her to talk about her late husband, but also wanted to know what she held inside.

"Well, that night was pretty awful...and the whole next week. Melinda cried in the back seat of her mom's car all the way home, while trying to not let on what it was about."

"Her mother still disliked him after all that time?"

"We didn't know for sure, John just was never talked about, and neither was Dawson - the two topics were linked. She didn't want to chance it. Anyway, she was a wreck..."

◈◈

Melinda went directly upstairs to her room when she got home that Saturday night, leaving Gwenn and her mother at the foot of the stairs. Gwenn was staying over that night in June, and she would definitely be needed for the breakdown that followed. It was the most upset she'd ever seen her best friend – even worse than the day John had been taken away – and she could only watch helplessly as her emotions ran the gamut.

There was an inconsolable sadness at first, as she threw herself on her bed, burying her face in her pillow to muffle her sobs. Following that, she composed herself long enough to show her bitterness and utter contempt for John Chapel, spouting off words like "betrayal" and "cowardice", followed by a string of curse words she said in a low voice.

Finally, after settling down and listening to Gwenn, who tried being the voice of reason, she used words like "humiliation" and "desperation" and collapsed on her bed again. Her best friend left her to sulk in her room and told her that she had two choices: stay angry the rest of her life and never see him again, or swallow her pride and hear what he had to say.

The following day, John drove back down to the city to take up his case with Gwenn, and they had a long talk about the situation. She advised that he call and smooth it over with her, but to steer clear of the Malowski house. In the meantime, she would make her best effort to act as a go-between and try to talk her out of being so stubborn.

After a week of hanging up on him, and trying to ignore Gwenn, she decided to finally hear him out. He'd written and called her after all, but her mother had never let him talk to her, so he imagined that the letters had suffered the same fate. Melinda held tears behind closed lids as she listened to his voice on the other end of the phone that first night they talked. He spoke his heart and told her that she was never far from his mind, and told her about etching her name under his bed so that it was the first thing he saw when he woke and the last he saw when he went to sleep.

She laughed and the tears came flowing, though she had to quickly hide them so her mother wouldn't see them. By the end of that call, she had forgiven him and wanted to see him again as soon as possible. Her parents, of course, would be a problem, so they enlisted Gwenn's help again.

As he and Gwenn both had guessed, Margaret had tossed out his letters, and she insisted that he write her more of them. He did so, and Gwenn agreed to deliver them to her at school. She would read them over and over and then call her best friend, giddy with excitement. It went on like that for almost a month, until she felt brave enough to risk meeting him.

It was going to happen at Gwenn's while her parents were gone out of town. They planned all week for it, right down to what they would say, what they would wear, and what movie they watch. The whole day was planned down to every last detail, but when he roared into the driveway in his old Ford coupe, all of those details disintegrated.

It was a cooler summer night in late July, and he stepped out of the car wearing a leather jacket, jeans, boots, and a warm grin. He didn't rush up the driveway as he'd wanted to; instead he leaned against the warm fender of the car, waiting for her. Inside the house, two girls giggled and screamed - one as excited as the other.

Melinda composed herself and walked out the front door, closing it gently behind her, with Gwenn staring through the peephole. It was like seeing him for the first time, and she understood how nervous he'd been a month before, knowing that it was her but not having any idea what to say. She didn't have any cool lines this time, and her sense of humor abandoned her, leaving her with crippling anxiety as she stood frozen on the porch with her arms folded. She could hardly move, and completely forgot everything that she had wanted to say, every rehearsed line dissolving in her mouth like candy.

Behind the door, Gwenn was yelling at her, encouraging her, "Go to *him*, Melinda! *You* have to move off of the porch! Quit being a stubborn bitch and walk halfway to him!" It was muffled but she heard what she said, shushing her with a hand gesture behind her back.

This was the meeting they should have had. This was the one she had always thought about; him showing up in her drive one day, coming to get her and take her away from everything. He looked a lot older standing in front of her than what she'd pictured in her dreams, though those had been old dreams, ones she hadn't had since she was a little girl when she remembered him as a little boy. He looked so different; the little boy was gone now and a man was in his place.

She moved a quivering leg off of the porch and placed it firmly on the driveway, as if it wasn't solid or would crack beneath her and give way. He finally moved away from the car and took his hands from his pockets, walking towards her. It was slow at first, waiting for her to take another step, and as she did, he picked up the pace. Both of them broke into a short run and John scooped her up in his arms and lifted her from the ground.

It felt good being held by him again, even better than the last time, for this time she knew who it was holding her, and she felt every minute of those ten years they'd lost returning. The emotions came then, and she couldn't stop them, burying her face into his chest to muffle her sobs. He could feel her shaking and moved a hand up to coil his fingers in her blonde locks and cradle her head. His strong arms pressed her tightly against him as her body shook from the tears that had been waiting to erupt for a decade.

She dug her nails into the back of his leather coat, holding him close, and took him in. He smelled of leather and fresh cotton, with a hint of oil from his car and a slight, spiced perfume smell. They were all different "man" scents - things she had smelled before on her brother, father and grandfather - and they were all rolled into one person. He kissed the top of her head repeatedly and told her how much he had missed her and that he was sorry.

She lifted her head and stared at him with black streaks on her face that had once been meant to make her beautiful. He laughed and wiped her eyes with his fingers, as her own fingers followed suit, getting tangled in his. They pressed the black mascara between them as she squeezed his hands so tightly that they turned red.

"I missed you too! So much..." She whispered and cupped his face in her hands.

Her eyes stared into his, still probing for that little boy that she missed, and finally she caught a glimpse of him just beyond the deep blue windows, and she smiled.

"There you are..."

Her fingers were outstretched on either side of his face, and she moved them back behind his head to play in his hair as she pulled his face towards hers. She didn't know what to say. There was nothing else that she could say to describe how she was feeling, so she had to show him.

She had to show him her happiness, her relief, her aching that was going away now, and all of the years of sorrow and loneliness. She showed him all of those things as her lips touched his, warm and welcoming, moist and loving, in a kiss that she'd been waiting a decade for. There was joy there, but sorrow too, for all of the years that she had missed him, all of the years that had been ripped away from them, and when he kissed her back, she knew that he felt exactly the same.

Gwenn watched them from the open door of her house and smiled. It was bittersweet, in so many ways, to watch them kiss. She was happy for them beyond elation, knowing how many nights Melinda had been sad and cried over him, knowing how much she wished that he would return, and now there he was. It was a moment to celebrate and always remember, as she watched all of the hurt and loss melt away in his arms.

She also couldn't help but feel a pang of jealousy as she watched them kiss, wishing that she had been the one who had someone like John who loved her in that way. She knew that no matter where her life took her, or what boys she had met or would meet, that she would never have a story like theirs. She hung her head then, feeling so awful for being jealous at a moment like that. Melinda was her best friend, and she deserved this. She had been so miserable and lonely most of her life and treated so badly by her family, she deserved at least this moment of relief and joy. A smile broke across her face as she watched them.

The little boy and the little girl she used to know were standing in her driveway making out. John Chapel and Melinda

107

Malowski were kissing each other in *her* driveway, in front of *her* house. It was so strange, beyond anything she ever thought she would see happen, and she leaned on the railing just beaming at them, feeling their radiating happiness wash over her.

Chapter 9

That was the beginning and the end of it. It was the end of any quarreling, fears, doubts, or regrets, and the beginning of "Melinda and John". They were inseparable after that and together nearly every single day for the rest of the summer. John would drive down and pick her up at Gwenn's to go for a drive or he would just come and sit beside her next to the small lake that Gwenn's family home was nestled on.

They spent the summer just talking and catching up, sometimes going for walks, but would always end their evenings beside the water, where they would kiss. Gwenn would retire for the night and leave the two of them to their kissing and laughing at the water's edge. Almost the entirety of John and Melinda's first summer together was spent beside a lake, and that was precisely where it would end as well.

For the last trip of summer, the Lawsons took the girls up north. Gwenn was excited to spend some time with her best friend, but for Melinda it seemed like a prison sentence. She hadn't been away from John for more than a day since he'd returned, and their goodbyes sounded like he was going off to war. She would kiss him, walk away and then run back to kiss him again several times until finally Gwenn had to drag her off to the car.

She pressed her hand against the car window and the look in her eyes tore at him. He was reminded of the day that his own mother dragged him away. He knew she wasn't going forever, she would be back, but it would seem like a lifetime to be without her for even three days.

That Friday night, Jeremy stopped by the house and interrupted his moping. "Come on John, you're not sitting on your bed all weekend waiting for that girl to come home! Our summer is slipping away and the guys are meeting us at the old skate place again!"

John only frowned. "I won't be much fun...not much of a wingman."

Jeremy leaned in his doorway and gave him his best smile and puppy face. "You're going! She's just a girl! There are *dozens* more down there, or didn't you see them? The guys have been asking about you and I keep making excuses for you!"

"I saw the girls. I just didn't look at them. You have no idea who this girl is to me Jeremy."

"Quit calling me *Jeremy*, you're getting out of the zone Cap! Who's going to lead the group tonight if you don't go? We'll fall apart without you...we've *been* falling apart without you! You've been with this girl every day for a month now! You're like a ghost."

"I'm a *happy* ghost though," he joked and couldn't suppress a smile.

"This is our last summer together, remember? Don't you remember complaining about how you hated sitting around doing the same thing and how you wanted this summer to be great?"

"This summer is great," he said, almost offended.

"For you, maybe, but not for the rest of us. Everyone is going to college but me...you're all moving on to greater things and I'll be stuck here, the *last Regulator*. How can I be a *Regulator* by myself?"

"Why can't you just be *Jeremy?*"

"See? You're already thinking negatively! We're Regulators until the last one of us goes, Johnny! You're pissing away your summer - *our* summer - on this *one* girl! When the other guys leave, you're going to regret spending every last minute with this girl."

"You don't understand...I've spent enough time away from her. *Time* is something we lost too much of. We'll always be friends, but I don't want to lose this girl again."

Jeremy sat down on his bunk bed with him and looked at an old photo of them in their fifties outfits, sighing. "I'm not Josh and I don't know the history man. He's been your corner man on this one, told us to leave it be, and to leave you alone. I don't understand it, I wish I did, all I know is that our days are numbered buddy. *My* days are numbered...you guys are all that I have. There's no college for me, no money, no other friends, and definitely no special mystery girl from my past coming back to haunt me."

John looked up and felt sorry for Jeremy for one of the first times that he could ever remember. Usually it was some con game with him or him trying to sell the other guys on something by putting on an act, but not this time. He was scared, and John could see that. He knew that Jeremy Connelly took his friends seriously because they were the only family he had. Once they were gone, he would be completely alone, and he was truly afraid of that.

John nodded and stood up, grabbing his jacket. "Okay Con, this will be a good weekend, we'll make it good! Call up Hunter and tell him to meet us there with the others."

Jeremy broke into a big smile and picked up the phone in John's room to make the call, and then hurried down the stairs out to the garage. The Ford coupe was painted a shiny black now; the open house had provided enough money for John to get it painted. John tossed him the keys and let him drive. The car purred out of the garage - the exhaust also legal - and they sped off towards the interstate.

The late summer air was cool in John's hair and it made him feel very alive. He hung his head out the window and Con laughed as he noted that the wind didn't even move his hair a bit. He cranked the radio up when an old rock and roll song came on and John worked the air guitar as Jeremy played air-drums on the large steering wheel.

Halfway to their destination, the sun dipped beyond the dashboard and turned the sky pink before it completely disappeared from sight. The moon was high and full and John felt charged and refreshed in the crisp night air that hinted at autumn's arrival. It hadn't seemed like a month had passed already, and time always seemed to go quickly when he was with her, but too slowly when he wasn't.

Jeremy's smile was lost when he turned to see the look on his friend's face, staring blankly into the night sky through the window. He checked his watch then looked back over at John, sighing and fixing his bottom lip over his teeth in a frown. He gripped the wheel and signaled to exit at the next green sign.

"What are you doing? We're not there yet...this isn't the exit." John said, looking over at the fuel gauge which still indicated they had half of a tank.

"I think you're right about the girls at the old skate rink...they're not really that great."

111

"Then where are we going?"

Connelly nodded. "I thought we would go north instead of south…"

John's face broke into a huge smile, "You sonova…you serious?"

Jeremy nodded. "I've gotta' see what this gal is all about anyway right? You're not going to do us any good with that lost puppy look anyway."

"You want to turn around halfway to Troy and drive to Port Austin? That's like…well, I don't know how far it is, but it's far!" John was in disbelief.

"Hey, there will be other days and other girls, right? Besides, she has a *friend* right? Gwenn? She wasn't all that bad…"

John grinned big again, "Oh I see…your sacrifice isn't as noble as I thought. Gwenn *is* hot isn't she? You *are* into her!"

"I'm not *into* her…I just figured since we were going that way, I may as well right?" Jeremy tried to play it cool, but John knew that he had been calling Gwenn since he had met her that night at the arena.

"Whatever you want to tell yourself man." John smiled and leaned back in his seat, folding his arms across his chest to enjoy the long ride.

It was almost a whole hour back north just to their home town, and then another two hours beyond that. Neither John nor Connelly had ever been to Port Austin, and needed to stop halfway at a rest area to check one of the giant maps. Jeremy wasn't happy when John returned to the car and told him it was another hundred miles.

John shrunk into his seat as Connelly cussed and moaned about them not sticking with their original plan. His adventurousness suddenly left him as well as the tiny shred of romanticism that he had shown by his turning the car around to find the girls. John took the wheel and let him vent in the passenger seat for the next twenty minutes as they left the last signs of civilization behind them.

There were few houses along the way, and even fewer gas stations. They barely made it to the next station, where John filled up the car with his last twenty. He didn't want to ask Connelly for the other twenty to get them home until later - hopefully Gwenn would make him forget that he was mad. Hopefully they would even find the girls. He also didn't want to tell Connelly that he didn't know, exactly, where they were staying. Port Austin looked like a small place on the map, how hard could it have been to find them?

Four hours later the two of them were walking through their second campground with flashlights, investigating every tent and camper window trying to find them. This was, of course, after they had exhausted all twelve hotels and motels. Connelly hadn't spoken much to him after the fourth motel yielded no results. *I can't believe she didn't tell you where they were staying*, he kept repeating after every dead end. It wasn't until the last hotel that John remembered that Gwenn's folks were taking a camper. Connelly went berserk and threatened to walk back home, leaving John to find her on his own.

After much apologizing and playing on his sense of adventure, reminding him several times that they would look back on this and laugh, Connelly calmed down and decided to pitch in. That's when they bought the plastic flashlights at the corner gas station and took the search to the next level.

John had been a little apprehensive about shining his light "into" the tents, but Jeremy berated him, "You dragged me all the way up here, having no idea where she was the whole time, and we checked every damned hotel and one whole campground already! You'd better believe that we're going to use these lights and find them now, I don't care if it is one in the morning!!"

He shrugged and followed his lead, shining the light and then subsequently apologizing to each family that they woke up. It went on this way for another forty-five minutes until they had covered the entirety of the second campground. John met back up with Connelly at a cluster of trees with his head down.

"I don't get it...I *know* she's here, Con! Do you think we missed her somehow at the last campground?"

Jeremy frowned. "I don't know man, let's just go home. I'm exhausted from running tent to tent and people chasing me off."

"Yea, I had a few of those too," John said, laughing.

"You're sure it was here? You're sure it was Port Austin? Camping?" Connelly ran back down the checklist of facts to be sure they were even close.

John nodded, "Yea, I'm sure of it. They're *here* somewhere...I'm sure of it. Is there another campground?"

Jeremy shook his head, "No, the guy at the gas station said there were just these three major ones; two state parks and then Duggan's park...that anyone goes to anyway."

John had also asked the same info of a patron leaving the station, and his look told Jeremy that he knew something he wasn't sharing.

Jeremy sighed and hung his head in frustration, "There are *more*? How *many* more?"

"Technically *five*...there are five. But one is some kind of trailer park...they're not there, I'm telling you!"

"Then where in the fuck are they Johnny?!" Jeremy was losing his patience, as he rarely swore directly at him.

John leaned against the nearest tree and slouched, his exhaustion sinking in. "I wish I knew! Don't you think that I would go straight to her if I knew *exactly* where she was? Do you think this is a good time for me? Do you think that I would let you come with me all this way just for us to turn around and go home empty-handed?"

Jeremy put his hand on his shoulder and nodded his head at his friend, "I'm sorry, we tried John. I wanted you to find them. I thought you could find them..."

John clicked off his flashlight then and stood in the dark, squeezing his eyes to hot tears. He didn't know why he was crying, probably from just being exhausted, defeated, letting Con down and dragging him all the way up there for nothing. Maybe because Jeremy Connelly was right; this was one of their last weekends together and he had wasted it chasing after a girl. He had missed a lot of the past weekends not only with him but with all of his friends when she came back into his life.

Storming off through the tree line towards the beach, he wiped his face discreetly as he went, so that Con wouldn't see. Night was closing in on them, time was slipping away, and he felt helpless. When he was halfway to the beach and he could hear the lapping of gentle waters, it was then that he heard something else echoing through the trees around him; a girl's laughter.

He turned to look at Connelly, who seemed as surprised as he was, and he exhaled, "No way...wouldn't you die if it was...?"

Con just pointed, "Go, man!"

John broke into a run and Jeremy was right behind him, crunching in the sand. As he climbed a small dune of sand, covered in swaying reeds and cattails, he slowed and caught his breath, composing himself.

She was sitting just beyond the dune among the blowing reeds, her knees tucked up to her chest, and hair whipping across her face. When she turned to see him, he could see that brilliant smile even from as far away as he was. Standing slowly, staring in disbelief, she tried to brush the hair from her face so she could get a better look at the man cresting the small hill. It was as surreal a moment as they'd experienced a month before when he was standing at the end of Gwenn's drive.

Her legs found motion then and she moved towards him, shrieking, and nearly knocked him to the ground when she leapt on him. She held his face firmly in her hands, kissing it, in total disbelief that he was there. She kept repeating, "What are you doing here? How did you find me?"

He could only beam at her, as she draped her arms around his neck, pulling him closer. Her hair tickled his nose and it smelled of lilac, and her skin smelled like the beach and tasted the same as he pressed his lips against hers.

There was the same tingling and feeling of weightlessness, like the kiss from Lyster Lane, but they'd had time to perfect the kiss since then. It was gentle but eager, wet but not sloppy, and devouring but not greedy. Not only had they perfected the kiss, but the embrace as well, finding a way to fit even closer together than the time before. She put her arms around his waist, inside of his leather coat, and found shelter, heat and safety there. His body warmed her against a night that can only be found near a lake, so chilly and damp.

"Actually," John whispered, when he was finally able to speak, "it was Jeremy's idea...partly."

He indicated the shadow standing at the edge of the wall of cattails. She gave a small wave and hugged John tighter as she peeked at Connelly, smiling at him. "Thank you Jeremy...umm...*Con man?*"

"*Jeremy* is fine...we're off-duty tonight."

Melinda took John by the hand and led him back to the spot she'd been sitting; the most perfect spot for viewing the lake and the moon above it. Her eyes reflected the moonlight at him like

115

twin black pearls, but they sparkled at him as brilliantly as they did in the light of day.

"I can't believe you're here…this is the most incredible thing…no one has ever…"

He just kept smiling at her and nodding in agreement, "I know."

She squeezed his hand as it was suddenly going to turn to water and slip through her fingers. He'd held her hands dozens of times over the past month, but she had never felt as real to him as she did that night. In between words of disbelief, she leaned in and kissed him over and over, savoring each one with a brush of her tongue over her lips.

John retold his story of how they turned around halfway to Troy and a night at the arena again, to drive three hours there, and spent over two more looking for them. He laughed as he told about how he and Con had covered the Ford on the side of the road with tree branches to camouflage it, as if they were on some covert mission. She laughed as he told her about shining their lights into every single tent and camper, and that some of the people chased them off.

Her eyes grew wider as she realized that he'd come all that way, braving those angry campers and fighting exhaustion just for her. She listened with a skipping heart as he retold how he sat miserably in his room missing her, and how he had no desire to go to meet other girls.

They interspersed talking, touching and kissing for almost an hour before she stared up at him and with her soothing and sweet voice she said, "Stay the night here with me."

"I can't stay…I have work in the morning. And it's a *two* hour drive home."

She only looked at him with a sad expression.

"Please don't look at me that way, I can't stay Mel, I wish I could…"

"I know, but it would be wonderful if you could. We *never* get time alone - not real time alone. I'm beginning to wonder if we ever are. This is the first night ever, really, where it's just you and me."

"Someday, I promise, we'll be together for good."

She leaned up against him, resting her head on his shoulder. "It seems like we never get a moment to just sit and talk, or just

116

relax together without someone interrupting, or having to sneak around," she complained, stroking his arm gently.

He bent in, kissing her head, and said in a low but serious voice, "This is *our* time, Melinda, right *now*, right *here*. If we never get another day like this, think back to this one."

He knew what was on her mind and he had been thinking about the same thing. Their time would be growing shorter just like it was with his friends, and it would become more difficult for the pair of them to see one another once school started back up. If not for weekends with Gwenn, they might not have seen one another at all.

"How much do you love me?" She asked in a peculiar tone.

"I'm not going anywhere Melinda. I already decided to work full-time with my uncle and not go to college this year."

"You already decided that *before* you found me again, John."

"Yea, but I wasn't sure until now. I can't go away just yet, because I think it would make everything harder than it already is."

"You think we would fall apart if we didn't see each other as often?"

"Nothing will ever keep us apart again – I promise you!"

"My parents…they won't approve if they find out about us. I'm just worried that we can't keep using poor Gwenn forever. Eventually, I have to tell them…"

"We don't need to talk about this now, Mel. I've come a long way to be with you tonight, and I just want to enjoy this night."

She stared quietly out at the rolling tide of Lake Huron, still going over the logistics of their situation in her mind. Neither of them was even certain what the "situation" was that they were trying to preserve. All they knew was that they were happy – happier than either of them had been in a decade – and they didn't want to lose it again. They were just content rediscovering one another, and hadn't thought much about how they would continue on in a normal relationship.

They were just "Johnny and Melinda" and every waking moment they took every moment they could steal away. Questions had never been asked about the finer details because they had never been concerned with those things until that moment, when those questions loomed over them like the full summer moon.

"Why did you stop?" She said finally.

"Why did I stop *what*?"

"You stopped calling and writing the letters. Why? Why did you give up on us?"

"Mel, I wrote you almost three-hundred letters...and called three times a week for a year. What did you *want*?"

"I *wanted* you to keep writing them until my mom got tired of throwing them away, and to keep calling until I knew you were still out there."

John sighed at her. "We've been through this before; I told you that I was sorry that I couldn't reach you. Why can't you let it go, and just enjoy the time we have now? We still have our *whole* lives!"

"*Do* we? Not the way I see it," she snapped back.

"Why do we not have time?"

"Johnny, you've graduated and I'm still stuck in school! I have *two* more years to go! You're going to go to college – maybe not this year, but possibly the next - and there will be college girls and parties..."

"And before I met you, there were older girls and parties. I left one of those parties to come and find *you* remember? I skipped a party tonight to drive three hours to find you! What is this really about Mel? It's not about *older girls*..."

"It's about *everything* that's out there that can rip us apart again! I'm going to have to tell my mother about us soon, and I'm scared to death of what will happen! I have to know that you won't let them stop you again, and that you'll come for me no matter what!"

John gave her a solemn look as he let her words sink in. He was reminded of a day when he'd promised he would never leave her side, and also the day he understood the heartbreak of watching promises fall apart. From that day forward, he'd made no more promises, expected very little of people, and when things went his way, well, that was just good fortune.

He looked into those big blue eyes of hers staring expectantly at him, begging for another promise, and one that he could keep – no matter how simple. He'd promised to storm the gates of Heaven for her and he couldn't even escape his own mother that day. Now she was just asking for something in-between, and he wasn't sure he could even give her that. She was right to be afraid and to question their future, and it reminded him that he hadn't questioned it enough.

"Melinda, we're not kids anymore and neither of us has to be afraid of your mother. She's *not* going to chase me off again!"

"You don't know my mother...not the way she is *now*, Johnny," she said with a heavy sigh. "She's not going to like this one bit and I don't even know if I can face her."

"Just use the approach I used: be very vague about the details about the boy you're dating."

He laughed but she gave him a scornful look and he immediately stopped.

"This is *serious* Johnny! My mom isn't going to let me go running around with some guy she's never seen; she's going to want to meet you. Once she sees you and connects the dots, she'll *know* it's you! Sneaking around and being deceitful isn't going to work forever...or weren't you planning that far ahead?"

"What does that mean?"

"I need to know that you want to be with me...before I hurl myself into the lion's den."

"Are you kidding? After everything we've been through? You don't have to worry about *me* going anywhere. It's *you* I'm concerned about."

"*Me*? I'm talking about sticking my neck out with my parents just so we don't have to make out in Gwenn's backyard anymore, and you're worried about *me*?"

"Well...I'm more bothered by the idea of you being in school still, surrounded by those friends of yours, and tons of guys your own age."

"You're only a year-and-a-half older than me - for one - so that makes you *my age*. My friends have nothing to do with us, and I don't care about any of the other guys at my school either."

"So you're going to be content being the girl sitting at the movies alone, while all of her friends have their boyfriends next to them? Or walking through the hallways of your school for the next two years watching them holding hands with someone and yours are full of books? What about parties? You're just going to go and sulk in a corner by yourself and ignore any guy that approaches?"

"I never said that it wouldn't be hard, but nothing will ever be harder than what we've had to do before. We were apart for ten years, wondering if we would ever see each other again! I would rather have a few dinners by myself and know that I'll see you at some point, than believe I'll never see you again."

He looked away from her, staring out at the moonlit lake and thinking about the months that would come. The first two had been difficult - more difficult than any relationship that he'd ever had - and every day for them had been an accomplishment. Even the simplest of tasks, like a phone call, was a major undertaking. He couldn't call her when he wanted to, for fear of being discovered, so he had to route them through Gwenn and leave messages with her. She would then walk down to her house and relay the message, and the girls would have to collect change and walk to a payphone so that she could call him back. That was just phone calls; making plans to spend time together had almost required a spymaster to execute.

"The fact that you want to risk our relationship already, by telling your mother, says that you're already tired of how things are."

"What do you mean?"

"What I mean is that your mom is *never* going to go for it and you *know* that. That's why you're trying to prepare for it, prepare *both* of us for it, when it goes south."

"You don't know what she'll say for sure. Why are you giving up on us already?"

"I'm not giving up, Mel, I'm being a *realist*. I don't like having to sneak around all the time, and not being able to call or see you when I want. But I'm telling you, it would be a *huge* mistake to tell her now. You're not even sixteen yet, don't have your own car or a license, and would have no way to reach me if she flips out and refuses to let me see you."

"So what do we do? What's your *plan* for us, Johnny?"

"Why do we have to talk about this *now*? I just want us to enjoy tonight...because we never know what tomorrow will bring."

"So you're planning on us failing? You already know that we won't work and that something will go wrong for us? Thanks for having faith!"

She stood up, brushed the sand from her shorts, and stormed off. He let her get thirty feet down the beach before he reluctantly stood to follow her. Placing his hands on her shoulders, he kissed her neck and felt the tiny hairs rise to meet his lips. She yielded, falling back into his arms.

"Kissing on me isn't going to make me forget that I'm scared to death of losing you again or that I hate not having you there all the time," she said, playfully yet serious.

"How about just for tonight?"

"Just promise me that you won't let them pull us apart."

"Your parents?"

"Anyone. Anything. Parents. Friends. Girls. Boys. Don't ever let anything come between us. Even if I slap you across the face again and tell you to go to hell, don't stop coming for me."

"You tried that once, and I didn't give up on you, did I?"

"No, but things won't always be this way; I have a feeling that everything will harder for us soon, and that this is as good as we're going to have it," she said, her voice cracking.

"No matter what they throw at us, no matter who tries to get between us, I won't ever stop," he whispered over her shoulder. "Even if I have to come creeping in your bedroom window and steal you away in the middle of the night, I'll be there."

She reached a hand behind her to stroke his face and whispered, "This will all be worth it in the end right?"

"Anything worth having is worth a fight, my dad used to say," he said, kissing the top of her head. "While your friends are burning through guy after guy, tired and bored with them, we'll still be here Mel."

She started to say something, but he leaned in and kissed her deeply. He didn't want to talk about their difficult situation or the even more difficult tomorrows they faced, and knew that it would be impossible to reassure her anyway. They kept the talk to quiet whispers between kisses, and kept it light, deciding that they should just enjoy their time, as John suggested.

The minutes passed too quickly however, as it always did. He felt the drops first, striking his head and running down his cheeks, though he tried to ignore them and continued kissing her, enjoying the indulgence of her warm mouth against the cool night. As the water came down harder and harder, they kissed more passionately, knowing that they would soon be interrupted by more than the rain.

"They'll be coming to complain about the rain," Melinda said between kisses.

"Jeremy doesn't like to get his hair wet," John laughed, not relenting.

He dipped her head gently to the sand and kissed her more ravenously, rolling atop her. Her chest heaved as she relented to him, and he knew that he could take her there, inches from the waters of the tranquil lake, if he'd wanted. She knew that he hadn't wanted to, and that they weren't ready, but her body tingled in every place and the question came involuntarily.

"Please stay with me tonight...just for a while," she moaned.

He finished kissing her and stood up, pulling her up by her tiny wrists, and noticing every wet curve of her as she stood. The soaked thin shirt was pulled tautly over her breasts, showing every curve, dip and protrusion, leaving very little to the imagination. Her deep breathing made her chest swell and recede, the shirt clinging tightly despite, and her hot breath was a fog in the chilly air. He brushed the curtain of dripping strands from her face, to reveal the twin, black pearls that were trying to enchant him.

He took a hesitant step back, as if it would protect him from the power of that gaze, or allow him a moment to collect himself. It did neither. She pressed the attack and locked her fingers behind his head, pulling him down to consume him again like a lioness finishing her kill. He could feel her heart pounding against his chest through hers, which was pressed quite conspicuously against him. They could both hear their friends coming in the distance, and she knew that it was her last chance to break him.

As she kissed at his neck, she whispered to him, "How much do you love me?"

It was another invitation to stay the night, and there was nothing more that he wanted at that very moment. Visions of her pulling the wet shirt off over her head and climbing atop him beneath a heap of blankets in a tent were already flashing before his eyes. Her unspoken suggestion and her fingers playing in his hair made him swallow hard, his muscles tense, and a chill taking hold of him.

"Mel, we can't do it like this. I want to stay the night with you, just..."

"Stay with me, just for a little while."

"I have work in a few hours…I have to get on the road soon and it's pouring out."

"You'll still have time to get back before light," she said as she gnawed at his ear.

"Melinda, not like this…not tonight."

"I know that it would still mean something. It would mean something to *me*."

There it was; the offer had been placed on the proverbial table. She played with his bottom lip with her finger, those eyes boring through him.

"This is the perfect night, this is *our* night…even you said that. What are the chances that we could ever have a night like this one again? You drove here without even knowing how to find me, but you did find me, and there's a reason for that, Johnny. All the planning in the world couldn't make a more perfect night for us, and you know that. I'm ready…"

He hugged her close, pressing his lips to her eyelids, and she had her answer. That was always what he did when he was saying goodbye, and usually it was accompanied by "everything is going to be fine", but tonight it was just the kiss on her lids. It had always ended small arguments or worries on every occasion before, but on this night it only served to infuriate her.

"So, you're not staying - not even for a while? I want you to stay…we'll have the tent to ourselves, no one will know." There was panic in her voice and she was tightening her arms around him.

Her big eyes were streaked by dark lines from her mascara, and he couldn't tell if it was from the rain or if she had been crying.

"You said you *loved* me…and I love you *so* much! I want you to be the *one* John! Don't you *want* that?"

"Yes, I want that, but we don't need to do this just to be together! Our relationship isn't based on sex, and I don't want it to be!"

Melinda burst into tears then, the rain couldn't cover her any longer, "You don't understand! If we don't do this now, we might *never* get to! There won't be any more up north weekends without my parents for a long time! I won't have the freedom to just come and go with friends. We're going to lose one another Johnny and I'm scared!"

123

"I'm scared too! I'm scared that if we do this tonight, that it won't mean as much. I don't want tonight to be the night we *did it* in a tent because we had nowhere else to do it!"

"You think that you won't do it right? I don't care! I know you haven't been with as many girls as your friends, and I don't care!" She said, wiping the makeup from her cheeks and lowering her voice as they saw their friends waiting for them on the dune above.

John grew red-faced then, as an awful taste suddenly appeared in his mouth. "What is this about? Is this you being afraid of us falling apart or is this about your friends pressuring you? They've been pushing you for details haven't they? Well, I'm not going to give them anything to talk about!"

Her mouth turned down and her eyes went wide. "No! It's not *them*! I'm not trying to impress them! I'm worried about *us*..."

"They haven't asked you *one* thing about me huh? They haven't asked you anything about how I *perform* yet? Are you behind schedule for putting out with your little clique of tramps?"

"My friends aren't *tramps*-they're popular!"

"*Popular* means they put out more than the rest! Hunter and JB are *popular* too, for the same reason, but I'm not with them, I'm here with you tonight! I don't give a shit about what they say Melinda, and if I did, I wouldn't be here!"

"They don't control my relationship - I do!"

"Really? Have they asked if we've been together yet or not? Yes or no?"

She went silent and hung her head. They *had* asked her, almost every time they saw her. They'd been the ones that told her she had to hurry up and get with him if she wanted to hang onto him; guys left girls who didn't give them a reason to stay. They convinced her that two months was too long.

He shook his head at her, in disgust. "So, they *have*...that's *exactly* why I don't want to do this. I'm not doing it so you can compare notes or fit in with them. You have to be *grown up* enough to live outside the influence of your friends. When mine find out I blew them off to come see you, I'll never hear the end of it! The difference is I don't *care* about what they say. I love you too much to change anything about us just because *they* tell me I have to!"

124

"You *don't* understand! I'm not doing this because of them or because I'm afraid of my mother, I'm doing it because I hate being the only one without a guy around. You're right, it does suck when they all have someone with them at the movies and the seat next to me is empty. I don't even enjoy myself, because I'm sitting there wondering where you are and when I'll see you again."

"Melinda..." He said her name like an apology, but she wouldn't listen.

"And they all look at me with this face...pitying me...and then they try to convince me to leave you and move on, but I won't! I make my own decisions and I don't care what they say about us, but yes, it's breaking my heart to be away from you! And they say that you won't wait around forever..."

"They're wrong! And you don't need to lure me into your tent to keep me around!"

"I don't know how long I can do this, and I need to talk to my mom. I know you're afraid of what will happen if I try talking to her, but I'm more afraid of what will happen if I don't."

He nodded, taking up her hands in his as he spoke, staring unflinchingly into her eyes. "I'm not staying tonight because that time will come when it comes, and I won't let it be dictated by fear, friends, parents, or anything else. It will happen when we decide it happens, and that isn't why I'm with you. You asked how much I love you?"

She nodded, smiling up at him with anticipation.

"I love you enough to walk away tonight, though everything in me tells me that I want you right now, at this very moment. I'm walking to prove them all wrong, and to show you that we will make it through without having to be pushed into something. I'll go with you to talk to your mother, if you want, and if not, I'll support your choice."

"Thank you," she whispered.

That ended their first big argument, and though they had come to an understanding, voiced their fears and intentions alike, that wouldn't be the last of it. They both knew, as they said their goodbyes and parted reluctantly, that the worst was yet to come. Neither of them looked forward to the confrontation with her mother, any more than they looked forward to more ridicule from their friends – the ones who didn't understand anyway.

125

Both of their truest friends were each waiting to collect them with somber, but welcoming faces, knowing that something bad had just transpired. John watched as Gwenn threw an arm around Melinda's shoulders, expecting her to turn back around to look at him once more, but she didn't. He just stood there, Jeremy at his side, letting the rain fall on his face, and mouthing the words *I love you* to no one in particular.

"You okay man?" Connelly finally said.

He contemplated running back over the hill to grab her up and tell her he was staying, but his principles kept his feet rooted in the sand. Instead, he just stood there watching their shapes disappear in the rain.

Chapter *10*

Gwenn let out a long breath that she'd been holding for some time, once the tape of her husband's retelling of Port Austin stopped. She was there that night, but had never heard what was said between the two of them and couldn't fill in the blanks, so Campbell had obliged her. She wished now that he hadn't.

There were many reasons why the sound of his voice was jarring, and the fact that he was speaking from beyond the grave wasn't top on the list. There was a tone in that voice when it spoke of Melinda Malowski that she didn't care for at all. It was a tone that he'd never used in her presence whenever they had discussed her.

The man she'd known always spoke of the woman as though he despised her, but the voice on that tape had nothing but unbridled compassion, empathy and (she could swear) a sense of longing. It made her physically ill to hear it, and she'd set her last cracker down before finishing it, her appetite ruined. That tone confirmed not only that her husband hadn't been completely honest with her about how he'd felt about Melinda, but even worse, it was beginning to confirm Campbell's theory about John's condition.

"I *still* don't think that this is all about her, Jim," she finally said, her tone heavily-laden with denial.

"The story sounds a lot different when you hear it from him and not from his journal doesn't it?"

Her scowl dipped lower, but Campbell pretended not to notice and turned his attention to his notebook where he scribbled with his pencil.

"So, did *anything* I told you about Port Austin help?"

"You mean did it change my opinion about John's case? Not really. It was illuminating, however, in understanding the persona of Melinda Malowski a bit better. It gives me better insight into the dynamic between the two of them, and how it shaped John."

"I'm glad I could be so helpful," she snipped.

"I understand that this may be difficult for you, but you insisted on staying to help with this."

"It's hard enough hearing his voice again without having him prattle on about *her* in such a way. I just need a minute to process it, but I'll be fine. So why do you think that this is still all tied to her?"

"The better question is: why do *you* think it *isn't*? I know you hated listening to that, but you had to hear it so that you can see where I'm coming from. I'm already convinced that John's manufacturing of the other place and the other woman was based on this exact blueprint."

"Nice metaphor, but if we're talking about him following blueprints, there must be another set he was following because there are things missing still."

"Every good builder deviates from the plans now and again, Gwenn, especially when he sees something that can be made better once the construction begins."

"Can we forego the colorful language and just lay the facts out there?" She said, rubbing her temples. Fatigue was setting in and the fifteen minutes of tape had taken its toll on her, draining the color from her cheeks.

"Okay, just lining up the facts? A young man and woman, barely old enough to understand the raging hormones within themselves, trying to find their places in the world and with each another, discover their first love together beside a lake…"

He stood and stretched his legs before kneeling beside the fire to inspect it as he talked. They sounded like words he might have been reading from cue cards from somewhere in the fireplace, and that he might have rehearsed or spoken before in that very room. Perhaps he had said them to John, or maybe he just had time to memorize his notes in the event that he would need to spar with his widow on the phone again.

"…at some point, they realize that there are outside forces preventing them from pursuing the course they've embarked on together, and have some harsh realities to face. They have to decide if they will continue struggling through it together, or finally confront the thing that's been ever present in the background, and be able to move forward. How does this sound so far?"

128

"Are you talking about John and Melinda or John and Nicolette?"

"Both," he said in an oddly chipper tone, lifting a fresh log from the pile. "The two stories, at this particular junction, are almost mirror images of one another. The story varies and goes in different directions in many places, but here, it's the same story no matter what people we're referring to."

"But Melinda's particular obstacles aren't just parents. We're talking about her very influential group of friends and how her image with them is affected when John doesn't come around for their approval. Nicolette isn't worried about reputation or being chastised."

"Tell me about how that night affected Melinda, specifically, and what it meant to her," he said, prodding at the fire and trying to get the fresh log in just the right place.

"Well...she was just as upset that night as she was the first she had seen him again. She just couldn't accept the fact that they might fall apart, and it didn't help that her other friends weren't supportive in the least. Their advice was for her to lose her virginity to him, and that she should prepare for the inevitable anyway."

"Which was?"

"They would go their separate ways no matter what they did. They acted like they were such experts, and she was young, impressionable and foolish enough to listen. John was right about them, and what he said about them; they were a bunch of shallow, insecure girls who slept with anyone they could."

"You were her best friend, why didn't she listen to you?"

"She did, to an extent. But there were *five* of them and one of me, and I was *boring old Gwenny Lawson*, they were beautiful and got lots of attention. I think Melinda missed that the most, with the way she was ignored at home. It was almost as if she needed it for her very survival after a while."

"That's when the two of you began to grow apart as well?"

"It wasn't long after that night that she wouldn't listen to a word I said. I think she knew, deep down, that those girls didn't have her best interests at heart and they gave bad advice, but I think she was so desperate to keep John around that she would've done anything."

"So…they put her up to it at Port Austin? What happened when he rejected her?"

"She was angry, and became more desperate. It wasn't that she was mad at him, though; she talked about him all that night and you'd have thought that the ground John walked was holy."

"Interesting turn of phrase. She started to pull away from him?"

"She thought she wasn't good enough for him, the same way her mother made her feel about herself. That stupid little test that her friends put her up to only served to shatter her self-image that much more. They put her into a no-win situation…"

"I'm pretty good with human psychology and even group behavior, but you'll have to forgive me if I'm not up to speed with teenage girl head games; please explain."

"Well, they told her that if he refused her, then he didn't want to really be with her and she was to get rid of him. And if he gave in, well then they would've told her that he didn't respect her. Melinda never wanted to push John into that situation, but *they* put the whole thing into her head, and that begun her induction into the *council of bitches*."

"I take it you weren't friends?" He said.

"They taught her how to be shallow and manipulative just like they were, and they didn't just take her from John, they took her from me and most importantly, from herself. She was looking for an identity, she was vulnerable, and they exploited that."

"It sounds as if you almost don't hate her…that you felt sorry for her?"

"I never *hated* her, I *loved* her…but she let them control her, and she, in turn, controlled John…until the day he died. I *resent* her for it. I resent her for being so weak."

They both jumped when the heavy log tumbled and scattered embers, nearly singing his eyebrows. The fire returned to life, angry that it had been disrupted, and slowly consumed the cedar flesh of the fresh sacrifice. Campbell brushed off his hands and plopped back down in his seat, then gave a disappointed look at his empty glass.

There seemed to be a quiet negotiation taking place in his head as he stared at the full bottle on his desk, unable to decide if it was worth giving up the comfort of his chair for the journey. With a long exhale he decided to put off another trip from his seat for the time being, deciding to let the fire warm him instead of the brandy, and turned his full attention back to his guest. With a nod and a click of his pen, he told her that he was ready again.

She gave the same disappointed glance at his pen and pad, then up at the clock on the wall, stifling a yawn with her fingertips. Her host mimicked her, glancing over his shoulder at the clock face as he suppressed his own yawn with a closed fist pressed to his lips.

"I didn't realize the time; you must be exhausted after the day you've had?"

"It just sort of hit me. I think the adrenaline has finally worn off. Can we--"

"Of course," he cut her off. "How about you have lunch with me tomorrow?"

"Lunch?" She asked.

"Unless you'd like breakfast? I just assumed that you'd like to sleep in, and besides, I make the best corned beef sandwiches in town; your husband's favorite."

"So I've heard. That sounds wonderful," she said with a warm smile, and then added, "The sandwich and the sleeping in."

Campbell escorted her to the door and retrieved her long coat from the rack. Always the gentleman, he held it for her as she slipped her arms into it and she gave a little shiver as the still-damp collar grazed the back of her neck. The rain had stopped an hour before, but it's cold fingers could still be felt on the coat.

"I should've hung this by the fire an hour ago," he said apologetically.

"It's fine, it's just a little damp still. At least the rain stopped…"

He opened the door for her and she hesitated at the threshold, peering out into the crisp night air, a look of apprehension on her face. There had been doubt in her statement about the rain, as if she wasn't altogether convinced that it had stopped, just because it wasn't pattering on the windows any longer. Extending her palm outward, she showed it to the sky as she might an animal with a questionable temperament. There was relief in her face when she withdrew it and saw that the invisible beast hadn't so much as brushed it with a damp tongue.

Campbell pressed the journal back into her hands, saying, "Take this with you and take a look at the next passages before you stop back by tomorrow. That way, we can dive right back into the discussion. I think you'll see many parallels between what we just spoke of and what's written there."

She nodded, staring down at the notebook, as if she didn't recognize it at all. Campbell had begun translating the secrets hidden within its pages and the book had been transformed into something more than a memoir. With its cryptic passages that could be interpreted dozens of ways and eerie accounts from the unknown beyond, only a rich leather binding or possibly velum pages separated it from other tomes of arcane or 'holy' knowledge.

She held it away from her body, not cradling it lovingly as she had a few hours earlier and carefully negotiated the steps, remembering the abrasion on her knee.

"I'll be sure to take a look at it in the morning," she said, looking over her shoulder at him. "Tonight, I just want to crawl into bed and shut the world out."

"Sometimes that's better than a glass of expensive brandy," he joked. "I'll take a look at those letters and see what sense I can make of them."

There was something ominous in his tone as he mentioned the letters, an aura in his words as unsettling as the tome dangling from her fingers. She wondered if perhaps there wasn't something that he'd already seen in his quick review that had disturbed him. Had he seemed too eager to corral her out the door? Was there a reason he'd insisted she not come over first thing in the morning, besides trying to sell her on his corned beef?

Trying to push the paranoid thoughts from her mind and shake the chill from her shoulders, she stepped back into the safety of her black sedan. Tossing the notebook into the passenger seat, she fumbled through her pockets for her keys and the cabin came to life. Reflections of various green and blue numbers and symbols were obfuscated in the fogged glass, until the rush of heated air from the vents slowly revealed them.

She stared at the reflections of the blinking system messages in the glass as she waited for the car to warm up. Beyond them, still watching from the doorway, was the man who'd been uncovering the foggy messages in the book more efficiently than the heater vents. As the windows were finally cleared, allowing her to back out of the long drive, she wondered if he would continue to reveal as much to her in the coming days.

Chapter 11

It was early on a Saturday morning, and the sun was just rising over the lake in the woods. Normally, the light beams peeking through the branches of John's primitive domicile woke him, but this particular morning it was the sound of footsteps crunching through the underbrush. They stopped at the overgrowth that was his front door, hesitated, and then a knock came from one of the trees.

Through the low-hanging branches and thick foliage he could see flesh tones trimmed in a faint blue and highlighted with gold. He pushed his way quietly through the back "entrance" of his tree home and made his way around the side to get a better look at his visitor. The light blue was the fabric of a pretty yet simple dress, the gold was the sunlight reflecting from her hair, and the flesh belonged to a young maid of about fifteen seasons with pink lips and cheeks. She waited expectedly outside of the front entrance still, rocking on her toes and looking nervous.

He straightened his tangle of hair and adjusted his only shirt, then appeared from behind the dome of tree branches with a smile. "Hello there."

She gave a start, but quickly collected herself and smiled back. "Hello John...I brought you some food...I thought you might be hungry."

There was a small cloth tucked under one arm, and she held it out at arm's length offering it to him. He approached slowly and took the parcel from her eagerly, feeling the warmth radiating from both her and the cloth bundle. Inside, he found three large pieces of freshly-baked bread, and he tore a piece from one of them to satisfy a rumbling belly.

He smiled at her politely as he enjoyed the delicious bread, saying, "What are you doing here? I thought you couldn't help me?"

She turned red-faced, either from being insulted or embarrassed, and replied, "Well it's just bread. I had extra, and I was doing the wash anyway. I thought I would see if you were still here."

"That was very kind of you. I still am." He chuckled.

She watched him devour the first piece and then the second before he seemed satiated, and wrapped the cloth back over the last piece to save it for later. "It's nice to have something besides fish for breakfast…or smoked venison."

"You are welcome. I'll need that cloth once you're finished with the last piece. It's no hurry…I can get it the next time."

"*Next time?*"

Her cheeks glowed again but her words were unwavering. "I have to do the wash more than once a year. I am here every Saturday to do work, and if you are still here then you can keep me company."

"I thought you weren't coming back to this side of the lake? You decided that maybe I wasn't as bad as the gossiping washer women after all?"

"Perhaps. If you begin gossiping or become an annoyance, I will take my chances with them. For now, you'll help me with the wash."

"Help you?"

"Yes, if you help, I'll finish my chores more quickly."

"Why would I help you wash your father's clothing?"

"Because it's more time I get to spend visiting, and consider it a fair price for my company. If you're going to take care of yourself, you need to learn how to wash anyway."

"So that I might make someone a good wife someday?"

She looked around, as though looking for someone, "Oh, you already have a wife who does your wash sir? My mistake! If my services aren't needed, perhaps I can find some other gentleman that needs them?"

"You are a tease!"

"I assure you, I am not! Your shirt could use a good washing by the looks of it. You'll never find a suitable woman in that filthy thing as it is!"

"I suppose you'll have to do until I find a suitable one then. I think one might be more forgiving of the condition more than the style."

"You are bold sir, to speak so of a gift, and one I risked my very neck to deliver to you."

"I am grateful, but you mock a shirt you gave to me? It's not as though I have a full wardrobe hanging about in my tree fortress there, nor do I have a seamstress or the coin to pay one."

"You have one now, if you pay her," she said in a playful tone.

"Do you prefer fish or colored rocks from the lake bed?"

"You do *all* of the wash, and I can sew you something more to your liking."

"All of the wash? I would be here for a week beating shirts on the rocks."

"Then you will learn how to become efficient," she said.

"That will take some time," he replied.

"And do you have more pressing matters? I can always go with the washer women…"

"You're here to humiliate me aren't you? Is this because I saw you in your bedclothes?"

"Humiliate you? Have you a reputation with the fish I should be concerned with?"

"No, but the squirrels will have much gossip to spread."

"I feel as though my company and my offer aren't appreciated."

"I suppose your company will have to do. Why are you here anyway?"

"Maybe I'm curious about the man from the forest. Maybe I just want to hear different stories from a different face than the same old nonsense I endure every Saturday."

"If you came for stories, I am sorry to disappoint you, I only have one good one about a bear. I told you that I don't remember anything from my past, my family, or where I came from."

"I would love to hear your bear story, and then you can make stories up for all I care. Maybe you could just listen to mine, because the good Lord knows that I have never been able to get a word in with those women across the lake."

He smiled, nodding, "I would be happy to hear your stories Nicolette."

"Finally," she joked, "some sincerity. At least…it *sounded* sincere."

"It was. So I get to listen to your stories, learn to wash clothing, and eat fresh bread for breakfast once a week with you?

135

In exchange…I help you with the wash and make up interesting stories to tell that aren't true? I think that sounds like a fair trade."

Just like that, when he least expected it, he'd found a friend and a cure for his terrible loneliness. And not just anyone, but the most beautiful girl he had ever seen who had more stories to tell than he ever would have guessed, and he loved every one of them.

There were simple tales about trifles between neighbors, trips to Rouen with her father, and how to prepare her favorite stew. There were also more serious stories about war, sweeping famine, and loss as well. Either she trusted him more than she let on, imparting her deepest secrets with him, or no one had ever really listened to her. In either case, he was glad she was sharing with him.

He learned that her father had spent many years off on campaigns to the east and that she had never really known him until her mother passed of the fever only a few seasons past. The two of them had to adjust to her death, and having only each other to rely upon, adjust very quickly. As a result, he spent more time at home and turned back to farming, as well as to the bottle. She had to learn to become a woman in short order, taking on the burden of her mother's responsibilities, and parted with the last remnants of childhood. Her father also became more overprotective of her and his temper was legendary in that small village.

A drunkard had made lewd comments once in his presence, the story goes, and was nearly beaten to death with a horsewhip as a result. For that reason, many steered clear of the only child of George of Avandale, even some of the women. Men of any age were never allowed to associate with her or even make eye contact, with the exception of Pelleon on occasion, because all men had ill intent according to him. And so, it seemed Nicolette's fate as a spinster had been decided for her.

By her fourth visit (she started doing wash twice a week just as an excuse to visit with him by then), she had exhausted only half of her stories and John was working on his own storytelling and his laundering skills. He was accounting for almost one quarter of the load and for a little less than that in their discussions. She was surprised that he really didn't have any stories of his own, but she enjoyed his tales of things that he'd made up.

The way he told them, she was almost convinced that he had seen the fantastic things he talked about, and she was

136

entranced by his tales. She would become so entranced that she would lose track of time and not notice that the sun was dipping into the lake behind them. In a panic, she would gather up the clothes that were drying on the grass and scurry away, as though she was in fear of her very life. John hated watching her go, and always counted the hours until she returned.

They spent that entire summer together, two days at a time, doing her own wash and the neighbor's just to get more time with him. Besides his stories, he shared with her all of the things he had done in the forest to pass the time. There was skipping stones, spearing fish and hunting for the right kind of stones that would spark just the right kind of moss. She was as adept at the fishing as he was with doing the wash, and they both laughed until their ribs hurt as she scared every trout from the shallows with her clumsy throws.

Later on, when she felt comfortable enough, she let him teach her how to swim. She'd never had the time for it as a girl, and he had all the time in the world and the benefit of a lake. He held her hands and pulled her along as she kicked her feet and churned the water, which he teased her about, saying that she scared even more fish away with her swimming than her spearing.

By the last week of summer, she was quite a bit more graceful, and would try to race him, but would always lose. One of those afternoons she'd been laughing and having so much fun that she had forgotten their ritual of modesty when getting in and out of the lake, and walked right up the beach in all of her glory.

She realized it too late and suddenly froze in place, covering herself with her hands and turning red, retreating back into the water and asking him to turn his back.

"Well I think it's hardly fair that you've seen every inch of me by this very lake, the first day you found me. And it's not like the water has helped any with modesty."

"That was different - you were hurt. I wasn't paying attention." She said, retrieving her dress. "And I cannot believe you would not tell me all this time that you could see...me...under the water!"

"You weren't *paying attention*? How could you not pay attention?"

"No, I do not mean that...I noticed, but..." She became flustered.

"I would certainly have noticed you."

"I think you've done quite enough of your noticing. I was just more concerned for you," She stammered, hurriedly dressing, and keeping one eye turned towards him.

"Concerned with what?"

"I was worried that you were…"

"*Dead*? Then it wouldn't have mattered if I was naked if I was dead?"

"No. You don't think those things of the dead…I mean…you…"

"What things? So you would be attracted to me if you saw me without a stitch on now, but if I was dead that would be disrespectful to think anything of it?"

"Well, of course that would be disrespectful!" She finished lacing up her bodice and said, "You can turn back around now."

"I'm curious about what kinds of things you were thinking that day."

"I wasn't thinking anything! I was thinking 'here's a man who looks like he's dead, I should see if he's still breathing.' You're just being foolish."

"So you didn't notice me at all? Your father doesn't have anything to be concerned with then – you are truly on the right path to becoming a spinster if you take no notice of naked men whatsoever."

He laughed but she didn't find the comment amusing, and her face suddenly turned serious, and her fists turned into little balls as she shouted at him. "I don't want to be a spinster! I don't plan on waiting on my father hand and foot for the rest of my life! I want to be married and have a family of my own!"

He stopped laughing and forced a very serious face then. The usually pleasantly-pink cheeks were blazing like the overhead sun, and her eyes were as wide as he had ever seen them.

"Of all the stories you've ever told me, you've never once told me a single one about yourself, did you realize that?"

"What do you mean?" She huffed, eyeing him warily as he approached.

"I mean that everything you've ever told me has been about your mother or your father, how much you love them and want to please them, but you've never once said anything about what you want for yourself. Not until now."

138

"What of it? Doesn't every girl want to be married and have a family?"

"I just always envisioned you as this girl who was dominated by her duty and I never asked you a thing about any of your desires for a future of your own."

"I want a life of my own, that's why I come here to spend time with you, because it's something I like to do. Don't you have things you like to do or that you dream about, besides the odd dreams you fashion your stories from?"

"Well yes, I have things I want…"

"And what is it that you want?"

He was standing just a few feet short of her, close enough to reach out and touch her, but he kept his hands on his hips, as if coming any closer might startle her like a doe. She had subconsciously backed away as far as the trees would allow her to, though he didn't press forward any further into her space.

"I suppose I want the same as any other man: to get my hands dirty in the fields or in battle, fighting for a home that I've built with those same hands, find a good woman…"

He took a step nearer and he watched as she tensed up and stopped in mid breath, watching him like that frightened doe watches a man. Slowly, his hand moved towards hers and she felt the warmth and softness of it as it brushed against her skin. Hairs stood, muscles tensed, and head was poised as all senses were focused, ready to dart away.

"…fall in love…start a family," he continued on, braving another step.

His fingers danced in between hers and it sent a chill up her arm as far as her shoulder, and the fingers followed that impulse along its trail. Up her arm, across her shoulder, and brushing the flesh of her delicate neck ever-so-slightly as it finally came to rest on one of those blazing cheeks.

"Those sound like wonderful things," she said in a raspy voice. "Someday I hope all of those come true for you…and me as well."

"I've already found a *home*," he said in a whisper.

"That's not much of a home…or one suitable for a wife."

"Home isn't wood and thatch, mud or stone, it's flesh and bone. It's the person you want to return to when he sun falls beneath the trees at the end of the day. You said that you come here to have a life of your own? Well, for me, when you come here, you make this place like home just being near. When you leave…this place is empty…and it becomes just a forest again."

She cupped the hand that rested on her cheek and closed her eyes to his touch, resting her head in his hand and listening to the sound of his words. No one had ever made her feel more necessary just by being there, and her entire body had never tingled at the sound of a man's voice before like his.

"What are you saying?" She asked in a breathy voice.

"I'm saying that I need you, Nicolette, and I have loved you since I set eyes on you."

The tingling intensified, every muscle stiffening and making her whole body rigid, until everything let go the moment his mouth closed around hers. Taking her first draught of pure euphoric bliss that can only be found in a first kiss, she drank deeply and eagerly, savoring every second of it. More satisfying than the words that had prepared the way for that kiss, she lost herself in it, and in his arms, for an eternity all her own.

The heavy sun, hovering so close above the water, reminded her that their day and their moment were at an end. She squirmed out of his arms, collected her basket, and kissed him once more before she hurried off towards home. He was left standing there, watching her disappear within the forest that was already thick with the shadows of dusk. The kiss lingered on his lips as well as the curiosities which follow an impromptu first kiss with a beautiful girl.

Chapter *12*

She did not return to visit him the following Saturday and he became worried. Pacing up and down the beach, tossing stones for hours, he ignored a rumbling belly that had not been filled with her bread that morning. His defiance lasted until the end of the evening, when necessity took over and he was forced to catch a fish and make it his supper begrudgingly. He lay awake all that night, wondering what became of her, and hoped that she would show the next morning. She did not.

Three more days passed, and on the fourth, she finally appeared with her basket of clothing but no bread for him. She also chose a spot further away from their usual place and commenced to doing the wash as if she didn't even know he was there, watching her.

"Nicolette?" He called from the edge of the forest, not certain if he should approach her.

His call went unanswered and unacknowledged, and she continued on in her chore. John's face went flush and the hairs prickled on the tops of his ears as though there was danger nearby, but he could see nothing. Never once did she look over her shoulder to acknowledge him there, though she must have known he was there, and she simply collected her articles and made her way back along the trail towards her village.

John pursued her, keeping to the cover of the trees instinctively, but calling out her name every few feet until he got her attention.

"I cannot talk to you today, people are watching me."

"Watching you? Nicolette, what happened? I was worried about you!"

"I cannot be seen with you today. I will come back and explain when I can."

"When will that be? Why are people watching you?"

She didn't answer, keeping her eyes straight ahead and trying to hold back tears and her quivering lips pressed firmly together. He could only watch her helplessly as she left the forest and made her way over the crest of the hill, disappearing again and leaving him with a confused aching in his chest.

It was finally in the middle of the night, more than a week later, that she came to him. Half asleep and groggy, he barely stirred from his dreams before she was already atop him on his bed of skins, her own skin pressed against his, chasing away the chill of the night. He was assailed by kisses and she wrapped herself around him as she whispered unintelligibly to him.

"I'm so sorry...I've missed you so much...my father...I couldn't see you..."

"Nicolette? Slow down! What's happened?"

"John...I wanted to come to you but he's been watching me and he's had people watching me! I couldn't get away, and he's even hired Pelleon's sister to do the wash with the others on the other side of the lake!"

"What? Why is he doing that?" He asked, sitting up and rubbing the sleep from his eyes.

"I think he knows something, or at the very least, suspects something. That last day I came home late and he was home from the tavern waiting for me. He was drunk and...he said awful things to me. He forbade me from doing the wash or leaving his sight - I had to sneak out tonight just to see you. If he wakes up and discovers I'm gone..."

"Nicolette, calm down. He's not going to find you here in the forest - you can barely see this grove in broad daylight."

"John, I don't know what to do! I can't just sneak out every night and hope I don't get caught, but I need to see you! I haven't been able to stop thinking about you...and there's so much I want to talk to you about."

He pulled her down beside him, draping an arm around her, as he settled back in to resume his sleep.

"John! I can't just stay here with you and act like...everything is okay! We need to figure out what to do about my father!"

"What *can* we do? Either continue seeing me in secret, or come stay with me here for good."

She sat back up and was trying to compose herself, starting to hyperventilate again just like she had been after her harrowing escape from the house. Tugging at his arm, she forced him to sit back up so that she could talk with him.

142

"None of those things will have a good outcome, John! If my father knew you were here, he would come with every man in the village and hunt you down. If he caught me sneaking out...well I don't even want to think of what he would do then. And if I came to stay with you here...well...that's not even a possibility."

"Why isn't that a possibility?"

"Because I can't just abandon my father, for one, and you live in the *forest*, for another thing! How would we live? I can just hear my father: *You are marrying a man who lives in the woods and catches fish?*" She imitated her father's deep baritone voice. "That's not the kind of life I want for myself, John, or for you!"

"What kind of life do you want Nicolette? The one you have now? Living under your father's thumb? Letting him make you feel guilty about your mother so that you have to take care of him forever? You already said that you wanted a life beyond that - well, *now's* your chance!"

"I love my father, and I help him because he needs me!"

"He's hired another girl to do the wash because he doesn't trust you! Does it sound like he needs your help? I love you because of how you make me feel when you're around, not because I need someone to cook and clean for me! What about that?"

"That isn't fair, John! That's not at all fair of you to say!"

"What? That your father just wants to keep you around because he's afraid to be alone, or that I want you around for different reasons?"

"Both! You're making me choose between you and my father, and I just can't do that!" She broke down into sobs.

"I'm not the one making you choose! It's *him*! He's the one being unreasonable! Most fathers know that their girls will eventually want to make a home and a family of their own, and encourage their daughters to do so."

"My father and I come from a different home, John! It would be fine if my mother was still around to take care of him, so that I would be free to pursue my own dreams, but that's just not the plan God had for us. He isn't ready for me to be gone yet."

"*He* isn't ready or *you're* not ready?"

"What is that supposed to mean? *Of course* I'm ready! Do you think you're the first boy to try to steal me away from my father? Do you think I haven't dreamed about being a grown

143

woman and having my own family? I've always given up on it and dismissed it as foolish daydreaming until now and until you! I wouldn't have risked everything I have for nothing."

"Then we'll run away together and start our own life and then when your father calms down, we'll return and talk to him about it. Once we're married there isn't anything he can do about it."

"He would still kill you, whether you were my husband or not! And where would we go, John? How would you even make us a home? How would you provide for us?"

"I've built what I have with my own two hands and a hatchet - I need more tools to build a proper home! I can build us a cozy place here in the woods, and catch us fish until we are eighty if need be!"

"What a stupid thing to say - no one lives to *eighty*! I'm not eating fish every day either…"

"Then *forty*, or *fifty* - what does it matter? And we don't have to always eat fish, it was just an expression. It means that I love you and I don't care where we live or what we eat, so long as we're together. I don't care if I don't remember my family or where I came from, I just need you."

"I know you do…but there is more to this than you've given consideration to."

"All I've thought about is you for the past week - that's all the consideration I need."

"John, *I* gave you the axe and that was my *father's*! Where will you get tools? Building a house takes more skill than you'd think. What about farming? Do you even know how to plant or harvest?"

"I can hunt game until I get the planting thing down…I figured you could help with that."

"Did you even know that in most places, if you kill a doe, the lord of the land will arrest you for it? You're very fortunate no one has found you out! These are things you should *know*, but you don't, and without those other skills…you won't ever be able to get us away from this patch of trees!"

"Nicolette…home is more than just wood and thatch…"

"Yes, it is…but you also can't keep out the cold winters with dreams or keep your belly full with prayers. If I didn't love you I wouldn't be laying awake at night crying or thinking about

144

how I can make this right for us. I wouldn't have risked my father's wrath coming here to see you tonight! But if I was *ever* to consider facing him, and making a life with you, I need to know that you can take care of us both...and *children*."

John hung his head, and though she could barely make his features out in the dark, she knew that hot tears ran down his face the same as hers. He shared her impossible choice now, and he understood just as well that there was no choice that wouldn't be heartbreaking for one or both of them.

After a long silence she whispered, "I almost wish you hadn't kissed me that day...because I do not know how I will go on without you in my life."

"So you've decided already...that this is over before it's begun?"

"I didn't decide anything, it was decided for us long before I was ever foolish enough to come looking for you. It isn't your fault that you're here or that you don't remember anything about your life before this place, any more than it's mine that my life is the way it is. It's my fault for coming back here...for being curious about you...for not being able to control myself and thinking about what had become of you. I blame myself for that, and I never should have come..."

"Don't talk that way," he said, stroking her cheek. "Don't ever regret coming here or giving me the best days of my life. Even if I don't make it through this winter, and it's the end of me, warm thoughts of you will keep me until that last breath."

"Now you're the one talking foolishly. You're not going to die out here. I wouldn't be able to forgive myself if something happened to you! You're going to pack your things and you're going to go somewhere else!"

He shook his head, "No, I'm not leaving you, even if I die here! This is *our* place and I have to stay here in case, just once more, you can sneak out and visit me!"

She cradled his face in her hands then, becoming very stern and choking back her tears, "No, you listen to me! If you stay here then you'll die and then there is no chance that we'll ever be together! You need to go away, and you need to stay in the city for the winter! My uncle...he's a blacksmith in Rouen...I can give you his name..."

"Nicolette..."

"Listen to me please! I have given this many nights of thought. I want to be with you and I want us to do this the right way. If you go and meet with my uncle, he would at the *very least*, give you a place to stay that's warm this winter. Pay attention to his craft and you could become his apprentice, and then he would surely give you a proper introduction to my father then. We travel to Rouen about once a month for supplies, and will be there at the end of harvest. We stay with my uncle and I would be able to see you then..."

"That's *two* months away! I would go crazy without you! And if you're coming with your father, how will you even get away to see me?"

"My father takes an entire day just negotiating prices for the crops he sells, making sure he doesn't miss a single coin. I usually go with my cousins to the market and watch the ships come in, or just browse the merchant tables. I could spend the entire day with you..."

"So we get one day...twice a year to be together?"

"You don't think this is awful for *me* as well? We have to do it this way, or no way at all! Once you are properly introduced to my father and he sees that you are a successful, upstanding man, he would be more apt to let us be married. By then, you can save some money and build us a home. Maybe we could even live in the city..."

John rubbed his temples; his headache was growing at the thought.

"You're talking about us being away for months and then *possibly* that there may be a *chance* that we can be together? You're asking me to go away to make a life for us...when there's a likelihood that we may not be able to be together because, in the end, your *father* may not approve?"

"We have to put this in God's hands, John..."

"There it is again! What is with you people and that expression?"

"It's true. We can only change so many things; the rest isn't up to us."

"So, you want to try this plan of yours and suffer through months without seeing each other, all in the hopes that your father comes to his senses some day? What then? What if he refuses?"

She cracked a smile then, saying, "Then we take matters into our own hands. If we do everything properly, ask God and my father for their blessings and they still turn us away, then we'll run off together."

He could only laugh and shake his head at her, "I have your word?"

"Only if you've learned a trade and have saved up enough money to do so!" She interjected, holding up a finger that said she was quite serious.

"You believe this much in us – in me – after one summer together? After one kiss?"

"It was a *really great* summer and a *really great* kiss! I know that it's you I'm supposed to be with, and I know that we will be together someday."

"You don't really know all that much about me…"

She put a slender hand to his face and smiled up at him. "I *do* have faith in you, and that is why I want you to do this for us. I know enough about you to know that you *will* be a great man, a good husband and father to our children. You are the man that I love and I am not going *anywhere*. I will wait for you."

"Nicolette…I don't know what to say," he choked out.

"Don't say anything else," she whispered, and pulled him close to kiss him. "This is our last night for a while."

It was like the first kiss but there was so much more behind it. It was just as passionate, but a sort of quiet release as well, as she turned her life over to the boy she loved the most and to her God above who was ever watchful. She knew, somehow, that he would never fail her and that, in turn, God would preserve them and lead them back to one another. She told him these things and many other secrets in breathy whispers as they lay together beneath the autumn canopy of their cozy little sanctuary.

She left just before daylight, with final instructions on how to reach Rouen and a prayer that she would see him safely there soon. Standing on her tiptoes, she kissed him again deeply, then handed him a bundle wrapped in a leather strap that she'd brought, telling him not to open it until he was on the road.

He lay alone inside of his small tangle of trees, trying to fall back asleep, but the place was eerily quiet and empty without her there. It was then that he knew he couldn't stay there if he'd wanted to, because she wasn't ever coming back to that place to see him. He packed up his few belongings, rolling them into a deerskin, and decided not to waste another moment there in the forest. Saying goodbye to his lakeside retreat, he set off into the early morning light towards the city.

As promised, he didn't open the wrapped bundle until he was several hours along the road. Inside was a considerable portion of her fresh bread, and a folded piece of paper. He chewed on a piece of the bread as he unfolded the paper, trying to read the words she'd written without success. Apparently reading was just another skill he didn't possess, and would have to learn in the city. Folded within the parchment was a small bit of braided rope, as thin as one of Nicolette's fingers, and long enough to fasten about his neck.

It had been woven by intertwining hemp, a strip of his favorite blue dress, and several strands of her golden hair, and was adorned by small pieces of bone carved into beads. In the morning light, the strands shimmered like gold and the beads gleamed silver. There were words etched into them as well, but he could not read those either.

The bundle itself was actually a shirt she had been working on for him for some time, dyed black and considerably more fashionable than the one he was wearing. He buried his face in it and it smelled of her and of the loaf of bread she had packed with it. He pulled the shirt over his head and fashioned the leather strap into a belt, tucking his hatchet into it, just in case the road to Rouen wasn't as easy to travel as she'd made it sound. Surviving the road would be the easy part; it would be surviving without the girl he was leaving behind that would prove most difficult.

Chapter 13

Gwenn closed the journal, tucking the loose, yellow notes inside that had Campbell's translations on them, and set it on the side table beside her chair. Across from her was the expectant face of her old college professor, waiting for some verdict. She swallowed the bite she was chewing, dabbed at the corner of her mouth with the cloth napkin, and leaned forward in her seat to share her decision.

"Well...John was right about the sandwich; I can't remember when I've had better. You have to tell me where you get this dark rye from, and the gourmet mustard."

His eyes lit up, eager to share his deepest culinary secrets. "There's a little place not far from campus called Zingerman's where I pick up a loaf, and the mustard is my mother's recipe – I'll give you some to take with you."

The smell of the grilled onions and toasted rye still wafted into the room from the hall, mixing with the pipe tobacco and she recognized it as the same aroma she used to smell on her husband's shirts after a visit with Campbell.

"Maybe if I'd kept some of this bread and a bottle of your scotch around the house, John would've spent more time there," she said with a lighthearted tone, unable to disguise the hurt in her eyes.

"I don't think I lured him here with the corned beef or my store of Calvados, and I wasn't quite as pretty to look at as what he had at home," he reassured her, taking her plate and setting it on the mini bar in the back corner of his study.

Pouring himself a glass of that famous apple brandy and grabbing up his notes from the desk, he returned to a quietly reflective guest. He'd hoped that she was pondering the pages she'd just read (or perhaps the recipe for the mustard) and not letting self-pity get the best of her before they even started.

In a chipper tone, shuffling the notes he began their discussion. "So, you've had a chance to read the passages I assigned...sorry, it's an old habit to use the word 'assigned'...what did you think?"

"I still think of you as 'Dr. Campbell' anyway, and that outfit doesn't help any either," she said, giggling. "Anyway, I didn't see any compelling evidence that linked this Nicolette with Melinda, other than the basics wants and dreams every young girl has."

"I suppose that's fair to say," he conceded. "Every girl needs to know that her emotional and financial needs will be met, but some put more of a premium on that than others. I'm referring to the very specific challenges they faced; there was a 'trial' of sorts that had to be passed before they could be together."

"I married for *love* and nothing else, Jim," she said proudly. "And we went through a trial of our own – many couples do. Despite how we felt, we couldn't be together until it was the right time. John wanted the same out of life, yet he kept finding these girls who were more concerned with money and status."

"Most young men and women are attracted to those most like their parents. John's mother followed the same principles – if you'd call them that – as Miss Malowski. Of course he belonged with someone like you, and eventually figured that out, but not until he'd struggled trying to make things work with girls who were more like his mother."

"I suppose that makes sense; I loved John because he reminded me of my father. We never had much money, but my dad loved us all in a way that Melinda's father never did."

"Well, there you have it then; Mr. Malowski was the ideal archetype for a man to Melinda: wealthy, successful, ambitious, and not without his influences in the right circles. She responded to that, and though I believe she saw some of her father's other virtues in John, she couldn't accept a man she considered incomplete."

"And Nicolette? You believe that she turned him away because he was *incomplete*? I didn't see that...not from what I've read. I think she was different than Melinda and she was less selfishly-motivated, but you think she was just as awful?"

"*Awful* is a matter of opinion. Does wanting security and some sort of normalcy in a relationship make a man or a woman awful?"

"I suppose it depends on the lengths one will go to in finding what they need," she said. "What about her influential friends who were putting ideas into her head? Nicolette had no friends, and she acted alone in pursuit of her ambitions with this boy she loved."

"Did she? There were no physical advisors to steer her, no, but I think Nicolette had her own counsel of conscience. That's what those friends of hers were, after all, isn't it? She couldn't make decisions on her own, so they served to guide her, almost like an external conscience."

"I suppose that's an accurate metaphor, but how does that relate to this girl?"

"Melinda isn't mature or experienced enough to make these decisions on her own is she? Before John, there really weren't any boys who were older or whom she felt the same way about as John correct?"

Gwenn nodded.

"So who does she turn to? Not Gwenn Lawson because she wasn't an expert in matters of love either, was she? The other girls were no better, but they gave the illusion of being more experienced and so she turned to them, desperate to know what the "mature" girls did in her situation."

"I'm not disagreeing with you about any of that, it's pretty black and white, but what has it got to do with a girl like the one in John's dreams?"

"Nicolette is also at a delicate age and in a delicate situation. All she knows is that she wants to be with this boy, and she follows her heart for a time, but then realizes that there's more to it than just a summer flirting. She desperately seeks counsel on what to do next, from the only place she can."

"There is no counsel, Jim. Why won't you just admit that this is a point where the two of them diverge and are different people?"

"Nicolette has a counsel...but not one that's obvious. She looks to the wisdom of those who know about relationships - about real relationships that are meant to last. She's a woman of faith, old enough to remember her mother and the values she instilled in her, and she was a victim of the gossip of the older washerwomen of her village. This is her counsel, and this is what she draws upon in making her decision about John."

"You got all that from that short passage? You really had to dig for that didn't you?" She said.

"The other option is to say that Nicolette had the presence of mind to just know how to handle her relationship with John. We can say that she had no need for any counsel or influence of any sort, and she just knew, as if by instinct alone, precisely what to do. That would make her a complete opposite of Melinda, and every other impressionable teen girl who walks the earth, and would have to mean...that she didn't exist!"

"So if she was the *same* as Melinda, he made her up? And if she was *different* than Melinda, he made her up then too? That's convenient!"

"Then give me something else that proves she was real! Give me something that you know about John or Melinda or their relationship that I can't use to reinforce my argument! So far you've given me a story of a girl who wants a bit of security and who has difficulty in putting her emotions in check to pursue that security. That describes the girl in this notebook."

"The girl in the notebook could just as easily be *me*, if that's your argument. I wanted something too, and I had to put my feelings on hold for many years, doing what was right."

Campbell nodded, "I had considered that as well, and it's not something I've eliminated as a possibility Gwenn. But I believe that this other place was created for the purpose of John finding closure with certain individuals, and I don't think he needed to find forgiveness with you."

"I don't know if I should take that as a compliment or something else."

"You should feel fortunate to be one of the few constants in John's life and that he looked to you as his anchor when things started to fall apart. I think that there are parts of your own personality in this other woman he wrote about as well, and that he subconsciously desired her to be more like you than Melinda. The minor differences you see between the two of them are taken from you, I believe."

"That's flattering...in some ways. You're saying that John made a hybrid Gwenn-Melinda character because we both lacked things he desired?"

"That's oversimplifying again, but yes, that's what I'm saying. That's why similarities and differences between the girl in this journal and Melinda aren't really valid enough points to prove that she existed or that, in the bigger picture, the entire world he created was a real place either. The things that were different about this other girl I can easily link to you and other women he knew."

Gwenn Chapel stood from her seat and took her own glass over to the desk to help herself. It was an excuse to get another look at the pages tacked to the wall, certain there was something missing and obvious that she should've seen before. She poured the brown liquid slowly, scanning the drawings, pages and colored notes. When she'd finished, she snatched up her glass and took a triumphant draught as she turned to face him again.

"Okay...so you need something that's *irrefutable*? If you're making a list of people he needed to set things right with, what about his *mother*? There's not a single mention of a mother or a father in connection to the other John, is there? She's nowhere on that wall behind me, and she should be!"

Campbell could only sit quietly contemplative, as if trying to recall the information from memory. When that seemed to yield no answers, he referred to his pile of notes again.

"You know the story as well as I do, and translated parts that I've never even had a chance to look at, yet I know that there's no mention of his mother anywhere in the story. If this other place is some type of...*purgatory* for the liberation of all my husband's ghosts, then why isn't *she* there? She caused him as much aggravation as Melinda ever did!"

He gave up on his notes and met her expectant gaze finally, though reluctantly, and his voice was an odd pitch as he struggled to put something together that made sense. "Not everything translates over the same way...the story is very difficult to follow sometimes...there are a couple of possibilities..."

Gwenn gave a satisfied grin over the rim of her glass, "Just admit that you don't have a *perfect* answer for that one either, and if you do, I'd like to hear it."

The Professor cleared his throat, pushed his glasses up on the bridge of his nose and scoured his yellow legal pad again. He was either seeking an answer there for her, or trying to buy himself time as he looked internally for one. Neither place yielded anything satisfactory and he finally shrugged at her.

"John never said much about his mother. With the exception of the incident at Rain tree, and a bit later on when she finally called him from out-of-state, there really is nothing…"

"My husband never said much about *Victoria Chapel*? The woman who he blamed for the ruin of his relationship with Melinda and who almost ruined our own? I'm quite surprised by that, Jim. That woman was more wicked, destructive and selfish than Melinda ever thought of being, and he didn't share this with you?"

Campbell shook his head and clicked his pen, giving her his full attention. "Please, spare no details about Ms. Chapel, and her part in all of this. Do you think that she would be available for discussion at some point?"

"Vicki has been too busy feeling sorry for herself since the loss of her son, and she and I aren't exactly on speaking terms. She wouldn't be sober long enough to give you a coherent statement anyway, Jim. But I can tell you plenty about her and how she not only ruined every relationship he's ever had, but how she started him along a path that…ultimately destroyed him."

WARM GLOW IN WINTER

*"In the depth of winter, I finally learned that within me
Lay an invincible summer."*

~Albert Camus

It was Christmas, and a bitterly cold wind bit at the cheeks of the lone figure standing on the porch, causing his eyes to water and blurring his vision. There was nothing new about the place to miss anyway, and even through the watery lens it looked the same as the last time he had seen it. Time hadn't disturbed the place, leaving it as intact as the unbroken carpet of snow in the front yard. As soon as the first heavy steps crunched across that carpet, however, the wind blew the white coverings from the trees, and the place came alive again, like a clock that had just been wound.

The young man wrapped up in three layers of wool, cotton and leather hadn't wanted to return to that place, or be the one that started that ominous clock ticking again, but she insisted. He'd promised her that he would come, and much had happened between that day and this one. In fact, he wasn't sure that he would ever be fulfilling that promise, the way things had deteriorated after Port Austin, and he couldn't say that he wasn't at least somewhat relieved by the prospect of not having to face her parents ever again.

Standing there on that porch, feeling the stare of the illuminated eye of the doorbell, he was overcome by a mixture of dread and exhilaration. He hadn't seen her face in two months, and they had all but called it quits, which was the longest, most miserable eight weeks he'd had since the days he'd first been separated from her. A tear-stained letter had informed him that things had come to an impasse, and that she just couldn't see him anymore, and then, only two nights ago, the phone call came that told him that she couldn't be without him.

That same night, he drove hastily to Gwenn's for a teary reunion that involved lots of make-up kissing and a very uncomfortable discussion detailing her failed attempt at dating two other guys that culminated in her realization that she wanted to be with him again. This, in turn, resumed the full-scale war with her parents, and she wasn't going to concede until they agreed to talk with him. To her, it was a hard-won victory, but to him it was one of the most stressful, dreadful situations he'd been put in since the day her little brother passed.

He only had a day to prepare for his visit with the Malowskis and to put together an argument so brilliant that they would have no choice but to give their blessing. It would've been easier preparing a brief for Clarence Darrow himself in the Scopes trial, than arguing against Mrs. Malowski in the case for her daughter dating him.

So he sat up all the night before, eating very little, and throwing up more than he'd forced down, in preparation for that meeting. Now, he found himself standing frozen by the terrible wind and the prospect of failing the woman he loved again, and he couldn't recall a single word of his prepared speech. His gloved finger hovered above the illuminated button, running through a dozen greetings he'd rehearsed on the drive down, but not satisfied with any of them. Shivering from the cold, his finger involuntarily pressed the button, and he shuddered realizing that he'd started the countdown.

A moment later, he heard heavy footsteps approaching and the porch light flipped on above him. , He let out two long, icy breaths trying to prepare himself as he watched the handle turn and the light from inside spilled out onto the porch. A man who'd been middle aged for as long as he could remember stood before him, dressed in a plaid cranberry sweater and wearing a smile.

He welcomed him inside, "Come on in John, I have a fire going in the basement – you look like you could use it."

The bundled young man nodded and managed a nervous smile as he entered, kicking the snow from his boots. There was some small relief in the fact that Dennis had answered the door and not his wife, and he was thankful that he still had a few minutes to prepare before he met her. Perhaps they had engineered it that way, and she wanted the suspense to overwhelm him before they came face to face. Or, quite possibly, Melinda had insisted that her dad answered the door to make him feel more comfortable.

"Merry Christmas! It's good to see you again," he said, shaking his hand and taking his jacket.

"You too, Mr. Malowski," he said, managing his warmest fake smile.

"Melinda is downstairs too, I'm sure she'll be excited to see you. Marge is finishing up with dinner, I hope you like ham."

"It smells delicious!" John said, with more genuineness than his handshake.

The house really did smell more inviting than it had appeared from the outside, and he was assailed by a mixture of cooking spices, baked pies cooling somewhere in the kitchen, and seasonal candles burning from every corner of the house.

Taking off his boots, he descended the stairs into the elaborately-furnished basement. There was the same bar with the same old bar stools he remembered sitting on to drink root beer with the other kids, and the same billiard table in the corner with the dusty green lamps hanging over it. The old television had been replaced by a fancy new big screen, and he stopped to admire it. He had never seen a T.V. so large, and he said as much to Mr. Malowski who followed him down.

Melinda was seated on the old couch watching a show, and she gave John a little wave, pretending not to be too eager with her father standing right behind her. He snatched up the intricate-looking remote and offered it to him. "You can watch whatever you kids like before we get dinner on the table and while we're waiting for everyone to arrive."

John stood frozen with the sleek thing in his hand, studying the buttons and thinking on what he had just said. There were *others* coming. What did that mean? Melinda hadn't said anything about there being a dinner or a huge production at the house, and he wondered what that signified. Was it just a simple, friendly dinner, where he could meet the rest of her family, or had Marge invited everyone over to watch as she destroyed and humiliated him?

Dennis walked over to the brick hearth to poke at the fire, thinking the already-eighty degree room wouldn't quite be warm enough for their guest. Perhaps he was trying to make him sweat more than he already was, and it was part of the plan to soften him up before he met his old nemesis. When Mr. Malowski turned around, he smiled warmly at John again with his perfectly-off-white teeth, and he noticed by the light of the fire how much older he looked.

He looked much older than he had originally thought upstairs. His hair had grayed more, and he wore thicker glasses on

159

thinner frames. The creases in his face had deepened, and there were more shadows in the pits of his sunken cheeks that were cast by the flickering light. His eyes had always seemed sad, but now the once-brilliant blue was faded like an old magazine cover.

Time, indeed, had touched the Malowski family and the house.

"I'm headed up to help Marge, would you like some egg nog or warm cider, John?" He always called him *John*, not *Johnny* like the others, even when he was a boy. He had always liked that, because it had made him feel more mature and likewise respected.

"No, thank you Dennis," he said with a more genuine smile than before.

The small talk and the presence of Melinda in the room had allowed him to relax somewhat, and the knot began to unravel in his stomach as well. His dry mouth began to water at the thought of kissing her as soon as he left the room, and he almost forgot that her mother was only one floor above, waiting to begin her inquisition. Her father nodded and gave them both a look, like a friendly warning, and then turned to head upstairs.

She waited until the door closed before leaping from the couch to smother him. He hadn't anticipated that her greeting would be so eager, and it took his breath away for a moment. Hands gripped his face, holding it in place as she went to work on his lips with her own, as if he might try to escape. After a few minutes, he tried to halt her unrelenting advance, reminding her that the floors and walls weren't as thick as she thought.

"I'm just happy to see you and glad that you came," she said with a pouty expression.

"I'm glad to see you too, but we have to be careful with your parents right upstairs," he whispered. "It sounds like you're sucking the juice out of an orange."

"Oh, it does not!" She insisted and resumed her kissing.

Maybe she was right and he was just overly-paranoid and jumpy. He decided to enjoy her greeting, and tried to push the thought from his head that it might be the last time he would ever kiss her if things went badly. Her mouth was warm and moist and lips soft, her tongue playing gently in his mouth, just the way he had remembered from their last kiss. He'd kissed her two days before, but he still missed it.

160

He backed her against the couch and went on the offensive, locking her fingers in his, holding her hands at her sides as he reciprocated her aggressive kissing. For several minutes, he played and teased at her lips with his own, then moved in to gorge himself on her tongue, sending chills through her body. Just as things were getting intense, he broke off the kiss and took a step back, a peculiar look on his face, as if he'd just done something wrong.

"What's the matter?"

"I just *missed* you-that's all," He tried to give her the fake smile he'd given Dennis.

She grabbed him by the arms and pulled herself away to get a look at his face. "What's wrong Johnny? You just stopped kissing me, and you've never done that…like that."

His head dipped and he let out a long breath, "Everything is wrong…"

Her fingers went slack on his arms and she took another step back, sitting back on the couch, pulling him down beside her. "What do you mean *everything* is wrong?"

"I don't know…just…things are different," he tripped over the words.

"Different how? You don't like kissing me anymore?"

"It's not that. It's…when I think about you kissing those other guys…it bothers me."

She frowned at him, folding her arms across her chest, "I don't want to be with those other guys, and I can't believe you're bringing them up tonight of all nights."

"You asked! That's what's on my mind. If you didn't want to know, you shouldn't have asked me," he grumbled and stood from the couch.

She grabbed his arm and pulled him back. He let out another long breath and plopped down beside her again, but stared into his own lap, not wanting her to see his face. There was hurt there, and he'd tried to keep it masked for her benefit, but he'd simply had too much time to think about the things. Initially, he'd just been incredibly happy that she'd called him and that he was touching her and kissing her again, but after that wore off, the other things started to preoccupy his thoughts.

"Hey," she said, lifting his chin. "You're here right now because I chose you over those other boys. I explained that to you the other day. I couldn't bear to be away from you any longer, and I sacrificed a lot to have you here tonight."

"I understand that…and I know how hard it must have been for you, but I can't get the image of you making out with another guy out of my head. My mind gets carried away…and I don't like thinking of you letting some guy put his hands all over you…"

"It wasn't like that, John! I know you think I'm like the rest of my friends, but I'm not! My mother wanted me to be, and they wanted me to be, but I couldn't be that way! I could only think of you, the entire time. No matter what I was doing or who I was with, you were always the one I wanted there! Please don't turn me away now…"

"I'm not turning you away. I'm just having a hard time with this on top of everything else. You just left me, and sent me a *letter* to say goodbye. A one-page letter was all I got."

"We've been over this! I said I was sorry and that I didn't know how to say goodbye. I couldn't face you because I wouldn't have been able to…do what I had to do. My mother forbade me seeing you at all, once I told her, what did you want me to do?"

"I don't know, Mel. The whole thing was just…awful. I went for months thinking that I wouldn't see you again. And when I finally do, I have to hear about your other boyfriends and the things you did with them. You didn't have to tell me all that!"

"I've never lied to you, Johnny, and I'm not about to start! I wasn't going to leave anything out, and I didn't want there to be secrets between us to come back and cause problems down the road. That was the right thing to do, and I'm sorry you're having a hard time with it! My friends told me to lie to you, but I told them that you would be understanding, and that they didn't know you."

"I'm sorry…you're right…you shouldn't have kept anything from me. It's just hard…this whole thing is hard…and now, I have to face your mother and if I screw this up, this could be the last time I see you!"

"You want to know what's hard? Hard is listening to your brother go on and on about all the girls you talk to when the two of you go hang out! That's what's hard! But I never once criticized you for that did I? I never once asked who you were with or how many girls you'd made out with, did I? You know why? Because I love you and the only thing that's important to me is us being together!"

She looked very hurt and she was the one to stand from the couch and cross the room to sit closer to the fire. Her arms were folded and she glared down at her feet as if she was dissatisfied with them. John sat by himself on the couch for a few moments as he gathered his thoughts and tried to push his jealousy further down into the pit of his stomach, thinking on what she'd said. He thought that he was well within his right to be angry at her for the way she'd left and then carried on with other guys.

She had been forbidden from seeing him, but Dean wasn't, and John had deliberately reignited that friendship in the days after they fell apart, so that he could keep in contact with her. Dean knew that he was nothing more than a relay person in the beginning, just like Gwenn had been, but he understood how John felt about his sister and didn't fault him for it. Spending time with him helped John to make it through those months, and eventually they became good friends again, and got his mind off of her.

"You must've forgotten that I had to listen to you and my brother carry on whenever you called the house, or that there are stories I know about you from people who saw you out places? I couldn't very well hold those things against you when I was the one who broke things off, but it still *hurt* Johnny! Yes, I kissed boys, but I was thinking of you when I was doing it; who were you thinking of when you were making out with girls at parties?"

He frowned at her and realized that despite being ambiguous about his own behavior since their separation, she must've known quite a bit about where he'd been and what he'd done. Keeping good relations with her brother had been instrumental in keeping a channel open to her, and had been quite intentional, but he also wasn't aware of just how much information she'd gotten out of him.

"Okay, fair enough. Yes, I'm angry and I'm hurt, and yes, I spent more time with your brother deliberately because I wanted you to not forget me…and to also regret letting me go."

He assumed she would be upset by his admission, but she instead walked back towards the couch and cupped his chin in her hand as she stared down at him with those Mediterranean eyes. "I regretted it the moment I did it, but I didn't have much of a choice. And you really are stupid if you think I would ever forget you, Johnny."

163

She leaned over to kiss him and he pulled her over the back of the couch and into his lap, using the time they had to make up for their foolish mistakes. As the smells of dinner and Christmas crept ever closer down the steps, they whispered heartfelt apologies, kissed away their bitterness, and tried to concoct a plan together for approaching her mother when the time arrived.

"Why did she invite the entire family over tonight, I don't understand?" He said, playing in her hair as she laid her head in his lap.

"I don't know, she didn't tell me anything about it until today. This is usually the day we have our family dinner every year for Christmas, and maybe she couldn't do it any other day. It's odd that she had me invite you tonight though."

"Yea, that's what worries me," he muttered.

"Maybe it's a good thing? I mean, why would she have you meet the rest of my family if she planned on never letting you see me again? That has to be a good sign right? Maybe you won't have to talk at all, and my dad convinced her to let us see one another?"

"Dennis? I didn't know that he was such a huge fan of mine?"

"Well…he's more of a fan than my mom. Plus, Dean talks about you all the time and says what a good guy you are. No matter what happens with us, it's not like they can tell my brother to stop hanging out with you right?"

"I suppose not. Maybe they just won't let me into the house anymore, and Dean will have to come meet me somewhere, like you and I used to do with Gwenn."

She giggled, "Well, let's hope that no one has to sneak around anymore to do anything, and that someone finally got through to her."

"Let's hope so…"

The door upstairs creaked open, as if on cue, and Mrs. Malowski's voice called them to supper from the top step. She sat up fixing her hair and adjusting herself to make sure she didn't appear as though she'd been fooling around on the couch with a boy. He did the same and then they kissed once more for luck, and she led him up the stairs to introduce him to the rest of her family.

Both sets of her grandparents were there, including the grandmother that talked to him at Dawson's funeral. She seemed pleased to see him again and commented on how big he'd gotten.

Marge's sister did the same, and seemed to be the only other one that recognized him from years before. The rest of them shook hands and gave pleasant introductions, whether they had seen him before or not.

Once pleasantries had been exchanged, they all took their seats around the elaborate dining table, and bowed their heads in anticipation of Marge's saying grace. Her sons rolled their eyes and shared grins in preparation of her overly-emotional dinner prayer, and gave John a silent warning as it came. It was a long, drawn-out prayer, including an exhausting list of people she wanted to personally thank - both present and not - and then ended, as always, in her breaking down at the mention of Dawson.

All heads stayed down and waited for her to compose herself, with the encouragement of her husband (who seemed as annoyed as his sons by her display), and she finally was able to wrap it up with an "Amen" to announce the beginning of dinner.

Heaping dishes were noisily passed around, and Dennis's mother took charge of pouring beverages for everyone, having to raise her voice above the others to ask each person what they preferred. John thanked her for filling his glass with milk, and listened to one of the five conversations going at once around him. He had his choice of politics, the price of Christmas gifts, which of them had the longest drive to the house, Super bowl picks, or a bad bit of weather that was approaching.

John sat in the center seat just listening to the voices of the family, took in the smells around him, and would check to make sure Melinda's hand was still firmly placed on his leg under the table every few minutes. She would rub his leg each time he touched her hand, and gave it a squeeze for good measure.

He finished his plate and the second helpings that each grandmother heaped upon it, insisting he was too skinny, and then finished off his glass of milk. Afterwards, the ladies cleared the table and he was served a slice of both apple and pumpkin pie, and his glass was refilled. When he was done gorging himself, he excused himself to the family room.

There was another large screen television and a larger, more comfortable couch there for him to relax on. Moments later, Melinda entered the room and flopped down beside him, nuzzling her head into his shoulder. She had changed into a sweatshirt and loose-fitting jeans, and pulled her hair up on top of her head. Dean and Steve unbuttoned their dress shirts and rolled up the sleeves and their father did the same. They each took their places around the family room and pretended not to notice Melinda draped across John on the couch.

Their fingers played, interlocked beneath a large couch pillow as they watched a cheesy Christmas special that her dad was so engrossed in. The boys talked of football still, and bantered with their grandfathers for a while, as the women finished up with the kitchen and commenced to playing cards and gossiping.

The first boring special ended, the clock chimed ten, and the women collected their men from the family room, reminding them about the bad weather and how far each of them had to drive. They said goodbye to the grandparents and aunts, uncles and cousins, and John got more cheek pinches from the women, except from the old Polish woman who had been so kind to him before.

She was helped by her husband with her long wool coat as she spoke to John as she had before, with her odd but cheerful tone, "I am glad to see you again and it is good to see that you have taken such good care of my granddaughter."

It made his face turn red as well as Melinda's, and Marge had heard what was said, but only gave her mother a perturbed look. The old woman placed a veined, wrinkled hand on his shoulder and leaned in to whisper to him, ignoring her daughter's glare.

"She is taken with you, anyone can see it. Don't pay any attention to her mother, and don't let her scare you off."

The old woman patted his shoulder and chuckled, then took her husband's arm to be escorted to the waiting sedan in the drive. No one else had heard the words she'd imparted with him, and no one had asked, not even Melinda. It was as if they had a little secret all their own, and it made him feel better about facing Margaret later on, whenever that would be. After they saw everyone out, they all returned to their places in the family room and suffered through another Christmas special.

Dennis was called into the kitchen by his wife at ten minutes to eleven, to some mild grumbling, and he shuffled in to see what was so important that he miss the end of his show. Steve and Dean shared a look and then instinctively glanced over at John sitting beside their sister. The towering, older brother walked over to him and shook his hand, saying, "I should be headed out too, before the roads get too bad. Good to see you again, John."

That left the three of them, Dean, Melinda and John, to share nervous glances and try to communicate in whispers and by reading lips.

Dean kept reminding John that he would be fine and John kept asking him what was going on with his mother in the kitchen. He knew that there was undoubtedly some heated dialogue transpiring on his behalf, and he would be called in at any moment to stand trial. Melinda squeezed his hand and scooted closer to him, just in case things went badly. After what seemed an eternity, Dennis's voice sounded and made the pair on the couch jump.

"Good night John, Melinda, Dean...I'm headed up to bed, don't stay up too late okay?"

"Okay dad," Dean said, giving him a half-wave, half-salute, and Melinda copied him.

"Good to see you again, Mr. Malowski," John said, his voice full of nerves again.

"You too, John...I think Marge wanted to speak with you in the kitchen."

There it was; the announcement that there would, in fact, be a confrontation still. Though there was nothing in his tone to indicate what was waiting for him there. His stomach turned upside down and he suddenly wished he hadn't had the extra slice of pie, or maybe it was the milk. He swore he heard the giant hand of the invisible clock make a loud "clack" as it moved forward again, and reminded him that his time was almost up.

He nodded quietly and he swore that Dennis gave him a look of sympathy before he turned the corner and disappeared. John stood from his comfortable place on the couch, and Melinda finally released her grip on his hand as he pulled away. Dean patted him on the shoulder and excused himself to bed, not wanting to get into the middle of it, much the way his father didn't. He was rooting for John, but he was still living at home until he finished school in the spring, and that meant he had to remain neutral for the time being.

John looked back over his shoulder at the only remaining person in his corner before he left the room, and she mouthed the words 'I love you' and made a gesture crossing her heart. He smiled and collected himself as he made his way into the darkened kitchen where his old nemesis awaited. There would be no one else in the room but the two of them, and she wouldn't have to keep up the façade she'd had at dinner.

Chapter 15

She was seated at the small breakfast nook table and was cradling a glass of wine in both hands, watching him like a cat studies her prey. He stopped a few feet from the table, waiting for her to offer him a seat, but she did not. He swore that she wore a thin smile as she looked up, though it could have been one of the long shadows of the room, dimly lit by a single lamp over the sink. There was a small frame sitting on the ledge above the nook, and in the frame, a picture of a smiling little boy.

She indicated the picture as she spoke, "He's been gone for ten years now...the same length of time that you've been gone."

There was almost a sad satisfaction in her voice, and he nodded reverently.

"I never thought that I would see either of you again, and for a while, that's the way I wanted it. You reminded me of him, John, and that's why I couldn't bear to look at you."

He nodded again, "Yes ma'am."

"You expect me to do a lot of yelling, break down like I did at the dinner table, and tell you that I want you to turn around and never come back, don't you? You're expecting me to tell you that I don't want you to come into my home ever again, talk to my daughter or my son, and that I don't want to see your face at my door again?"

"That had occurred to me," he said simply.

"Then why did you come? If you knew that was what might happen, why would you even show up here? And once you knew that my entire family was here, why didn't you leave? If I were in your shoes, I would have thought the worst, and I never would have wanted to come out of that basement to face a woman that hated me, much less her entire family."

"I came because of your daughter, and because she asked me to come."

"But you knew that we'd have this talk? And you knew it probably wouldn't go well?"

"Yes ma'am," he said proudly.

"Did you do it simply to defy me, or did you have other reasons?"

"The only reason I came is because I love Melinda, and I came to say my peace."

She took a long draught from the fancy wine glass and stared up at him over the rim, as if unimpressed by his statement of intent. Finally, she pointed at the seat beside her.

"My husband, my son, my daughter, and even my own mother...have all spoken on your behalf John. They speak highly of you, of the things you do and say, of the man you've become, and have all reminded me that the fact you even showed up here tonight speaks volumes about your character. I can't say that I disagree with them, and if I do, I'm the bad guy. But I'm the only one who seems to remember that day in the park, and seeing your face at my table tonight reminded me of him."

"Mrs. Malowski, you're not the only one who remembers him--"

"Let me finish. I was reminded of him when you stepped foot in this house, because of something I did a long time ago. It was something irrational, spurned by my own guilt, and completely unfair to you. I never kept you from Melinda or this house to punish you...I kept you away because I couldn't be reminded of him. Do you understand?"

"I don't think I do..."

"I pretended that he never went to that park and that my children never played there. I used to drive around it so I wouldn't have to look at it, and I had to avoid everything that reminded me of that place and you were part of that. I blamed you, and that was irrational and awful of me to do, but a grieving parent doesn't deal in the rational. I hope you can understand that...and forgive me?"

"Excuse me?" John wasn't sure what he was hearing, and the discussion wasn't going at all like he had planned.

"I'm apologizing to you and telling you that there is no discussion to be had between us, other than this. You showed up here tonight when I never thought you would, and that was all that you ever needed to do to prove how much you care for her. I've watched her fall apart so many times, and I never cared before because I was too self-absorbed to notice, but I can't watch her do it anymore. She needs you here, and I know it took everything she had to face me and tell me about you...just as I know it took everything you had to come and support her."

"You don't need to apologize..."

"Yes I do. You have to let me apologize and you have to accept it, or we cannot move past this!"

"Okay...I forgive you..."

She reached a hand across the table and placed it atop his then, her eyes threatening to burst from their sockets with the water pressure building there. Her hand was oddly cold and clammy, and it was uncomfortable, but he didn't dare pull away.

"I expect to see a lot more of you around here. It makes her happy, and when she's happy, everyone else is happy. The house has been gloomy with her moping around, and I never understood why. For years, she's just moped around and barely talked to me, and then all of a sudden, this summer, she brightened up the entire house. No one knew why until she finally told me that you'd come back. I...was furious with her...because she was so happy and could smile that way, and I could not. I want my daughter to smile again, John."

"I would like that too," he said, wiggling his fingers under her grip.

"When she smiles, the whole house smiles...it's something that Dawson used to do...a power that he used to have over this place. Now she has it, and in a way, your return caused the house to light up and it's like he's come back. So...I never expected to see either of you again, but here you both are."

She finished, pulling the picture down from the ledge and smoothing her fingers over his small cheeks behind the glass. John sat motionless, waiting for her to finish her private moment with the memory of her son, and said not a word. Setting the picture on the table, she smiled warmly at it and then at him.

"Merry Christmas, John, and welcome to our home again. I'm off to bed, and I'm sure you two have lots to talk about. The weather is going to turn nasty tonight and I know you have a long drive. I've had Dennis make you up a place in the basement on the couch if you'd like to stay."

"Thank you..." he said, as the churning ceased in his stomach.

The hands of the unseen clock moved forward again, but more slowly than before, and the ticking in his head dropped to a subtle, gentle rhythm once again. For ten years the hands on that hidden face had remained frozen – as frozen as the waters of Rain tree and the awful images of that day that plagued them all – and now they were beginning their steady revolution again. Margaret Malowski had decided, somewhere between seeing the anguish in her daughter's face and the brave return of the boy she'd cast away, that enough time had passed in stagnation in that house.

She would never forget her son, never forget the light she'd lost that day, or the ability to feel true happiness. But she'd finally recognized her irrational persecution of those around her who weren't responsible for her loss, and would try, little by little, to correct it. There was a little bit of that sunshine in her house again, and it had been delivered to her by the warm hand of love that she'd turned a bitter shoulder to for so long. She was ready to feel that love again, even if it was seeing it through her daughter's eyes.

That daughter waited on the final verdict and fate of her love, pacing the family room alone, almost to the point of making herself physically ill. When she saw him appear in the alcove, a broad smile on his face, she knew that everything was going to be okay. An assault that made the one earlier pale in comparison ensued then, as she wrapped her arms around his neck and stood on her tiptoes to welcome his lips to hers again, and celebrate their victory.

"What did she say?" She asked excitedly in between a flurry of kisses.

"Well she said…" he began to explain, but she wouldn't let him finish.

"It doesn't matter what she said! You're here with me and we can be together right?"

He nodded and was subsequently engulfed in her arms like the quiet house was engulfed by the winter storm everyone had been talking about. It pelted the large picture window in the family room with giant flakes and the howling wind rattled the place. She gave a start and retreated with him to the safety of the basement, nestling beneath the blankets left on the couch and into each another's arms. It wasn't the pile of blankets, the popping fire or the heat of their bodies that kept them warm however, it was the glow coming from deep inside each of them; the glow Margaret Malowski said had returned to her home.

Chapter *16*

Campbell studied the old photograph that had been snapped of the pair that following Christmas day. They were seated at the bottom of the steps in the entryway, both wearing big smiles, and couldn't have been sitting much closer to each other.

"They looked…"

"Happy? They *were* very happy back then," Gwenn finished the sentence he'd hesitated with. "It's okay… you can say it, Jim. I'm supposed to be objective right?"

He nodded, "Yes, we are supposed to be objective, to the best of our ability. I can understand how something like this," he said, holding up the picture to her, "might be upsetting though."

"Yea, considering he would never throw the thing out, even after we were married and long after he'd stopped speaking to her. I would just get upset with him and yell at him about it, and he would take it and proceed to hide it somewhere else. Eventually, I just gave up."

"That Christmas was pretty much it for them for a while?"

"Yea, but I don't get why you wanted to talk about that before we discussed Vicki."

"I'm sorry, I sort of steered the discussion that way, didn't I? I wanted to get any details that John left out about that Christmas before his mother called, in case I'd missed anything."

"Pretty much what you just heard on the tape was how I remember Melinda telling me it went. I didn't really know many of the details about what went on in the basement, so that's new I guess," she said, sneering at the small tape player on the table.

"I apologize; I forgot that was on the tape. I really was looking for the overall mood and climate of their relationship at that time, before Vicki disrupted things."

"Things had never been that good for them; they were 'Port Austin' good again. They were like a regular couple that did regular things, and she wasn't sitting next to an empty seat at the movies anymore."

"What is *Port Austin* good?"

173

"Emotions running high, savoring every moment, kissing every time you turned around to look at them, and non-stop laughter…about nothing in particular. It was obnoxious."

"I can imagine that was pretty irritating for you. What about Margaret?"

"Oh she was on cloud ten - which was a cloud above the one Melinda was on - every time John came to the house. The giddiness and the uncontrollable laughing would start after she would hang up from his call. Next, her mother would start making a pie or a damned cake just for him, and her father would start browsing the cable guide trying to find a good movie that the two of them could watch together."

"Well that's good that her parents had a change of heart and that they included him in the family isn't it? I mean, after everything they'd put him through, don't you think he was entitled to a little ass kissing on their part?"

"A little? Yes. But, as with everything else the Malowskis did, they went over the top with it. Between Dennis's tendency to overdo everything, and Marge's over-dramatics, they smothered him. They all but had their wedding planned out, and she hadn't even finished high school yet. Even Dean was sick of their behavior after a while."

"So John was their *golden boy* for a while, I don't really see the harm in that, considering. He was a regular fixture at the house then?"

"He was there at least five days a week for dinner, and on the weekends, they would do a family outing somewhere with him. Even I didn't get to see Melinda that much…I suppose I was just a little bitter because…I don't know…"

"They'd used you as a go-between, and you had all of your time with her taken away as soon as they didn't need you any longer?"

"Well, yes…I used to spend two or three nights at her house, and I couldn't because he was always there. He practically lived with them, and the couch in the basement had been mine long before it was his. It didn't last long, though, and it was inevitable that they would fall apart."

"So the phone call comes and everything turned upside down?"

"Yea, that was the final straw, but the wolves were already gathering outside their door, waiting for one of them to slip up. I was irritated by my replacement, but not half as much as her council was. That was the one good thing that came of them being together so much; he got her away from those idiots for a while."

"So they were already having problems before the call?"

"Not really *problems*...just *pressures* I would say. It had been building up for a while, and when everything happened, it all happened at once. He was the only thing keeping those wolves at bay, so when he told her that he was leaving, they fell in on her...and the end result was awful."

"This was in January?"

"The twenty-fifth," she said before he could check the date in the book. "But the first call came a few days before. He swore to her that he didn't know anything about it earlier, but he looked like he'd seen a ghost when I saw him a few days after her birthday. She knew something was off with him as well."

"That was about a week before?"

She nodded, "Her birthday was the sixteenth, and it fell on a Thursday, and I saw John with her the following Tuesday and I could tell something was wrong then. She was having a party with her friends at a hotel the following Saturday, and he was helping her plan that night."

"I remember reading about that, but John mostly glossed over it – it's nowhere on the tape."

At the mention of the tape, she glanced over at the recorder again, listening to the faint whine that only she could hear - too high-pitched for Campbell's aged ears to detect. It was the sound the small gear that spools the tape makes when it's held firmly in place by the pause button. It sounded much like a helpless rabbit screeching, trapped under the talons of a large hawk, and it was both satisfactory and irritating. There was a satisfaction in not having to hear his voice, especially when it spoke of the girl in the photo, and that Campbell was relying on her for what she knew.

There was almost a power over him as he would sit on the edge of his chair, hanging on her every word, when she was the one in control. In their debate over the fate of her husband, he had been winning thus far. This was finally her opportunity to score some points and present her argument, so she was savoring the moment. But that small gear kept clicking and whining, driving her

175

to irritation, until she finally leaned forward to silence that rabbit with a finger.

"We won't need the tape for this part anyway," she said with a smile. "You have your best eyewitness to that whole affair sitting right here."

He was already scooting forward in his seat, probably not even aware that he was doing so, and she had to moderate the size of the grin that yearned to split her face in two. There were few moments that she'd ever recalled having the great Dr. Campbell's full attention.

"I would like to hear about the entire incident then," he said, preparing his yellow legal pad, limbering up his wrist. "Tell me about that call and about his mother, and what followed. There's an interesting event which takes place at about this same time that John did share with me, and I think it's connected to something that happened during this time."

Gwenn's expression was one of puzzlement for a moment until suddenly a look of recognition crossed her face. "You're talking about the incident in the pool?"

"He said he had a mishap with a swimming pool where he'd almost drowned, yes. It was the same night he had his first episode."

It was her turn to sit forward in her chair. Something he'd said made her uncomfortable in that seat and she seemed to be fighting either to recover her composure, her breath, or both.

"That's when he started having his nightmares? I never made the connection."

He turned the journal around in his lap, sliding it forward so she could see the date at the top of the entry. There weren't many of those earlier entries with dates, except the most significant of events, and that seemed to be one of them. She scooted back in her chair, wearing a thoughtful expression, and tapping a finger across her lips.

"It wasn't a mishap; there was a fight...one of the most awful fights I've ever seen. John was nearly drowned that night, and when we pulled him out of the water, he was talking about things that...didn't make any sense."

Campbell nodded, his attention focused on the legal pad and whatever he was writing as he spoke. "Why don't you start at the beginning; take me back to the night of her party..."

176

John sat in the corner booth of the small diner where he, Dean and Connelly had spent many Saturday nights. It was his favorite place to eat as well as being a happening place to meet girls. After things had been patched up with Melinda, he'd taken her there a few times for his favorite burgers and to split a milkshake. At least once a week, he would stop there on the way to her house on the drive down, and pick up some take out for them. The *Metro Coney* held a lot of good memories for them, and that's why he'd chosen it to sit down, gather his thoughts, and write her the letter.

He sat back sipping a chocolate milkshake and clicking his pen, trying to find the words to write on the blank sheet. It was two nights before he had to go away, and he'd tried to tell her what happened to her face, but just like her, he found it impossible to confront her. He'd criticized her for being a coward back then, for not being able to face him and tell him why they couldn't be together, and now here he was, following that same cowardly path. John finally understood the anguish she experienced in trying to say goodbye.

The call came in a week prior, as he was trying to plan for Melinda's party, and he had Marge on the other line, trying to decide cake flavors. The voice on line was familiar, but sounded like it was coming from a million miles away. It was his mother, and they hadn't spoken for a very long time. He'd kept in contact with her through phone calls, but hadn't physically seen her for more than two years.

Victoria Chapel was something of a gypsy who never stayed in one place for too long. It was fortunate that John's father intervened and filed for custody, or who knows where he might have ended up, or how he might've turned out. Her priorities had been: the bottle, the most popular recreational drug of the day, men, and then John - in that order.

South Florida was a great environment for young people who liked to indulge in self-gratification, or for middle-aged people who thought they were still young. His mother fit the latter category, and she made a new life for herself there that didn't leave much room for raising a teen-aged son. Once he'd turned eighteen and graduated, she'd called to offer him a place with her, and he'd refused without putting much thought into it. Now, she was calling again to make another offer that he couldn't turn down.

She was calling from the hospital that day, and she was in bad shape as a result of her most recent bad decision. It scared her badly enough to call her son and remind him that she loved him, and that began him prying to find out what had caused her moment of sobering clarity. The story came out in sobs next, and John listened to the awful details with a stone face, saying nothing. He told her that he would take care of her soon and hung up the receiver.

Afterwards, he made a series of desperate calls to the Broward County Sheriff's office, his aunt, and his friend Hunter.. The Sheriff's office told him that there was nothing they could do unless she filed a formal complaint against the guy who'd put her in the hospital. His aunt had no more money to loan his mother, because she had borrowed thousands for her habits already and not paid any of it back. Hunter was presently attending school at Florida State, only a few hours from John's mother, but he didn't want to get mixed up with that mess, and he couldn't blame him.

Out of options, the only thing he could do was go down there and handle it personally. Even if he'd had the money to send her, there was no guarantee that she wouldn't piss it away on booze or drugs, and she was too afraid to leave the guy who was abusing her on top of it all. John couldn't just let it go, like he'd done so many times before, because inaction on her part to change her situation would certainly land her in the hospital again or worse.

It was an impossible choice, but the *only* choice, and it couldn't have come at a more inopportune time. Things had been going too perfectly with Melinda, and he should have known that it wouldn't last. It seemed that it was his lot to never know happiness for too long and he posed the silent question to whomever was listening: *when will this end?*

He drove to the Malowski home and stood on the front porch sometime after Midnight, contemplating throwing stones at her window to get her attention and talking with her face-to-face, but thought better of it. The house was peaceful and he knew that she was sleeping upstairs in her room, probably having pleasant dreams of her coming birthday or even about him. He didn't want to disrupt that, so he slipped the letter in the door jamb and then snuck back to his car to steal away quietly into the night.

The next day came and the phone call he had dreaded with it. The voice at the other end sounded as far away and shattered as his mother's, and he could barely make out her words. There was anger there, absolute terror, and pain the likes of which he'd never heard in a voice. There were few things to say to her that he didn't painstakingly inscribe in that letter to her, so he didn't even try. He reassured her over and over that he would return as soon as he was able, and made it sound like a simple roundtrip excursion.

She was afraid for him and knew that he was needlessly putting himself in danger, and tried to talk him out of it, but he had his mind begrudgingly made up. There was a total breakdown and then the phone was handed off to Dean, who needed to be caught up to speed on the situation. After John explained the dire situation, there weren't many words that could be said between them, except his friend wishing him luck and to come back safely. It was decided that he would set out the next day and that he wouldn't stop to say goodbye to her, because it would only give her the impression that he wasn't coming back.

It was Gwenn who called a few minutes later, after having talked with Melinda, and pleaded with him to at least stop by her party and that it would mean a lot to her if he did. He said he would give it some thought, but that he didn't think it was for the best, because it would disrupt her birthday party.

The next day he started out in the early afternoon with a couple of bags packed in the back seat. As he approached the green road signs warning him that he was abut to pass her exit, he cringed and wrestled with his conscience. He wanted to see her so badly, but it would only make things worse for both of them. Odds were that he would only be gone a couple of weeks until his mother got back on her feet, and he would be back before she even missed him.

As his car approached the last sign before passing her exit, he tried to stare straight ahead and ignore it, but the glaring green billboard seemed to taunt and berate him for being so cowardly. He jerked the wheel causing the tires to scream, and the coupe cut across three lanes of traffic, nearly causing an accident, and tearing up the grass by the ramp. He screeched to a stop at the traffic light at the cross street, and his hands began to shake.

The loud engine grumbled as he idled two drives away from her house, still contemplating going in. He slammed the door (because of the sticky handle) and walked up the pristine drive to the front door. He pushed the little button whose eye had grown dim in the daylight, and waited nervously.

It was Marge that answered the door and welcomed him with a more overbearing hug than normal. When she had finished mauling him, she wiped the tears from her cheeks and gave him a stern but friendly smile.

"Melinda…told me about the letter. She's pretty upset…"

He could only imagine how the news had impacted the entire household. There was nothing she could say to change his mind, and they both knew it, but as her mother she had to try anyway.

"I know…I spoke with her. Is she here?"

"No, she's at Gwenn's…she's been there since last night."

"Gwenn is a good friend," was the only thing he could say.

What he wanted to say was that he was glad she wasn't taking refuge with the council of evil bitches. They both knew how upset and fragile Melinda was, and knew that Gwenn was her best chance to cool off and get some good advice, and she wouldn't turn her against him. Marge left the room and returned with a small, yellow slip of paper that was folded in half.

"She left this for you…in case you stopped by. I think she knew that you would…and I hoped the same…"

The woman stared at him expectantly, but John only stared down at the paper with his name messily scrawled on the front. She'd always had neat handwriting before, and the chaotic forms the letters had been written in worried him. There was an uncomfortable silence between the two of them, as he suddenly felt like a stranger in that house again, just like that first day he'd returned with the knotted stomach and shaking hands. The house was in chaos again, like it was before, and he could hear that clock slowing to a deafening stop, preparing to go backwards.

He was already expending all of his energy in trying to find the right words for his next stop, he didn't have anything left for the disappointed woman before him. She still had expectations of him, still needed an explanation, and deserved as much. The young man standing in the doorway had brought life back to her household, and now he was threatening to take it away again, without so much as an apology. She didn't mean to blame him, to put it all on him again, and had absolved him once of those sins that she'd burdened him with, but she couldn't help feel as though he was betraying the trust she'd put in him.

Margaret Malowski had fought a long, hard internal battle before she'd abdicated to her compassionate side, and to all those voices that spoke on behalf of forgiveness and the boy standing before her. She'd opened that door to him again, welcomed him with open arms for the sake of her daughter and the sake of her family, and now he was slamming that door in her face.

"Make me understand, John..." she finally said through quivering lips.

"I'm going to have to have this same discussion with your daughter, and I'm sure she'll explain it to you, Marge," he said in a surprisingly cold tone.

"Then maybe you could use the *practice* running it by me first, to see if it makes one bit of sense before you try to pass it off on her. I guarantee you that she will be less understanding," she warned.

"She's not the only one who's upset and torn apart by this, Marge..."

"You're right, she's not! Do you even *know* what this will do to our household again?"

"I explained to her that it wasn't going to be forever! I'm going for a week or two at the most!"

"She held up the letter he'd written and thrust it in his face. "Then why would you write something like this? I've read it. This isn't the kind of letter you write when you're taking a short vacation, John!"

"Because it's not a *short vacation*...my mother is in a lot of trouble and mixed up with something bad. I'm the only one who can help her!"

"Let the police deal with this! You're an eighteen-year-old boy who can *barely* take care of himself! You could be seriously hurt going to tangle with someone like *this*...haven't you thought this through?"

"I've thought it through plenty, and the police will do nothing unless she files charges, which she's too terrified to do. If I don't go, she could end up dead!"

"I don't understand why you're doing this for her, John! I *get* that she's your mother, but she's never done a damned thing for you! I used to be the one to make sure that you had eaten and that you were dressed for the weather when you were little because she was too busy to be bothered with those concerns! Why would you put your life in danger like this for her? Never mind Melinda or the rest of us worrying about you."

"She's *still* my mother and she has no one else!"

"Your mother doesn't have anyone else because of how she's treated everyone! She's put herself in this situation, and you need to let her find her own way out of it or she'll just keep using you!"

"Sometimes parents use their children as a crutch, even if unintentionally, and there comes a time when that has to end. It's an *adult's* responsibility to realize their mistake and make things right...but sometimes...it's the child that has to say 'enough' and find the strength to extend a hand through the darkness and reach them, because they don't realize that they're lost."

Marge could only stand with her mouth agape at the audacity of his character and the wisdom in his words. As one who'd been pulled back from that abyss by her own daughter, she could not condemn him for trying the same. Melinda had faced no less danger of being hurt or ruined than he presently faced, though he faced real, physical danger. If her own child had failed in her task, there might never have been an awakening for her, never feeling anything in her stone heart again, and she could not deny the woman she'd once called a friend and her son that peace.

She pulled him close in a long embrace, wiping her fingers across her eyes as they faced away from him. "Melinda will be fine...because someone like you loves her, John. I realized that the night we spoke in the kitchen. If you are half as dedicated to her as you are to someone less-deserving, then the two of you will be just fine, come what may. I know that in my heart."

"I'm coming back, Marge, no matter what it takes," he uttered over her shoulder, patting her back.

"You make sure that you do! Go and get your mother and bring her home, John, and we'll be waiting right here for you. All of us will be here waiting."

"I'll be home before she realizes I'm gone."

"I don't know about that, she feels as if you're already gone. Are you going to stop by Gwenn's to see her before you leave?"

He stared down at the paper again and nodded slowly at her, knowing it would be much more difficult to do so, and that not even his most clever words, metaphors or anecdotes would work for her. He turned and left the Malowski house standing on its perfect, snow-covered lawn, and had sworn that he'd left his footprints there, but there wasn't a single track there. Perhaps he'd been mistaken, or perhaps the clock was already erasing his existence.

Sliding the worn key into the ignition and firing up the old coupe, John accelerated slowly through the quiet, residential development - as he always did - and then gunned it as soon as he reached the main road. At the next light he was stopped by another glaring highway sign, this one colored red. The upright messenger was telling him to stop, as if it could read his mind, knowing that he wanted to just leave the city and not face her. There was not an easy road waiting for him in either direction, he knew, and so he slowly moved the wheel to the left.

He leaned on the hood of his car and stood in the drive listening to the engine hiss and cool down from its short jaunt. His hands were still shaking, even in the warm pockets of his leather jacket. The cold was no more responsible for his chattering jaw as it had been the first time he sat in that drive, waiting for her.

The door opened and it wasn't his Melinda, it was an imposter with long blonde hair and a pretty, triangular face staring sadly back at him. At first, he thought it could have been her, with her streaked eye makeup and the scowl she was wearing, but the chirping voice gave her away.

"Johnny...come on inside," she squeaked as she walked out onto the snowy porch in her socks, just to welcome him in.

"Hello Gwenny," he said in a voice that issued forth like air leaking out of a tire.

He took special notice of the imposter's hair, and saw that she had colored it since the last time he'd seen her. Almost all of the red was gone now and it was streaked blonde like Melinda's. Her makeup was done the same as hers also, he noticed, and from a distance, she could have almost passed for her best friend. She led him through the kitchen towards the family room, and stopped before they reached the alcove, to give him a word of warning about what waited for him in there.

Gwenn waited in the kitchen, taking her place behind the counter, as if preparing for a tank battalion to come rolling up her street and start shelling her house. That would've been mild compared to the explosive situation in her living room, and she gripped the granite countertop and held her teeth tightly until it was over.

There was a lot of screaming, incoherent words mingled with sobs, and the sound of flesh cracking on flesh, as she was giving him hell in that other room. Then there would be a lull, and she'd lean over the counter, straining to hear the whispered voices, until the screaming would start again and she'd back away from the counter.

At one point, he stormed out the front door into the street with her hot on his heels, the argument being carried to her driveway until she delicately tried ushering them back inside so the neighbors didn't call the police, or worse, tell her dad.

When it was all over, an hour later, Melinda hadn't managed to convince him to stay, but she had won two small victories: one was convincing John to take Connelly with him to Florida, so that he wasn't going alone and she wouldn't worry as much, and the other was convincing him to delay leaving long enough so he could attend the party. It couldn't have gone that badly, for he kissed her on the eyelids as he always did before setting out to retrieve Jeremy, promising to be back later.

Once John was gone, she began discussing her plan to keep him there, and Gwenn reluctantly listened. The party would go until midnight or so, and once all of her friends were gone (that was going to be her job, making sure that they all were ushered out by twelve) she would have the hotel room alone with John. It would be her once chance, she explained with a hopeful tone in her voice, for her to finally give herself to the man she loved, and he would have no choice but to stay with her then.

Gwenn thought it was a terrible plan – as terrible as it was the first time when her idiot friends had suggested it – and she told

184

her as much. In her desperation, she'd utilized every available resource, including those five idiots who'd given her the same bad advice six months before. She pleaded with her best friend not to resort to that, reminding her that John would react very much the same way as the last time, and it would only strain their relationship even more. Not wanting to hear it, she gathered her things and went to prepare for her big night with friends that were "more supportive", and that's what led to her bad plan becoming an even worse plan.

Chapter 18

Just after eight, John and Connelly arrived at the hotel and parked around back. It had taken very little convincing to get him to come along for the party, and even less to make the trip to Florida with him. Connelly didn't have any family to worry about him, or any girls to go into a tizzy about his comings and goings, and he liked it that way. His face had brightened up a bit when John told him that Gwenn would be at the party, and it would be just the four of them staying the night.

John unfolded the paper and read the number Gwenn had written down, and the boys easily found "226" at the top of the first flight of stairs. He could have found it without the paper, by the noise coming from behind the door. A guy with greasy hair answered the door and looked them up and down.

"Yea?"

"We're here for the party." John said in a friendly tone, though Jeremy eyed him suspiciously.

"Aint no party for you here, maybe you got the wrong room?"

He tilted his head to the side and looked down his hooked nose at them. Connelly was an inch or two taller than John, who stood at five feet, ten inches on a good day, and the man at the door was a full three to four inches taller still. Neither of them recognized him, and John couldn't recall his name from the guest list.

"Who is it Shannon?" A familiar voice called from somewhere inside.

Gwenn pushed past him and gave John a hug, then Jeremy. "These guys are cool, they're my friends."

The tall man never cracked a smile as he stepped aside to let them in, never taking his eyes off either of them. John didn't notice, but his friend kept a watchful eye on the doorman.

"Who the hell is that?" Connelly whispered.

"I don't know, but I hope it's not who I think it is," John muttered.

Inside the small hotel room, there were about twenty people jam-packed from wall to wall - filling every chair and both double beds. Acrid smoke hung in the air that John had smelled before, and it was rolling out from beneath the bathroom door that was closed. He scanned the room and saw about ten guys and maybe seven girls - five of which he recognized as the "council"- and he scowled at Gwenn.

"I know," she whispered apologetically.

Another darker-complected guy handed John and Jeremy a beer in red plastic cups, and greeted them, but John paid him little mind as he surveyed the room looking for Melinda. He raised another brow at Gwenn. She bent close, keeping her voice low so as not to be heard over the music. "They're Chaldeans! That's all her clique hangs with - they're *obsessed* with them."

"They look like Arabs," Connelly snarled.

"They are – they're just not Muslim."

"What's the difference?" He said, twisting his mouth into a frown. "They're still Arabs."

"I thought there were just going to be a few people here? I helped her call most of them the night we planned this...what happened?" Josh asked, bewildered, looking around.

Gwenn took a drink of her beer and looked around the room at the snotty girls she hated. She locked eyes with one of them that she hated in particular, Michelle, the ringleader, as she got him caught up from the few hours he'd missed.

"As soon as you left today, we got into an argument and she took off to go hang out with her other friends. By the looks of her, she's been drinking most of the afternoon, and they told her to invite all of these guys. I asked her what she was doing when I first got here, and she told me about some idiot plan of hers to make you jealous."

"Why would I be *jealous*? These guys are tools!"

"Because she's *dated* two of them! The guy that answered the door is Shannon - he's the first guy she dated after you. He was the biggest asshole, and just like the rest of them; arrogant, vain, and they treat women like property! Melinda's friends eat it up."

"I don't understand...why would she invite him here? She knew I was coming..."

"I know. I didn't know until just a little while ago. She had it in her head that she was going to try to sleep with you tonight, try to make you feel guilty about leaving, and I told her it was a bad idea."

"Yea, it is," he confirmed.

"So her brilliant friends took it a step beyond and told her that the best way to make you stay was by making you jealous and seeing what you were going to be missing."

"I'm going for a week or two! I thought we were fine this afternoon? I even changed my plans for her and delayed my trip! Jesus, what is wrong with her?"

"I know! We've all told her. The other guy is Sallah Nussein – they call him *Sal* for short. He's actually Shannon's cousin, and he's less of an asshole, and treated Melinda a lot better. I don't like either one of them, though. I think if you just talk to her, this whole thing will blow over and she'll see how stupid this is."

"Where is she now?"

It was Connelly who figured it out before she said anything, "This is a setup Chaps. All these guys...your girl playing head games...she wants you to start something so we can get our asses beat. There are at least eight or nine guys, maybe more. We need Hunter and JB here, maybe some others..."

"No! No one is fighting here tonight! This is stupid!" Gwenn warned them.

"So what do we do? Just fucking smile and sing *Happy Birthday* to her? I'm not staying here for this bullshit! This is unbelievable!"

John happened to be leaning in, talking very close to her ear, and one arm was coiled loosely around her shoulder at the time Melinda decided to come out of the bathroom. Gwenn saw her and took half a step away from him, so as not to make things more volatile than they were. Her body language caused him to turn and his eyes met with hers, fury burned through the air in both directions. She stumbled slightly as she crossed the room towards him.

"You and Gwenn, huh? I always knew she had a thing for you, but you're kind of out of her league aren't you Johnny? That's okay, because I'm done with you!" She jabbed her finger into his chest, and her words reeked of alcohol and pot.

"You're already smashed? It's eight thirty! Having a good birthday huh?"

189

"Yea, I've been with my new boyfriend all day. He doesn't have a problem staying tonight and I figured that you wouldn't mind since you hate sex for some reason, and never want to sleep with me."

John's face burnished like a brazier, and she could see it even in the dimly lit hotel room. "You're unbelievable, Melinda! Obviously, today was a big drama scene for you and nothing I did or said got through to you. You will never grasp what it is that we had, and I feel very sorry for you, because you'll end up just like those shallow, clueless whores in the corner over there!"

"*You're* the one who doesn't grasp what we were about, and have no idea what I sacrificed for you! You still threw me away, and I blew off my friends for you!"

"I blew off my friends too – *real* friends, not people who use me! Those people don't care for you, and someday you'll figure that out once they're finished with you. It sounds like you have a *big birthday* night planned, so I guess I'll be on my way!"

"Don't forget to take your *girlfriend* with you...she will probably even go to Florida with you Johnny. I know she'd jump at the chance to be with you!"

"Knock it off, Melinda! You're being ridiculous," Gwenn said, stepping between them. "You're going to regret this in the morning, when he's gone!"

"I'm not going to regret it...*you're* the ones who will regret it! You just lost your best friend and *you*...you lost the best thing that ever happened to you," she said, jabbing her finger at John.

"I don't want Gwenn, and you know better! You want to be angry with me, be angry with me! But this isn't going to solve anything! I understand that you're hurt still, and I don't blame you, but there's a different way to go about this...would you come outside and talk to me?"

"I'm not going anywhere with you! Why don't you just fucking go? This is my party and you said you were so worried about not fucking it up...but here you are, causing a big scene."

He just shook his head at her, and felt the others watching him from the corners. Shannon was on the edge of the bed, the slutty Italian ringleader of the "bitches" was sitting on the bathroom counter glaring with her black-rimmed eyes, and the others were watching him from the table where a card game was going on.

Jeremy put his hand on his friend's shoulder and told him, "Let's leave this party Johnny, this bitch is just trying to get you jumped. All these fuckers are watching us. I can't fight this many guys... maybe if we had Brennan and Hunter...not just us."

John turned in a half circle, sizing them up. Almost every one of them was olive-skinned and had greasy black hair. Almost every one of them was staring at him, waiting for him to make a move. At the back, standing by the bathroom door, was the biggest of them. He was sure that was Sal, staring the hardest at him, arms folded as he leaned coolly against the bathroom countertop. John wasn't sure how he'd missed him, being the tallest guy in the room, and possibly even as tall as their friend Pete. The giant man left his corner and pushed his way through the crowd towards him.

"You want to say something? You weren't invited, so why don't you fucking leave?"

"I set this fucking party up and paid for the fucking room," he replied. "So why don't you take your friends elsewhere so I can have my hotel room back?"

"They probably want to be alone, Sal, him and his girlfriend," she spouted off from behind.

"Knock it off Melinda! I'm not his girlfriend," she shouted.

"This is *your* hotel room?" He asked, taking another step towards him.

"Yea, and I can have the cops come and sort this out! *My* name is on the room, and I see a bunch of under-aged kids drinking and getting high, and I'm willing to bet *most* of you will spend the night in jail."

"You want to *sort it out*? We can sort it out right now." He reached in his pocket then, producing a roll of money wrapped in a rubber band. Pulling a few twenties from the roll, he flipped them in John's face.

"There's enough to cover the room, now be smart and get the fuck out of here! Leave shit be and just let her enjoy her party. I'm only gonna' say it nice once, you get me?"

He looked a lot bigger up close, and John studied every inch of him, just in case things escalated. Even under the dark blue jumpsuit, he could tell the man was built of solid muscle, and had several inches on him in reach as well as stature – there wouldn't be too many soft places to choose from. Though his facial features made him attractive to women, a sharp chin and ridged cheekbones

191

formed a nearly impenetrable defense. Only his prominent nose made a favorable target, but a missed shot meant a shattered hand on those bone ridges.

Gold adorned his ears, hung around his neck in thick chains, and covered almost every finger of each hand. Tearing one of those hoops from his ears or strangling him with those chains would be a good start, but the gold on his fingers made him think twice about it. Those fingers were attached to hands that could be turned into gilded wrecking balls, and John's face wasn't as strategically constructed to withstand them.

There were few men that intimidated John Chapel, and he couldn't recall the last time he'd wanted to back down from one, but the one that towered over him wasn't just a man. The broad lips spread into an overconfident smile, while dark eyes twinkled like black stars down his hooked nose at him, and his very presence commanded the attention of every soul in the room. With a bit less gold and minus the tracksuit, he would've passed for a modern day Pharaoh.

He did not want to fight this man, and even if he'd wanted to, he didn't know where to begin tearing the giant down.

"I don't want your money, Sal," John finally said, still running through combat scenarios in his head. "And if this turns ugly, we can go ahead and add some assault charges while we're at it. I'm sure I'll be back from Florida before you get out of jail. *You* be the smart one and take you and your clowns out of here."

He had to try a bit of intimidation of his own, hoping it would diffuse the situation, but it only made things worse. Sal seemed not at all moved by the scenario John had just described, but he didn't reply or even take his eyes from him.

It was Shannon that seemed most stirred up and he got into John's face, yelling, "Can't you hear? My cousin told you to get the fuck out! You better do it before he kicks your fucking ass! We don't care 'bout no motherfucking cops dumb fuck! All they'll find here is two dead motherfuckers by the time they get here!"

His cousin was all talk, he could tell; the loud ones were never a threat. It was the very quiet and serious stare from the regal Arab man that he was most concerned about. He wasn't going to yield, wasn't going to lose face to the outsider, especially when he had the superior numbers.

But neither was John, despite being hopelessly outmatched. He wasn't about to let it go, wasn't about to turn and walk away and let this stand. He'd been more than fair with her, and she had started this bullshit. She wanted a war. She wanted him hurt. John didn't want either outcome, but even less he couldn't stand giving her the satisfaction of humiliating him the way she was. The more he thought about it, the more it burned and burrowed into his brain, a singular, white-hot thought that ignited everything inside of him.

John took one last look at Melinda, Sal, Gwenn, and then Connelly. All eyes watched him still, and there was a premature sigh of relief from the crowd as they assured themselves that the confrontation was over. Only Sal and Connelly were still on alert, ready for anything, as the rest broke into jeers and curses in their native language. Amidst the loud din of voices, party music and adrenaline-charged senses, everything moved in slow motion suddenly, like a record player being switched so that the voices sounded slower and funny.

In his right hand, he'd been gripping a brown paper sack during the entire exchange, and no one had noticed until that very moment. It was a gift for her, a bottle of expensive rum to celebrate her birthday, but he hadn't had the opportunity to hand it to her. He was glad that he hadn't.

In one fluid movement, the immense rum bottle slipped from the brown wrapper, and he caught it up in his opposite hand by its thick neck, arm coiled like a spring-loaded trap. As he spun back to face the gloating giant, a hot ash traveled up his arm, lit the fuse, and the whole contraption exploded.

A sound like a muffled shotgun blast erupted from somewhere in the middle of the room, and the party stopped. Some of the people on the bed and even a few back at the bathroom counter felt the shower of rum and glass shards. They pattered on the mirror over the sink like gravel being poured in a bowl.

The bulk of the glass formed a jagged, circular design in John's hand, and the rest was resting in Sal's face and hair. The force of the blow snapped his head back, causing him to stumble backward over the bed. The god-king was falling.

Brandishing the jagged cudgel, he prepared to finish the battle as others looked on in horror. His famous temper had assumed complete control, and his limbs moved mechanically, fueled by pure rage. The white-hot flashes in his brain were accompanied by brief images of Melinda and the man beneath him doing unspeakable things together. They were things she'd promised him, and things that were being torn from his bloody fingers.

Even if he beat him, left him battered and bruised, it wouldn't prevent the inevitable once he was gone. The superficial wounds would heal and she would, no doubt, dote on him even more. He would have to utterly destroy him, keep him down long enough until he returned home, or even longer. That was the only way, and he fully intended to bring an end to that affair before it could even begin.

Connelly and Gwenn could see it in his face. He had been pushed to the edge, backed into a corner, into a no-win situation, and he wasn't going to be the only empty-handed one when the dust settled. Neither of them could move quickly enough to intervene, and their mouths were frozen into an open position, completely uncooperative. They just watched as the light flashed from the broken pyramid of glass, raised high, poised to bring an end to everything.

It was the loudmouthed cousin who intercepted him, leaping in the way and taking the shot intended for his Pharaoh. He yelped as the bottle sliced neatly through the sleeve of his vinyl jacket, and gashed his arm. A second man tackled him and slammed him into the long dresser, knocking the wind out of him and the bottle flew from his hand. Shannon moved to repay him for the slashed arm, but Connelly was already there.

A stiff right knocked him into the man who was grappling with John, and both men landed squarely into the mirror above the dresser. A small crack split the glass in two where the back of Shannon's head struck, and a second right jab from Connelly caused it to shatter completely, leaving bits of glass in the back of the Arab's head.

Three men were down, but five more were making their way towards the pair of them. Five on two wasn't great odds, but if they hit them fast and hard like they did the first wave, they might make it out that door in good shape. Those odds took a sharp dip when Sal got back to his feet, ready to take command of his army again.

John tried to scramble for his weapon, but there was little time to prepare for the enraged, bloodied locomotive steaming

194

towards him. He was hit harder than he'd ever remembered being hit, and the pair of them went through the front window with an ear-shattering crash.

He was still recovering from being put through the window, when he was suddenly being battered by the gold rings, crushing and tearing with each devastating blow. Shielding his face from the onslaught was nearly impossible in his present state, and they were coming so fast and so hard that they were unstoppable.

As he was being punched in the face, he was trying to recall fighting strategies that had been passed onto him by Pete and Hunter, from their days of sparring in the basement.

Always protect your face; you don't want them landing one on your nose...your eyes water...you can't see what the hell is goin' on, and the fight is done...yea, and you don't want your brain getting scrambled either...I'm trying, but the punches are coming too fast...use your elbows...for defense and offense...get in close...most people don't know how to fight close up...

The voices of his friends called to him from somewhere in the darkness that was waiting to overtake him, and he was trying to follow what they were saying. He had his elbows up, just like they told him, and made it more difficult for the punches to find their way in. Trying to see through the blood and haze, he slipped an elbow through the punches to land a solid shot in the center of his face.

His large nose erupted and the barrage stopped for just a few seconds – long enough for a second and third elbow to force the giant off of him, and to roll out from under him. Fingers clawed at the tear in his face and he let out a cry, while the other hand risked the bone defenses to work at the nose.

Sal's knees were starting to buckle under the brutal hammering, and either they would completely give out or John's knuckles would first. One was shattered for certain, and the rest had ripped through the skin, bloodied and exposed, but he wouldn't feel them ache in the cold night air until the adrenaline stopped and the fire died down.

He still had enough bone, flesh and determination to finish the demolition and then some, but he wouldn't get that opportunity. From the corner of his eye, through the haze of red, was a haze of green coming towards him. He didn't see the guy's face, and couldn't remember which of them had been wearing green. It wasn't important. He was being hit in the face again, and being hit in the back of the head by someone else. No, not someone else, by the steps he was tumbling down.

John was starting to breathe hard and the fire was starting to go out, making his limbs heavy without the steam to power them. The boy in the green shirt was lying face down at his feet, and he hadn't remembered even hitting him with his hand that was starting to throb. He was starting to wear down and he was losing his taste for this fight.

As he steadied himself on the rail and thought how the stairwell looked like an overwhelming climb, he'd contemplated making his way to the car instead. Connelly was still up there, as was Gwenn, Melinda and of course, the broken giant. He couldn't abandon either of his friends, couldn't turn away without confronting Melinda, and most definitely couldn't walk away from the most incredible fight he'd ever been a part of.

Halfway up, he stopped when he saw his challenger standing again, waiting for his return. The conclusion would come to him, and it wouldn't be the one he'd expected. John was certain at this point that he was, in fact, facing a god-king. Though his nose was broken, blood running over his lips, he smiled at him, teeth outlined in dark crimson. He charged and tackled John about the waist, and the impact lifting him high off the ground and into a fence, which buckled beneath them, and the pair went tumbling through, right into the swimming pool.

His right hand was ruined, hanging limp and useless, and his fingers wouldn't respond to his commands when he felt his adversary's close his own meaty hands around his throat. It was only seconds before the darkness crept in again, and his throat burned as he was swallowing the icy chlorine water. There had been a tarp over the outdoor pool, but their hard landing had put a large tear in it, and the two of them were being swallowed up by it.

He felt the freezing water all around him and the icy air bite at his exposed arms, his face hurt and he could taste the blood coming from his mouth and corner of his split temple. The combination of the pain and the freezing water pushed him further into the arms of the darkness, dragging him further down. He thought of Connelly at that moment, taking his own share of beatings from the others, helping him fight the good fight. He thought of his mother too, thinking that he wouldn't survive this battle to reach her, and he wondered who would take care of her.

The last face he saw, though, was that of a curly-haired blonde girl, who he recognized from long ago. She looked much like she did that day by the water's edge, watching him struggle to get the small boy ashore, frantic to get him away from the water. John knew how that boy felt at that moment, the icy water all around, the air being choked out of him, and no one coming to help, no one knowing that he was down there.

As he was overtaken by nothingness, dragged further downward, he saw the boy again. His lips were moving as he slowly sank to the bottom of the clutching deep, his small fingers flailing, just out of reach of John's outstretched hand. He was trying to tell him something, trying to shout something through the murkiness to him, but John could hear nothing. Down they went, and the boy seemed to be descend faster towards wherever they were headed, enveloped by the black water, until he could no longer see him. There was only the quiet darkness then, and though he still unconsciously struggled for his survival above the surface, there was no struggle in that black night beyond.

Chapter *19*

John found himself standing beside eerily still waters, staring at a reflection that was not his. The man in the dark pool wore a sad expression, his eyes lifting up towards him beneath heavy lids, weighted by despair and loss. His face was familiar, as familiar as his own, but there were subtle differences like the heavy stubble and the long hair that was being tossed about in the icy wind. That arctic gust howled through the naked trees, disturbing the tranquility of the pool and scattering the reflection.

Turning from the water, he pulled the hood of his cloak back over his head and made his way towards the barren tree line. He remembered that these trees had once been lush with thick green leaves, forming the roof of his home in the glade, but his roof had since fallen to the ground. It had turned brown and lifeless, and lay beneath a thick layer of snow that he crushed beneath his feet as he walked.

He could not recall how long he walked among those trees, or how he had even come to be among them, he just opened his eyes and there he was. That was how the dream went, like most dreams do. Time passes too quickly, jumps and skips over minutes or even hours, and then slows almost to a stop, so slow that you can hear your own heart beat and your own private thoughts within that dream. He was thinking of a girl, a beautiful, fair-haired girl waiting for him just beyond the trees.

His legs pumped and his heart raced, out of breath, cheeks frozen but the blood pumping behind them still. The road before him was long still, but then time did its funny thing, skipped, and he had moved an impossible distance in an impossibly short span. There was her home, just as he'd left it, and he was standing in the road beside the wagon again, hurling stones. No, he wasn't hurling them, he was weighing one in his hand, contemplating. But she wasn't inside there. No one was inside there; the house looked as desolate and ruined as the one he'd left behind in the forest.

The roof had begun to collapse, and the window sills were deep with snow. The door hung off of its hinges and a drift had taken up residence in the main room, like some homeless squatter. John kicked at it and spat, but it would not be chased off, much like the stark emptiness that hung from the rafters of the place. It was still furnished with a crude table where she and her father had taken their suppers, and the crockery was still piled neatly beside an iron pot, unwashed.

He feared the worst, but there was nothing disturbed or upturned. Nothing was broken. Nothing was out of place. Everything was left behind in the delicate way a child leaves a toy on a shelf when it no longer serves its purpose. It is lovingly tucked away, goodbyes are spoken, and it is only afforded a smile now and again as the years pass. There was no blood trail to be found, only a few tears dripped upon that floor perhaps, and the only thing foul there was the neglect of a broken-down, forgotten place.

Leaning in the open doorway, he rested his head on his forearm, hot tears on his face. His beautiful girl no longer waited in this place for him, she had moved on. Where would they have gone in such a hurry, without taking anything with them?

In the distance, the old tower laughed at him, perched atop its steep hill. He felt it leering, with its smug stone face, delighting in the fact that it knew the answers he sought but would never speak them. John cursed at that old, broken stone sentinel, slamming his fist against the door post, spitting on the cold ground.

Looking up at the top of the hill where the tower stood, he tried to get a good look at the decrepit thing. He'd never been close enough to it before, and only noticed its bleak silhouette the night he scoured the small village looking for Nicolette. Even from the distance he'd seen it from before he could tell that no one had bothered with the old place for probably a century or more. She had told him that it had stood for many years before her people built atop the ruins and renamed it Avandale. There hadn't been a lord in that tower in many generations.

But there was life there now, and the scattered stones had been collected from the hard earth and were returned to the places from which they had fallen. At the tower's base were more stones and building materials, as well as recently-used tools. Footprints were all around the place, fresh impressions left in the snow and mud, by the dozens. Who would rebuild this place and why? There couldn't have been more than a hundred residents of the small village, who would bring them together for such a task?

As ascended the hill admiring the handiwork of those humble residents, he happened to look beyond it at the sprawling valley below. There were more than a hundred freshly-built homes in that valley to the west that had not been there before. This was where the workers were coming from, and he could see the tracks leading down the hillside towards the new homes. Avandale had grown four times its size in only a few months of his absence. Something was happening here, and he knew that Nicolette and her father were somehow involved.

Was George one of the workers involved in the tower project? Was that his big break? He couldn't see the old man hefting stones or mixing mortar with those tools. Soldiering would have been less physically taxing than heavy construction. Had he been an engineer then, and directing the workers? Nicolette had never mentioned such a thing, and George didn't seem the architectural type. What, then, was his part in the rebuilding of the tower and the sudden population boom?

As he stood scratching his head, staring out over the valley, then up at the tower, something caught his eye. The tower was flying its own colors, emblazoned upon twin banners and fluttering from two pikes placed atop the structure. He couldn't make out the design in the darkness, but he was certain that they were colors flown for war.

Avandale was becoming a staging area for an army, and John slowly began to realize that terrible truth as he noticed the banners, the homes built in uniform fashion, without space left for plots between them. They were built to house soldiers, like individual barracks, and the harvest from this year, he would wager, was being used to feed an army.

What was Nicolette's father's part in all of this? Had he returned to the fight, at his age, or was he functioning as some type of advisory position for another man? Could her father be the new lord of the tower, or did someone else welcome him there? No matter the details, Nicolette and her father were inside that tower, he was sure of it. That was why they left their home and all of their belongings in it.

The old iron portcullis was a bit rusty but it had been the first thing put in its place in the restoration project. The stones

201

around the opening looked newer than the others in the tower face, and there was fresh mortar pressed between them. There would be no way through that entrance, and John needed to get inside and find the girl he had come for.

Looking up at the nearest window, he decided that tossing stones was out of the question this time. The lowest one was a full ten meters over his head, and quite inaccessible. As he paced back and forth beneath them, he scanned the area, trying to find a way inside. Just beyond the veil of the night sky, he saw the outline of another building. As he approached, he realized that this was the chapel that Nicolette had talked about, and spent many hours in her dedication to her faith.

The old chapel looked as ancient and decrepit as the tower, and must have been the only other building remaining from the time of the earlier inhabitants of the village. The roof appeared to be folding in on itself, and the old crucifix of iron atop the steeple was leaning to one side, threatening to break free. The structure was simple, but it might have just sufficed for his needs, especially with the sprawling oak not far from its cornerstone.

Time skipped again. He was weightless as though swimming, his arms and legs flailing, and far below him was the stony earth waiting to receive him. The leap from the tree to the roof of the chapel had been easy. The one from the chapel to the open window of the tower had been suicide. He never made it to the edge to even attempt that jump, however, for the ancient timbers cracked, giving way beneath his weight, and the roof swallowed him up. The whole process had taken fourteen minutes, but it had been skipped right over in less than a heartbeat in the dream.

He seemed to hover in midair for an eternity, before the sensation of falling gripped him and slammed him downward into something solid. A long table broke in two, sending candles flying and the crimson tapestry which rested there was set ablaze. John lay on the ground, the breath knocked from him, staring up at the ceiling of the chapel, seeing the stars through the portal he'd left. He was surprised that the fall hadn't killed him, or at the very least, shattered several bones. His arms and legs followed his commands and his back seemed intact.

Finally, he stood, and stomped out the small blaze, as he got his bearings. He looked around to find himself in a generously decorated chamber, which belied the outside appearance of the place. There were several ornately carved statuettes set in recesses in the walls, a multitude of candles and polished brass lanterns illuminating them. A beautifully crafted pulpit was inlaid with silver and bronze trimming, and a large crucifix with a likeness of the savior was fixed to the front.

Hand carved benches, upholstered with worn cloth sat in rows to accommodate the worshippers, and a large chandelier holding four dozen candles, hung from a substantial chain attached to a beam. He sat on one of those benches, replaying his failed infiltration of the tower, and tried to recalculate distances, staring up at the hole in the ceiling. It would have to be done over, using the mighty oak, the scaffolding, careful footing on the shingles, and then around that pitfall.

Just as he reached the massive front doors, one creaked open, and a moonlit shadow swept across the floor. A hooded figure entered, the light of a lantern mingled with that of the quarter moon, but would still not penetrate the darkness of the church. He couldn't be certain that the watchman was armed with anything but a lantern and a voice loud enough to warn others, but that was enough of a threat. The intruder grappled the investigator from behind, putting the edge of his hatchet against his throat.

"If you value your life, you'll not scream," he whispered.

There was no cry, and none needed, as the hood fell away to reveal golden ringlets and the fairer features of a woman. John immediately moved his grip from her throat to her arm and turned her around to face him. She looked as beautiful as ever, in the soft glow of the lantern, despite the weariness in her eyes.

"What are you doing here?" He demanded, grabbing her by the shoulders.

"I should ask you the same, John", she replied. "This is my home! You are fortunate that I was the one to hear you banging around out here and not one of the guards!"

"Since when has Avandale had guards, or a standing army Nicolette? You were supposed to meet me in Rouen two months past, but you abandoned me there," he growled. "And your uncle is dreadfully sick; I've been apprenticed with a man named Harold – who spends more time drinking and telling stories than he does swinging a hammer."

203

Harold the bald was her aunt Elizabeth's brother, and she knew him well. Under different circumstances, she might've laughed at his description and proceeded to tell him stories of her own about "Uncle Harold" and his adventures that she used to love hearing as a girl. But there was nothing joyous about this reunion, and it wasn't the occasion for fond memories of any sort.

"A lot has happened here since you left, John," she said with a heavy sigh. "I could not get away to see you, and for that, I am sorry. I am aware of my Uncle William's condition, but I have not even been able to leave to even see him, as we have our own illnesses to deal with here."

"What is so pressing here that you cannot come to Rouen as you promised?"

She pulled away from his grasp and set her lantern down, closing the door to the church so that they would have privacy. Taking his hand, she led him gently to one of the long benches and began her story. The dank shadows hid her face well, but he could still see the sadness there in her eyes as she spoke.

Much had transpired since he'd been told to go and make a life for himself in Rouen, just as she'd said. His assumptions about war coming to the small village had been correct, though he couldn't have guessed how strong that grip was and how deeply it had penetrated every aspect of that place he loved.

A man named Hugh had been installed in the tower, under the orders of the king himself, and plans had been put in place to turn Avandale into something greater. A lot of money and manpower had been invested over the past several months to take full advantage of the strategic benefit of her home, and its proximity to Rouen. Apparently, that city and its people had allied itself with the king's son, and that had prompted the king to notice the small valley place.

The grand political schemes of kings and princes didn't interest him as much as the new players who were involved in those schemes. Hugh was an interesting new face in Avandale, and he was the talk of the village, as the man who would single-handedly elevate their status and political importance. He brought with him the coin and support of the king of England, as well as a slew of soldiers, workers and engineers to begin the transformation.

The tower was being brought back to life, after being abandoned for two centuries, and from the ramparts, Hugh would oversee the next stages in the plan. That plan involved a barracks, a blacksmith shop, a renovation to the old church, and the residences quadrupling in number. Nicolette told him that she would champion John as their resident blacksmith, once the shop was completed.

His apprenticeship with her uncle and her father's relationship with the new lord of the tower would ensure his return to Avandale. George wasn't a stranger to either Hugh or King Henry, and he'd eagerly accepted the position of military advisor and master-at-arms. That was how an old soldier and his daughter had been able to leave their lives behind as struggling farmers living in a cramped and drafty home, moving into a more spacious and drafty tower.

Everything had been going according to plan, and she had only a few more months to wait until the smithy shop was ready for occupancy. Her father had been to Rouen to visit with his brother, to tell him of the news, and he'd brought back word of the promising new apprentice working the shop in his absence. She'd suppressed a smile and any interest in the news her father brought about the young man, but her heart had leapt in her chest. She also pretended not to hear her father talking him up to Hugh and dulled her excitement as she realized that John was as good as coming home to her soon.

Things were going even better than she had envisioned for them: Her father would no longer struggle to make a living for them; she no longer had to wait on him hand and foot and had more free time; the man she loved was coming home, and had the approval of her father as well as Hugh. Good things would happen for them soon, and she gave her thanks to God prematurely.

George had brought more than good word from his visit to the city; he'd also delivered his brother's illness to his household. Nicolette was overwhelmed again by taking care of not just her father, but Hugh as well, and she watched her plans fall apart as their health declined. George was a man of strong constitution and fared better against the illness, but Hugh's condition was cause for concern. At death's door, his only son was summoned from Paris, and that was when all of Nicolette's hopes had been dashed.

Reginald was a young man of considerable education and refinement, having been raised in the same courts as the likes of Richard and Philip of France. He was as charismatic as the former and attractive as the latter, appealing to men and women alike. His true gift was in getting what he wanted from either, using his charms and a well-oiled tongue. At twenty-two, he was a court favorite of the most beautiful women and most influential men from Alsace to Aquitaine, and his presence even overshadowed his father's in many circles.

It was no surprise that a young, impressionable and desperate girl would fall helplessly under his influence and charm. Reginald de Poitou – as he liked to be called – was a bigger happening to Avandale than his father, and all eyes turned to him as Hugh's health wavered like a candle flame in a storm. His immediate attention was to his father's condition, but after several whispered discussions in his bedchamber, he took over his father's duty to his king. With Avandale's prosperity and advancement in Reginald's hands, it meant Nicolette was his servant as well as his father's.

In the beginning, she doted on him for the benefit of her father, her home and her absent love, and she'd tried hard to hold to those motives. An exceptionally hard winter, a household in chaos, and emotional vulnerability had made her lose sight of those things. She began to dote on Reginald for the same reasons that other young maidens in his presence did – because he had that indescribable quality that drew them in, and didn't allow them to escape. The emotional climate in the tower, with both of their fathers so near death, only drove them closer together.

John saw through it as soon as he had to bear every awful detail. He knew those types of men, and heard plenty of awful stories about them from Harold. This, by far, surpassed those others as the worst he had heard yet, because it was a story that completely overwrote his own. The tale she was sharing with him in that church wasn't a continuation of their own, it wasn't a new chapter for John and Nicolette, but the place where his name had been replaced in her book and the rest of the pages from his were being torn out and tossed into the wind.

The hurt and anguish in his face made her turn her own away. He rose from the old bench and stumbled a bit as he moved away from her, as if he'd been stricken with that illness that had caused him so much grief. It was that plague that was responsible, the awful, faceless thing that had changed everything. The sickness created an opportunity for him, but it created one for his hated, unseen adversary as well. Like God's own hand, it had both given and taken something away.

His gaze was drawn to the gilded likeness of that God, suspended on a cross of wood on the front of the ancient pulpit. Her words kept playing over in his head, the words that he whispered to himself every night since he'd left her: *The rest is in God's hands*. The carved face stared back at him, and the crudely carved expression of pain and martyrdom seemed to twist into a grin, taunting him. One of the benches suffered his wrath only because it was tangible and solid, unlike those other culprits that he blamed.

"John, what are you doing? They will hear you for certain, and I will not be able to stop them!"

He whirled on her, the broken and toppled bench not satiating his rage, screaming at her, hoping the master of the tower and that house might hear him, so that he might settle up with the both of them.

"Let them come! I do not care!"

She placed a hand gently on his arm, trying to calm him like a spooked stallion, "John…please…"

But he snapped his arm away and continued to prance about nervously, nostrils flaring, and eyes wide and full of fire. "Let them come I said! I would prefer to face this Reginald and fight for you, than allow him to steal you away in my absence!"

"John, there's nothing left to fight for…there's no reason to fight anyone! I decided this on my own, nobody has decided this for me."

"You've decided *nothing*! This has *all* been decided for you! Your father's ambitions and your over-eagerness to appease him have pushed you into this!

"My father wanted a better life for us! He didn't want to die watching his daughter work her fingers to the bone in the fields!"

"So he whored out his daughter for better meals and some meaningless title instead?"

The small hand cracked the air like a bullwhip and stung his cheek, drawing the blood to the surface. He barely felt it, but didn't care for suffering another, so he caught her wrists in his hands as she struggled against him. She had to look away so that he wouldn't see the tears welling up.

"You have *no idea*...you have no idea what I've been through and the difficult decisions I've had to make!"

"I have yet to hear of a *single* difficult decision you've had to make yet! All I've heard is how the grand opportunity that was laid out before you and your father didn't quite go how you thought it would. What is that like? What is it like to hope things go one way and then they go another, Nicolette?"

"Nothing was *laid out* for us! This *grand opportunity* you're referring to was delivered at our door with fire and blood...lots of blood. The fever wasn't the only thing that followed my father back here, John! The eyes of the king weren't drawn to this place without cause..."

"Avandale was attacked?"

She hung her head, and the shadows parted from her face.

"Nicolette..."

"Just go..."

"What happened here, exactly?"

"I spared you the details of the attack. People...were killed. The women were..."

John's heart fell with a splash in his stomach and the bile crawled up the walls of his insides. His skin grew cold and clammy and the shadows rippled around him as his head spun.

"There was nothing that you could have done...if you'd been here...they would have killed you. The only men they spared were the old and the very young. Any boy over twelve, who could pick up a sword, was slaughtered...and even some who couldn't..."

"Who was it?"

"What does it matter? They were men who carried a banner and who fought under another man. It doesn't matter if they were English, French, Flemish or from across the sea. They did what they came to do. Hugh happened across the burned out homes...helped bury the dead. He and my father appealed to King Henry...the rest is exactly as I've told you."

He became the spooked stallion again, pacing the inside of the church, the nostrils flaring again. Another bench almost felt his wrath, but he assailed the wooden man instead, sending him clattering across the floor. She kneeled and picked up the cross,

208

cradling it lovingly, giving him a sheepish look. He shook his head at her as if in disbelief that she would give such reverence to the god that had looked the other way as her home and her people were ravaged. Strong hands that were supposed to bring them back together became loose fingers for them to slip through.

"So...Reginald...the two of you..."

"Not by choice but necessity. His father...before he died...brought security to this place and promise. Reginald is the only hope that this place has now...he has all of his father's resources and connections, as well as a few of his own. He's not a bad man, John, and he wouldn't turn me away...despite what's happened."

"You think that I would have turned you away? What happened wasn't your fault!"

"As it was happening...I took some comfort in the fact that you were away from this place and safe under Harold's watch. I thanked God that you weren't lying face down in the fields with the rest, and that I might see you again."

"I am here now, Nicolette. Come away with me tonight and leave this place. I have learned so much and William is making me his assistant when he returns to the shop! We can have a life in Rouen, just like we talked about!"

"I am not the same girl you knew, John. I was changed forever by that night...I lost my faith in men and struggle with my faith in my God every day. I do not love Reginald as I loved you...I don't think that I can love any man ever again...and you deserve better than what I can give."

"What are you saying?"

"I didn't come for you because I wanted you to be happy and not be burdened with this...and to forget about this place and me. I didn't want you to come looking for me, but somehow, I knew that you would."

"I can protect you..."

"I have no doubt that you can...but even if I could make things as they were, even if I could quell this bitterness in my heart and be with you like before, I cannot leave this place. Reginald is the reason that my home is protected, and I am the reason that he protects it. There is nothing here for him but me...and he says that I am its beating heart."

"So he keeps you here against your will?"

"No, it is my will that my father, my home and the people in it are safe. I am well-taken care of, and Reginald has not been the same since his father passed."

"Your father would not want you to stay here for his benefit, Nicolette!"

"This is the only home I've ever known...my mother is buried here, and her mother as well. Avandale is going to rebuild itself, become better than it was, and never fall victim to men like that again. I will be happy watching all of this happen...I will be happy knowing that you are still out there and thinking good thoughts of me."

"I can come back here and help you rebuild it! We don't need Reginald! I know something about war and fighting and your father and I..."

"Harold has been telling you his war stories, putting ideas into your head, and that is noble of you, but you cannot offer Avandale the protection that it needs. We need an *army*, John, not just a blacksmith. If I abandoned Reginald, I fear that he would leave and we would be fending for ourselves again."

"So...you send me out to find a trade and make a living for myself, but it's not enough because I lack the power and entitlement of one born into it? You send me out again?"

"I am not sending you out for my benefit, but for your own! Make your own way in this world John, make a reputation and do good works for yourself, not for me or anyone else! I ask only this of you...I beg you give me this one gift. Leave this place behind and give it not a glance or second thought, you are destined for something greater."

John crossed the room towards her, approaching with such a certainty in his step that she thought he intended her harm. Stopping an arm's length away, he looked upon her with eyes that smoldered like the coals from the furnace he labored over day after day. Her eyes did not burn that way any longer, and that glow that he loved had been extinguished.

She pulled his face towards hers and gave him her best goodbye kiss. But she was right; it was empty and hollow and there seemed to be no warmth coming from those lips any longer. She had tried to tell him, tried to explain, but it was that kiss that made him understand. It was like brushing his lips against the cold metal of his idle hammer before he started his day's work. Never had a kiss to that icy metal ever been as cold as those lips.

There was nothing left for him to say, and so with a smoldering bitterness, he turned from her and made his way back out into the winter night. The wind kicked up and spat its icy saliva in his face, forcing him to turn his head and shield his face. In the blurry gust, he saw shapes there that looked like men, saw arms grabbing at him, and felt them dragging him down.

Those hands continued to drag him downward, and then he felt himself rising out of that icy cold nothingness, as the hands dragged him from the water. John coughed and sputtered mucous and burning fluid from his mouth and nose, trying to gasp for air that would not come. His rescuers dragged him to a lawn chair and deposited him like a doll, where he fell face down and ejected water and food onto the cement.

"Some party Caps, thanks for inviting me," Connelly groaned.

John rolled over and took deep breaths before sputtering, "What happened?"

It wasn't a question about the beating he'd just taken at the hands of Sal, but about the things that he'd just seen as he'd been nearly drowned. He was disoriented from a lack of oxygen but also from the episode he'd experienced, and he was shaken by both.

"The big guy kicked your ass. I would've stopped him but I was getting beat up by four more of them. Gwenn told me she saw you down here in the pool, so we headed down just as the sirens started blaring. The party got broken up and everyone bailed."

John stared up at him and then at the figure just beyond, with a strange expression on his face, as if he hadn't seen either of them in years. The girl approached then, and he'd thought, just for a moment, that she was somebody else. He began to call her by another name, but then forgot that name, and called her something else.

"Hey Gwenn...I suppose I owe you...for not letting me drown."

"Yea, I was pretty worried. The cops showed up pretty fast and Sal dropped you immediately. I know he doesn't want to be involved with this, given his reputation, and if you pressed charges..."

211

"I'm not pressing charges," he snapped. "I don't want anything to do with him or her!"

"That's probably for the best," Connelly said as he helped get him back to his feet.

"Where are we going?"

"Back up to the room, you still have it for the night. We may as well use it."

"I could probably use a little rest before we head out."

Connelly opened the door to the room and deposited John on the bed nearest the wall, then collapsed himself on the other one. He could hear them talking as he dipped in and out of consciousness, and felt a cold rag on his face, dabbing delicately at his seams.

How is he doing?

About as good as he looks…I'm sure that he'll be alright in the morning.

We shouldn't take him to a hospital?

Naw, he just took a few good lumps – nothing that won't heal up on its own.

He fell back asleep, after hearing the professional assessment of his friend, and certain that he wouldn't expire in his sleep. There was an unusual, familiar comfort then, being with the two of them, but with Gwenn especially as she tended to him the entire night. He dreamed of the other woman that he'd seen in the strange episode, but he felt her presence as he slept.

In the morning, John examined his swollen face in the mirror, washed the rest of the dried blood from it, and combed his hair. He woke Jeremy who was snoring and looked very uncomfortable on the other bed, telling him that it was time to go. They let Gwenn sleep and closed the motel door behind quietly as the icy morning air greeted them. It made his face hurt more, but woke him up enough to begin their journey south.

They put on sunglasses, more to hide their faces than to block out the dingy January sun, as they eased out of the parking lot onto the highway. He looked up at the motel room window and said a silent goodbye to the girl that was inside, and to the one who wasn't. He ached from every bruise and seam where he'd been split, but pride shone brightly through those seams, making him forget that he ached. He had stood his ground against impossible odds, and fought for the woman he loved, and though he had lost, he couldn't stop smiling. As he set out on that long voyage south, he wondered if he would ever see the faces of that girl or that other man again.

KINGS AND MADE MEN

"He who reigns within himself and rules passions, desires, and fears is more than a king."

~Milton

Chapter *20*

James Campbell had laid out quite a spread for breakfast for his returning guest, and she could smell it from the front door as soon as he opened it. Down the long hallway he escorted her, always the gentleman, across the expensive rug, beneath the beautiful high ceilings of his foyer. They passed the closed doors to the den that they'd used the night before to proceed deeper into the 'Campbell estate' (as he jokingly liked to call it).

There was a surprisingly modern kitchen, complete with mosaic-topped counters and brushed steel appliances, he gave her a brief tour of, more for the benefit of her familiarity to access at her leisure later on. Campbell had money, and he had a few snobbish tastes, but he wasn't snobbish in the least. She'd expected the dining room to be modern and roomy like the kitchen, but it was actually quaint and just large enough to accommodate four or five people if the table had been pulled from the wall.

He explained, intercepting the obvious question that all guests had asked, "I don't like to trip over myself in the kitchen – I need room for my culinary masterpieces. I don't like to be reminded that I'm dining alone in a big house when I'm eating, however."

Campbell had been working one of those masterpieces that morning before she arrived, and it almost overwhelmed the modest table. There was an arrangement of plates heaped with flapjacks, English sausages, spiced potatoes, quiche, and freshly cut fruit. In the center was an antique silver platter that held a tea service, a pitcher of juice and coffee, and all the essential spoons and sugar dishes. Gwenn was admiring his presentation as he pulled out her chair for her.

She hadn't realized just how hungry she was until her stomach grumbled at the sight of the food. Eating and sleeping, the most basic of human needs, had seemed like luxuries to her over the past few months. Guilt had afforded her little of either, and she felt that they were comforts that could wait until she'd had answers about her husband's fate. For the first time, she'd had a good night's rest, and for the first time she had an appetite.

The man pouring her the steaming cup of coffee was responsible for that, even though they'd made very little headway the night before. She had faith in James Campbell and in the plan they had established for the day. The first stage of that plan involved a hearty breakfast, and it hadn't sounded like much of a plan when he'd suggested it, but after her first bite of his quiche, it sounded like the best idea she'd heard yet.

Campbell finished a full plate of flapjacks and three sausages, washed it down with a glass of milk and poured himself a cup of Earl Grey before he said a single thing about the next part of their plan. She looked up from her plate and noticed that the morning paper was in front of him and not his notebook and found it odd.

"You're reading the paper?"

He glanced up at her and smiled over the top of the paper, "I find that it helps to get my brain primed before I tackle the more difficult puzzles if I work something simpler...like the crosswords."

"You're doing the *crosswords*? Without a pencil?"

"I do them in my head," he said from behind the paper.

"How do you keep them straight if you do them in your head? Don't you have to know which letters intersect?"

Campbell chuckled, "I find that if you know the answers to the questions, it doesn't really matter how they're organized on the paper, or if they fit with the other words."

"That's kind of contrary to the entire way you do things isn't it, Jim?"

"In unraveling any mystery, you start filling in the blanks with the facts and things that are known, much like a crossword puzzle. Then you look at the blanks and open spaces that remain, and start guessing at every answer that fits into those spaces. Historians are no exception, and we fill in those blanks to the best of our ability, but those answers aren't infallible, because we never see leftover boxes. So long as every question has an answer, and it seems rational, no one usually checks that answer."

"Until something doesn't fit and new information is discovered?"

He nodded, taking a sip of his tea and folding the paper before setting it down. "That's why new History books are published so often; the story changes every time one of those answers changes, and everything shifts around that one bit of information. I should have gotten into the damned publishing business."

"So how does that apply to John's story? Are you saying...that the system you were using is wrong? Is there a better way to find the answers?"

"I'm saying that if we know the answers the first time around, and stop guessing or just finding ones that seem to make the most sense then we don't have to keep rewriting the story."

"You lost me...how are we supposed to know the right answers if not by process of elimination?"

"Process of elimination isn't necessarily wrong, but only if used in conjunction with knowing exactly how many boxes need to be filled. The answer has to fit with the others in such a way that no other possible answer can be right, and to do that, you have to make sure that you have all of the intersecting letters correct."

"And how do you do that? How can you turn a fill-in-the-blank into a crossword puzzle?"

"That's precisely the system your husband and I were working on, using his journal pages. Those pages affixed to the back wall of my study, with all of their interconnecting lines and notations, are like one giant crossword. We decided to turn blanks into boxes, using the irrefutable answers that we did know."

She wrinkled her brow at him, "But you're saying that...you're abandoning the system?"

"I'm saying that there may not be enough of those surrounding boxes filled in correctly, and I need to go back and look at those."

"Aren't those supposedly *irrefutable* facts?"

"When we first started this, John and I went over the facts together, starting with the most basic like names, dates and places. I assumed that these things were hard data, not open for interpretation, but lately, anything that's in that journal...I have to question."

"Because you think John had a personality disorder?"

"I can no longer assume that even the basics were right. Just in talking with you last night, I see a different angle on the things he was absolutely certain were fact. John obviously couldn't know what was happening behind the scenes with Melinda, and formed his own opinions, which he wrote in the journal."

"So what does that mean? You have to wipe out everything and start from scratch?"

"It means that I need more hard data that doesn't come from John."

"That's why I'm here, isn't it?" She asked, refilling her coffee cup.

"That's exactly why you're here. Well, that and I just like the company," he said with a wink.

"But you want more data? You need another source to check the facts?"

"There's no hiding anything from you," he said, scooting his chair back and producing a pipe from his inside jacket pocket.

He seemed to have a full wardrobe of expensive Scottish tweeds, and he was never seen without one. This particular morning, he was wearing a handsome gray, single-breasted one with two hacking pockets. Coupled with his lighter gray slacks and the sky blue button down, it gave him a softer, more approachable look – not that of a stuffy college professor. If there was the perfect brunch ensemble, Campbell had nailed it as easily as he had selected the perfect décor for his dining room.

"Do you mind?" He asked, indicating the pipe.

She shook her head, "It's your pipe and your home."

He deliberately packed the thing with such a slow precision so as to buy himself some time, thinking of how to approach the topic she'd just brought up. He'd been up for several hours before her arrival and had lots of time to think ahead to the next part of his session with her.

"You said that you had some new angle…some plan…what other source are you talking about?"

"I'm adding someone else to the discussion," he said, taking two stout puffs.

"Who are you talking about?"

"The next entry in John's journal is dated late nineteen-ninety-four: more than two years after he left for Florida. There are no details of his time there, Gwenn."

"John never talked about what happened there and I respected his choice."

"I need to know what happened there for John's sake."

"Only *Connelly* knew what happened there, and I haven't spoken to him since the funeral."

Campbell quietly savored the taste of his pipe, and nodded slowly, thoughtfully. He was still thinking of his approach, but when her eyes met his, she knew what had already been done in her absence.

"You spoke with him? When?"

"This morning. He agreed to meet with me...with *us*."

"How did you even know how to find him? I had a hell of a time reaching him myself. There's no guarantee that he'll even tell you what you want to know, Jim."

"He sounded very cooperative on the phone."

"How much money did you offer him?"

Campbell raised a brow, "Connelly was one of John's best friends, and I explained the situation...he wanted to help."

"I've known Jeremy Connelly for years, and I know his situation Jim. He wouldn't be coming to meet with either of us – especially me – unless you made it worth his time."

"Oh," he said simply.

"So how much did he extort from you for this?"

"If I had known months ago, when this began, that all I had to do was retrieve my checkbook to get the right answers for John, I would have eagerly done so."

She pushed her plate away and sat back in her own chair, folding her arms and staring over the juice carafe at him. It was a bold move on Campbell's part, and she wasn't sure how she was feeling about it. As the man her husband had personally charged with the task of taking on his unusual case, it wasn't as if he didn't have a right, but she still felt it was something that should've been discussed, given her history with the particular source he'd chosen.

He sensed her discomfort and the pleasing colors of his ensemble and the breakfast he'd prepared were losing their intended effect.

"Let's worry about Mister Connelly when he arrives. For now, let's touch on what we discussed at the close of last evening. We agreed to take a break until this morning and reconvene after a good night's rest, when our heads were clearer."

"That was the plan."

"So? Did you have some thoughts about what we discussed?"

"You said the words *near-death* experience."

"I did, indeed. John was nearly drowned in that pool at the motel that January eve. You said yourself that you were concerned that he'd been under for too long and that you and Connelly both thought he had…well…you thought the worst."

"We did. Everything was happening so fast, and I may have lost track of time, but he was under that pool tarp for a minimum of three or four minutes. John wasn't exactly a professional diver trained in breathing techniques, and anything over that amount of time can be dangerous."

"No argument there. Is your assessment that some type of brain damage may have brought on John's episodes?"

"I had initially thought that there was some correlation between a lack of oxygen and the hallucinations. He was tested for sleep apnea, because it was the only thing that made sense at the time. Then I thought that it might be psychological and the simple sensation of being submerged was enough to trigger them."

"That would explain the rain."

"It would, but he was perfectly fine taking showers and was an expert swimmer."

"So that leaves us what option?"

"My husband had a brush with death when Sal was holding him beneath the water, and that experience…could have opened him up to something."

Campbell frowned. It was Henry Marshall joining them at the breakfast table, though he wore a much prettier face and less-boring ensemble. He imagined his colleague at home, meditating and using some sort of new-aged channeling technique to speak through his adept student. He wanted to tear into her and really give her a piece of his mind for bringing up such an absurd thing so early in their pleasant Saturday morning breakfast talk. He really had tried his best to get off on the right foot with her and not have a rehash of the prior evening, but she had spoiled it and the mood would soon deteriorate.

He decided against any lectures warning against the dangers of Dr. Henry Marshall, and instead decided to play along in an attempt to steer the discussion back into the realm of the possible.

"What are you suggesting that it opened up?" His tone was still like soured milk.

"Jim, I realize this isn't your area and you've discouraged me from jumping to this type of conclusion, but I am a *medical doctor* – I deal in science and facts as well – and I've exhausted every resource at my disposal in explaining what happened to John. Traumatic experiences account for extreme psychoses, but they also account for other phenomena that can't be explained."

Gwenn pulled a small yellow pad from her purse then and started flipping through the pages, reading off names like Kenneth Ring, Raymond Moody, Elisabeth Kübler-Ross – each followed by several PhD's - explaining their contributions to the study of near death experience – or "NDE".

"Moody interviewed over a thousand people who all gave very similar accounts of their experiences while they were clinically dead, one of which was Dr. George Ritchie, who was dead for nine minutes."

Flipping a page, she cited her notes with earnest and enthusiasm.

"Dr. Gregory Shushan did a cross-culture study on NDE. His findings were that Old and New Kingdom Egyptians, Pre-Colombian Mesoamericans, Mesopotamian Babylonians and even Vedic Indians all shared the nine most frequent elements of the NDE model – despite their cultural differences."

He nodded, puffing at his pipe and holding his pen slightly above his notepad.

"Dr. Kübler-Ross wrote the book on death and the dying--"

"I'm aware of history of the religious beliefs of those ancient cultures as well as the Kübler-Ross model for dealing with death," he interrupted, in between puffs. "You didn't mention *Kinseher* or *Strassman*."

She knew the names and she gave him a poorly-camouflaged scowl.

"Strassman did some pretty incredible work with the drug Dimethyltryptamine, or DMT: the same chemical released from the pineal gland at or near death."

"I'm aware of Strassman's work, and if you'd read up on him you would know that only a couple of his test subjects reported similar auditory and visual experiences to those of a NDE subject. The rest reported nothing more than the standard

223

experience one would expect from experimenting with psychedelic drugs."

"Indeed, you are correct, and it wasn't Strassman who I was particularly impressed with, it was Kinseher and his work on the sensory autonomic system and how it's applied to the NDE phenomenon."

"The 'Paradox of Death' theory? I've read it."

"It's an interesting concept and I think it makes absolute sense. I'm sure at some point in your life - perhaps when you had your accident - you've experienced the same thing? Where your whole life flashes before your eyes in an instant, when you think death is near?"

"The auto accident that I was in was very traumatizing for very different reasons, as I'm sure John explained to you."

"Not to bring up a sore subject, but in the moments before the impact, you didn't experience anything similar to what Kinseher described? Where the brain seeks out a similar event, reviewing the entire episodic memory in an attempt to cope with what was happening? I'm not using his theory to argue against yours, Gwenn, I'm actually on the same page with you as this applies to John."

"So you think when John almost drowned, his brain was trying to cope with his impending death and that's what caused him to be transported to an entirely different world?"

"When the brain performs this scan, looking for any stored experience which it can relate to the paradox of death, and the individual is able to see the entirety of his stored memory at once, old things can be retrieved. It's believed that this applies to even prenatal memories, and I find this to be an amazing testament to the power of the human mind. The brain then takes the sum total of those stored memories and creates a mental overview, projecting them into the surrounding world. This is the out-of-body, dreamlike experience these subjects report seeing and feeling."

"Yes, I read all of that. But how does this explain John's dreamlike state? If you believe that he was recalling stored memory and then projected those memories into some auditory and visual hallucination…where did those memories come from?"

"I've spoken with Dr. Marshall at length about varying genetic memory theories and the possibility of the human mind accessing those memories lying dormant in the brain. It's one of his less nonsensical areas of study, but I don't know that I want to stand on that platform just yet."

"If there is such a thing as genetic or ancestral memory stored in our DNA, and John's accident allowed him access those memories, wouldn't that explain his condition in a more scientific context?"

"It's borderline science *fiction*, and even Parapsychologists agree with the biological view, and contend that genetic memory applies only to dispositional things; how the person reacts to stimuli, not actual memories. It was in my studies on this particular topic that I found something very interesting that I thought applied to John's case, however."

"Relating to NDE?"

"You recall the name 'Stephen LaBerge'?"

"He wrote quite a bit about lucid dreaming. I studied his work extensively and so did my husband, but it just didn't seem to fit the bill. Lucidity implies that the subject has some awareness of being in a dream; John walked around the house flipping light switches and checking clocks to see if he was awake."

"Those are the standard tests many lucid dreamers perform to validate the fact that they're in a dream. Digital readouts tend to be inaccurate or jump ahead on clocks for the dreamer, and light switches will rarely affect the volume of light in an imagined space. The same applies for looking in a mirror; the image will usually be distorted."

"Right, so what does this LaBerge have to do with John?"

"Dr. LaBerge stated that the two phenomena – lucid dreaming and NDE – were very similar in that they each seemed to so realistic to the subject that they were almost indistinguishable from reality."

Gwenn studied her notes in the small tablet in her hand and gave him a puzzled look, saying, "Neither of his two models for lucid dreaming applied to John, though. Both dream-initiated-lucid-dreaming and wake-initiated-lucid dreaming also required some type of preparatory methods."

"I don't disagree. However, John suffered from both 'DILD' and 'WILD' by every other definition of the terms."

"Besides the deliberate steps required by the subjects to enter either of these states, like counting or reaching a meditative platform first, he also wasn't reaching REM sleep. There were no eye movements whatsoever when he was in his trancelike state, and his dorsa-lateral prefrontal cortex was still quite active when he attacked me."

"The working memory center can be inhibited by stress, Gwenn, and would explain his sleepwalking episodes."

"I have pages and pages of notes on hypnagogic visual and auditory hallucinations and he didn't meet the criteria for those--"

"I'm not even talking about hypnagogia, Gwenn, I'm talking about an offshoot treatment method involving lucid dreaming called narrative therapy."

"*Narrative therapy*? What is that?"

"It's the closest thing to a treatment I was attempting for your husband, which was a relatively new technique employed by a man by the name of Dr. Michael White in treating people suffering from ADHD, sleep disorders and schizophrenia."

Gwenn referenced a separate folded sheet of paper she kept tucked in the notepad then. She nodded and folded it in half again, tucking it back between the last pages, saying, "Yes, my husband has his book."

"You keep a list of John's books he kept in his study?"

"When you're running out of options, you start looking in the least likely places for answers. He and I both accumulated dozens upon dozens of self-help and psychology books over the course of a few months, and we read every one of them. When he finally came to you, we'd exhausted just about every other resource."

"Which was why he insisted that his problem wasn't psychological," he said insightfully. "But in trying to diagnose and remedy his own condition, I fear that he made it worse."

"How do you know that he'd made an accurate diagnosis?"

"I don't, with any certainty. Narrative therapy involves the therapist acting as a sort of 'investigative reporter' to discover the source of the subject's affliction, and then help that subject re-write their own narrative – hence the name."

"Wait…you re-program a person to believe something that isn't true?"

"Truth is subjective, Gwenn, and that was a huge argument against Dr. White's work, as well as the fear that the therapist could interject his own personal beliefs into their subconscious minds."

"You're talking about *brainwashing*?"

"It's not so much 'brainwashing' as allowing a person to see their problem in a new light. The primary principle of narrative therapy involves externalizing the problem from the patient – separating the two – and then diminishing the issue by re-working the narrative or overall story about how that problem came to exist."

"So under this lucid state, you steer their perceptions of the story relating to their individual life problems? And this is accomplished by digging into their past, just like you did with John? Were you attempting this treatment with him…without his knowledge?"

"My methods were similar to those used by Dr. White, admittedly, and I don't think John was aware of what I was doing, no. But you know, as well as I, that he would've refused treatment if he knew what I was trying to do. He was already getting angry that we were taking a detour in his journal and discussing things from his past."

"That's highly unethical, Jim…"

"I was trying to save his life!" He growled, leveling a hard stare at her. "We were running out of time and out of options, and as I reminded him many times; I'm not a licensed Psychiatrist. So, if you'd like to take it up with the A.P.A., by all means…"

"I'm sorry…you're right. He went to see you and Marshall because your methods were unorthodox and he trusted the both of you. What did you mean by saying he tried to *remedy his own condition*?"

"As I said, separating the problem from the person is the key to this externalization. In John's case, the problem was a girl. We can argue all day about the identity of the person or persons in question, but we can both agree that John gave a face to this thing that plagued him; a very *female* face."

He pointed his pipe stem towards the wall behind her, out of habit, but realized that the face he was referring to was locked away in another room entirely. She seemed to catch his meaning, regardless, and gave him a nod or understanding.

"So this girl he fabricated is the embodiment of this externalized issue that was causing his episodes? The 'Girl in the Rain' isn't a real person, but a phantom of sorts that he just assigned a random name to?"

227

"I'm not one for ghost stories, but if this theory holds any water – pardon the pun – then this mystery woman is nothing more than an *idea* that your husband gave an identity to."

"But an identity that haunted him nonetheless," she added.

"I believe he was well-aware of Dr. White's method and either deliberately or subconsciously followed through on it, and it got away from him at some point. Haunting him would probably be the best description, yes."

"His externalizations...giving identities to his regrets and issues...became an entirely new world for him? He re-wrote the stories surrounding these things, and the end result was some...entirely new life he became lost in?"

Campbell nodded and took a long draught from his pipe, seeing that he was finally reaching her; his eyes twinkled as he spoke.

"White says in his book that these identities can become stronger than what the subjects can deal with on their own – without realizing exactly what they are. They can become dangerously obsessed with and overpowered by these personalities, just like John was. He became so protective and attached to this phantom woman that he refused to be cooperative when I suggested that she wasn't real."

"His mind just took over like that? Implementing it's own sort of self-repair that he wasn't even aware of? Is that something that's even possible?"

"As we said earlier; there are areas of the human mind that we are just now beginning to understand," he said in a low voice. "Something may have been damaged in that incident in the pool with Sal, some type of failsafe for the brain that keeps it from doing self-diagnosis and repair or from slipping easily into states of lucid dreaming."

"So your initial *Dissociative Identity Disorder* verdict wasn't just one diagnosis but several?"

He nodded, "One of many parts of a larger whole. I'm still open to more suggestions, and I can't even rule out every component of your NDE theory. Many subjects exhibit post-NDE behavior similar to what your husband did. There is often a shift in motivations, attitude, beliefs, and personality."

The amber eyes of his guest seemed to brighten at the prospect that he had given serious consideration to what she'd said.

Their prior phone conversations had been fraught with condescension and disdain; this seemed like real progress.

"There tends to be less fear of death in the individual after a traumatic experience like that; a sense of invincibility, and one of importance or destiny. I read the passages you and my husband both had begun translating and this seems to explain the transformation this other John goes through as well."

Campbell was already turning pages, looking for the passages she was referring to, as if he needed to use them as reference. There probably wasn't another person – living or dead – who knew every word on every page of that journal, yet he still liked to keep it on hand for levity.

"While neither of us have the details of what occurred there, there was a definite change in his attitude and even his writing style in the journal. I only had the pleasure of a very quiet, pre-Floridian John Chapel in my classroom. We didn't begin our friendship until much later, after his return."

"He was a much different person when he came back, and I attributed it to the blowup with Melinda and his fight with Sal – never thinking that something more serious had happened to him in the aftermath."

"While we're waiting for Mr. Connelly to arrive – which should be shortly – I'd like to go over this passage about his 'journey from home' that he recorded here. I think it's a good indicator of what was going on inside the mind of John Chapel at this period in his life, and there was indeed reckless behavior, an unhealthy fearlessness, and the beginnings of his belief that he was something more than an ordinary man."

She nodded solemnly, "I think there was a part of him – part of the man I knew that returned – that believed he would live forever. If only that were true…"

Campbell gave her an uncharacteristic look of compassion then, and in his gentlest tone he reminded her, "John was mortal like the rest of us Gwenn; a man who could hurt and feel pain, but it was that pain that he used to transform himself into something greater and became more than a man…"

Chapter 21

The Anglo-Norman capital that overlooked the river Seine was exactly as Nicolette had described; it was large, noisy and had more bodies moving through the narrow streets than he could have ever imagined. Rouen was to Avandale what Avandale had been to his small place in the forest, not only in population but in architecture as well. The buildings that made up the skyline here, some three and four stories tall, were constructed of stone and fine wood. At the end of the avenue was a magnificent cathedral that dwarfed every building that surrounded it, and could have housed a hundred of the tiny chapels from back home.

It was the largest and most beautiful building by far, built in the exact center of the city, standing like a sentinel over Rouen. Every time he passed that structure, he would stand and stare up in awe at the stone faces of angels watching over the city, always believing that Nicolette had sent one of them just for him. That stone sentinel watched him all the way down the avenue, and even beyond the wooden bridge that spanned the Siene, carrying him into St. Sever quarter, where most of the tradesmen could be found.

The more prominent taverns were located there as well, and Nicolette had told him to steer clear of those, for they could be dangerous. St. Sever quarter faced the harbor, and as a result, the taverns drew in many sailing men who could be a raucous bunch. George had frequented those taverns whenever he went to visit his brother, and he would never allow Nicolette to enter one of those places.

William's shop was there in the northwestern quarter, just the other side of the bridge, and residents of the city could hear the noisy clanging echoing from across the water. One could easily follow the sound of the ringing metal to a row of tightly-packed buildings, down the narrow cobblestone street, and find the smithy shop at the very end.

The shop consisted of three standing walls covered by a heavy roof of thatch with a cutaway to allow for the chimney, forming a large open bay facing the street. The floor was dirt covered in blackened straw, except a portion that was inlaid with blackened stone where a heavy anvil crowned the center of the open space. Surrounding the anvil were several long benches and racks where tools of all varieties rested, and behind it was a brick furnace full of glowing coals.

That shop was being manned by a single apprentice smith who could be found that early June evening – like most evenings – fully engaged in his work. The loud crack of thunder jarred him from his lethargic, semi-trance state, ringing loudly above the soothing din of his hammer. He was working late in the shop again and fighting against fatigue as well as the pelting rain that was blowing into the open space.

Harold used to complain about the way his brother-in-law had built the shop, with three standing walls and only a partition where the fourth should have been. Even though the sweat spilled from his shiny, bald head in torrents and dripped from the ends of his long moustaches as it was, he always said an enclosed work space would've been more practical – despite the heat.

He said that it took too much effort to keep one eye on "the steel" and one on the shop to prevent folks from walking off with things. With a man of Harold's stature and hard features, powerful arms knotted with muscles making his hammer ring like that of mighty Hephaestus himself, few would be foolish enough to attempt to steal from that shop. With Harold gone on campaign, it fell to his own apprentice to keep an eye on things, while he kept both on the "steel".

John hadn't minded working with the open shop in the dead of winter, because the physical exertion and hot furnace kept him warm. In the first days of spring, however, when the rains came, they flooded the ground and turned it into mud, and threatened to cool the metal too quickly. John had an inexplicable dislike for the rain as it was, and hated the feel of it on his face. He deliberately stayed up long hours into the night, finishing his work, because he couldn't sleep with the sound of it tapping on the roof above his room.

The nightmares came when it rained, and he saw the phantom woman who'd first visited him by the lake in the forest. If it wasn't her, then it was the girl of flesh and blood who used to visit him in the same forest, but only came in dreams now. He

232

subconsciously fingered the bone necklace around his neck as the rain attempted to reach his own bones.

"You look worried, John?"

The voice startled him and he'd forgotten that he wasn't alone. Wiping the rain from his face and setting his hammer down on the anvil, he turned towards his assistant. The boy had been watching him for some time – watching his hammer swings get heavier as he stared out into the rainy night.

"I don't care for this weather…it threatens my fire."

"I told you that I would help you build a more solid partition; those curtains will never do."

There were curtains of heavy sail cloth hung from the awning that were doing very little to keep out the rain, with the way the wind tore at them and threatened to bring them down. Like a limber cat, he shimmied up the side of the wall and hooked one leg in the rafters, hanging there effortlessly as he worked at the cloth, trying to secure it.

Pelleon had grown into a young man and come a long way since he'd first met him in Avandale two years before. In just that time, he'd grown a full head taller, his shoulders had begun to broaden like a man's and his arms and legs were long and awkward for his body.

His sandy-colored hair had lightened and became almost as fair as Nicolette's. He especially hated the compliments about his hair, so he'd used ash from the pit to keep it darker and smear it purposely upon his face so that he looked a little more rough-edged. Pelleon had his mother's features, and might have been mistaken for an eleven-year-old girl and not an eleven-year-old boy if he'd stayed clean and kept his hair washed.

There was no better companion or assistant to be had, though, and he could count on the boy to do anything he'd asked – even keep secrets that Harold wasn't privy to. That allegiance was formed on the very night that John had returned to Avandale to find Nicolette, and found much more than he'd bargained for.

Reginald's men found him in the chapel that night, dragged him from it, and commenced to beating and kicking at him in the snow. She'd tried to stop them, shouting and crying from the door of the church, but it was Pelleon who'd gotten their attention.

He discovered his old friend receiving a thrashing that would make old George envious at the hands of the new Avandale

233

guard. Many people didn't care for the strange men moving into their home, taking up with the widows of Avandale and eating their crops. Pelleon was one of them, and was never one to keep an opinion to himself. Once cursing and hurling stones at the guards went ignored, he plunged his dagger deep into one of their shoulders, and it turned serious afterwards.

One of the men turned his weapon on the boy and left him with a nasty gash on his cheek as a result, but that man wouldn't get a chance to come at him again. John recovered from the assault and flew into a rage, killing the man that had struck Pelleon, and then turned on the others. Before any of them knew what had happened, there were five dead men at the doors of the chapel, a stunned woman left weeping uncontrollably, and a boy tugging at the avenger's hand, telling him that they had to flee.

They ran away from that place and never turned back, neither of them having anything left to go back for. Since then, Pelleon had been indispensable in the smithy shop and as a friend. John had taken over Harold's role when he left on the campaigns, and Pelleon fulfilled his, performing duties of the apprentice smith.

When William regained his health that first spring, he'd worked very closely with both of the boys, and taught them as much as he could – sometimes from the corner, resting on his stool. He may have even sensed that his return to good health and to his shop was temporary, and that prompted him to pass on his trade secrets while he was able. He liked John almost as much as Elizabeth and the girls did, and treated him like the son he'd never had. It wasn't just his shop that needed a skilled set of hands, and he'd made John promise that he wouldn't run off with Harold and leave them behind.

He and Pelleon held to that promise, and had their work cut out for them. It seemed there was something needing repair or a quick patch job in that old shop daily, and his young friend had become quite handy with the upkeep.

Pelleon prepared to hop down from the rafters, the curtain secure once again, but hesitated when he saw a figure approaching in the rain. He signaled to John, who instinctively placed his hand on the hatchet at his belt beneath his long apron and shirt. There wasn't usually trouble in Rouen, only the occasional drunk making his own sort, but as of late, there was something in the air besides the weather and both he and Pelleon sensed it.

The figure finally reached the protection of the awning and the curtains that strained against the wind, and stood dripping on the muddy stone floor. Pelleon watched from his perch above as the hood was pulled back to reveal dark blonde curls.

"What are you doing here on a night like this?"

"I wanted to see you and bring you something to eat...I figured you would still be awake because of this weather, and you didn't come home for supper."

"I'm sorry Elizabeth, I only keep you up when it's like this anyway. It's best if I sleep here."

"I don't mind that you wake me, John. I miss you being there."

He took the food from her that had been wrapped inside of an apron to keep it dry and warm. Unfolding it, he found some of her fresh biscuits, a bit of cheese, and two chicken drumsticks. These he set on the warm anvil beside his hammer for later and then moved to greet her. She was always apprehensive about such displays in public, and withdrew from his touch. It was a silly notion, for every one of the neighbors had seen him at the house and probably heard their late night antics through the windows, yet she kept up pretenses for her brother's benefit.

"You didn't have to bring me anything; I could have gone to the tavern for some soup and ale. I don't want you out in this weather and catching fever on my account. It does look delicious though."

She gave him a mild scolding then about the tavern food and how a hardworking man needed better sustenance than that. It made him feel uncomfortable when she approached him in that way and she became more mothering like she'd used to be. It reminded him that she was older and more experienced and he was still just a young man with not too many seasons behind him.

He studied her face, as she fussed over him and his eating and sleeping habits. She turned thirty that month but looked no less beautiful or youthful than girls Nicolette's age. Her skin was healthy and free of blemishes, and the only wrinkles he could see were those in the corners of her eyes and mouth when she smiled at him. She kept herself in fine health, eating not too little or too much, and her constant walking between the house and the shop kept her properly fit and her figure well-defined.

Elizabeth was a woman with a near-endless constitution and one that could stay ahead of two children and a man many years her junior. She stayed up late with him into the night, either talking with him about one of his nightmares or putting that well-defined figure and reputable constitution to good work, and yet she was still always up before him making breakfast for him and the girls. The woman was tireless and always greeted him with a bright and chipper expression, not a trace of fatigue in her face.

"How is your hand?" She asked, taking up his right hand in both of hers.

Immediately he pulled it free, feigning a pained look. "It's still tender, but healing."

It was a lie, and only Pelleon knew that beneath the linen wrapping his hand bore not a single mark, blister or scar. He and Harold both watched him stumble over the shield that had toppled over from its place beside the bench, sending him towards the hot coals. Instinctively, he thrust his right hand into the fire to catch himself, then quickly retrieved it. Harold gave him some dressing, but said no more about it. It was his sister who asked about it incessantly.

"What is it, Elizabeth? You're not just here to bring me food or ask about my hand."

She shook her head, but tried to maintain her smile, "My brother will be returning in the morning - perhaps even sooner. The widow Gilda's son came back this evening, and he had news of Harold's return."

"We should give thanks to God for his safe return, though I know it is difficult for you to keep up the pretenses when he is home," he said, stroking her cheek. "We will do as we always do."

"I was hoping...that you would come home tonight and stay with me and the girls before he arrives. I know this weather...disturbs you, but I think we could manage for one night."

"Harold has been home before, this is nothing new."

"The widow's son brought news..."

"What sort of news?"

"My brother is coming to conscript more soldiers. The campaign did not go well for Richard this time and they suffered heavy losses. I am worried..."

"I promised you that I would not leave you and the girls here, Elizabeth. I'm not going off to fight this Prince's war. I am a blacksmith and my talents are needed here for the war effort. I cannot see them trying to press me into service and leaving this shop empty."

She held his hand tightly against her cheek and closed her eyes before the tears came. "There are other smiths in this city John, but not as many fighting men. Harold will come here and he will ask you to go, not because he wants you to go, but because it will be his duty to do so. How will you refuse him or the Prince?"

"I will just look him in the eye, as I'm doing with you, and I will say no," he chuckled.

"John, this is serious! The fact that he is sending my brother here for conscripts means that the war has taken a turn against our favor. There are whispers that the barons rising against Richard are now allied with the young king Henry and his father. I am terrified by the implications of this, John!"

"I'm not leaving you or the girls, Elizabeth!"

"This is what you always wanted, and this is a day that you prayed for...a day that I knew would eventually come. You can't stay here with us forever..."

"I don't want to have this discussion..."

She reached her slender hands out towards his face, then hesitated and dropped them towards his chest, hooking them around the piece of leather about his neck. Turning the smooth bone over in her fingers, she stared at the words there that he'd never been able to read, but that she'd understood only too well.

"She knew the truth as well, John," she said, indicating the delicate bone pieces. "These aren't just the words of an old lover."

As a godly and spiritual woman, Elizabeth never ignored signs, omens or prophecies of any sort. She was a woman of faith, attended worship services and had taken the lord Christ as her savior, but she hadn't forgotten the old ways that her grandmother had taught her. The art of deciphering one's future from the "bones" had been fascinating to her as a child, and it was art that she'd kept hidden from most except John.

She was with him the night of the first hard spring rain, when he'd awoken flush and speaking in odd tongues, clutching the bone artifact around his throat. He told her about the odd visions, and she shared with him her grandmother's knowledge of *sortilege* with him. Turning the pieces over and over in her fingers, studying them intently, she prophesied the great destiny that awaited him, and his odd visions only enforced that. She told him that all things were tied together; numerology, signs of nature, the stars in the heavens and even dreams, and if one knew how to read those things, then that person would gain insight into the plans written for them.

John dismissed her grandmother's superstitions and had as little use for them as the church, for each was designed to scare people and control them. He would never tell her as much, but Pelleon shared his vision of organized faith and foolish pagan traditions as well, and he was certain that he was snickering in the rafters at that moment.

"I will be waiting for you at the house, if you change your mind," she said, then prepared for the night ahead by crossing herself, kissing him on the cheek, and pulling her hood up.

After she'd become part of the rain again, Pelleon hopped down from the rafters and scrunched up his face at him, pointing a thumb over his shoulder in the direction of the woman that had just left.

"What was that all about, John?"

"Which part?"

"Harold is home again and he's recruiting soldiers?"

"You heard the same as I, Pelleon."

"What you told Elizabeth wasn't true. You wanted to go fight..."

He'd all but begged Harold not to leave him behind and to take him off to war. When he'd returned from Avandale, there was anger coursing through his blood and revenge pumping in his heart. Someone had to pay for what had been done to Nicolette and to Avandale, and Richard's army would lead him directly to that someone. Harold wouldn't allow it, however, and told him that he was needed in Rouen.

He remembered the bitterness of that day well, the day Harold left him in charge of things at home, and how he hated being treated like a helpless child. Things had changed since that day, and now he finally had the opportunity to settle the score, but something else coursed through his veins and into his heart. He'd become quite content there in Rouen, and embraced the task

Harold and William had set before him more eagerly than he ever thought he would.

"We're not going to fight, Pelleon," he snapped, taking his apron off and tossing it on the bench, brushing past him to walk out into the rain.

"So, should I clear your side of the room tonight?" He called after, but received no answer. "You could've asked how Ann was...for me..."

John stood and let the rain mat his hair and sting his face, turning his head slowly to look both ways up and down the cobbled street. His nostrils flared and he looked spooked, sniffing at the wind. The same odd sensation came over him that he'd only felt in the moments before falling into one of his fitful dreams. There was something odd about the weather, about the way it fell or how it sounded – he wasn't quite certain.

The rain stopped suddenly and the dark heavens gave a mighty sigh, light flashing on the horizon, and the air tingled with something that felt like electricity. John continued to stand in the middle of the street, staring up at the sky, holding his breath along with it, waiting for the eruption to return. It didn't come from the sky, the storm exploded somewhere in the distance, announced by a thunderclap of screams and horse hooves.

Chapter 22

John ran back into the shop and past Pelleon, shouting orders at him as he made his way to the small entryway that led to the back. Crouching down and using a metal bar, he pried up the heavy boards that covered the floor to reveal a shallow recess beneath. He pulled a bundle that was wrapped in oiled cloth from the compartment and carried it to the long bench as his apprentice ran with a saddle to the back doorway.

This had been planned for months, and they had rehearsed the plan until it could be executed without a single misstep. Two young men maneuvered in the small entryway in choreographed steps, like a dance, so as not to impede the other even for a split second. The apprentice prepared the mount in the back lot as his master readied the items in the bundle. A heavy shirt of mail he pulled over his head, the thousands of small, interlocking rings jingling as he squirmed into it. It and the long sword had belonged to William, but were left to him just for such a situation.

William had fought under Henry with his brother-in-law when they were younger men, and that was the way in which he'd been introduced to Elizabeth. Even back then, he'd been a large, broad-shouldered man, and the shirt was still loose on John despite alterations he'd made. The old thing had begun to rust on a peg in the upstairs room, and it was in considerably poor condition when it was bequeathed to him. In the late hours, when he could not sleep, it had become a project repairing the more brittle and rusty rings, and required a most skilled hand.

The sword was in much better shape, and had only needed to be sharpened on the large stone, which had been done so zealously that the blade would split a man's hair in two lengthwise. That wasn't true, of course, but Pelleon bragged it up to Harold and the girls that way. They would only giggle and give their patronizing looks, thinking how foolish and unnecessary a thing that John kept such good care of those things that he would never use.

As he strapped the scabbard at his waist, Pelleon ran back in from the back lot, informing him that he'd finished his task and in record time. All that remained was the lacing of the heavy leather cords at the back of his mail shirt, and he did so as John fussed over his sword belt. The cords had heavy oil residue, which made them difficult to hold, but kept them from drying out. The young squire walked his man to the back door and presented his mount to him, as it pranced about the small plot of grass.

Napoleon was the name John had given her, and it was an odd name for a mare. The small horse had been William's as well, and she'd been acquired from a boarder who'd never returned. The horse wasn't any good to William and he tried to sell her to every customer that came through his door, but they hadn't any use for her either. She was much too small to be trained as a warhorse, and too skittish to be fitted with a plough. One man had almost bought her, but she reared up and delivered the man squarely on his back. So, William kept her for the girls primarily, and even they didn't come by to pay her much attention.

John loved that horse, though, and it seemed that he was the only one that the horse would behave for – like they two were made for one another. Pelleon had the task of keeping her fed and watered, and she sometimes snipped at him before he could leave her pail and run out of the corral. She loved to be ridden, though, and when she saw the saddle, she held perfectly still. That night was the exception because the creature had also smelled whatever John had on the wind and the weather had been bothering her.

Seated and trying to calm her, John waited for his apprentice to carry out the last stage of their plan. Running from the shop, he bore the shield that his master had been working on. It was a plain, round shield of wooden planks and covered in a solid sheet of metal, like the Saxons had used. The leather straps had just been riveted in, and there was no standard painted on the face, but it would do what it was designed for. John slipped it over his forearm and kicked his heels into Napoleon, urging her up and over the fence before Pelleon could even unlock the gate.

John was more anxious and skittish than that mare as they barreled down the middle of the cobbled street. Her rider pressed his thighs too tightly against her, and wouldn't ease up on the reins, and she seemed to sense his awkwardness in the saddle. Picking up speed, she changed course and cut across the field off the stone path, weaving in and out of buildings so closely packed that he scraped the flesh off each knee, and that seemed to sober him enough.

He hunched down into the saddle, let the reins slacken, and adjusted his feet in the stirrups, letting her know that he was in charge again, and they continued forward, until they cleared the outer ring of buildings. John could finally see the heart of the storm that had come to his home and destroyed everything in its path.

There were at least a dozen riders in chainmail, wearing the same brilliant red surcoats, emblazoned with the same coat of arms: three black swords, one turned up beset by two downward turned. He wasn't expert in heraldry quite like his mentor, and had only been able to identify a small handful of the symbols by those who had left their shields for repair at his shop. Those had all been loyal to Richard, however, and these men obviously weren't allied with the Duke.

It mattered little who they were, only that they were running innocents down in the streets. Some of the merchants and residents from the quarter had assembled in an attempt to defend their neighbors, but they stood little chance against heavily armed cavalrymen. Most of the professional soldiers and veteran knights had left months earlier like Harold had, and there were few left behind who even owned a decent sword or knew how to use one. The riders cut them down with ease and the dead were already starting to pile in the streets.

Everything turned to black for the lone horseman, his face tightening into an awful grimace, eyes nearly rolling back into his head, and he shrieked as he urged his mount into a full charge. The impact he hit the first man with sounded like a thunderclap, and no one could be certain if it was the sound of the round shield being split in two or the sound of the man's neck when his face met that shield.

His head snapped backwards and he was thrown from his horse, dead before he hit the ground, crumbling there among the splintered pieces of wood that had taken his life. Discarding the remainder of the ruined shield, John used his free hand to draw the hatchet from his belt, and with both weapons, worked like a whirlwind through the rest of them.

Napoleon pushed her way through the middle of them, not only undaunted by the chaos but seeming to thrive on it. She nipped and kicked at the other horses as she shouldered her way through, scattering the horsemen in no particular direction, and John took advantage of the chaos. A second man fell forward with his neck torn wide open, and a third fell atop him when the hatchet struck again, deep into the side of his skull.

John's own brain was running through every combat tactic Harold had taught him over the past two years, and he was following them expertly, no longer hindered by the fear. He recalled the series of numbers, measurements and crude mathematical equations that Harold had imparted with him concerning the science of defeating a swordsman with a hatchet. The length of each weapon, design, proper positioning and angle of striking as well as the necessary force applied were all factors his mentor had made him memorize.

Harold was a simple and brutish man in all other matters, but in the art of combat and forging weapons for combat, he was a brilliant scholar. *The cavalryman's blade is easily half a toise, some are up to four pied in length, because they are mounted and need the extra length. The trick is to get up close so that they can't swing effectively, and you move in with your hatchet and the swordsman loses.* He remembered the words as if he had spoken them that very morning, and used them to his advantage.

His mentor hated using Frankish units of measure, being from Wales himself, but knew that John dealt in those measurements everyday as a smith. The toise was the length between a man's fingertips with his arms outstretched, and a pied divided that number by six and was equivalent of one of Harold's "foot" measurements. The English were odd and measured things in barleycorn, hands, digits, shaftments and other equally odd terms. John had understood these terms, and some were even practical, but they only confused him as a resident of Rouen, where few used them.

He was thinking of these measurements as he was fixed in bloody combat, calmly using his eye to trace arms, weapons and distances with invisible lines, much the way he did when marking steel in his shop. There was a simple math and a simple science to warfare, much like anything else, and it was John's first lesson on the streets of Rouen that night.

A sword came at him from the left, measuring three-and-one-half pied, or ten-and-one-half hands, and he leaned forward to avoid the swing by only half a digit – which was one-eighteenth of a pied. A horseman moved within a yard of him, and John pressed himself within that span, knowing that he was too close to swing. Approximately thirty stone of force was his response, and ample to cleave the bottom of the man's chin in two and sink the hatchet into his mandible.

As he killed each man, he recalled Harold's math that he had perfected in twenty years of butchering men. He knew exactly where to strike a man, with how much force to cripple, maim, and kill. He memorized the tensile strengths of all the pertinent bones in a man's body, and the proper application of force with each particular type of weapon. That was dangerous knowledge and he had passed it along to his favorite pupil, who now demonstrated his comprehension in a final exam of sorts, being administered by a council of his peers.

Those faces stared at him from all sides, watching, judging and evaluating him. They took measure of his abilities in every category: strength, agility, courage, martial prowess, and efficiency. They did not find him lacking. As each of those examiners tested him, they gave him their final, passing marks in their own blood.

Chest heaving, John stood among the carnage, inspecting his handiwork the same as if he had just finished with some metalworking task. It was like that now, his arms burned from swinging the steel, and the saltwater ran into his eyes and over his lips as his eyes scanned every inch of his latest piece. There were no flaws; master's hands had performed the execution. None had been left alive.

His first instinct was to head towards home - Elizabeth's home, rather - but the road was congested with the frightened, dead and wicked. The closer he got to her house, the more chaos blocked the streets and they were near impassable. He turned Napoleon round and round, looking for another way through, but half of the quarter was already aflame, and the narrow streets between the buildings would offer him no safe passage. The only route remaining was directly up the main street, through the bedlam that had been created there.

There was a chorus of steel and voices ringing through that borough like the announcement of Christmas morning at the cathedral. Sharp blades meeting shields and rings of metal in different pitches joined screams in soprano, alto, and tenor to form a haunting orchestra. Communion was given and taken beneath flaming arches, as blood fell upon parched lips and flesh was divided among the sinners for their consumption. A baptismal was also taking place in that holy place as one among them was welcomed to the fold, his forehead streaked by blood and water doused upon his head.

The storm began again, making the raging fires hiss, washing the blood from the streets, and the tears from the faces of the dying. At the end of the block, there was one place the rain seemed to not touch, however, and the newly-baptized man added his voice to the chorus of the lamenting when it finally came into view.

There was black smoke rolling from the ground floor windows and doorway, and orange light flicking its tongue at him from somewhere inside, taunting him. His way was still not clear, though, as the chorus seemed louder ahead of him than it was behind him, and there was still one more street to fight to before he could reach the place.

His blood flowed slowly like a winter stream, thick with ice, and his breath came in cold puffs as though he was suddenly drowning in that flow. Panicking, he turned Napoleon about to take full measure of the crossroads he'd currently arrived at, trying to find another way through. The street heading to the east, away from the river, was just as chaotic as the one he was on. Some of the merchants had pushed wagons and carts into the street, firing spears and arrows at the horsemen from behind the cover of the barricade.

The street leading back towards the river was no better, almost a mirror image, except the horsemen had created their own barricade out of the heaping dead. Napoleon pranced around and round, as her indecisive rider tried to formulate a plan and use his numbers again, but the numbers wouldn't come.

All plans began to fall apart in his head, the numbers and the math became jumbled, and there was no contingency for this scenario. As he sat paralyzed by indecision, people were dying, buildings were burning and Rouen was slipping away. He couldn't make the choice of who to save and who to let die, it was a decision that no one man should have to make, and it only served to overwhelm him more.

...sometimes, when there isn't a simple answer, a simple approach, ye have to make yer own...just put yer head down, get a firm grip on yer sword, and ride yer mount fer all she's worth...right into the middle of hell...

It was Harold's all-purpose strategy for when things went to shit, and it was all he had left to fall back on. He squeezed his fingers tightly around the reins and the hilt of his sword, lowered his posture, and dug his heels in as he turned Napoleon towards the flaming house. With a bloodcurdling yell, he prepared for his bloodiest ride yet, and rode the mare directly into that gaping maw of hell.

Faster and faster he moved, building momentum with every fallen soul, as if the blood of the dead propelled him forth. It seemed nothing would halt the onslaught, until it suddenly hesitated of its own accord. Something had disrupted its path, made it change course, and spared those who'd waited to meet their end with prayers on their lips.

Astride the largest horse he'd ever seen was a man of equally impressive size, roaring like his namesake as he hacked at the swarm of men around him with a great long sword. In the light of day, the surcoat and shield would shine a more brilliant crimson than his enemy's and both were emblazoned with lions of gold instead of the blades of black. Though matted with blood and pieces of flesh, his hair and beard were that of a king, and his eyes blazed like twin blue stars as they locked with his through the crowd.

Richard Cour de Leon – the Lionheart – was on the other side of that thick wall of men crammed into the street, and John now understood why it had been so congested. The Duke of Aquitaine was at the eye of the real storm in that city, and he raged in such a way as to all others seem minor squalls.

As he cut his way through the wall of flesh and steel, he noticed that there were other faces within that he recognized. There were sons of Rouen, like Edward the tanner and his own mentor Harold, as well as the regular patrons of his shop, like Andrew de Chauvigney, John Marshal, and Roger of Glanville, who were men of considerable reputation. All of the champions of Richard's army were cornered in the middle of that street and fighting like enraged bears against impossible numbers.

John could only assume that they'd followed their enemy back to Rouen, and had arrived just in time to prevent its utter destruction. He couldn't help but feel overcome by the sight of these men - true warriors and veterans in their craft – leading the heroic charge into the city and trying to drive out the invaders. On any other night, in any other battle, John would have had his courage restored and felt proud to stand against the enemy with men such as these, but on this night, fear and disgrace began to creep upon him.

His mentor had returned, and he would see that his apprentice had allowed his city to burn and failed to protect those he'd sworn an oath to. Duke Richard and those others he'd worked hard to impress over the past two years would surely know how he had failed defending Rouen as well. They would see how Harold's apprentice was not worthy to bear the name or reputation, and how all of his training had been for naught. Even more than he feared disappointing great men like those before him, he feared what Harold would say once he saw the smoldering house, if he hadn't already.

Catching glimpses of him through the mass of bodies and the intense fighting, he couldn't discern any sort of expression other than the frightening war face that Harold wore into battle. He fought ever closer, trying to push his way through to those men and the house beyond, at each step trying to catch a glimpse of Harold's face. The apprentice sought guidance there from his master, some indication of a plan or instruction for his next move.

His best friend and the very best fighting men of Rouen were beset by superior numbers and might fall if he did not intervene, and that meant the fall of more innocents and possibly the city. Yet if he did stay and fight, the flames would grow brighter and the smoke would rise higher into the sky, as the chances of survivors in the house beyond them dimmed.

John screamed his name into the night, but the voices of the living and the dying drowned it out. Three more fell under his hatchet and blade, he edged Napoleon closer, closing the gap between them, and still Harold did not look. Again, he cried out his name, and again it was washed out by the clamor of battle. At last, he resigned himself to the fact that he would have to make the most crucial of decisions alone, and live with the consequences forever after.

He laid his sword across his lap in exchange for one of the torches from the hand of the dead man closest him, and went to work with fire and the close quarters steel. Neither was an adequate weapon for penetrating a shield or blocking an incoming horseman's blade, but he wouldn't need to do either.

A good warhorse weighs about a hundred twenty stone or more, and that's enough to crush a man's legs or break his neck if they end up beneath it. I know what yer going to say...but all of that gentleman's code for fightin' does ye' no good if yer facin' down a mounted man and yer on foot. The Welsh and the Scots have had their share of English horsemen on their land, and aren't too proud to bring those horsemen down with a good spear...

John remembered the words of the man who was locked beyond the wall of horsemen, as he pushed through it, cleaving and burning horseflesh. That wall crumbled and broke apart, smaller pieces of it falling in bloody clumps on the street and the larger portions crushing the men just the way Harold had promised. Some of the men trapped beneath their horses had their screams answered with a quick drop of the hatchet, others did not scream, immediately killed by the fall. The horses that were shown mercy fled in all directions, suffering only a burnt patch or a deep gash, carrying their riders off despite their commands.

He finally reached Harold, who was screaming like an enraged bear, crushing bones with his mace and tearing gaping holes in the enemy with his blade. John helped to fell two men he'd been engaged with, and moved to his flank to protect him as he shouted to him.

"Elizabeth!"

"I see it! What the hell do ye' think we've been trying to do? We were cut off from the rest!"

"What do you want me to do, Harold?"

"There's nothing that can be done! We'll never make it there alone! Our duty is to Richard!"

There was his answer: he'd made the right choice in coming to their aid, but the heavy, sickening feeling in his stomach told him otherwise. He continued to fight against the men that came, against the urge to try to break through the line, and against the tears that burned in his eyes.

249

Though no blade had drawn blood and no arrow had pierced his skin, a more grievous wound had been struck, and he felt his life draining from it as he pressed on. No matter how many he killed that night, no matter if he sent every one of those men to hell, the life that he had known had already been taken. His place in that city was gone after this night, and every reason he had to stay there would be turned to so much ash.

The man beside him bellowed like a dying bull, tears streaking his face, and John knew that he would never be the same either. He would be consumed with revenge and there would be a never-ending campaign against every enemy of Rouen and of Richard from which Harold would never return. The other man at his side, the one who'd brought this war to his home, was promising him that fulfillment and signing God's name to that contract.

By God, I swear we will hunt these men to the ends of the earth Harold, he said, as if he could guarantee that any of them would even survive long enough to see that fulfilled. They were hollow words, and no one could even be certain that Harold had heard them, consumed by bloodlust as he was. John was certain of one thing though; Harold the Bald didn't need Richard's or even God's assurances – he would bring justice to those responsible by his own hand.

Within minutes, dozens more lay dead, still clutching at those useless and shattered weapons, the rest turned to flee for their lives. Some were pursued by Richard and his men, cut down that night; others managed to prolong the inevitable by a few days before being hunted down. Despite the efficiency in their dispatching, however, the fire had been twice as efficient in its devastation of the house at the end of the street. The entire thing was engulfed in the blaze, yet both men approached it fearlessly.

He steadied the shuffling bull with an arm, saying, "Your leg…you've lost lots of blood…"

"The next man who lays his hands on me gets them cut off! I'm going inside!"

"How do you plan on getting them out with that leg if they are alive? Let me go in!"

"Twenty men couldn't stop me, this leg will not slow me," he boasted.

"I can get to them, Harold, you know I can! You have to trust me…"

"I *did* trust you…and they're up there because I did so…ye've done enough."

John would have knocked him to the ground just then if his legs hadn't given way. Andrew caught Harold under the other arm before he reached the hard stone, and nodded at the young soldier. He let the knight take the burden from him, and giving one last look back at them, charged through the front door of the house.

Chapter 23

The entire first floor was full of black smoke and the only light was the faint red glow of burning embers. He did not need to see to navigate through that main room, however, and had his eyes melted in their sockets from the heat, it wouldn't have mattered. That heat was so intense that the blood covering his arms bubbled and the chain shirt became very uncomfortable, but it did not burn his own flesh. His blood-soaked hair was even steamed dry almost instantly, but it did not ignite either, and he knew that the powerful hand upon him was still there as he walked through that blaze.

It was in that front room, on the kitchen floor that he found his Elizabeth. The fire had charred her flesh badly and she was no longer breathing, but it wasn't the fire that had taken her. She lay on the floor, legs spread at an awkward angle, and the blackening flame was unable to hide the tears in the dress and in her womanhood.

Her eyes were turned upwards, staring towards the stairwell, and her mouth was stretched wide to release final pleas that went unheard. He held her shriveled, blackened hand in his and rubbed the only remaining smooth part of her thumb with his. Adjusting her legs to a more modest pose, he smoothed the ruined dress that had been his favorite. The hot tears came and sizzled as they fell over her, and he said goodbye.

Heading towards the stairs, he found Mary not far from her mother, in much the same fashion. She was lying face down and her dress had been torn up the back, exposing her flesh. When he gently turned her over, he could see that she had gotten the worst of it and fought back harder than her mother had. Elizabeth had probably not resisted so as to not make things worse for her and her girls, and knew that was her best chance for survival. Mary hadn't the courage to do the same and would have been absolutely terrified, making every effort to get away from them.

She had made it as far as the first step where she most likely received the blow to the back of the head. Her hair was matted and crusted over with blood that turned into an awful scab under the heat already. On her torso were several smaller cuts and she had been stabbed to death because she would not cooperate. They had violated her before she exhaled her last breath and probably even after that, he guessed from the extent of her wounds. The men who did this to his girls were less than human, and Richard's words echoed in his head.

By God, I swear we will hunt these men to the ends of the earth...

He was snapped out of his daze by the sounds of squealing coming from somewhere up the stairs and he sprang from his crouched position, running up as fast as he could. In the bedroom, there was a large chest at the foot of her bed that she used to house blankets and other heirlooms. Lifting the lid, he found something much more precious inside, and he hefted the small child into his arms.

He burst from the front door as a fireball shot from a downstairs window, and the house began to fall in on itself. Harold limped towards him with his arms out to collect his niece in his large arms, who was shrieking unintelligibly and stretching her small hands towards the house. John's eyes met his, red and wet, and he shook his head slowly to indicate that the others didn't make it. Harold sat hard back on the ground with Ann and stroked the back of her hair with his bloody hands.

John took a few steps up the street and found that wound he had suffered deep inside of him sapped his own strength, and his legs buckled. The world around him was burning, screaming, smoking black and spinning around. So much had happened that night, so much he never expected, and never anticipated battle to be like. His first taste of the fight had been an awful thing, like rotted meat in his mouth that he kept trying to spit out. It made him sick and he ejected vomit onto the stone street near him.

The battle in Rouen lasted less than an hour, but in that hour John had seen enough bloodshed, inhumanity and indignation to last him a lifetime. There was nothing glorious about what men like Harold and Richard did, and he wanted no part of it, though he knew that it was far from over. When the last fires of Rouen burned out and the dead were buried, they would go after those responsible and pay them in kind, there would be a reckoning that he would be a part of. He was one of those men now, just like

Harold and the others, and he could never go back to being the man that he was.

John the blacksmith was dead, and there was only "John the butcher" now.

Richard and his knights had regrouped and chased out the rest of the invaders before returning to the square where he'd left Harold and his blacksmith friend. He put a large hand on the weeping bull's shoulder and told him to stay and bury his family, promising to return in a week's time to seek out those who had attacked Rouen. There were few words between those men, but there would be many between Richard and his newest champion.

"I expect that you'll be coming with us this season then?"

"There's nothing here for me now, milord," John said in a hoarse voice.

"With the gift you have...a skill I've rarely witnessed on the battlefield...there never was anything here for you anyway, son. Those hands weren't meant to swing a hammer or any other tool but a sword, and God has truly blessed you."

"I took no pleasure in the fight, or in killing those men, I did what was necessary."

"What I saw was a man who is master of his craft, and a man who puts his heart into it, not a man who was simply doing his duty to protect his home."

John sat silently for a long while, staring towards the flaming rooftops at the end of the street. He couldn't remember what he'd felt, if anything, when he claimed those men's lives. He turned his eyes up at the man who towered above him and shook his head slowly, denying his accusation that he'd derived as much satisfaction in warfare as he.

"Nevertheless, you would not refuse me your service if I ask?"

"I want those men dead the same as Harold, because it's no less than they deserve."

"You are Harold's squire?"

"Harold trained me in the art of combat and other trades, yes," he said simply.

"Rise to your feet and take a knee if you are able, squire," he commanded.

John's knees still shook from the terrifying experience he had just been through and now trembled doubly so from what the

Prince was asking of him. As he wiped his blade clean with a cloth, preparing for the impromptu ceremony, the unprepared neophyte swordsman realized what was being asked of him, there in the middle of the street for all eyes to see.

He barely heard the words to the oath spoken by Richard, words which he repeated mechanically as he stared up into his fierce blue eyes. Harold had explained the oath of the knight to him many a night over ale and in the back lot practicing their swordplay, but he'd never taken them to heart, because the life of the knight was one that he'd never aspired to. He wasn't like the rest of those men, not brave or wise in the way of their politics. John could barely identify most of the standards that were emblazoned on the shields he repaired in his shop, and cared little for the men associated with those standards.

Now, he was staring at those three golden lions and knew that he would be forever lorded over and watched by them if he finished his oath. John wanted to stand and tell him he wanted no part of it, but the strength was gone from his legs and there were so many watching expectantly. Their hopes were with the new champion of Rouen, with the man who'd driven out the enemy single-handedly and rescued their future king.

He could not stand for their benefit and for the benefit of the girls he'd loved who would have been so very proud of their John being knighted by Prince Richard himself. Elizabeth had always known the day would come when he went on to greater things and leave the old smith shop and Rouen behind, and Nicolette had told him the same. If it had come any other way, on any other occasion, John would have been ecstatic to be welcomed into the ranks of great men like Richard and Harold. He felt as very little joy in his heart as he'd felt about the slaughter of his enemy, however, because his promotion had been paid in blood.

The bulk of the words spoken to him were lost in the haze clouding his mind that night, and only the slap of the blade across his face snapped him awake long enough to hear a single thing Richard had said.

"Do you understand your oath?"

"Yes milord," he replied. He did understand it, but not because he'd heard it from him.

"Then rise as a knight, Sir John, and remember it always, as well as your service to God."

There was applause and cheering for their new favorite son, but John afforded them little more than a weak smile as he stared around at the carnage, disgusted by the simple-minded commoner. How easily they forget tragedies that befall them and their neighbors if there is some entertainment to be gotten out of the whole mess. Husbands, wives, sons and daughters lay dead on the streets and there they were, cheering for the man who was too late to save them, because he was now some type of celebrity among them.

He watched Richard walk away; glaring at his back, realizing that what had just taken place was nothing more than a clever maneuver. A terrible thing had happened that night and the expert politician enters to use him as a distraction, convincing them that a great victory had just occurred, and from that victory, a hero had been born. That was the way the speech went that he addressed that crowd of simpleton idiots with. They stood, smiling and swelling with pride, in the blood of their neighbors, and hung on Richard's every word as he sold them something other than the harsh truth.

When Richard finally ended his ridiculous speech and the crowds dispersed, John was finally free to check on Harold and Ann. The child did not raise her head of matted curls to look at him, and the man holding her pretended not to take notice as he approached.

"Harold...I did not want any of this," he whispered.

"Ye' wanted it John, and ye' begged me for it before I left. Well, now ye' get it."

"It's worse than I ever imagined..."

"We bury our dead, and then honor them with the payment in blood we will exact from our enemy. After we are done, ye' can do as ye' like with yer newfound status, as for me...this will be my last fight."

"You're just going to stop being a soldier? Just stop fighting for Richard? What about all the talk about backing the prince and making sure that we support the best man for the throne?"

Harold forced himself up with much effort, struggling with the bad leg and the child he had wrapped around him. Without a word, he started up the street, pushing his way through the crowd of people that were tending to the dead.

257

"Harold…"

The old soldier whirled to face him, and snapped at him like a frightened dog, "This war is done with me, John, and I am done with it! The price of political ambitions and for putting men into power has become more than I am willin' to pay!"

"So what will you do?"

"I'm going to help you find these men and make sure they never again step foot in Rouen, and then I'm going to finally answer that calling. We do not get to choose what we are, John, just as Richard told you, we are what we must be, and what is chosen for us! You will make a great knight and this is your time; this is a younger man's fight, and I will stay and be what I must to this little girl."

"I can't do this without you, Harold," he said.

"Ye' don't need me anymore, boy. Richard was right about you, about what I always suspected; you were born for greater things than swinging a hammer and wasting away in that shop. There is no place for you here anymore John; your place is at Richard's side now."

Harold gave him a heartbroken look, the way a father looks upon a son that has lost his innocence, and realizes that he can no longer protect him from the evils of the world. He did love John, but what he spoke was truth; things between them would never be the same. As much as losing a majority of his family had broken him, watching John become Rouen's new champion and knowing that he was no longer relevant was just as devastating.

There was much pride and also great trepidation as he watched the boy he'd considered a son fight as a man. It was like watching a younger version of himself pitched against those men, but there was something even greater about John that he had never possessed himself, a presence that he'd never had, and a skill that exceeded even his own, not taught by his master. The others called it that, they called it a *skill*, but Harold knew differently and that's what scared him. He watched the swords glance off of him and the arrows miss him, as if deflected by a mighty hand, just like the fire that should have taken the boy's hand in the shop.

He was certain that Richard had seen it as well, and had deliberately placed him under his banner, realizing what a great weapon he now had in the boy from Rouen. Under Richard's auspices, John would know glory and a reputation greater than his mentor, and possibly even greater than the Lionheart himself. A man with John's ability would take the Duke of Aquitaine to the throne and beyond, the kingmaker of all kingmakers, but he could also lead to his ruin. Duty, honor and idealistic allegiances would only go so far with a man like John, and could easily become secondary to something as foolish as love. It was love that would return to ruin the best-laid plans of kings and made men.

Chapter *24*

Campbell had just finished transforming more of John's jumbled notes and voice clips into something as easily digestible as the breakfast he'd prepared. Gwenn was just beginning to roll the words around in her mouth, preparing her questions, ready to begin dissecting the story, when the knock came from the front door. Those questions would have to wait.

He stood and extending a hand towards the hall, as if to offer her the honor of answering the door in his stead. She shook her head, using the excuse that she had to use the restroom, and he escorted her halfway down the hall on his way to receive his guest.

Locking the door behind her, she leaned on the beautifully-tiled countertop, letting out a sigh as she studied her face in the ornate mirror. The small smudge of jam at the edge of her mouth was the least of her worries, she thought as she washed it off. Her eyes looked tired still, despite a good night's rest and the earthy colors she'd painted them in. The wrinkles at the corners were still as evident as the lines at the far edges of her smile had once served to accentuate her best features. Now they drew attention to how much those features had deteriorated.

She wasn't sure why she was so concerned with her appearance under the circumstances, or even why her hands shook as she tried smoothing out those lines. It was just Connelly, the man she'd been in a brief relationship with more than ten years before, and not a very good relationship at that. Things had been so bad with him that she'd decided - in the end - that she would prefer to be "second best" with John than to continue putting up with his antics.

At least she'd had security with John and the assurance that he would be coming home to her at the end of each day. There was a reason he was called the "Con Man", and she found out firsthand after months of his an on-again-off-again nonsense. Whenever he was around, he really put on the charm and made her feel like she was the most important girl in the world, and at times, she felt like she was on a higher pedestal than Melinda Malowski.

It was Connelly that first noticed her eyes and her smile that she was fussing over in the mirror, not her husband, and the first to notice that she was a woman. That was probably the reason she'd given him chance after chance, always taking him back when she shouldn't, and why she was self-conscious of her appearance whenever he came around – even years later. Old habits were hard to break, even irrational ones, and it wasn't the first time she'd disappeared to the powder room when one of Connelly's last-minute calls came.

Whenever he was a guest in their home, she remembered what it was like to feel flattered by flirtatious gazes. It was exhilarating and the rush would last for days after he left, but John never seemed to notice the difference, or if he did, he never mentioned it. She would wrestle with her guilt afterwards, trying to justify her behavior by reminding herself that her husband never looked at her that way and she deserved that kind of attention.

The voices passing just outside the door snapped her out of her reminiscing, and she made last minute adjustments to her hair, smoothed out her skirt, and adjusted her top to reveal more cleavage. Frowning and feeling that tinge of guilt, she decided that was too much and hiked her bust line up a bit before stepping back into the hall.

As she walked confidently back into the small dining room, she was greeted by two raised brows from Connelly and only one from Campbell. His attention to detail apparently wasn't limited to history research, and he noticed the ridiculous drop in her neckline and bolder eye makeup.

"I believe you two have met," Campbell said, pouring him a coffee. "Can I offer you something to eat?"

"Yes, of course we've met. That's a lot of food you have there, so I won't feel so guilty asking you to share," came the chipper voice that made her cringe.

She took her seat across from him, never taking her eyes from him, as though he might disappear the second she did. Jeremy Connelly had never been hard on the eyes, and he hadn't been plagued by wrinkles or the need to cover them with makeup. John had that same quality – always having a youthful face – and she hated them both just a little for it.

He had the same perfect hair that he'd spent too much time fussing with (a trait he'd taught John, and annoyed her to no end), his smile was just as straight and only aged a bit by his cigarette habit, and he was dressed in an outfit that belied his financial situation, as always. Somehow he always managed to appear like he was on top of the world and things were going in his favor, despite constantly asking John to borrow money to get out of trouble.

Campbell noticed her glaring at him as he politely accepted the dish of spiced potatoes, and he could feel the tension emanating from her side of the table. She politely poured him a cup of coffee and the honey for his biscuit, and he smiled at her just as politely, but for some reason, the observer felt like a parent of two children that were waiting for him to leave the room so they could begin antagonizing one another. He finally took his seat once his newest guest had a full plate and set to eating, certain that Gwenn would not be able to start in on him with a mouthful of food.

He was quite mistaken.

"Would you like me to make you a plate to take with you, Jeremy, or did you already put some in your pockets?"

Connelly looked up from his plate and stopped chewing his food, offering her a cynical smile. Campbell gave her a scornful look and she looked in her lap, fidgeting with her napkin, looking much the part of the mischievous child who'd been scolded. Campbell excused himself and asked her to accompany him into the hall. Once she was in the hallway, he led her back to the study and closed the heavy doors behind them.

"What is *wrong* with you? Whatever history you have with that man in that room, you have to let it go for the time being, if you want the answers you came here for."

"I wouldn't leave him alone too long in that room, Jim, you're liable to end up missing your silverware and most of your expensive brandy," she said, not taking his tone seriously.

"That man is a *guest* in my home – as are you – I expect that you pay him the same respect as I give you!"

"You might've had a few pleasant conversations with him, but you don't have any idea what he's capable of. He's been a guest in my home as well, and that didn't stop him from taking advantage of my hospitality. So please don't lecture me about cordiality!"

"I'll draw him a map to my safe upstairs if it means we get what we need from him! You were starting to really make progress

263

on leaving your feelings and personal grudges out of the way, what happened?"

"Melinda Malowski is gone, Jim, so I don't really have to worry about her anymore. But Connelly? You can't turn your back on that man for a second! Trust me, you'll regret it!"

"You mean the way you and John turned your backs on him?"

"We never turned our backs on him!" She said indignantly. "He was our friend and we did everything we could for him! Telling you his poor victim story is just the first step as he cons you out of house and home."

"You did everything you could for him until it became an inconvenience and an embarrassment, and then decided you'd done quite enough. The man in that room down the hall hasn't breathed a single word about his shaky past; it was your husband who told me everything. He said that he suffered from the same addictions as Melinda, yet no one came kicking in doors to rescue him the way everyone did for her."

"We tried to help him, we gave him money, a place to stay, but he wouldn't quit doing it!"

"What was Melinda's excuse? Did she quit? Did you throw money at her to make the problem go away, or did you and John actually try to help her? What was the difference between Jeremy and Melinda? Why did she deserve to have everyone falling over themselves to help her and not him?"

"You don't know anything about him!"

"I only know what's written in that journal and what John told me about him. He was a young man without the same advantages as either of you, who considered you both the only family he had, and who would do anything for either of you – and did. He was more than eager to talk to me about John – without being offered a single dime."

"You're not going to lay a guilt trip on me. John and I were his family and we both went out of our way for him – John more than either of us. But every single time he extended a hand to him, it nearly got bitten off."

"So John gave up, but what about you? Didn't you still care about him?"

"Of course I did! I was the one that still talked to him."

"Did you? I don't think John mentioned that...did John know about that?"

Her eyes dipped to the floor, "No. He didn't know."

"Why didn't you tell him? Because it would have upset him?"

"It probably would have yes," she nodded.

"And you were always about pleasing John, weren't you? Even if it meant you sacrificing something you cared about, isn't that right? You supported John all that time as he chased after Melinda, time after time, pulling her ass out of trouble when she was in deep, because you thought that it pleased him didn't you? But you never dared to go out of your way to help Jeremy, because John would've been mad, and assumed something, isn't that right?"

"John knew about our history..."

"But didn't he have as much history with Melinda? That was okay? It was okay for him to help her time and time again, and for you to stand there quietly at his side and pretend you didn't hate every second of it, but it wasn't okay for you to do the same for his best friend?"

"John loved him and he did a lot for him! How dare you say that he didn't try...he did."

"I know he tried...he sat right there in that chair and said how he'd regretted not trying harder or doing more. He blamed himself for all of his wasted efforts on Melinda and not enough on his best friend who had no one else to go to. Melinda had lots of friends and lots of family to support her, but Connelly...he lost everyone didn't he?"

"The other guys...they didn't talk to him anymore because they said he was a loser. He never went to college, never did anything with his life, never had any ambition, and they didn't have much in common with him after a while. They all got married and had families; John and I were the only ones that ever gave a shit about him, even when he was going through hard times."

"So you gave him a place to stay...a recovering drug addict...and John, with that huge ego of his, thought he could pull him from the brink like he'd done with Melinda? He failed him and you're surprised that he disappeared in the middle of the night with John's wallet? He needed real help, Gwenn, not an opportunity to slip back into the place he was!"

"Is that why he's here now? You're going to get him some real help? Get him checked into a rehab center and sponsor him?"

"We *both* know that's not why I asked him to come here. But I've spoken with him at length, Gwenn, and I don't believe that he's the same man you used to know either. He was just as apprehensive about coming here, but agreed to help us regardless, and I would hope that you could put whatever is between you aside long enough to work through this."

"Just like you have with Marshall?"

There was an uncomfortable silence in that room for a long ten seconds as he stared at her with that expression that had no classification. It wasn't anger, it wasn't surprise, it was just empty and it was the most unnerving thing when he stared at her that way.

"Henry Marshall and I have been in contact via the telephone many times over the past few weeks and I spoke to him this morning. I've made great efforts for the good of bringing your husband's story some resolution. If I can offer an olive branch to a man I've hated for three decades, then certainly you can do the same with a man you once loved."

"I didn't realize…"

"We're making progress, Gwenn, and neither of us can allow personal grudges or grievances to derail us. We have to be objective and stay focused, even if those people who have caused us to carry old wounds are the only ones we can turn to."

"You're right, I'm sorry," she said, letting out a long sigh.

"It's not easy to sit in the same room with someone you have a history with, Gwenn, but he may just surprise you. I think Mister Connelly has come not just to help us with John's story, but to share some of his own as well. I think it's just as important for him to finally open up and tell you about some of those things that maybe he's been too ashamed to talk about with you until now."

"That may be, but this isn't about him, it's about my husband," she said, crossing her arms.

"This is about all of us, Gwenn, and the reason we've come together for this is so that we each may find some kind of peace and resolution. I believe everyone in this house has lost their fair share of sleep because of the things they cannot lay to rest."

She nodded in agreement reluctantly and Campbell opened the door for her to exit the room. The hallway that led to the breakfast room at the rear of the home was generous enough in its span to allow her to compose herself before seeing him again. She'd even had time enough to don her best fake smile again and greeted him with it when she entered. Jeremy looked up from his plate and didn't know what to make of that, but smiled back just for good measure.

"Did you get enough to eat? We are ready to begin whenever you are," she said with a polite but professional tone.

"I won't need to put any in my pockets to take with me, that's for sure," he joked and Gwenn rolled her eyes.

"Would you be more comfortable in the study or here in the breakfast room?" Campbell asked.

"I'm used to the sunshine. This is just fine with me."

Campbell politely pulled her chair out for her again, refilled her coffee cup, and then took his seat at the other side of the table. She and Connelly sat in awkward silence, fidgeting with their silverware and napkins as they waited for the storyteller to lead them in discussion. He repacked the pipe that had been sitting on the table, checked the clock on the wall to determine the appropriate beverage selection, and gave a little scowl as he poured more tea into his cup. The good stuff would have to wait another hour.

"Mrs. Chapel has been so kind as to give me a thorough narration of the events leading up to the twenty-sixth of January of nineteen-ninety-two," he said, igniting his pipe with a wooden match. "Could you take us from that day forward, and give us an account of what happened immediately following that morning?"

Connelly sat back in his chair and tossed his napkin into the center of his plate. His eyes rolled slightly upwards, but not the way they did when he was putting together one of his elaborate lies. Gwenn frowned impatiently at him, as if irritated that he wasn't as sentimentally attached to dates as John had been.

"Seriously? It's the morning after the big hotel fight, Jeremy!" She huffed.

"Oh yea...that was quite a scrap," he chuckled remembering it fondly. "That was the morning John and I headed south to go after his mother."

"That's precisely the date we're referring to, Mr. Connelly."

"You said John never talked about it? Never told you about Florida?"

267

They both shook their heads in unison, leaning across the table towards him, giving him their full attention. Connelly smiled and took his time in the retelling, taking a long draught from his coffee, and then deciding it wasn't to his liking, added three more cubes of sugar from the fancy dish in front of him. The sound of his spoon lightly clanking as he stirred was the only thing that could be heard in that room as all ears waited on him. Taking another sip, he seemed more satisfied and gave them a look as though he never could have begun a story of this magnitude without the proper drink.

"I don't exactly know where to begin…"

"Damn it, Connelly, John is dead!" She said, slapping her hand on the table. "It's not like I'm going to yell at him when he gets home! We need to know *everything!*"

Campbell shot her a stare and revised her statement, "There's nothing you can say that will make us think any less of him, Mr. Connelly. As I explained to you on the phone, we have quite a mess to untangle, and we need you to be as forthcoming and frank as possible – sparing no details."

As Campbell had said before, Jeremy Connelly was a loyal friend to John, even after his death. A disclaimer before offering up the secrets only he knew was fully expected, if not trying to deviate from the truth altogether, out of respect for him and his widow. The way he looked at the both of them, Campbell knew that he wasn't quite sure why they were so intent on digging up the past, and why it had sounded like a matter of life or death over the phone. He'd deliberately not told him everything, hoping not to taint the objectivity of his one remaining control subject, but a man like Connelly couldn't be kept in the dark for long.

He eyed Campbell warily as he asked, "So, what information is it you want, really? You don't want to hear about John and me spending drunken nights on the strip in Lauderdale I take it?"

Smoke swirled from the corners of a smile, and he replied, "You guessed right. I need to hear about what happened with Victoria and the events – and people - that transformed him in that place, Mr. Connelly."

"I suppose I should begin with the *Island Pub* then…"

Chapter 25

The *Island Pub* was a small bar that used to be nestled on a quiet corner only a few yards from Hillsboro beach and under the shadow of the Days Inn Oceanside. The proprietor of that small pub was a man named Gary Polidoro, who had a thick New England accent and a thicker moustache that was ten years out of style. His Pub was likewise trapped in the same time period as his moustache and floral shirts, but it was a happening spot regardless, and no one ever complained.

Seated at one of the small tables in a corner beneath a broken neon sign, were two young men down on their luck and trying to hash out a plan to get back on their feet over a couple of beers. The good thing about the Pub being so small and run by a guy like Gary Polidoro was that guys like John Chapel and Jeremy Connelly could order drinks without being hassled. One of the regulars, Danny, who had his own special seat at the bar had ordered them a round one night, and that was better than showing ID to Gary.

It was sometime in mid-February – only a few weeks after they'd left Michigan – but so much had happened since then it seemed like they'd been gone longer. After a grueling road trip down, the duration of which he'd had to listen to John whine and complain about Melinda and the incident at the hotel, they ran into more trouble with John's mother. Trying to intercept her after her release from the hospital, they found her right back at her boyfriend's place, trying to gather up her things. He showed up before they had a chance to leave, and they found themselves in their second brawl in a forty-eight hour span.

As badly as they'd gotten beaten by the superior numbers at the Knights Inn, they'd fared much better than they did against the six foot five, two hundred-forty pound brute. Those guys they'd fought at the hotel party had been just kids, and even Sal was more imposing physically, but wasn't a professionally-trained fighter. The guy that sent John sprawling to the pavement with one punch had built a reputation for splitting guys' heads. Connelly knew better than to try to square off with him and had to improvise if any of them were going to walk away from that mess. Improvising meant using a steam iron to bash the back of his thick head in until he stopped beating on his friend.

It was several days before he could get out of bed, and a week before he could even leave the small efficiency apartment in Boynton Beach they took him to instead of the hospital. Vicki was worried that her boyfriend would come looking for them there and insisted that her son would be fine. John probably needed some stitches in his cheek and have his hand looked at, but the scar wouldn't become too noticeable and his hand was usable after a while. His hand and face were the least of his worries on the third morning when John discovered that his mother had abandoned them and taken the rest of his money.

Now, three weeks later, John's face was still swollen pretty badly on one side, his knuckles on his right hand still purple, and he was too worried about their situation to think about either. Connelly had to sell the car once they realized that they were out of options for money. John's dad was their last resort and he was too angry with John for blowing his college money on his "useless" mother. It was his contention that his son should learn from his mistake and figure out things for himself before hanging up on him.

They'd been talking about options that night at the Pub, asking Gary about odd jobs and telling him that they were in desperate need of work. There probably wasn't a guy around who had a better line on the happenings around town, or who had more connections. Hundreds of people sat at his bar everyday and felt compelled to share their story with him over several drinks, so if there was something going on from Boynton to Lauderdale, Gary knew about it.

The Pub seemed their best chance, but each night they stopped in to check with Gary about any leads, he still came up with nothing – nothing that a couple of eighteen-year-old kids were qualified for anyway. It would turn out that the Pub was, in fact, the right place to be, but an opportunity would come for them in a way they never would've expected.

On that Saturday evening, the pair of friends was enjoying the last of Gary's happy hour specials, trying to maximize their limited cash. Connelly had been able to negotiate five-thousand for the old Ford coupe – which was way less than he could've gotten from a serious dealer – and the beater car he paid too much for had only left them with thirty-eight hundred. Two weeks of groceries, beer dwindled their funds to thirty-three hundred and some change, and when that was gone, there wasn't any more.

It was that roll of hundreds that John kept pulling out of his pocket to pay for their drinks that drew the attention of two girls to their table, though he warned Connelly not to wave them over. As the tall brunette and the busty blonde made their way over, he continued to berate him under his breath, telling him that they couldn't afford to buy drinks for a couple of bar tramps. Connelly only reminded him that it would help him get his mind off his mother, Melinda and the fact that they struggling.

The beautiful brunette seemed to make him forget about all three, once he got a good look at her. Connelly would've preferred talking to her instead of the fake blonde with the vacant expression, but John really needed to snap out of his funk. The shorter girl with the boobs practically lying on the table wasn't a bad choice either, and he seemed content stare at her and at them as she blathered on about herself. Either one of them was more attractive than what they'd left back home, and that fact wasn't lost on John.

The tall brunette was probably the most beautiful girl either of them had ever seen – even in magazines – and they kept sharing puzzled glances, wondering why the hell they were sitting at their table. It was a fairly busy Saturday, even for the Pub, and there were a lot older and better dressed guys than them who would've been more than willing to buy them a few drinks. Girls like that belonged at the table in the far corner where the Island Pub's most prestigious "regular" sat.

They didn't know much about the guy and they left him alone, per Gary's friendly advice. They knew his name was George, he wore expensive Italian suits that cost more than what John had in his pocket, and he liked to drink alone unless you got a special invite to his table. Girls like the ones sitting across from them that Saturday night were the type that were usually given that invitation, not the kind who sat with a couple of underage losers from out of town. Neither of them could piece that puzzle together under the influence of several more glasses of beer and the intoxicating looks of their companions, so they just continued to stare.

The girls made small talk and feigned interest as they ordered their expensive drinks with umbrellas and half a fruit salad in them. They told them their names, but they were most likely fake, just like the names Connelly gave them. Jack and Julian were brothers from upstate New York who had wealthy parents and were in the middle of a month-long trip up the Atlantic coast aboard their yacht. They were only in town while their parents had gone to Nassau for the weekend, and they were staying with friends.

The story sounded solid, even to John who knew every word of it was a lie, and the girls suddenly became a lot more interested in them. The wad of hundreds that he kept pulling from his pocket seemed to solidify their cover as a couple of trust fund brats. They left for the restroom and left the boys to work out the finer details of their story. John used the opportunity to complain about Jeremy's strategy.

"What in the hell are you doing? These girls are going to figure out that we're frauds. I don't know the first thing about upstate New York or yachts!"

"Those girls don't know about New York or yachts either," he said calmly.

"What happens when they see us here next weekend and figure out that we're either full of shit or our parents forgot to come back from Nassau to pick us up, *Julian*?"

"It will be too late by then."

"Too late? For what?"

"Look, these girls are professionals. They probably find a couple of schmucks like us at a bar five nights a week to get fawned over and as much free booze as they can drink. After those schmucks drop a few notes on them, they go home empty handed. I'm not going home empty handed, *Jack*!"

"Are you serious with this? You're trying to out-con them? You're unbelievable!"

"It's working isn't it? You'd rather have the brunette play footsies with you under the table for the hundred you're blowing on her or did you want to get your money's worth?"

"You make them sound like prostitutes," John said, shaking his head.

"No, prostitutes at least put out for the money they take. These chicks are used to getting what they want and walking free and clear. The trick is to make them think there's more in it for them if they ante up something first."

"You're referring to the yacht we don't have and a free trip to the Bahamas that we're not taking them on?"

"Exactly! But they're not going to know that until it's all over."

"You sound like you've got it all worked out?"

"And they don't? They are in that bathroom right now working out the next phase of their plan, trying to get over on us, John!"

"Why the hell would they even bother with us? Why wouldn't they go after bigger fish?"

"We *are* bigger fish as far as they're concerned. For all we know, they've already tried to run their game on George and he's wise to them. So, they see you pulling out your roll, don't recognize us, and decide to go after something easier. But they're going to regret it in the morning when they realize they've been taken."

"Sounds like you've got it figured out, Con."

"Don't sound so glum and don't look at me that way. That girl is the hottest I've ever seen, and you can't tell me that you'd ever regret a night with her."

"We're supposed to be figuring out a way to make money, not get chicks into bed."

"Well, I don't see anyone around here offering jobs tonight, Johnny, so this is the next best thing. We've seen nothing but bad luck since we got here and the both of us deserve a break. It's going to happen tonight if you follow my lead and don't screw it up!"

He did exactly as he was told and did follow Connelly's lead, and found himself in the parking lot an hour later; making out with a beautiful woman, and his troubles seemed to be melting away. Connelly was standing beside their Mercedes with the blonde, doing the same.

For several minutes everything was going perfectly. There was a warm breeze blowing in from the east, accompanied by the soothing sound of the ocean only thirty feet away, and the rustling palm fronds above them. They would soon be in the Mercedes

Benz, driving up A1A towards their condo, which was probably as exquisite as the car and the two girls. Once there, they would have one of the most exciting nights of their young lives, and in the morning they would slip out and take a cab back to the Pub.

That's how it was all playing out in Connelly's head at least, and how the blonde girl (he still couldn't remember her name) was selling it to him as she nibbled on his ear. He was so relaxed and distracted by the dirty things she was telling him that she was going to do to him, that he didn't hear the shuffling of feet coming towards them.

Gentle fingers had been playing in his hair and relaxing him, but he didn't realize that they had been getting him relaxed for a reason. Suddenly, a much stronger hand pulled his hair and jerked his head back towards the car. Everything happened so fast that he didn't even have time to react, and he'd been too relaxed and drunk to even tense up in preparation for the attack. His head bounced off the rear door of the Mercedes and a fist caught him in the nose, making his eyes fill with water.

The next thing he knew, he was on the ground being kicked repeatedly, trying to cover his face with his good hand. He could hear scuffling and grunts coming from the other side of the car and assumed John was getting the same treatment. They'd been set up.

As he was being kicked, he wondered how he'd missed all the cues that these girls were looking for more than just drinks. If the Mercedes in the parking lot didn't tip him off, or the expensive clothing they were wearing, then just the simple fact that they chose their table in the first place out of all the others in the bar. He was regretting being so sloppy and not seeing the con that was being run on them more with every stiff shoe to the face. He regretted even more convincing his best friend to put his trust in him, and was reminded that his entire purpose for coming along was to make sure nothing happened to him.

The brutal beating ceased abruptly, just as he was about to slip into unconsciousness. Through the one eye that wasn't filling with blood, he saw Danny, the wiry, leathery-skinned regular giving a hell of a beating to the two guys that had jumped him. Apparently, before he became a permanent fixture in the Island Pub, he'd been Danny Vincent, Sergeant in the 101st airborne division of the United States Army. A dishonorable discharge, lots of drugs and alcohol, and a streak of luck far worse than John's

274

had taken all of that away. Despite being a bit rusty, he was a man of ample ability, and made quick work of the two assailants.

His Army training and military wasn't the most intimidating thing about Danny Vincent, however, it was the other connections he'd made over the past eight years in south Florida. He'd brought more than a couple of quick fists and a healthy curiosity to that parking lot; he also brought the man from the corner table.

He looked a lot bigger standing up, and was so intimidating that he didn't even have to lay a hand on the man beating on John. Calling out a couple of racial slurs at the fleeing Hispanic man in his heavy Boston accent, he helped John get to his feet.

"You okay kid?"

"Is he okay? Con..." John mumbled.

"Yea, he's gonna' be fine...a few bruises and some pavement scuffs. I think they took your roll, though, and it's no wonder the way you were flashing it around the bar."

John spat a bloody wad of saliva onto the ground in disgust. "I wasn't flashing it."

"Everyone gets rolled now and again kid, even me," he said, as if the beating they'd just received was some sort of rite of passage and no big deal. "How much did they get you for?"

John checked his pockets, "Ugh! God damn it! I had thirty-three hundred bucks!"

Connelly shuffled over to check on John as he was cussing, "They got everything?"

John nodded and sat hard on the curb, hanging his aching head between his legs. He looked like he was going to vomit right there, not because of the beating he'd received, but because they were truly screwed now without a penny to their names.

"He's right; everyone gets taken now and then," came the gravelly voice standing behind them. "Especially when you are trying to pull a score and it backfires."

Danny couldn't help but chuckle, as he'd watched the two young con artists work from across the bar, and knew that if it had been any other girls they would have pulled it off. He offered up his condolences, "Yea, those were the wrong girls to be messing with fellas."

"Someone might've mentioned that they had giant Mexican boyfriends waiting for us out here!"

"They were *Colombians*, not Mexicans, and they weren't their boyfriends," the larger man snorted. "Those chicks are bad news, and you got rolled by the best."

"Yea, those guys are animals, and not the kind you want to be mixed up with," Danny chimed in.

"What are we gonna' do about our money Johnny?" Con moaned.

"You mean *my* money? What do you want to do? Go after those guys and let them finish the job?"

"I wouldn't recommend it," the balding brute warned.

"Look, you guys probably see this thing all the time, and I'm sure that it's a Saturday-night's entertainment for you, but for Johnny and me, it wasn't a real good time. We're broke and soon-to-be-homeless now, and about a thousand miles from home, so if you don't mind?"

The man in the expensive suit stopped laughing, not because he'd been asked to be sympathetic to their situation, but because the smart-mouthed one was really starting to rub him the wrong way.

"I was gonna' offer you guys a way to get your money back, but if our help isn't appreciated, we can go back inside and let the two of you cry like little girls out here," he said.

"You know how to get those guys?"

"Forget those guys! They're gone! Your money is long gone - let it go! I said I could get you money back in your pockets, are you interested or not?" He said, annoyed.

John looked up at Jeremy and gave him a look of warning. This Danny, who mopped up the floor with two of the Colombians, and his friend with the heavy Boston accent were probably more bad news than the last guys. He didn't like their present situation, but he liked even less that one of their prospects might be living in the pocket of some shady characters they didn't know. For all he knew, the Colombians were working with them and they were all in it together.

"It's your call, Johnny," he conceded.

"I'd prefer to weigh our options, Jer," he said in a low voice, as though the others couldn't hear.

The big man pulled a card from his inside jacket pocket and handed it to him, saying, "No one is holding a gun to your head kid, and I just thought I'd be nice because you seem like ya' got a good head on your shoulders. I don't like to see anyone in a spot like this, and if we can help each other out, then it's good for everybody."

John stared at the card in his hand, and turned it over to read both sides. It was one of Gary's business cards and on the back, written in sloppy ink, was the name that he would never forget for the rest of his days - *George Gallianni* – and a number scrawled beneath it.

"I take it you don't work for the hotel?" John said sarcastically.

George shook his head.

"I'll be in touch," he said almost as sarcastically.

"It's your call, kid. Do what you have to do."

Danny and George walked to a vintage Mercedes Benz across the lot and the pair of boys watched them drive away. Jeremy plopped down beside his friend, and they looked quite a pair, with their torn shirts and bloodied faces. For a long while, they just sat there in the parking lot of the Island Pub, staring out at the lights of the city, not saying a word. They each knew that the other was thinking about the offer that the intimidating man had made them, and trying to run through every other alternative option at the same time.

Chapter 26

Within three months of that terrible night at the Island Pub, John and Connelly had almost forgotten all about it. George promised that they would get their money back and they'd gotten every penny and then some, and the work wasn't as bad as they'd thought it would be. There had been a lot of guesses between them as they lay awake all that night, trying to figure out what kind of things the large Italian man was mixed up in. Most of what they knew about the business conducted by scary Italians they'd seen in mob movies with Pete, but none of those portrayals was even close.

They called the number on the card and it was a direct line to Gary's office at the Pub, and it was Gary who answered. He took their number down and called them back within a half an hour, telling them to be at a particular address at a particular time. A man they'd never seen before was waiting for them, standing beside an old Cadillac, sipping a Coke from the can. He wasn't much older than them, maybe twenty-one at most, but dressed much better than they were. Jeremy guessed that he was Sicilian like their new boss, because of his prominent nose and dark hair, John guessed something Middle Eastern or Mediterranean by his complexion.

The man didn't smile or make small talk beyond confirming they were "George's guys". He handed them keys to the Cadillac and explained that everything they needed was in the glove compartment. Before they could ask him a single question, he disappeared around the corner of the building where there was another car waiting to pick him up. They shared a curious look and then checked in the glove compartment as they were instructed. Inside was a small envelope with a folded piece of paper and two fifty-dollar bills. On the paper was an address and nothing else.

They delivered the car to the address, where a second man drove the car away and a third waited in a car to drop them back off at the place they'd picked up the car. It was good pay for an hour's worth of work, and they didn't have to break anyone's legs, get shot at, or rough up shop owners for their "protection money". It was easy work with minimal risk and there were a lot of those cars to move and a lot of fifties to line their pockets with.

Those fifties paid the rent, kept them fed and paid for their weekends at the Pub. Even that changed, though, once Gary knew that they worked for George, and they never had to pay for a drink (even a happy hour drink) after that. They were given their own seats at the actual bar, too, which they discovered was kind of a "round table" of sorts for George's regulars. If you had a chair at the bar, it meant that you were "taken care of", but it also meant that you were "on the payroll" of George Gallianni.

There were a dozen stools at that counter, and though there was no gold name placard on them, the same guys always sat in the same seats. Once in a while there was a "mix up" when a vacationer would inadvertently take one of the "regulars" seats at the bar, and they were given a friendly suggestion that they might be more comfortable at one of the tables on the floor. Only once – according to Gary – was a guy thrown out and given a beating when he refused to give up his seat for one of the regulars. That regular was Ray the Indian.

Ray was a full-blooded Sioux Indian who was two fingers short on his left hand because of an "alligator incident". The story went (the way Gary liked to tell it) that Ray used to work at a gator farm and one of them had gotten a hold of his hand, pulling his two fingers off. Not "bitten off" or "chewed off", but "pulled off"- because that's what gators did. The story gets better at this point, because Ray the Indian (the badass that he is) calmly wraps his own hand in a towel and drives himself to the hospital without showing a bit of concern.

That made "Ray the Indian" the last guy at the bar you wanted to get into an argument over a seat with, and that story was Gary's favorite to tell the out-of-towners who selected that chair by accident. John and Connelly would chuckle as they watched more than a handful of them scramble out of that chair for the safety of one of the "guest" tables.

Of the others, Danny Vincent was about the only guy Ray liked or would talk to, because Danny was the only guy who could match him drink for drink. At about six feet, seven inches and two-hundred-seventy pounds, it was hard to drink as much as Ray. Those two usually spent the bulk of their money on drinks (George refused to pay their tabs and cash on top of it) and by Sunday, they were broke and passed out in Ray's van in the parking lot. For that reason, George knew that the early part of the week was the best time to put Ray and Danny on jobs and not to come looking for them after Thursday when had drinking money.

Gary Polidoro didn't need the money; he just worked with George mostly so that he could impress the girls with his "tough guy" stories. There was something about a "connected man" that the women responded to, and since he wasn't a particularly attractive man – with his bad eighties moustache - he relied on the mystique.

There was no real official "title" for Gary, or specific task that he performed, other than providing a safe haven for the rest of George's thugs and functioning as a messaging service. The phone in the back was always ringing off the hook and he was usually too busy answering it to tend the bar, so one of his girls helped out in the front. The messages he wrote on napkins and then handed them off to different people. Usually it was Danny or Ray, but sometimes it was one of the other guys who John and Con didn't know.

The rest of George's "crew" kept to themselves and they came and went at all hours, so the newest additions never learned their names. Some of them, Gary warned, were "Vincent's guys" – George's brother – and they didn't like to associate with the others. Polidoro didn't have very good things to say about Vincent Gallianni, and told them to steer clear of him at all costs. He was the guy they wrote books about and portrayed in the mob movies, and cut from a different cloth than his older brother.

George stayed out of his brother's business, and his brother did the same, for the most part. There were times when extra muscle was needed for a job and George loaned his guys out, and whenever those jobs came up, Vincent's messenger made an appearance. Gary referred to him as either "the handler" or "the Slav", and he made the entire bar nervous whenever he was around. He never addressed anyone but George or Gary directly, and wouldn't even make eye contact with those who sat around the bar.

Gary and the rest of those guys outright hated him for that reason, but weren't stupid enough to voice their disdain openly for fear of repercussions. The Slav, it was rumored, was more than just

281

a handler and a messenger for Vincent. There were more stories floating around about him than George and his brother combined, and they were the kind that were preceded by a glance around the room and a few drinks for courage before they were uttered in whispers. They didn't want to be numbered among those lying in the murky bottom of the everglades, or one of those who'd come home to find their families chopped into pieces, so they avoided the cold stare of the stone-faced Slav.

John didn't believe any of those stories, however, and wasn't intimidated by the Slav. In fact, he was intrigued by the man, and couldn't deny that there was a mystique to him even if the stories were bogus. He referred to him as the "Lancelot" of the Island Pub "round table" (it was more of a three-sided rectangle). The cavalier had mysterious origins, would disappear on quests for his King for long periods, returning to his chair in a place of honor beside that King. Most notably, the knight had never been bested in combat, much like George's champion, and his reputation as a formidable opponent was not comprised of exaggerated tales.

Even Ray and Danny, George's two best brawlers, didn't want to tangle with the Slav, for they'd both seen him fight and said it was unlike anything they'd ever seen. Danny said that some of his tactics were straight from the Green Berets, and some he recognized from a tour in the Middle East where he'd witnessed the Mossad in action. The strange thing, Danny puzzled over, was that their "Lancelot" couldn't be more than twenty-four, yet he'd had more training, and from more places around the world, than any of his Ranger buddies.

For that reason, he insisted that the Slav was a "spook" who'd been sent by a covert agency for reasons they couldn't even guess at, and they gave him a wide berth whenever he came into the Pub.

Everyone else followed suit except John Chapel, the new kid at the table, and there was quite an uproar the day he was invited to George's table by the Slav himself. For four months, he and Connelly had been busting their asses running the cars, doing courier work, and any other odd job George had for them. And just when Connelly thought they were getting somewhere, that they were starting to fit in with the rest of the crew, all of it fell apart.

The first thing that changed was their living arrangements. John wasn't going to stay at that "slum hole" anymore – according to George – and he was given a suite on the top floor of Gary's hotel, across the hall from the room George had. For some reason, he wanted him to be more accessible and available around the clock. Connelly complained, even though he was a regular guest in the suite with his best friend, because he felt that he'd worked just as hard (sometimes harder), but had been passed up for whatever promotion John had been given. He couldn't even be sure of what kind of promotion it was, because he never told him what kinds of jobs he was doing for George.

It sure as hell wasn't driving cars, dropping off envelopes full of cash, or even picking up George's dry cleaning. John was getting paid a lot more than the standard fifty (or occasional hundred) that he'd been getting before, and Connelly noticed one of the thick envelopes sitting on the dresser one morning. It was the same kind he was still delivering to the important guys in the organization, and he stared bitterly at it, counting the hundreds inside, realizing that he was one of those important guys he was delivering them to now.

It wasn't as if John didn't share the wealth, letting him stay in his suite on the top floor and paying for drinks when they went out to clubs in West Palm or Lauderdale, but it still felt like a slap in the face to him as well as the rest who'd worked with George for years. Because of this division at the "round table", John frequented the Pub less and less, and only showed up for the messages that came through for him in the back office. Even Gary thought something was "off" about the whole thing, and told the others that he'd never seen anything like it in his sixteen years with George.

John Chapel and Jeremy Connelly were just a couple of eighteen-year-old kids that happened to get rolled in "his" parking lot, and he felt partly responsible for helping them get back on their feet. George was no fan of Connelly – that was for sure – and if not for Gary's fondness for him, he might've cut him out of the group long before. Neither of them understood why George disliked the one guy who was good at running cons and why he'd taken to the doe-eyed Midwestern kid who never had a dishonest bone in his body. Ray and Danny, who believed that the Slav was tied in with every conspiracy in the world, blamed him for it, and they probably weren't far off the mark.

On occasion, John was in the company of the Slav when he came to meet with George – which they found odd. In the three years he'd been coming around, he'd never arrived at the Pub with anyone else. All eyes turned discreetly towards that doorway when they showed up, following them to the table in the corner, and ears perked up, trying to listen to what was said between them. As soon as the trio left together, all eyes turned to Connelly and demanded answers about his friend, who'd somehow weaseled his way into the good graces of a man who had no good graces.

He was just as confused by the whole situation as they were, and more alienated than any of them. As the summer sun burned so unforgiving above them, their friendship seemed to dry up. They used to close down the clubs and bars on Climatis Street in West Palm, or those along Ocean Drive on the outskirts of Miami every weekend together. When Sunday came, they would head to the gym to sweat out their hangovers, doing some lifting or sparring. Weeknights, when they weren't on a job, they had dinner together and a few beers at Charley's Crab or Boston's in Delray Beach. He was lucky if John met him for a quick drink just to receive his envelope of pay from George that first winter.

John Chapel wasn't going to the same clubs he used to go to with his best friend, instead, he was seen by Orlando Perez frequenting the higher-end places in South Beach and Miami with a whole new group. At the head of that entourage was Vincent Gallianni himself, and John had somehow become his new favorite as well. John was also his dinner guest at exclusive restaurants that had month-long wait lists, and Sundays at the gym were spent with Francos Kovacs – the Slav.

Apparently, they had become good enough friends that John had been allowed to call him by his name – a name that few even knew – and he'd let it slip one night while telling Con how cool he was. That was three months after his virtual disappearance, when he suddenly decided to show up at his suite at the Days Inn Oceanside, to the surprise of Connelly. He'd been staying as a guest of Vincent's or Kovacs' for the duration of his disappearance. When he showed up that night in October, he looked so different that Connelly barely recognized him.

Physically, he looked good, and had never looked better. His face was taut and void of any trace of fat, much like the rest of him, making him appear much older. He seemed to stand an inch or two taller, but this was just because of his renewed confidence and "Frank" breaking him of his slouching habit. There was definitely more definition in his musculature and he looked like he'd bulked up about fifteen pounds since only December. Whatever routine Kovacs had him on was working much better than anything they'd done in the gym the months prior.

Connelly was most concerned with the expression in his eyes – that same cold, empty stare that Kovacs wore – and the abrasions, bruises and small cuts on his face and his hands. His right one looked as bad as it did when he'd broken it trying to protect his mother, and his left didn't look much better. John didn't seem to be concerned with his hands or his face; he just kept going on about Kovacs and Vincent and how things were so much different with them, and how he felt like he was on top of the world. The expression in his eyes told him differently, though, and he knew that there was something he wasn't telling him.

John waved away his concerns that night and told him that things were going to be different from that point forward. He was coming back to do some work for George again and John was going to get Connelly in good with Vincent and Francos, so that he wouldn't have to be running cars anymore. Jeremy expressed his apprehension about bailing on George, letting him know that he wasn't exactly happy that his brother had already snatched up one of his favorites. John shrugged it off and said that he wasn't afraid of George, and that he was protected by more important people. That's when he really became worried.

John's first night "back" seemed almost like it had been before, with some minor differences. That first Saturday night, they sat and drank at the old "round table" beneath the hotel, cracking jokes and laughing with the other guys. They enjoyed listening to his stories about how the "other half" lives, and some of the jobs they pulled together. It was more than they'd ever heard about Vincent's exploits before, and it sure beat the hell out of making up stories and spreading rumors for entertainment. Connelly listened to something different altogether though, and he heard anger, pain, angst and suffering in the words of his best friend.

When he talked about busting guys' heads for Victor, or just for the hell of it, it drew a laugh from the group, and they wanted to know every detail. Connelly listened to him describing the sound it made when someone's jaw shattered or when their femur was cracked, how pleasant it was to feel a wrist crumble or a windpipe close off in your hand, and chuckled along with the group as his stomach turned. Those dark eyes glistened as he gave them every sickening account of the men he'd destroyed in his scourge across south Florida, and Connelly's cheeks burned hot.

They'd done this to his friend - Victor and his soulless killer had made him just like them - and he felt his heart split at the seams when he saw what they did to him. Those men took a gentle soul like John Chapel's and they exploited all of the hurt, all of the humiliation, and all of the anger inside of it, until they twisted it into something unrecognizable. There had been something festering deep inside of John for some time, ever since they'd left Michigan, and none had known about it except Connelly.

The girl he loved more than any other had betrayed him in the worst way, the woman who should have loved him more than any other did the same, and as he was trying to come back from those defeats he'd been handed, just as he was trying to get back on his feet, another woman came along and kicked him while he was down. Dwelling on those things hadn't been a luxury at the time, and he had to push them somewhere deep within himself and turn his attention to survival.

Now that he felt like he was "on top of the world", working with Vincent and Kovacs, pockets full of money, driving nice cars and having pretty much anything he wanted, he turned his attention back to those things he didn't have. They were things that couldn't be fixed by money or by two of the most powerful men in south Florida, and they started to eat at him once again. He'd overcome those setbacks, kept getting up after being beaten by each of them, but they still hadn't been set right. John Chapel had been given power, but for all that power, he still felt helpless to change those things that had been done before.

Helplessness turned to frustration, frustration to anger, and anger to violence. Jeremy Connelly knew why he was busting people's heads in clubs all across Miami and Lauderdale, and it wasn't because someone looked at him funny or spilled a drink on him. When he was splitting some guy's nose open, he was busting open the nose of Sal and the muscle-bound guy who'd put his mother in the hospital, and when he was cracking ribs of some mouthy kid, he revisiting the night in the parking lot with the

Colombians. There was a rage there inside of his friend that he'd only seen the beginnings of at the motel fight, and had since grown into something terrifying.

That same night John returned and bought drinks for all the "old crew", they took the party back down to Lauderdale, and Connelly got to see some of that rage firsthand. They weren't there an hour when some guys interrupted his discussion with a girl he'd been talking to, and there was an explosion like Jeremy had never seen before. There was no juvenile mouthing off or bumping chest to chest, trying to intimidate the other guy, he tore into him like a starving dog into a piece of bloody steak.

Connelly had seen John fight before, and he and Hunter had been the ones to teach him most of his moves, but the guy he watched fight in that club wasn't the awkward kid he'd trained. He was the living embodiment of the rumors that had flown around the bar about Frank Kovacs and his unconventional methods. There were elements of basic striking and arm locks, like Danny Vincent had told him about, mixed with the fluidity, deadly accuracy and pressure points that only a martial artist would know. It was like watching a graceful dance with sporadic, violent spasms interspersed.

He didn't even have time to step in and "help" by the time he knew what was happening, John had all three of the mouthy toughs incapacitated, groaning and coughing on the floor. That was just a "warm up" fight for the two follow-up matches at the Irish bar and the dance club on A1A that would come before the night was over. The others cheered him on as he traded blows and the beer and the blood flowed, while Connelly quietly watched his friend destroying himself.

The next morning, he went directly to George, trying to get him to intervene, but he only laughed and said that it was about time that Johnny "cut his teeth" in the business. He didn't get involved when he had to bail John out of jail several times over the next few weeks, or even when he had to shell out money to keep a couple of college kids quiet that John busted up, or pay for the broken patio window he tossed them through at the bar in Lauderdale. It was only when his favorite protégé started going after the wrong guys that he was forced to step in.

A meeting was called by Vincent Gallianni – an informal deal over dinner at Charley's Crab in Deerfield Beach – where

George, Kovacs and even Connelly were present. It was his first time with the "big fish" and he was a little confused as to why he'd been picked up in Vincent's limo and ordered to the meeting. It was the first real discussion he'd ever had with George, and the only discussion he'd ever had with his brother or the mysterious "Slav" about anything. They all were concerned about Johnny, they said, but the truth was that he was causing problems with another organization after he'd busted up some Colombians in a dance club.

Jeremy had no recourse but to tell the three of them about the events preceding their move to Florida, the girl he'd left behind, his mother's betrayal and his anger over the incident with the guys who'd robbed them. After hearing Connelly's story, the three wise men each came up with a solution. The older king was more sympathetic, and he suggested more distractions – more women, more money, and higher-profile jobs. The younger king's solution was harsher; simply order him to correct his behavior or have him removed. Surprisingly, it was the great Lancelot who came up with the plan to save their lost man.

Chapter 27

The widow of John Chapel was understandably stunned. Her husband had never spoken much of his time spent in south Florida, besides the few stories he reminisced with Jeremy about whenever he came to visit. They were mostly stories about this girl or that girl, crazy nights of binge drinking and closing down the bars and clubs at four in the morning. That kind of stuff was what a wife expected to be kept "on the hush", and she didn't really want to hear about the sophomoric antics of her husband long before they exchanged vows.

While she'd always guessed that there were some harder times that he'd faced while he was gone, she never would've imagined the full scope of what John was involved in. Sure, he was going to retrieve his mother from the hospital after a violent encounter with a possessive boyfriend, but she had just prayed that he would be safe and then put it from her mind.

He called her and Dean after being gone only a few days, but was always vague about what he was doing and where he was staying. Neither of them would have ever dreamed that the boy on the other end of that line was speaking to them with eyes swollen shut or holding the receiver with his one good hand. Neither of them could tell by the tone in his voice, when he was asking Melinda, that he'd been shattered to his core and was hurting in that way.

She watched the way Melinda hurt and her own method for driving the pain away and just always assumed that John retreated to a bottle, partying and dating a slew of women to forget her. Never would she have pictured him hurting other people the way he was, constantly looking to dispense his pain on others as violently as he was. The thought of him losing himself in that way, not caring anymore about even himself, sickened her as much as it had when she watched Melinda do the same.

"Things were pretty bad by that point," Connelly's voice called her out of her haze, and she sat upright in her chair. "And we had to come up with something."

289

"That's when you called me," she recalled. "Things weren't much better at home either, I remember."

Campbell scratched away with his pen, not looking up from his notebook as he spoke, "So Melinda wasn't the answer, I presume?"

"She didn't want to hear anything about John or Florida. He wasn't the only one dealing with anger and bottled up issues. Melinda didn't run around town starting fights or pulling hair though, she took a different route," Gwenn said bitterly.

"That's when she turned to drugs," Campbell said, continuing to write.

"She wasn't just doing recreational drugs; she was on a mission. She couldn't sit still long enough or stay away from them long enough, because then she had to deal with real life and the situation she put herself in."

"Doesn't sound much different than John; the more heads he bashed, the worse he got and the more unsatisfied he was," Connelly added.

Campbell looked up at each of them from behind the pad that was resting on his knee, his pen hovering above it as he decided what to write next, waiting on Connelly.

"Tell me what happened, Mr. Connelly…tell me about the *girl*," he said coyly.

Gwenn gave a confused look at Campbell and then at her old flame, as if she'd left the room and missed a big part of the story. She sat forward in her seat and leaned on her elbows, staring across the table at the storyteller expectantly.

"What girl, Jeremy?"

He gave a sideways glance at Campbell, seeming to be equally lost and confused, but answered her, "He's right…there was a girl. That was the solution to the problem…for the time being."

"This Kovacs was meticulous, calculating and methodical in everything he did," Campbell gave his assessment. "That's why those men kept him around, because he was the perfect fit for that sort of work. In what I've read about that world, they also called 'handlers' by the term 'fixer' isn't that correct?"

Jeremy nodded, saying, "You've been following along pretty well."

"I can relate with this Kovacs because I understand how a man like that thinks. He doesn't let his emotions get the best of him and his mind works like a computer, processing every piece of information before taking action."

"Yea, he sounds like someone else I know," Gwenn said, raising a neatly-trimmed brow towards him, and then her face lost all color as something suddenly seemed to occur to her. "The Slav...Kovacs...the name is..."

"Hungarian," Campbell finished her stuttered revelation. "I'd picked it up as soon as he mentioned it in his story."

"Connelly's story," she said, remembering the cryptic line in her husband's journal. "Con man...*the deceiver*...there's something John wanted us to know about this man."

Connelly could only look from one face to the other, looking thoroughly confused by whatever secret thing had passed between them.

The professor nodded, folding his hands across his chest and sitting back in his seat and gave her a satisfied smile. When she wanted to be, Gwenn Chapel could be as logical and astute as her husband. That keen intelligence had been balanced and tempered by an intense flame that burned hotter in her than in most, however, and wherever that sharp intellect struck, it was usually followed by a burst that would char that clean mark.

Campbell knew that fire was coming as he grinned, clicking his pen and turning his eyes back towards the pad, "If I was in Mr. Kovacs' position, I would work backwards through the problem and find the source. He was the one that suggested you contact Melinda?"

"Yea, he figured that was the biggest 'cog' that was stuck – so to speak."

"And when she wasn't an option, he turned to the other girl."

Again, it was a statement, not a question.

"What *girl* are you talking about?" Gwenn asked, still thoroughly confused.

"I'd wager you every tweed in my closet that I could guess at her name."

"Keep your tweeds, they're not my style, but I'd love to hear anyway."

"Tell us about *Nicole* Mr. Connelly..."

That sharp blade of reason slipped from her fingers as elbows lost their structural integrity, causing a heavy chin to slip from thin hands and nearly be torn open on the breakfast table. Campbell settled his shoulders back into his chair and savoring a long draught from his pipe, giving a satisfied smile.

She suddenly looked disoriented and turned a shade of green, forcing herself out of her chair, as if just getting off an amusement park ride. Steadying herself on the edge of the table, leaning on her knuckles, she tried to catch her breath. Connelly noticed the quiet exchange between them and suddenly felt as if he'd said something very bad.

"You didn't know anything about her?"

She shook her head, still unable to speak, trying to hold down her breakfast.

"I don't understand why she's so important," he said innocently, staring wide-eyed at each of them.

"Please indulge us," Campbell said, jabbing his pipe stem at him. "Tell us about this mystery girl, and then I think Mrs. Chapel will be able to fill you in on what we were discussing before you arrived."

❦

On the warmest October night Connelly had ever experienced, he found himself on the balcony of a club in Lauderdale, overlooking the ocean. He was sitting with Johnny and Kovacs in plush loungers, sipping daiquiris, talking the night away. John was sure that he was in for a night of serious drinking and rough stuff when he received Frank's message at the hotel desk. He had no clue that he was walking into a setup.

It wasn't the sort he'd acquired a bitter distaste for, where some woman lures him into the middle of an ambush to get beaten, robbed and humiliated, but still the sort where a guy walks into a place expecting one thing to happen and something completely different goes down. John was definitely surprised that night, watching the plan unfold that he never realized had been put into place, but not quite as surprised as those others who were the real targets of that plan.

When John saw the third familiar face pass by the patio entrance that night, his blood ran cold and he realized that something was afoot. A less-than-subtle stare was answered by a subtle nod as the Hungarian man leaned forward on elbows to explain the uncanny coincidence. He left out the part about the private meeting where John's fate had been decided, and began the story with the fortuitous hot tip he'd gotten from an informant. From there, a little more footwork uncovered the names of two of the three Colombians, as well as the brunette who was involved in the Island Pub incident.

Finding them was easy, once he had the names, and getting the "okay" from Vincent was as simple as a phone call and having the right plan – a plan Connelly had already been privy to. John wasn't thrilled that he hadn't been let in on the plan from the beginning, but knew better than to second guess Frank Kovacs. When he put something together, it was airtight, well-thought-out, and accounted for every conceivable variable, so only foolish men or dead ones strayed from the plan.

John's face took on a different hue once he realized that they were on a job, and not just any job, but the kind that he'd dreamed about. His eyes glimmered as he listened to the Hungarian's plot, and Frank shared a knowing look with Connelly from across the table. When he finished with the mini-briefing, he made sure that both of them understood their parts, John in particular.

"So I have to hit them *before* they can leave the club."

"You have to hit them preferably before they make you, but most importantly in a place where you're sure of your surroundings – remember what I taught you?"

"Yea, so we don't know how many they're here with and we don't want the attention here anyway."

"When did you start worrying about attention?" Connelly joked and both of them gave a sour look.

"This is serious," John scolded him. "Following them to their car could be a worse idea, because things can get messier when there isn't a crowd around, and they could have more guys outside."

"I don't think they do, but it's better to be safe - you're starting to get the right idea."

"So where then?"

"*You* pick the place. You always need to select the battleground for the advantage, Johnny."

"How am I going to get these guys to meet me at a place I pick? They rolled me for three grand, as soon as they make us, they're going to scatter."

"How did they get you to meet them in the parking lot?"

He left John on the balcony to ponder his words, taking his drink inside to get into position for the next part of the plan that John hadn't discovered yet. They followed him through the crowd, keeping out of sight of their targets, discussing their next move. It was at the edge of the dance floor that he spotted the beautiful brunette talking to a well-dressed older gentleman, when he finally figured out what his mentor was getting at.

She looked great, even better than the last time he'd seen her, and rightly so; she was trying to pick up a higher class of sucker that night. John got to see her working her "A game" instead of slumming it at some small pub in Deerfield Beach, and she was really turning heads in the crowd just by the way she walked. It didn't hurt that she was wearing a painted on dress and expensive jewelry that reflected the lights on the dance floor to dazzle those poor saps.

Connelly and his partner watched her as she did her signature half-dance half-flirting routine, making certain to touch him as much as possible while she talked and laughed with him. Within five minutes, she had him leading her to the bar, fishing out his wad of money – which she studied and counted thoroughly in a glance – and ordering an expensive drink. There was more flirting, touching and fake laughter, as she pretended to be interested in him, as they finished their drink, and then she pulled him back onto the dance floor to move in for the kill.

That's when John decided to save the poor slob about five grand and a bitter Saturday morning in the hospital. As he walked by, he caught her firmly by the arm and dragging her in the other direction, leaving her confused potential victim to stare after, thoroughly confused. Connelly intercepted him and offered to buy him a drink, explaining the disaster that he'd just narrowly escaped.

He watched John pull her across the dance floor and down the narrow hallway leading towards the restrooms. Once they were out of range of the blaring speakers and tightly packed bodies, he pressed her against the wall and cornered her there with his own body, appearing to be an intimate couple to the casual observer.

294

Connelly could see the fire in his eyes even from where he was standing, and didn't envy her at that moment.

After he bought a drink for the older gentleman and sent him safely on his way, he watched the pair of them from his corner of the room, making sure they weren't interrupted and that John didn't do anything stupid. He could see that finger of his wagging in her face, really giving it to her, pressing her further into that shadowy corner. The fiery brunette wasn't taking it lying down, though, and her finger was flying right back at him. No one took notice because they looked like the typical couple who'd had a few too many and were having a lover's spat.

Though Frank hadn't left anything to the imagination about his plans for the Colombians, he hadn't really been clear about the fate of their co-conspirator. He was obviously leaving that in his hands, though Jeremy wondered if that was wise as he watched the two cons putting on a show that looked too real.

"You don't look so happy to see me," he said with a wicked smile.

"*Jack* right? Look, it wasn't my idea...the whole thing..." She looked incredibly nervous.

"Save it! I've been watching you work the crowd for the last fifteen minutes. I just saved that poor sucker's ass and he doesn't even know it yet."

"What do you want? Money? I have money and I can get you your money back," she said weakly.

"Oh, I'm going to get my money back, don't you worry about that."

"Then what do you want with me?"

"Let's start with a name...I never got yours that night."

"Nicole. What's it matter?"

"I'm *Johnny*, not Jack, and now that we've formally met, I'm going to tell you about the deal of a lifetime. I'm giving you a chance to leave right now, and quit pulling scores with these losers! They're going down tonight, and I'm giving you the opportunity to put distance between yourself and them."

"What are you, a cop?"

"No, I'm no cop! Do I *look* like a cop? Your friends are going to wish I were a cop at the end of tonight. Walk away now!"

"Why? Why would you do that? They beat you pretty badly and took your money, and that was my fault! Why would you not just take me down with them?"

"Because *maybe* I don't think you're as bad as they are and *maybe* no one else has given you a choice to do anything else but what you're doing right now. Maybe there's something else out there for you and you just haven't found it yet."

"You don't know anything about me, let me go...you're hurting my arm," she pleaded.

"I'm not letting you go until you've heard what I have to say," he pressed his face close to hers and she could smell the sweet alcohol on his breath.

"You going to try to save my soul, *Johnny*? You going to try to tell me to go straight and clean up? Go get a real job and not to wear so much makeup because I'm prettier without it? I've heard it before."

He laughed. "No, I'm not going to tell you any of that. Whatever makes you the way you are makes you the way you are, and I don't expect you to change. I'm telling you to be smarter about what you're doing. You want to live this life? Don't hang out with bottom-feeders like those guys. Yea, I'm telling you to get a real job, I guess, one where you're not working suckers out of their money with a bat of your eyes. And I've never seen you without makeup, so I couldn't tell you how you look, I got my ass beat before I got to go home with you, remember?"

She gave a nervous laugh, and wasn't sure why. As she looked him up and down, her mind tried to wrap itself around the man she'd never thought she would see again. She had stood by and watched him get beat up for a couple of thousand bucks, and here he was, telling her that was all amateur work and that he might have a better offer. And she couldn't be sure, but she was pretty sure he was flirting with her. Was he insane?

"What is your program, exactly?" She finally gave up trying to figure him out on her own.

"My *program*?"

"Yes, your program. What is your malfunction? I mean, I guess I know mine is an abusive dad, an alcoholic mom, a long string of bad choices in men looking for attention, and all the usual shit. That's what makes me tick, but you...I don't get you. Please explain to me why you wouldn't want to beat my ass or, at the very least, have me arrested after what I did to you. And…why you're looking at me like you were that night, before you realized I really didn't like you and just wanted your money?"

"I'd thought about what I would do to you if I ever found you again for many nights after that last one I saw you, and yes, beating your face in had occurred to me. But then I realized if I beat your ass and take your money, then I'm just perpetuating the problem…I'm just like you. It won't change anything. It won't make you stop taking scores and rolling naïve men who think you're hot. You'll just keep right on doing what you're doing."

"So far you're on a roll…"

"I figured. So what would be the best answer? What's the best thing to do to you to make sure nobody else has a run in with you like I did? You'll never stop the best crooks, and who wants to? If you're smart, you'll employ them, just like the government does."

"And you're not a cop?"

"Nope, just a guy who uses his head."

"Okay…why do you keep looking at me that way?"

"Because I think that you felt bad about that night and you really did like me."

"If I liked you, I wouldn't have let them take your money," she said, perturbed.

"It wasn't up to you, Nicole, it was up to them. You stood by and watched, and I could see by your face that it bothered you. Sometimes nice guys get hurt because of what you do, and you act like it doesn't bother you, but it does. You might be tough, you might be good at what you do, but somewhere in there is a conscience," he continued with his barrage.

"You were a *job*," she insisted.

"You didn't kiss me like I was a job," he fired back, moving his face even closer to hers.

"Sometimes I enjoy the kiss. Doesn't mean anything…"

He pushed his body closer against hers and finally pressed his lips into hers, meshing them together into a tight seal and eagerly tasting her tongue. There was only the faintest of resistance before she yielded to him and then reciprocated the repeat kiss they shared from months before. There was no doubt that she had liked it before and that he'd seen through her.

Con looked around nervously, wondering if anyone else could see them, Kovacs in particular. He was still standing halfway between the door and the bar, making sure that the Colombians weren't slipping by them, and the Colombians were just beginning to notice that their partner had lost her mark. They would find out where she'd gone soon enough, and he had to make certain that John wasn't caught off guard.

He'd heard most of the discussion, but just watching the two of them together, he couldn't tell if she'd seduced him or if his friend was still in control of the situation, and it was part of his plan. Just to be sure, he made his way across the dance floor to give him fair warning that the others would be coming.

"Am I interrupting something?"

The brunette seemed less surprised to see him than she had John, and seemed to be genuinely perturbed that their make out session had been interrupted.

"It seems that we've come to an understanding," John said as he turned to greet his friend. "This is Nicole and she's decided to be cooperative."

Connelly looked her up and down, though not in the flattering fashion the other men were, as though she was actually able to conceal any kind of weapon in her ridiculously-revealing dress. None of her curves seemed out of place and there weren't any bumps that didn't belong.

"So she knows the score and what we're here to do?"

"I'm right here and I understand English, so you can talk to me," she snapped at him.

Connelly's eyes narrowed at her and he pressed his own frame towards her, though not in the pleasant way that his partner had. "If I had it my way, I'd drag you out into the fucking street by your hair and bash that pretty face of yours in. You might've conned my friend into sparing your worthless ass, but you won't fool me twice!"

"I'm not afraid of you--"

"Enough!" John stepped in between them. "You're not off the hook yet, Nicole! Whether you walk away tonight from this depends entirely on you. We talked and I decided that it might be more practical to have her on our side – for now. If she crosses us, I'll be the *first* one to put a fucking bullet in her face, believe me!"

298

He looked from John to their uncertain ally, still not convinced, and the look in his eyes was a warning to the both of them. If he messed this up, it was his ass. If she messed it up, it was her life.

"Look, I know we're not best of friends but I can help you. I know how many of these guys there are, where they're at, and what their plan is. Without me, you might not get very far, so you either trust me, or you try to go it alone. Good luck if you do!"

He frowned at the both of them, giving them a disgusted look and then growled, "Let's go!"

They signaled to Frank at the bar as they made their way towards the door, Nicole in tow, making sure that they walked slowly enough for the two Colombians to notice them. According to her, there was another one outside the bar, watching from across the street, and another waiting by the car in the parking garage. She helped them navigate past the one at the door and to the black Mercedes they recognized from that night at the Pub. The man standing guard at the car was blindsided by Connelly, who came from the other direction and sent him sprawling to the pavement with a haymaker to the back of the head.

As he kicked him a few more times just for good measure, Nicole took his keys and handed them to John. The three of them squealed out of the parking garage, making sure that her two friends were still following and Frank right behind them. They hopped into a green BMW, tearing off after them, and Frank was a bit more subtle in his own BMW, staying a few car lengths behind them as they raced up A1A towards the express way.

"So what's your plan?" Nicole asked, watching the car behind them in the side mirror.

"To enjoy the ride, enjoy the scenery and play it by ear," he said calmly.

"So you don't have a plan? Do you at least know where you're going?"

"Somewhere familiar," he said, changing lanes and whipping around a silver Mazda.

"So you *do* have a plan? There are three of them and they have guns, just so you know."

"I can handle it. What's your connection with them?"

"What do you mean?"

"Are you with one of them?"

299

"As in dating? Not exclusively, no why, what's it to you?"

"Because this might get messy once we stop," he said with an odd finality in his tone.

She looked quietly out the window and her cool and calm demeanor crumbled into her lap. There was a silence then in the cabin of the vehicle, and though it was her car, she seemed incredibly uncomfortable there. She wouldn't let it show in her face, but her hands fidgeted and her leg swayed gently from side to side. John reached his right hand over and placed it on her leg to steady her.

"I can let you out anytime. You don't have to come with us."

"I can't believe I let you talk me into this," she said, her voice wavering.

"You've let worse men talk you into doing far more."

"How do I know you're any better than them? You work with the Galliannis?"

"I didn't buy this suit on a McDonald's salary."

"Well, they're not good men either."

"I asked you if you wanted to get out from under the Colombians. This is how you get out. If you would rather be back there with them, working small scores, say the word."

Connelly couldn't believe what he was hearing. Johnny had worked some kind of deal with her, promised her something that wasn't his to promise, and negotiating on the behalf of the Galliannis. If they survived the night, Vincent would probably shoot her in the head and have Frank dump her in the everglades, George would probably do the same. They didn't work with the Colombians or anyone that associated with them; even a small time guy like him knew that. Johnny had to know that, and if he did, then how did he plan on making good on his promises to her?

"I told you I would set you up and get you away from those guys."

"But why would you do that? Especially for me...someone you should hate?"

"Why do you do what you do? You keep pulling these scores hoping that you'll forget about that hole in the middle of your chest, and it does for a little while, but it never really goes away. You find yourself busy destroying yourself most days, and every once in a while, you find something that's a…worthwhile distraction."

Connelly rolled his eyes in the back seat as he listened to his best friend reveal far too much of himself to a complete stranger. It wasn't as though he didn't know exactly what was going on with him, but he'd never been as candid or open with him.

"I'm a worthwhile distraction?" She asked.

"Don't take offense."

"I don't…I think that's the nicest thing anyone has ever said to me," she said, grinning at him.

She stopped fidgeting with her hands and wrapped one of them around his. Connelly studied her from the back seat as she did the same to the driver, each trying to peer through hardened layers to find something more vulnerable and more honest. Whether or not she could see that in John, he couldn't tell, but he knew it was still in there and the people who'd tried breaking him – her included – hadn't succeeded. He wasn't as corrupt or empty as a Vincent Gallianni or a Frank Kovacs, and he hoped that day would never come.

Watching her eyes searching for that man only he knew, Connelly wondered if she was looking for an opening to exploit like before, or if she just wanted reassurance that she could trust him. What reason did she have to trust him? That slender hand that rested comfortably atop his had once worked to undo him, and by rights, he should've returned the favor instead of giving her a second opportunity to do the same. That's how he knew that the old Johnny was in there - the one who had a talent for finding goodness in most everyone, and forgiveness for the rest, no matter the situation.

This girl, who was at the center of Frank's plot, would either bring him ruin or she would fix the damage that she'd caused. Those were Frank's words, and he thought on them deeply as he watched her every move, trying to determine which outcome was most likely. She was trouble – that much was certain – but was she as lost as those other men too, or was she lost like John and still reachable?

Those questions tumbling over and over in his mind would have to wait, as they were suddenly replaced by new ones as they veered off the expressway. The hotel was just at the end of the street, less than a mile from where they were, which meant there was little time to prepare. He hoped that Frank hadn't gotten too far behind and that he would arrive in time for his part, or things would go very badly.

It was a quick sixty seconds, as John raced up Hillsboro Boulevard and came tearing into the parking lot on the south side of the hotel. Ray's van was at the back corner and he pulled up right behind it, waiting for the Mercedes to arrive. The car pulled in seconds later, and sat idling at the entrance for a long while, making the occupants of the BMW more on edge.

"What the hell are they waiting for?" John grumbled.

"Maybe they're spooked and thinking about running," Connelly suggested.

"Maybe they're loading up for a quick drive by," John snipped.

"What do you want to do?" Nicole finally asked.

"I want you to stay close to the van. If the shooting starts, I want you to let yourself inside."

"What's in the van?"

"Ray…"

"Who's Ray?"

"A guy who won't like Colombians knocking on his door asking about a hot brunette girl."

Nicole slid across the seat to exit from his side and stayed low, making her way towards the back of the van, just as she'd been told. Both front and rear doors opened and four Colombians got out, but didn't appear armed. They stood beside their vehicle the same as John, in case they needed to make a quick exit. What happened next surprised John as much as it did those four guys in the Benz.

From the side of the van came Ray with a shotgun that looked as big as he was, and he didn't appear to be staggering like was his usual Saturday ritual. He approached the Mercedes with the shotgun leveled at the four men, and John could tell even from where he stood that the color had drained from their cheeks. They knew, at that moment, that they'd been set up and this had been planned from the start.

From the hedges at the east end of the lot that separated it from the beach, a second gunman appeared. He was much smaller and had skin as tanned as the Indian, but his size wasn't a concern, it was the assault carbine he was waving at them. Once he was in place, only ten yards from the Mercedes, a third man came from the south. He was the one they'd seen at the club in Lauderdale with the sharp suit and the slicked black hair. There wasn't a small sub-machine gun in his hands like there was now.

The last man to appear was George Gallianni himself, stepping from the front door of the hotel, hands in his pockets, but no doubt, armed just the same.

"You fucking wetbacks are in the wrong parking lot – again!"

One of them was brave enough to speak, "Your boy took one of our friends from the club."

"So what if he did? This aint fucking Colombia! It's a free country and you don't own her!"

"We came to take her home."

George turned towards the van and called out, "You want to stay or go with these guys?"

She appeared from the back of the van and stood very close to John saying, "I'm staying, Carlos."

"The fuck you are!" He snarled and moved towards her.

George buckled his legs with a ham-fisted shot to the nose.

"You don't fucking move until I tell you to! She says she's staying! That means you fucking leave and never come back here again! I won't tell you a third time!"

"We'll be back!" The man said, holding his busted nose. "And we'll bring a fucking army!"

"Well now you just said the wrong thing. Seems we have a…predicament don't we?"

George just looked at him and shook his head. Connelly would never forget that gesture for as long as he lived, because it was just like the Emperor at the coliseum giving the thumb – their fate was sealed in that subtle nod. The trio moved in on them like wolves and started tearing them apart right there in the Island Pub parking lot. They didn't give it a thought; the lot was their territory and they were protecting that territory, just like wolves do.

John came late to the feast, and found that all four of the men were already on the ground, bleeding badly, and the fight was mostly gone out of them. The alpha stepped back and offered the pup some of the kill, once he'd already had his share. He grimaced at him in recognition. It was the one that attacked him and kicked

303

him in the face. He repaid the favor, stomping the man furiously until he stopped screamed for mercy, the way the rest of them had before they were silenced.

Breathing heavily, John leaned over the one called Carlos and rooted through his pockets, producing a roll of cash wrapped in rubber bands. Tearing the band away, he thumbed through the bills, counting out thirty-three hundred dollars. He bent lower so the man could hear him.

"I promised myself that I would get this back from you one day," he said, waving the money in his face. "Thirty-three hundred dollars that you obviously needed more than I did, so you left me bleeding in this same lot, wondering what I'd done to deserve being beaten that way and left with nothing."

George held a fistful of his hair so that he was forced to stare into the face of the man who'd sealed his fate that night many months before. John could only stare down in disgust, shaking his head, holding the price of the man's life in his right hand, still contemplating the final stroke of his revenge.

He crushed the money into a wad and crammed it into his mouth as he condemned him, "Are you wondering what you did to deserve this Carlos? Is your memory hazy? I'm going to let you keep this money so that you can think about it while they're burying you! Thirty-three hundred dollars that you'll never get to enjoy."

Frank signaled to Connelly then, indicating that he should leave and take John and Nicole with him. One last glance over his shoulder was enough to tell him was what going to happen next, and he didn't need to see the rest. Kovacs and the others loaded them into their own car - two of them into the trunk and the other two in the back seat – Danny got behind the wheel, and George slapped the roof of the car before it disappeared up A1A.

Chapter 28

Gwenn had left her seat at the table about halfway through Connelly's commentary. He'd been very thorough about the details, and she'd asked him to spare her none. It was one thing to hear about her husband getting into bar scrapes or even having to do some things that weren't "above board" to get by, but being involved with murderers was too much for her.

He'd spent years putting men like that away, and John Chapel was one of the "good guys", or so she once believed. While she and John had their own blend of troubles, she'd always prided them on the fact that there were very few topics that they felt were taboo, and with the exception of work cases, there were almost no secrets between them. When his hand had been forced and he had to kill a suspect in self-defense, Gwenn was the one confided in and broke down in front of; not some police shrink.

She'd watched her husband actually cry that night, weeping for some piece of murdering garbage whose life he'd taken. That was the sort of man John Chapel was, not the sort Connelly was describing. He wasn't the kind of man who would watch with indifference as four men – even bad men - were sent to their deaths, and he certainly wasn't the kind that was implicit in a plot to take lives out of revenge.

Over the last three days, she realized just how much of a stranger John Chapel was to her, and that the thing she'd prized most about their relationship never existed. She'd been his champion for as long as she could remember, and her absolute faith in him had been unwavering, despite every logical argument Campbell had thrown at her – arguments that she was beginning to accept.

That was the worst part of it all; while the mysterious girlfriend wasn't the worst of his secrets coming to the surface, she served as the final nail to hammer the lid closed on his theory about her husband's fate.

"I know what you're going to say…and I don't want to hear it right now," she choked out in a quivering voice as she stared out the window.

"Then you already understand the implications of Mr. Connelly's story?" Campbell said quietly, smoothing his palms over his slacks.

"I understand that my husband…kept a lot of things from me," she said, still facing the window.

"I'm sure John never meant to hurt you, Gwenn," Connelly interjected. "He wanted to forget all about that life and leave it behind."

"But he didn't *leave it behind* did he? It caught up with him…"

The reference was lost on Connelly altogether. He'd only been told the basics of John's condition and that it stemmed from repressed memories and other clinical terms that were foreign to him, not the more intimate details. Campbell decided that it was finally time to let him in on exactly why he'd been asked to come and why Gwenn looked as though someone just walked across her grave.

"John suffered from recurring nightmares and delusions about people that existed only in his subconscious. Gwenn and I have been drawing parallels between John's reality and his fantasy world, in an attempt to arrive at some conclusion about his condition. One of the central figures in this alternate reality was a girl named Nicolette, and there were still a few questions pertaining to her origins…until now."

"There are so many complexities and nuances about this girl that he hasn't mentioned yet…"

She tried to argue still, yet knew that she didn't have a leg to stand on. The girl she'd never known was just another face to add to the list. Not because he necessarily had some torrid, heart-rending affair with her like he did with Melinda, but because he'd kept her hidden from her. He'd kept all of it hidden from her, and like Campbell said, it was that guilt that eventually shattered him.

Campbell shook his head sadly at her, "It seems that discussion is now at a close, Gwenn, and maybe now we can turn our attention to other things."

"So that's it?" Her voice sounded very hollow and empty, as if coming from the bottom of a well. "This *girl in the rain* was his anthropomorphizing of his guilt and regrets and he gave her this woman's name?"

"I would wager that when John initially began having dreams about the blonde woman from Avandale, she had no name at all, just like his mysterious man of the forest and some of the others. I think that assigning this name in particular to her was his own way of opening up and exposing his own secrets that were eating at him."

"And he changed the names later; randomly assigning them to the people he had the nightmares about?"

"Sometimes these alters take a long time to take shape and assume identities of their own. It's common for them to not have names at all in these beginning stages."

"I don't understand any of this…" she whimpered, her voice trailing off. "But what makes the least amount of sense is him not telling me about this girl if she was just some ex-girlfriend. He wouldn't have gone to all of this trouble to hide her from me or need some weird closure with her by writing her name in a journal…if there was really nothing between them."

She continued to pace the small room, and her mounting anxiety and frustration were as palpable as the bitter drink sitting in front of Campbell. There was really nothing more to debate, and it seemed that she was just splitting hairs over minor aspects of the story, looking for some small victory to save face. He sipped at his drink as he patiently waited for her to concede and finally admit defeat, not wanting to upset her further by pushing the issue.

Seeing that he had nothing more to say, she looked to Connelly for an answer to the question she'd not really asked of anyone directly.

"The whole Johnny-Nicole thing wasn't exactly your conventional relationship, Gwenn," he explained. "She was a criminal and had more issues than Melinda and John put together. They argued a lot and there were some pretty big fights, so I'm sure there's a list as long as my arm of reasons he might've had regrets."

Gwenn stepped closer to the table, leaning on the back of her chair, studying his face. She'd known Jeremy Connelly a long time, and though he'd made a living out of being a professional liar, every once in a while she could pick up that small twitch of his eye or curl of his lip. There was something he wasn't telling her.

"What happened between John and this girl, Jeremy?"

"Melinda…"

Chapter 29

Things were good again, at the cost of only four lives and the procurement of one girlfriend – an acceptable cost to have John "back" to his old self. He was hanging out at the Pub again, with Danny, Ray, Gary and Connelly, and they were glad to have him back. Nicole was a regular fixture there as well, and she was easy on the eyes as well as a serious drinker (giving Ray and Danny a run for their money). She seemed happy there and was part of a family, not just part of a crew that pulled scams on people, and there wasn't a safer place for her to be in all of south Florida.

She was just what John needed, and he was just what she needed. They shared John's suite upstairs, and Jeremy finally ranked enough to get his own room, which gave them some privacy. They needed it with all the intense fighting and making up they did; there was probably never a more dysfunctional "couple" than those two, but they were crazy about each other.

Gary deliberately kept the top floor clear and frequently had to move other guests and compensate rooms that had to overhear one of those battles. It would start in the Island Pub attached to the hotel, usually over some girl flirting with John or Nicole having too much to drink, and they would take it upstairs where anything went. Lamps were broken, TV remotes were tossed through the sliding patio glass, and mirrors were ripped off the walls. Then, in the aftermath, among broken glass and tipped over chairs, they would make up just as intensely as they had fought.

The next morning, John stopped by the front desk and left an envelope of money for Gary, who would use it to hire some guys to fix the room up again. It was actually profitable to have weekly repair bulls, because John always paid far in excess of the damage, and compensated him for the money lost if he had to comp rooms.

For all their fighting and intensity, there was a softer side to the both of them that only seemed to come out when the other was around. Anyone who saw them together would have thought they were newlyweds, and anyone that heard them upstairs would have no doubts about that at all.

George put Nicole's talents to good use, primarily because he could use another dependable person on the payroll, but also to give John some breathing room. If they were left together too long, they probably would have burned the Oceanside down to the ground. It also made Nicole feel as if she served a purpose and was pulling her own weight. He was just as generous with her payoffs as he was with John, but she earned it.

Instead of rolling out-of-towners from up north and luring them into parking lots to get beat up, she was rolling much bigger targets. One of George's favorite "scores" to pull was knocking over Semi trucks or warehouses full of goods, and then moving the product through his drop off cars. He used to send a couple of heavies like Ray and Danny to rough up the truck driver or security guard in the old days. Now that he had a knockout girl like Nicole on the payroll, he used her to "distract and extract", as he called it.

Things had been great with Nicole and working with George, there was talk of more permanent relationships on both fronts. She and John had been together almost a year by the summer of 93', and were even shopping condos in Delray Beach. George was talking about a partnership with Johnny, giving him a bigger cut, and working more jobs with his brother. He felt that with a sharp guy like him, there would be opportunity with the bigger players.

This was all discussed one night in July at their regular table at the Pub, long after closing time. Everyone seemed to be in good spirits, old animosities fizzled into the air and it crackled with something else. Only John seemed not to notice, his attention captured by some faraway place beyond the glass patio door, and he excused himself to catch some air. It was Connelly that followed him, being the only one who could read the well-disguised worry in his face.

"What's going on man?"

"Feels like...rain," John murmured, taking a drink.

"It's south Florida, it rains every five minutes," Con joked.

"Not like that...see the lightning over the water? A storm is coming."

There was fear in his voice, and it was something he rarely heard in John Chapel's tone.

"Things are good with Nicole? You guys are shopping for condos…"

"Things couldn't be better with her," John said, staring out over the water.

"George? He's talking about taking things seriously. Are you worried about that?"

"A little, but that's not it."

"You're ready for this man! You've worked hard for this…for this whole thing. You've come a long way since that day we were bailed on, Johnny."

"I have worked for this…but I'm not sure that this is what I want, Jer. This is something we did short term, to survive, so that we could go home. Is this the life that we always thought we'd have? Working with guys like George and living in hotels? I had something else planned, Con, and this isn't what I saw for myself at all when I graduated from school."

"Yea, you're right…most of the guys who graduated with us had mommy and daddy pay for college and about now, they're starting their third year of college, eating Ramen noodles and scraping together beer cans to get to their next party. In another year, they'll move back home and be pounding the pavement for a job that starts out at thirty grand a year, if they're lucky."

"I've heard the George speech before. I know how much money we make."

"Then what? Nicole? You getting cold feet? I don't think the girl wants to settle down right now – not a girl like her – but what's wrong with a move in that direction? She's crazy about you and you could do a lot worse. You have done a lot worse…"

"Nicole is a mess…and I'm a mess…and together we're okay with that. I don't ever see us really settling down and starting a family. I don't see a life other than this one for us, and if things ever changed, I see myself waking up to an empty bed one day beside a 'Dear John' letter."

"Well, your name is John…it makes sense."

"You're an idiot."

"Trying to lighten the mood. Do I see her as the stay-at-home mom type? Not really. I can't even imagine that, but she's only twenty-one, she has a lot of living to do, maybe she'll want that someday. You need to talk to her about it, not me, man."

"I've tried…she changes the subject when I talk about kids. I don't think that's in the cards for us man…and I don't want to waste my time or hers."

"You're barely twenty, Johnny, why the hell are you talking about this shit? Every guy we know back home would kill to have your life right now, why are you trying to sabotage yourself?"

"This ride can't last forever, Jer, not for me. George and Nicole are talking about the next step, and that scares me on both accounts. If I take that leap, I'm in this life for good, and this isn't the life for me."

"And do what? Punch in for a nine-to-five and work your ass off for scraps? Come home to a nagging wife who's miserable because she stays home all day and takes care of some snot-faced kids?"

"That sounds kind of nice…kind of normal."

"Your mom screwed you up brother, and you just want to make up for her fuckups as a parent. It's not your fault, Johnny…"

"I don't want to be anything like her, Con!" He snapped at him and slammed his drink down.

She probably hadn't given John a single thought since she abandoned him, but Connelly knew he still worried about her. Victoria Chapel was partly responsible for that "hole" in the center of him that he'd once mentioned to Nicole, but she wasn't the one he was most worried about or who he was even talking about at that moment. He saw that old look in his eyes again as he stared out at the rain falling into the rolling tide – the same longing, far off look he had the night dragged them to Troy.

Nicole put Melinda to shame in a side to side comparison. She was more attractive, had a body that wouldn't stop and she was a woman, not a childish little girl. Nicole wasn't without her problems, but she owned up to them and made no excuses for them, while Melinda was just a mess without a beginning or an end. Despite all that, and defying all logic, there was still something there, deep down, that was unfinished with her.

Kovacs thought he'd fixed the problem by putting a Band-Aid on it – it was a pretty Band-Aid, but a Band-Aid nonetheless. Nicole was a temporary fix, and that hole was growing daily and eating him from the inside again. There really was only one solution, and unfortunately, it was a solution that wasn't an option.

His friend was going to fall apart and there wasn't a damned thing anyone could do about it.

After a long silence, he finally said, "I talked to Gwenn yesterday."

John sounded homesick and he thought news of home – any news – might either cheer him up or make him less homesick.

"Oh? I haven't heard from her in a while, what did she have to say?"

"Things are about the same. She's still going to OCC for Medicine; Dean is going to U of M for Engineering. Family is about the same."

"Melinda?"

"The same...things haven't changed, Johnny, and they're not going to."

"I should've stayed there. I should never have come here," he grumbled.

"The point is home isn't what home used to be, Johnny. All the guys have moved on, our friends back there have moved on, and *she* has moved on. We have to learn to move on."

The talk of home didn't seem to help. There was an expression on his face as he looked out at the black ocean even darker than the starless night sky. It wasn't a look of misery, it was just a look of complacency and that was something much worse for a man like John Chapel.

"She hasn't *moved on*, Jeremy; she's living under the thumb of a fucking drug-dealer! That girl is destroying herself because I made her feel like she's worthless, and now he continues to make her feel the same!"

"What about Nicole? She was doing the same thing until you came along. Do you want to undo all of that? That girl is finally happy, man, and you want to throw it away? Do you know what that would do to her?"

"It's not my job to keep her alive," he said coldly.

The look on Connelly's face as he stared over John's shoulder drew his attention towards the sliding door of the balcony. He didn't need to look to know she was there; he felt the long shadow fall across his back and felt the harsh silence that fell with it. He didn't want to look beyond that shadow, for shadows don't wear expressions that make you regret something terribly stupid that you've said. And shadows never weep.

313

He called after her as she disappeared from the doorway, and would've chased her out into the parking lot and across A1A in the rain, but he was stopped by the very serious expression of Gary Polidoro, barring his way. Connelly watched as he whispered something to him and John followed him from the front door towards the back office. There was a call waiting for him.

Connelly took a seat at the "round table" just outside the office, waiting for John to fill him in about the call. It was very brief and there were few words exchanged before he sat hard in Gary's desk chair and the receiver fell limply from his fingers.

John didn't bother looking up at the shape that filled up the doorway and cast a long shadow over him. There were too many other shadows dancing in his cold eyes for him to notice.

"That was her?" He asked nervously.

"Gwenn," he replied simply.

"Something's happening back home?"

In a voice that sounded a million miles away he replied, "They found her in the park…they found Melinda at Rain tree…"

Transcript of recorded session with John F. Chapel
November 7th
Dr. James Campbell

Campbell: "I suppose you could say that it's kind of poetic that a phone call from a woman took you far from home and another brought you home."

John: "Things weren't going so well down there anyway, and I knew that the time had come to head back and leave that life behind...it just wasn't for me."

Campbell: "Evenings on the town, beautiful women, and lots of sunshine and tropical breezes sound like a terrible way for a twenty-year old man to live, John."

John: "Everyone has to grow up eventually, Jim. Well...except maybe Connelly. That sort of place was perfect for him, and he really had no attachments to either place. As for me, I'd left too many things unfinished when I'd left, and I never planned on being gone as long as I was."

Campbell: "You'd only gone to retrieve your mother, and that didn't quite go how you'd planned? You're sure you don't want to tell me the details? It might help to talk about it."

John: "Like I told you before; there isn't much to tell. In classic Victoria Chapel fashion, she let a man bail her ass out of trouble – this time her own son – and then she turned and ran the other way. I have no regrets about her, Jim, or making the decision I made back then."

Campbell: "Even though it seemed to cost you Miss Malowski?"

John: "I think that it was inevitable that I was going to lose her anyway – even if I'd stayed. Our mothers did their share of ruining us long before that day."

Campbell: "It sounds as though you've found forgiveness with your mother at least?"

John: "Some people just don't change, Jim, no matter how much you try to change them. So, you have to accept them for who they are...or just walk away."

Campbell: "But you had hoped that maybe they would change didn't you?"

John: "I'm not going to lie; I thought maybe after twenty years and enough bad situations, my mother might've finally come to her senses. It was more than just going to help her out of a bad spot..."

Campbell: "You were hoping for a reconciliation?"

John: "I was, but in the back of my mind, I kind of expected to be let down just like I was when I came home."

Campbell: "More specifically we're not talking about cries for help that lured you away from home and back again, but opportunities for setting things right?"

John: "Gwenn always accused me of trying to play the *hero*, but that couldn't have been further from the truth; I only wanted to fix the things I'd felt that I was responsible for breaking."

Campbell: "But neither of those women was 'broken' as a result of anything you'd done, John. Why did you feel so compelled to keep trying then, if what you say is true?"

John: "I understand that now, as a grown man, but back then I felt differently. My mother made it clear that I was constantly holding her back and that I'd changed the course of her life negatively from the moment I was born."

Campbell: "She guilted you? So you felt as if you owed her something?"

John: "It's irrational to think that way, but as a young boy, I didn't understand."

Campbell: "And Miss Malowski?"

John: "Same thing. Even though I recognize every outside factor that influenced our young lives now, at the time I had a much simpler view of things. I left her and I chose my mother over her – just like she accused me of – and I carried that guilt with me all the way to Florida and it ate at me for two years."

Campbell: "And every bit of it came bubbling back to the surface when you received that call that day? I can only imagine what was going through your mind."

John: "I was devastated. Not only because I'd felt that what happened to her was my fault, but because I'd lost the opportunity to ever go back and fix things with her."

Campbell: "But you were given another chance weren't you?"

John: "That's a difficult question to answer. When I called from Tennessee on our way home to see how she was doing, I breathed a sigh of relief when Gwenn told me the news. But that relief was cut short when I realized what I was walking into."

Campbell: "You wrote here that everyone thought that she wouldn't pull through the first night, but she not only survived, she was unfazed by what had just happened?"

John: "Gwenn and Dean both told me that when they saw her at the hospital, she looked like she was already dead. But by the time I'd arrived, less than thirty-six hours after the call, she had already checked herself out and ran back to Sal."

Campbell: "It sounds like you had your work cut out for you."

John: "I was walking into the fight of my life...and was completely unprepared. It would've been easier if I just had to walk in there and bust a couple of heads – Connelly and I had done some of that in Florida – but I was up against an enemy I couldn't beat with my fists."

Campbell: "It's far easier for men to destroy than to build, and you weren't just trying to rebuild this shattered girl; you were trying to rebuild your home."

John: "It definitely wasn't the place I'd left two years before...I hardly recognized it."

Campbell: "Yes, I read something about a very distraught young man's homecoming and a battle to save a girl from herself and the man who'd brought ruin to his home...to his *sanctuary*."

John: "You're doing it again."

Campbell: "I'm doing only what you asked me to do. This is your story, your journal..."

John: "This other man's return home was nothing like mine, Jim."

Campbell: "Nothing like it at all."

John: "You're not very good at the sarcasm."

Campbell: "So I've been told. I'll give it to you straight then. I see very little variation between your homecoming and this blacksmith's; the stories are almost identical."

John: "I'd love to hear exactly how you think they're identical..."

SANCTUARY BROKEN

"Where thou art, that is home"

~Emily Dickinson

Chapter 30

Harold and John had buried Elizabeth and her child, left Ann in the care of the neighbor widow and Pelleon, and amassed a small army of fifty men to track down those responsible for the massacre at Rouen – all in the span of one week. Richard had not been as generous as initially promised in supplying men for the task, but he had provided the intelligence necessary for finding the origin of the invaders. His spies tracked the survivors back to their home, several miles to the west, to a small village of Normandy.

The same red banners that were emblazoned upon their shields were flying high from the ramparts of the old tower that John instantly recognized. He hadn't noticed them that night under the shroud of darkness and the single-minded mission of finding the woman he loved, but Harold assured him that they'd been flying there for some time. Avandale had been turned into a glorified war camp for the enemies of Rouen and of their patron, the Duke of Aquitaine.

When he'd last seen that place, a few extra homes had been added just beyond the tower, where the valley dipped sharply, housing the new military force brought in to protect Avandale. Now, those homes had tripled in number and the tower that watched over them all had been restored to a fully-functioning fortification for the business of war.

Additions had been made to the base of the tower, connecting it with the chapel and the new blacksmiths shop (which put his to shame back home), and there was a fortified wall running the length and breadth of the top of the hill, that was at the highest point of Avandale. It was no longer a simple, broken-down tower, it was a small fortress and it looked out of place in the sleepy, mist-covered valley. The tower seemed to scowl at him and he scowled back.

He turned his horse and pushed his way through the men, and they gave him a wide berth, for every one of them respected the "butcher of Rouen", and feared him just the same. Harold was already surveying the valley and forming one of his plans, so he hadn't noticed John until he was some distance away.

Prodding his horse back down the hill, he called after him, "John, this isn't a one-man battle, I need ye' to wait until we've prepared a proper strategy."

"I wasn't planning on riding in first," John said, not meeting Harold's gaze.

"Well good, we don't need heroics on this one; we'll need every man to make sure that no one leaves this place."

"I wasn't planning on riding in at all. I'm sitting this one out, Harold."

The old knight would've looked less surprised if his friend sprouted horns. "What do ye' mean, yer sitting this out?"

"Most of those people down there are innocents, and I didn't come to slaughter innocents."

"There are no *innocents* down there, boy! Ye' knew what this was when ye' agreed to come along! Ye' knew there would be bloodshed, and ye've talked of nothing since we buried the girls."

"I won't ride down peasants beside you and those others! Show me a soldier, a fighting man with a sword in his hand, and I'll be the first to put his head on a pike...but not those people!"

"Those soldiers didn't spare a soul and play by gentleman's rules, they cut down everyone in their path – they need to suffer as we have!"

"So we burn their homes down? Slaughter their children? Just so they know what it's like to come home to nothing? That makes us no better Harold!"

"Better or not, they are our enemy!"

"Are they? What of George? He is a friend! He is your family!"

"So that's it? Ye' don't have the stomach to kill anymore because of a girl?"

"That *girl* is Elizabeth's niece and technically *your* family too!"

"That's right, and she betrayed her own family when she bedded down with our enemy!"

"You don't know what you're talking about, and I'm not having this discussion with you! Take your men and go slaughter defenseless women and children, just like the animals that came to Rouen!"

322

"Those animals took Elizabeth and Mary!"

"They're gone now, and no amount of blood spilled on the ground will bring them from it!"

"Yer judgment is being clouded by some foolish whore, and she's nothing to me...just so ye' know, I won't hesitate to cut her down!"

"And *yours* is clouded by your foolish bloodlust and pride! I'm not letting you hurt her! Take the rest, but leave her be she's been through enough!"

"Ye' don't get to give orders here, boy! I'm the one that gives the orders, and I say that every single one of those people down there is going to be buried by the end of this day!"

John placed his hand on the pommel of his sword and gave him a fierce stare, "*Orders*? Who's going to enforce that order, you? Which of you is going to stop me from defending this place?"

"T'would be a grave mistake siding with the enemies of Richard," he threatened, circling John. "Especially protecting the life of a worthless whore who sent ye' away and wants nothing to do with you!"

"I'm not trying to save these people for *her*! There is nothing between us any longer!"

"You were *infatuated* with her; I remember you bellyachin' and crying in your ale, and here ye' are again, acting like a foolish child instead of a man!"

"I'm trying to protect these people for Elizabeth...and for Mary. Neither of them would want this and you know it! We're not butchers, Harold, we're better than this!"

"Oh, yer a butcher, alright, I watched you kill those men, John! Ye' bathed in their blood and ye' embraced it like no man I've ever seen before! Yer a killer and we've come to do killin'! And don't ye' dare preach to me about what those girls wanted, they're dead now because of you!"

"Because of *me*? Where were *you*? You had an entire army - I'm just one man! How was it that you missed those soldiers exactly? How did you let them slip past you? If you'd done your part we wouldn't be having this discussion!"

"That's *my* sister and niece you're talkin' so reckless about! I would've cut down any other man for speaking of them that way," he snarled.

323

"Yes they were your sister and niece, and they were *your* responsibility not *mine*! You left them there with me and you left me to do *your* job - which I gladly did!"

"What does that mean?"

"It means I loved them too! They were *my* family too! You forget that I went home to them every night! You didn't. I'm the one who will miss their smiles and laughter. I'm the one who will miss suppers waiting for me! How many nights were you there for that, Harold?"

"I won't stand here and listen to this! I won't let ye' dishonor their memories!"

"Nor will I! She would never stand for taking more innocent blood to appease innocent blood! As sure as I stand here, I know that she would never condone this!"

"You didn't know anything about my sister!"

"I loved your sister and I knew her as you never did!"

Harold stepped from his mount at that point, thick fingers gripping his pommel so tightly that they were turning white. His face glowed red, and his forehead became a crisscross of knots and deep valleys, as pure rage took hold of him. Circling John, he hesitated and kept his blade still housed for the time being. Either he shared the sentiment of the other men or there was still some other sentiment holding him at bay.

"She never had the heart to tell you Harold. I'm sorry, I wanted to, but she wouldn't allow it."

"Never would she have dishonored me or William in that way..." He choked out.

"William himself told me to take care of his family – he knew he was sick. And you weren't there...you were off fighting a war. She was left alone with two girls to bury a dead husband. How do you think she got along so well over the past year Harold? How many lonely nights do you think she endured just to keep her brother happy?"

"My sister was a strong woman and she didn't need a man to get along!"

"She was *miserable* being alone in that house and with you gone, she turned to me! You and William pushed that responsibility on me, and at least *he* saw that. She was vulnerable and heartbroken, and you wanted her to be alone the rest of her days like you?"

324

"So she turned to a nineteen-year-old boy? Now I've heard it all! She would never have lowered herself to be with a man like you," he said, laughing uproariously.

"A man like me? One who listened to her and talked to her about things besides war and blacksmithing? A man who helped her with her daily work and with the girls – not just bringing coin home and expecting supper for it?"

"She would have told me!"

"It was more important to her that your feelings and your pride were spared. That's why she had to hide her happiness when you came home. She had to pretend not to love one of the few things that gave her any joy!"

"She wouldn't have hidden anything from me."

"She hid a lot of things from you Harold, and from William. She spared you just like I spared you! I ran into that blaze after the woman and the family I loved! *I* was the one! *I* saw what they did to them so that *you* wouldn't have to! I *protected* you just as she would have wanted. Don't tell me I have no right to speak of them!"

"You're a liar!" He screamed, finally loosing his blade and leveling it at him. "That girl isn't worth this, John!"

"This isn't about her, I told you that! But she is among the innocent here, and I won't allow you to harm any of them!"

"There are no innocents here! Reginald of Poitou sent those men who cut down Elizabeth! He is allied with the barons who work against Richard, and your whore lies on her back in his bed! That makes her the enemy!"

"Nicolette did what she had to for her father and her people, she is not to blame!"

"Her father? George isn't here in Avandale; he's gone to his cousin's in (place). Reginald and his whore decided that he was no longer useful, and had him replaced!"

"I don't believe you!"

"Let's go to the tower together and see for ourselves then."

"You're not stepping foot in that tower, Harold, so long as I breathe!"

Harold roared like a grizzly and brought down his sword in powerful overhead sweep, and the epic battle between master and pupil had begun. John intercepted his blows deftly, but the sheer force of the attacks drove him backwards towards the onlookers.

They whispers flying among them favored Harold, and had they any coin, it would've exchanged hands in wager. Despite some of the outlandish rumors about the 'butcher of Rouen', Harold's fearsomeness and martial skill were legendary, and they knew better than to wager against him.

John lasted much longer on his feet than most of them had given him credit for, however, and some of those more superstitious among the group began to fear for their leader. Harold came at him with the ferocity of a raging beast, wielding his sword with more skill than all of those men had put together, but his protégé lost little ground and seemed tireless as he matched his opponent blow for blow. After several minutes, the larger, more skilled fighter seemed to be wearing down and his movements slowing, but John appeared as agile as he was at the start of the fight.

Harold was well aware of his waning vigor as well as his opponent's seemingly endless reserve of the stuff, and knew that he had to change his tactics to defeat him. Drawing him in with a feint, he lowered his shoulder, gripped his shield as hard as he could, and trampled him like a berserk elephant. John flew backwards with such a force that the wind was knocked from him, and the spectators were certain that the fight was over.

He writhed in the wet grass, trying to catch his breath as Harold stood above him, trying to catch his own. The angered bear-man stared at him with beady eyes and studied his prey, deciding whether or not he was worth engaging again. He turned slowly and called to the other men to resume their course.
But the man would not be stopped. He righted itself and spat on the ground at his larger opponent, challenging him once more. There was determination in his eyes, though none could be found in his step as he still wobbled from the impressive blow that had been dealt him.

"Why don't ye' stay down John? Why don't ye' just stay where ye' lay, and let those of us with the stomach for what needs to be done go about our business?"

John's knuckles creaked as they tightened into fists. Knees locked and shoulders back, he righted himself and inhaled deeply to puff up his chest and get his blood flowing again. He'd left his sword and hatchet on the ground where they'd been knocked from his fingers – he wouldn't need them for what came next.

"More than stomachs are needed for what needs to be done here," he said hoarsely. "Men of conscience are needed, and it looks like I'm the only one."

"Fair enough," he grumbled, annoyed. "If ye' won't stay down, I will put ye' down. Again and again I'll take ye' to the ground, boy, and I'll hold ye' there until these men are done doing what we came to do. I don't want to hurt ye', but ye' have given me no choice."

John approached with a renewed purpose, unarmed, and that made Harold hesitate in his swing, just long enough to give John the opening he needed. He fired a solid, bone-shattering blow directly into his bulbous nose, forcing the man lurching backwards, arms going limp just long enough for John to press the attack.

He was on top of the roaring grizzly, firing blow after punishing blow into the center of his swelling, bloodied face, unrelenting and unforgiving. Fists, elbows and even knees fired at the old bear-man seemingly from all directions, as though he was being assailed by six men and not just one. John fought with the ferocity of the berserkers of legend, yet his strikes had the precision of a master of martial combat.

The bloodied and defeated man finally fell heavily in the grass, crushing it under his mass as he rolled down the hill. No man stepped forward to go after their fallen leader that lay motionless at the bottom of the mound.

"Anyone else?" He growled at them. "Are there any among you who would defy me?"
There was a long silence, and then from the bottom of the hill a voice called weakly.

"I will defy you...until you have given up," came the words gurgling from ruined lips.

John and the others turned and stared with amazement at the shambling mass making its way back up the incline. They watched him struggle with every step, his thick legs shaking and hands trembling, and every one of them couldn't help but feel the swell of pride within their breasts.

"Damn you Harold, I'll give you the same mercy you offered me: stay down in that grass and let this be. This will not end well for you, because I will not stop or be stopped."

"And I will give ye'...the same answer ye' gave to me in reply," he said, spitting up blood.

"You cannot defeat me, Harold, and everyone here knows this. I do not want this! You will keep coming and I will keep beating you until you don't get up! Only your blood will spill here today!"

Despite the warnings he kept calling out, the defiant man kept coming, only more determined with every word to reach the arrogant boy and teach him a lesson. He gave his own warning as he got closer,

"Ye' still have time to get your sword, boy. I will not hesitate this time. I will give ye' no quarter."

"Damn you, Harold! This has gotten out of hand! I'm not picking up my sword!"

"Pick up your sword! I'm not tellin' ye' again!"

"I'm not fighting you anymore! I'm taking these men back home!"

Harold found strength in his legs once again and charged up the remaining few feet of the hill, dropping his shield so that he could take up his sword in both hands. Bringing it high above his head, he ran straight at John, and brought it down just as he'd promised: without mercy and without hesitation. He'd meant to kill his apprentice.

The sword hit its mark, and John hadn't even tried to evade the blow or sidestep him. He could have, because Harold had become slowed significantly by the beating he'd received, but he chose not to. It was the only way that he might end the fight for good, one way or another. Either the blade would cleave his head from his shoulders, and he would die on that grassy mound in defense of the innocents in the place he loved, or whatever force had protected him on every occasion prior would find a way to do so again.

The sound of steel rang in his ears and the force of the blow dropped him to one knee, almost toppling him completely. Harold finished his downward killing blow, and like the rest, he waited for the head to roll and the blood to come issuing forth from the neck. But it did not flow and his head was still attached. Calmly he stood, and turned to face Harold and the others, rubbing his sore neck and exposing it for all to see.

Many of the men fell from their saddles to their knees and begged mercy. Some even wept and called out the names of their savior and the Holy mother. A few of them crossed themselves, spat on the grass near John and fled back to the east as fast as they could. Harold only let his shoulders droop and the sword fell from his fingers, un-bloodied and as useless to him as the men lying prone around him.

"She was my sister," he mumbled, dazed and defeated. "We owe this to her..."

"I can't believe that you tried to kill me...you were my best friend," he said in disbelief.

"Ye' are not the man I once knew, John," he said with moist, red eyes. "Ye' have the hand of God on ye' for certain, and ye' serve a greater king than any man here. Forgive me..."

He fell to his knees and bowed his head in reverence, and there was such a fear in his eyes the likes of which John had never seen before. It made him uncomfortable, standing there in the center of that circle of humbled men, honoring him as if he was greater than them all. He certainly didn't feel like a great man, having bludgeoned his best friend and humiliated him so, and yet there they were, terrified by him and paying him homage that he didn't deserve.

"Please stand and save your penitence for God," he said, flustered. "I will not have men I've considered friends kneeling before me; it's insulting. We have other concerns to address this night."

"Greater than the miracles worked here?" One of them spoke up.

"We came to this mount to plan an attack, not so that I could give a sermon," John scolded. "I'm no Holy man, but certainly God has worked through me to deliver a message: and that message is that we should show mercy upon these people."

"Then we should ride back to Rouen and share this message," another piped up.

"Yes, God would have us protect this village not destroy it!" The first man spoke again.

"No! We speak nothing of what we've seen this night. This message was intended for us and us alone! We must still bring justice to those who have fallen and not let their murderers go unpunished, but the rest we must spare. There is another way..."

"What is your will, milord," one standing close to him asked, bowing his head.

329

"This once peaceful place has been turned into a military outpost because of the ugliness of war that was brought here by other men. I fear that an outright attack on this place will only cause it to become more determined in its new course."

"As I said," Harold reminded him, "we should raze it to the ground, and leave no one standing."

"And as I said, there is another way," John snapped at him. "They've spent the last two years building this place up, making it defendable, training soldiers, and stockpiling arms…that would be a horrible resource to waste."

"With due respect, John, this isn't the fortress of Taillebourg," Harold said, ever the tactician.

"With due respect, Harold, this isn't Richard's army and neither of us is Richard. This is a clandestine attack to render one of his enemies' outposts useless, and strike a blow for the fallen of Rouen. But it could be *our* Taillebourg, and we could do something unexpected, just like the Duke did."

"You're suggesting we take over this outpost and the tower?" a voice called from the crowd.

"It wouldn't be half as difficult as Richard's feat on that impregnable fortress, even with this number of men. I can get inside that tower myself and negotiate for its surrender, and after that, the rest will follow suit."

"How are you so sure?" Harold rumbled. "Trusting enemy converts is always a bad idea."

"These soldiers here care little for political allegiances, only coin, Harold. Most came here two seasons ago and the rest were residents of Avandale, trained by George. If what you say is true, we already have George in our camp, and I believe that I can sway his daughter."

"The soldiers here take orders from Reginald, not her. How will you persuade him?"

"You underestimate the community of this place. With Reginald gone, they will serve her because she is one of them, and I would be willing to bet that without her, his coin would not hold so much sway over the people here. I don't plan on persuading Reginald; I plan on taking his head."

Harold became very serious as he explained the dangers of tangling with a man like Reginald de Poitou. "It isn't so easy just to kill a man so deeply entrenched in French high society, and with ties like his. Even if you can reach him before he slithers away back to his French allies, and even if you could best him in single combat, the repercussions of such a thing could be…disastrous."

"You're so cautious now, the man who'd planned on razing Avandale to the ground?"

"Razing the village, yes, but killing Reginald wasn't part of the plan. With this place destroyed and its people dead, he would abandon it and go back to Poitou or even Paris. A man like Reginald doesn't care about this place or its people, and he would gladly leave them to move onto his next endeavor. But if you go after him personally, and you fail in killing him, he will never forget your face and he will never stop coming after you."

John was thoughtful, pacing atop the grassy mound and staring at the tall, black shape in the distance. He had failed to penetrate that place two years before; a grave misstep had been his downfall – literally. Reginald had only briefly seen the face of the intruder in the chapel that night, and Nicolette had told him that he was a transient seeking shelter. If she'd told him the truth, those men would have beaten him more severely and he might still be sitting in a dungeon.

"I can make it inside, overpower his guard, and finish this tonight," John boasted. "Once he is dead, I will signal you and the rest of you move in to take care of any remaining men who still wish to be loyal to a dead man. Take the rest captive and offer them terms. Those who resist? Burn their homes to the ground…with them inside."

Harold nodded and again gave a smile; there would be bloodshed after all.

They prepared for the assault and made final preparations as the last vestiges of daylight were dragged down into the black sea of a moonless night. A small fire was lit far beyond the mound, so that it could not be seen from the tower, and torches were prepared for the second phase of John's plan. The men whispered amongst themselves and only Harold was brave enough to approach or make eye contact with the "Holy man" leading them.

"I hate the way they stare at me, Harold. I know they're speaking of me."

"Do ye' blame them? They're more afraid of you and of failing you than they are of dying in this place tonight. Ye' are certain this is the way ye' want to do this?"

331

"Just give me time enough to reach that tower, find her, and disembowel that sonovabitch!"

"I wish I was going with you...this should be *my* day...*my* revenge."

"You need to lead these men, Harold. Take satisfaction in knowing that there will be justice this day, not revenge. For God said vengeance is mine; let's leave it to *Him*."

Chapter 31

John headed toward the tower on foot, so as not to alert anyone of the presence of an incoming rider. Swiftly and silently, he made his way towards the old Oak just the other side of the chapel. He would try the same point of entry, and also try to avoid the same pitfall as before. He tried to replay that night in his head, in an effort to recall his exact steps from before, and recalculate distances and numbers.

From his perch on the stout branch of the Oak he'd used last time, he could see that the corner of the old steeple had been patched. He wondered if the roof of old chapel had received a full renovation like the rest of the buildings, or just enough to cover the hole. He would just have to pray that he'd already found the one weak spot, and take a "leap of faith" as he sprang from the Oak.

Thankfully, it held, and he landed as nimbly as a cat not far from the repaired portion of the roof. He couldn't resist taking a peek through a small gap at the beautiful interior of the church, remembering the last time he saw her standing there. A shiver took hold of the back of his neck like a chilly hand, as he thought about the words she'd spoken to him then, wondering if there was any truth in them.

He would discover the truth soon enough, he told himself, looking up at the nearest tower window and gauging the distance from the corner of the chapel. It was a nine-foot span from the edge of the roof to the tower stone (French measurements annoyed him), and the opening was another four feet above his head. There were no other openings below, which made sense from a strategic standpoint: most towers and citadels had only small windows on the upper levels for archers to rain arrows upon the heads of would-be infiltrators. At least he had the small benefit of the window being unguarded, but the distance would prove difficult regardless.

Looking back at the length of the rooftop, he was already making his calculations, trying to decide if it wouldn't just be better to knock on the front gate. Not only was the opening a nearly impossible distance to jump, it was no more than two or two-and-a-half feet in width – just wide enough to get an archers shoulders through. Taking a few practice steps back and forth on the rooftop, he unfastened his sword belt and knotted it around the handle of his hatchet, fashioning a makeshift grapnel.

He took a deep breath, focused on his target, and ran as fast as he could from the far edge of the roof. Kicking off with his legs at the last moment, he hurtled through the air and tossed his grapnel towards the window above. His heart fluttered as he thought his throw was too clumsy, feeling himself fall, but the hatchet wedged in between the stones of the window ledge, and the belt was pulled taut as he held fast to it. He hung suspended beneath the window for several moments, thinking that the sound of his back slamming against rock may have alerted someone, but no one came.

Once he'd pulled himself up and squeezed through the window, he stood to scan the room and get his bearings. He was in a fairly-large chamber of the second floor, and if Harold's teachings on standard towers and keeps were accurate, the living quarters were on the upper levels and it was best to avoid the ground floor. That's where the bulk of the guard would be, and while they would present little in the way of an obstacle for him, they would alert those upstairs and he couldn't risk that.

He maneuvered through the darkness of the floor he was on, and discovered that it must have been the dining hall. A large table was placed centrally in the chamber which seated probably twenty people or more, though there were only enough seats to accommodate possibly twelve. Besides a fireplace, a threadbare rug, and a giant tapestry hanging from the west wall, there was little in the way of decoration. He'd begun to wonder if this was truly the tower of a wealthy and privileged warlord that had organized a competent army.

Climbing two stairwells, which ascended in a circle to the topmost floor, he finally discovered where the decorating budget had been spent. The entire top floor, more than fifty feet in diameter, was the personal chambers of the lord of the tower. No expense had been spared in its lavish decoration; from the exotic tiger and leopard rugs that had been brought from lands far away, to the gold and brass appointments.

Large bureaus and armoires adorned almost every section of wall, filled with rich dress no doubt, and they were of the finest wood and fitted with handles of polished brass. Atop these dressers were perfumes in glass bottles, expensive ivory hairpieces and brushes, incense and lit candles issuing intoxicating aromas. Beautiful tapestries were hung from every wall, so that no drab stone could be seen, and even the chamber pots were gilded with gold and precious stones; a sign of true conceit.

In the center of the room, stood the most absurd piece in the collection; four immense, hand-carved posts of oak, suspending a richly-dressed canopy over the most ridiculous bed he'd ever seen. Heavy drapes of fine linen were drawn on all sides, and plush pillows surrounded the whole things like a moat around a castle. He heard laughter and giggling behind those drapes, and John swallowed hard, preparing himself for quite a confrontation.

He saw them moving as dim shadows behind the curtains, frolicking and whispering nonsense as lovers do. Tightening the grip on his hatchet, he reached towards those drapes, as his heart pumped faster and his cheeks burned like hot coals. In his head, he formulated his plan: throw open the sash, bring down the hatchet on his most hated foe, and offer the woman terms for the surrender of the tower. It was a simple and straightforward plan, and the only thing he had to concern himself with was being accurate and swift with his blow.

His fingers tightened around the soft fabric, knuckles white, sweat on his brow, and justice ready at the edge of his hatchet. He closed his eyes and listened to their sounds, knowing them so well that he could predict exactly where they were in their carnal course behind the curtain. He'd taken that same course many times himself, and heard the shallow breathing in anticipation of the moment right before the sweet release of two lovers. He remembered then, as he was forced to relive his own pleasures with the woman he'd loved, that he would never again know that sound from his Elizabeth.

That cold and bitter thought took hold of his heart, chilling it enough and numbing him so that he could proceed in his dark task. The curtain was torn from its post completely, and hatchet was poised, waiting only to make visual contact with a target. He would end their pleasure as they had ended his, more violently and more abruptly than his had been taken from him.

He didn't recognize either face, for it had been many nights since he'd seen them both, and that had been a starless winter eve, draped heavily in shadow. As a result, John hadn't seen much of his features, so he kept his own version of the man who'd stolen his Nicolette in his head. He was short and hid his flabby torso beneath exquisite shirts, and he wasn't unattractive, but had a feminine frame to his face and slight features like the "fancy lads" that Harold talked about being popular at the courts.

The man sitting upright, blinking at him, didn't fit that description at all. His chiseled chest and midsection were exposed, as were his broad shoulders and powerful-looking arms, just so John could hate him that much more. There was nothing at all feminine about his sharp jawline or Roman nose, or the way his brow extended over his perfectly-shaped eyes just enough to hide them in shadow and give him a mysterious appearance. In fact, the only thing flawed about Reginald was that a bit of his hair was tussled from his romp in the bed with the woman beside him.

What was revealed by the flickering candlelight of that woman was only vaguely familiar, and as different from his mental picture as the man's. Had he not seen the unmistakable hue of those eyes and the recognition playing in them, he would've thought he'd barged into the wrong chamber.

The bedclothes covered small parts of her, but the rest was in full view in the flickering light for him to see, and it was not flesh that was familiar to him. Her once dainty breasts were much fuller and rounded; her hips, a bit broader than he recalled; her belly, no longer flat as a board and her legs had become thick in the upper thighs, no longer curved and agile-looking like the yew bow. He remembered every detail of her so well, even from two seasons past, and the girl before him wasn't the one he knew.

There was also no shame left in her, for she didn't move to cover herself like she would've when she'd come to the lake. She just sat upright in the bed beside her lover, her only concern seeming to be in discovering the intentions of the hatchet-wielding man standing at her bedside. She eyed him and the weapon as he studied her with as much caution.

The man beside her seemed more mindful of modesty and of the fact that there was an intruder standing beside their bed. He shouted, "I beg your pardon, but who are you and what are you doing in my tower? I will have my guards hung for allowing you entrance and at this hour!"

"Good evening Reginald, I apologize for the intrusion, but I bring a message for you and your lady," he said, finally remembering why he'd come..

"A *message?*" He shrieked, leaping from the bed and pulling on his breeches and scrambling for a weapon. "You've a message for me that couldn't be given to one of my men or waited until morning? You've a similar lesson to learn as my incompetent guard!"

"Your guard knows nothing of my presence here," John said, circling around the end of the bed.

"What is this about? How did you get in here and what is it you want?"

He kept a cautious eye on him as he moved towards one of the bureaus, still seeking a weapon. John circled around and pointed the hatchet at him, so that he blocked his path.

"That's far enough!"

He could only stare at him in disbelief, his face showing the complete loss of comprehension of who this man was and what offense he'd given to warrant such an attack. Behind him, his wife moved from the bed and found her modesty, draping a blanket around her shoulders, taking her place behind him.

"You know me, Reginald of Poitou," John said, stepping closer so that his face became illuminated by the same flickering light. "Two years ago, in the chapel...you found me there. You believed me some downtrodden unfortunate seeking shelter, and your charity was a merciless beating."

Reginald laughed, albeit nervously, and said, "You've come seeking revenge because you sought the wrong shelter two years ago? I commend your resourcefulness and tenacity sir; I could use a man like you to fight for me. Perhaps we could find some mutually beneficial arrangement?"

"I have no doubt that you could use a good fighting man, as I personally buried twenty of those you sent to Rouen! The only *mutually beneficial* arrangement I'm interested in is repayment for the lives you destroyed! There's an army outside waiting to collect that debt, and what I offer you is much better than what they will."

There was finally a hint of recognition in his eyes, and the blood drained slowly from his face as he got down on his knees.

Whether it was a ploy to stall for time or a genuine plea for forgiveness and his life, John was not certain, but he would give him neither. Reginald of Poitou was out of time and would find little mercy from the butcher of Rouen.

"This is Richard's doing then? What are his terms?"

"No, these aren't Richard's terms, these are *my* terms: one life in exchange for dozens."

"You're a mercenary then? I-I can pay you double...triple of whatever he's giving you."

"I wasn't given coin to come here, Reginald. If you're the great savior of this place, as people say you are, then spare them this debt."

"I will do no such thing! You are a fool to reject my generosity! I can make you very wealthy and I have powerful connections as well!"

"Save your bribes, you have nothing I want," he said, sneering and preparing his dark hatchet for the final stroke.

Nicolette hurled herself in front of the prone man, shrieking at the axe-wielder. "I won't allow this, John! Take my life for his! Take my life for theirs!"

Reginald's face was contorted in disbelief as much by what had transpired as the face of his would-be assassin, and both stared at her with mouths agape.

"You know this man?"

She nodded, not taking her eyes from John's. "He is no beggar, Reginald, he is a man I once loved...and I meant to spare his life by concealing his identity from you. I see that my sacrifice was made in vain, for he has refused my generosity and returned here despite my wishes."

The man standing before her was no longer the innocent boy she'd found by the lake, nor the one whose heart she'd shattered and sent away that winter's night. She almost wished, at that moment, that she had never sent him away, or cursed herself with the prophetic words she'd last spoken to him. She'd wanted better for him, and implored him to do something great with his life both times she'd sent him off. She regretted that now, for she could see that he truly had become something greater.

"It was not my hand that slapped away your generosity, Nicolette, it was your own! The soldiers that set upon my home carried the same banner that flies from the battlements of this tower!"

"My husband and I were not involved in this massacre you speak of, John! I swear it to you!"

Reginald got to his feet and pushed her aside, his eyes narrowing at the stranger, and the muscles of his face shifted from a look of confusion to one of rage. "Save your words, Nicolette! We do not have to answer to this brazen child! There is a war afoot – a war that your Duke brought to our doorstep – and we repaid the kindness he extended to us, slaughtering our people and burning our homes! Neither my wife or I have a quarrel with Rouen, but it is allied with the traitorous Prince, and thus, makes itself a target for his enemies!"

"At least he makes himself accountable and accepts the just outcome of his actions. Perhaps there is a true martyr in this room after all," he said, giving her a look of disgust. "I almost believed your noble sacrifice was genuine, but you counted on me not being able to bring an end to your life, and hoped to manipulate me once more."

"I would gladly give myself for him or for the people of Avandale," she said, letting the blanket fall to the stone floor, extending her arms and offering her flesh to him to do as he pleased. "I did it before, and I would do so again."

"You are a liar!" He screamed, pointing his axe as he accused her. "If you sacrificed for Avandale before, like you claimed, then where is your father? Where is George? Where is the *better life* that was afforded to him because of your sacrifices? Is that his gilded chamber pot there? How about that extravagant armoire? Did he forget to take that with him when you sent him away?"

He spat at her feet and his eyes burned with more fire than his hated nemesis, cursing them both.

She just stood there helpless and exposed as he berated her, making a most piteous face that put him to mind of the one she'd worn in the chapel. He wanted to believe her, and he almost did, but he didn't know this girl anymore, and she didn't know him. This was not the place or the girl he'd left behind; neither was his sanctuary any longer.

"That's what I thought." He spit the words out with disgust. "This was *never* about George or the people of Avandale; this has always been about you! I wasn't sent out because you wanted better for *me*...I was sent out because you wanted better for *you!*"

She didn't get a chance to protest or address his accusations like she'd wanted to. They all heard the rumble of stomping feet ascending the stairwell, and realized their discussion had come to an abrupt end. Reginald, the modest one, snatched up the fallen blanket in an effort to cover her before the guards arrived. John, seeing an opening, lurched forward in an attempt to take his head before he missed his opportunity. Nicolette, who'd never taken her eyes from him, finally found a taker for the flesh she'd been only too willing to give.

To the horror of both men, her lithe body nimbly maneuvered in between them. John's reflexes were quick, and he twisted the axe quickly to the side to avoid cleaving through her throat. It bit into her shoulder, scraping the top layer of her smooth flesh, and possibly her collar bone as well. She let out a cry as she clutched at the spot, and the blood seeped through her fingers, staining them.

Reginald cursed at him as he caught her in his arms, watching the guards quickly fill the room, taking their places around the intruder in a tight semi circle. John ignored the wall of spears and blades, trying to catch a glimpse of Nicolette, but all he could see were swatches of pink brushed with thin strokes of crimson. All around him, the men shouted in his face like they'd done on that bitter winter's night, and their words were drowned out by Nicolette's pitiful cries in the distance.

And just like then, they fell in on him with their weapons, beating and slashing at him as he tried to stay focused on her face in the chaos. Her life was spilling upon the stone floor – the life that she'd gladly given for another – and he regretted the words he'd said to her in anger and distrust. He regretted most of all, allowing doubt to seep into his heart like the precious blood that was seeping into those narrow stone channels.

He'd taken a stand in defense of the innocents of Avandale, like Richard had made him promise in his oath, and at the end of a hard-fought battle, believed that Harold had actually yielded to him honorably. The wizened old knight had deliberately placed doubt in his mind, though, knowing that he was turning a more dangerous weapon loose on that place. Harold, the one who'd warned him about how dangerous and slippery Reginald was, had done his own maneuvering to serve his own ends.

One of the younger guards called from the window at that moment, "Milord! There are men outside with torches! They're headed towards the homes in the north valley!"

John clenched his teeth, not because of the guard who had him in a chokehold with his spear, but because he realized at that moment that his friend had betrayed him.

Reginald moved from the bed where, he'd laid Nicolette, to the window where his guard was watching the army below. With a frown, he turned his attention towards their captive and commanded them to stand down.

"I want this fool alive so that we may negotiate different terms," he said, stepping towards them.

"Sir?" One of them said with a wavering voice and pointing at their captive.

The lord of the tower stopped in his tracks, a look of absolute terror spreading across his face, unable to speak anything but partial questions and fragments of what sounded like prayer.

"Not a scratch...not a single cut," the Captain gasped, wide-eyed, crossing himself.

"I will not stand for incompetence," Reginald shrieked, snatching the Captain's blade from his hand and running it through the side of their prisoner, so as not to give him a wound he couldn't survive.

The blade glanced harmlessly off of his chain shirt, so he ordered those gripping his arms and legs to lift the shirt to expose his bare flesh. A second and third thrust of the long sword was just as ineffective, and the hand which held it was rendered the same, allowing the thing to clatter to the floor. His legs quivered as he backed away, retreating to the bed where his wife lay, and those he'd abandoned to the bedeviled man lost their nerve as well.

John broke free of the frail circle holding him prisoner and picked up the blade Reginald had dropped, turning it on those frightened men who pleaded for mercy. He spared only two, who'd had the presence of mind to surrender their weapons and fall to their knees like the soldiers of Rouen had done earlier. His tabard was stained and wet, his face streaked and spattered, and he'd caused those stone channels to become flooded riverbeds. As the grisly butcher approached, his feet pattered wetly on the stones and he stained the fur of the exotic creatures covering them.

Sheer desperation and the desire to flee that horrible place overpowered all reason in Reginald's frantic mind. Throwing back the linens, he grabbed his wife by her bloodied arm, and dragged her from the bed. She cried out in agony and her legs flailed as he lifted her by the throat, producing a dagger from his bedside table and drawing beneath her chin.

"This woman has brought this plague upon my house and she is surely damned! Turn back from this place and take your men with you, or I will open her throat and send her condemned soul back to hell!"

He was beyond "terms" now, beyond reasoning, and he wouldn't understand that John had lost control of those men outside as much as he'd lost control of things in the tower. Fear was the beast that governed that chamber and they could all feel its grip upon their shoulders, its hot breath on their necks. Perhaps there was something more sinister and wicked that had taken hold of them all, as Reginald insisted. Whatever awful thing had come to Avandale, it couldn't be reasoned with and couldn't be stopped, and John knew that it would end very badly for them all.

Chapter 32

Campbell sat back in his chair, a look of satisfaction on his face that always came with a story well told. He always gave his audience time to absorb and reflect on what they were being told, whether it was a large auditorium or a small classroom full of students. In this case, it was a lecture built for two, and they were both attentive, sitting at the edge of their chairs. He'd told the same story once before just down the hall, and he hoped that it would be received better than it had in that room.

"Sanctuary," Gwenn blurted, bravely leading the discussion, "is an interesting word you used, Jim. I think it fits perfectly in this context – in both contexts – and I'd never really thought of it that way before."

"What does the word mean to you?"

"I remember this look on John's face when he first got back into town that was almost… heartbreaking," she recollected.

"The place looked so much different just since we'd graduated, and I know that it probably wasn't all that different, but it didn't feel like the same place anymore," Connelly added.

"I think the expression is 'you can never go home again', Mister Connelly?"

He nodded, "Yea, like I said: I don't think it was 'home' that changed so much as we had, and I think he took it pretty hard when he didn't feel the same about it."

"That's not quite it, though," she interrupted, "but you're on the right track. I felt the same sort of thing when I moved back home after college, before I married John, like I didn't belong there anymore. You should know better than anyone, Jeremy, just how John felt coming home and why it disturbed him so much."

"What do you mean?"

"I mean that John never really felt *attached* to his home or any particular member of his family. He was on the outs with his father, and let's face it – they'd never really been that close anyway. Mr. Chapel did his best to provide a roof over his head and keep food on the table, but it wasn't like my relationship with

343

my father. His mother was even more distant, and they were on worse terms when he came home that year."

Campbell smiled and folded his fingers across his lap, watching his "slow processor" finally get up to speed and really dazzle them with her insights.

"So what was it then?"

"Remember back to when we were discussing that summer day when John felt restless and that prompted him to drag the rest of you out of town in search of something he wasn't even certain of? He was technically 'at home' that day, and still, he didn't feel like he belonged and didn't feel comfortable."

"You're not talking about a *place* then so much as you are a *person*, or a group of people? Like for me, my friends were really my family back then, and even though I was far away from home, I still felt the same so long as John was around."

She nodded, "You felt pretty empty when you realized that the last of them had abandoned you – not to bring up a sore spot – and even though you went back and forth from here to Florida, you just never felt like you were where you belonged, isn't that right?"

"Once John and I had our last falling out, I felt like I had no more direction," he admitted.

"You were John's best friend, and he loved all of you, but for him 'sanctuary' meant something else – someone else."

"Melinda?" Connelly rolled the name from his tongue as easily as his own.

"And don't forget Gwenn and Dean," Campbell chimed in.

She gave him a puzzled glance across the table and he nodded at her, saying, "I think if we refer back to the story about Rain tree, the place where he found his first family, where he felt he first belonged, that Melinda wasn't the only member of that family. You three were the ones who remembered him before everything changed, and I think that's what he went looking for that day he was becoming restless, not so much Melinda in particular."

"Maybe you're right," she conceded reluctantly. "Dean and I may have been part of that place he was looking for too, and who knows, maybe that's why he always said that he *needed* to be with me – because I was the last piece of that place for him."

"Very insightful Gwenn," the Professor complimented her. "That goes a long way to explain why, at the high point of his

344

young life, when he's seemingly on top of the world, he confesses to his very best friend that he's still unhappy and he's still missing something."

Connelly finally seemed to understand what they were getting at, adding, "Yea, I think John sensed somehow that things were falling to pieces back home with those people, just by the few calls he received from them. At the very least, I think he feared that they would forget him or leave him behind someday if he didn't return. Even if Gwenn had never called, I think he still would've left eventually."

Campbell did more of his scratching on his pad, as he gave his own assessment, "I think this is very evident in what's written here as well. There is a fear that Nicolette has outgrown him in this other place, and she's moved on and left him behind. She represents the only link to youth and innocence – the only person who knew him before he goes through this transformation to become a man – and he feels as if she's slipping away."

"John striking her with his own hatchet, even unintentionally, I think is important," Connelly chimed in, scrunching up his face, deep in thought. "I'm not so good with the metaphors and comparative thinking like you guys."

"What it means – if this was all a product of John's subconscious, as I believe it was – is that he blamed himself for not only the loss of Melinda's innocence, but also the ruin of their relationship and losing her in the end. In classic John fashion, he tried to fix things, but he made a critical misstep and shot himself in the foot," the self-appointed authority on John Chapel explained.

The sound of breaking glass made the both of them jump and they looked towards Connelly to see what the ruckus was about. The small handle from his coffee cup was still in his fingers and had snapped off in his hand, causing the cup to crash to the table. He was already dabbing the spill up with his napkin and apologizing to Campbell.

"Vanessa had a set large enough to serve two dozen people, Mr. Connelly, and I don't foresee myself ever entertaining that many people in one sitting," he explained, waving away his apology.

"Are you okay?" Gwenn asked with concern in her voice.
He shook his head, obviously shaken, but blaming his poor dexterity for the breakage and spill.

"Guess I wasn't cut out for tea time. Do you maybe have a coffee mug with a baseball team logo or possibly a state bird or catchy phrase on it, Jim?"

He rolled his eyes," I'm afraid I do not collect those sorts of things. I can get you another cup."

Connelly put his hands up, "I tell ya' what, I could probably use one of those 'afternoon drinks' now anyway, if it's no trouble."

The Professor obliged him and stepped to his bar service to fix him a drink (and of course, to get himself a refill while he was up), continuing with the discussion. "Good catch on the imagery in John's journal passage, by the way."

"Yea, *nice catch*, Jeremy," Gwenn said slightly annoyed.

Campbell appeared to ignore her jab as he took careful measure of the brown liquid as he always did. Once his masterpiece was complete, he creaked back over to the table and handed Connelly his glass, then retrieved the recorder from under his chair before settling back in.

Placing it on the table in front of him seemed to elicit the same response as showing a spray bottle to a pair of cats. Gwenn recoiled further into her seat and Jeremy watched it nervously behind his glass. He was aware that neither of them was used to the voice on that cassette yet, but it was sometimes necessary to call upon that voice to settle questions that they could not.

"What else can you tell me about this passage and how it relates to John's return?" He asked, fast forwarding the cassette, in preparation for the next part of the discussion.

"Well, like you said," Gwenn began, eying the recorder warily. "He's undergoing a transformation of sorts. The John I saw that summer had changed quite a bit; He'd been out to see the world, had more money and a little bit of ego, but there were still traces of the boy I knew. It was much different than the second time."

"Yes, he was still in the process of learning about who he was at this point, caught between his boyhood and something else. It was the first journey away from home to see other places, allowing him to grow and change, but he was still clinging to some of those old things, and like Mr. Connelly said, that's what brought him back."

"What's the recorder for?" Gwenn finally dared the question.

"I just want to have it on hand to address this particular topic. John is the only one who can tell us about his first meeting with Miss Malowski, so that we can better understand in what ways it is similar or different from the dramatic reunion we just discussed."

"You mean so you can drive your point home, crushing any doubts I still have the best way you know how? The parallels aren't lost on me, Jim, but I still stand on my faith."

"It's not meant as a punishment for you, Gwenn, but that is why we're here – to eliminate doubt. Let's just set the recorder aside for now and begin with Mr. Connelly's version of the events of June of nineteen-ninety-three..."

Chapter 33

The old "Metro Coney" was transformed into a reunion hall of sorts on that warm June evening that John and his 'Regulators' returned. As each new face arrived in the door and the bell jingled to announce them, he hopped up from his corner booth to greet them with a hearty hug and a big smile.

Dean was the first to show because he lived the closest, and he was there within ten minutes of talking to John on the payphone outside the restaurant. He arrived in a big black pickup, looking very much the part of a guy who drives a big black pickup, just like John looked the part of a guy who drove a black Mercedes. Dean poked fun of his "Guido hair" and he made fun of his mullet. John made fun of his simple black tee and he laughed at his black silk shirt. After sizing one another up, they embraced again and slapped one another on the back loudly.

Josh Allen was the next through the door, and as always, he brought his sense of humor with him, giving his friend the same ribbing that Dean had.

"Hey, I didn't have time to change into my *hillbilly* wear, sorry man."

"These are 'board shorts' and this thing here is called a 'tee shirt'," he said sarcastically, pulling the printed tee out so that he could read the logo. "I designed this shirt myself; I didn't have an Italian tailor custom-make it for me!"

"I buy my clothes at this place called a 'store'...you guys have stores here right? I don't buy my shirts from hippy burnouts taking liberal arts credits so their parents don't make them move out of the basement."

"I didn't buy this from hippies, man. It's more of a *grunge* crowd."

"Cobain is dead, tell them to move on. You look like a hippy with that hair!"

"Hippies don't dye their hair maroon! What's up with yours?"

349

"Never mind my hair. It's good to see your ugly face anyway."

"You too, man! If you want to talk about ridiculous getups, you should see Hunter…"

On cue, a second black pickup truck came tearing into the lot, leaving black streaks in the road and a cloud of smoke. "I dunno' what the hell Florida is doing to all of you guys, but you might want to consider moving away from there," he said as they watched him get out of his truck.

Chad Hunter's ridiculously perfect smile was the first thing they noticed, and it was more ridiculous than they'd remembered him having before. Maybe it was the absurd George Hamilton tan he had, or he'd spent more at the dentist than he had on accessories for his obnoxious truck. He was wearing baggy, designer shorts, military boots, and a tight black tee to show off his chest and arms that he'd spent way too much time on as well.

"I thought you were in Florida for the past eighteen months, man? Why does Josh have a better tan than you?"

He gripped his hand, squeezing it so his arm bulged deliberately.

"Some of us *work* Hunter, and don't have time for fake tans."

Chad grinned, "Doesn't look like you've seen a beach at all, by that outfit. What the hell is up with that? It's summertime, Johnny, you want me to loan you some shorts?"

"I have shorts, but I'm not home to go swimming or surfing."

"I still have to get my ass down to see you guys; I hear South Beach is incredible!"

"We've only been there for a year-and-a-half," he said, sarcastically.

"Hey, I'm just a poor college student, maybe you could front me and I'll make the trip."

"If you hadn't spent all your money on that ridiculous truck and hair care products, maybe you'd have enough money to come see your friends who only live four hours from you!"

"Well, we're here now, so what's the big occasion? You missed the girls and the ice cream shack didn't you?" Chad teased.

"Not exactly, but yea it's kind of like that…" John shared a look with Josh, knowing that he would understand. "Come on and sit down to eat something – it's on me!"

As Chad went to their old booth to greet Con and Dean, the boys at the door noticed a third pickup truck, even louder than Hunter's, rumbling through the parking lot.

"It's Bren! Pete just got back into town yesterday," Josh explained. "He's on leave until next Saturday."

"What is this, 'redneck truck' weekend?" John snorted, laughing at Bren's truck.

It was even more outrageously outfitted than Hunter's, and instead of green neon gracing the bottom, he'd opted for the semi truck horns mounted on the top. Chad was also missing the gun rack, the off-road mud tires, and the plethora of Army stickers in the back window.

"Can it, Chappy! This truck would eat your little German piece of shit car and have Hunter's lady truck for dessert!" Brennan said in his usual monotone voice.

"When did you become Schwarzenegger's stunt double?" Josh teased.

Pete Brennan had always been a big boy, even before he hit puberty, but almost two years in the Army had made him broader and thicker than before. His arms looked like swelling pythons that had swallowed small dogs, and his once-chubby face had slimmed down into something resembling a chiseled block of granite. His head was shaved almost bald, with the exception of a small patch on the top, and he wore classic police-issue mirrored shades.

"I'm not sissy-hugging you girls either!" He barked, extended a giant hand. "I haven't talked to you since you called me drunk from some bar down there, Chaps! How are things with you?"

"Could be better, but I'm glad you're here. You're the guy I like around when the shit gets hairy."

"Ooh, we gonna' bust some heads? Point the way!"

Pete was always up for some muscle work, or at the very least, intimidating people. He'd always been the self-appointed bodyguard of John Chapel, primarily because John had never been an imposing figure as a boy, but also because he knew that he had a good heart and shared some of the same ideals as he did. Pete would never let anything happen to his "little buddy", even though John could more than take care of himself now.

"I'll tell you about it later," he said, checking his watch. "Let's grab some grub!"

"What about J.B.? Did you get a hold of him?" Pete asked.

"Beck didn't come home from school this summer. He got some perfect job out there and some *perfect* girlfriend there."

"Sellout punk," Pete grumbled. "We're better off without him anyway."

Neither of them disagreed, and John was glad that he wouldn't have to spend his entire visit home having Jeremy's cousin trying to take the spotlight from him. None of them would really miss him this time around.

Dinner at the Metro Coney went pretty much the same as it always did; two malts and two cheeseburgers a piece, for starters, and when they ran out, John just ordered more. As they gorged themselves, they shared lots of laughs revisiting old stories and sharing new ones.

Hunter gave his own rendition of Florida life, which consisted mostly of college girls, non-college girls, and with what time he had left, a little bit of college. He also told some good stories about deep sea fishing, surfing, jet skiing and his big upcoming trip to the Virgin Islands for some art-study program. He kept reminding them that he'd formally changed his name to just "Hunter" – which was how he signed his paintings – but the guys just laughed and called him "Chad" on purpose.

Josh's story wasn't quite as exciting, having just finished high school, but he found common ground with Hunter to discuss art and the classes he was planning to take that fall. He gave him some good pointers and the rest teased him about having a crush on Hunter now that they were "art buddies". The jokes kept rolling in until they got out of control and Josh's face turned red, prompting John to put an end to it by putting Pete on the spot.

Brennan's story would've been the most interesting, but he always had a way of taking the most fantastic stories and making them boring somehow. He and the Army had been a better match than any of them had imagined, graduating top of his class in basic and advanced infantry training, then being accepted into Ranger school. That was quite a feat for any of them, but he made it sound like it something as simple as winning first place at a pie-eating contest.

John and Connelly had arrived in a very expensive Mercedes and were both likewise dressed in expensive clothing, but they underplayed all of it, and made their Florida experience sound like the most boring time ever. There were a few stories about some of the clubs, the nightlife, and the girls, but it seemed like they were deliberately leaving things out. Hunter tried to drag more out of them, but Pete shot him a warning stare across the table.

They knew that something big had been going on there, and that there was something even bigger that had brought them home, but none of the rest of them wanted to pry. Dean went last, and he had everyone's attention, because they knew that he knew exactly why John was home. Before he could even get through his stories of college life and get into the grittier parts, he was interrupted by a figure he noticed from the corner of his eye.

She was a petite, auburn-haired beauty, with bright amber eyes and a wicked smile. John had not seen her in over a year, and had no idea she had grown so much. John never would've pictured her looking anything like that when he'd talked to her on the phone. The once slightly-annoying, pencil-thin girl had flowered into something not in the least annoying. Gwenn Lawson turned every head at the table, and he never thought he'd see the day.

She leaned down to give John a big squeeze, whispering something to him that none of them heard, and then flashed Dean and Connelly a big smile before introducing the two girls she had in tow. None of them paid any attention to those other two, despite them being attractive, as distracted as they were by the one in the middle.

"What are *you* doing here? I told you I'd call..."

"You might *look* different Johnny," she said, looking him up and down, "but you're still *predictable*. I knew this would be the first place you'd go, just as I knew you'd call *Dean* first."

"Sorry," he shrugged. "I just kind of wanted to wind down before everything got crazy. I just drove thirteen hundred miles and--"

"Don't worry about it," she dismissed his apology. "Maybe I just wanted to see you, *I* missed you too."

353

She flashed him a flirty smile, and the guys carried on in their juvenile snickering and looks, prompting him to introduce the others at the table.

"You know Con and Pete, do you remember Hunter, and Josh? They were at the rink that first night...you guys remember Gwenn?"

The boys jumped over each other to shake her hand, and even Pete seemed excited to see a girl for once. John shot them each a stare as he was embarrassed by the way they were looking her up and down, especially Connelly.

She was wearing a half top that was low cut and her breasts threatened to spill out as she reached over the table to shake the eager hands reaching for her. They'd gone from 'hardly noticeable' to 'unable to miss', and most of them were staring directly at them. The other half of the table was gawking at her legs, which weren't stick-thin like John remembered. They'd always been long, but now they were proportioned properly, and the shorts she was wearing showed every curve and muscle as she stood before them.

"Nice to meet you," she said, smiling, trying to ignore their invasive stares.

"Why don't you and your friends have a seat, we can all catch up," Hunter offered.

John gave him a fiery stare, but scooted back into the deep booth to allow room for them. She plopped down next to him and scooted close to allow the second girl to sit on the outside, the third taking a seat next to Dean. As soon as they were situated, the boys assailed them with their flirtatious looks and a revamp of the stories they'd told – making them much more interesting than the first time they'd told them. Even Pete was able to jazz up his Army stories, making them sound exciting for once, and the rest of them shared puzzled looks.

Only John was quiet, feeling his exhaustion all of a sudden, slouching bit, trying to avoid having to rehash his stories. Gwenn could tell that he seemed uncomfortable, and that it wasn't really the proper forum for discussing the things they needed to discuss. For conformation, she shared a knowing glance with Dean, who was also quiet and fidgeting with his straw in his milkshake. He seemed even more uncomfortable just being physically close to her, and winced each time the bare flesh of her leg brushed against his hand under the table.

Gwenn tried to break the somberness between the three of them, forcing a fake smile and announced, "So there's a party tonight...you should go. You can just take a night to unwind."

She wasn't addressing anyone in particular, but they knew it was directed at John.

"Yea you should go!" The girl seated beside Dean chimed in, the other repeating her.

John looked across the table at Dean, then the others, and finally at the girls. He hadn't been to a good party in a long while, not one without pretentious people anyway, or one where he was working a potential mark with Nicole or Frank.

"That might be just the thing we need..."

"Where's it at?" Hunter asked.

One of the girls pulled a napkin from the dispenser and wrote an address on it with an eye pencil that looked abused. Probably the same one that Gwenn had used, John thought to himself, noticing how thick her lids were with the stuff. She watched him from the corners of those dark lids, trying to gauge his reaction and level of enthusiasm, as her friend scratched a series of letters and numbers down. When she was finished, she left it in the middle of the table for the boys to fight over. Gwenn scooted out of the booth then, and the girls followed suit.

"Where are you going? You just sat down," John asked.

"We don't want to crowd in on your guy time, I just wanted to say hello. We can catch up later if you guys show up at the party. If not, I'll see you around," she said, winking at him.

Every eye at the table was focused on her as she walked, and John looked away after only a few seconds, scolding the rest of them, as though they were staring at his own sister.

"What?" Three of them said in unison.

"Not cool," John said, shaking his head.

"Tell me you weren't undressing her with your eyes like the rest of us," Hunter said laughing.

"Even *I* was undressing her, and I've seen her naked before," Connelly laughed.

"I forgot you haven't seen her in a while," Dean said, smirking. "She really blossomed in her last year of school, and she pretty much ran the other crowd - the one my sister didn't run."

"What the hell was up with that hit-and-run?"

"I thought you were like the chick expert? She obviously wants you to come to the party."

"You mean she wants *me* to come to the party," Hunter corrected him. "Didn't you see the way she was eyeballing me?"

"She didn't even notice you *Chad*," Josh exclaimed. "She was burning a hole through Johnny though – that's for sure."

"Johnny isn't here for *Gwenn*," Connelly said in an ominous tone, and the others quieted down, looking at each of them nervously, waiting to hear what the rest of it was about.

He just stared across the table at his friend, gnashing his fries with his teeth, and waiting for Connelly to say something else. There was suddenly an uncomfortable tension at the table, and none of them dared say a word, for fear that it would erupt into something very bad. Connelly finally withdrew from the stare down, looking down at his milkshake and making some comment about it melting.

The boys made small talk amongst themselves as they finished their food, Hunter and Josh trading jabs at Pete for the show he put on for the blonde girl. Pete wore his usual stone-face as he chewed his burger like it was made of rawhide, his cheeks turning slightly pink. When he finished his burger and the assault from his friends had died down, he asked the obvious question, "So is your sister going to this party?"

Dean looked up at the only man at the table bigger than him and smiled. "If Gwenn and her friends are going, then I'd have to give a firm 'no' on that - they don't hang out with my sister or her friends."

"I say we go then, I'm in!" Josh was excited to hear the prospect of drama was slim.

"You know I'm going!" Hunter said with a devilish grin.

"It's up to Johnny," Connelly said, nodding towards him in supplication. "I think he just kind of wanted to do a quick dinner and catch up since all you guys are in town--"

"We can go to the party," John cut him off. "There will be time for sleep tomorrow."

He slugged down his milkshake and slammed his cup down, "Let's roll outta' here!"

"No *Regulators*?" Josh gave a feigned frown.

"We can't *technically* do the Regulators call without JB," Hunter mumbled to him.

"Well then it looks like we have a slot open in the Regulators for Dean," Josh said, smiling.

"Where do I pay my five bucks for registration?" Dean joked.

"Is it *that* much now? I got in for the price of a comic book," Josh cracked wise.

"Inflation, man," John laughed. "I think we can waive the registration for Dean – he's been around a long time."

The boys stood in the parking lot joking around about Dean's initiation process and deciding on the driving arrangements. John laughed and said they would look ridiculous with a procession of 'hillbilly' trucks following a Mercedes around Troy, so they decided to pile the bulk into his car, and Hunter rode with Pete in his truck. The followed Dean in his truck back to his house to drop it off and let him get cleaned up.

The house still stood exactly as John had left it over a year before, and he realized that the hands on that unseen clock had not moved since then. It seemed empty, void of the vibrant life it once held, no longer emanating that inviting feeling that had once been there. When John used to walk up the steps to the front porch, the door used to practically open itself for him, but now an air of foreboding hung over the entrance to the old place. Even though it was late afternoon, everything seemed to have a gray tinge to it like on a rainy overcast day.

He parked his car in the drive, and followed Dean up the steps, holding his breath in nervous anticipation as he opened the front door, not knowing what to expect inside.

The inside looked as dark as the outside had. A single lamp sat on a small wooden table by the door trying to pierce the shadows with a soft, forty-watt glow. Dean headed up the winding staircase, and told the guys to get comfortable in the family room and to help themselves to the beer in the basement refrigerator. Hunter headed downstairs to grab drinks and John cautiously navigated through the hallway towards the kitchen and family room.

The room, like the rest of the house, was quiet. There was no television or radio playing to interrupt the silence like usual. The big screen sat silent, staring at him with one giant, dark eye of

357

glass. The stereo system that usually was lit up like a Christmas tree behind glass, with all of its LED indicators, was resting peacefully. He'd sat in the room so many times watching that TV or just enjoying the music which resounded in crisp tones from the four corner speakers. It seemed unusual for the electronic voices to be stilled, and the immense leather sectional sofa to look so empty.

That was the way it had been as of late, according to his discussion with Dean over the phone. His sister brought turmoil to the family, and caused a rift between her mother and father, so that they rarely even sat to dinner anymore, most meals ending in a feud.

John stood at the edge of the family room, staring into the kitchen, remembering the last time he'd sat there with the family. It looked nothing like he'd remembered either. The home was normally so clean that it reminded him of a hospital, and Mrs. Malowski had a near-obsessive compulsive cleaning habit. There were piles of dishes in the sink and on the counter top, and the table had stacks of mail and magazines heaped on it.

Hunter returned with a few bottles of beer and handed them to Pete, Josh and Connelly who'd made themselves comfortable in the den. John returned and gave him a puzzled look.

"Sorry dude, there were only four left down there. I figured you would wait until we do a beer run. We're the guests after all!"

He sighed at Hunter and went to meet Dean at the foot of the stairs to give him some money for the beer run. At the top of the steps, he swore he heard voices arguing, and then a door slamming closed. Peering up, he could only see Dean carrying his wallet in his mouth and pulling on a clean shirt, hurrying down the hallway.

At the bottom of the steps, John handed him a fifty and gave him a curious stare when Dean asked what kind of beer he wanted.

"Just get whatever...what was that about? I thought everyone was gone?"

Dean bit his bottom lip and nodded, "My folks are out of town with friends, and she's not supposed to be here while they're not home. They don't even know what happened yet."

"She's here?"

"Yea...she's up there getting a change of clothes or something. You want to go with me to the store?"

"Should these guys be here?"

"Yea, they're fine. This is my house, not hers. I'd feel better if someone was here anyway, to keep an eye on things. Maybe they want to take it into the basement and chill while we're gone?"

"I think we'll be okay here. Why? What's going on?"

"She's expecting company, and it looks like she's going out tonight. I just don't want any shit going down at my parent's place while I'm gone, man."

"That motherfucker is coming here? After everything that happened? What's wrong with her?"

"I don't know. She's not welcome here, but whenever they're not home she shows up to collect her stuff or just hang out. I can't make her leave and I just ignore her."

"Does she know I'm here?"

As if on cue, the blur of a figure appeared briefly above them, moving quickly from the bathroom and then back down the hall. A familiar voice called out, annoyed, "Yes, I know you're here. Make yourself at home, Johnny, and don't listen to my brother – I'm not here to steal anything, and I feel perfectly fine."

Just the sound of her made his face lose its color and his palms immediately became clammy and the room grew warm. He'd expected their reunion to be so much more dramatic, not just a quick glance over the upstairs railing and an indifferent greeting. For months, he'd thought about what he would say to her when he saw her again, and he couldn't think of a single thing to say to her cold welcome. It made him flustered, and he knew that she'd done it on purpose. She'd ruined his grand entrance.

Dean gave a worried glance at his friend and then at the top of the stairs, then left to get the beer and John promised that he wouldn't confront her just yet. It was something the three of them – Gwenn, Dean and him – had agreed upon in the flurry of calls that followed the first one that day at the Pub. Gwenn kept him updated on her condition and Dean would call and brainstorm about ideas about how they would approach her in an intervention.

It was Gwenn who'd gone driving around looking for her the night of the strange call she'd received that was just the sound of a woman sobbing uncontrollably on the phone. She knew it was Melinda, despite not having heard from her in months, and she immediately called Dean to help her track her down, knowing she was in bad trouble. She found her first, lying beside the river running along the perimeter of Rain tree, and she called Dean after calling an ambulance.

Two days later, she signed herself out of *Beaumont*, and they were unable to hold her since she'd refused treatment and she was an adult. Dean hadn't called his parents to let them know, and they decided instead to call John, hoping that he would know what to do. They'd put it all on him, expecting him to fix things, and now he was standing less than a hundred feet from her and told not to intervene.

Like hell he wasn't going to intervene.

Chapter *34*

He headed up the stairs with purpose in his step and finding his second wind. Once he reached the top, he could hear the faint music playing from behind her closed door. He ran his fingers on the smooth banister, glancing at the old family pictures which hadn't been updated since the last time he'd been there. Twenty years of the family's history had been proudly displayed on that wall at a time when the framer of those pictures had been proud of her family. Now dust and traces of cobwebs covered them and they'd been untouched by their curator.

At the end of the hall was her door, still adorned with all of the adolescent markings he'd remembered. A "Do not disturb" sign hung on the knob, beneath a "Get Lost" poster with a cute puppy on it, and a faded, handwritten poem that he knew was about him. It was horribly plain and too angst-ridden for a girl her age, yet a part of his memory of her from those days gone by, and he couldn't help but feel nostalgic when he saw it.

He gently knocked at the door as he prepared himself for his grand entrance, trying to find just the right expression and posture to impress her with. She called for him to enter, as inexpressively as she'd greeted him. Nudging the door open, he found himself walking through a portal into a room that time had also not touched. It was the lavish interior of a teenaged-girl's room, complete with carpeting made of teen magazines and dirty clothing, walls painted by posters and photo collages, and at the center, the old four-poster bed still resided.

Beside the bed was the old bureau with the antique mirror and in that mirror was the reflection of the young woman who sat on the velvet chair doing her make up. John sighed softly and leaned against the door jamb, watching her. Her hair had grown considerably longer, and had been straightened. No longer did she wear the luxurious natural curls that he so loved. The straight locks fell like a yard of silk over her smooth bare back.

His eyes traced the golden strands down to her round behind, which was the only part of her skin that was covered. A silky black outline accentuated and divided her hips, legs and ass in neat segments. Her panties formed a black arrow shape which pointed down and showed him the way to her long legs. They were crossed and her foot danced as it dangled over her knee to a sultry techno beat. One slender arm worked in smooth lines, applying a deep crimson to her lips. The other moved more sporadically, wiping and smudging.

The small, round bureau mirror teased him as much as her rounded shoulders did at hiding her breasts. From behind, he could only see the slight curve of soft flesh, and the mirror only revealed the crest of the pair of them at the base of her slender throat. As her arms worked, they moved in a hypnotizing rhythm, undulating like the underbellies of plump serpents, moving to charm and beguile him.

John had seen several, larger breasts on the women who danced at the clubs in Miami. He had seen women with faces as perfect as their bodies, and seen them far closer and more revealing than this. But the way she sat and just the *idea* of her nudity caught his breath more than the first time he'd seen one of those dancers as a naïve boy. He lost his innocence in that city, and thought he'd seen it all, but there was, thankfully, at least one thing in the world that could still hold his gaze.

He stood and looked at her for what seemed like hours before his presence became more obvious to her. She twisted fully on her velvet chair and stared with her ruby mouth hanging half open. She seemed not to care for her exposed parts, and he also gave them little consideration, glancing at them briefly before moving his eyes to her own and keeping them there.

Her beautiful face held more power over him than any other part of her body, like it always had. Melinda was like the Helen of old Troy, whose beauty separated her from other women and caused men to do foolish things - even make war.

The two old lovers could only stand and stare at one another, while their minds both searched for the most intelligible and appropriate thing to say for this moment. Neither realized that their silence was the most fitting thing on this particular summer night. It would've made a perfect dialogue for the moment they had both secretly waited for so long to happen, but she had to ruin it by speaking.

"You look…different. I didn't get a good look at you in the foyer," she said apologetically, is if it would've made a difference in how she'd greeted him before, or that she's mistaken him for someone else.

"It's been a while," he said simply. "I'm sorry; I didn't know you were here."

"I'm usually not here, and I won't be here long. I have a date tonight and I don't really have the time to talk about *this* right now."

John's smile tugged into a smirk then. She had said "this", implying that his appearance there signified a special moment which needed ample time to be dealt with or worked out. Maybe she was referring to their year-and-a-half silence, or perhaps she'd caught wind of Gwenn and her brother's plan somehow, and knew why he'd come.

It was the mention of a 'date' that had prompted him to confront her, though, and caused the cauldron to boil in his bowels. Not because she had a date, or that he was jealous, but because of whom she had the date with. He couldn't mention it or even show that he disapproved, though, because she would just be that much more determined in her course. He did his best to showcase his indifference with his reply.

"It's good to see you Melinda, you look great. I just wanted to say hello, and I'll be around for a little while. Maybe another time?"

She stopped applying her makeup, wiping off her lipstick dissatisfied, and gave him what looked like an irritated glare in the mirror over her shoulder. He knew that giving her such a bland, generic compliment on her appearance would upset her sense of excessive vanity, and begin planting doubt in her mind. Melinda Malowski knew that all men – especially John Chapel – wanted and desired her, and for him to not look at her like the rest, even seeming distant, was insulting.

He continued to watch her calmly, as she waited for something, for some reaction or verbal response to her cold shoulder treatment. It didn't come and she finally turned, somewhat surprised, to see if he was still even in the room.

He could see how this agitated her, and prompted her to study this new person who wore an old face. It wasn't in his character to remain quietly expressionless in such a dramatic

363

moment; he'd always liked to make an entrance after being gone for long periods, at which point she would rush into his arms and fulfill his ego. But looking at him now, he appeared to expect nothing from her.

"Are you alright, Johnny?" Her concern almost sounded genuine.

He smiled at her and nodded. The curious young woman fully expected that to be enough of a prodding to get him to spill his troubles.

"Are *you* alright, Mel? You look tired."

Saying that she 'looked great' was insulting enough, but telling her that she looked 'tired' was going over the line. Trying to keep her composure, she stood and approached him, forcing a smile upon her face as he knew she struggled with his last comment.

At that moment, he knew that she was being assailed by a hundred questions at once. Why does he seem so disinterested? Has he become disenfranchised with me? Has he found somebody else? Has he stopped thinking about me? Is his infatuation gone?

She shuffled through those questions, looking for the most direct ones to prod at him with. "Do I look *bad* to you, Johnny? Do I look fat?" The last she said placing her hands on her hips and cocking a hip to one side to allow him a full view of her figure.

He looked her up and down as if still disinterested then replied, "No you look fine. I told you that. You look the same, but just a little…exhausted."

She frowned at this: 'looks the same' was worse than 'great', and 'exhausted' may as well have been a slap in the face. He could see the curiosity drop from her expression and replaced by something resembling indignation. Her John had lost interest. Her John didn't think she was extraordinary anymore. Her John, who'd shattered her heart long ago, wasn't back and begging for her forgiveness.

"How was Florida, Johnny?"

John knew that she really meant to ask, "Who is this other girl?"

Another short answer agitated her further, "When you have the time, we can grab a drink and I'll tell you all about it."

"Just grab a drink…and catch up?" Her tone changed and she was becoming rattled, which was exactly what he wanted.

"You stopped calling me Johnny...you expect to walk into my house, and just...pick up where we left off?"

There it was: she was the one to finally crumble and come right out with it. He looked down at his shoes, letting out a silent breath, and then raised his eyes to meet hers again. They were smoldering blue, like the center of the hottest flame, and there was so much ignited within them: implacable fury, unmistakable disgust and judgment, and passion that had been corrupted and turned into something terrible.

"I called...you stopped answering! Can't blame mom for this one, no one threw the messages away! You decided not to call back. I moved on."

There was something in his tone that frightened her – something beyond anger and accusation – like a voice that was completely void of emotion, despite it resounding like thunder around her. He wasn't yelling at her like he'd done so many times before, it was something much different, something much colder and detached, and she squirmed at the sound of it.

"I just couldn't bring myself to talk to you...but I wrote to you every day."

There was something odd in the way she said it, like it was a secret she'd been harboring for a long time and she was parting with it as some kind of offering. She wanted something from him in return, she wanted a secret of equal value, a foothold inside of him, and a place to start where she could work her way in deep again. There were far too many things he wasn't sharing and allowing her to see, and that would never do. She used to be able to read John Chapel like a book, every expression, every tick, she knew what each meant. Now she was staring at a blank screen and she hated it.

"I never received a letter..." He replied as she gave him a playful smile and sat down on her old bed, patting it and indicating that he should sit beside her.

She slid off of her bed onto the floor and got onto her knees, bending forward beneath the bed, looking for something. John tried hard not to notice her round ass wagging teasingly from side to side. There was certainly no need for her to move her body so much while searching beneath the bed. She was *trying* to seduce him, and was playing dirty.

Finally, rocking back and sitting on her feet, she had a jumbled stack of papers and notebooks cradled in her arms. She patted the bed again, laying the offering there for him to examine. It seemed harmless enough, but this was Melinda Malowski, and she could not be trusted. He took a step towards the bed so that he could get a better look at the pile of papers, and confirm what she'd told him.

"I'm not going to bite you, sit down and read them...they're yours."

He sat on the edge of her bed and sorted through them, shuffling them into as neat a pile as was possible, noticing the mismatched dates at the top corners of each. John skimmed the first lines of each, as if verifying legal documents. He nodded at each one, flipping through the stack, and then looked up at the girl sitting on her knees, waiting expectantly for his approval.

"You never sent these...why?"

She pushed herself up on her knees, and leaned across his lap to take a look at what he was holding. For the second time that day, he'd had breasts dangled in front of him, and for the second time, he'd tried not to stare at them. Gwenn's approach had been a little less conspicuous and it was more believable that her invasion of his space had been "accidental", which was the sign of a true expert. Melinda wasn't holding anything back, rubbing them across his lap as she pretended not to remember what each of the pages said.

In a few seconds, the letters could have been scattered across the floor and he would be mounting her right then and there, with his friends downstairs and her brother on his way back from the store. He could've taken her; the offer was in her Mediterranean blues, and in the gentle touch of her body against his. Nothing good would come of that, though, and he knew it. She would win, she would be back in control, and worse, she would probably use it to renew the war between him and Sal.

Seeing that she had his full attention, she replied in a soft, sultry whisper, "It wouldn't have made a difference."

"How do you know? It might have made all the difference in the world."

The irony of her handing him a stack of letters he'd never known about didn't escape him. He wondered why she'd gone to so much trouble just to torment him.

366

Melinda came closer, sitting on the bed beside him, so she could get a better look at the pages in his lap and so that he could feel her breath on his neck when she spoke, "You'd already made up your mind. What did a few letters matter?"

Now her fingers were resting gently on his shoulder, and he noticed that she'd aroused herself, rubbing her breasts against his legs. She sat beside him, resting her chin on one knee and letting the other leg dangle from the bed. He glanced down at the pages, trying to ignore her breasts in his line of sight, and instead, caught a view of the small area that she knew would be exposed by the placement of her legs and underwear that fit just a little loosely.

Again, he thought of giving in, but he remained vigilant, realizing that this was what she did professionally. Whether she wanted drugs, money, control, whatever the case, Melinda got what she wanted. It turned his stomach again and, thankfully, ruined the mood for him so that he could stand again, but he wasn't free of her yet.

She locked eyes with his, and he saw how the light played about them as though they were sapphires. "Yes...yes I guess I did. But thanks for these anyway, I'll take a look at them."

Now the two old lovers could barely speak words over the strong presence of physicality and sexuality. "Why did you come back?" She finally braved, standing from the bed to press herself closer.

"I'm needed," he said without hesitation.

The inference was as blatant as the desire for her that he kept choked down like a bad wine.

"Are you?" The pink grapefruit lips quivered in answer.

"That's what I'm told," he countered, never moving his eyes from hers, trying to back away.

"It's nice to be needed," came her breathy whisper.

It was that last damned whisper and the way she was looking at him that broke through his icy calm. He embraced her, his sleeves tickling and arousing her naked shoulders and arms. While their lips, noses and chins drew together, he uttered, "It's nicer to be wanted."

As their lips were almost pressed together, he was taken back to that day in front of Gwenn's house, two years before. The kiss of this pair was to be envied. There were none among their companions or past lovers who could compare to the magnitude and perfection of their kisses. Every crease and fold of their lips seemed made to fit within the other's, and moved in a beautiful synchronization like ballet dancers. People disappeared and time stood still when they closed their eyes for a kiss, with all sound being drowned out by reverberating hearts in their ears.

It was going to be like that again, all of their pent up aggression and longing would melt away in that one sweet release. Their words had been contrary to the emotions that had been welling up in the both of them, and the kiss they would share would be all of the apologies and things needed to be said between them that they had wanted so badly to say. They had both practiced clever lines and speeches they would make when this day came, but all words were soon to fall to the wayside before the power of the kiss.

But the kiss would never be. The precious few moments they had together were always disturbed and interrupted at their apex. As her top lip yielded to his bottom, and their breath was already beginning to mix, Dean came gently tapping at the door politely before he pushed it open with his shoulder. "Mel, your date's here. Johnny, the guys want to roll somewhere else man."

There was more emphasis on the last part for John's sake. His friend tried to make it sound as though they had to leave her before she had to leave Johnny. It was like being the first to close a phone conversation with someone whom you'd just started talking to; it was all about appearances. He didn't want for his best friend to be left standing there looking desperate, while she got dressed and went out on the town.

They had important things to do, and she would be the one left first. It was juvenile, but it was the etiquette of the fickle and popular. Mel stood looking over John's shoulder at her brother, her skin well draped and covered in the folds of his shirt and his arms. She wore a slight crease in her eyebrow. It was half for his rudeness of entering her small, personal palace, and half for interrupting her moment of victory.

"He knows to wait in the driveway, but tell him I'll be down shortly anyway, and close the door on your way out."

John cracked a smile as he saw Dean give a playful curtsy and bow his way out of the doorway.

She turned her head quickly toward her bureau, allowing John to smell the lavender of her hair as it flipped at his nose. Quickly she re-applied her lipstick as she bade him goodnight.

"I have to go; I made plans a long time ago," she explained almost apologetically. "But I want you to...take me to dinner. I'm eager to hear all about Florida."

John wiped the faint trace of lipstick from his lower lip with a thumb and replied, "*You* buy *me* dinner...good stories don't come cheap you know."

She paused and gave a little chuckle at him. Melinda had always loved his humor. Even in the tensest of situations, his wittiness could change the mood. She wiped away the lipstick that she had been re-applying so vigorously with a cloth, seemingly dissatisfied again.

"I have to get *dressed*, John," she said as though she was going to get undressed, and that he would see something he wasn't supposed to.

He let her walk him to the bedroom door where she gently patted his butt to get him into the hall. There he turned and looked at her once more as she slowly began to close the door. She reached a slender arm through the shrinking crack of the doorway and grabbed the back of his neck, and rewarded him for his vigilance. It wasn't a last play at seducing him - she knew that she'd have to concede that round and they'd simply run out of time - it was just a kiss, and a promise that their game was just beginning. He understood then why she'd wiped the lipstick off.

He felt her tongue play lightly inside of his mouth just long enough to remind him of what it was like, and to warm him up to the idea that he would want more soon enough. She tasted of mint toothpaste and menthol cigarettes - that was her flavor.

"Call me John, you still have the number?" He nodded even though she knew that he did.

Finishing her kiss, she hovered at his mouth for a few moments as though she might change her plans, but then playfully pushed him away and closed the door. The whole while, she looked at him through the crevasse, until only one dark-hooded eye and half a pouty lip were visible. Then there was nothing but the sound of her music and the smell of lavender mixed with jasmine.

Dean was leaning against the banister, waiting for him. "Well?" He inquired.

John walked past, not wanting to talk about the whole fiasco in the bedroom.

"I told you not to go up there. *She* ran the whole show didn't she?" He asked jokingly.

"I had it under control," John tried to sound cool.

"Yea, it looked that way," The stocky man muttered disapprovingly.

"I was cool until she tried kissing me. She didn't even have to say a word...she just knew I wanted it so bad...you pretty much saved my ass back there."

Dean stopped at the top of the stairwell, his fun-loving attitude changing, "I think it's good that you're intimate, that means she knows you still have a thing for her, but you have to get it under control. You're the *only* one who can get through to her. This is a game to her and you can't let her win."

"It's a game...mostly...but there's something else there. I felt it...and I saw it just for a moment. I saw the old Melinda in there, Dean...just for a second."

"Well, that's a start. Did you talk about anything?"

"She wants to get together over dinner and talk...I suppose that's good."

"That is good. That's an improvement from *I never want to see his face again.*"

"She said that?"

"All the time. So that's progress, and progress is good. So long as she still thinks there's a chance of you getting back together, she'll straighten up. It worked last time."

John shook his head, "But we're *not* getting back together, she's still seeing what's-his-name...and I'm with somebody. Even if I wasn't, I can't get back with her after everything that's happened. I'm not in love with her anymore...I don't know if I could even feel that way again."

"I don't have the answers, John. You're pretty much our last hope. You have to find a way to get her away from this guy, and from this life. Take her away with you to Florida if you have to, so long as she isn't mixed up in this shit anymore."

Dean was almost in tears, and John hadn't seen him cry since Dawson's funeral, hadn't seen that desperation in his face since the day at the park. The danger was just as real, of him losing another sibling, of watching her drown and being helpless to stop it again, and John recognized that. He didn't want that to happen, and he would've done anything for Dean, Melinda or their family, but this was asking too much, and there was no guarantee that he could even pull it off; no guarantee that he could keep this Malowski from drowning.

"I know you can do this, Johnny…if anyone can do this…you can," he said in a quivering voice, then patted him on the shoulder and left him standing at the top of the stairs alone, contemplating the depth of the situation he was now in.

Peering down the hallway, he swore that the bedroom door was opened a crack, and that he could see a single, dark-lidded eye watching him. He hurried down the steps to rejoin his friends in the family room, and explained to them why they had to leave again, after they'd just gotten comfortable and made themselves at home.

Grumbling, they finished off their beer, took care of their empties and followed Dean out the front door. As John was the last to leave, he closed the door behind him, but hesitated for a moment as he caught sight of Melinda standing at the rail and watching him leave. Her hand lifted from the railing to give him a little wave and the look she wore him reminded him of the day she'd given him the letter at the end of their first summer.

As he closed the door, he knew that she'd heard everything that was said in the hallway, because he knew that look well; it was the one she'd worn the day she first broke his heart, the day they realized that maybe they didn't love each other the way they'd thought. Just like that day, he thought that was the end of it and that he might never see her again, and he'd wasted a trip home. But as he passed by the waiting Porsche, meeting the eyes of the man he despised above all others, he discounted all of his fears and doubts, and vowed that he would get her away from him, no matter the cost.

Chapter **35**

I had finally returned home...

    ... after a long absence only to discover that the place I'd once loved lay in ruin. The old structures stood empty and abandoned, and new ones had been built where none had been before, changing the landscape of that place, so as to almost make it foreign to me. The faces I once knew were gone, save a few exceptions, and the place felt even more deserted and alien without them.

    The one face that I'd thought would be my last remaining connection to home had changed just as much, and stared at me with eyes equally as empty. I longed to see that face, dreamed about seeing her again after being gone so long, and when I finally did, I'd wanted to crawl back into those dreams and never wake again. The reality of our reunion was a dousing of icy cold water on my head that made me realize a hard truth: that girl had gone with the rest, and she was just another empty structure to add to the gloomy landscape.

    It was like I was looking at everything through a cracked and water-drenched window, distorting my beautiful memory of her and my home. Outlines and colors were still there, but the finer details were muted like a painting splashed with acetone by a malicious hand. That malicious hand, in this case, was that of my most-hated enemy – the man who'd taken her from me once before and left my precious sanctuary in ruins as a result.

    The girl and the place were one in the same, inseparable in my mind, and when one had been ruined and trespassed upon, then the other suffered as well. Home had become a gloomy, miserable place because that girl had been made gloomy and miserable, and was brought to ruin. To save one, I would have to save the other, and that meant confronting the man who'd desecrated my temple, my sanctuary, and the thing I'd loved the most.

~ Journal of John Chapel

The entry in John's journal told of that malicious and meddling hand, as it attempted to hold an army at bay with the pointed edge of a single blade. It was pressed to the throat of the ruined girl mentioned in the same passage, threatening to bring an end to her misery and begin a new misery for the man standing only a few feet away. The passage goes on to say that it seemed an eternity that all the players involved were held immobile and powerless under the threat of that malicious hand and only a most difficult decision made by the author of the passage would break them free.

Outside, the situation was different and the players continued on in their role. Men with vengeance in their hearts, bent on destruction to satiate that vengeance would not be hindered by ruined girls or malicious hands. It seemed that there was nothing that would stop them in their course, not even a man they feared only a little less than their own, unseen God, for they had disobeyed him in favor of satisfying their own pride. That was the way men were, though, and they were foolish and simple creatures, fueled by the most simple of desires: love and hatred, lust and pride. One could not fault those men for giving in to their weaknesses, for those same weaknesses had taken hold of those in the tower as well.

Pride was a central player there, always given top billing in the more foolish acts of men, as well as love and hatred, who had lesser roles but were given equal speaking parts. Vanity, selfishness and selflessness were also bit players, but gave quite a performance in the second act of *John, Nicolette and the Wicked Man in the Tower.*

That wicked man tightened his grip on the bloodied shoulder of his hostage – who'd once been his beloved wife – and she gave a squeal and writhed under his blade. It was still part of the show, but the opening of a new act, the old act closing when Reginald made his desperate move. John was now watching a man so consumed with self-preservation and vanity that he was using his wife for protection, no longer a very well-rehearsed act, where the victim was not a victim at all, but a key player.

374

She had certainly put on a show for him only moments before, when he'd first entered that stage, in an attempt to preserve both of their lives and their livelihood. But the roles had changed and the lines had been rewritten, even completely improvised in some parts, as the lead players competed for the spotlight. The blade was real and his intentions just as plausible; the blood running from her injured shoulder was most definitely not a prop. Improvisation had brought them to this, and improvisation would have to save the show.

The girl was supposed to play the helpless damsel, and wait for her fair hero to rescue her from the tower prison, held against her will by a tyrant. She wasn't supposed to turn against him, allying herself with the villain, and sacrifice herself for him. Josh wasn't supposed to be the one who'd dealt the damsel a grievous wound and watch as the villain and hero roles were reversed. It was supposed to be a simple part: climb the tower, save the girl, and kill the wicked man. Instead, he had possibly doomed the girl and become the wicked man, making Reginald the hero.

He had to find a way out of his predicament now, had to find a way to end this without it turning into a complete disaster, but he did not know this man. It was the first time he was really meeting him, face-to-face, and he could not gauge his next move by studying him. Harold had given him fair warning, told him not to make a single slip up with this man, and he had. Now, he had the upper hand and the curtain would come down with this man as the last performer standing to applause.

"Let her go Reginald!" John demanded.

"I gave you my terms, John," he said firmly. "Tell your men to leave this place!"

"I've explained this to you; I gave them their orders and they disobeyed! Obviously, they're not going to listen to me now! Your only way out of here is to let her go and escape with your life!"

"I'm not stupid! As soon as I release her, you'll do to me what you did to them!"

"Let her go and you have my word that I will let you go free."

"What assurances do I have other than your *word*? You killed almost every man here with so little effort, what chance would I stand?"

"I have the same assurance that you'll release her if I let you go. I cannot prevent you from cutting her throat either...if you so choose. But I promise you, that if you hurt her, there is *no* chance that you will walk out of here with your life."

He edged towards him, keeping his hatchet from view so as not to excite him, keeping his open palm upward, indicating that he wanted a peaceful solution. Nicolette's tears and her fear were as genuine as his, causing every inch of her body to shudder uncontrollably. The blood from her shoulder had trailed down the side of her arm, falling from her fingertips, and also ran into the shallow valley above her collarbone, spilling onto her breast, painting it in deep crimson. She was losing quite a bit of blood from that wound, and if he didn't do something soon, she would collapse anyway.

"Come another step closer and her blood will run in the valleys of these stones as well!"

"She's bleeding badly Reginald...let her go for God's sake! She's your *wife!*"

"I'm not letting her out of my sight; she's the only thing keeping me alive! If your men will not follow orders, then you will escort the both of us to the stables and see that they do us no harm. Once we are gone, you can burn this place to the ground for all I care."

"I can't let you take her with you Reginald, she cannot make that trip! There isn't another place for her to get the proper attention for a half-day's ride, and if those men see me leading you to the stables, they will try to kill all of us. Your only chance is to leave her here, let me tend to her, and try to slip away under the cover of darkness."

"No!" He screamed, closing his hand more tightly around Nicolette's throat, squeezing out a garbled scream and causing her eyes to grow wider with fear.

John hesitated and looked from those frightened eyes to the desperate ones behind her, trying to read them. He could still not tell if it was all an act or if he really meant to kill his own wife just to go free. Harold described the man before him as someone more level-headed and calculating, and his behavior fit neither category. He seemed intent on leaving with her, despite her condition, and if he couldn't, he would condemn the both of them to death in that tower.

376

Nicolette, on the other hand, had not changed her behavior much since he'd first entered the room. She was trying to side with the man who represented her best chance of survival and continuing on with the life she had enjoyed, and she'd presumed, albeit foolishly, that man was Reginald. Once she'd realized the seriousness of her injury and of her situation, everything changed. Her best chance now would be staying in Avandale, if she had any chance at all.

"If you don't see to that wound, if the bone was shattered... the marrow will spread infection. She will lose her arm - if she's lucky! You'd be doing her a service to kill her quickly," he said bluntly.

Reginald's eyes fixed upon him, filling with hate, watching him take the lead from him. The man playing the frantic captor could not very well reassure the woman playing captive that she was going to be alright, without spoiling the act. He had to convince the man opposite that she was still his hostage, and that he wasn't concerned for her at all, even though she was starting to unravel and forget her lines.

"Reginald please...," she choked out, real panic in her voice.

"He's not going to allow you to be harmed...it's a façade," the lord assured her. "He overstates the extent of your injury, my love. I will have the finest surgeon in Poitou attend to you."

"You won't make it to Poitou, Nicolette," he continued to fan the flames of her fears. "He will carry you only so long as you are useful to him and then dump your body in a ditch for the crows."

"I don't want to die!" She shrieked. "Please let me stay!"

"Shut up! Stop frightening her!" Reginald snapped.

"I'm not the one holding a blade to her throat! You're threatening her life, yet you're promising her a surgeon? There is certainly a façade afoot here...you won't kill your own wife!"

"She is my wife, and I have a duty to protect her! Better to put her under my own blade and offer her a peaceful death than leave her in the hands of barbarians! She has had to endure that horror once before, and I will not allow her to do so again! Her life has been threatened by your own careless savagery, yet you would convince her that you're her deliverer?"

There, finally, was that cleverness Harold warned about: he was the one putting fingers in the wound now, and twisting them. Not even he would stoop to reminding her of the day she'd lost her innocence and a piece of her soul to the savage invaders.

"And you would convince us that you're defending the Roman Empire against the invading Visigoths? The only real danger here is your deliberate savagery, Reginald, for no other man here will bring her harm."

"Out my very window, men prepare to satiate their bloody lusting on the unwitting people - men whom you claim you can no longer control. On my chamber floor lie the victims of a practiced killer, delivering his message of vengeance, and you claim that she is safe?"

Though he could see through his manipulation, the woman caught in his grasp was too frazzled to do the same. His words were sufficient enough to twist and redirect her fear towards John, where it would have the most effect. The whole ordeal had pushed her to the edge, and it only took a small tug from one man and a gentle push from the other to send her spiraling into a place of despair. Nicolette pulled her arm free of his loosened grip, and stepped forward to slap John in the face.

"Why are you doing this? I spared your life and this is how you repay me; by taking everything away that I love?"

"If you're referring to your armoires, your fancy dresses, your coin and this dreary tower, no I didn't come to take those things, but those who came with me did. If you're talking about your life, or the lives of the innocents here, those men also came to take those things, but I bartered with them to leave those things untouched. If you're referring to the murderers that this place is harboring, then yes, those men will be taken."

"What about those men there? Did they not deserve your mercy?" She indicated the men on the floor, the ones that had tried to flee and had been cut down without hesitation.

"I did not come here to give mercy to those who do not deserve it. I did not come here to take lives, as he claims, but to *preserve* them!"

"*Preserve* lives? You've killed *ten* men so far, John, and you intend to take two more…while you do nothing to stop those men out there…with anything more than empty words?"

"I told you that they disobeyed me, and as we stand here bickering, I'm being prevented from intervening on the behalf of the innocent I came to protect!"

"No one stands in your way! Go forth to defend the innocent then, if that is why you truly came!"

"I cannot do so and knowingly leave you in peril! I came to protect you as well!"

"And a fine job you've done of that..." She said, holding out her bloody hand to show it to him.

"This man is wicked!" He screamed, growing red-faced. "And his wickedness has surely plagued you if you cannot see how he works to deceive you! I came here for you and for those who could not defend themselves, yet he turns me into a monster with his words and himself a savior!"

"Reginald is a *good* man and he has protected me and Avandale from our enemies! That happens to include your precious Rouen, which has invaded us many times before! It is unfortunate that you lost someone you cared about, I am truly sorry for your loss, but would you have me suffer her same fate? Am I to lose my life and my home simply because I was caught in the path of warring men?"

"I am not like those men...had there been only one among them with a conscience, one among them who tried to protect the innocent, then my girls would have been spared! I did not come here to rape and murder people for sport, and take pleasure in the lamentations of the dying!"

"They did no such thing! The men of Avandale were sent to deliver a message to Rouen: that we will not continue to be brutalized or intimidated by them, and we will no longer live in fear of them! I was beaten and then held down and raped repeatedly by men who wore colors from your home, John! And when we were finally strong enough to retaliate, when those men rode off to fight for our honor – for my honor – you slaughtered them! You protected the very people who ruined me...and destroyed us..."

"*Honor?* Those men knew nothing of *honor* and acted no better! I was there! I *watched* them! I had to cover the bodies of the girls who had been ravaged, and one of them was a child – your own cousin! And you believe that is was some mission to restore the honor of Avandale? This man makes a career of lying!"

"Those were men my father trained himself! They were loyal to him, followed his ideals and his standards, and they never would have done such a heinous thing!"

"And where is your father now? The truth is that Reginald sent him away, and he no longer has a place here in Avandale, isn't that right Reginald?"

"My father has been on a diplomatic mission for us to plead our case in the courts of Poitou, and Anjou...to request aid and support from our allies," she said defensively.

"Is that what he told you? Harold just saw your father in Rouen two days ago...and the two of them had a very different conversation. Your father learned of the nature of the mission of those loyal men...and he refused to be a party to it, so Reginald removed him from his station!"

She shook her head slowly and pressed her lids tight against the hot tears, trying not to let John's words seep into those gaping holes in the story that Reginald had told her. He had told her that it was a diplomatic mission of utmost importance, and that he'd had to leave at once, without even bidding his daughter farewell. She had thought it odd that the man most capable of negotiation and diplomacy had chosen to stay home to defend it and the man most capable of defending their home had gone on a mission of diplomacy. She had also thought it odd that every time she'd asked if there had been any word of her father or his progress, that Reginald had avoided the topic.

"My father...Reginald...he's on a mission..." She stammered, not having enough conviction to finish a single sentence.

"He *uses* people Nicolette...and he will continue to use you until you stop him. He has become so adept at twisting the truth that it sounds genuine as it pours from his forked tongue. Now you don't know what to believe or whom to trust, and he turns you against me...but you know that *something* isn't quite right..."

Her head was spinning and she was conflicted like never before, and the two voices of the bickering men were drowned out just for a little while. A man she'd thought never to see again suddenly appeared at the foot of her bed only a little while ago, threatening to take everything from her in one swift stroke of an axe. She would again descend into a life of hopeless destitution, and become a girl with nothing, and that terrified her as much as the possibility of death itself.

He wanted to murder her husband, who was a good and caring man, and he was the one who'd made him resort to most desperate measures. He'd only been trying to protect her hadn't he? Her Reginald would never act so cowardly would he? She thought that she knew him well enough to answer those questions with certainty, before the stranger returned.

She could not answer any of those questions with certainty about that stranger who'd barged into her chamber, making wild accusations and demands. And though she could obviously not trust such a man, there was something about him that made her question if she really trusted Reginald. It wasn't just mistrust that the stranger had stirred within her bosom.

It began when she'd stood with the sharp blade beneath her chin, holding what was possibly her last breath, entranced by the magnificent fighter's dance. For a moment, she believed that he danced just for her, and that he'd come for her, and for a moment, she felt her dead heart leap in her chest. Perhaps it was all the excitement, the thrill of having all of those men fighting just for her, or just the subtle, quiet reminder that death often brings with her when she enters a room. People forget to respect her sometimes, and she has to give them that cold, unsettling stare or touch her fingers lightly on their shoulder, and that's usually enough to get their attention.

She hadn't realized just how numb and bored with living she'd become until that very night when the boy from the lake returned like the storm that had first brought him to her. As that room slowly spun around her, she took note of all that she'd amassed over the past two years, filling every nook and empty space in that tower, in the hopes that she would forget how empty she was. Collecting those pretty things and stockpiling them in that place was a desperate attempt to fill that void that was left when she'd been robbed of everything.

Reginald promised her that no one would ever take these things from her, and she would be safe in this room full of her pretty things. But now that John had returned, a more pleasant reminder to lay her eyes upon than the dark mistress, she remembered what true happiness had been about. She suddenly wanted nothing to do with those pretty, unfeeling things, or the room that she'd locked them and herself away in. Reginald had lied to her: someone had come to take those things from her, make her hate them, and she no longer felt safe in that room, no longer felt safe with him.

"Why...why did it have to be *you*? I sent you from this place...prayed that God would keep you safe...that you would find a good life elsewhere...but here you are. I never dreamed...to see your face again...or to feel any joy in that sight...but here you are."

Her voice was trailing off and she was doing a little swaying dance, teasing both men and making them each think that she might fall at any moment. She eyed each as she seemed to hover above the ground like a gentle bird trying to find a solid branch in a wind storm. Back and forth she swayed, appearing drunk, barely lucid, yet still trying to piece together the truth in her head.

She finally lurched forward, with the last of her strength, and fell into his waiting arms, at last making her choice. As he held her, Reginald looked helplessly on, inevitability finally realized and materializing before his eyes, like a picture being etched on glass, it would be burned there in his memory forever. He would never forget that night or the man who'd made him as obsolete as her father. He couldn't help but remember the night he'd sent George away, telling him, so coldly, that he had fulfilled his purpose and should move on. He'd broken that man's heart in two, crushed his pride, and forced him away, promising that Nicolette would be in good hands.

Reginald was haunted by his own words and, at the same time, marveled at the humor of those three bitches at the loom, forever weaving their private jokes into the tapestry meant for men such as him. They took her from him as much as the man standing before him, and he was as helpless to fight against them as he was against that clever performer who'd outwitted him.

"Well-played..." He uttered to no one in particular, and John barely paid him any mind as he carried the limp woman to the bed.

He only noticed that he was still there when he looked up to find the necessary materials for dressing and mending her wound. "Are you still here then? Did you not hear what I said? I gave you my word...and I gave her my word. I promised that I would not

382

squander precious minutes to fight you, and instead try to save her life."

"You're just going to let me go? You must know that I will return? That I will bring an army larger than you have ever seen to-_"

"Are you quite finished? Either stay and help me with her or make your way to the stables and be on the fastest horse you have away from this place! It's your decision, Reginald."

He stood, dumbfounded by the audacity of this brave bastard who had just walked right into his tower, dispatched his guard (who were still lying in a pool of blood and piss, not ten feet away), took his wife, and was now acting as though *he* was the unwelcome guest in his own home. He wasn't sure if he liked the brazenness of such a man, or if he truly despised him – like a bittersweet wine he swished in his mouth, uncertain if he should spit it on the floor or savor the taste.

John ignored him and tore strips from the curtains into bandages as he was quietly admiring and cursing him at the same time. He moved efficiently and seemed to be as versed in the medical arts as he was at swordplay and word-smithy, fetching the necessary materials. From the bureaus he procured spools of thread and needles, as well as more clean cloth, and from the corner stand, the washing bowl. At the fireplace, he put on the kettle and left the iron rod in the center of the coals.

"What do you intend to do with that?" He asked, as he grabbed up a few of his things.

"Cauterize the wound where the stitch won't hold," he said, annoyed.

"So you are a surgeon?"

"I'm a *blacksmith*," he snorted. "I've had to use the iron on many a soldier fresh in from the field."

"This isn't the field, and she's not a soldier! You're going to scar up half her body--"

"I'm going to do what it takes to save her life!" He growled, standing from the bed and baring his teeth like a guard dog. "I think I hear the men getting closer...you'd best be off!"

"What will become of her?"

"Suddenly you're concerned? She'll be quite safe here as she recuperates. I need to mend this wound, make sure there is no infection, keep her fed and make sure she gets rest. She should be well within the week, provided that she doesn't take with the fever--"

"I meant…she is my *wife*…I'm not a perfect husband…but I have loved her."

"When she regains her strength and is well enough, she'll make that determination," John said.

"I will be in Poitou, and I will send for her within the week once I am established there. Perhaps we can avoid any unnecessary unpleasantries in the future if--"

"You can send for the *Pope* if it pleases you, it doesn't mean he'll come running! If you are trying to intimidate me or threaten me, let the ten dead men behind you serve as a reminder that I do not scare easily," he snarled again, annoyed that he was taking up his precious time and hers.

Reginald backed away, "I'm leaving! But so you might be prepared, Henry will hear of this and this will not stand!"

"Henry cannot even control his son right now, or the rebellious barons, or his wife for that matter, what will he care for a small tower in a military outpost? This place is under Richard's protection now, Reginald, and mine. Don't presume that I will be as incompetent as its former lord in protecting this place or its people."

Reginald turned red again, finally spitting the bitter taste on the floor, deciding that he indeed hated him more than he admired him. "This isn't the last day you'll lay eyes upon me, John of Rouen."

"It's a short distance to the roof," he reassured him. "From there, take the old oak down and slip around the side. You'll be safe there from the others. Now go, before I change my mind."

Reginald took one last look at the woman resting peacefully on the bed and then to the man whose capable hands he was leaving her in, and finally took his leave. He wished him success and John secretly wished for him to lose his footing during the jump and go crashing through the chapel ceiling like he did. Letting him live was a huge mistake and letting him leave was an even bigger mistake. He remembered what Harold had said about missing an opportunity to kill him, and knew that it wouldn't be the last he'd see of Reginald of Poitou.

He remembered Harold and their agreement then, and after he'd prepared the bowl of hot water and let the iron heat up more, he climbed the ladder in the chamber up to the roof of the tower. Taking a torch, he set one of the crimson and black standards hanging from the ramparts aflame and waved it in the air for the others to see. That was the signal that the tower had been taken and that they would not need to bother with it.

He saw Harold's signal from the valley north of the tower, where the new houses had been built for the soldiers. They had already set most of those houses ablaze, despite John's insistence that they wait for his orders. He'd hoped that he'd at least offered those poor souls an opportunity to surrender to the new order before putting them to death, but there was no way of knowing. There were more pressing matters at hand, and a precious life was now in his care, so he would have to hope that Harold's rampage would be limited to the north valley.

Chapter *36*

He scrubbed his hands repeatedly in the scalding water, turning it pink, and then dried them thoroughly on strips he'd torn from the bed curtains. Examining the jagged gash, he saw that it would require a steady hand and lots of thread, but the gleaming white collar bone seemed to be intact and he said a silent prayer of thanks. The stitches weren't pretty, but they would hold and stop most of the bleeding. Just to be sure, he pressed the very tip of the red hot bar on the wound and her flesh sizzled.

She winced and let out a moan but didn't stir otherwise from her unconscious state. After she was soundly resting and he wrapped her wound in fresh dressings, he sat on the end of the bed and finally had a moment to collect himself. He'd had to hold himself in check, emotionally, through the whole ordeal that had only lasted less than twenty minutes. Confronting Reginald and facing his old love, seeing them together in bed, and fighting with his old feelings about that girl had been draining – more so than the ensuing battle and standoff which had almost cost her life. She'd almost died because of him, and he was just now playing that scenario out in his head, how he would live with that for the rest of his days.

He hadn't seen her in almost two years, and she'd been pushed far from his mind, though he hadn't been able to push her from that other place somewhere between the shadowed corners of his heart and the deepest pit of his stomach. Losing Elizabeth had been devastating because he'd truly loved her, but losing Nicolette would have been so much more so, because he hadn't been allowed to love her. Things had been unfinished between them since that night two winters past, and it had left a hole in him larger than the one in her shoulder. Had she died, that hole never would have closed and such an infection would have overtaken him that he would have died a slow, painful death.

He grasped her limp hand and wiped the water from his eyes to smear the crimson on his face, and then stood to take his leave of the tower to confront Harold. He wouldn't have far to go, for Harold and two of his men entered from the stairwell, weapons drawn as if expecting to meet resistance. He looked around at the pile of bloody rags, the bowl of pink water and the other odd things strewn about the room and gave John a puzzled look. The amateur surgeon indicated the sleeping woman and shooed them back down the stairwell, where he met them to discuss what had taken place as well as the status of their captive.

"The men downstairs are what's left of the guard...the girl was injured in the fight...she's lost a lot of blood but she will live."

"What of Reginald?"

"Reginald...is gone," he said, as if surprised that he didn't know. "You did not see him?"

"Should we have?"

John was already having a hard time composing himself after the small meltdown he'd just had, and would have as much difficulty telling Harold the lie.

"While I was fighting the others, a small detachment covered his escape. I killed all but one of his guards." It was mostly true, and the rest he made look good by feigning disgust. "He would have ridden right past you and your men! You did not see him?"

"We didn't. I warned you about the consequences of letting him escape!"

"Had you kept your word and not went on your murderous rampage before I gave the signal, you would have seen him and been able to end his miserable life! But you defied me and went chasing after men who were only following orders, instead of killing the man who was truly responsible!"

The men with Harold backed away and lowered their weapons, not wanting to be involved in another confrontation between the two of them.

"What are you talking about? Those men killed your brethren and might have been the ones responsible for Elizabeth! They will never again harm an innocent in Rouen!"

"Yea...about that..." John said, wiping the blood from his forehead with a palm, "Who was in charge of the first attack on Avandale, two winters past?"

"What kind of nonsense was she filling your head with?"

John's brows knotted like they did when he was both angry and working a puzzle in his mind, and he stepped closer to Harold, checking the hatchet at his belt. The soldiers stepped further back, fearing that they would end up on that pile in the room.

"There was an attack...right before harvest...two seasons ago. Men came and murdered the people here, raped some, and left Avandale in ruin. She was among them," he said, pointing to the girl on the bed. "She said they came from Rouen. The men who began this war...came from Rouen! Tell me you weren't there, Harold!"

"No one from Rouen would bother with a worthless hole like Avandale!"

"So she's a liar? She lies about being raped and beaten? She lies about the attack that brought her home under the protection of Henry and Reginald's father, Hugh? Why would she lie about that? I have often wondered, many nights, why anyone would single out a place like this...why a place like this would send soldiers to Rouen. Now I realize...that there was a past with Rouen that I had no knowledge of!"

He was screaming now, and didn't realize it, had his hatchet in his hand, and did not feel it. Harold now decided that backing away with the others wasn't a bad plan.

"John...I have not been involved in the affairs of this place or its people, only George would know these things. We can talk to George as soon as we return..."

"You've already spoken to George, and you already know what has taken place here! He trained those men that we've both killed...the men who killed his sister-in-law and his niece...and he found out about it, didn't he? That was why Reginald sent him out, wasn't it? Did he warn *them*, Harold? Did he warn you?"

"Yer makin' a lot of accusations boy! Yer not thinkin' clearly and I understand that yer upset, but think about what yer' sayin'," Harold nearly tripped over every word as he tripped over the bodies behind him as he backed away.

"Did George come to Rouen to warn Elizabeth of an imminent attack? Answer the question!"

Harold dipped his mighty head, "Yes...he knew that it was coming. But he never trained those soldiers to unleash them on Rouen...he was *never* told why they were being trained! Reginald sent them, and George tried to stop him, but he wouldn't hear of it!"

389

"You *knew* they were coming? You *both* knew...and you said nothing to me?"

"We tried to stop them...we tried to follow their trail...keep them out of the city...but it's more complicated than that!"

"Explain it to me! What's so complicated? 'John, men will be coming to Rouen, get Elizabeth and the girls out of the city' (he mimicked his baritone voice) – that seems like a fairly easy thing to say!"

"There was an ambush waiting for us, John! Reginald has connections in lots of places, and an army from Poitou fell on us before we could intercept the one from Avandale! We couldn't stop them in time...Reginald planned the whole thing from the beginning!"

John gripped the handle of his hatchet and studied each man, as if selecting his target, making each more nervous than the next. Finally, he swung it with a cry like a wounded bear, and buried it deep into the bed post nearest him. He stormed off down the stairwell and left the stunned and frightened men alone in the chamber with the sleeping girl and the dead.

Harold was the brave one that followed him down the stairs and out the front gate to find him standing beside the chapel. His friend had vomited in the grass and rested his face on the cool stone of the church wall, leaning his forehead on an arm.

"John...war is an ugly thing...I've told ye' that many times, son."

He only had called him 'son' on one other occasion, when he'd had a very heartfelt conversation with him about protecting his girls and how solemn a duty that was. That same solemnness had returned to his face and the fearful seriousness to his voice.

"This...none of this is *your* fault...these are games and maneuvers of other men...and we are only soldiers carrying out orders."

"Who are you making excuses for, Harold? For me? For Richard and his father? Or for yourself?"

"There are no excuses or answers that will make it right..."

"Only *blood* right? Isn't that it? Enough blood drowns your guilt? Did you get enough this time? Did you take enough blood from this place to forget what happened to her? Does blood wash away the lies and the politics of those men handing out the orders?"

"John, this is why I'm only a soldier...why I don't make these decisions...why I cannot send men to carry out deeds such as this," Harold said. "I never wanted to be a king, just a man who fought for a king and fought for an ideal"

He picked up the blackened banner that had fluttered to the ground nearby, and held it up for him to see. "*This* was an ideal, Harold, this...right here! This was a place that had taken enough of being oppressed by someone and they decided to take a stand! And we came to teach them a lesson for it. Why? Because we're just fighting men, just stupid, mindless soldiers that blindly follow orders!"

"We took a stand! We came here for revenge and to let this place know that we will not tolerate murderers running rampant in our streets!"

"We didn't take a *stand*; we came to do another man's dirty work! Richard told you where those men came from didn't he? He was supposed to ride with us! Instead, he just pointed his favorite war hound in a direction and set him loose, thinking this would satisfy his thirst for blood. Did you give *any* thought as to why he didn't show up personally or even send a single man to help as he'd promised?"

"Richard is busy fighting a war with many fronts, John; he did not feel that a small--"

"Do you even know if they were sent from here?" He cut him off. "How do you even know if the men we killed in Rouen were from Avandale, Anjou, Poitou or somewhere else?"

Harold was silent, mulling over what John was suggesting, and the squeamish look on his face said that he didn't care for his suggestion.

"The truth is that you don't know - any more than I do - and we just came here to slaughter those who we *think* were responsible! That's just what we were *told*! This reeks of something sinister, and I do not trust Richard any more than I do Reginald!"

"What are you trying to get at, John? That this was all some insidious plot...by Richard?"

"Well he's not here for us to ask him, is he? He sent his obedient fools to punish this small, insignificant village, and we

391

carried out those orders without question! Men were brought to this place from the outside to be trained by George, most of the soldiers here were not born and raised here, and we don't even have an accounting of how many more came through here to be trained, or where they came from! The man who trained them isn't even here? The man who ordered the attack isn't here either, and I would wager that he never was!"

"What do you suggest, John? We question Richard and ask him to produce evidence of his spies' information? We accuse him of what? Staging an invasion of Rouen? Placing the blame on a small village? For what purpose?"

"I don't know what *purpose*, but it's time that we start asking! It's time that we started to make decisions of our own and time that we become greater men than this!"

"You want to become lord of the tower, is that it? Rebuild the army? Take on barons and kings like Richard and his enemies? You don't know the first thing of politics or their kind of warfare!"

"I don't need to know one banner from the next, or which lord I should address by which title, I just need to have a conscience and an ideal that I pay more than lip service to!"

Harold shook his head and let out a long sigh, "I cannot follow ye' in this, John. If there is any truth at all to what yer suggesting, and ye' get yerself embroiled in the plots of men such as those, they will ruin ye' John!"

"You wanted Reginald's head, this is your opportunity. Stay here and help me rebuild this place, Harold, help me train an army. There is nothing in Rouen for us any longer, nothing there to go home to...you can't be someone's war hound forever."

"We all have someone to answer to, John. I answer to Richard and I have to give him an accounting of this place."

"Then tell him we've taken Avandale and never again will any of its people set foot in Rouen or any other place loyal to him."

"And if he brings an army here to see this place laid waste?"

"Then God help him...for that will only confirm his guilt. Avandale is under my protection now, and you will not change my mind in this! God help any man who would bring this kind of bloody destruction here ever again!"

Chapter 37

That was how the act ended, with a long look over a heavy shoulder at a seemingly insignificant tower. For one of the lead players on that stage, it had represented a simple military target and the stronghold of the enemy, for another, it was home and a second chance at love and a new life. For both of them, it was a pivotal turning point in their story, a dramatic end to one act and the exciting beginning of another, where friends were potential enemies, enemies lovers, and the roles of every other player were rewritten. The tower changed everything for all of them in just one night, and the significance of that place would never be forgotten by many of them.

It was home to many, the place that they looked to for security and protection from enemies both real and imagined, whether they were watched over by the tower or were looking from its ramparts. When it was occupied by pretense and many luxuries, it seemed very empty, but when pretense was deposed and luxuries were cast out, it seemed fulfilled at last. It's funny how a place full of many faces and possessions can seem the most desolate place, but the same place with but a single face can seem like a sanctuary. Such was the case in another place far away, on another stage, filled by much different players.

The story was the same though, and transcribed by the same hand. A young man is called back to the place he calls home to find that it has been corrupted and changed almost beyond recognition. He discovers that the very thing that defines that place as home, the beating heart at its center, has been poisoned by his mortal enemy. The face of every player seems darkened as well, overshadowed by darker skies above, and there, a storm looms. Some of those grey faces he calls allies, yet he feels unaided in his task and the burden of saving that home and its poisoned heart lies with him alone.

As the curtain draws, the stage is still being set and all of the players have yet to arrive. The ladies have all gotten into makeup and costume, all done up for their biggest performance yet, and the men are going over their lines together, seated comfortably in a black Mercedes Benz. None of them are aware of the size of the venue just yet; they just have the playbill, with the location and time, scrawled on a napkin with an eyeliner pencil.

The black sedan sat quietly beside the curb, parked behind a long procession of cars, and a large truck wheeled in behind him. In between arguing over the directions on the napkin, they'd been taking turns trading shots at one another, just like old times. It felt almost like a typical Friday night after school, complete with a case of beer in the back seat that Connelly had split open and handed them each a can from, and the noise of a house party coming from up the street.

They chugged their beer as they let Dean in on some of their old school day antics, getting him up to speed on the history of their little group and mutual friend, John. Dean fit right in, having polished off his third can since they'd been parked, and tossing his most recent empty in the back seat with a loud belch.

"Geez, I thought I could put em' away," Connelly said, laughing. "We need to take this guy with us to some of the spring break parties – I think we could make some money betting on him."

He handed him another can and then grabbed two more to take to Pete and Hunter, leaving Josh to feel out of place in the car with John and Dean. He could sense the tension in the air and that same murkiness that John felt, and he knew that there was a discussion waiting on the lips of the two men in the front seat. He excused himself, saying something about checking on Connelly, and left the two of them alone.

John sat quietly sipping his beer for a moment, and then pulled the stack of pages from the console that Melinda had given him. Dean watched him glance at the top page of each and neatly organize them by the dates written in the upper corner. He rattled off each date aloud to Dean, as if he was supposed to know the significance of them.

"Ah...August third...November fifteenth...where was I then? Hmm...July eighteenth...don't remember." And it went like this until he had them neatly organized in chronological order all the way back to the very first. "January twenty-fourth...that's the night before I left."

Dean finally gave him a nod of acknowledgement, recalling that night very well. Melinda had been a screaming, blubbering mess, and no one could calm her down. That had been a year-and-a-half ago, and things hadn't changed much.

"What's it say, man?"

John shook his head looking back down at the letter, "Probably that I'm a rotten sonovabitch, she hates me and never wants to see me again."

He set his beer on the dash and leaned closer to the illuminated display to read the pages. A moment later his face seemed to absorb more of the green light from the dash than what seemed possible, and he set them down in the pile.

"What does it say Johnny?" He dared the question again. "Why the hell did she write all of those and not give them to you?"

John glanced up at his friend, then back into his lap. "It doesn't really matter now. These are old...these are all old. She wrote them...to torture me. It means she never got over the fact that I couldn't reach her when we were kids. I wrote letters. She never got them."

"It's not your fault that she never got them, Johnny! Why the hell is she such a bitch?"

"She didn't do it to be a bitch, Dean...she was hurting...and this was her way of letting me know that she was hurting. That's good!"

"It's *good* that she gave you a pile of useless letters she never sent?"

"It's good that she admitted that I hurt her, it means that she wants me to know, and that she wants to talk about it. If she wanted to just hate me, she'd have kept these tucked away forever, or just thrown them out. There are two types of angry, Dean: being angry and keeping it to yourself and being angry and doing something about it."

"But she gave you these to...hurt you. It's some kind of weird...poetic thing."

"She's acting out, which means she wants me to notice, and if she wants me to notice...it means she *can* be reached and she *wants* to be reached."

"I think she just wants to screw you over, like the night at the motel...I would be careful."

"Your sister can't hurt me any more than she already has…I have that to my advantage."

"You're fooling yourself, Johnny. Remember what happened back at the house? If I hadn't walked in…it would have been all over."

"But it's not all over; it's just beginning…but not tonight. Tonight we have fun and forget about your sister. Tomorrow we'll open this discussion again."

Dean nodded, clinked his aluminum can with John's, and the pair of them toasted with hopes for a nice relaxing evening. Four car doors slammed and six shadows crept up the long drive towards the house on the hill. It was a tri-level, spacious Rochester Hills home, too nice to belong to any of the kids standing along the drive or packed inside, most likely one of their parents' who were far away on some vacation. They could hear the music blaring from the end of the drive and it got louder as they got closer to the front door.

Two knocks later and a tall Arab guy sporting a Michigan sweatshirt and a backward baseball hat pulled the door open. He looked them over, not recognizing them, and was about to turn them away until one of the girls from the diner spotted them and came to give them a personal escort.

"It's okay, I invited them!" She had to yell in the man's ear, and then led Dean by the arm.

Once inside, they had to shove through the crowd of sweaty bodies and squint through the haze that was giving them a contact buzz. Every square foot of the place was occupied by someone, and every piece of furniture had two or three couples climbing on top of each other, oblivious to their surroundings. From somewhere, a jolly and robust man handed John and Dean a beer, then disappeared into the fog once again.

John inspected the large red cup as if expecting it to be filled with something else, but found his beer to be in good order. He turned to look at Dean who already had his half gone, and so tipped his own cup back. They were led through another yard of bodies before they spotted another familiar face, and she waved them over as she flashed them a big smile. It was Gwenn's and she looked even better than she had earlier at the diner, wearing a slinky party dress and having done her hair up and adding a bit more eyeliner – as though that were possible.

396

John locked eyes with hers and smiled at her, and just as he was about to push past the last couple of sweaty obstacles, Connelly and Hunter brushed past him in a race towards Gwenn.

"You guys…" He shouted after them, but was drowned out by the music.

As he was about to go to the defense of the poor girl and shoo away the jackals, he felt a hand grab his and smelled the jasmine perfume a moment too late. A familiar body suddenly came between his and Gwenn's and stood with big eyes looking into his. "Hey Johnny, did you come to see *me*?" The beautiful blonde asked, swaying a bit as she talked.

"How are you doing Mel? I didn't know you'd be here…" He replied, trying to recover from the sudden shock of seeing her there.

"I'm doing great now that you're here…"

She reeked of alcohol and her eyes showed hints of red. Even so, she still looked hot in her tight shirt and skirt, which wasn't at all the outfit he'd remembered laying on her bed. She was moving to the rhythm of the electronic beat that was playing and draped her arms around his shoulders. He stood like a rock as she gyrated around him, trying to gently push her away and appear disinterested.

Gwenn, Hunter and Connelly turned to watch him. The guys had a big grin on their faces, but Gwenn wasn't smiling at all. John kept his eyes fixed on Gwenn as he spoke to Melinda.

"This isn't the time or the place, Mel…"

"This is the perfect time – it's a party! Come and dance with me…and then we can talk," she exclaimed, grabbing him by the arm and trying to pull him away from his watchful friends.

"How about we go grab some dinner tomorrow night and we can talk then?"

She gave a pouty face, "Johnny…I think we need to talk now. I've been thinking about a lot of things…and there's a lot I want to say to you."

Of course she'd been thinking after that bomb he'd dropped in the hallway upstairs. It was probably the only thing she'd been able to think of all night, and she'd become borderline obsessed with it. Nobody told Melinda Malowski that they weren't completely into her anymore, especially John Chapel.

"Let's just have fun tonight, Melinda…and tomorrow we can talk," he said, barely looking at her.

She wrapped her arms around his neck then, pressing her breasts against him for the second time that day. "I like where your head is at…okay…let's have fun then."

"I didn't mean together," he said, fixing a harsh stare on her finally. "I came here to be with my friends tonight, I haven't seen them in a long time. I'll call you tomorrow and we can talk."

With that, he did something that Gwenn, Dean, and especially Melinda had never seen him do. He gently pushed the seductress to the side like a curtain, and moved past her to put his arms around Gwenn in a huge embrace.

Dean wasn't sure whose eyes opened wider, Gwenn's or his sister's. It was common knowledge that John Chapel had always been wrapped around the certain pinkie finger of a girl standing in that room - the same girl who'd completely stopped dancing to gape awestruck and be put well into her place. If John was trying to get her riled up and play games with her, it appeared to have worked. But, by the size of the smile John's face as he talked and laughed with the auburn-haired girl, he seemed to have cared less.

Melinda glared first at her old best friend and then at her brother, one ignoring her and the other giving her a shrug, then she stormed off. Her brother secreted a smile behind the protection of his large red cup so she wouldn't see it and whispered, "Good for you, Johnny."

Pete and Josh even shared an unusual moment where they slapped discretionary hi-fives, having enjoyed the scene, and then disappeared into the crowd. Connelly and Hunter were irritated that their secret competition was over before it began, but Connelly patted his friend on the back still, and he dragged Hunter off to start their eternal contest anew. Dean, finding his cup empty, made the excuse that he was headed to the kitchen for more, and left the two of them alone to talk.

"You came," was all she could manage, still reeling from his grandstand move.

"Of course I came; it's a party, my friends needed to unwind, and I knew you'd be here."

"I'm glad you came," she sputtered out, not able to think of anything clever to say.

He was standing close out of necessity, but she liked his proximity and the occasional brush of his arm against her bare shoulders. It made the tiny hairs at her neck rise, but it also made her blush and dried up her mouth, making it impossible to talk. So she just listened to him make small talk and nodded, smiling bigger and bigger, until she thought her face would split. She'd hoped that she wouldn't have to actually respond because it felt like she'd swallowed a cup of sand, and also hoped he wouldn't graze the inside of her palms by mistake, which were growing clammy.

"I need to get a drink, "she finally choked out. "Do you want to come with me?"

"Sure," he said, putting a hand on her shoulder again, and making her need for a drink even more urgent.

Dean had arrived in the kitchen a few minutes ahead of them to refill his cup and try to find a girl to talk to. As one of the frat guys pumped the keg for him, he thought he saw his chance. It was the other girl who'd been in the diner with Gwenn earlier, a bit prettier than the one who'd greeted them at the door. She was talking to another girl and waiting to get her cup refilled apparently, because it was dangling loosely from her fingers and she was playing with it.

Sipping at the foamy head of his beer, he made his way towards her, but then changed direction when he'd noticed the tall, tan-skinned guy standing near to her, who threw his arm around her. The man had his back to him, but he had looked familiar to Dean, and he made a half circle to get a good look at his competition's face. The long, greasy black hair and the white running suit was nothing to distinguish this guy from all of the others, but his unusual height gave him reason to pause.

Dean took a large gulp form his cup as an excuse to refill it, then bending down and working the tap, he turned his head slightly to get a look at the man's face. For a moment, his eyes met with those black eyes, and his blood ran cold.

Sal stared back at his girlfriend's brother with indifference, as if he didn't recognize him or just didn't care that he saw him. He only looked at Dean briefly, smiled, and then turned his attention back to the girl he was flirting with. With a full cup, Dean stepped back and continued to stare at the arrogant man over his beer. About that time John and Gwenn came through the door, and he caught them and pulled them into the corner to give them a briefing.

"Dude, it's Sal," he said in a low voice to John.

"Who's he with?" Gwenn whispered, trying to look over Dean's shoulder. "Oh my God, is that Melissa? I can't believe she'd even talk to him!"

"Keep it down," John warned, his eyes burning into the back of his hated foe's head.

"This happens all the time, just never in the same room with my sister," Dean explained. "If we could bust him...if she could see it with her own eyes...that might help our case."

"Well that rules me out," John said. "I don't think she'd believe me if I said the house was on fire at this point."

"And I'm pretty sure she wants to stab me with a shank the first moment she has alone with me," Gwenn joked.

"Okay then, you two stay here and I'll go grab Mel. Keep your eyes on him and keep him here if you can," Dean hashed out his plan.

"I'm not staying here," John protested. "If he sees me, it could be world war three!"

Dean nodded, "Agreed. Okay Gwenn, you stay here – you're Melissa's friend anyway, you have a reason to go talk to her."

"Why do I have to be in the same room with that piece of trash?"

Dean kissed her cheek and prepared to drag John from the kitchen so they could find his sister, but sometimes things work out better than the best laid plans. Melinda came stumbling into the kitchen at that moment, almost running into her brother and John, and they had to catch her by the elbow to keep her from falling.

"Oh...it's you...that explains why *he's* here," she said, jerking her arm away and not realizing how loudly she was talking.

Her awkward entrance and loud mouth had caused enough of a scene that Sal turned around to see what the commotion was about. He noticed John immediately and his bottom lip coiled under in a frown, and he started towards him, not seeing the blonde standing beside him. Before he could engage his hated enemy, however, he was stopped by the very angry stare of a very jealous girlfriend.

Dean decided to duck out of the kitchen, having seen that look on his sister's face once or twice before, and tugged at John's shirt. It meant things were soon going to be hurtled about the kitchen like some poltergeist had taken possession of it. Though he wanted badly to observe the confrontation which would follow, he didn't want to stand in the kill zone.

Gwenn was the only one brave enough to stand in the door, watching and narrating to the others tucked behind her. Within moments, the shrill screaming came spilling forth in a string of near-incomprehensible obscenities. Sal had taken a step back, letting her have her tantrum, and knowing that he was caught. He'd hoped to diffuse a physical situation, but stepping out of melee range only caused her to switch tactics, and plastic cups, ice cubes and an empty pizza box became ranged weapons.

These bounced harmlessly off the apologetic man, but the next volley didn't. Two glasses broke on the cupboard doors above Sal's head, followed by a cordless phone which hit its mark. He cursed back at her in Arabic and he lunged forward to grab her by the arms to stop the missile attack before it got out of hand. Dean stood at the ready, just in case he wanted to get rough with his "little sister", but Sal was on the defensive, only wanting to protect himself from showering glass. He and Gwenn kept looking back at John, expecting him to go bursting into the room at any moment, but he stood expressionless.

Gwenn turned back to peep through the crack in the door, and unable to suppress a smile. Maybe Johnny was really over her, she thought to herself, and for one night, Melinda's drama wouldn't spoil her fun. The man she knew before would've gone charging in there to leap on the giant and pummel him, and she'd wager too, by the looks of him now, that he would give Sal more of a run for his money.

The screaming died down to loud voices, and Melinda's siege was weakening as he continued to convince her that what she saw was a misunderstanding. It made Gwenn cringe and almost wish that John would flatten that liar's face and teach him a lesson. This was as close as they'd been to exposing Sal for the cheating piece of trash that he was, and now they were losing their opportunity. She felt a bit guilty then for hoping that the Melinda "problem" would just work itself out just so she could enjoy her party and possibly get closer to Johnny.

401

Gwenn turned to John then and gave him a scolding eye, "Why don't you go in there and say something to her? You're not going to let him lie his way out of this are you?"

The two boys looked puzzled by her statement, especially Dean. He knew that Gwenn always had a thing for John and saw exactly how excited she was when John had snubbed his sister to go talk to her. Now she was trying to throw him on top of a grenade.

"What would you like me to say? She saw him with her own eyes and she's buying into his bullshit," John grumbled, suddenly looking very uncomfortable and wanting to leave.

"You have to say something to her – she'll listen to you! If you get her riled up enough, tonight could be the end of them!"

"Yea, because she thinks that there's a chance with me and I'll be stuck with her!"

Gwenn suppressed the smile this time, and liked the sound of John's tone when he'd described being "stuck" with Melinda Malowski, as though it was on par with getting a root canal. Still, she had to put her friend first, and she gripped him by the arm and pushed him towards the door.

"Then make her think that there is a chance so she gets rid of him! The two of you can sort it out later…we need to help her Johnny, and she won't listen to either of us right now!"

He looked to Dean who nodded reluctantly, "I think this is our only chance…she'll see me or Gwenn as only meddling if we go barging in there. I'm just her brother and Gwenn she just thinks of as a jealous girl who wants everything she has…but you…you're the one she'll listen to."

"I just blew her off earlier," he protested.

"All the more reason she'll want you now!" Gwenn said.

"Why do I feel like this is a bad Scooby Doo cartoon and you're using me as bait in a trap that's going to completely blow up in my face?"

Gwenn sighed with disgust and turned from the door crevasse, "It looks like it already has…."

She pushed the door open a little wider to allow the boys to look inside. The yelling had stopped altogether and they hadn't noticed over their own plotting. The pair in the kitchen was embraced in a kiss, and that signaled the end of the fight as well as a closed window of opportunity. They walked away from the door, defeated, and watched from an alcove as Melinda led Sal from the kitchen by a hand towards a set of stairs and then disappeared to the second level.

Dean cursed and shook his head in disgust, saying, "Why is she so damned stupid?"

John frowned and shared his look of disgust, staring off towards the stairwell, "I should've done something...you were right. Maybe I should go up there...and talk..."

"It's too late now, Johnny...just wait until you can get her alone. Maybe tomorrow," Gwenn said, and disappeared back into the haze and packed bodies of the party.

"There went my chance with Melissa too!" Dean complained.

John slugged him in the arm, "You're an idiot! Go get us some beer!"

Dean went into the kitchen, which looked more like Beirut after his sister had been there. While he was left standing there, John stared through the crowd, catching glimpses of the auburn-red hair as she got further and further away. He looked back towards the door to the kitchen, and then dove into that sea of bodies to follow the girl.

Chapter 38

"Wait...I need to talk to you," he said, grabbing her wrist and spinning her around.

"Johnny? Hey I didn't know you were behind me..."

The college guy stood expectantly, as if John was just passing through, until he stared him down and the guy took the hint. Then he led Gwenn away from the mass of sweaty bodies into a side room populated with kids who'd had too much to drink or smoke and were crumpled on the couches. At least it was quiet, and that's what he was looking for.

"Do you want to get out of here?" John asked, once they had privacy.

"What do you mean? Leave everyone here? Our friends?"

"Yes, that's what that means. I thought I would have a nice time just unwinding here...but I've been here for exactly twenty minutes and I've had one too many run ins with *her* already. I shouldn't be here."

"Yea, I understand how un-fun that can be; I've been babysitting her for months at parties until I just...gave up. Why don't you gather up your friends? I'm sure I can find us another party."

"I don't want to go to another party with them, I asked *you*. I want to go somewhere with you. Like...maybe just go grab some pie at the diner?"

"You mean like...a date? *Tonight*?"

"Yes, that's what I mean...and yes, tonight. Right now."

"Johnny...I can't do that...I can't leave my friends and...Melinda...what about her?"

"You're acting like we're together, Gwenn, and we're not," he said, pushing her hair behind her ear with a finger and smiling down at her. "I haven't even been home for two winters...I've been living a life without Melinda Malowski...and after only being here for a day, I can see why. She's no good for any of us, Gwenn! Not you, me, Dean, her parents..."

405

"I know you're not together, but...you will be. You're Johnny and she's Melinda, and even though you're not together right now, at this moment, that's how it will end up. I know that about the two of you...if I don't know anything else...I know that."

"We're not the same anymore, Gwenn. I'm different....she's different...you're different. When I talked to her earlier tonight..."

"Earlier tonight?"

"Yea, I saw her at the house for a few minutes. It wasn't the same. I always thought...when I came home finally...there would be this big reunion...this big, emotional production. But there wasn't. There was nothing. I felt nothing."

"I know you, John Chapel, and I know you could never feel *nothing* towards that girl."

She tried to take a step back, out of his reach, feeling strange being so close to him and having the sort of conversation with him that didn't involve him pining for her old best friend. It was like he was really talking to her just to talk to her, and she wasn't a messenger or a relay person for once, and she liked it. She liked it too much.

"She and I...we have a history...and nothing will ever change that. But we're different people, Gwenn, and we both tried to make things work out the way we thought they were supposed to work. Melinda said before that maybe we weren't meant to be together, but that we were never meant to be apart either. I think that makes sense. I could never see my life without a Melinda Malowski in it, but I also can't see my life with her at its center."

"What are you saying?"

"I'm saying that she's wrong for me, in that way. I'm not meant to be with her, just because we shared a traumatic experience and I've been guilted into this...never-ending nightmare of fixing her every time she's broken. My life is more than fixing a broken girl, Gwenn...and I want more."

She cracked a big smile, "Well that's something I never thought I'd hear you say: that you want to live your life and be happy."

"Doesn't everybody?"

"But do you know how? Does John Chapel know how to be happy all on his own?"

406

"I've been on my own for a while now, and I've been pretty happy..."

Although the music was a bit quieter in the smaller room, he had to talk closely into her ear so that their private conversation wasn't overheard by the others nearby. His chin hovered above her shoulder as he spoke warm, breathy syllables that tickled her earlobe. That, coupled with his hot breath on her skin, made her chest rise and fall more deeply. She no longer resisted his closeness or the touch of his skin against hers.

"So what's your plan then? If you're not here to save the day...to fix Melinda again...what now?"

"Well, it's too late to just turn around and go home isn't it? So...I thought we could leave here."

"If you're really asking me on a date...then why don't we do it another night? That way, I know that it's not just a last-minute, alcohol-induced kind of thing. If you really want to take me out, call me tomorrow and ask me out, like a guy who is really interested in a girl?"

"I've had two drinks, but okay, I'll call you tomorrow...will you say yes?"

"I might. I might be busy and I might not be," she teased.

As they'd been talking, he'd been leaning his face down closer and closer to hers, and she was no longer backing away. She couldn't break his basilisk's gaze; her feet felt heavy like stone, rooting her in place, and the breath in her unmoving chest was frozen there as well. Despite all of her rational defenses, they would all crumble the moment their lips met. A kiss was inevitable.

She closed her dark-lidded eyes to it and was involuntarily taken back to Lyster Lane, standing in her doorway and watching this exact moment happen all over again. That kiss was something she'd replayed in her head many times since that day, sometimes – most times – superimposing herself into the spot her best friend had been standing. It was something she'd always wondered about, the secret of that kiss, and something she was sure she'd never have the opportunity to discover for herself. Melinda had tried to describe what it was like, but she knew, just by watching them that day, that she would never understand it unless she had experienced it first-hand.

She hesitated just as her lips pressed against his, but it wasn't her physiology that delayed that discovery – every part of her physical body wanted it to happen. It was something that came bursting from the deepest parts of conscience, memory and her somatic identity that made her withdraw. Gwendolyn Lawson was a young woman of strong conscience, resolve and logic, and often times, these overrode her equally strong emotional desires and passion. Images of a beautiful, impassioned kiss were blotted out by images of inevitable heartbreak, abandonment and of another woman.

"What's wrong?" John breathed.

"This is *all* wrong…Johnny…I can't do this," she choked, struggling for air.

"I'm sorry…I don't understand…"

"It's her…Melinda…you're not here for me. I want to be with you but it's not the right time," she stammered over the words, her eyes threatening to burst.

"Why can't we just stop talking about her for one night?" He sighed, agitated.

They might've both truly wanted to forget her at that moment, push her from their minds altogether and not constantly be reminded of her at every turn. There was no conversation between them without her being involved, no dialogue they'd ever had without her inclusion, and a moment that they'd both wanted had been overshadowed by her as well. There would be a comparison, a constant fear of not measuring up, and a never-ending, unspoken competition for his affections with the omnipresent Melinda Malowski.

As though sensing her very thoughts or the event that had almost taken place, Melinda suddenly materialized not twenty feet from them. Neither of them had noticed the drama unfolding on the stairwell, being lost in an embrace and the bliss of possibility, until the screams and the crying became too loud to ignore.

They both turned towards the commotion, catching sight of Dean and Melissa in the crowd first, thinking that the noise was coming from them. Gwenn grabbed John by the hand and led him from the room, pushing through the crowd to get closer to her friends and see what was happening. Just as they broke through the front of the group of onlookers right beside Dean and the girl, they found themselves on the very stage where the drama was unfolding.

Melinda was crawling on her knees on the bottom three steps, trying to get away from whatever was coming down after her. Her face was streaked with black lines and her mouth was bleeding from a split lip, tears mixed the blood and makeup together on her chin in an ugly, thin grey beard. She was wearing only the shirt they'd all seen her in earlier, and the flimsy black panties that had lured John in earlier in the night. There was nothing sexy about her now, as she crawled towards them, sobbing and screaming for help.

Sal emerged from the stairwell then, shirtless, wearing only his jeans and a wicked scowl, and he hesitated at the bottom step as he noticed that a crowd had gathered. He stared at them all like a frightened animal feeling cornered and braved a step towards the girl at his feet. John didn't move to interfere, and only squeezed the hand of the girl standing closely at his back, as though he was more concerned for her safety. It was Dean who stepped forward to extend a hand to his sister as the tall Arab continued after her, cursing in a hybrid of English and Arabic.

John withdrew back into the crowd, an unreadable expression on his face, and led Gwenn back away from the fight that was about to take place. She reluctantly followed him, not turning her worried gaze from the terrified face of her old friend, as they left her behind.

"Where are we going? We can't just leave her there," she called after him.

"Watch me," John said coldly. "I didn't come here for this and I'm not allowing you to get hurt."

"Johnny, I believe what you said earlier…I know you meant it…but she's our friend and we can't just turn our backs on her now."

"We can call the cops after I get you out of here. There are about twenty of those Chaldeans in there, maybe more, and a lot of them I recognize from that motel. If I stay, things will only escalate, and that means you both could be hurt."

He passed two of those guys on his way towards the front door, that seemed to recognize him like the doorman earlier, but couldn't place it. They were headed towards their leader to see what the commotion was about. They also passed by Hunter and Connelly, who stopped to ask him what was happening.

"Dean is trying to keep Melinda from getting her ass beat! Go and check on him and make sure he doesn't do anything stupid."

"Sure, man, where are you two going?"

"I'm getting her out of here before this gets hairy," he said calmly. Connelly knew what he meant and he gave him a solemn nod.

"Want me to come?"

"No, go with Hunter. Keep Dean out of the way if you can."

Gwenn scrunched up her nose at him, wondering if there was some secret conversation between them that she'd caught part of. "So are we leaving her here or not? What was that about?"

"What was what about?"

"You and Connelly...keep Dean out of the way of what?"

"Never mind," he snapped and yanked her out the front door.

Inside, things were already beginning to escalate, just as John had predicted. Sal had reached Melinda before her brother could get her away from him, and snatched her up by her hair, pulling her up to her knees. He continued to curse at her through gritted teeth and a bloody lip. Dean noticed the fresh scratch marks on his cheek and lips; apparently their fighting had gotten out of hand this time, and things were about to go too far.

"Dean...please..." She pleaded, seeing her brother through tears.

He took a step towards his sister, eyeing the group of Sal's friends who were now gathering around and watching. Their faces said that he ought to think twice about approaching Sal, but he paid them little mind. He grabbed Melinda's arm and tried pulling her towards him.

Sal glared at him, "Let her go now Dean, this isn't your business."

Dean's lip curled up, like it did when he was really angry, and he replied, "It *is* my business, she's my *sister*." He gripped her arm tighter as a display of his resolve.

At that point, one of the jackals from the crowd had to butt in, "Hey man, back the Hell off!"

410

Another cursed at him and stepped closer, "Yea, you don't start shit at our party!"

Dean didn't look at him, fixing his stare on Sal. "I'm not starting shit! I'm taking my sister home."

Sal shook his head with that arrogant smile, "You're not taking her anywhere. Leave if you want to leave, but she stays with me."

The muscular ex-state champion wrestler held firm to his sister's arm, proclaiming, "If any of you guys have any kind of influence on your buddy, you'd better tell him to let go of my sister's fucking arm!"

He started to raise his voice, which meant he was all business now. More and more of the 'cousins' started appearing from the crowd around them and started to circle him, each too afraid to do anything on their own, but getting more brave as the group grew larger.

Hunter and Connelly had also taken their spots in the crowd, per John's request, and were trying to talk Dean down, knowing that it wasn't going to turn out well, "Come on man...let's just leave."

Dean only shot Connelly a glance, and said again, "I'm *not* leaving my sister here."

Another one of the cousins piped up again, "Are you fucking stupid man? We're gonna' fuck you up if you don't leave!"

It was Connelly that caught a glimpse of something bulging under his waistband and knew things were about to get serious.

Chapter 39

Outside the house, John and Gwenn were almost to the car when they realized they were being followed. He whirled around to confront whoever was doing a poor job of shadowing them, and he was relieved to see that it was Brennan.

"What the hell is going on in there, man?"

"Sal is getting rough with his girl and Dean is right in the middle of it," John explained.

"Where are the other guys? I saw Josh but not Hunter or Con," he said mechanically, working a strategy in his head already. "There are about twenty of them, Chaps. We're going to need everyone."

"You want to fight them? Fist fight? They outnumber us four to one, Pete!"

John stopped at the passenger side of his car to open the door for Gwenn and ordered her to get in. She reluctantly sat in the car as she was told, not wanting to argue, and he reached in and handed her the keys after using them to open his trunk. "Here, slide across and start the car and get ready to pick us up."

"Nice car." She commented, and then asked, "What are *you* going to do?"

He called Pete around the rear of the car and repeated, "Just be ready to leave." Then he turned his attention to Brennan, "They're armed, Bren, at least *three* of them. I'm not going into this shit outmanned and unprepared again!"

He lifted the trunk and reached in, producing two very nasty-looking shotguns, handing the larger one to Pete, "This isn't going to be a fist fight. This is going to be an all-or-nothing deal. Hopefully the shotguns scare them into being smart enough not to draw down on us."

"Whoa, Chaps! That's a shotgun, man! It's a nice shotgun...but it's a shotgun. This isn't something you want to do. I say we walk back in there, hit em' hard, and we walk out with this girl before anyone knows what's going on," Pete pleaded, trying to reason with his friend.

"You don't know these people, Pete! We go in swinging and they pull guns, someone is going to get killed! I thought they taught you how to do all this shit in the military? Of any of those guys in there, I thought I could count on you to be on board with this?"

"Chapel...I'm trained for this, but pulling this kind of shit here, against civilians, can land us both in prison for a long time! This isn't a war!"

"This is a goddamned war, Pete, and they started it! This is the only way to reason with them; we have to be crazier than they are and willing to go farther than they are! The only other one who is willing to go that far is Dean, and he *will* take a bullet to save his sister! I'm not leaving him in there alone, and I wouldn't leave you either Pete!"

"Damn you Chappy...you *had* to say that didn't you? Gimme' that eight-seventy!"

Pete grabbed the modified Remington from him and some shells from the box in the trunk, loading them into the magazine as he admired the hardware. "Jesus Chaps, where did you get these?"

"They came with the car..." He said, loading his own shotgun.

"These aren't hunting guns...these are breach weapons!"

"Well it's a good thing we're not going hunting then," he said with an odd grin.

Gwenn had stepped from the car, not believing what she had been watching in the side view mirror. "Johnny, are you serious right now? Are you planning on going back in there with...*those?*"

"I know what I'm doing, Gwenn. If this goes the way I think it will, they will back down. These people are cowards and if someone has the drop on them, they'll back down. You have to trust me!"

"Someone is going to get killed...oh my God...please just call the police!"

"Remember to have the car running and be waiting for us!" He racked the action on his Mossberg as an exclamation point to his order.

He walked with a measured and deliberate stride back up the drive towards the front door, Pete Brennan hot on his heels. Taking positions on either side of the door, they both took two sharp breaths and nodded to one another. He signaled to Pete that he wanted him to break through the door first, given his larger size, and he would make a more impressive entrance. The door gave way to his heavy, booted foot and John moved in swiftly behind him, covering his back.

They walked in on a standoff that had gotten much worse, just as John had predicted. Sal had Melinda's hair wrapped around his fist and had her standing now. Dean still had a firm grip on her wrist, which was turning red, and wouldn't let go. The Arabs had all began to shout and curse at him, and some were beginning to shove him and get in his face to yell or just spit at him. It looked as though one had even punched him in the head, causing blood to run down his temple onto his cheek.

The sight of the blood had only stirred them up more, like the animals that they were, and the whole thing was sobering to Melinda. She stared at her brother, with wide terrified eyes, and she seemed to finally realize that there was going to be a reckoning this night for her long string of bad decisions.

The music and screaming was still so loud that only a few noticed the shotgun-wielding men at the front door, and it wasn't the entrance John had hoped for. One of them was the doorman who'd struggled each time he saw John to place his face. Just as the carbon-fiber stock came crashing into his nose, there seemed to be an epiphany forming there in his ruined face, and a look of recognition in his watering eyes. This was the dangerous man they'd tangled with before, the one who wasn't afraid of anything.

Brennan brought down the second man – another veteran of the *Knight's Inn* battle - with a snap of his elbow, catching him in the solar plexus with the stock of his Remington. The wind and the fight gone from him, he fell to the ground nearly vomiting and trying to find his air.

Finally, all eyes turned towards them, just as John had wanted. Brennan racked home the first shell for effect, making sure that they had their undivided attention, and leveled the barrel at the most vocal among the cousins. He'd never seen the guy before in his life, but he certainly chose the best target. It was Shannon, Sal's number two man and closest family member, and the guy who was probably just as dangerous as he was.

"You don't want to do this," Sal tried the bluff anyway, in his most intimidating voice.

415

"You want to play crazy?" The voice was smooth and unwavering, but forceful. "I'm just the guy to play crazy with you," he said, walking steadily towards the center of the bodies where Dean was standing his ground.

Halfway, he stopped and surveyed the faces of the jackals, daring just one of them to twitch or get into his way. He was mapping out the immediate area, taking an accounting of every player in the game, and assessing the level of danger from each one. Keeping his gun loosely trained on Sal, he weaved in between those others, studying them. He hesitated over the shoulder of one of them that he'd identified as a potential problem. With his free hand, he jerked a pistol from the waistband of his track pants that had been concealed there.

"Con!" He called out, getting his attention before tossing the pistol to him.

Jeremy snatched up the gun and trained it on the guy nearest him that he'd already been eyeing. He'd noticed the bulge under his shirt ten minutes earlier, and he'd kept a careful watch on him. Mimicking John's maneuver, he snatched the pistol from the man's pants and handed it to Hunter, who took it reluctantly.

"Your guys came pretty well-armed for a little college party, Sal," John said, not taking his eyes from him. "By my count, only you and Shannon are still armed. We have four men with tactical superiority, all ready to put you down before you can even reach your guns. Be smart about this!"

"You might be a good shot, but the two of you have shotguns – you'll hit Melinda!"

"I am a good shot, Sal, and Pete is a better shot! Good thing we have these loaded with slugs, not shot, and I can take half of your face off from where I'm standing. So I'm going to tell you one time: let go of her hair and back away!"

Sal shook his head slowly, "I'm not letting go of her! As soon as I do, I'm a dead man."

John raised his shotgun to a less-casual position, staring down the barrel at his most-hated foe, showing that he meant business. "I didn't come here to kill anyone, Sal. I don't want to have to shoot anyone, especially in front of all these people. But I absolutely will if I have to. You let her go and you have my word that we all leave here and you go free."

Pete pushed through the crowd towards him to enforce John's command, holding the shotgun in one hand and using the other to grab Sal's wrist. His muscles flexed as he closed the vice on the bones of his wrist, threatening to snap them. His strength was impressive, and it was a display as much for Sal's benefit as it was the rest of his gang, to keep them from getting brave.

"If you don't let go of her hair, I'm going to break your fucking arm and my friend is just going to shoot you in the fucking face – you'd better believe that!" Pete threatened in the loudest, scariest voice any of them had ever heard.

Sal finally released her hair and Mel went to her brother's arms.

"Dean, get her out of here," John growled, not looking at his friend, but staring straight ahead.

As Dean made his way toward the door, the hot-headed Shannon pulled his gun from his belt. "No way are you walking out of here!" He screamed, waving the gun at them.

Brennan was right on top of him, pushing the shotgun in his face with one hand and backhanding Sal across the face with the other, sending him sprawling. The rest stepped back, witnessing this brute's strength. John was glad he was on their side.

In an instant, John was straddling Sal, pressing his shotgun into his forehead. "You go ahead and squeeze that trigger Shannon! I guarantee you that he'll die first and then you! My friend there will paste your brains on the fucking wall before you can blink! He's a fucking Army Ranger - Special Forces!"

All of the Chaldeans turned their head towards Pete now, and sized him up. They believed the last statement, as Pete proudly wore his dog tags and combat boots with every ensemble - plus he looked like he knew how to handle a gun.

"Put the fucking gun down Shannon!" He half pleaded and half demanded of his cousin.

The cousin eyed John then Sal nervously, then at the faces of his companions as if looking for the right answer. The faces were all solemn and most looked at the ground, none of them indicating that their loyalty included dying foolishly, except Shannon Nussein.

"I count eight gunmen to our four, and if we're doing simple math, you would have the drop on us," John said, still very composed, "But in that first hail of bullets, I count four of you dead, including you and Sal. Now, maybe the guys left standing won't be pissing their pants and actually get a shot off, or maybe they'll just stand there and Pete and I will drop those guys too. But despite all that, all of the strategy and bullshit we're all thinking about right now, the real question is: are you willing to die here and now, over a girl? A girl you don't even care about? Will your cousin die for her? Because I will...I will go that far."

He subconsciously glanced through the crowd and caught a glimpse of a familiar face he'd left behind. The adoring eyes were glistening at him once again as the black water drained from them, revealing the Mediterranean hues. There was forgiveness in them and an appeal for his, which she knew he'd given with a nod of his head. This was the reunion they'd both longed for, something more appropriate for John Chapel and Melinda Malowski, but it had come too late and they both regretted every minute that had been spent in bitter anger.

She wanted to break free of her brother and run to him, embracing him one more time and tell him how she'd never stopped loving him. But she wouldn't need to; she could see that unmistakable look in his eyes again; he still loved her, despite what he'd said in that hallway outside her door, and that would be enough just to know the truth before they died.

Sal noticed that quiet exchange between them as well, and he gave them a knowing look before he conceded. He couldn't win out against John – not where Melinda was concerned – and though he'd beaten and humiliated the man and he'd been gone for a long time, that strange bond between them was something that he couldn't shatter.

"Shannon it's over...for now. Johnny get the fuck out of here, take that bitch with you and I never want to see either of you again."

He nodded to his adversary, slowly stepping away from him, and then to Pete, who released Shannon less delicately. There were some curt words and promises that the score wasn't settled yet, but the standoff was over that night. John escorted Dean and his sister to the door, where she collapsed and had to carried the rest of the way to the car, her arms around his neck and face buried into his chest, sobbing.

Gwenn was waiting in the Mercedes, just as she'd been instructed, and she'd pulled right up to the front door. There was a look of relief on her face, seeing that everyone had made it out safely and that no one appeared to be bleeding. Relief turned to a nauseating feeling in her stomach, however, when she saw Melinda coiled in the arms of the man she'd almost kissed earlier.

Dean took the passenger seat, Josh got in the back beside Melinda, and the other three were already hoofing it down the drive towards Pete's truck. They followed them slowly to make sure they arrived safely, and when the truck was loaded up, Gwenn mashed the accelerator and squealed the tires as they sped off. All eyes were turned towards a window, keeping watch for any pursuers – cops or otherwise – and the cabin was dead silent except for the whispers coming from the back which made Gwenn cringe.

Just as she'd predicted, she knew this would come to pass and she heard her own words echoed in those whispers; *You're Johnny and she's Melinda, and even though you're not together right now...that's how it will end up...*

RETURN TO FIELDS OF GOLD

"All things truly wicked start from an innocence"

~Ernest Hemingway

Chapter 40

John had never been to the Malowski summer home, but it looked exactly as Melinda had described to him many times; was set off of the road and down a gentle slope, appearing to be resting on top of the water itself. It was a small place, very rustic, and not at all what he expected from the Malowskis, who usually had extravagant tastes. It wasn't much more than a small cabin, sided with yellow painted aluminum, and he had a hard time imagining five of them being crammed into the small, three-bedroom place.

He also had a hard time picturing Dennis in anything but a suit or a nice sweater out on the back dock fishing, or Marge in gardening clothes tending to the flower beds. He chuckled when walked around back and saw the wooden, two-person swing suspended from a tree branch. He just couldn't imagine Dennis and Marge being romantic and watching the stars, they weren't very affectionate from what he had seen and heard of them. It was nice to see this other side of them, and it made them seem less-stuffy and preoccupied with their possessions. The Malowskis were human after all.

After his reconnaissance, he returned to the car and found Dean and Gwenn still standing beside it, waiting for his direction before they disturbed their cargo. Gwenn held the door for him as he leaned in and scooped Melinda up to carry her to the house. Dean ran ahead to get the front door and held it wide for him to step through sideways, being careful not to wake her. He deposited her on one of the double beds in the first bedroom, and then closed the door behind him.

Dean retrieved a small armload of blankets from a closet and distributed them to Connelly and Gwenn, giving them their temporary arrangements for the evening. Jeremy seemed a bit disappointed that he wouldn't be sharing the only queen bed with Gwenn, but he didn't argue and settled on the couch in the main room. Gwenn retired to the Malowski's room, passing by John without a word, and left Dean and John to fight over the last two beds.

"There's another room that used to be Melinda's across from the bathroom down the hall, but there's just one bed in there. I suppose that leaves you the recliner…or the other bed in my old room."

"I'm not tired at the moment…I think I'll just grab some coffee and sit on the back deck for a bit."

"That actually sounds good. I'll put some on," Dean volunteered.

John opened the back sliding glass door and found a semi-comfortable folding chair facing the lake. He leaned his head back against the plastic covering, closing his eyes and filling his lungs with the tranquility of the night air. It was the first time he'd been able to sit down or rest his eyes in what seemed like days, and he was exhausted but too wound up to get any rest. He'd been awake since Friday morning and his watch was telling him that it was the first hour of Sunday morning already.

Thirty-nine hours didn't seem like time enough to drive thirteen hundred miles, have a reunion with old friends, engage in an armed standoff, and rescue his old flame from peril. Some people couldn't pull that off in a month. Hell, some couldn't pull that off in a lifetime, but for John Chapel, that was all just a typical day for him.

He gave a start when Dean appeared suddenly behind him, handing him a cup of steaming coffee, and hadn't realized how long he'd been sitting there with his eyes closed.

"You awake?"

"Yea, just resting my eyes. Thanks for the java," he said, taking the '#1 Dad' mug from him.

"I don't know how you're still going, man."

"Yea, I was just thinking that myself…"

Dean leaned his elbows on the railing, setting his own mug down to let the night air cool it down some. The pair of them quietly stared out at the lake, letting the conversation die out, each too exhausted to make more than small talk. There were many things to discuss between them, the most obvious topics attached to the two women sleeping fitfully inside, but neither wanted to tackle those bigger questions yet.

"Good fishing on this lake," Dean finally said.

"Oh? I took a charter a couple months back with some of the guys to go Snapper fishing."

"Nothing as exciting as that here; some small mouths and perch, but the perch are delicious."

"Haven't had fried perch since I was a kid; that does sound good!"

"Yea, me, Dad and Steve used to catch a couple dozen and fry them all up. Mom has a great recipe for some fry mix, I should see if I can find it."

"Put it on the list and we'll run into town tomorrow and grab some with the rest of the supplies."

"How much stuff do you think we'll need?"

"Well, I assume mostly food...I would guess that Melinda has some clothing for--"

"I meant, how long do you think we'll have to stay up here?"

He hadn't thought much further ahead than getting them all somewhere safe, and as far away from Sal as possible. It was Melinda who'd mumbled something about Merrill Lake and that Sal had never been there, while she was fighting sleep, comfortably resting in his lap. After dropping Josh off at the Metro Coney and saying his goodbyes to the rest, it was straight to the lake for the rest of them. Figuring out what the rest of the plan was from there would have to wait until the morning.

"I hadn't really planned that far ahead," he finally said. "Everything just went kind of fast."

"Yea, I guess I owe you big for that one. Thanks for pulling my ass out of that mess."

"I couldn't leave you to face those guys alone, man."

"The way you just walked in there and took control of the situation, like it's something you just do on your regular Saturday night; that was pretty impressive shit, Johnny."

"You mean scary?"

"Yea, that too," he said, giving a nervous laugh. "I guess I just don't see that kind of stuff, I'm just a college kid who sees the occasional brawl at a frat party. I suppose whatever you do – in your line of work – you see that kind of stuff a lot?"

John quietly sipped at his coffee, staring out at the dark lake, the look on his face telling him that it wasn't a topic he wanted to discuss. Dean took his silence as a cue to drop the discussion and leaned back on the railing to stare at the lake with him, trying not to feel awkward.

"It didn't exactly go the way I thought it would."

"You think Josh will be alright? He seemed to be pretty shaken up on the car ride back."

"I don't know. You and I have seen some fights, been in a few too, but that's just not his thing. Pete always used to give him a hard time about being 'soft', but that's just his way. I think this might've been a little too much for him."

"Yea, he looked pretty pale and didn't have much to say to you. At least we had Pete there," he chuckled. "He really laid Sal out! I wouldn't want to tangle with that guy."

"I wish I had a camera for that one," John laughed. "Still, I know I put Pete in an uncomfortable spot too. He's got all that training, and that's just the sort of thing he lives for, but he's never had to put it to use."

"They're your friends, Johnny, and they'll always be your friends – just like I will – you just have to give them a little time to digest it."

"You're probably right. My primary concern is Melinda…and Gwenn."

"Yea, she didn't seem too pleased with you. What's going on there?"

"We were just talking about some things before everything went down tonight, but your sister put an end to that pretty quick with her big scene."

"You have a thing for Gwenn now? Man, I can't even fathom that."

"That's what she said. Pretty much doomed me to a life shackled to your sister."

"I don't know man, it just seems like that's sort of the natural order of things. The four of us have this balance together, and being friends with my sister and an item with Gwenn seems like it messes up that balance."

"So, I'm just stuck with Melinda for the rest of my life?"

"I wouldn't wish that on my worst enemy," he chuckled. "But maybe it's good that she at least thinks there's a chance with you, until we get her straightened out. She's pretty fragile right now, Johnny, and it might be best just to play along, even if that's not how you feel anymore."

"I don't know how I feel anymore. When I saw her at the house earlier tonight, it wasn't the same as it used to be. But then,

426

when I was looking at her across the room at that party, thinking that Shannon might…I guess…everything just kind of came back to me. I still don't know if it was just the situation, though, and maybe it was the same way for her. She might think differently when she sobers up in the morning."

"Well, I guess we'll cross that bridge when we get to it. I think the whole thing might've scared her straight – at least for the time being – and we can't lose that momentum."

"I'm doing my best, Dean."

"I know you are, man. I just wanted to say thanks…for everything. You might not hear it from either of those girls in there, but I appreciate you coming back for us. I think I'm going to head in to bed. You should probably get some sleep too."

He nodded quietly. "Good night buddy. I'll be in after a while."

John wanted to follow him into the house and follow his advice, but the sleeping arrangements and the nagging feeling of paranoia wouldn't allow it. Gwenn occupied the only queen bed, and he'd been guilted out of sharing that with her, Melinda's room had a spare bed, and he'd been guilted out of that bed by Gwenn. He didn't feel right about sharing a room or a bed with either of them, and he wasn't sure that sleep would come anyway.

He walked to the end of the old dock and stood, staring out across the lake at all the other houses and to get an idea of their surroundings. There was some comfort in the fact that there were two large clusters of birch trees on either side of the dock, which hid the house from view from anyone driving along the lake. There were many patches of trees all around the lake, and it made it hard to even see the water, much less other homes, from the winding road. Anyone who didn't know exactly where the house was located would have a hard time identifying anyone from both the front and back sides of the place.

John sat down and took his shoes off then, realizing he'd been wearing them for the past thirty-nine hours as well, and thinking how refreshing dipping his feet in the water might be. It was better than he'd imagined, immersing his tired feet in the warm lake water, and it helped to relax him somewhat. He leaned back, kicking his legs slowly back and forth, just staring up at the moon and feeling like he had finally arrived home.

He hadn't recognized the small town he'd grown up in or half the guys he used to run around with, but here, despite never having seen the place before, he felt at home. He was in Michigan, sticking his toes in a warm body of fresh water, teeming with freshwater fish, and there was the old summer moon above that he hadn't seen since Port Austin.

He went from leaning back on his elbows to folding them behind his head, fingers interlocked, and lying flat on his back to stare up at that moon. It was the most welcoming face he'd seen since returning, and it was beautiful as it smiled down on him. Listening to the sound of the lapping, gentle waves and the reeds swaying in the wind, he blew a kiss to that pale face in the sky and closed his eyes.

The next morning, he awoke very much the same way he'd dozed off: to the sound of the gentle water, blowing reeds, and a beautiful face staring down at him.

"Good morning," she said, as his eyes fluttered open, trying to adjust to the bright morning sun.

"Hey there…"

"There was another bed up there to use…I see you chose the dock instead. How was it?"

John sat up with a groan, "A lot more comfortable last night than this morning. What time is it?"

The auburn-haired girl grinned at him, "It's about ten. Don't worry, nobody else is up yet, you're not missing anything. Everyone had a long night."

He scooted forward to put his toes back into the water, as if it would wake him up the same as splashing it in his face. Moving his shoes and socks, he cleared a place for her to sit, and she scooted beside him. It shouldn't have surprised him that she was wearing the same black dress from the night before, but his exhaustion and disorientation made him blink at her outfit anyway.

"I didn't really get to pack a bag," she explained, as though he'd forgotten.

"It looks nice on you still," he said, stretching his arms out and taking a deep breath.

"Thanks. It's not really suitable for outdoor activities."

"Well…you don't have to roll up your pants to put your feet in the water," he joked.

She was kicking her feet playfully already and he was staring at them as they moved beneath the water. He'd never really noticed her feet before, and noted how delicate and attractive they were. Melinda had stubbier, squared toes, and it was her least-attractive feature, but she kept them well-manicured and usually strapped in expensive shoes. Gwenn had nice, long, thin toes that were shaped almost perfectly and didn't need any paint or shoes to disguise them.

She caught him staring at her feet and said, "Did you lose something down there?"

He looked up at her and wrinkled up his lip in a half-smile, "Your feet...they're really cute."

Gwenn frowned, lifting them from the water for him to get a better look, "You're not one of those weird fetish people are you?"

"Why do I have to have a fetish just to compliment your feet? Just never noticed."

"Let's look at yours," she said, snaking one foot under his and lifting it up for him.

"Not as cute," he said, apologetically.

"I don't think they're bad. You should see Dean's feet – he looks like a troll. They're short, stubby and all hairy, like the rest of him. Yours aren't too big or too small – guys with small hands or feet creep me out! And your second toe...it's longer than the rest, which is supposed to mean you're smart."

"Okay, I felt weird staring at your feet, but I didn't give you a dissertation on them."

She held up her hands and pressed them against his, taking a measurement. "See? Your hands are much larger than mine; that's good."

He scrunched up his face at her, not sure of what to make of her odd, random monologue about hands and feet, or why she thought that his having bigger hands was favorable. This didn't seem to be the same girl from the night before, the one that passed him by without a word and seemed like she'd wanted to choke him. Perhaps a night's rest had done her some good, and she'd gotten over being mad at him. As she suddenly changed subjects, though, he realized she hadn't.

"So, why did you sleep down here?"

"I didn't really feel comfortable sleeping in the house."

429

"There was another bed in Melinda's room."

"I know; I didn't want to sleep in there."

"There was a queen bed in the other room."

"You were in it," he shrugged.

"So? I wasn't laying in there naked or anything."

"You slept in your clothes?"

"No, I slept in my underwear."

"Do you think that would be appropriate given our…talk from last night?"

"Probably no less appropriate than anything else that happened last night."

"Fair enough. You're still mad then?"

"I don't think *mad* quite describes it," she replied sarcastically.

"That's why I didn't come and sleep in the room with you…or Melinda, for that matter," he admitted, studying his own feet in the water.

"Well, at least you didn't go crawling into bed with her right away," she huffed.

"I'm not sure what I'm supposed to say or what I'm supposed to do up here, Gwenn. I had quite an uncomfortable discussion with Dean last night about this same, awkward subject, and I told him about the talk you and I had."

"What do *you* think you should do, John?"

"I have no idea. I thought I knew what I wanted to do but you both got huffy with me and told me that I can't break free of Melinda. You both have your reasons, but you're on the same page, and you're mad at me even though I haven't even made any real decisions yet."

"What are *my* reasons for giving you that advice?"

"I don't know…because I guess…you don't want me to hurt you?"

"And what are Dean's reasons?"

"Because he doesn't want me to hurt you either…and because he sees me as the only one who can straighten out his sister, and the rest of his family, by proxy. He says I'll upset the balance and we'll all be ruined if I don't just act like good old Johnny and come to Melinda's rescue, as always."

"But you *did* come to her rescue," she said.

"Who else was there to step in?"

430

"So Dean isn't wrong in what he said? You're taking it personally, and it's not personal John, not with me at least. Sometimes things just are the way they are, and no matter how much we would like to change them, we can't."

"I don't believe a person can't just change their mind. Melinda doesn't have to be a mess her entire life. You don't have to be the stoic martyr who pushes her feelings deep down to spare her friends. I don't have to be the guy who goes against all reason and logic to keep bailing out the same stupid girl."

Gwenn gave him a thin smile, patted his hand and said simply, "Yes we do. That's just what we are, Johnny, and I wouldn't change you for the world, or Dean, Melinda or myself, for that matter."

"I thought I was here to change things? I thought that was why you called me?"

"Change *little* things, not the *big* things. If Melinda doesn't change some of the things about her life, I fear what will happen to her, yes. You need to reach her and pull her just far enough out of the misery she's gotten herself into, but no one expects a miracle. No one *wants* a miracle. I don't think Dean or I, or even her parents, would know what to do if she just did a complete one-eighty and straightened up."

"I'm going to go with 'heart attack'?"

"See? No one would know how to handle that. Melinda will always be that girl who causes trouble. I'll always be the girl who stays out of it. You'll always be the boy who keeps her balanced…and keeps me hoping that there's another boy out there, just like you, for me."

"Why did you have to say that?"

"Just because I told you to go away and I expect you to go away, doesn't mean that I'm not hurt that you listened and you did what I expected of you. I'm a girl – girl's don't make sense most of the time."

"So you *are* mad?"

"I said hurt; hurt is different than mad, but sometimes has the same outcome."

"You didn't have to come…I could've dropped you at home on the way."

"There's a lot of bad blood between her and me, but I wouldn't dump this off on you to do alone. Just because I got my hopes up for one night and got my feelings hurt, doesn't mean you and I aren't friends either. I'll get over it. I need you to do whatever needs to be done to fix this, even if that means I have to watch something I don't particularly like. It's not like it's anything new."

"I could've gone without knowing that too…"

"Like you didn't know? I know you're not stupid, Johnny, and when you were with me last night, you had to know how it was killing me not to make out with you."

"We can still make out," he teased.

"Not without toothbrushes! Put that on your list when you go to the store. And make sure you get floss and Listerine!"

"Are you planning on doing a lot of making out?"

"Hey, you never know! Connelly is here," she teased back.

"I could've also gone without hearing that," he said, frowning.

"Connelly is a pretty good kisser, maybe someday I can find out who is better."

"You love to torment me, don't you?"

"Oh, let me have my fun! I said maybe *someday*; it will give you something to look forward to!"

"I'll hold you to that," he said, giving her a flirty smile. "You know that I meant what I said last night? When we were in that room together, I wasn't thinking about her, I was only thinking about you and…you were the only one I wanted…"

He thought for a moment that she might forego the Listerine and toothbrush, and he could smell her bitter breath as she leaned in towards him, thinking she might kiss him there on the dock. It was all an act, or perhaps a last-minute recovery, and she pulled away, giggling.

"That wasn't very nice of you to say. Just keep it up and see what happens."

"What will happen?"

"Keep flirting with me and brushing up against me, paying me compliments and saying sweet things and you know what will happen. It will eventually drive us both crazy, so that we do something really stupid that we'll regret."

"Like what?"

"Like…me sneaking into your room at night and having my way with you."

432

"And that's something we'd regret?"

"Not until at least the next morning. You're so bad. Please stop looking at me that way."

"What way?"

"You know *what* way. As much fun as it would be to see what *Gwenn and Johnny* would be all about, we just can't do that right now. We'd be acting on a whim and a desire to be *temporarily* free of Melinda and you know how that would end; with us resenting one another and not being friends anymore. I couldn't handle hating you or not seeing you again, and we both know that's what would happen if we did this."

"You're probably right…"

"I know I am. So, if anything you said last night was true at all, and you really want to give us a shot, see this through to the end first. Do whatever you have to do with her, and if that means you end up with her in the end, then that's what it means. But if you leave these things unresolved with her…it will catch up with you someday Johnny, and you know it will."

"Doesn't sound like you're giving me a choice then either?"

"Nope," she said, playfully hopping up from her spot beside him, and extending a hand. "Come and help me get breakfast on and wake up the rest of those bums."

He followed her back up to the house, letting her pull him along by the hand, enjoying the touch of her fingers intertwined in his. When they reached the porch, she let his hand fall away, as if suddenly ashamed or reminded that she wasn't supposed to be touching him. They were greeted by a groggy and disoriented man just waking up from the couch, who gave them a strange look as they walked in together.

The eggs and package of frozen bacon would have to suffice; the milk had spoiled and the bread had started growing green spots, which limited their options. It still smelled good enough as it was sizzling in the skillet to rouse the other two guests of the lake house.

Dean came shuffling from his room, scratching himself and trying to fix his hair, and Melinda followed, each seeming more disoriented than the man on the couch. One of them complimented the aroma coming from the kitchen, the other complained, claiming that it made her stomach queasy. She tried to stay out of range of the odor, flopping down in her father's recliner, and her brother seemed drawn to the source, making his way to the kitchen to investigate.

"Smells good, I'm famished," he said, inspecting the skillet over Gwenn's shoulder.

"You're always famished. Sorry, it's not much. It's all we could find," she said.

"I'll head into town later and pick up some more food," John added.

"And an outfit for Gwenn?" The girl from the chair said, snorting.

Melinda had somehow found the presence of mind in the middle of the night to change into sweat pants and a tee shirt. That was how she was though; even when extremely inebriated, she was conscious of her appearance. Gwenn rolled her eyes at John and didn't respond to Melinda's comment.

"We didn't have time to shop last night, sorry," John said, coming to her rescue. "I'll pick up whatever you guys need in town. Make me a list."

"Maybe you could offer Gwenn something?" Dean said, giving her a dirty look.

"I don't have much in there, and I don't know if it would fit her anyway."

"I'm comfortable in the dress until later," Gwenn said, with a fake smile. "It's supposed to be hot today anyway."

"Breakfast is done! Come and eat!" John barked, trying to change the subject.

Connelly and Dean wasted no time in finding their seats at the small kitchen table, and helped themselves to the plates of eggs and bacon. Gwenn waited until the boys had their fill and took a smaller plate, taking only two small scoops of eggs and one strip of the crispy meat.

"Is that all you're going to eat, Gwenn?" John asked before helping himself.

"Gwenn keeps her girlish figure by not eating – like the supermodels do," came another comment from the living room.

They ignored her and continued on with their breakfast, each trying to talk about something else besides the obnoxious elephant in the living room. First, it was the accommodations from the night before, each laughing about John's choice of passing out

434

on the dock, and then they discussed the weather. Melinda made a sour face from her chair, and they pretended not to see it, not wanting to encourage her attention-seeking behavior by making eye contact.

She made several sighing noises and even tried saying derogatory things about each topic they brought up, but still, nobody would give her the attention she demanded. Frustrated, she jumped up from her chair and made her way out the back sliding door. Everybody quietly ate as they waited for somebody else to get up and go after her.

"I'm not doing it," Dean said with a mouthful of egg.

"I'm *always* the one," Gwenn protested.

"I don't even know her," Con said, gnawing at his bacon.

That left John, who was volunteered by default, not able to come up with an excuse fast enough. He chewed his food and tried to ignore the eyes watching him expectantly in unison. As he took his last bite, he knew that he would inevitably have to acknowledge their stares, and either come up with a good excuse or be the one to go after her. He swallowed hard and still hadn't come up with anything, so he excused himself and reluctantly followed the elephant onto the back porch.

Chapter 41

The trio inside heard the first part of the dialogue easily from their place at the table, though they tried hard to start up their own discussion to drown the other one out.

"Something you want to say…to Gwenn?"

"If there's something I want to say to her, believe me, I'll say it to her face," she said coldly.

He leaned on the rail beside her, staring back out at the lake, just as he had the night before with her brother, looking considerably less comfortable.

"We all need to try to get along. It's been a long time since the four of us have actually been together, and I understand that it's difficult, but we have to try our best."

"Is it difficult? I don't have a problem with anyone inside that house, but they all seem to have a problem with me. You seemed pretty comfortable yesterday."

"No, I don't have a problem with you at the moment, but I've been gone for a while. They've had to put up with you and your behavior all this time, Mel, do you blame them?"

"My behavior? What would *they* know about that? They haven't been around."

"They know enough to be afraid, and to know that something had to be done."

"I'm fine; they're exaggerating!"

"Cut the bullshit, Melinda! If last night was an example of *fine*, then I'd hate to see when things aren't fine with you. All three of those people in that house put their lives on the line for you, so you should cut them some fucking slack! You can be a bitch to me if you want to, and you can make shitty, smartass comments about me all you like, but you don't get to be that way to *them*! Your brother refused to leave you last night and this is more uncomfortable for Gwenn than anyone, but she stayed here for you!"

"What's *Gwenn's* deal?"

"You know what Gwenn's deal is," he said, lowering his voice for the benefit of his audience.

"Oh that's right; she's always mad that she can't be me," she snipped. "Did I ruin a special moment for you guys last night? Maybe I should let her know that John Chapel isn't everything she thinks he is, so she doesn't get wrapped up in you like I did."

He cringed, knowing that Gwenn could hear every word, and tried to redirect the discussion.

"I asked the wrong question. There something you want to say to *me* then?"

"No, I already said what I was going to say."

"There must be *something*. There must be *pages and pages* worth of stuff you want to share, now that I'm here. Or are you only brave when you're writing letters that you'll never send?"

"You would know all about not sending letters," she said with a scowl.

"What the hell is wrong with you? You seemed perfectly fine last night, and seemed grateful that we pulled your ass out of that mess."

"I *was* grateful, until you started trying to get on Gwenn! If you want to be with her, then be with her, Johnny! I don't need you to patronize me and I don't need you here unless you *want* to be!"

"I'm not trying to 'get on' Gwenn! Even if I *wanted* to, she wouldn't let it happen because she knows better! All she keeps talking about is how I need to be here for *you* and how *we* need to resolve things – and *that's* the girl who you're trying to start shit with."

"Do you *want* to?"

"I don't know what the hell I want or even what I'm doing here, Melinda! I get a call a couple days ago telling me that I have to come home and that you're a fucking mess! I get reamed out by my girlfriend and my boss, drive twenty-four hours straight to get here, just to find myself in the middle of a fucking armed standoff, and now you're up in my business about Gwenn and we're fighting - *again*! I didn't just go through all that bullshit for the fun of it, I did it for *you*!"

She stormed off the porch then, making a beeline for the dock, swinging her arms in exaggerated arcs and taking broad strides. John leaned heavily on the railing, letting out a long breath as he watched her march off angrily. He felt the eyes on his back and when he turned to look over his shoulder, those faces urged him to go after her.

"Just go back to your girlfriend and your boss! I didn't mean to put you out," she snapped as she saw his shadow creeping across the old planks. "I'll be fine without you, Johnny."

"You're not *fine*, Melinda! Keeping company with drug dealers and a man who beats on you isn't a recipe for a long and happy life! Snorting shit up your nose, shooting up and drinking until you need to be admitted to the hospital isn't an okay lifestyle!"

"It's *my* lifestyle, and I'm fine with it!"

"It's not fine with *me*!"

"Then what are you going to do about it?"

"I'm going to do whatever I need to do. You saw how far I'll go, already, why don't you believe that I came back here to help you?"

"Because as *soon* as you think everything is okay, you'll be gone again – just like always!"

"I never left you in the first place, Melinda! That was *you*, remember? *You're* the one who pushed me away – both times! You wrote me a shitty letter telling me you were confused and we needed time apart, and then I needed a few days to go after my mother and you try to have people beat the hell out of me! But I just keep right on coming back like an idiot, don't I?"

"Why? Why don't you just give up? Why didn't you just stay away?"

"Because you need my help! No one else can do it apparently, so it has to be me!"

"Oh, so I'm a charity case? That's the only reason?"

"You know better. You know why I keep coming back!"

"Apparently I don't," she said, staring down into the water.

"You know how I feel about you," he said, lowering his voice.

"Yes, I *heard* you in the hallway outside my door," she said, looking up to meet his gaze. "You didn't come home for me; you came home for *them* and for yourself. It's the same reason you left in the first place; because you have something to prove!"

He shook his head at her, "I don't have anything to prove with anyone in this place! I was content to stay in Florida and live my life there!"

439

"I know why you came, John, even if *they* don't: you love the *fight* and playing the *hero*! You're not here because you want to fix things for *us*; you're here because you need to fix things for *you* - just like you did with your mother."

"You know I loved you and you broke my heart both times that you pushed me away!"

"I pushed you away for your own good! We weren't healthy for each other, Johnny! We got into a relationship because neither of us knew how to handle everything that happened to us! You felt guilty and I felt lost without my best friend, and ten years later what do we do? We think that we needed to be together and we got so carried away."

"If you're the expert on the Johnny and Melinda dynamic then what the hell are you giving me so much grief over? What have you got to be mad about?"

"What have I got to be mad about? I'm mad because you won't be honest with yourself or with me! I'm mad that you tried to sell me and yourself on the idea that you left here for your mother when you left here for yourself! I'm mad because you're still standing here telling me that you love me and you don't even believe it yourself!"

"It's not like that...I still love you!"

"You love me...but you're not *in love* with me," she said, sadly. "You don't even know what you want...you don't even know why you're here...or what you came back for."

She was crying now, and unable to maintain her composure in front of him any longer. There was no strength left in her to hold up that wall that she'd erected so many months before, when he'd left her.

"I thought that you finally understood...I thought...at the party..."

"You thought that coming to helpless little Melinda's rescue was enough to prove anything to me? It proved exactly what I've been saying; John Chapel came back to play here, not to really fix things!"

"What do I have to do then?"

She shook her head slowly at him, the tears streaking her cheeks, "If I have to tell you...then you can't fix anything. If *ever* there was a time to say or do the right thing, to prove to me that you really loved me, it would be now..."

440

She turned and started back towards the house, and left him standing helplessly behind, the wind knocked out of him. He was trying to run through every right thing to say in his head at that moment, but nothing would come. The only thing that kept forcing its way to the back of his tongue were the words that Dean and Gwenn had shared with him, reminding him that he had to be the one to save her and get through to her. But he couldn't say that.

He stood there, growing more and more frustrated with himself, angry that he hadn't prepared for this and that he hadn't been given more time before he'd had to confront her. When he walked through that glass sliding door, he never imagined that it would be "this" conversation that he'd be walking into. He felt as blindsided and ambushed as he did the night he fought Sal and his cousins, and holding his ground about the same as he did that night – which was hardly at all.

John wasn't losing this fight.

From the large picture window, they watched him following her, hastily enough to close the gap between them and not let her get away, but pacing himself enough to stall for precious time that he needed.

Don't be the hero. She doesn't want you to save her. She wants you to love her.

He might have been whispering the words, but his lips didn't move as he approached her.

She's mad at you for always having something to prove. You left her for that.

There were only twenty boards between them now, and his mind worked faster and faster.

You have to know what you want by now. What did you come home for John?

The blood carried the oxygen even faster to his brain as it beat hard against his ribs.

Remember when you knew what you wanted? What did you say to her? What did you do?

The images of days forgotten started firing in rapid succession in that revived brain.

A water fountain. A girl walking towards him from the porch. An embrace and a kiss to be envied.

I didn't say anything. I didn't say a damned thing to her. Say nothing.

441

He grabbed her by the arm, finally three boards away, and spun her to face him. Pulling her close with one hand and cradling her face in the other, he took her back to Lyster Lane.

They soon discovered, as they stood on that dock eagerly consuming one another, that no one could ever recreate that kiss, not even them. There was a brief moment when each of them realized this fact, when they closed their eyes and tried pretending they weren't on a dock, and hoped to become lost in the memory of a street far away. There was a shared sadness, just for that moment, when they realized they could never go back there, but in the next breath, there was elation, for they understood that they were creating an entirely new moment.

It was the Merrill Lake kiss.

Even though they would never compare with the two lovers from that quiet street, those two would have still envied the kiss of the pair by the lake. The distance they'd each braved to reach one another again had been greater than a few porch steps and a driveway, and couldn't be measured by the span of whitewashed boards. Overprotective, meddling mothers and intercepted letters had been replaced with dangerous men and letters deliberately never sent, and no one had stood in their way this time but each other.

The kiss is a promise that he will love her and not try to fix her or save her. Even if she's broken and unable to crawl out of the hole she's created for herself, she will only try to crawl out of it if he keeps that promise. There are no expectations for change and no promises except to do their best for each other. They will rediscover one another in that place only through these simple things, and through stripping away the things that they've hidden behind. For the first time, they will see each other.

They hovered above those boards for a long while after the kiss had ended. Neither of them saw the faces in that window or the mixture of expressions they wore. Connelly was smiling; a big, genuine, oblivious smile. Dean wasn't smiling; it was something closer to a grimace one might see on the face of an onlooker at a traffic accident, knowing it would end in a loud, inevitable crash. Gwenn wore a smile that she forced to stay alight like a kite on a breezeless day.

They hadn't heard the words spoken on the dock, but they saw the kiss and they knew what it meant: It had begun again.

Chapter 42

John Chapel's voice ceased being channeled from the great beyond by a thick finger depressing a black plastic button, and Campbell commanded their attention once again. Gwenn seemed to be as anxious whenever he stopped the recorder as starting it, and he gave her a concerned look. She managed a weak smile and leaned back in the chair she'd been sitting at the very edge of.

"The rest is probably redundant; things you've already heard," he said apologetically. "The private discussion with Miss Malowski was something I was pretty certain neither of you had been privy to."

She and Connelly nodded in unison, "I never really knew what John said to her, exactly, but I noticed a huge change in his behavior after."

"His behavior?"

"Well, that first two weeks with her was the worst, and John wasn't just cool under pressure, he actually asked the rest of us for help. That's something he rarely did – admitting he couldn't do something by himself – and we were all surprised. It makes sense now: he did it for her."

"Helping someone through a heroin withdrawal isn't something just anyone can do either," Connelly volunteered. "John knew not to try to play hero with something like that – not as delicate as her situation was."

"Jeremy was actually our saving grace. He was kind of our coach and we each had our specific jobs in dealing with her," Gwenn admitted, and it almost sounded like a genuine compliment.

He seemed as surprised as Campbell, and repaid the compliment, "Gwenn actually had the hardest job – being the only other girl – she had bathroom duty, and none of us envied her."

"That doesn't sound pleasant," Campbell said with a grimace.

"About as pleasant as it sounds; the body of a heroin addict goes through quite an ordeal through that process. Vomiting, dehydration, and diarrhea, in addition to lots and lots of showers - both cold and hot – were part of the daily routine."

"Dean and John took the night shift with her," Connelly continued, "which was no picnic either. Night terrors, the shakes, and insomnia are the worst in the first thirty-six hours. I used to sit up with my mom when she tried to go clean, multiple times, and Melinda was much harder to deal with."

"It sounds like it was quite a trial for you all, and you pulled through it together," Campbell noted.

"We still have to give credit to John, though; he was really the pillar that held that roof up and kept everything from collapsing on us. There were times we were at each other's throats, and he really did a great job of playing mediator and relieving us when we'd had enough. He was tireless and I've never seen him have that much patience with anything or anyone."

"We also had good times," Gwenn said, smiling sweetly. "Our night watches together were precious to me, full of long, intimate talks, and really…that's where I discovered that man I would fall in love with. We all sort of reconnected on that trip, and some of the old wounds went away."

Campbell listened to them intently, scribbling on his pad, and his mind was working over something that he hadn't shared with them yet. They had both talked with him enough to realize when some epiphany was coming or when one of the bigger questions was taking shape in that brilliant mind.

"John made a promise to her, but I think he knew it was as much for all of you, because he knew what was at stake and he knew you were all in it together. I see this as a sort of…redemption for him, and for all of you.

"I suppose," Gwenn said in a whisper, staring beyond them at a blank spot on the wall. "It was almost like the ordeal at Rain tree, all of us scrambling to hold onto her, trying to keep her from…drowning."

"Correct. And John knew that he couldn't exclude the rest of you from finding that, and from dealing with your own issues with Melinda Malowski. He knew that the house wouldn't stand for long without the rest of you, just as he knew the Malowski house wouldn't stand without her."

"Dean and I expected him to disappear with her once things were back to normal, but he was good about including all of us, even if she didn't like it. They still had their moments, and we didn't begrudge them that, because what you said was right; if they weren't strong then everything else was off."

"The balance Dean referred to?"

She nodded.

"So what came next? Everything went back to normal?"

"After those first grueling weeks, we all spent the rest of the summer talking about what we were going to do once we went back to the real world. Connelly had to head back to Florida, and I know a small part of John regretted not being able to go with him, but I think he knew that it wouldn't be an option."

"But he wasn't staying because he felt obligated? He stayed because he was able to follow through on his promise? Something changed between them, and the old John-Melinda formula was rewritten, wasn't it?"

She arched a brow at him, studying his expressionless face. She was certain he'd just asked three questions, but his inflection made those questions sound more like statements of fact. A subconscious glance at the recorder prompted him to show his hand, ruining his poker face.

"Yes, it's on here. I stopped it deliberately."

"I would like to hear it," she demanded politely.

"As I said, it's mostly redundant material," he insisted.

"I know they were together that day, Jim. We all knew, but they just didn't tell us."

"Then there you go; it's redundant to play it."

"It's not redundant! They talked about something that day - there was some big secret between them, and I'd like to know what it was."

"The secret was that they finally consummated their relationship; there's no great mystery to that. After all the times she tried to lure him in, and him rejecting her, telling her that it wasn't the right time, the right place or the right moment, they finally found their opportunity. It's as simple as that."

"It's not as simple as that. I knew them both better than either of you in this room, and I know it wasn't just sex. I was there for the Port Austin discussion, so I know how much words played into everything that defined them, Jim."

445

"There were words, but nothing that stands out in my mind, but I'll play it for you all the same," he said with a sigh."

❧❦

It was just a small patch of sand, broken up by reeds and bits of coarse grass, with a C-shaped cluster of trees all around them that kept prying eyes out. There were no houses nearby, just an abandoned wooden structure that had once been a small church. The place hadn't seen a fresh coat of paint in probably two generations, and the brittle glass of the narrow windows that faced the lake had long since been broken out. It would've made for an eerie eyesore, had the pines and birches not been so thick and shrouded its existence from the casual passerby. Only those explorers who discovered the small stretch of sand behind it knew that it was still there, forgotten among the trees.

Melinda and her brothers used to paddle their rafts to that place when they were young, and had claimed it as their own personal "island" (though, by definition, it was a peninsula), and would spend hours there playing. It was their little secret, even from their parents, and John was the first to ever be welcomed to "Malowski Isle". They found a spot close to the southern edge of the trees, and sat down to rest from their trip across the lake.

"This is so perfect…almost like Port Austin" she breathed heavily.

"Kind of looks like it," John commented. "I think it's the cattails and the way the sand is piled up behind us in that little dune. Like that first night I came over that rise and saw you sitting by the water…"

"I think we were meant to sit staring at a lake…forever," she said in a queer tone.

"I used to sit by the ocean some nights and think the same thing. I was a thousand miles from this place, but yet…there I was, sitting beside the water and thinking about you. There were tall grasses there too, and I would just close my eyes and listen to them blow, pretending I was still on that beach in Port Austin."

"I did the same when I came here last summer, and just sat by myself, remembering that night and wondering what you were doing at that moment. I wish we could go back to that night sometimes and just hit a pause button, and stay there forever."

"I thought you hated me that night…you were so mad that I wouldn't stay," John mused.

"I wasn't mad at you…I was disappointed that you had to go. I was disappointed that our time was so limited…and I thought that if you stayed that night that you would never be able to leave me."

He gripped her hand, locking his fingers in between hers. He'd held his share of hands since that night at Port Austin, hands of all shapes and sizes, but none felt as soft or as much "at home" as hers. Gwenn's had been long and slender and hers were more squared, but there was just something different about touching them that he couldn't describe in physical terms. It was just a certain way that they made him feel; like he was eight-years-old again and his innocence had returned on the wind with the smell of sweet lilac.

He didn't just smell it coming from her hair that was blowing across his nose, it seemed to be all around him, and coming from the beach itself. He pulled his nose away from the tickling strands and tried to spy the lilac bushes in question, but there were none to be found. It quite possibly was just a scent linked to a memory that had been stirred up by her presence or the familiar scene he felt he had returned to.

"I don't know if I was right about that night, Melinda…maybe if I'd stayed just one night…"

"What would've happened? We would've slept together and then what?"

"I just…I should've stayed here…I should have never let out of my sight."

"Who can say if things wouldn't have still gone the way they did? It put too much on you…always looking to you to figure my mess out and fix me, and the more I did it, the more guilty and self-destructive I became over it. I just couldn't do that to you and it's why I felt you deserved better and I pushed you away the first time."

"And what makes *this* time different? How can you say that you'll be okay now?"

"Because you came and pulled me out of *Hell*, just like you promised you would."

The reminder of the eerie promise he'd been asked to make when she was six made him shudder and caused every hair to rise

447

at once on his body. He'd never thought about that promise since the day he'd made it to her, and never thought there would come a day that she would actually ask him to make good on it. It wasn't actual Hell, of course, and she hadn't experienced true death, but it was probably the closest that she would ever face either.

"Jesus, Melinda..." was all he could utter.

"Well? It's true; I was miserable and so lost, ruining myself, and if Gwenn hadn't called you...you might very well have seen me at a funeral instead of a party. I know that I said that I wanted to do it for myself, and that I wouldn't let you play the hero...but really...it was all *you*. I was only able to go through that because of you and there's no one else I would have done it for. I didn't want to live for myself...I wanted to live for you and for *us*. So...I know we'll be okay."

"So...what do we do now?"

"I want to pretend that the last two years never happened..."

"What about Christmas and the good times?"

"Christmas reminds me that I hadn't seen you for weeks because we were having problems before that. It reminds me, too, of the last good days, right before everything fell apart. It makes me sad. I want to just continue on where we were...right after that second night at Port Austin."

"Okay...so this is night number three...and we're at Port Austin," he whispered.

"I like the sound of that..."

He leaned in towards her, whispering, "It's not raining anymore...and I just walked over that dune again. I've changed my mind...about staying the night with you..."

"And Jeremy isn't going to show up to complain about his hair being messed up in the rain," she whispered back.

"Jeremy's halfway to Florida by now; his hair is no longer my concern."

They playfully pecked at each other's lips in between smiles and hushed conversation, to keep whatever they were saying a secret from the pines.

"Kissing on me isn't going to make me forget that I'm scared to death of losing you," she said, echoing the line from that night they were reminiscing about.

448

"Fair enough, but you should know…that even if you slap me across the face again and tell me to go to hell, I won't stop coming for you," he countered with the words he'd never forgotten.

"I'm glad you remembered what you're supposed to do…can we just make out now?"

He turned his head slightly as he recoiled, measuring the precise angles of her lips, and then attacked it like an adder might go after a soft, fleshy beast in a field of grass. Her chest rose as their lips met, and her fingers went limp in his. She pulled him into the sand, and she was inviting him again, but this time there was nowhere to be and no excuses to be made. They had both anticipated this night for so long, and though it hadn't happened quite how they'd imagined, it still seemed perfect.

Just like he had taken her back to Lyster Lane on the dock, he took her back to their place at Port Austin on that secluded stretch of sand. John had a way of making her forget how complicated her life was whenever he was around, and he made things simple and straightforward again.

They both lay on their backs in the sand afterwards, looking straight up and letting their breathing slow and their hearts with it. It took a long time for them to compose themselves, physically and emotionally. There were so many things to say, so much to talk about that night, but they decided not to spoil it with words until later, when Gwenn and Dean heard the whispers and giggles coming from their room.

That next Sunday morning she rejoined the world at the breakfast table wearing a big grin. She'd even taken a shower on her own and put on some makeup to hide some of the telltale signs of the struggle she'd endured. Connelly and Dean commented on her improved health and Gwenn could tell that she wasn't just in better health; she had the old Melinda "glow" she used to have whenever things were good with John. He had the same aura, but was trying to suppress it.

It was Dean's turn to make breakfast that morning and he was doing his best not to catch the entire kitchen on fire. The guys were laughing at him and Gwenn had to rescue him more than once, going behind him to make sure burners were turned on the right temperature and keeping a towel handy to waft the smoke away.

"I thought you guys were trying to help me get better, not put me in the hospital?" Melinda remarked as she smirked at her brother, turning over the rubbery eggs to inspect them.

"Hey! If you guys don't like my eggs, you can all go to the nearest restaurant which is about twenty miles away - or cook them yourselves!" Dean snorted indignantly.

"It's not that they're that bad, buddy, it's just that I don't know how these are classified; are these scrambled, over-easy, or *both*?" John had to contribute and the girls snorted, choking the eggs down.

"We're out of bread again after John's French toast feast from yesterday, so there's no toast to dip in your eggs anyway! I thought you would prefer scrambled," Dean grumbled, scraping one of the pans.

"Yea...*scrambled* would be nice," Gwenn teased. "These still have the yolk in them."

"I'll make us some pancakes tomorrow morning." Melinda volunteered. "It's my turn right?"

"Oh you guys *are* brave if you're going to eat *her* pancakes!" Dean laughed.

Melinda replied by throwing some of Dean's eggs at him, which stuck to his hair. She laughed and eggs came out of her mouth, which caused John and Gwenn both to laugh. Gwenn knocked her juice over on the table as a result, and that just caused more laughter to erupt from the table as the entire contents spilled onto John's crotch. He tried to avoid the spill and stood so fast he cracked his knee on the small kitchen table and the whole group was brought to tears as he stood holding his knee with the wet crotch of his pants.

John picked up some of the blackened potatoes and threw it at Connelly, who seemed to be laughing the hardest at him. They were all still giggling as the girls helped clear the table and John was plucking egg from everyone's hair like a monkey searching for mites. Dean grabbed the broom and helped clean up the floor, still chuckling. They hadn't had this much fun together since they had been children, and it seemed to hit each of them as the laughter faded into smiles and they looked around the room at one another.

For a few minutes, they'd forgotten why they were there, and that they'd spent the last week at one other's throats and one of them had just struggled through a drug withdrawal. John wondered

450

if it was only a temporary respite before the bickering and the tension began again, or if the change in Melinda's disposition meant a change in the happiness of the entire household. Like him, she'd been the alpha in her own little circles and those circles spun around her like gravitational fields, being affected by every little thing that she did. Perhaps those forces would be realigned so long as she was spinning the right way again and everything was exactly as it was supposed to be in her cosmogony.

Just as Dean had said, when John and Melinda were together and strong, everything else seemed to fall into place and everyone else was happy too. They weren't quite up to "old times" strong as of yet, but watching them together in the kitchen that morning, and the days prior, he was sure that they were well on their way. He was glad that the tension was being lifted finally from that house and that it would soon have a ripple effect at his own house, once word reached his parents that Melinda had been brought back from her dark place. He didn't envy John, however, and the fate that he always seemed destined to follow, being at her side.

Gwenn also didn't envy him, but like Dean, she accepted it. She probably understood it better than any of them, having watched it unfold and play out over the past thirteen years. For that reason, though, she hated it the most. She hated that he was just stuck with her, forever being necessary to her happiness, and by proxy, all of their happiness. She hated that he'd wanted to break free, believed that change was possible, and that she lied to him and told him that it wasn't because it was what was best for everyone else. Everyone else except her and John.

John seemed relatively happy though, and his smile was infectious and spread through that room as much as Melinda's glow. She knew that it wasn't just her and the battle they had just fought together, or even the fact that they'd reconnected in a way that they never had thought possible; he was smiling because he had found home finally. He was among friends – his very best friends – and they'd all made it through one of the worst times together. All that remained was making the days ahead the best summer of their lives, and he meant to do just that.

Chapter *43*

The five friends were seated around the campfire, laughing and reminiscing, telling more stories and poking fun of each other (as they did best), as was their evening ritual after dinner. Melinda was cozied up beside John, leaning against his arm, fighting sleep as she listened to the soothing way in which he told stories. Gwenn was seated on a log at Connelly's feat, and they'd spent their own days walking the lake and taking paddle boat rides since things had calmed down. Dean was in charge of the fire and the hot dogs (which might not have been the best idea, since they'd watched him eat seven of them that night).

"When do you all have to get back?" John asked in a serious tone after the laughter died down.

"Well, I have a job I'm supposed to get back to," Gwenn explained. "I already called in sick the last two days. I don't know how much longer they'll keep me on if I call in again."

"Same here. I'm supposed to show up tomorrow on a new site. I've been working construction with a friend of my dad's, and it pays pretty well for a college guy," Dean said.

Melinda laughed, "Well, I don't really have any source of income except Sal...and I think I'm fired already. So I suppose I'll have to do the honorable thing and get a job like you poor slobs."

Connelly nodded at him, "You know me John; I roll where you roll."

John grinned, looking around the room at all of them, finally enjoying the fact that they were all together in the same place. "I say we all stay up here until we absolutely have to go back. I have some money put away and I think we all could use some time to catch up before school starts up. Dean, you and Gwenn are headed back in the fall right?"

They nodded, the smiles fading and being replaced with puzzlement.

"And Melinda, you're going to school starting this semester..."

If it was supposed to sound like a question, John had used the wrong inflection. She looked up at him and then to her brother for confirmation of what she had heard. "Umm, I was thinking about it…"

"No, I think this would be a good time for you to go."

"I would love to go, but I can't this semester, I haven't gotten any scholarships, no loans, I'm not prepared…I don't really have the money. Mom and dad cut me off basically…Sal was all I had if I wanted to go…and he never encouraged it."

"He's gone, Melinda! It's time for you to start thinking that way…and thinking for yourself." Gwenn was stern with her.

"We start things new from here on out. I will front you. I stake you from now on. You go to school and you keep your grades up…" John began making his offer and she couldn't accept it. She had just come from under one man and didn't so quickly want to be pushed under the thumb of another, even one as well-meaning as John Chapel.

"No! I can't accept that. I'll go to work and save some money and start in the winter - I promise!"

"I was going to say…you stay in school, you keep up your grades and I will *help* you. When you finish with school you will pay me back *every penny*. This isn't charity, it's a loan. I don't expect anything in return, you lead your own life, do what you want to do…with a few exceptions of course: stay away from the drugs and stay the hell away from Sal Nussein." John put his counter-offer on the table and his tone and expression said that it wasn't up for negotiation.

Melinda nodded softly, touched by his generosity. He had said the magic words; "*Do what you want to do*". That implied that he wasn't expecting her to be joined at his hip or anywhere near his thumb in exchange for his generosity. That was *John* though, and that's what made him different than Sal. She smiled up at him and grabbed his hand in thanks. It was settled, Melinda had some sort of future laid out before her, and they breathed a collective sigh.

"What about you? Are you going back to Florida?" She asked, swallowing hard.

He'd made it clear that there were no promises in their present arrangement, but the thought of him disappearing again wasn't something she was ready for yet. His offer sounded too good to be true, and it implied that he would be spending the remainder of the summer there and then leaving. Why else would he stake them all just to spend some time with them, if not to get in one last hurrah before he left again? How would he come up with the money to front her for school if he wasn't going back to work for the mysterious George?

"I don't know yet...not just yet. I planned to stay for the remainder of the summer, just to make sure everything goes smoothly until the weather turns cooler, and then we'll see. In the meantime, we can have one hell of a summer together, and I think we've all earned it."

Melinda looked to her brother, who looked to Gwenn, and Gwenn back to John as they all considered the offer. There were about six or eight weeks left before the Malowskis came to close up and winterize the home, and they had already used all of their vacation time in the beginning of summer, as they did every year, so they would have the place to themselves. They knew that it was really John and Melinda time, but he genuinely wanted each of them to stay as well, because he had missed time with them all. They also knew that it wasn't just about having fun, it was about strengthening the bonds they had with Melinda in the event that he had to leave again so she had a network of friends to fall back on.

"I've got to get some things from home first, if I'm going to do this - look at these awful clothes man, they're like from tenth grade and they barely fit. This ugly flannel is my dad's!" Dean protested.

"Don't get us started on the fashion. Look at Mel's awful sweatshirt collection!" Gwenn teased.

"If it wasn't for my ugly sweatshirts, you'd be wearing your cocktail dress still," she fired back.

"No way!" John cut them off. "If you head back, you stay. I can't risk Sal or one of his goons following you back up."

There was the awful reminder of why they had come there in the first place. None of them had given much thought to Sal or his gang of cousins, being so distracted by their own issues at the lake. But John was right; he was probably still out there, looking for her and possibly for all of them. He was probably driving by their houses nightly, or had some of his goons posted at the end of their streets, waiting to report in.

"John...we have to go back to the civilized world eventually...you know that. We can't go into the witness protection program or flee the country because of him or what happened. Some of those guys go to the college, and we're going to see them again. It's inevitable," Dean complained.

"I know that, but sometimes time and distance help people to forget things. I'm banking on them not being like buzzing hornets the next time we see them. We stirred up the nest, and we just need to give them time to cool off. That's all I'm saying."

"I don't know if guys like Sal or Shannon cool off, Shannon especially. He was notorious for his bad temper - that's why Melinda broke it off with him," Gwenn expressed her concern.

"Yea, she's right. He was a maniac! He beat some guy's ass once over a parking space and I would have left him there but it would have been a long walk home," Melinda chimed in.

John was quiet and thoughtful for a long time. He knew that he had begun something that wouldn't just go away. He knew that somewhere down the line there would be some retribution for what had happened the week before, and they would be made to suffer because of his actions. Sal hadn't forgotten him and it had been more than a year since the last time they'd had their encounter. Something bad would happen, he could sense it, and he would be off in sunny Florida when it did. That's when he made his decision.

He went to grab another soda from the house and asked Connelly to join him. Jeremy could see by the look on his face that John was about to make a rash decision and he was already trying to think of the words to talk him out of it.

"John...you said you weren't going to save her, remember?"

"I keep hearing that. But we can't just leave them here to deal with the mess we started."

"The mess *we* started? We didn't start this!"

"No, but we certainly changed the game, didn't we?"

"Let's bring her with us," he pleaded. "Just take her out of this place for good."

"She wouldn't be able to handle that place, Con, and you know it. What are we gonna' do? Put her on George's payroll and having her pull jobs like Nicole? I want to keep her as far away from that life as possible!"

"You stay here with her and keep an eye on things. I'll go back to George and send you cash each month to keep things running smooth."

"You know that's the *dumbest* idea you've ever had," he said, grimacing.

"I think between the two of us, it makes the most sense," John concluded.

"Because George likes you more and because you don't think I'll send you money?"

"No, because of the two of us, like it or not, I'm able to pull the bigger jobs and make enough to cover the both of us. And you have no obligation to send me money, Con. This isn't your problem, it's mine. You'd be doing me a huge favor by staying with her."

"And do what? I'm not a one-man army. I can't tackle Sal and his boys on him own, John! And you're like a brother to me, no matter who George likes more, I would still send you money. *Your* problems are *my* problems, remember? I stuck by you when everyone else bailed remember?"

"I can't stay here, Con, I have to get back to George," he said.

"Why? What's back there? You have nothing back there that you need, everything you need is right here. This is your home...she is your home...and you belong here."

"I can't just bail out on George like that..."

"You're like a son to that man and he's always telling you that you're better than the rest of us, and that you shouldn't be mixed up in shit like that. Stay here and go to school, stay with this girl, make something better of yourself."

"It's not that easy..."

"Johnny...she's going to forgive you. This is the time to stop playing hero and trying to fix everyone, like Melinda asked you to. If Nicole falls off the wagon down there then she falls off the wagon, and that's nobody's fault but hers. I'll go and keep an eye on her."

"I'll bet you will," John said, smiling.

"Someone has to, and besides, she's not your type anyway."

"Yea, you're probably right."

"So what's keeping you? You afraid to go get a regular job and be a regular guy? You too good to hang out with these people now? You have to be rolling around in fancy cars and wearing your nice clothes? That life wasn't forever Johnny – not for you. That life is for a guy like me...and that's probably as good as it's going to get for me, but not for you, brother."

"Con...you can come home and go to school too...do something different..."

"College isn't for me, man; it's for guys like you and Josh and Dean. Is that what you're worried about? That I can't handle working for George on my own? I'll be just fine, I've been the one taking care of you remember?"

John slapped him on the shoulder, "Yea, I wouldn't have made it without you, Con. I just want something better for you...for both of us."

"Who says I'm not enjoying my life? I love it down there, Johnny! Don't feel sorry for me. I feel sorry for you having to stay here and sort out this mess...but it will work out...the way it's supposed to."

"What if it doesn't? What if I can't make it work this time? This is the last time I'm doing this, and if we don't make it this time, it's over for good."

Jeremy Connelly grabbed his arms in both hands and stared him straight in the eye, saying, "Then if you don't turn things around with that blonde in there...there's a redhead who is dying to be next in line. You make it work with her!"

"I'm not doing that to Gwenn," he snapped. "I'm not asking her to wait for me."

"You won't have to. I see the way she looks at you and so does everyone else. Melinda is a firecracker, man, and she turns heads for sure, but Gwenn...Gwenn is a keeper. That's the kind of girl you can come home to every night and never be surprised."

"What's that mean?"

"It means what it means. I regret letting that one go, but my time with her is passed. If things take a nose dive with Melinda, you put everything into that one."

"Jesus, Con, you sound like you're walking out the door tonight and I'm never seeing you again. We haven't even decided what we're doing yet."

458

"Yes we have," he said, as his head dipped to the floor. "You're staying and I'm going back to George. You get an honest job here and I'll send you your cut every month to help out. That's all your money anyway; you set up most of those routes and made the deals to get the business. You'll see me again, real soon…"

"You're thinking about *Josh*? You think that this is it for us too?"

"No…that was Josh…this is *me* and *you*. We've been through too much shit together to call it quits. I'll probably be home at Christmas…"

"You have no reason to come home for Christmas Con."

"You're right…then you bring your woman down to get out of the snow for a while. There will always be a place for you there."

John nodded, conceding to Jeremy's plan. It made the most sense, and he wasn't sure what it was that he felt he was giving up by not going back. A life of unorganized crime? A bunch of ex-con nobodies? A girl who he could trust even less than Melinda? The mysterious Hungarian who'd warned him about this very thing? He couldn't help but think of Frank Kovacs at that moment, remembering being pulled aside at the Island Pub and being given a warning that sounded almost like a death threat. He had been more against his leaving than Nicole was, and though his reasons were cryptic at best, there was something dire in his tone. Under no circumstances, he said, should he leave and return home.

He didn't share the odd conversation with Connelly, though, and dismissed it as Frank being overprotective as he always was. He was John's unofficial bodyguard, among other things, and it hadn't been the first time he'd tried to steer him away from trouble. Kovacs had known some of the details of the situation at home, most likely thanks to Connelly and his big mouth, and he was probably just being overly concerned.

Finally realizing that there were no more arguments to make against his case for staying home, he picked up the phone and made a long distance call. Connelly returned to the campfire wearing a smile, in an attempt to camouflage the nature of the discussion that had just taken place, but the rising and falling of John's voice in the house told them that something serious was taking place.

John hung up the receiver heavily and returned a few minutes later, looking a little a bit anxious but smiling. "It's a done deal...I'm going back to school this semester. I just called George. He needs you back there within the week, Con...*with the car*...and he doesn't sound happy...that it's *you*."

They all knew who George was and the type of work that John did for him, either hearing it firsthand or through one of the gossip sessions in the house, and so, none of them asked a single thing about that particular situation. Gwenn and Dean liked to pretend that a man like that didn't exist and that John did something else while he was away. Melinda knew men like that, and thought she had a pretty firm grasp of what John had been involved with, so she acted like an authority on the subject (though she had no clue what George Gallianni was all about). Connelly had just never talked about it around outsiders out of habit.

They decided that the next day would be Connelly's last, so they made the most of it. John helped Gwenn make omelets (Dean and Melinda were the worst cooks) that weren't burned, rubbery or filled with questionable items, so Jeremy would have a good sendoff meal. Afterwards, Dean and John took him out in the aluminum boat for a final round of perch fishing and their secret beer drinking sessions (it was important not to let Melinda see them with beer), and they came back for a big lunch.

John said goodbye to his friend, and it felt almost like saying goodbye to the others weeks before, unsure of whether or not he would see him again. Connelly gave him that crooked, reassuring grin, slapped him once more on the back for luck, and hopped in the Benz to reach the expressway before dark.

It was odd not having him around for the last couple of weeks they were at the lake house, but it was also strangely refreshing. It was back to just the four of them again, the Rain tree group that preceded all of the silly groups John had been in since, and it seemed to bring those four even closer together. Gwenn didn't even miss Con as much as she thought she might, or feel left out, because Dean, John and even Melinda reserved time just for her.

John insisted on her being his breakfast partner, saying that it now fell entirely up to them to keep the house from burning down and prevent the spread of botulism. Dean filled in for Connelly on their afternoon walks, freeing John up for time with

Melinda, and Melinda took her on paddle boat rides for girl talk (though they steered clear of Malowski Isle). After lunch, it was an epic game of Monopoly, which had always been a Malowski tradition, and sometimes went well beyond dinner.

Afterwards, John and Dean would get the fire going in the fire pit in preparation for their other ritual that they followed every night. There were tons of marshmallows and chocolate for dessert, which they would melt in the fire and get their hands gooey as they shared more stories about the times they'd missed. Of course, Melinda was the most overdressed because she'd taken advantage of John's generosity the day they went clothing shopping. She wouldn't be the same if she wasn't the best-looking one there, and had applied full makeup and did her hair for the event.

The others didn't mind, particularly Gwenn, because John had included her in the secret beer club that held meetings on the fishing boat and in the garage after Melinda fell asleep. So, they let her be pretty and they tolerated it because they had their own fun without her once she left the fire pit. John missed out on a lot of "secret beer club" because he was dragged off to bed with her most nights. Dean and Gwenn let him off the hook on that one, because he really was making a solid effort to spend quality time with each of them, and there was more beer for them.

When the last day came, and the call came from Dennis to let them know he was coming to close the house up, the foursome packed their things and said goodbye to the place. John found Melinda standing on the end of the dock, and he wrapped his around her waist and shared a last, longing look out at the lake that they would miss, promising that they would return every summer after that one. Just across the corner of the water was the strip of beach where they had made love in the tall grasses in the shadow of the old church there. They both stared at it and remembered that day, and she squeezed his hands to get his attention, just in case he wasn't looking out at the same thing she was.

Mr. Malowski showed later that afternoon and was greeted by both of his children with a large embrace. Dean had given him a few details about his sister's ordeal over the phone and they gave him the rest of the details when he'd arrived. After listening to their story, he approached John with a firm handshake and a hug. "Thank you" was all that he could muster, and he fought hard to not lose his composure. His eyes twinkled at John as they never had before, and he finally saw acceptance there, as well as respect.

He embraced his daughter again, as if he hadn't seen her for years, and checked her over to make sure she was alright. She looked like his old Melinda, and he believed that she was ready to finally come home.

"I'm fine dad. Really...I'm fine." She reassured him.

He smiled and nodded slowly.

"Dean, will you and Gwenn grab the plastic from my trunk and start covering the windows? And Melinda, go ahead and put your things in the trunk after they take out the materials."

He then turned to John with a solemn expression, saying in a hushed voice, "I know that my wife and I were never your favorite people and that we blamed you...for what happened..."

"Dennis, I had this discussion with Marge, it's okay," John interrupted.

"Yes, I know you did...but you and I haven't had this discussion...and a lot has happened since then. What I'm trying to tell you is that when we received word that Melinda was in your hands again, Marge and I both breathed a sigh of relief and thanked God. You're not a father, and it's a difficult thing to explain this through the eyes of a father..."

John watched his face twist up the same way he had seen it the day of Dawson's funeral, twelve years before, and it was unnerving. He hadn't understood those emotions then, as a young boy, and could only appreciate them just a bit more now. John wasn't a father who'd suffered the loss of one child and the slow destruction of another, but he knew how the sight of Melinda and her suffering had first affected him. It must have been a hundredfold worse seeing her in that condition through the eyes of the man who raised her from birth.

Teary-eyed, he composed himself and continued, "I was watching her die and fade away...as helplessly as I watched my son do the same...and there was nothing I could do. You have no idea of the guilt I have lived with, and I cannot imagine the guilt you have lived with, because we were both helpless that day to do anything. But you did it this time...you got there in time...and you saved our child. I cannot express, in words, my gratitude..."

He embraced John then, and he could feel Dennis shuddering the way a man did when there were no words. He broke off the clinch after a few moments, and wiped his foggy glasses on the corner of his shirt as he composed himself.

"Welcome home, John," he said in a shaky voice. "Now I could use some help, the more of us the better. We can have this place closed up in an hour or two and be on the road. Marge will have dinner ready and I hope you'll stay."

They got the old cottage sealed up tight and winterized in no time, with the five of them working together. When everything was ready and bags were packed, the five of them said goodbye to the lake house, each in their own way, and rode in relative silence towards the Malowski house. Melinda sat in the back, sharing a smile with John as they looked out at the fields of tall grasses tinged in the golden light of the last rays of summer.

THE LOST CRUSADE

"Lost causes are the only ones worth fighting."

~Clarence Darrow

The master storyteller and his apprentices had withdrawn from the breakfast nook for the more spacious study down the hall. With the passing of midday, the sun had decided to retire early to a bed of dark, swirling gray cushions that loomed above, painting the nook in similar gloomy, gray tones. Still donning his tweed, Campbell wouldn't have noticed the chill that settled over the room if not for Gwenn rubbing her bare arms and Connelly frowning at his cold coffee.

Heavy curtains covering the thicker panes of glass helped to insulate the room, but Campbell took the precaution of building a fire just to make sure that his guests would be made comfortable. Gwenn whispered to Connelly about how he looked out of place hunched over the hearth, placing the logs perfectly like a survivalist but dressed more like a boat captain. He didn't seem to get the Hemingway reference, or he was simply too engrossed in the Cincinnati roadmap on the back wall.

Connelly gave her a confused frown and Campbell managed a chuckle and an encouraging smile, delighted that she was still able to find any levity at all, given the weight of their most recent discussion. That discussion had ignited something behind those amber eyes again, and he felt that he was on the brink of hearing one of her fiery discourses.

The move to the study served in some strategic capacity as well, for that reason, and he thought it best to let those questions smolder and allow some of them to burn out before they re-opened their dialogue. He'd remembered well the folly of trying to engage her when her eyes blazed that way, and knew it would become an emotionally-charged exercise in futility.

So, here they were, back in the room it all began, and the stage had to be set again for the mood and subject matter of the newest controversy. Campbell would need all of those faces in his corner, peering over his shoulder at her, so that she could feel the weight of those stares and not forget them. Like John, she'd forgotten the place they'd once resided – deep in his subconscious

– and that they were nothing more but a series of abstract thoughts transformed into a series of abstract charcoal lines onto paper.

He'd given those characters too much life, just as he'd been guilty of many times standing at his lectern, and for that reason, he'd used slides and visual points of reference for his listeners, so that they could see that those figures only existed in stories. The key difference was that those faces immortalized in paintings and frescos had once been living, breathing people, each with fascinating stories; the people on that wall in his study had never lived but still had fascinating stories.

The other reason they'd returned to this stage was for the benefit of his newest guest, who'd insisted that he be let in on the rest of the story. Campbell argued that it was best that he didn't know the other half of that story for the sake of objectivity, and that his testimony might become skewed as a result. This threw the small breakfast room into chaos, Gwenn erupting and Connelly following suit, saying that it was unfair and accusing him of the same subjectivity that he claimed to fear. The story, she insisted, had already been tainted.

Campbell wanted to end it right then and there, but he was already invested in the story, feeling as though he was so close to a resolution and Gwenn had him backed into a corner as it was. She'd already hinted at accusations that he'd 'manipulated' the information for his benefit, so ending the debate prematurely and asking his guests to leave would've only appeared an admission of guilt.

Like an attorney preparing his brief before the case of a lifetime, Campbell gathered up every loose note and journal page from his desk, every line of transcribed from their discussions over the past two days, and fixed himself a stiff drink before taking the 'stand'. His opposition studied the patchwork of pictures and script tacked to the wall, the interconnecting lines, and every scrawled sticky note.

Gwenn glanced over her shoulder, squinting at the single available seat across from him – John's chair – and it didn't look quite as comfortable as it had the day before. There were no other seats nearby where Connelly would be accessible to her for support or a look of encouragement; it was just that single, empty seat, and she would be facing the great Dr. Campbell alone. It would be far worse than those mornings in his classroom where he'd put her on the spot with some question and all eyes watched her with trepidation.

The teacher-student guidelines for conduct were off the table, there would be no help from anyone else in the room, and the questions needing answers were much bigger than any she'd ever faced. More was on the line than a passing grade, the respect of her classmates, or even the respect of the man she'd worked so hard to impress. The reputation of the man she'd loved more than any other was now in her hands, along with her wavering faith, and if she lost this fight, both would be lost.

She chose not to cooperate, not to take the stage he'd set for her, and to not allow him to take her newly-discovered adversary out of play. There had also been a subtle accusation that Connelly's presence there hadn't been so much for the benefit of the information he possessed, but as a sort of psychological warfare, to throw her off balance.

Initially, that had been the case, but when they listened to the disembodied voice reminiscing about the "good days", they both joined in, laughing and sharing stories of their own. The awkwardness between them seemed to melt as they were reminded of how close they'd once been, and that they were both indebted to their friend to discover the truth. An oppressive hand brought a swift end to the affair, turning off the recorder, and their smiles switched off as well.

That's when Connelly insisted that he hear the rest of the story, and Campbell felt the shift in alliances. During the course of their many phone discussions, he'd briefed Jeremy Connelly on the emotional state of his old friend and warned him about being drawn into her personal crusade. There had been an agreement, like Gwenn had insinuated, and there were terms to that agreement – terms which Jeremy Connelly was dangerously close to violating.

It had never been his intention in offering compensation as a means of manipulating the man, just controlling the flow of information. There were very specific things he'd needed from him, only a few empty spaces in that 'complex crossword' that needed to be filled and he didn't want to have to start erasing boxes he already had answers for. But there they were, the pair of them, leaning on his desk with their smug faces, trying to rewrite the very *questions* in his puzzle that was almost complete.

He'd warned Connelly about being succinct with his answers, to address only the topics they were discussing, and above all, not to give any credence to the paranoid theories that Gwenn Chapel would attempt to champion. She'd accused him of manipulating the data to suit his needs, but he was well aware of her ability to manipulate things too; her best friend growing up was Melinda Malowski, and she'd dated Jeremy Connelly – the "Con Man".

He watched them cautiously as she prepared to make her opening statement, standing a bit too close to her unlikely ally, who was in danger of ruining everything.

"So, would you like to get Jeremy up to speed on what he's missed, or would you like me to tell him?"

"It might be more practical for you to give him a summary of the things we discussed last night, so I can see if we're all on the same page – to coin a phrase."

"Fair enough," she said, walking back to the road map. "John suffered a series of...episodes...which involved visual and auditory hallucinations, night terrors, and his eventual complete and total break from reality. The origin of these episodes, Jim believes, stems from a series of tragic events, the first of which was the death of Melinda's brother when John was seven-and-a-half."

She pointed to the illustration of Dawson Malowski and looked to Connelly for comprehension and Campbell for acceptance. They each gave her a nod and she returned to her reconstruction of events.

"He was forced to go live with his father for the next ten years and completely lost contact with Melinda, burdened by guilt over the death of her brother and for feeling like he'd abandoned her. This is about the time you met him," she said, addressing Connelly.

"Fast forward ten years. They stumble upon each other again, purely by chance, and what follows can only be described as two messed up kids trying desperately to make up for lost time and define where, exactly, they fit together. A torrid summer romance comes next, followed by a couple of devastating breakups, more guilt from *her* mother, more guilt from *his own* mother, and a string of people who treat him like a punching bag and a door mat."

Both men continued to watch as she traced her fingers across the dotted lines connecting the pages and pictures posted to the wall, nodding each time she confirmed that they were following along.

"Which brings us to Merrill Lake – the place where, in James Campbell's own words, John found *redemption*. That *is* what you called it, wasn't it Jim?"

He gave his fake smile, not certain where she was going with her line of questioning, but relinquished another nod.

"Jeremy, you were one of those people at the lake that summer, would you say that John looked like a man racked by guilt? Or would a better definition – Dr. Campbell's definition – be that he looked like a man who'd cleared all debts and was making a fresh start with the woman he loved?"

Campbell tried to interrupt, "I think you're oversimplifying the outcome of the events of Merrill--"

"Oversimplify?" Gwenn cut him off. "Your exact words, not more than a few minutes ago, were that 'the old John-Melinda formula was rewritten' and things had changed between them. Are you changing your statement?"

"Well no," he said with a sigh. "But with any *formula*, there are many variables to consider."

"There always are, aren't there?" She replied with her smug expression. "The bottom line is that there was nothing left for them to discuss or fight about, other than regular 'couple type' things: Leaving the toilet seat up, being late to pick her up at school, or just nitpicking as couples do. All of those things that fueled their constant struggle before – the things I just mentioned - were laid to rest after Merrill Lake"

"I think it's a bit overzealous to say that John walked away from Merrill Lake an entirely *new man*. I believe that it began an entirely new chapter in all of your lives, and I won't argue that point."

"You're absolutely right; that chapter was brought to a close by the fulfillment of a *promise* he made to her as a boy."

Campbell raised a brow and hid within his notes, Connelly looked lost, scanning each of their faces.

"You didn't think I'd caught *that*, did you? There was a reason that you were so reluctant to let us hear the rest of that tape, wasn't there?"

"As I said, I thought the information was redundant. You asked me to help you find conclusive answers, Gwenn, and getting sidetracked by information that isn't pertinent--"

"Isn't *pertinent*?" She exclaimed, her voice climbing two octaves. "John fulfilled the biggest promise he'd ever made to her! He came through for her in her *darkest* hour, and you say that's not *pertinent*?"

"You're being as melodramatic as a young Melinda Malowski," he scoffed. "She was a frightened, six-year-old child with no concept of what she was asking him to promise her."

"And yet, he still managed to keep his word didn't he? It may sound melodramatic, but you know as well as I do what that meant to the both of them. You think John didn't talk about your *crusades* with me?"

Connelly's puzzled expression said that he was feeling like the outsider once again and more so by the knotted brow creasing Campbell's forehead. The Professor locked eyes with hers and the way he shifted his jaw slightly forward, he thought that Gwenn might've insulted his honor or possibly his mother.

"What crusades?" Connelly dared disturb the cold silence between them.

"Do you want to hear Campbell's version, or John's? They're about the same, aren't they Jim?"

There was that smug expression again which seemed to only shift Campbell's jaw ever forward, drawing his brow downward until the knot grew larger.

"This is the first I've heard of it," Connelly said, almost apologetically.

"Of course it is; it's the entire basis for my argument for John's sanity, and Jim wouldn't bring something like that up."

James Campbell's face changed like a television with a broken remote; switching sporadically back and forth between a channel with a fuzzy picture and one with a foreign movie playing – both hard to interpret.

"We would need an entire evening dedicated to covering that topic, Mrs. Chapel, and it didn't apply to John in this case--"

"My husband died chasing *your* goddamned crusades!" She exploded, slamming her fist against the charcoal face of a very scary-looking character with black eyes and a terrible grimace. "Don't tell me that it didn't apply to him!"

472

Her outburst caused even the grim-faced professor to start, and Connelly took a precautionary step back from the desk, thinking she might hurl it at him next.

"*My* crusades?" He asked, calmly.

She came around the desk then, marching directly at him, and Campbell gave Connelly a concerned look, wondering if he might come to his aid if she suddenly decided to begin bludgeoning him with one of the artifacts he had scattered about the room. Stopping behind the empty chair he'd left for her, she jabbed a finger across the back of it at him.

"*Your* crusades!" She slapped the back of the chair and it resounded like a bullwhip. "I've heard the story a million times! He sat in *this very* chair to listen to your stories about bygone days when men were still men and women were helpless damsels waiting to be rescued! And you wonder why in the hell he lost his mind chasing these things? Because he *idolized* you and he took to heart every conversation you ever shared with him!"

For a moment, James Campbell was speechless. That was no easy feat, winning a verbal spar with the master orator, and as he stared up at those blazing, amber eyes, he silently applauded her.

"Yes, we often spoke of bygone days when people used to fight for what they wanted and what they believed in – not expected everything to be handed to them like they do now. This was something we talked about at length, a bond we shared, and I'm not so naive that I believe that he wasn't influenced by me in some measure. But John Chapel made his own choices and he followed this through until the end because that's the sort of man he was...long before I met him."

Gwenn's expression softened and she dipped her head, nodding slowly in agreement.

"John sat in that seat over there and told me...that he wasn't certain if this crusade of his was at an end or not, and this was when things had never been better between him and Miss Malowski. Why would he say something like that if he'd truly been able to let go of everything as you suggest he did at the lake?"

"I was there! I spent plenty of time with the both of them for months after we returned home, and I was a party to every little fight they had in that period of time. They acted like two regular people, fighting over being late for a movie date or picking her up at college, and the entire 'magical formula' to the John and Melinda dynamic changed, Jim. They relied on the regular things that couples do to keep them together."

"That formula didn't seem to work very well, did it?" He said with a biting sarcasm.

"They fell apart like any two people who can't make it work. It doesn't matter if it worked or not; that's not the issue! The issue is that my husband supposedly had a complete disconnect from reality because of unresolved affairs buried deep in his subconscious – affairs that had been resolved ten years ago!"

"This is another one of those questions that, unfortunately, comes down to faith and not facts," he replied coldly. "The problem is that your perception of things, of John's mental state during this period of calm, is being factored into your argument as absolute fact."

"It is a *fact*! I told you that I was *there*! My *perception*, in this particular matter, is the closest thing you're going to get to absolute fact! *Connelly* wasn't there, *you* weren't there, and unless you have John's testimony on that tape, stating something contrary, then it's all we have to go on!"

Campbell shook his head politely, and in his most inoffensive tone, replied, "All that I was able to gather was that there was a pretty violent and terrible breakup?"

"It was the worst breakup I've ever seen, but it doesn't signify that it was anything but John being angry with Sal and Melinda. He had a right to be angry!"

"So you're telling me that it wasn't a buildup of anything eating at him? If John had truly cleared all debts between them, let go of hard feelings and all that, then what you're saying is that John just had a violent temper? That afternoon in front of Oakland wasn't the straw that broke the camel's back, but the first on a fresh camel?"

"You're trying to portray him as a violent and dangerous person now," she shrieked at him, "instead of a man dealing with guilt and suppressed issues?"

"So how would you describe what took place between those men?"

"Whatever was leftover between John and Sal was between them, not John and Melinda. He hated him and that's to
474

be expected – they were *mortal enemies*. What I don't accept is that there was anything left on the conscience of my husband that caused…whatever happened to him."

"I think you're underplaying it a bit, don't you?"

"And you're overplaying it. It was a fight!"

"The *Knights Inn* was a *fight*," Campbell said with a smug grin. "The parking lot of the Island Pub was a *fight*. This was a battle that shook the heavens…and that students still talk about to this day! It's a fight that John sensed was coming, because he *knew* that things wouldn't last forever with Miss Malowski."

"Then how do you explain the fight?" she sighed.

"John buried all of those things at the lake, the sum of all of his guilt, put down like a sick animal. Sometimes…those animals go quietly, and others, they let out one final scream before you know it's finally dead."

"How poetic."

Connelly finally braved stepping in between the two scratching cats in their alley brawl.

"What you said about John, being torn apart by guilt, was probably pretty accurate. He felt guilty about not telling you about Nicole, and it started to eat at him…well, I'm sure there was a lot more guilt pertaining to that whole situation that he wasn't able to come to terms with."

"What do you mean, Connelly?" Campbell asked, raising a brow. "You said there wasn't much to that relationship? What would he have to come to terms with?"

They could both see that he'd immediately regretted opening his mouth without thinking first, and he edged forward in his seat, trying to conceal his expression.

"Well…John wasn't like the rest of us and I just think Florida weighed on his conscience more. I think he regretted a lot of his behavior – beating people up, living a life of crime, things like that – and he sought redemption for those things too. That's probably why he became a cop; to set those things right."

"Inevitably, he faced those same elements on the right side of the law," Campbell chimed in. "He discussed having to take lives and how he had nightmares about those faces too. Who knows? Maybe some of the faces on that wall behind us belong to those men? Maybe those people are the ghosts that haunted him?"

"So my husband was still crazy, no matter how you slice it? If it wasn't Melinda Malowski who drove him over the edge then it was the slew of criminals he resented working for and those he put away?"

Connelly approached her, patting her gently on the shoulder in a display of tenderness neither of them expected.

"Why can't we just say that John struggled with his conscience and to find absolution for the things he did, instead of calling him crazy? Why couldn't he have created this place to discover those things, to find his way along that road, as a means of clearing the slate one last time? Call it a religious experience or coming to closer to God if you want, what does it matter?"

"Devout Christians tend to work in metaphors and allegory, yet when someone outside of their exclusive club tries to speak in non-literal terms, they become outraged, and see it as an attack on their faith," Campbell snipped.

Gwenn softened her grip on the back of the chair and her expression seemed to soften with it, looking from Connelly to her opponent.

"I think metaphors would be a start...and something I could digest a little easier," she confessed.

Connelly smiled at her, and Campbell was trying hard to suppress his look of utter surprise. The least educated among them, a man who'd never stepped foot inside of a classroom a day in his life, was the one who'd managed become their adjudicator.

"Now that we've found our manners again, and arrived at some mutually-agreeable resolution pertaining to the question of John's...condition, can we proceed?"

"I'm not certain of what more there is to discuss," Connelly said with a frown.

Apparently, he'd thought that would be the end of it, stepping in as the great mediator to find an answer that appealed to the both of them. But he underestimated Gwenn Chapel if he believed that a fitting epitaph for her husband's case would be enough to bring her closure and send her merrily on her way back home.

"I believe we have a dying animal to discuss, before we then move onto this whole new batch of issues you made reference to," Campbell said with a sly smile.

"You still want to talk about the fight?" He asked with a long exhale.

"I do. Your contention is that it was a sort of 'death knell' of a beast that had been gnawing at John's insides for many years. While I don't entirely disagree, there remain a few questions about the incident of course."

"Of course," Gwenn echoed sarcastically. "And then I want to hear about these other things John was struggling with."

"Of course..." Connelly trailed off. "That's why I'm here."

Chapter *45*

The universe had shifted back into that "balance" that Gwenn spoke of once more, and things were right again between John and Melinda. Beyond her complaining about not spending enough time with him, and trying to balance their busy schedules, there was really nothing else to complain about.

Finding that balance had become crucial to their relationship; spending too much time together could be disastrous and not enough could be the same – as was the case with many couples – but moreso with them. So, the plan had been to take things slowly, in moderation, and follow the gradual path together.

As Melinda was famous for, she'd often changed her mind, and began rethinking the plan. She began talking more and more about pushing the envelope and believing that they were ready for the "next step". The next step was moving into his place and not just doing weekend trips.

They'd agreed to see each other on the weekend and devote the weekdays to school and studying. He knew that, if given the chance, she would look for any distraction to get out of studying – so he'd been firm on their "weekends only" policy. On occasion, there was a weeknight dinner at her house, and she always tried to drag those nights out until he had to pull himself away.

It was all she could do to wait until the last class on Friday night ended and their weekend together began. She would rush through the halls, working hard to suppress the smile that would play on her face all morning, and then finally let it loose once she was in her car, speeding ever so slightly to get her weekend started.

Going to John's house for the weekend was one of her favorite things to do, more than eating out or going to spend money somewhere. It was like a preview of a movie, a brief glimpse at the best parts of a life that waited for them at some point in the future, and she was always disappointed when the clip stopped playing.

Sunday night always came too quickly, and she tried to enjoy every moment, whether they were making something in the kitchen together or just studying on the couch.

John's house wasn't anything fancy – just a three-bedroom rental he'd found for a fair price – but it was their own little space. After setting aside money for Melinda and himself for school, picking up two cars, and some new clothing, there wasn't a lot left in the budget for housing.

His uncle had promised him a job at his store again, despite his strained relations with his father, and he made enough money to cover normal living expenses. It wasn't as glorious or lucrative as his job in Florida, but that chapter was closed for him and Melinda both.

They'd promised to be "regular people" again, and forgo the luxuries of flashy cars, expensive clothing and being seen at high profile nightclubs. Their regular Saturday nights now entailed a modest dinner, possibly a movie, and on occasion, drinks either alone or with friends somewhere low key. Neither of them minded leaving the trappings of their old lives behind for the benefit of the other, and they were simply happy to be making up for lost time.

It was a Saturday morning, eight days before Christmas, so that afternoon had been spent shopping. John carried an armload of bags in the house, dumped them onto the kitchen table, and they collapsed on the couch to take a break before breaking out the wrapping paper.

He'd noticed that she'd been distracted all that day, and didn't seem at all excited when they were shopping – which was highly unusual.

"What's eating you, Mel?"

She fidgeted with her fingers, like she did often when she was nervous. "I was just thinking what we talked about a little while ago. About *us*...and where we're headed."

"I think we're doing okay, and this is probably the best things have been with us. Why change it?"

"I don't want to change it...really...I just would like to know that we have some sort of...plan."

"A *plan*? What sort of plan?"

"Maybe I'm just being paranoid. Forget I said anything," she said with a long, measured exhale.

"Well something is obviously wrong with how we're doing things, and it bothers you, so I'm listening. What about 'us' isn't making you happy?"

"I'm not unhappy – not at all – it's just that I love our weekends together here, and then I get kind of bummed out when I have to go back home and wait another week to have any kind of quality time with you."

"Melinda, we discussed this; even if you were here all the time, we wouldn't see much of each other. I have work and school, and then there's homework and I like to work on the car and spend some time with my own things too. You have your friends and your family, as well as a pretty busy schedule with this semester too."

"I know. This is what I asked for, and it's been really nice having some space for once. But some days I just…want for it to be over."

"Over? You want us to be over?"

"No! God no! I mean…the waiting. I want to be older and finished with school and have careers and be…*with* you every day."

"Be with me every day? You pretty much are."

"That's not what I mean…I mean…oh, you know what I mean," she said, flustered.

"Like a couple?"

"We are a couple, I just mean…like…*together*," she said, trying to find the right words.

"They have a word for that, and we're not ready for that are we?"

She looked at her feet then, embarrassed. "I don't know. I didn't think so. But I think about it a lot lately. Some days I want to just be somewhere I feel like we're safe and that neither of us is going to ever leave. I still worry about that."

"Melinda, even if we were married, it doesn't mean that we're immune to the problems that married couples have or that we're immune to those things. Married couples fall apart the same as people who are dating, and wouldn't we rather be together because we *choose* to be and not because we feel obligated to be?"

"You know I do, but sometimes, when things are bad, married people try harder to keep the marriage together. Look at my parents."

"A piece of paper can't save everybody Mel. I'm not going anywhere," he said, gripping her hand. "You're not even nineteen yet and I'm not even old enough to drink legally, we've got lots of time."

"I know...I'm just being stupid and a bit selfish. It's just that I wait all week long for our weekend time and then it's gone before we know it, and I want more sometimes. I should be thankful for what we have, like you've said a hundred times, but it's hard some days to wait for us to have alone time."

"I would be more than happy to have you move in here, and I would feel better about you being here, but...we talked about it before, and one of our biggest problems was spending too much time together and smothering each other – remember?"

"Yes, I remember...but we were just stupid kids then and we hadn't seen one another for ten years. We didn't know what we were doing, we didn't know what we wanted, and now...we know what we want, don't we? I mean, this is a relationship now, not two people trying to overcompensate for lost time, right?"

"I think we know what we're doing and what we want, and I like what we have. But isn't what you're saying that you feel like our time goes by too fast and we need to compensate for that by speeding up the process? I'm just...afraid of what that might do to us, Mel," he said, swallowing hard.

"But I've given it a lot of thought...and I want this for us John. I hate being away from you. I know we might not get necessarily more quality time together, but at least I'll know that you're here even if you're in the other room, studying or whatever you're doing."

He let out a sigh and stopped rubbing her fingers, letting her hand rest in his very still, and lowered his eyes to her lap, not looking at her as he spoke. "You're talking about being obligated, and obligated is an ugly word. Your parents are obligated to come home to one another at night, and you were obligated when you were under Sal's thumb to come running when he called. I don't want that for us."

She stood up then, letting out a frustrated groan, stomping into the kitchen. There, she pulled a beer from the refrigerator, uncapped it, and stood to drink it alone as she fumed. He let her stew and sat by himself on the couch, listening to the low murmur of the television newsman, and the faint sniffling coming from somewhere in the kitchen. They were about to have a fight again, and he braced himself as if he was getting ready to drive headlong into a wall.

"I'm telling you that I don't want to act like we're *children* anymore," she shouted her battle cry as she emerged from the kitchen. "And you're not listening to me!"

"How are we acting like children? We're just trying to take things slow..."

"You said to give it six months before we decide to talk about anything else, and it's been almost six! I've been working my ass off in school, behaving myself, and I don't go out to the bar and get crazy anymore! I spend almost all my free time with you! What more do you want me to do to prove that I've changed, Johnny?"

"I know you've changed! I see it with my own eyes! You've been doing great, and *we've* been doing great, but why do we need to take such a huge leap and risk all of that falling apart?"

"How will it fall apart? How will spending more time together be bad for us? You don't want me here? You want to keep your options open? I don't understand!"

"Absolutely not! I don't want to be with anyone else but you, now or ever! I just don't want us to fall into the same patterns that we have before, where we resent one another or decide, after the fact, that we really don't want what we think we do! I can't take that again, Mel! I can't take losing you one more time!"

"How much more do I need to do to prove to you that I'm not leaving you again and I love you? Give me some credit, please! Don't compare what we have to what my parents do or what I had with Sal, because that's just insulting! We're better than that, even on our worst day!"

"I wasn't trying to be insulting, and I know we're better than that! What the hell is wrong with taking a little more time to do things the right way?"

"And what's wrong with knowing something in your heart already, without needing another five or ten years to figure it out? I know I was stupid before and I hurt you, and I can never take it back, but please don't continue to hold that against me...please don't judge me as that person anymore!"

"I'm not *judging* you, Melinda; this is something we *both* agreed to when we first started this – this isn't something I came up with on my own, and it wasn't meant as a punishment!"

"How much more time do you need, then, to figure out what you want? How much more time do you have to see that I've changed and I want to be with you for good? Another six months? A year? Two years?"

"No…I don't need that much time…"

"How much time do you need, Johnny? Just give me a *date* or a *number* so I at least know how long I should wait…"

He set his beer down and stood from the couch, walking over towards the doorway, and she thought that he was about to walk out on her, and her face lost color. Instead of leaving, he pulled his long, wool coat from the closet, produced a small package from the pocket, and tossed it onto the couch in kitchen table. It was a black velvet box, and she immediately realized what it was and the mistake she'd just made in starting up a discussion that would've come if she'd just been patient.

"You want a *date*? I was thinking Christmas would be a good time to ask you…but since you're so impatient, I guess today will have to do. Not exactly the way I wanted to do it."

She approached the table hesitantly, with eyes fixed on the small box, biting her bottom lip anxiously. Resting her fingers lightly on the plush box, her eyes immediately filled with tears, and she looked up at him with a pitiful expression.

"I'm so sorry…"

"Don't be sorry; it's obviously something we both have been thinking about lately. Go ahead."

"I don't want to open it yet. I'm so sorry. I'm such a bitch. I spoiled Christmas didn't I?"

"You didn't spoil Christmas. I don't even know if I was going to ask you then. I was going to ask you to move in with me, see what you thought about that, and then maybe ask you on your birthday."

She lifted the small box, cupping it in her hand and handed it to him, "I can't open this yet, then. I don't want to see it until you're ready to give it to me. Johnny…I'm sorry…I just wanted to know that *this* was in the plan. It doesn't have to be now."

He grabbed the small, velvet container from her and said, "Well, when you know...you just know I guess. So it may as well be now."

Every young girl dreams of that moment, plots and plans every detail extensively, long before she's even met her first love. It still never prepares her for the moment it happens. The tears fall and the hands shake uncontrollably, each breath is a shudder, and she feels as if she's in a haze when the words come. She just stared at him wide eyed and he shook his head, grinning, confirming what he'd just said.

"Are you...asking me? Are you *asking* me right now?"

He held it out in front of him and split the clamshell box into two halves, revealing the shimmering thing inside. It was silvery and shone so brightly tucked in its black protector, glittering brilliantly even in the faint light from the overhead lamp. He pulled it free and slid it onto her shaking finger, and it was a bit tight going over her knuckle but fit perfectly once it came to rest.

"It's heavy...what is it?"

"It's platinum. It's rarer and more durable than silver or gold, and it's going to replace both as the most popular metal for engagement rings - that's what the guy at the store told me anyway."

She held it out in front of her and examined it in the light, and a big smile crept across her face, the reality of what was happening finally hitting her. He was almost tackled him over the back of the couch in an embrace, and he was pretty sure he heard her say "it's beautiful" and "yes" between sobs and squealing.

They spent the rest of that evening on the couch making out, giggling, trying to contain uncontainable smiles, and making plans for a date that was still more than two years away at the very least. It didn't matter to her, though, she had her ring and he'd given her a plan, and she would be able to put her paranoid mind at ease for a while. She rested that head on his chest and fell asleep that night, listening to the rhythmic lull of his heart and dreaming of dresses, flowers and beautiful churches.

The weekend seemed to go by just as quickly, but when Sunday came, she didn't feel that sadness that normally came with it. They'd decided to use their winter break as an opportunity to move her things in, which didn't take more than a couple trips because she hadn't amassed much in the five months she'd been back home. Somehow she'd managed to fill her closet and her makeup cases, though, and he didn't know if there were enough closets in the house just for her things. They definitely would need a second bathroom at some point, as well, as it became cluttered with her "girl" things.

He liked that her things filled the place and it made it much homier than before. Pictures filled every wall - lots and lots of them - mostly of them together. One of their first, the one of them snapped on the steps two Christmases before by Dean, was their favorite and it sat on the sofa table. She also covered his stack of men's magazines on the coffee table with a pile of her own wedding catalogs, and part of their 'lazy Sunday' ritual became picking out colors and styles of dresses. He would remind her that fashions would most likely change by the time their day came, but she just liked to sit with him and make plans, regardless.

The only one who seemed more excited making plans and talking about wedding dresses was her mother, and John was relieved when she took his place on the couch to flip through her magazines. He didn't think it was possible for either her mother or father to dote over him more, but it almost got to the point of being uncomfortable. At Christmas, it was the worst, with grandparents, cousins and family members all making a fuss over the newly-engaged couple. It became more of a 'John and Melinda' celebration than a religious holiday, and they were so engrossed in discussing the event that they almost missed the midnight mass.

The excitement didn't die down much after Christmas, for Melinda's birthday approached, and they planned to do an "official announcement" at her party for the benefit of their friends. Almost everyone had already cooed over her ring and congratulated them by that point, but John didn't want her to feel "cheated" out of a proper engagement that he'd had planned for her. She was no less emotional at the event, surrounded by all of her friends and family, and with John making a speech and formal display for everyone to see. It was the most memorable birthday she'd had in years, and she couldn't remember a better one.

They were finally able to resume their normal lives as February approached and the flood of cards, letters and calls stopped coming in to congratulate them and drill them about every detail of their big day – which was still quite a ways off. It had become exhausting just being in the spotlight for a full month, and they could only imagine what it would be like in a year, when they really began serious planning. Melinda even gave John a moratorium on 'Sunday magazine day' because even she was overloaded by wedding talk. Her friends and family had given her a good indication of how much work was really involved with a wedding and the marriage that followed, and she wondered if she hadn't made a mistake in pushing John into something.

She tried not letting it bother her, but it was something that was constantly on her mind with each day that passed and brought them closer to that deadline she'd insisted upon. It began with little bouts of anxiety, and turned into full-blown nightmares by the beginning of spring, and eventually consumed her every waking moment. Eventually, she worried more about the commitment she'd made and pushed John into than she ever had worried about not having that commitment. She should've listened to John in the first place – just like always – because he was always right in the end. The problem was that she was just too damned stubborn to admit he was right, just like always.

In classic Melinda fashion, she tried to find a way to make John take the fall for her impulsive decision-making and her stubborn pride, and that usually ended terribly. Even though he'd told her many times that there was nothing she couldn't come to him with, and despite giving her an 'out' many times from that December day until the end of their school semester, she still would not resort to admitting she was wrong. She'd wanted a commitment from him, she got one, and now there was a deadline looming on the horizon that she felt she could not get out of. So, she did what she did best; she pushed.

By the time finals were approaching, things had already begun to take a turn for the worst, and John knew something was wrong despite her denial that anything had changed. She no longer rode home with him every day after class, and insisted that it was to spend time at the library catching up for finals. John didn't understand her sudden desire to spend time at the library all of a sudden, as she seemed to always prefer his help with her studies over doing it alone. Gwenn or Dean would bring her home afterwards, and he saw nothing wrong with that, but when her 'circle' friends started delivering her later and later, he knew something was wrong.

The calls started coming in later and later, letting him know that she would be going out with her friends to 'unwind' after studying, and in the last week before finals, she wasn't coming home at all. She'd been gone for two days straight and finally came home late Saturday night after being at the bar. He couldn't even talk to her then, because she was too drunk and passed out on the couch and slept half of Sunday away. When she finally got around and began getting cleaned up to start her day, he tried confronting her and it didn't go well.

Another big fight began, which they hadn't seen the likes of since the 'old days', and just like the old days, it took John completely by surprise. He didn't know why she'd been acting out or withdrawing, and he wouldn't ever find out, because she wasn't discussing it. The wedding magazines were hurled at him from the table, followed by picture frames, and then a string of curses which he couldn't make any sense of whatsoever. One of the frames shattered on his forearm and the glass cut it up badly, imbedded in his skin like shrapnel. He finally lost his temper – just as she'd wanted him to do – and said some things that he would regret for the rest of his life.

She slammed the door and left him standing there to nurse a bloody arm and trying to sort out what had just happened, feeling terrible that he'd allowed her to get the best of him. He'd resorted to some low blows and threw her past drug addiction in her face, as well as Sal, and told her to go back to him, and he wasn't sure if that's what she wasn't doing at that very moment.

He slammed his fist into the wall, leaving a deep impression in the drywall, snatched his coat, and went to go find her. They had come so far and done so well, and in the matter of a few weeks, completely fell apart and he had no idea why. She'd wanted him to fight with her, and he should've known better, but if he didn't say something and get to the bottom of whatever was happening between them, he would lose her anyway. He just wished that he hadn't let her get to him and make him behave the way he used to when he was a different person; when he dealt with people violently and a 'take-no-prisoners' mentality. That had been the wrong thing to do with a girl like Melinda, and he knew the backlash would be terrible.

Chapter 46

He would never have imagined how terrible, or how far they'd already drifted before that awful day came. Driving around all the rest of that afternoon, stopping at every conceivable place she would've gone, yielded no results.

He recognized the car that picked her up as her friend Michelle's (the one he'd hated the most), and she'd told him that she was going to study with her right before the fight began. Neither of them was at Michelle's house all afternoon or in the evening, and he must've driven by the place twenty times. They weren't at the Malowski house, or any other place he was familiar with. He finally gave up looking at midnight, and tried to get some sleep, but was unsuccessful.

It was no surprise that John was a volcano ready to explode that Monday morning when he finally saw her, getting out of a strange car that was dropping her off at college. Running on almost no sleep, charged with adrenaline and spending an entire night worrying about what had become of her was a recipe for something akin to nitroglycerin and far more dangerous.

His face turned to red-hot stone and his heart did the same when he saw the white car pull into the large circle drive of the college. She stepped from the car and her eyes went cold and her face ashen when she saw him, and she tried to push past him, pretending he wasn't there. She was grabbed by the arms and met with such a fury that she felt as if a tornado had descended directly upon her. The sky had turned dark moments before, and the first drops of a storm had begun to fall, but there was already a tempest waiting on the front lawn.

Every bit of love that he had felt for her was suddenly twisted by that tempest into hatred and rage. She'd betrayed him in the worst way, with the worst person, and the girl he'd loved was gone. She walked out of his door the day before, and simply disappeared forever. The girl that crumpled at his feet, sobbing and screaming at him, wasn't someone he recognized anymore, and he couldn't hear anything that she was saying to him, nor would he listen. There was just blame being cast, failure to be held accountable, and some thin excuse as to why she'd fallen back into the arms of the man he hated the most.

He had seen this exact scene before, the night that Sal stood over her, at his wit's end with her, and John had been the hero then. Now the roles were reversed, and John perhaps understood for a brief moment the anger and sense of betrayal that filled his enemy that night at the party.

Maybe they weren't so different after all, and they'd both been the victims of her manipulations and lies, but he wouldn't have the time to discuss it with him, for the giant Arab was rushing towards him from his car at that moment. As the sky broke and the rain began falling in torrents, John readied himself for war.

As adrenaline coursed through his body, he heard Frank Kovacs' voice echo in his head from the night they'd had their revenge on the Colombians.

Some men won't listen to reason and you have to put them down, or they'll just keep coming back around. We can beat them and break them repeatedly, but men like these won't stop, until someone is dead. This has to be done John...

He left Melinda sobbing on the ground and screaming at him to stop, and rushed to meet the freight train head on this time, to let him know that he wasn't going to be run over this time. The last time they'd gone toe-to-toe, he was forty pounds lighter, sloppy and unskilled, and far less angry by comparison.

He'd been trained by some of the best scrappers he'd ever seen in a fight, and he'd fought meaner men than Sal since then. He was still hit harder than he'd been in a long time, and knew better than to underestimate this man.

His opponent's longer arms reached him first, and drove rigid knuckles into his cheek, but John hardly felt the blow that tore open a cheek and bloodied his nose. Three blows came quicker than Sal could see, and snapped his head back like he'd been hit with a steel pipe. He'd underestimated this man as well, and never recalled him ever being able to hit that hard. The punches staggered him, and kept coming in short but powerful bursts.

They were precise and more surgical in their application than before, and he realized too late that the opponent he faced wasn't the same one from two years before. He'd prepared for this

490

day to come, for those punches had been practiced and delivered as accurately as an actor rehearses and delivers his lines in the performance of a lifetime. There was such perfection in the timing and the execution was so flawless that there was no doubt that this scene had been rehearsed over and over in the man's head.

A solid right stuck him in the left temple above the eye, followed by a quick snap of the left to the jaw, loosening it and snapping the head back to the right, so that the brain was jarred inside its cavity. The third blow came from the right and slightly below, the jaw was dislocated from the force and the wind pipe was crushed. That was only the first three strikes, the second and third series of threes proceeded in devastating other parts of his target. Solar plexus, xiphoid process and the trachea inferior were in the second batch. The third included the top of the ocular cavity, and two strikes to the nose.

The tip of calcified cartilage of his metasternum was sheared off and pierced his diaphragm, and the fingers to the jugular arch, near his supraclavicular nerve, in addition to the solar plexus had stopped his breathing altogether. The crushed nose made his eyes water, and the shattered bone above his eye was painful and would ensure the blurred vision for the remainder of the fight.

These were all things he'd learned from Kovacs, and things that he'd used before to end a fight quickly, if the correct power was applied to each technique. He didn't want it to be over just yet; he wanted to savor every excruciating moment with his hated foe.

Sal stumbled to the ground, trying to catch his breath and recover his eyesight, but he found no more mercy on the ground than he did above. A solid kick to the mouth resounded in the crunching of loose bone, and further dislodged his jaw, and the fight was over at this point. It was just beginning for John, though. He continued to curse and kick at the man, who was trying to roll away from his attacker, fracturing several ribs and turning his booted foot into a wrecking ball.

Melinda continued to scream at him as he beat the man savagely, and he ignored her pleas, fully engrossed in the task that was set before him. He meant to kill Sallah Nussein there in front of everyone, and only three of the onlookers realized it, one could actually do something about it. From across the lawn, Dean had watched the fight unfold with the other students that had gathered round, and cheered John on with the others. When he saw the fight turn into something else and Sal crumble to the ground, he knew that someone had to do something.

He dropped his books there on the grass and moved as fast as he could towards John before he beat the last of the life from the man at his feet. He grappled John around the waist, knowing that he would have to hit him as hard as he could to get his attention and interrupt the melee. The pair of them went rolling onto the sidewalk and they both suffered some minor scrapes. John rolled with the attack and was atop Dean ready to give him his share, when he finally recognized who he was sitting on, and stopped himself.

"Dean, what the hell?"

"John, it's done! He's down! Let it be!" Dean shouted at him, covering his face with his arms.

"Like hell it is," he growled and stood to let his friend up. "This is far from being over."

Sal had managed to scramble a bit further away, and pulled himself up onto the hood of his own car, but John's temper wasn't satiated yet, and he commenced the beating with renewed vigor and his rage loosed again. Sal put his arms over his head to defend himself as blow after blow hit him like a shockwave. Luckily, he was too consumed with rage by that point to make the shots as deadly accurate as they had been before, and most of them glanced off the top of his skull or his arms. Just as Dean got back to his feet to grapple his friend from behind, John got off more last good shot that knocked Sal over the hood of his car, spraying blood all over his own windshield.

The bloody Arab shuddered and shambled, trying to get back on his feet, and Melinda continued to scream at them both, hoping the whole thing would just be over with. By now, a large group of young college men had gathered and begun cheering the fighters on. Among them were some of Sal's cousins, who attended the college, and they were screaming at Sal, demanding blood, whipped into a frenzy.

Everyone watching was impressed by the large Arab's constitution and his dedication, and even John had to give the guy credit for being able to stand after the beating he'd doled out. His mouth hung loosely and he was unable to talk, his right eye was swollen shut and the lid was turning black and filling with blood, and he knew that he was bleeding internally. But still, the fallen giant rose to his feet and returned to the fight, not able to ignore the cries of his cousins.

Ignoring Melinda's cries for him to stop the fight, he charged John again and tackled him and Dean both to the ground. John's arms were tangled in Deans so he couldn't protect his face from the flurry of punches that came afterwards.

John Chapel had been taught to be an offensive fighter and to press the attack, hit hard and fast, and end the fight quickly. Sallah Nussein had been taught to do just the opposite; take everything they can throw at you, wear them down, and finish them off when they can't fight any longer. In any fight, whether a street fight or boxing match, it's usually that contender who can take more punishment who is left standing at the end. He'd made a grievous error holding back on his initial offensive, wanting to drag the fight out, and punish his enemy. As he was being pummeled, he wondered if even his strongest hits would have had an effect on the juggernaut.

The man was broken, bleeding, unhinged and unraveling, and yet, there he was, still ready to go ten more rounds with him. Six devastating punched landed square in the middle of his face, and he felt his nose shatter and more of the skin over his cheek bones split. Six more came before he could untangle himself from Dean, and he felt the blood in his right eye and knew that he was going to lose consciousness soon. He was becoming incoherent and thought for a moment that he might have been back at the hotel pool two years before with the same guy pounding his head into cheese.

It wasn't until that moment, when he was in that place in-between consciousness and darkness, that he remembered seeing the face of that other girl flashing in his memory. There had been water then too, all around him, just like there was now, washing the blood and the pain away. From somewhere beyond the approaching darkness, that old, familiar voice was speaking to him again, telling his that it was okay to let go. He still clung to the pain and to the voices calling his name, though the water was pulling him further down and down into the murky depths.

Chapter *47*

John awoke on the cool, stone floor of his chamber, and though the chill of winter was still in the air, his naked flesh was dripping in sweat. He'd had the dream again, about the other man, and it was always a terrible omen when he dreamt of him.

The last time he'd had the dream was the night before the terrible storm when the invaders came to Rouen, and before that, they preceded every significant event that had happened in his young life. He didn't know who the man was, but he brought with him the visions that he could never quite explain, as a warning of things that would come to pass.

There were visions of things that went beyond explaining; a bizarre place with tall, glass towers and houses large enough to hold five or six families each, horseless wagons of steel that roared loudly on streets of black stone, and torches that burned beneath glass through the night. These things fascinated him pondering them whenever he woke and remembered them. Then they would disappear completely from his mind, emptied once again like a bucket, and refilled with the things he was familiar with.

Lately, however, the things that were supposed to be emptied were staying behind for longer periods of time. He scrambled to get his footing, still too disoriented to get his bearings, in an attempt to reach his bureau beside the bed. There was parchment in the top drawer, and that was where he'd recorded the cryptic messages from his visitor, before they quickly faded as he returned to the waking world. Pulling himself up to the drawer, he retrieved the rolled parchment and the bottle of ink, and collapsed back to the cold floor.

"Campbell…he said something about crusades…"

John sputtered the nonsense fragments, hoping that repeating them would help him retain them. He spread the paper out across the floor and fumbled for the stained rooster quill that he'd been using to write with. His eyes surveyed the previous entries, written in messy columns, in some type of order that only made sense to him. Dipping the quill, he began to write as fast as he could, before the rest of the pieces slipped away.

"Dean is a friend...he helps the man...fight his enemy. Who is the enemy? The dark man...is the enemy..."

He continued to write sloppily and in broken sentences, as he always did, in the hopes that he would be able to sort the whole mess out at some later date. Eventually, all of the pieces would have to fit together, and something would have to click. Scouring the parchment, he saw the names written there that belonged to strangers he had never known. They were the people the other man knew, and they were somehow important, and played a part in the message that he was trying to relay to him.

Nicolette had watched him write on the parchment more than once, and when he would sit up late nights and try to decipher the things written there, before the next dream came. She didn't understand what was written, for Reginald had only just begun to teach her to read, and she couldn't grasp John's odd handwriting anyway. Most of the letters were familiar, but he arranged them in such a way that she doubted even a literate person could read them. She dismissed them as gibberish, and told him that he was wasting his time trying to understand the things that only God knew.

The truth was that his visions and violent dreams frightened her, and she didn't like discussing the strange things that he saw, because she feared what might become of them. The church frowned on behavior that was unexplained and people who saw things that they shouldn't be seeing were often subjected to punishment by the church. John understood how it must have upset her, being a devout woman of faith, and he agreed not to discuss the matter with her anymore. But she knew that he still wrote on that paper, and that the dreams hadn't stopped.

"The enemy..." He hesitated, struggling with the words, as though someone was trying to pull them away from him.

"The enemy..." His pen hovered in midair, dripping the fresh ink on the paper. "...has returned," he finally whispered, and let his quill fall to the floor.

A sense of urgency suddenly formed in the pit of his rumbling stomach, and he sprang from the floor to dash to the narrow window. Something was wrong, and he could sense that even if the messenger hadn't visited him in the early morning hours. There was an unusual silence that hung over the rolling hills and misty meadows of Avandale, and he hadn't noticed it until just then.

Normally, the moment the sun came up, the sounds of livestock being tended to and of servants bustling below would penetrate even his deepest sleep, to let him know that a new day had begun. Nicolette liked to rise early every morning, long before he did, to help out with the chores and get breakfast on. If the sound of the sows fighting over their rotted vegetables didn't stir him from his sleep, usually her clanging and banging in the kitchen would. This morning, he'd either been too deeply drawn into his visions, or the day had not yet begun for some reason.

He felt the place in their bed where she'd been lying, and it was as cool as the stones of the chamber; she'd risen at her usual time. Peering out the window, he didn't see any of their servants or even Pelleon or Ann milling about as they usually did. The boy often skipped out on chores, but Ann was always around to help her cousin with the cooking, and Pelleon would show the moment breakfast hit the table. This morning, there were no plates rattling on the table downstairs or Pelleon complaining about his portion of pork.

John dressed in his breeches and long shirt, pulled his boots on, and strapped his sword belt on, then hustled down the three flights of stairs. The guest rooms where Pelleon and Ann stayed were empty, as well as the kitchen and dining table one floor beneath that, and he finally arrived at the old sentry hall on the ground floor. It sat empty as well, save for the one servant, Aelwen, who was leaning against the door and seemed to be out of breath.

"Aelwen? Where are the others?"

"Lord John," she panted. "I've come to fetch you…come quickly."

He pushed her aside and flung the heavy door open, stepping outside to be greeted by more than the morning sun and the sounds of livestock in the yard. A heavy fog had risen from the lake that morning, shrouding everything in a thick, cottony veil of grey, and only the jingling of metal stirrups told him that riders were approaching from beyond the next hill. His eyes scanned the immediate area for others, but he saw no movements from the fog, as if he and the servant girl were the only ones left in Avandale.

"Nicolette? Pelleon? George?" He called out, but received no answer save the whinnying of a horse from somewhere inside the mist.

Within a few moments, he could finally see the outline of those beasts plodding through the spring mud of the road, the men upon them, and the banners they were carrying. Crimson was the first color he could make out from one of those banners, proudly jutting up from the thick, swirling mass to announce those men and their intentions. The three lions of gold glimmered in the light, emblazoned upon that field of crimson, and John knew at that moment that Richard had returned.

He exhaled in relief and sent Aelwen to fetch water for the horses and to try to find the rest of the servants to make ready to receive their Prince. Aelwen did not move to follow his orders, and only stared wide-eyed, and lifted a finger towards the shapes coming through the fog.

"This can't be good...this can't be good at all," he murmured.

At the center of the small army was the grim face of Richard, jaw set tightly and eyes fixed as though he was dead and staring at nothing in particular. He couldn't even be certain that he recognized the man he'd knighted months before, or if he even was aware of where he was. The Prince looked drunk or drugged, and there were dark rings that circled his eyes, and his normally-rosy flesh was pallid.

To his left was Harold, who he hadn't seen much of since the night they'd taken Avandale together. There had been some harsh words spoken in haste that night, but he'd assumed that they'd all been forgotten when he'd received his old friend only a few weeks later, and they shared a few cups and a few laughs together. Harold's face was drawn and pale like Richard's, and he hadn't seen an expression like that since the day he watched his sister's home burn.

The only face that showed any sign of life or vitality, and seemed very much out of place with this solemn group was the one over Richard's left shoulder. The eyes were bright and sparkling in the morning light, there was a smile stretched across his perfect jaw, and he was the only one sitting upright and proudly in his saddle. The other men in the troupe seemed to be cloaked in dismal grays and the crimson seemed mottled by comparison to the crisp black and gleaming white of his dress, all neatly folded, tucked, and clasped together. Reginald of Poitou had returned, just as the dream had foretold.

His stomach shuddered again, reminding him that he was hungry, but a second snarl from another beast told him that it had found a home there as well. It was fear that had taken hold of his belly and made his hands begin to tremble, as it would any man who awaited news of his own fate.

The rest of the ensemble emerged from the fog, the entire body numbering close to forty men, and John wondered why they needed so many to escort Richard to Avandale if it wasn't a war party. He was certainly eccentric and liked to make an appearance, but the expression in his eyes belied any intentions of making a dramatic entrance. None of the others in his entourage made eye contact with him either, including Nicolette, who was being towed behind on a small charger. Her head was bent to the ground and her hair was like a shroud of pale gold.

He put his hand to his pommel, his muscles tensing and ready to cut through any of those men who would dare stand in his way as he approached his beloved. The mass of men began to separate and spread out, and a semi-circle formed from the left to intercept the man walking towards them. Those men would only slow him down, and they were well aware that they could not stop him from reaching her, and the fear in their eyes told him as much. Their Prince would have to intercede before there was bloodshed, and they all hoped that he would do it quickly.

"That's far enough, John," Richard bleated weakly.

"What's this about, Richard?" He growled back. "And why is *he* with you?"

"He is the reason we're here," he said, the words coming with hesitation. "It seems there has been some transgression that has taken place here, and...laws broken."

"I've broken no *laws*! We came to Avandale six months ago under *your* direction, how could any laws be broken?"

"John, please just hear him out," Harold now spoke up.

The lord of Avandale gave his old friend a sour look and a contemptuous one to Richard, whom he'd suspected of arranging the entourage for his benefit exclusively.

He, no doubt, assumed that there would be less trouble if there were friendly faces in that group like Harold and Andrew de

Chauvigney, who had frequented his smithy shop in Rouen, or Roger of Glanville who had been a regular at the tavern there and had traveled with Harold to Avandale only a month before. They figured wrong. There would be blood, no more or no less, if Reginald had come to exact some kind of vengeance upon him.

"Speak then, and allow the accused to hear these charges," John said, spitting on the ground.

"Avandale was Rouen's enemy, and my enemy, all those months ago, John. You were within your rights, under my direction, to act in a military capacity in capturing this place and even taking prisoners. You could have executed every soldier responsible for their transgressions against Rouen, or the people there. You could have ransomed the rest, if you so decided, even this man's wife..."

John's eyes narrowed and he shook his head in disbelief, "*That's* what this is about? This coward has asked for some kind of...pittance for the loss of his wife? She chose to stay here of her own free will, Richard! In addition to this, she'd suffered a grave wound by his own cowardly actions, and she was unfit to even travel with him if she'd wanted to!"

"Once she was in fair health, the proper thing to do would have been to make a reasonable demand for ransom and see her safely returned," Richard said, ignoring his outburst.

"Reginald and Avandale declared war on Rouen and on all of us, Richard! Or had you forgotten that? The tower, the land around us, the livestock, and any of the people who remained behind were part and parcel of the spoils of battle. Since when did our enemies have rights?"

"Since we are no longer enemies," Reginald said calmly, giving him a taunting smile. "The Duke and I have come to an arrangement: I no longer serve Henry, and I support Richard fully, and I've made him some advantageous allies in the process."

"And so you've come here looking for 'payment' for your good will, is that right? You expect me to turn over this village and its people to your rule again, and just allow Nicolette to suffer the sight of you again? She hates you! She despises you!"

"Regardless, she is my wife! You do understand the penalty for adultery, don't you, John? It's even worse for the woman than it is for the man, and the married party suffers stiffer retribution than the non-married party as well. I've been gracious enough to

500

forgo any of those unpleasant proceedings if you will yield in this matter."

John had heard enough and he drew his blade, challenging the first man who was brave enough to stand against him. Harold was the first to dismount and he approached his old friend. He should have known better, and remembered how the last negotiation on this soil had gone.

"John...please put your blade away," he whispered, placing one of his gentle ham hands atop his. "We don't want this – any of us – we came to keep the peace. I don't like it any more than you do, and I assure you Richard likes it even less. But we are at war, and this alliance with Reginald can help turn the tide in our favor and bring an end to this quickly."

"I'm not turning Nicolette over to that slimy, belly-crawling coward!" he shouted over Harold's shoulder loud enough for Reginald to hear him. "If he was within his rights why didn't he just take her by force, Harold? Why is he here, rubbing it in my face, in front of everyone?"

"You know the answer to that question, John. He wants to humiliate you and to bait you into a fight. If you draw your blade on him and turn down his offer in front of all these witnesses...he has the right to have you arrested and they will take you and lock you up."

"Let them try," he snarled. "There's not a man here who can take me from this place in chains and you know it!"

"What are you going to do? Kill every one of us, including the Prince? You'll have every man from here to the Vexin hunting you down! If you won't do it for your own sake, or for mine, do it for hers. You know what they'll do to her John...she's committed adultery, like it or not!"

"They can't take her from me..."

"They can and they will, and if you try to stop them, Richard can declare her charges and her sentence on the spot! There are near forty men out there...you won't be able to kill them all before they set the sword to her."

"He won't kill her...she's his wife!"

"You think that matters to him? You think he came back here because he's madly in love with her? He doesn't give a damn about her, and every man here knows that! This is about you...this is about getting back at you and taking something away from you.

He will make her suffer just to make you suffer, and the more you fight it, the more you show him that it breaks you in half, the more he will delight in it."

"He'll get no such pleasure from me...or from her," John snapped.

"You're right in that; look at Nicolette. Look at her face. She's showing no emotion, and she sheds not a single tear in front of you or him. She knows that if she makes this a big display it will only excite him and make him feel as though he's won. Don't do this. Don't fight him on this or you let him win!"

"What's the answer then, Harold...I just give her up?"

"Live to fight another day, John, like I've always taught you. When this is over, and it will come to an end soon, the rules will change as they always do. There will come a day when Richard will no longer need men like Reginald and will remember who were most loyal to him, and on that day, those men will get their just desserts."

John squeezed the blade in his hand so tightly that his fingers turned white, and his eyes smoldered with hatred at the man over Harold's left shoulder. His friend was right; there was no way to win this fight now.

He loosened his grip on the sword then and finally met the very serious gaze of Harold, who had his arm in a vice-like grip, and he reiterated, "There will come a day when you're sitting on that horse up there, looking down at him, and you'll take everything from him. I promise you..."

The defeated man looked from Nicolette to the men then back up at Reginald who smiled down at him, trying to get a reaction from him.

"She has been *very* eager to negotiate the safety of her home and those within it, John. You should show her some gratitude. I wanted to bring torches to this place, but she convinced me to leave it standing. I question the wisdom of showing mercy to my enemies, though, because an enemy soon forgets compassion. Wouldn't you agree?"

"I spared your life and I could have taken your worthless head," John said through gnashed teeth.

"And that weighed heavily in my consideration for sparing yours," he said in a sharp riposte. "But the laws of the land must be upheld, and this affront cannot go unpunished. Put him in chains!"

It was Harold who reacted the loudest and with the most surprise, "Richard ye' cannot allow this! This was never part of the deal or what we'd agreed to!"

"You were brought along as a peacekeeper, Harold, and you have been most effective," Richard reminded him calmly. "I'm afraid that the terms of the punishment to be carried out are at the discretion of the offended party, especially a man of a higher station. You could be dancing at the end of a rope if you were still a commoner and not spoken highly of by men of considerable reputation."

Four of the men dismounted on command and produced manacles at the end of heavy chains and approached the condemned. Harold stepped in the way, pushing John behind him and looked defiantly at them and his liege.

"I did not come here to help ye' throw this man in chains. Taking the woman away is punishment enough, let it stand at that, and let this matter be at an end!"

"The matter is at an end when I say it is, not you Welshman!" Reginald exploded, turning red-faced. "It will be enough once I've decided that it's enough for him to endure! He will face the same humiliation which I faced, and he will learn his place here and know that every action has a consequence! I am showing great clemency by not imprisoning you and her father as well, for your implication in this offense, Harold!"

With a curse and a bellowing roar, Harold drew his own sword at that point and leveled it at the young men who were nervously edging towards him and the man he was protecting. It was John who put a firm hand on his arm this time, trying to get him to comply with a more peaceful resolution.

"Harold, there will come another time…just as you said," he said in a raspy whisper in his ear, keeping his eyes locked on Nicolette's, knowing that this would only make things worse for her. "We will never forget this day, my friend, and we will have our triumph over this enemy."

"Ye' should've gutted him this past winter when ye' had the chance," Harold grumbled.

"I don't disagree," John said glibly. "Another day will come when he's at the end of my blade…and when he finds that it is no longer Richard's shadow that falls over him, but mine."

He handed his sword to Harold, stepped forward with wrists extended, and let the soldiers clasp the manacles around them. Once he was secure, they delivered him into the hands of Reginald, and John realized that it was going to be a very long trip. It would never do to allow his adversary the comfort of a saddle on the long road ahead, and he would not be spared the humiliation and humbling experience of being dragged behind a horse, for all to see.

Harold scowled at him and then at John, "At least let him ride back, it's a day-and-a-half's travel."

Reginald gave another one of his not-so-genuine smiles, "I really preferred that he walk until his feet bled, just to prepare him for the rest of his sentence, but since you insist…"

He pointed two fingers of his gloved hand at the horse behind him, addressing them men who had just chained his prisoner, "Drag that whore from her horse and tie her to the saddle! Our prisoner is apparently too good to walk, so she will suffer for his laziness and vanity!"

"Damn you, Reginald!" John cursed at him as he watched poor Nicolette wrenched from her saddle and put up very little of a fight.

They'd already broken her, he knew, and there was little fight left in her. It had happened at some point between leaving her warm place in bed beside him and his waking to realize that he was sleeping alone. It could've been an hour or more that she'd had to endure the suffering that Reginald had brought for her, and he secretly prayed that it hadn't been as long as all that, or as bad as he imagined it was for her. Seeing her dress torn to the thigh and soiled with mud and her own blood, he knew that it had been every bit that bad and worse, though.

"Leave her be! She's suffered enough on my account! Let her have the horse!"

"So long as you breathe, she will suffer!" Reginald said coldly. "She has suffered since the day she was cursed to meet you, John, and yet, you keep insisting on making things worse for her. You just keep coming back and you won't stay away. Every time you come back into her life, something awful happens because of it. Maybe this will be a lesson that you both will learn from; maybe this time you'll know enough to stay away from her and stop torturing her."

504

John wished he hadn't allowed them to chain him at that moment, and he strained against them, just in case his odd "condition" afforded him super strength as well as invulnerability. It didn't, and he remained bound and helpless to defend his Nicolette, as seemed to be his lot. Maybe he was simply doomed to fail her again and again, like Reginald had implied, and maybe it was better that he was put in a dungeon somewhere and never saw the light of day. Perhaps that was better for her to never see him again, and cause her such torment.

"Give her my horse, for God's sake," Harold pleaded. "Take my horse and keep it as payment for a small kindness, Reginald."

"Whores need to learn to use their legs for more than parting them, Harold. She walks."

John had heard enough, he wrapped the chain around his forearms to tighten the slack, and leapt from his horse atop Reginald's. Looping the iron links around his neck, he pulled with all his might, jerking upward and back. The metal noose constricted and turned the suffocating man's face red and then purple, as he gagged and sputtered pleas in gurgled cries.

His own face had turned just as red, and everything around him was painted the same as the rage took hold of him. The clamor of voices became a dull buzz and all the men rushing towards him seemed to melt into one monstrous body with many arms grabbing at him. He was pulled back to the ground, landing on top of Harold, and they all closed in on him. The tiny stars popped in the air around him and then everything went black.

Chapter *48*

The powerful arms that had been tangled up in his finally uncoiled themselves and he was free. For all the good it did him though; the damage had already been done and the fight was finished.

Sal had ruined his face in the thirty seconds that John had been restrained, his eyes swollen shut, blood poured from both nostrils, lips and jagged seams, looking like some bloody jigsaw puzzle. His entire face had gone numb from the extent of the damage and he couldn't tell if Sal was still beating on him or not.

Through the heavy, bloody lid of his left eye, he saw the man towering over him, fists covered in his blood, cursing at him still as he was taking a break from his onslaught. Dean had gotten to his fist and placed himself in between them, trying to give John a temporary respite from the punishment that had just been doled out in a hefty serving. More of the cousins had gathered around and cheered their hero on, some swore in their native tongue at the "white boy" on the ground.

He had lost. Despite being in the right, despite fighting a good fight, he had still lost. Even if he got back up and endured more punishment, just for the sake of getting in a few more good shots, it wouldn't change things.

Through the haze, he could see Melinda taking refuge by Sal's car, and saw her eyes burning through the crowd at him. He was still going to lose her, and that was what the fight had been about. Not just today, but all of the days since that first confrontation at the party until this very moment.

He'd been fighting that whole time to keep her away from this man, keep her from going back to that life, trying to make life better for her and give her what she wanted. In giving her what she'd wanted, in yielding to her, he'd already lost. Whether he beat Sal on this strip of grass and concrete was irrelevant now, and it wouldn't change anything. He laid his head back in the grass and stopped struggling to get up, letting the rain clear the blood away, and wondered about that other man who'd been in the exact same predicament.

Who the hell was he, and why did he always come in times like these, giving him inadequate warnings of events that were about to happen or were in the process of happening? As far as premonitions or psychic abilities went, it was pretty much useless. What good was some spirit messenger warning you of things that were already happening? *Thank you very much, but I already figured out that I lost my girl to the asshole guy, and that fighting back was useless!* John laughed then, at the absurdity of the whole thing; getting beat up for nothing, constantly trying to fight against the inevitable, and the fact that he was mumbling under his breath to a man who existed only in his head.

He'd lost it finally – all of it – and there was no reason to try anymore.

Beyond the voices in his head, his own gibbering nonsensical talking, and the shouting of the people who'd gathered to watch the fight, he heard a single familiar call that was trying to pull him back to reality. Through the thick fog of pain and the encroaching unconsciousness he wanted to succumb to so badly, he heard her calling out to him, telling him to get up and continue the fight.

"You can't quit, Johnny...don't let her beat you!"

It was Gwenn's sweet little voice, and he knew it without even opening his eyes to see her there standing in the crowd. She'd said 'don't let *her* beat you', and she was referring to his true enemy, of course.

Of all the people there, only she knew who his real opponent, and it wasn't the man standing over him cussing at him. All of the others gathered around to watch a fight between two men, cheering on one or the other by name, and waiting for one of them to lose. But the fight wasn't with Sal, he was just a pawn in that struggle that seemed to never end, and he was being controlled just like John once had been.

The whole thing was a game, a contest of wills and of control, between him and the woman he'd loved. Only the man lying in the grass, bleeding, and the auburn-haired girl standing at the edge of the crowd knew that sad truth. Melinda had played him again, unable to ever feel like she was losing control, feeling trapped and cornered, she'd resumed her old role across the board from him and began putting her pieces into place again. Gwenn saw it coming, knew it would happen even before that incompetent phantom man knew, and hadn't warned him because he needed to see it happen for himself. It was the only thing that would free him from the game and from her control.

Beating Sal wouldn't bring her back and it wouldn't win the day, they both knew that, but standing to fight again was imperative. He had to get back up and face him, and by extension, his puppet master, simply on principle; he couldn't let her beat him again. John had to get up, as painful as it was, and fight for himself and nobody else, so that they could all see that he wasn't going to let her ruin him again.

"Get up, Johnny! You can't quit now...you can't let her do this to you!"

The pupils reappeared in the blank whites of his eyes, and his heavy lids fluttered like iron shutters in a hurricane. His arms and legs felt like they were made of the same, heavy iron, as he maneuvered them clumsily, looking like a baby giraffe trying to get to his feet.

"I told you to stay down motherfucker!" Sal screamed at him.

Dean tried to stay in between them, trying to just buy his friend a little more time, but any second, Sal wouldn't be corralled, wouldn't be contained or distracted, and he would make himself the next target. He tried to suppress a smile, knowing that John was rising behind him and that the fight would be far from over. The battle for his sister was over, but the fight for John Chapel was just beginning, and it was going to be a clash that would move the earth and the heavens.

John ignored the pain, tried focusing on his enemy and his new objective, and his own words he'd spoken to Gwenn his first night home echoed in his head as a reminder of that objective: *I'm not meant to be with her...my life is more than fixing a broken girl...I want more.*

He squeezed his fingers, making sure they were all still attached and ready to comply with his commands, and uttered the word "unfailingly" under his breath. Pushing Dean out of the way, he came flying at Sal like a rocket, and lowering his head, he drove it directly into his nose. Cartilage yielded to thick bone, and blood sprayed everywhere as he was launched backward by the impact.

John's ears were ringing from the blow, but he didn't need to hear the voices coming from all around to know that they cheered the contestants and demanded more blood.

The pair traded blow after blow, each drawing a cringe or a gasp from the crowd and another stream of blood from a fresh wound. There was no strategy any longer, no precise strikes, or an attempt to make it end as quickly as possible.

John could barely see or focus enough to land those types of strikes anyway, and he'd had to change his approach, relying on brute strength and unchecked rage. Both men had broken knuckles and their hands and faces were numb enough to continue battering away at each other until the sun went down.

These two would not stop until they killed one another, and the fight turned very dangerous. Someone had shouted from the back of the crowd, saying that the police had been called, and the cheers began to die down from most of them, replaced by cries of mercy and an end to the fight. Most had never seen anything so brutal or bloody, not even in a movie, and this certainly wasn't a movie.

Even Melinda, the master of the game, started to become concerned and worried that she'd made a terrible mistake in pitting these two against one another. She certainly hadn't wanted it to go this far, or for either of them to end up in the hospital or worse. She'd hoped that it would've been enough for Johnny to see her with Sal and that would be enough to free her from her obligations to him. Her only crime was that she'd been a coward about confrontations, and would've rather broken John's heart and have him be the "bad guy" in all of this instead of her. But this was not what she'd ever imagined.

Her voice soon joined those in the crowd who were trying to get the bloodied contenders to bring an end to their prolonged fight. She even put her own safety aside to rush in and try to break them up, when her pleas went unheard. Sizing up the both of them, she determined that Sal was receiving the worst of it, and she would have to try to contain John first. Leaping on his back, she was barely effective in subduing him, however, and she hadn't had the same effect as her brother had earlier.

Dean ran in to intercept her, pulling her from John's back before she got hurt, and walked into a right cross as a result. John used the distraction as an opportunity, and charged his enemy, screaming madly, and picked him up around the legs, lifting him from the ground. The muscles in his arms and legs strained beneath the weight of the heavier man, and his limbs felt like iron again as he carried him across the wet grass, but he would not falter. With a terrible crash, John deposited his cargo onto the hood of his own Mercedes, and the back of his head starred the thick windshield.

There were tiny fragments of glass imbedded into the back of his head, and blood began to gush into the cracks of the windshield, outlining the star pattern in red. Sal didn't move except for his legs and arms twitching, and everyone watching thought he was dead. John wanted to be certain, and he'd set his mind to the task of ending this particular crusade today, no matter the cost. Leaping up on the hood of the car, he straddled the limp body of Sallah Nussein and proceeded to pound in his face, just in case there was any question, turning the windshield more read with every strike.

Dean had to intercede again, and was more concerned for John getting into serious trouble than Sal's wellbeing. "Johnny! He's had enough man! The cops are coming and you need to get out of here!"

"I need to finish this...I need to *make sure* he never comes back...so she can't run to him..."

"Johnny...this is over man! Don't toss your life out for this piece of shit," Dean pleaded.

Some of the cousins had gotten brave and started to circle around them, and there was already talk of retribution for their fallen leader. They eyed John warily, seeing what he had done to their cousin, but also believing that he was too weakened to continue to fight all of them. He was still a wounded tiger and still dangerous, though, and none wanted to be the first to find out.

He was relieved to hear the sirens in the distance, though somewhat disheartened that Sal was being responsive when they'd helped him from the hood of the car. His head lolled to one side and his eyes blinked open to stare at John, though he didn't seem to register what he was looking at, for he didn't give him so much as a dirty look.

"The next time I see you Sal," John said through bloodied lips, "you *will* be a dead man."

He uttered the promise just as two uniformed officers pushed through the crowd of onlookers and were stunned by the amount of blood and carnage that they found that had been caused by two college kids. One radioed for an ambulance and paramedics while the other reluctantly put John in cuffs, after hearing the details of the fight blurted out by the onlookers, Melinda included.

"That man right there! He assaulted my boyfriend! Is he going to be alright?"

It sounded as phony and overacted as ever, but it was convincing enough to the officers, and they bought into her teary-eyed victim act. They only went easy on John because it looked like he wasn't much better off, and he would need to be taken to the hospital before they were able to book him or charge him with anything. The pair debated on whether they should move him or wait for the paramedics, but John insisted that he was in good enough shape to ride in the cruiser.

He didn't want to give any of them the satisfaction of seeing him carted off in an ambulance, even if he'd needed one. The story of the fight between John Chapel and Sallah Nussein couldn't end with both of them being carted off in a meat wagon; that would imply that there had been a "tie" and not a victory over his enemy. No, the story had to be retold with him riding in the back of the police cruiser, with his head held high and a smile on his face, while the bad guy was being carried away on a stretcher. And that's exactly how it ended that day.

UNTIL MY DARKNESS GOES

*I have a love in me the likes of which you
can scarcely imagine, and rage the likes
of which you would not believe. If I cannot
satisfy the one, I will indulge the other."*

~*Mary Shelley*

Chapter *49*

Gwenn waited patiently in the study, fidgeting and not making eye contact with the host of faces that stared at her from the far wall. She could feel them all on her, looking down at her in disapproval, and staring expectantly, as if waiting for her to address them.

It was foolish to let her imagination get the best of her, being a woman of education and good common sense (she was a doctor for Christ's sake), but she still had irrational fears of the mundane, just like most people. Some were terrified of snakes or spiders, others liked to sleep with a light on, and some, like herself, felt a bit uneasy about things like the rain and faces her husband used to see in it.

Campbell and Connelly had abandoned her in the room, left her alone with those disembodied heads on paper, to go take a tour of the garage. All of those boys had a fondness for cars and getting dirty wrenching on them, and Jeremy was no exception, but she couldn't help but wonder if it had been an excuse to stall the story.

Only Jeremy Connelly knew where the story went next, and as much as she'd begged him to give her the details surrounding John's "dark days", he refused. It was a secret that her husband had taken to the grave, and even the tears of a grieving widow hadn't worked in getting Connelly to part with the secrets he'd been privy to.

She'd told Jim about those things before, when he'd mentioned the gaps in John's notebook, and he'd dismissed them as "potentially of no value", and focused on the information they did have. She didn't like that they had been out there for a very long time – at least thirty minutes now – without her.

Her paranoid mind began to imagine scenarios in which Campbell was working his silver tongue on Connelly, slipping in seemingly-innocent questions between motor specs and automobile history. Once he had the information, he would promise Connelly that he wouldn't breathe a word of it to her, citing some nonsense about "respecting John's privacy", and the two of them would return as if nothing had happened.

Then, he would tell her that he'd reviewed the information and decided, all on his own (because he was the "expert" after all), that it in no way changed his original diagnosis. They would then resume the boring story that was laden with far too much medieval history, point out that John had taken every detail from his class and their discussions, and that would be the end of it. Case closed.

She tapped her fingertips on the arms of the leather chair, paranoia growing in direct proportion to her dwindling patience, and felt those eyes burning into her as she tried to look away. They taunted her and chided her for being such a fool, allowing Connelly to outmaneuver her to save his own skin.

Who does he think he is? She swore she heard one of them whisper.

You knew him long before he did, and he was your husband for God's sake! Another said.

Where was he while you were taking care of John? What right does he have?

She finally made eye contact with them, her amber eyes glaring back at each one of them, but not angry with them. They were right to ask those questions, and they were only reminding her of her duty to her husband and why she was there in the first place.

They'd come to her in her dreams and sometimes in the moments after waking from them, lying in the darkness by herself, crying out for her to be their voice. It was those faces that prompted her to renew her own crusade, and discover the truth, not only for herself, but for her husband and for those who'd been forgotten.

The faces on that wall staring back at her were real to her and she believed in them because her husband had insisted that they were. They went to him first, demanding that he help them, and when he failed, they turned to her.

Campbell didn't believe in those people, and dismissed them as creations of her husband's mind, and she'd even humored him and listened to his psychobabble, but the time was nearing when he would have to begin believing. They hadn't been able to reach him yet, so she would have to speak for them and make him listen somehow. It would take some logical and incontrovertible piece of information, however, and she believed that Connelly held that information. She would have to make him give it up.

516

Her fingers had gone from tapping heavily to gripping the rounded corners of the leather arms, turning her knuckles white. A scowl turned into a pained expression, and her perfectly white teeth were bared like an angry hound as she stared up at those many sets of eyes. A wave of anger and then guilt washed over her that she hadn't felt in a very long time, and she slowly whipped herself into a fury. She was going to make him give it up right now.

In the garage, Campbell and his fellow enthusiast were hovering over his Packard and looked like two boys peering into a candy store window. They both jumped when the garage door burst open and the girl with the fiery yellow eyes emerged, making a beeline towards them.

Campbell checked his watch, making sure that they hadn't lost track of time, and Jeremy smiled up at her, but the look in his eyes was pure confusion. She marched directly at him, not seeming to slow her pace once bit, and he braced for impact.

"I'm through screwing around," she screamed at him, grabbing up a handful of his sweater and slamming him against the car. "I know what you're talking about out here and I want you to tell me everything!"

Campbell tried to calm her as he moved to push Connelly and his coarse jeans away from the finish on his car, but she turned that fiery gaze towards him and gave him his portion, "And you! How dare you lure him out here to talk about me behind my back? I'm not some fragile China doll and I want to know everything he told you!"

"Gwenn...what are you talking about?" Campbell said, he expression now matching Connelly's.

"We were talking about cars!" The man trapped in his own sweater shrieked.

"Of course you were! Anything to stall right, Con? I've had enough of you dodging me!"

"I'm not dodging you! I've been sitting in there for the last four hours talking with the both of you!"

"You've told us *lots*, but not what we want to know, Jeremy. So far I've heard stories about mobsters, Florida nightlife, Colombians, a girlfriend I didn't know existed, and even a mysterious Hungarian - which is all well and good - but you're leaving something out deliberately."

517

"What the hell are you talking about? You insisted that I tell you *everything*, remember? You know that I didn't want to…but you insisted!"

"Don't act like you didn't enjoy dragging his name through the mud, Connelly! You've been waiting for this opportunity to bring him down to your level, and now you've gotten it!"

"John was my *best friend*…"

She shoved the piece of paper she'd retrieved from the wall of Campbell's study into his face. "Was he? Then you can tell me who this man was!"

He looked at the picture and wore an expression of indifference.

"Gwenn…" The Professor tried to calm her. "I know that you're upset right now, but screaming isn't going to--"

"This doesn't concern you!" She snapped at him like a ferocious hound. "This is something that *Connelly* and my *husband* knew about, and he's going to tell me what it's about!"

Taking the piece of paper from her, he studied the picture again. He looked as confused by whatever was on the paper as he was by her dramatics.

"It's a drawing John did of someone I've never seen! Just like half of those pictures hanging on the wall! Weren't you listening? *Those people don't exist!*"

She jabbed a finger at something written on one of the pages in her other hand then, "Just like these names? *Martin Bromm? Niccolos Callamassio?*"

He scrunched his face up at the paper and shrugged, "I've never heard of those men, who are they?"

"You *know* who they are…they're aliases for the same man."

"John's *shadow man*? We've been over this…"

"Then go over it *again*! The letters I brought from Merrill Lake have your name all over them, and they have Frank Kovacs' name on them! Are you denying that you were both at Merrill Lake?"

"You *know* I was there, and so was Frank…"

"But this man right here," she said, shaking the paper in his face again, "wasn't there? He was in my hotel room the night before, claiming that he knew John from Florida – of all places – and knew intimate details about him, yet you've *never* seen him?

He said he was a friend and he wanted to help him, but you had no clue as to who he might've been?"

Connelly continued to shift uneasily in his seat as she invaded his personal space, straddling over him and thrusting the pages in his face. There had been a time once, long ago, when he hadn't minded her being so close, but this was not one of those times.

"The man who came to see you was a *federal agent*, Gwenn, and he was involved in the case John was supposedly working on!"

"That's right, the case that had something to do with a man John knew from Florida, and something that was big enough to bring *Frank Kovacs* all the way to Michigan from whatever rock he was hiding under. I'm not a police detective, but even I can connect the dots Connelly!"

"I'm not a police detective either, which means I don't know anything about the case John was working. What I do know is that it's not a stretch to connect a fed from Florida with John or any of the rest of us; they were always snooping around and trying to nail Gallianni's crew. They probably had 'intimate details' on all of us!"

"This gets even better! So feds were tailing you, John and your whole organization almost twenty years ago? But they waited all that time to come around asking my husband about whatever happened in Florida?"

"I don't know!"

"What *do* you know, Jeremy? Want to know what I know? I know that *John* wasn't completely full of shit about this guy who came looking for him, but I'm starting to believe that *you* are!"

Connelly said nothing, staring up at her as she pushed her face closer to his.

"What happened in *Florida*, Jeremy? What happened there that brought all of this back on him all these years later? What was he involved with there that got him killed? You need to tell me the truth, you sonovabitch! I deserve the truth!"

She was raising her voice again, in between the sobbing, and she'd clutched his sweater again but more now to support herself than to toss him about.

"Jeremy, please," she whispered, her voice cracking like a splintered board. "I'm asking you to help me to understand what was going on with him, because I'm drifting towards that 'deep end' too...and I need to know."

The mediator finally stepped in, unable to watch her emotional state deteriorate any further, and the progress they'd been making with it. He led her by the hand away from Connelly to give him some breathing room, taking her aside to talk some sense into her.

"Don't you think you've heard *enough*, Gwenn? Do you really want to know about that part of his life? The part he tried to keep you away from, and with good reason? It doesn't matter who he was back then, or the things he had to do, it only matters what sort of man he became...the man you knew."

"But I didn't know him, Jim; I didn't know him at all. I need to understand what happened to him...what really happened to him, and I don't think narrative therapy gone wrong quite covers it at this point."

"You believe it was this man without a name? That someone was working to actively ruin your husband? What you're proposing--"

"Makes me sound as *crazy* as he was right? I came here two nights ago not knowing what to expect, and ready to even accept the fact that I lost John to Melinda Malowski – even though I didn't want to admit it. But some part of you has to see that something is *off* here, Jim, and theories about guilt and phantom women aren't enough to explain everything?"

He exhaled sharply, his shoulders slouching. "No, it doesn't account for everything...but as your friend, I have to advise you against this course, Gwenn. Are you sure you want to know these things about him?"

"Do you want me to sign a waiver or a disclaimer?"

"Even if this destroys everything you believed in about John? Even if it ruins your memory of him forever and you begin to despise the man you loved?"

"My husband came to you all those months ago because he trusted you to be thorough and to have some integrity! If you're going to help him hide these things from me, then who can I turn to for the truth?"

"Okay," he said with a heavy sigh. "Mr. Connelly...you're on your own."

Chapter *50*

On the afternoon of the fourth day that John Chapel had woken up in his cell, the county Sheriff appeared at his door and released him. He still looked a mess; his face was swollen and covered in scabs, his hair and shirt were stained and matted by blood.

When they booked him, they'd insisted that he be taken to the hospital, but John refused. One of the Oakland county boys mistakenly tried to force him to go to the hospital and he ended up going himself. It was as though John wanted to bleed and revel in the pain, and so they accommodated him. The three other uniforms took him in the garage and took the rest of the fight out of him and left him in a cell for four days.

A man in dark sunglasses wearing an expensive suit and wristwatch showed on the fourth day and posted bail, informing them that he was Chapel's attorney. They tried giving him the runaround because they'd decided that he hadn't spent enough time in the clink to pay for the humiliation their fellow brother had suffered.

The man in the dark glasses wasn't one to be jerked around, however, and words were exchanged. Whatever was said was sufficient to scare the uniforms into cooperating and releasing Chapel into his custody. They watched the pair of them get into a dark blue Aston Martin with Florida plates and that was the last they saw of their captive.

As soon as the Connelly had received the call from Gwenn, saying that no one had seen John for two days, Frank Kovacs left for Michigan to find him. Somehow, Jeremy knew that if anyone knew where John was, it was "creepy Kovacs" (as some of the guys called him).

The mysterious enforcer in the Gallianni army always knew things that nobody else did, and nobody ever asked how, they just put the information to good use. He had no doubt that when he returned two nights later that he would have John with him.

Not much was said by either of them when they came rolling into the drive of Vincent Gallianni's condo, where they had made their temporary residence for the past several weeks.

Frank showed John to one of the bathrooms so he could get cleaned up and the closet in the spare room where Vincent kept a few spare changes of clothing. Jeremy inquired about the trip but Kovacs was pretty vague and short in his answers, as always. All that he could discern from his friend's appearance was that he'd just been through a pretty rough spot and things most likely hadn't gone well with Melinda in the end, because, well, there he was in Florida again.

When Chapel emerged from the bathroom, he looked like a man reborn. Most of the blood had been washed from his face, and only a few bruises remained, and he'd shed the dirty clothing on the tile floor of the bathroom like an old skin.

They were all the things that had been a part of the man he was back home, the tee shirt and jeans guy, and he'd thrown that stuff in the trash bag Frank handed to him. It was as if Frank was telling him that he wasn't able to go back and that it was better if he just disposed of that life altogether.

He looked like his old self again, dressed head to toe in black, and had found a pair of sunglasses and an expensive, heavy watch like Frank's to complete the outfit.

Connelly had assumed that the both of them would want to take a nap after their long trip, but there was important business to attend to that he hadn't been a party to until two minutes before they walked out the door.

Frank slid behind the wheel of the sleek European sports car, John taking his usual spot in the passenger seat, making Connelly get in the cramped back seat.

They raced up I-95 towards West Palm Beach just as the ocean spat out the moon, and the tall glass buildings reflected its pale glow over the waters of the intracoastal, giving it a ghostly shimmer. As they took the Okeechobee exit which spanned the waterway to the city, the myriad of manmade lights began to ignite one at a time, like neon fireflies signaling one another.

On one side, a purple sign lit up to advertise the name of an upscale restaurant, and across town it was answered by a blue one with the name of the hottest dance club. Then, up the street, a pink one flashed to draw the attention of gentlemen seeking entertainment, and it was answered by a green one from the bank tower where they could withdraw money for just such a place.

Connelly noticed his friend's weary face in the reflection of the passenger mirror, even hidden behind the sunglasses, and knew he'd been through hell again. Gwenn hadn't said much, but the worry in her voice was enough to let him know that the worst had happened, if Frank's urgency in retrieving him had not.

Kovacs wouldn't tell him what had happened either, even if he knew, and he doubted that he even asked about the details on the long trip down. That was one thing that he liked about Frank; he respected a man's privacy and personal business. Somehow, he still knew an unusual amount of information about everyone despite that, and it was just another reason he was called "creepy Kovacs". Jeremy only picked up a little bit about their present destination and the evening plans, and it involved a visit to Vincent at one of the nightclubs he frequented in West Palm.

They hadn't been to see Vincent in months, and usually any jobs he had for them were passed along via a phone call to the house or a letter delivered by courier – a job John and Jeremy both used to do. An actual face-to-face was never good news, and it meant something big, a bawling out for a botched job, or possibly both. Most likely, he had news about whoever was responsible for the recent hits on their store fronts and employees.

In the past three months, six different locations had been robbed, looted, or burned to the ground, six locations that belonged to Vincent Gallianni in one way or another. After the second one, a pawn shop in Pompano Beach, had been robbed, he no longer chalked it up to random, unorganized hoodlums.

He had an enemy out there somewhere and they were trying to hurt his business. After the fourth one, an Italian restaurant in Lauderdale, was shot up and the owner caught in the hail of bullets, Vincent sent every available resource to the streets to find out who was gunning for him. He found out exactly who it was when informants spotted four Colombians leaving the scene of the nightclub in Boynton Beach where three employees had been beaten to death in the parking lot.

Connelly had a sneaking suspicion that Vincent would eventually find out exactly why the Colombians were harassing his businesses and associates once he talked with his brother, George. He knew that he would be less-than-thrilled that his brother had mixed himself up with some dangerous men by eliminating the four men who were after John. Obviously, one of those four was somebody important or connected to somebody important – that's how that kind of shit started – and Vincent had discovered exactly what was what in the whole mess.

Frank handed the keys to the Aston Martin to a valet in front of the club who knew him by name, and he led the pair of them through the doors past the line of people waiting to get in. On any other night, Jeremy would feel important and revel in the little reputation he'd built for himself as one of Gallianni's men, but tonight he was too distracted by whatever was waiting for them in the office upstairs in this building.

John seemed cool and collected as people moved out of his way and he crossed the dance floor, and Connelly wondered if he was just tired, oblivious, or just didn't care anymore about what happened to him. He had to know that a meeting with Vincent wasn't something good, but the guy just walked with his head in the air, shoulders relaxed and walking in a calm stride through the crowd of beautiful people, not paying them any mind.

Across the floor and down the hallway crowded with men and women waiting to use the restrooms (with neon signs of course), the trio made their way, ignoring the looks from both the women and the men as they went. Connelly brought up the rear wondering still if John was as calm as he looked and if he realized that he was probably the coolest guy in the whole place, like he did.

All of those eyes that followed them down the hall knew that they were in charge of that place and that they were more important than they were, and the men envied them and the women wanted to be seen with them. He wondered if John cared about that at all, at this very moment, or if he was somewhere else behind those aviators.

Frank knocked on the door at the top of the stairs, waited, and was let in by a guy three times the size of Pete Brennan, who eyed John suspiciously as he escorted them in. They were in a richly-appointed office that looked more like a living room, jam-packed with expensive furniture and post modern artwork on every wall. Vincent was seated in the middle of a large, kidney-shaped, velvet couch in the center of the room, talking on his cordless phone, and he indicated the couch opposite him with a commanding finger.

Connelly and John sat on the enormous couch, and Frank chose to stand and lean on the back of it, which made Jeremy nervous. Did he know something that he didn't? Had he brought them all the way up to the soundproof room to dispose of them? Did he pick up the Sig Saur pistol from his nightstand before they left the condo? Was Vincent blaming them for the mess with the Colombians and tying up loose ends?

All of these questions raced through his head as he tried to force a fake smile at his boss who was yelling at someone on the phone about money. Still John sat to his right, seemingly calm and unaffected by the large man who was blocking the door or the fact that Kovacs was standing right behind them.

He wanted to whisper to him, warn him that it was probably about the Colombians and that they were in trouble, but Vincent never moved his eyes from them as he was berating the man on the phone. Would they even be able to get out of that room alive if John had advanced warning?

Vincent cursed at the phone in Sicilian and tossed it onto the table, making Connelly jump when it landed hard with a bang, like a gunshot.

"Either of you gentlemen care for anything to drink?"

"None for me thanks," Jeremy said nervously.

"I'll take a glass of brandy," John said, seemingly more comfortable than he was in his own house.

"Jimmy, pour a glass of brandy for our friend here, and bring Frankie his usual," he ordered.

Kovacs hated being called Frankie, and it was a good way to get your head bashed in, but he let it pass with this man. The brute lumbered over to the bar service in the corner beside the desk and began to pour drinks as Vincent lit a cigar and settled into his seat. That was the only thing that put Jeremy to mind of George, the way they both lit their cigars and seemed to savor that first taste before beginning any conversation.

"You're wondering why I dragged you all here on a Friday night, I'm assuming."

John nodded casually while Jeremy sat perfectly still, watching his every move, and those of the men behind him from the corner of his eye.

"I don't know how much Frankie's told you about what's been going on the last few months, Johnny, but I would assume that he's at least mentioned some of what you've missed?"

Again, he nodded. Apparently Kovacs had talked to him on the trip down.

"Has he also told you that we've discovered the identities of the men interfering with our business?"

"He has," he finally spoke, though there wasn't even the faintest hint of a tremor or quiver.

"What do you know about these men, Johnny?"

It wasn't a real question; Vincent already knew every detail about them, how he'd been involved with them and his part in the "Colombian debacle" from almost two years ago. It was just a test to see if John was going to fess up and admit to fucking up royally, and bringing a war to Vincent Galliani's back yard. Maybe if he was honest about it and took some responsibility for it, the punishment wouldn't be as stiff. Or maybe, if he admitted responsibility, he would give him a quick death instead of having Jimmy beat the life out of him slowly.

The brute shuffled over at that point and handed a glass to John and one to Frank, and the man in the hot seat took a long, steady sip from his glass before answering. Maybe he was getting nervous finally, as he should be.

"There were Colombians sniffing around our territory a couple years back, causing problems, and your brother and some of his guys took care of them. The problem was solved, until now I suppose, when they came back sniffing around looking for their guys," John said calmly, not taking his eyes from Gallianni.

Jeremy almost cringed when he'd said *our territory*, as if John had some stake in the small empire of the Gallianni brothers. He hadn't feigned complete ignorance about the situation, but he had been smart about removing himself from the actual incident that resulted in the deaths of the four Colombians. That was really smart, and Connelly waited with a shallow breath to see how Vincent would respond.

"That's right...well...*almost* right. George told me that there were some minor problems back then and that he had it taken care of, and it seemed like he had cleaned up his own mess - as he *usually* does. He was very careful about the details - as he usually is - and nobody would have ever found out about that little incident if it wasn't for *one* person..."

Here it was; the part where he was going to tell them that *they* were responsible, and then Jimmy and Kovacs were going to take them from behind and put them in a trunk to suffer the same fate as those Colombians. Vincent's eyes studied them both, as if uncertain of who really fucked it all up, and waited for one of them to crack and give the other one up. A bead of sweat was already rolling down Connelly's temple and John was still as cool as the cubes in Frank's glass. Vincent was surely going to single him out as the one responsible, because he looked the most nervous and guilty.

Leaning forward and setting his drink on the table heavily, he asked, "Do you know a girl named Nicole?"

Vincent knew exactly who she was and even more, he knew that she'd been John's girl for almost the entire duration of his last stay in south Florida. Connelly exhaled and breathed a little easier for only a moment, glad that he was off the hook, but suddenly became very worried for John, knowing that Vincent was honing in on him and painting a target for his guided missile waiting by the door to strike at any moment.

"She did this? She's the one who told the Colombians?"

Vincent nodded, his fake hospitality suddenly fading and a solemn look crossing his face, "Yes, she's our little snitch, Johnny. After you left, she ran back to the Colombians to spread her legs for them, and while the little whore was lying on her back, she was whispering your dirty secrets to them."

John was quiet, and sat further back into the comfortable couch, finishing the brandy in one drink. He wasn't really appreciating the taste of it as much as he had in Campbell's study; he was just hoping that something about the taste would take him back to that place and the memory of a more pleasant conversation. Connelly noticed him staring at the empty glass, as though disgusted with it, before he set it on the table in front of him.

"Why in the hell would she do that? You're *absolutely* sure that she's your snitch?"

Even Frank seemed to shift nervously behind him, surprised by John's bold questioning of Vincent Gallianni. Their host didn't even so much as lose him temper, though. Instead, he waved Jimmy over to refill their glasses, because the conversation was about to become more difficult, and a bit of liquid heart never hurt.

"Absolutely sure, Johnny! I know that the two of you were very close and that things ended on a bad note between the two of you," he explained, glancing up at Kovacs subconsciously.

John was certain that it was information that hadn't been given up easily, but information that had been a necessity under the circumstances, so he didn't get too angry with Frank for sharing it with him. He could almost feel him wince standing behind him, and knew that he felt badly about being put in the position he was and having no choice.

"So she did this...to get back at me? She figured you'd tie this to me and I would take the heat for everything that's been going on," he said simply, still not bothered by the possible ramifications.

"It appears that way, Johnny. Your little bird sang and told them every detail. I've got *six* businesses that have been shot up or blown up, *eight* dead men – including two of my personal couriers – and too many people who are afraid to do business with me for fear of what will happen to them if they do. I have to assume they know about every business associate, every route, every safe house, and everything I'm involved in. She has done some serious damage to my operation from here to Miami, and I need to know what I'm supposed to do about this now."

John finished his second glass of brandy in three hard swallows, then set his own glass on the table next to Vincent's, and leaned back in his seat, running his hands over his face and back through his tangle of hair. The same heaviness returned to his face that had been there the night the phone call came from Gwenn. It was the burden that he had only temporarily freed himself from long enough to make the trip to Florida. He'd walked out of one mess he'd felt responsible for and right into another.

South Florida hadn't been in this much of a mess since Andrew ravaged her shores, and John knew it would've been easier fixing the aftermath of that disaster than this one. This one had left more dead floating in the waters of the intracoastal, and on certain avenues that Vincent Gallianni owned, it seemed there was far more property damage. He was staring across at him with those dark eyes, expecting that he had the answers, expecting him to be a one-man relief effort. No Coast Guard, Red Cross, National Guard, or Police could help on this one, just John Chapel and the two men standing nearest him.

"The damage has been done," he replied, slowly forming a plan in his head. "We need to stop the bleeding, plug the holes, and make sure we're in stable condition. Then we go after the source of the problem, and we inoculate against further exposure, then eradicate the source altogether."

"I don't know how you propose to plug the holes and all that, but one thing's for sure; when this is over, the girl goes too, do you understand? I'm asking you how to fix a major fucking problem, and you're thinking of protecting this bitch? Haven't you been screwed by enough bitches to understand you can't trust them?"

"Not protecting her; using her. She turned on them once, if I can get to her…"

Connelly thought his argument made sense; it was too late to do anything about her, and the Colombians were the real problem now, plus she might've still been useful as an ally again. John was trying his best to spare Nicole's life, but Vincent wasn't hearing it.

"Once an animal turns on you, it can never be trusted not to turn on you again. Stop thinking with your dick and start thinking with your balls! What's your move, Johnny?"

It was Frank who spoke up and diffused the famous temper of Vincent Gallianni, "Johnny and I were talking on the way up, and he and I are sure that we can hit them back so hard that they will be swimming back to Colombia!"

"Is that right? The two of you? You're going to scare these guys away all by yourselves?"

"Someone once told me that it's not how many guys you've got, it's what those guys are willing to do."

Vincent smiled. The flattery had worked.

"Okay so you've got your crew picked out, what's your magic play?"

"Mass retaliation…total war," Frank said with a finality like a guillotine blade dropping.

"Explain that to me…what does that mean?"

Chapter 51

Three days I sat in that hole...

... until a man came for me on the third night. The sound of the guard's neck snapping outside my cell had awoken me from a light sleep, and the man in the black hood explained that he couldn't risk loose tongues, so the guard had to die. A second man freed me from my manacles, and I recognized him beneath the shadowed hood as Andrew de Chauvigney. I should have immediately known then that my rescuer was Richard before he even drew his hood back once in the cell.

They hadn't come entirely out of charity, but with a business proposal that would be mutually beneficial. He'd apologized for being powerless to help with the Nicolette situation, and he was offering me a chance at retribution for the wrong that was done to the both of us.

Richard was well aware of my talents by that point, as well as my reputation as a man to be feared, and he was offering everything I wanted in return for my talents. His brothers had been working against him again, as well as men who had once allied themselves with the Duke of Aquitaine, and he wanted to put the fear of God into them.

Geoffrey and John were playing war games with their brother, not actually pursuing real war against him, neither of them had any clue what real war was all about. But Richard did and the both of them gave those brothers a lesson they would not soon forget. Mass retaliation was an understatement, and the pair regretted ever raising an army against Richard. Those who had foolishly pledged themselves to fight for those incompetent lords regretted doing so as well, for they got the worst of it. They were tortured, impaled, beheaded, drowned and worse.

None of those men ever saw their homes again once they marched onto the field against Richard, for they were slaughtered in the battle or after it – Richard did not negotiate for a single man's ransom or release. Taking no prisoners was a merciful gesture to those men, however, for if they had been allowed to return to their homes, they would've found only burnt rubble standing on scorched plots of land, strewn with charred bodies of their livestock and their loved ones.

I was in charge of these things, of seeing that fear was spread among our enemies liberally, and that they would be too terrified to raise arms ever again. My talents weren't just used on the battlefield, however, and fighting on the front lines wasn't my primary objective. Richard wanted me to lead a "secret forward guard", as he called it, though we were nothing more than a group of assassins and terrorists. There were only nine of us, in total, hand-selected from Richard's knights, archers and tacticians, and we rode separately from his army to carry out our mission.

Word spread across the countryside about the men bearing black shields and banners, and it became easier to acquire surrender without even fielding an army. The peasantry would no longer give refuge to any man serving in Geoffrey and John's army, the farms would not supply them, and none of the fighting men would dare reinforce their dwindling numbers.

The resistance eventually collapsed from lack of support and the "total war" strategy of Richard. His father, Henry, stepped in to make peace between the brothers afterwards, and for a time, the sound of marching feet no longer echoed through the valleys of the Vexin. My mission did not end despite the temporary cessation of war, and for two more years I traveled the countryside with my secret guard.

Ambitious men gathered in courts and halls in Poitou, Aquitaine and even Rouen to plot and whisper their strategies for their next big coup, and wherever these men gathered we were there. We became Richard's answer to Reginald's vast network of spies and assassins, and what we lacked in numbers we made up for in tenacity and efficiency. This was my true mission; building a greater reputation and a longer shadow than Reginald of Poitou, for it was the only way of finding my way back to Nicolette.

I knew that Richard had been powerless to stop my adversary from seeking his revenge, and I held no grievance against him for his position in the matter. I knew that he'd hated him nearly as much as I did, and he'd given me just the opportunity I'd prayed for in that dank cell. There really was only one way to defeat Reginald, and it was the same strategy we'd used against Geoffrey and Henry: cutting off his lines of support.

The only problem was that a man like Reginald was more deeply entrenched within his tangled network of allies, spies and people who protected him simple out of fear.

We had to intensify our campaign of terror and harassment against his allies so that they would be afraid to even utter the name Reginald of Poitou. Those Barons and Lords who'd sworn their allegiance to him, either openly or in secret, would soon come to regret their decision. They soon realized that Reginald could not protect them, their families or their lands quite as well as had been promised in exchange for their loyalty. Many returned to ruined homes and burnt out farms, murdered servants and men-at-arms, and in a few cases, found their wives and children swinging from the rafters of lavish dining halls and churches.

Some were stubborn and still refused to extinguish their allegiances with Reginald, so their lives were extinguished instead. Richard preferred to win back some of those Barons and lesser Lords, but he also did not want the allegiance of men who could not be reasoned with, he said. In the spring of 1183, an agitated and desperate Reginald appealed to Richard's brothers to make war against him again, feeling his power and influence being pulled away from him, knowing that the "black guard" was somehow connected to him. Reginald had tried to deny his involvement with Henry later, but I saw him personally escorting Henry's wife Margaret to the France with my own eyes, in anticipation of the impending war.

Richard had no desire to engage his brothers again, but was convinced to renew his fight when he discovered that Reginald was again behind the coup and when Henry and his younger brother, Geoffrey showed up at his door in Aquitaine. We hadn't expected so many of the nobles to join in the rebellion, as most had already been served warnings. I guess some men need to be reminded more than once, so that's what we did.

The accounts of the invasion of Aquitaine will recount how bravely Richard fought off the armies of his brothers and the rebel lords, and that's partly true, but the part that will never be written is the role we played in that victory. While they were fielding their men against Richard, our black hoods crept behind the enemy lines with our torches, blades and other implements of persuasion. As news of our operation reached ears on the front lines, many of them abandoned the campaign and fled home to see what we had done.

The victory at Aquitaine was more than a military victory for us; it signified a shift in power from Reginald and his lackeys to Richard and those loyal to him. I was one of those who could be counted among the loyal during those long campaigns with so many wavering allegiances, and when it came time to collect payment for our efforts, I was right there with the rest with my hand out. I wasn't fixing a purse of gold to my belt; I was rewarded with something far more precious.

~Journal of John Chapel

Campbell stopped reading, but continued to scan the remainder of the page he was on and a portion of the following one before he glanced up looking like a bloodhound that had lost the scent. Both of the faces in his audience stared back with a pained expression that said they were able to make the connection from that passage with the story Connelly had been hesitant to finish.

The names were different, the geographic locales, and even the time period, but they could see all too clearly that John had made a very detailed account of those things he had been too ashamed to talk about with either of them.

"I don't think that we should take what he wrote there too…literally," Connelly said, trying to stomp out the proverbial fuse before it reached the powder keg.

Looking over at Gwenn, he saw that he was too late. She had a hand pressed over her mouth, muttering the name of her god between shaking fingers.

"I should've been able to read between the lines and understand that this journal…was nothing more than his way of dealing with things from his past that he wasn't able to tell anyone…I need some air…"

She walked unsteadily away from the old Packard, where she'd been standing and listening intently as Campbell finished dismantling her fond memory of her husband. They both watched her struggle to keep her balance and her composure, and though they couldn't see her face, they knew that she was having a hard time seeing her way out through the tears. Campbell pressed the button on the wall and opened one of the large doors to provide her with a way out and a fresh gust of air that made her catch her breath. They thought for sure that she would collapse right there on the drive, but she steadied herself with a rigid arm against the garage and took in deep gasps of air.

They quietly sipped at their drinks and waited patiently for her to return in her own time, or to just turn and make the rest of the walk down to her car and disappear, never to return. Connelly fully expected her to leave, and thought she'd heard enough, and that she had reached her breaking point.

Campbell was surprised that he hadn't recognized that same fire flickering behind those amber windows that had burned behind deep blue ones prior. He'd been there in those last days with his best friend, saw the conviction and desperation in his eyes, and wondered how he didn't notice that the crusader's torch had been passed onto Gwenn.

And even though the awful truth swept through the middle of her like a mighty wind, it wasn't enough to snuff out that flame just yet. He knew that fire was still burning, even with torrents of water filling those small chambers and spilling over.

As he predicted, she stopped the waters from flowing, found her legs, her stomach and her posture, and marched back into that garage wearing the echo of a defiant smile. There was no apology or excuse given, and she refueled those lanterns with some of the good "fifty proof" stuff before lifting those shutters for them to see just how brightly they were burning still.

"Did my husband *kill* those men, Jeremy? *How many* did he kill?"

It was a simple and direct question, and they both knew it was coming. Their reaction shouldn't have been staring helplessly at one another like two clueless buffoons. But that's just what they did.

"*How many*, Connelly?" She shrieked the question again, in case he was suddenly only able to hear in pitches three octaves higher, bordering the supersonic spectrum.

"I d-don't know, Gwenn, I never actually *saw* him kill anyone," Connelly sputtered like a dying engine.

"John Chapel was out for revenge and given free reign to wreak havoc on the scum of the earth, and he didn't harm a single one of them, huh? Even Jim doesn't buy into that! Did you *listen* to

535

the passage he *just* read? It was all but a confession of running rampantly through south Florida and executing every man who stood in his way!"

"You don't know who these men were," he continued to babble. "They would've killed me, Frank, John, and the rest of us..."

"So my husband became a *murderer*, just like the rest of them, and you all slapped him on the back and called him a *hero*?"

"John Chapel killed *five* men in the line of duty, but since he was wearing a badge and paid with your tax dollars, that makes him a *hero*, right?"

"I know that you're a man without a conscience or scruples who fills his pockets with blood money, and you'll do anything for a few dollars, isn't that right? Even sell out your best friend and ruin his name?"

"You wanted the *truth*; I'm giving it to you! And the truth is that I didn't have to ruin John Chapel's name – he did that *all on his own*! In the end, *unscrupulous* guys like me were all he had left because he went off the deep end and turned on everyone else!"

"Connelly!" Campbell warned.

"It's okay; I understand now...why he was so haunted and overcome with guilt. You were right about him, you've been right this entire time, and I should've listened. These terrible things he did...they finally caught up with him...and he lost his mind."

Campbell winced when she looked at him. He'd been championing his theories about what happened to John Chapel since before he was even gone, but it didn't mean he wanted to be right about any of it. He didn't want to be a party to ruining a widow's fond memories of the man she loved above all others.

Jeremy Connelly seemed to be in physical agony at that moment, as if some giant serpent was devouring his insides, and his face was drawn and pale. Apparently he had more of a conscience than what he'd been given credit for, and the truth came spilling out.

"John wasn't a *murderer*," he said through clenched teeth. "He did it for *her*...they were going to *kill* her..."

Chapter 52

It was Saturday night in March, and John Chapel was seated at a table on the balcony of the *Iguana Club*, sipping a drink from a plastic novelty cup that had something about "Mardi Gras" plastered on the side of it. The drink itself had some clever name that he couldn't remember, but the cute bartender with the skimpy costume did, and she'd served him three of them so far.

For the price and the fancy name, there wasn't much to them – mostly fruit juice and some rum – but he wasn't here tonight to get drunk anyway, or to even mingle with the hordes of sexy, costumed creatures inside. He was there waiting for a very particular creature to reveal itself, and he would wait on that balcony sipping his drink until it did.

Connelly leaned over the balcony, listening to the palms swaying below and said something to John about how they sounded like static from a television. He didn't pay them any mind, or his friend's comment; they were the same rustling palms that cast long shadows across neon-streaked walks the last time they were at this place, two years before.

He slammed the rest of his third drink, chasing away ghosts from the past, and stood to join the crowd of new ones waiting for him just beyond the patio door. Connelly followed him as he brushed through the undulating bodies of the living and the dead, making his way back to the attractive bartender to refill his plastic cup with the drink only she knew the name of.

Setting the cup down on the bar top, it caught the overhead black lights and glowed bright orange and his gaze was transfixed on the glow as he waited for his turn to be served. When the bartender finally stopped in front of him, she had to ask him twice for his order before she pulled his attention from the cup.

"I asked what you're drinking?" She shouted a second time.

He shrugged, "I don't know…a *zombie* something."

"I don't know what that is," she said, annoyed.

"Where's the other girl?"

"Brianna? She's on the other side of the bar. Can I get you something else?"

"Just give me a Corona with a lime," he finally yielded.

He paid the girl with a five and let her keep the change for a tip, then headed back through the dancing dead, hoping that his informant had been more competent than his bartender, and that he wasn't wasting his time. Leaning against the back wall beside a man in sunglasses, he played with the lime wedge as he watched the dance floor and the front door, and the man struck up a conversation with him.

"See anything out there you like?"

"Half the girls are wearing face paint – it's hard to tell what they look like."

"She's not going to show here, Johnny, and if she does, she won't be alone."

"That's why you two are here," he said, not looking at the man to his right.

"This isn't going to go down like last time. You can't save this girl, and I'm not helping you. I *can't* help you…you know what Vinnie said."

"Something went wrong with her, Frank, and I'm going to find out what it is."

"Yea, you had a bitch go crazy and sell you out. You should be used to it."

"That's not really funny."

"I wasn't trying to be funny."

"I need to talk to her, Frank, and find out what happened. Nicole is messed up, but this goes beyond her level of messed up – someone got to her," he insisted.

"Yea, the *Colombians* got to her. It's not hard to figure out. You remember the guys we've been after?"

John raised a brow at him and stopped in mid-sip of his beer, "You and I know there was someone else."

"*Someone else*? You're paranoid…"

"You've made me that way. You know something and that's why you've been trying to talk me into leaving since we got here."

"Who do you think is working against us besides the Colombians, John?"

"I'm about to find out, she just walked in," he said, handing his half-empty bottle to Kovacs and making his way across the dance floor.

She was dressed in a devil costume, ironically. The bright red vinyl came in two pieces that (barely) covered her breasts and (very little of) her ass, exposing her midriff. Sheer, black thigh-highs matched the long fingerless gloves that covered her arms to the shoulder, and the thin strip that functioned as a choker. Red high heels, plastic horns and a tail completed the look, and all that she was missing was the mask, but she could've passed for one of the denizens of hell anyway.

There were two men with her, just as Kovacs predicted, so John hesitated at the edge of the dance floor, using the other costumed patrons as camouflage, waiting for his opportunity. He knew Nicole's habits well enough to know that her first order of business for a Saturday night out was heading towards the ladies' room while she sent someone to fetch a drink.

One of the men headed towards the crowded bar – which would buy him about ten minutes – and the second stood by the hallway that the bathrooms were in – which meant he would have to be careful.

Giving her a thirty-second head start, he motioned for Connelly to follow him down the long hall. John yanked the handle on the ladies' room door and walking in like he belonged there. There were only two other girls in there besides the one he was after and they were washing up and fixing their makeup and costume pieces. Nicole was in the center stall, and the two girls that scurried out of the restroom didn't pay any attention to the two men there.

Connelly stood guard at the door while John nearly tore the door off its hinges with a powerful kick. The girl inside jumped, spilling the powder all over her black nylons and onto the tile floor. She whirled to give some bitch a bawling out for making her spill her coke, but her face went as white as that powder when she saw John standing there.

He waved his pistol in her face warning, "In case you get any bright ideas to scream or in case anyone even hears you if you do. Get your ass out here!"

Grabbing her by the shoulder, he yanked her out of the stall, whirled her to face away from him and pushed her up against

539

the sink, keeping the gun trained on the back of her head. She glanced to her right towards the door and Connelly gave her a wave.

"We have about five minutes before anyone comes looking for you, which means you have less than two minutes to explain to me what the fuck is going on!"

"They'll kill you if they find you in here, John…"

"I'll kill you if you don't start talking" he said, cocking the hammer.

"You won't kill me…"

"You sound sure. The bodies they've been pulling out of the water? I've put half of them there. I won't hesitate for a second to decorate that mirror with your fucking brains! You didn't have a problem running your mouth to start all of this shit, so why suddenly so shy? A lot of people want me to personally bring them your head in a sack!"

"If you were so worried about me running my mouth, maybe you should've stuck around," she said, scowling at him in the mirror with her dark crimson lips and blinking her black-lidded eyes.

"Don't you *dare* pin this on me! There were a million ways to act like a slighted lover, and selling me out along with everyone who bent over backwards to fucking help you wasn't one of them! Cut your hair short and go on a drinking binge like every other chick!"

"I'm not everyone else, and you shouldn't have fucked me over, Johnny!"

"This isn't about a jilted woman trying to hurt her ex, and I know better. You were a *professional*, Nicole, and this isn't something you ever would've done on your own. There isn't anyone out there better than you at keeping business and emotions separate, so you tell me what the fuck is really going on."

She seemed to not care that he had a pistol trained on her and turned the water on to wash the residue from her hands as she started talking in a casual tone, "The Colombians that George had killed…"

"Don't give me that Colombians bullshit! I don't fucking buy it!"

She glanced in the mirror at him standing over her shoulder and shrugged, drying her hands on a paper towel, "That's who you've been after, Johnny, that's who's been shooting up Gallianni's places all over, from Lauderdale to West Palm. Who else would it be?"

"I know *exactly* who we've been at war with," he growled at her, turning her around to face him and pressing the hard barrel into her chest. "But I didn't ask you who we're at war with. I asked you why you sold us out. You have about sixty seconds left, and don't tell me the *Colombians* again."

He'd turned her to face him so that she couldn't lie to him. She'd been a professional liar most of her life, and had used that talent once to help him pull some big money jobs, so he knew exactly what he was dealing with. She was so good, in fact, that she could probably tell him a convincing enough lie so long as she only had to make eye contact with him in a mirror.

Facial expressions could be misread in a reflection, as well as body language or, most importantly, the tells that give away someone who is trying to hide behind a lie. But staring someone directly in the face, especially a man she once loved, afforded her no protection and too much exposure.

"John...you need to just go..."

"I'm not leaving until you tell me the truth, Nicole! Tell me who got to you!"

She tried to twist her face away from his, but he had her cornered against the sink, and she looked more uncomfortable with him standing so close than she ever had before..

"Please...get out of here...and get as far from this place as possible..."

"Who are you afraid of?"

"He'll kill me...there's nothing you can do to stop him. Please just walk out of here tonight, leave everything behind...Me, Frank, Vincent, Connelly...you're endangering all of them."

"Who the hell has you this scared Nicole?"

She tried wriggling out from under him again, as if his very touch was forbidden, and someone was watching her from somewhere in the ladies' room.

"You have to let me go, John. He knew that you would try to find me...that he could use me to get to you, and that's why you have to go. I never meant to hurt you, or any of the others, but I had no choice.'"

541

"The men you came with aren't working for Santos are they? They're working for this guy?"

"Santos still wants blood for what happened to his brother, but he's not the one doing this…"

"It sounds like I need to go ask him some questions then…"

"Damn it! You need to listen to me for once – just this *once*! If there ever was a time to put your pride in check and learn how to walk away from a fight it's right now!"

He backed away, seeing the absolute terror in her face, and knowing that it was genuine. He'd never seen her so frightened in all the time he'd known her, and it wasn't an act, that was for certain.

"Nicole, I'm going to make this right…I'm going to find out who this guy is whether you tell me or not."

She shook her head sadly, "I know you'll try, and that's *exactly* what he wants you to do…you should've stayed gone, John."

Touching his face gently with fingers cold like death and tipped in black paint, she drew his face towards hers and kissed him briefly but deeply. Leaving him with that revelation and the taste of her on his lips, she made a hasty retreat from the bathroom to intercept the bodyguard before he reached the door.

Waiting until they were clear, he and Connelly moved back into the narrow hallway and towards Frank as quickly as possible, watching the goons escort her across the dance floor towards the balcony. She was trying to distract them long enough for them to leave and they didn't hesitate to take advantage of her play – just like in the old days. Frank was already halfway towards the door, when he saw the coast was clear, and he ushered John past the bouncers and kept looking behind them as they made their way to the car.

Once they were half a mile away, headed north on A1A, John and Connelly shared what he'd been told.

"You know who she's talking about, don't you Kovacs?" John shouted as he pressed the accelerator and gripped the wheel so hard his knuckles popped.

"Settle down or you're going to draw unwanted attention. How the hell am I supposed to know who she's talking about? She just told you there's someone who threatened her and she said she's afraid of him?"

"She didn't have to say she was afraid, Frank, I could see it in her face! Nicole isn't a girl who easily spooks, and she used to work with Santos, so it's not him she's afraid of."

"We don't even know who this guy is, Johnny. Did she give you a description? An address? A name? How are we even going to find him?"

"No, she didn't say anything else about him – she was too terrified to even talk! But we can find this guy…we should go back there and wait for those gorillas to come outside and take them uptown."

'Uptown' was where they'd taken more than one of Santos's men to get information, and the place where none of them ever returned from.

"This war isn't going to end even if we get to Santos if there's another player! I knew she wouldn't just sell us out without good reason!"

"Vincent was *clear* on what he wanted: scare Santos out of town or eliminate him, and Nicole doesn't get a pass, Johnny, no matter what the excuse she gave you. We stick to the plan."

"Vincent doesn't know about this other guy I would wager. He has to be told, Frank…"

"What are you going to tell him? You have it on good authority from a scared girl – a girl you were *supposed* to put away – that she sold all of us out because of some guy you didn't bother getting the name of?"

"I don't give a damn what he says to that! This is bigger than he even realizes and if we're not going to at least tell him what he's up against, then we have to find a way to reach this guy and end this!"

"Always going after the impossible aren't you Johnny? How did that Melinda situation work out for you? How about standing up to Sal and beating the shit out of him? What did that accomplish?"

"At least I didn't run away from it and hide my head in the sand."

"Have you ever known me to play the hero? Know why you don't hear me running my mouth? Because eventually that guy

543

with the big mouth gets too much attention drawn to him and someone eventually shuts him down."

"*Too involved*? Don't act like you don't even know her, Frank – you're the one who helped me get her away from those guys and get her cleaned up! I know you looked after her when I was gone, because Connelly told me, and I know that you must at least care about her a little."

In answer, Frank could only turn his head towards the window, staring at his faint reflection that was filled by the starless night and the black ocean beyond.

"I'll do it alone if I have to," John finally said, after receiving the silent treatment.

"I'm coming with you," Connelly finally spoke up from the back.

"Like *hell* you will! Either one of you!" Frank jerked his head away from the window and his voice was like the crack of a bullwhip, causing them to start. "I'm responsible for you and responsible for seeing this through to the end."

"Just *once* I'd like to think like a man with a heart and a soul, Frank, not just a brain!"

"Men who think with their hearts end up dead, Johnny, and they make stupid moves like going up against someone they have no chance against."

John fell silent then and stared straight ahead at the series of green lights, readjusting his grip on the wheel so that the bones popped again.

"You *know* who this other man is. It's not that you don't believe Nicole...it's that you *refuse* to get involved...because you're *afraid* of him too!"

"I was never taught to be afraid of anyone, John, and I know that you were taught the same. That's one of the reasons I've always respected you. I've never run from a fight unless it was in everyone's best interests, and I'm telling you to run from this."

John suddenly became very hoarse, "You knew about this before I went after her?"

He nodded at his own reflection in the window.

"Why did you let me find her? You could've stopped me before we even drove down here," he said, slapping the steering wheel as something else occurred to him. "Sonovabitch! You *tipped the informant* didn't you?"

544

"You needed to hear what she had to say…and you needed to say goodbye to her," he replied somberly.

"What does that mean?" Connelly asked nervously.

"Say goodbye? You have to be out of your mind if you think that I'm going to pull the trigger on her now"

"That's *exactly* what you're going to do, Johnny…or *he'll* do much worse. You have to make the same sacrifice she's made for you, sparing you the pain and misery that she's endured on your behalf, and put an end to it. You should've pulled the trigger tonight in that bathroom, and you've only prolonged her suffering."

John jerked the wheel of the sports car sharply to the right and the tires screamed as he came tearing into the parking lot of an Italian restaurant. Turning off the engine, he jerked the handle of the door and flung it open, then leapt up from the luxurious leather seat like it was covered in spikes and on fire. He left Frank and Connelly sitting in the car to watch him pace back and forth like a hungry tiger.

"What in the hell are you talking about?"

"Johnny, get back in the car and I'll tell you what's going on…please."

"No! We're not going *anywhere*! You tell me *now*!"

"Stop being ridiculous and get in the car!"

"I'm tired of your goddamned secrets and your *mystery man* bullshit! I want you to get out of the car and look me in the eye and tell me everything you know right now!"

Frank didn't move and he only gave him his usual blank stare. All they had to do was wait about three minutes and he would lose his momentum and get back in the car, apologizing for losing his cool.

That's not what happened at all, and Frank actually look surprised as the pacing tiger lifted a large piece of concrete from the parking lot and hurled it at the front window of the Italian restaurant. That got Frank's attention and he stepped from the car as quickly as John had.

"What in the fuck are you doing?"

"The cops would normally be here in two minutes, but since we're in Lauderdale and it's a Saturday night, you *might* have five! If you don't start telling me what's going on, then you can explain it to them when they get here – you can explain the whole goddamned thing to them, because I'm done with it!"

"Whoah, Johnny! Let's think this through," Connelly called from the car.

"Are you out of your goddamned mind?"

"I'm tired of being lied to, Frank, and I want some answers for once! You *knew* what was going on all this time and you kept it from me! You know who's after me and after Nicole and you need to come clean right now, or so help me God, I'll tell the cops everything!"

"Where's your head?" He screamed.

"If this guy has you and Nicole this scared, then what chance do we have on our own? It's better if we take our chances with the Feds anyway!"

"You're talking about going to the *Feds*? They'll give us both the goddamned *chair*, Johnny! Connelly will get life, the same as Vincent, and probably Nicole too!"

"We can cut a deal, pin this all on Vincent!"

"Vincent would have you killed from the inside! Where's your loyalty?"

"*Loyalty*? If you were really loyal to him, you'd tell him what he was really up against! You don't give a shit what happens to him, I'm not stupid! What has Vincent ever done for either of us?"

"You're right, Johnny; it's just us out here, just like it's always been! You and Connelly are my responsibility and I'm supposed to protect you, but if you start losing your cool now, I don't know if I can do that!"

"Why do you keep saying that? Who decided that you're in charge of *my* protection? Who made you my personal fucking bodyguard? Because I'm pretty sure I can handle myself!"

"You can handle yourself? Just like you handled yourself against the first guys that rolled you in Pompano? Or how you handled yourself back home? You would be floating face down in the fucking river if it wasn't for me!"

"What the hell are you talking about?"

"You don't think Santos Vergara was looking for the guys who did his brother in three years ago when it happened? Who the fuck do you think has been cleaning up after you all this time? "

"What do you mean?"

546

"You think George Gallianni or his brother gave two shits about a *nobody* kid from up north? Do you really think *Uncle George* took a shine to you and felt sorry for some moron who just got his ass beat in a parking lot?"

"Are you trying to say that it's been *you* this whole time? You're the reason I got in good with George and his brother?"

"*Got in good*? George might like you *now*, but Vincent wanted to put a fucking bullet in your head over this mess with Vergara! *I'm* the reason he didn't! *I'm* the one who promised him that you and I would clean it up! So, you don't get to go barter for some girl's life with him, because you're lucky to have your *own*!"

"I knew it," Connelly complained from his place by the car.

John started pacing again, and the faint sound of sirens could be heard in the distance, probably only six or eight blocks away by the sound. Everything he was telling him made sense, and he'd always wondered how he'd found his way so easily into the ranks of the criminal underworld, even the lower ranks.

"Why have you been protecting me, Kovacs? What's your interest in a kid from the Midwest? What did I ever have to offer a guy like you: a guy who has everything and knows everything about everyone?"

"That's a longer story for a day when we have more time! I've told you enough for now, please get in the fucking car before the cops get here and really make a mess of things."

"I'm not going anywhere! You have about two minutes!"

"Are you trying to threaten me, you sonovabitch? After everything I've done for you? " He pulled his pistol at that point and aimed it at him, and John followed suit, circling one another, Connelly reacted and pulled his as well.

"Are you going to shoot me Frank? After all of this shit we've been put in together? There must be a *really* good reason you've gone out of your way for me all this time, and I'd really like to hear what it is before they get here!"

"I'll shoot that gun out of your fucking hand and then cripple you and carry you out of here if I have to! And I'll leave you face down in this parking lot Con! Put the fucking gun down!"

"But you won't kill me. I want you to tell me why it's so important to keep me alive and why you've been pulling the strings for the past three years, Frank!"

"If it was up to me, I'd put a bullet in your face you self-righteous sonovabitch! But I've been paid very well to keep you alive and to keep you out of danger!"

"By dragging me into the *mob*? You're not very good at your job are you?"

"I'm better than you know! Pulling you in with guys like Gallianni and his brother has kept you off the radar for a while, but I can't hide you with them anymore! That's why you need to get in that fucking car right now and listen to every fucking word I tell you if you want to live through the night!"

As he was weighing Frank's words and considered trying to say something stupid to bully him into telling him more, the sound of the sirens from just a block away and a ringing telephone made him reconsider. It was the car phone that Vincent kept in contact with them on, and he rarely called it unless it was something important.

"Yea? Yes we are. What? Police sirens. No, we're not involved. We'll be there in ten minutes."

Connelly hung up the phone and turned towards them with a pale expression, "Orlando and his brother spotted Vergara! We have to roll right now to catch him!"

Frank and John exchanged glances, nodding and making some sort of silent pact to finish their discussion later, then holstered their guns and hopped back in the car.

They shot back onto A1A and took the first right on 36th street and another right on Galt Ocean Boulevard to double back south as the cops were arriving via Oakland Park Boulevard. Frank watched the red and blue lights through the alleyways of the buildings facing A1A, and breathed a sigh of relief realizing how close they were to getting caught.

As they raced along Ocean Boulevard, not another word was said about the heated exchange, Nicole, the spook, or anything else that had just been shouted from behind the barrel of a gun.

From the back seat, the quiet observer watched the both of them shift in their leather seats like it was suddenly a hot July afternoon. They were about to go head to head with Santos Vergara and they would all have to be one-hundred percent on top of their game, and trust one another one-hundred percent. They were screwed.

Chapter 53

Everything that happened after that explosive confrontation in the parking lot of the Italian restaurant seemed like it was something out of a bad dream. A million things were running through Jeremy Connelly's head from the moment they'd arrived at the *Bimini Boatyard Bar and Grill* until he finally stepped foot back on the *Fountain Forty-Two Lightning*, docked behind Santos Vergara's villa.

It was like someone injected his entire body with Novocain and he could feel nothing, and all of the screams around him were muted and distorted. Frank was shouting something at the top of his lungs at him as he was starting the boat back up. No not at him, at John. *Where was John? He'd just seen him in the house hadn't he? He was right behind him wasn't he?*

Connelly scanned the courtyard again, trying to place him through the chaos of screams, gunfire, and smoke. There were bodies strewn across that lawn, many still dressed in their macabre Halloween costumes and ball gowns, but he wasn't among them either. Orlando Alvarez – the one who'd called them on the car phone only an hour before - was still slumped over the fountain, his brother, Victor, still sprawled across one of the long tables. There was still no sign of John.

He'd wanted to go with him in the first place, and he'd practically begged Kovacs to let him go back at the *Bimini* when they were first hashing out their plan. That's where they met up with Orlando and his brother, the guys who'd gotten the hot tip on Vergara in the first place. A couple of band members playing the *Bimini* had bragged about playing some gig for an after-hours party afterwards. They'd overheard the words *South beach* and *Santos* – that's when they called Frank.

It wasn't too hard for a smooth talker like Kovacs to get the rest of the scoop from one of the drunken and too-talkative band members. Not only were they playing for Vergara, the hot-shot guitarist bragged, they were delivering more than audio equipment and live entertainment. A few more drinks and some friendly chatter revealed exactly what their cargo was and how they were transporting it: they were moving about twenty pounds of coke inside the equipment cases and taking them straight up the intercoastal in a boat that obviously didn't belong to them.

They waited at the docks near the *Fountain Forty-Two Lightning* – a long-nosed racing boat with three 540 horsepower Mercruiser engines – until the band members arrived. While Frank and the creepy Alavarez boys took care of them and their heavy cases, Connelly was trying to talk John out of getting on that boat with them. He insisted that their fate would be the same as those unfortunate band members and that they should walk away while they had the chance. John wouldn't listen, though, and his mind had been made up since the restroom of the *Iguana Club*.

Once the large boxes of music equipment, speakers and amps were re-packed by the Hungarian and his shifty cronies, they were loaded onto the boat. The *Forty-Two Lightning* was forty-two feet in length – as the name implied – but despite its size, the cargo and five-man crew were packed pretty tightly in the small, open cabin.

Last minute addendums to the plan they'd hashed out on the docks were made as Kovacs guided the sleek machine through the channel out of the marina. All of the men sat with serious expressions, listening to the plan, but Jeremy only half-listened as he tried to make one last appeal to John. The loud boat engines drowned out most of what he said, and the rest was simply lost on him. The best he could do, then, was to stick as close to John as possible and hope they made it out alive.

There wasn't a provision in Frank's plan for them to stay together, though, and when he paired each of them up with one of the Alvarez's, Connelly gave his best friend a nervous glance. *This is it*, he thought, *as soon as we finish this job, those two gorillas are going to carry out Vincent's orders. That's what Frank said back at the restaurant, and he can't be trusted anymore.*

John didn't seem to make the connection or even seem to notice that Connelly was trying like hell to make eye contact with him. His expression was the most serious and as unreadable as Kovacs', not showing a hint of fear or trepidation about the plan. He was paired up with Orlando, who would be walking in front of John. *Good, at least he might still be able to get the drop on him if he tries anything funny.*

Jeremy frowned at the larger and more imposing figure he was paired up with, and he would be walking behind him all the way up to the house. *Damn it! They want to do me in for sure! If this Neanderthal wants to cave the back of my skull in, I won't be able to stop him.*

The place was lit up like the white house at night, and wasn't much smaller – all it was missing was the pillars. It sprawled across a large estate, encircling it like a large, pristine white pincer on three sides, and the Venetian courtyard in the center was as immaculate as the home itself. There were scores of hedges and trees – native and imported - neatly-trimmed and decorated with lanterns and lights, which complemented the ones floating in the large fountain that served as the centerpiece for the entire courtyard.

Authentic granite sandstone-colored tiles covered the base of the tiered fountain and a majority of the courtyard as well, and a likeness of Poseidon was placed upon the very top of the fountain to preside over the whole thing. Anyone who hadn't arrived by car might've believed that they'd been blown off course and were docking somewhere else altogether, if it weren't for the obnoxious yacht moored at that dock. The place belonged to Santos Vergara for sure.

As Frank secured the cases and bags they were carrying, Connelly got a good look at the ridiculous house facing the water and all of the ridiculously beautiful guests in attendance. Some of them looked like they'd spent almost as much in preparation for this party as their host did in turning the South Beach mansion into a Venetian chateau.

The costumes that some guests wore for the Halloween-themed soiree were like those that one would expect to see at the Carnival in medieval Rome. There were elaborate gowns with raven and peacock feathers, jewel-encrusted masks, headdresses and odd prosthetics such as giant angel wings, tails, and the sort. Scattered among them were the wealthy guests whose costumes were merely Versace dresses or tuxedos that cost just as much.

Watches were synchronized, final instructions given, and five heads nodded in understanding (one not paying attention whatsoever) before they split into three groups. John and the shorter Alvarez brother were met by one of Vergara's men, who led them right through the middle of the busy courtyard towards a

551

door in the south wing. Connelly and his man were escorted around the north side towards a large garage area, and Frank carried the rest by himself, following a man up a flight of exterior stairs.

Exactly three minutes later - the time Kovacs had worked out in his plan – an explosion rocked the south wing of the house, and all hell broke loose. That was John's case, and it had been packed with the most charges, because that, too, had been worked out in Kovacs' plan. He'd known the numbers before they even docked, scanning the grounds and the man balconies and windows of the house, running the scenario in his head. The bulk of the guards were in the south wing, and that was also where he'd suspected Vergara to be.

All of the windows facing the south lawn had been blown out by the force of the blast, and for a moment, Connelly wondered if Kovacs' had really packed the case with concussion charges and not something more lethal. Victor reassured him that it was all "bark" and no "bite" as he jammed his earplugs in, indicating that Connelly follow suit, and hit the small plunger on his own radio transmitter. The speaker case they'd just left with the guards in the garage erupted five seconds after the first, shattering every car window of Vergara's collection as well as the ear drums of the men inside.

Connelly barely heard the third explosion coming from the second floor through the ear plugs, the ringing in his ears and the gunfire. From his duffel bag, Victor produced a small sub-machinegun with a collapsible stock, and burst back into the shattered garage to clean up whoever was left standing. His partner hesitated, hanging back in the hallway, preparing his own weapon.

I'll let this sonovabitch go in there first; maybe they'll dust him and then I won't have to worry about what comes later.

There wasn't much offered up in resistance; the five men they'd left standing in the garage were scattered around the room like marionettes without strings, crumpled in odd positions. The aftermath of the concussion grenades left them with blood streaked across their faces from ruptured vessels and shattered ears. Victor put them out of their misery with a few short bursts from his CAR-15, shortened carbine.

As bullets flew and the screams of the dying echoed in the spacious garage, Connelly could only think about his best friend.

Was he the trigger man and doing the same, or was he standing back and being smart, watching Orlando do the dirty work? Did they get clear of the blast? Frank put more shit in his case!

There were many rumors flying around about Santos Vergara, and one was that he was a stickler about his "deliveries", and one of the stories said that he could tell if there was a single ounce missing just by weighing the bag in his hand. Another story was that Vergara always personally inspected his deliveries and dealt with inconsistencies in his own special way.

Kovacs counted on the validity of those rumors when he'd rigged John's case. The concussion grenades gave off a blinding eight million candlepower of light in addition to the 180 decibels of sound to displace the fluid in the inner ear, rendering anyone within about fifteen feet completely incapacitated. But this wasn't enough for Vergara, he insisted.

Six white phosphorous canister grenades were also rigged in sequence to ignite simultaneously, and in such a way that the blast would catch whoever was closest to the amp case. He explained that the phosphorous burned at somewhere near one-thousand degrees Fahrenheit, and could not be doused completely with water, thus the victim had to cut the chemical off his skin with the blade of a knife to keep it from burning through several layers.

If they were lucky, the blast would take Vergara's face off, if the arrogant sonovabitch inspected his delivery personally. At the very least, it would shake him up enough for Orlando or John to finish the job. *There's a lot of smoke coming from those windows. Frank said that stuff isn't good for your lungs; get the hell out of there Johnny!*

He was more entranced by what was happened across that courtyard at the south wing, with the white, billowing smoke rolling out of every window, than the gunfight he and Victor were embroiled in. More guards came to reinforce the garage and the bullets zipping over Connelly's head and Victor's string of curses temporarily snapped him out of his daze. He didn't remember giving a thought to what he was doing - he just squeezed the trigger like some automaton, the numbing coldness creeping into his chest and every extremity.

Connelly was still trying to recall how he'd gotten back to the boat from that hallway they were pinned down in, and still trying to remember where he'd last seen John. The entire back of

Vergara's villa started to glow a brilliant white, as if it were engulfed in a fire devoid of color. He shielded his eyes and continued to scan the courtyard for any trace of his best friend.

The movie reel stuttered and began playing again, and he remembered racing up a stairwell in another part of the house. He'd left Vincent dead somewhere between the Poseidon fountain and one of the long food tables, not looking back as he made his way towards those smoking windows. John was taking too long in there and when he said something to Victor about it, he told him to forget about him. That only confirmed his paranoid suspicions and he realized that he never should've let John go on this suicide mission.

At the top of the stairs, he found himself in a small room decorated in a nautical theme, complete with paintings of old Spanish Galleons, sailing paraphernalia on the walls, and even an antique captain's desk in the corner. A single door to the north led to the rest of the second floor, and the source of muffled screams that he'd heard at the bottom of the stairs.

As he charged through the door, the screaming turned into a whimpering, and he could plainly hear it coming from just up the hall now. Moving hastily, he paused only for a moment at each doorway, listening intently with an ear that had just stopped ringing, and then forward. It was at the fourth door on the left that he heard the soft weeping and the sound of men talking.

Stepping into the bedroom, he recognized Vergara immediately by the expensive suit he'd been wearing, even though it was slightly tattered and charred from the blast that he'd apparently survived. John was standing to the left of the door, pistol leveled at him and ordering him to step away from the large queen-sized bed. Besides a few scrapes and bruises, he seemed fine, and Connelly heaved a sigh of relief.

Vergara's hands were saturated in blood and there was quite a bit of spatter on the front of his white shirt and jacket. A chill came over him as he met the grisly, mangled face of the drug lord, who was, strangely, smiling at the both of them. One black eye glared at him, the other having been incinerated with his upper cheek and half of his jaw. The white phosphorous had burned deeply, and was imbedded in his face still, but he didn't appear to be in any pain.

John kept the gun pointed at that grisly mask, as he kept looking from the sharp, yellow teeth to the bloodied palms. The charred jaw only quivered with laughter, and the hanging bits of charred meat that had been his face jiggled as he did so.

"What the fuck are you laughing at? It's game over for you Vergara…if that's your name."

"Such a clever boy," he rasped through a ruined throat. "I'm no more *Colombian* than you are."

"What's he talking about Johnny? What happened up here?"

"I don't care where you're from. I don't care what your name is. You're dead."

He continued to laugh uproariously, and Connelly would never forget that cackle for as long as he lived, or the way he kept proudly showing the palms of his hands like a painter having finished his masterpiece. Jeremy edged around to the right, keeping him covered with his CAR-15, trying to see what was beyond his large frame.

As he moved closer to inspect the bed, the charred-face man gave him wide berth, hands still in the air, and still laughing. An expensive-looking comforter was tussled and heaped up, as if the maid hadn't bothered with making it that morning, and one of the side tables had been knocked over, the Chinese lantern-style lamp shattered in three pieces.

When he was only a few steps from the foot of the bed, the strength in his fingers and in his legs gave out and his eyes went wide. Seeing his expression, John asked him what was wrong. The room was spinning and he had the sensation of falling, and vomit burned at the back of his throat, making speech impossible. John called out to him again, but tears blurred his vision and his ears rang again, just like he'd been hit with a stun grenade again.

He saw the hues of black and chestnut brown painted across that canvas there, along with differing shades of crimson and red as they seeped across the plain sheet like spilled watercolors. The artist had painted a likeness of the beautiful woman in strange, bent angles with broad, precise strokes and broken lines. The only thing that was party recognizable was that face of hers, twisted towards him with eyes still glazed by the ecstasy of pain and stimulation.

You should've pulled the trigger tonight in that bathroom, and you've only prolonged her suffering

They were Frank's words, but he repeated them under his breath as he took in the nightmarish artwork. John circled around to the left side and the moment he saw her, the stun grenade hit him too. His pistol clattered heavily to the floor, fingers no longer able to hold the heavy chunk of metal. Using the same tactics they'd employed against him in his own house, the ruined-faced man made his retreat after his trap was sprung.

Connelly ran after him in the hallway, raised his carbine and fired, screaming a string of obscenities over the roar of the gun. Blood spattered the cool blues of the room and ruined the nautical theme. The horrible artist was sent sprawling through the shattered upstairs window, spat out like a charred piece of gristle.

Inside the bedroom, John hadn't even noticed that his friend had delivered swift justice to the architect of the awful scene there. He touched the woman's face gently then finally turned to acknowledge that his friend was there, with a face more shattered than the man who'd called himself Vergara. Connelly could only look at his feet, unable to look into those empty eyes of his.

He thought they were too late, but a horrible gasping came from the bed. She was still alive and fighting for her life, apparently not realizing how hopeless her situation was. John sprang into action, carefully scooping her up in his arms as he might collect a torn sack of groceries, holding her tightly for fear that if he relaxed his grip everything would spill at his feet.

She let out a moan and struggled with breaths that came in short, moist gasps – one or both of her lungs had been punctured, and they'd both heard that awful gurgle before. It was a gurgle that would soon be replaced with a death rattle, and then that would be the end of it.

"John...we need to leave her here," Connelly tried to reason with him.

"I'm not leaving her!" He howled, making his way towards the door.

"The police will be here any minute. We need to disappear, and they'll get someone up here to help her."

"By the time they get done screwing around with arrests...locking the place down..."

He didn't have to finish the sentence. Connelly knew he was right, but he also knew that she wouldn't survive the trip to the boat. Even if she did, Kovacs would never allow them to bring her with them and that would result in a worse standoff than what happened earlier.

Down the stairwell he struggled with her, leaving the heavy brush strokes of her colors as he went, along the walls, the carpet, and dripping on each step. She was losing a lot of blood, and they couldn't even be certain where she was bleeding from. The black dress Connelly had briefly seen her wearing before was clinging to her body, saturated in the stuff. He didn't even know what kind of instrument had been used to cause the multiple punctures, slashes and contusions on her body, as he didn't see a knife or any other weapon close by.

"Hold on Nicole! Stay with me!" John called out to her as if she were a mile away and getting further every second.

Connelly followed closely behind as they descended the stairs, covering his friend, expecting more of the guards to show up at any moment. At the bottom of the stairs, John gathered up his bundle again, feeling her slipping, and pressed her close against his chest as they made their way towards the last set of double doors.

Just beyond those doors was a war-zone they would be walking into, and Connelly gave his friend a concerned look. *We're not going to make it with her slowing us down.*

"John, I'm going to go ahead and give you cover," he explained his plan that sounded more suicidal than Kovacs'. "Just make sure you stay right on my heels!"

He nodded, though reluctantly, and in understanding. Any one of them might not make it back across that lawn to the dock, and Connelly, in particular, was making himself the biggest target. For a moment, he hesitated at the door, possibly contemplating their options, but they both knew the time for options was past. He wouldn't have left Connelly the responsibility of carrying the girl, and he was the best suited to give them the best cover.

Any of the bodies that were still capable of autonomous movement had cleared out, leaving behind the severely wounded and dead, which they had to step around as they made their way towards the fountain. It was difficult terrain, and Nicole gasping became more intense behind him. John still tried to comfort her.

"Hold on Nicole, I have you…just hold on!"

Connelly was relieved that the gunmen were all gone, from both sides, and that he didn't have to shoot his way to the dock. As he reached the halfway point at the fountain, though, he realized why there were no gunmen in the courtyard. Just like in the wild, when a bigger predator moves in, the smaller ones scatter, and that's exactly what had happened.

He heard the chopper blades spinning in the distance, and from the corner of the south wing, quite a distance across the carpet of coarse Florida grass, several men cautiously advanced. They were wearing the same logos and markings on their Kevlar vests and black "BDUS" – battle dress uniforms. They were feds, and the letters "DEA" were neatly displayed on their arm patches and breast plates.

"You have…to…let me…go," Nicole moaned, apparently coherent enough to see the bright lights and the men swarming the compound.

"No, we're only a few feet from the water…almost to the boat," he huffed, picking up speed.

"Johnny…please," she mumbled, and her head bobbed as she struggled with consciousness.

"I can make it…I can make it this time…I'm not letting you go," he choked out.

"You came…for me…and that's enough," she murmured in a whisper.

Connelly heard their voices trail off behind him and he turned to see him hesitate in the entryway where the smoke still hung in thick clouds. The feds were advancing and they would be on top of him any minute, yet he knew that John wouldn't leave her there. The rest of his trip across that vast courtyard had been involuntary, his legs carrying him against his will, and now he found himself standing on the boat beside Kovacs, watching John stagger towards them through the smoke.

There he is! What took him so long?

Frank shouted something from behind him about leaving the girl and that the feds were closing in. Connelly knew he was wasting his breath.

"We have to help him!"

"I'm not going up against *federal agents*! We're the only two left, Connelly!"

"I'm not leaving him out there by himself!"

He hopped out of the boat, back onto the dock and started firing at those closing in on his friend. They dove for cover, wherever it could be found, and those out in the open withdrew to the corners of the house. The icy numbness still gripped him, but fear for his best friend had restored motive power to his limbs. Frank cursed after him and he was sure that he would abandon them both, but he followed suit, laying down cover fire.

He complained about always having to pull John's ass out of the fire as he raced up the doc behind Connelly, and he thought to himself *It was you telling him that he'd never been able to do one goddamned thing on his own that's put him in this spot!*

The self-righteous know-it-all should've never told him that he'd looked after him behind the scenes or implied that John had never earned his keep. It was the last thing to tell John Chapel, and that stubborn pride of his would make him rush headlong into his own death before he'd let Frank Kovacs or anyone else ever help him again. Watching him cover those last twenty-five yards, seeing the determination in his face, he knew that this was his plan all along and why he wanted to come along.

This was the night he was going to do it all on his own - just this one thing - and he wasn't letting anyone stop him – especially those men swarming all around him. The chopper had appeared over the villa by this time, and Connelly could see every line, crease and pained furrow of John's expression illuminated in the bright searchlight. He knew that his blank eyes didn't see him and he was in another place at that moment.

"Johnny! Let her go! You're not going to make it!" He called out, but he knew there were other voices drowning his out from that other place. The wailing of a father, the shriek of a young girl, and her brother telling him "Go! You can make it!"

John heard the gunfire from behind, but didn't need to look to know that he'd just been shot, feeling the burning sting in his left thigh, just above the knee. He collapsed and his "groceries" spilled all over the sand as he fell facedown. The popping of guns was coming from all around, and they watched the dark tide come crashing in on top of him as they pulled away in the race boat.

Connelly couldn't tear his gaze away from the scene, and he just kept muttering "They killed her…they all killed her…"

He wasn't just talking about the feds who, as John predicted, were more worried about calling in the escaping race boat instead of the girl at their feet who badly needed medical attention. He was talking about all of them – every man who'd had a hand in her death; Vincent Gallianni, the black-eyed man without a name, and even the one man who'd tried to save her.

In the distance, lighting flashed on the black water, and dark clouds moved in as quickly as the feds had swarmed the house. He felt the first drops patter on the back of his neck, remembering how much John hated the rain, as his face became smaller and smaller in the distance. He'd never known why he hated the rain so much, and it was something as lost on him as the strange expression on Nicole's face that only John recognized.

Her mouth opened and closed, gasping for air as her body twitched, like she was a fish that washed up on shore, abandoned there by the cruel god from the fountain. Her fingers stretched towards his in the sand, and the colors swirled all around her, turning the soft, white sand a shade of pink. He moved his own to greet hers, and interlock with fingers that were already icy cold and void of life.

She gave one last smile through bloodied lips and with eyes that were no longer glazed over by pain, then she let go of that bottom rung she'd been desperately clinging to, allowing herself to fall into that gulf of night. He followed her into that darkness soon after, swept up in the arms of the storm and carried far away.

DOWN CAME THE RAIN AND WASHED THE GHOSTS AWAY

"For who can wonder that man should feel a vague belief in tales of disembodied spirits wandering through those places...when he himself...is forever lingering upon past emotions and bygone times...?"

~Charles Dickens

Chapter *54*

Jeremy Connelly was seated in the back corner booth at his favorite diner that he hadn't been to in well over a decade. He stared out the large window at the heavy night sky that had been dumping torrents upon the city for almost two days straight. Some of the streets of metro Detroit had even flooded, and there were half a dozen smaller lakes that formed in the old parking lot. The neon letters of the familiar place were reflected in one of those pools, and he gave a quiet chuckle to himself as he read them.

Old Carl still hadn't replaced the missing letters of the "Metro Coney" sign, and here it was, almost twenty years later: it still read "Money".

"Did you count the money?" The voice called him back from the past.

"I trust you," he mumbled, not wanting his thoughts interrupted.

"You don't trust *anyone* Mr. Connelly," the raspy voice reminded him.

"I don't. But I don't have a choice with you. If you wanted to short me, you would short me, and there's not a damned thing I could do about it is there?"

"You have a point," he said, taking a sip of his coffee. "I can't believe any of you could stomach the food – or the coffee – in this place."

He'd just seen him a week before, and the sight of him was still unnerving each time. It was those eyes that never looked directly at him, like those of some melodramatic fortune teller, always looking off into his "future" as they spoke. Otherwise, the man seated across from him looked like any other man dressed in a wrinkled suit and who seemed to shun a comb or any hair products at all. The only other distinguishing feature was the old scar on his left cheek that looked like someone had drawn a line with a cigar there.

"It's not the food or the coffee – we could probably get better at any place along this same strip – it's about the *company*. I

563

had a lot of good memories in this place, and somehow, it just makes everything taste better."

"Odd that you chose this place, that's all."

"It's the closest thing I have to a place I like to call home, what's it to ya'?"

"Well, now you can call anywhere you like 'home' I suspect."

"That's the idea. I'm making a fresh start after tonight. Never coming back to this place, so I suppose my visit here is a bit…sentimental."

"That's good to hear. You've certainly earned it," the man taunted. "You have a gift for storytelling, Mr. Connelly. Maybe you could look into that in Argentina…or Belize…or wherever you're headed."

"I'm retired from storytelling and everything else, thanks," he snapped back.

"I guess every man knows when to quit, doesn't he?"

"Except John Chapel…"

"Yes, well…we see where that persistence got him didn't we? I guess the question is: did it end there, or should I be concerned?"

"I'm no hero, and I have no desire to be where he is right now."

"I was referring to those who were taking up his crusade. You're certain that his wife and his friend were satisfied with what you told them?"

"Campbell was, and that's what matters. Once Gwenn felt like she was outmatched and no one was listening, she gave up. He already had her on the ropes and it didn't take much to take her down."

"I'm surprised with all the embellishing with the story about his internal struggles and all that nonsense that Campbell didn't take issue with your version of the truth."

"I was his *best* friend, and I was there through the mess from the beginning. If I can't speak to how his mind worked and what motivated him, what he loved and what he believed in, then who can? Campbell knows that I probably took liberties with the story, just to make Gwenn feel a bit better about her husband and the things he did in south Florida, but he's a smart enough man to sort out the facts from the bullshit."

564

"Let's hope he doesn't sort out the bullshit from the facts."

"*Campbell* called *me*, desperate because he had an unstable woman on his hands, and needed someone to reinforce his theories. I told him exactly what he wanted to hear, and he used what I gave him to shut Gwenn down completely."

"And how did she handle that?"

"I think that even if some small part of her wanted to believe there's something more to it, she's been broken and has nowhere else to turn to find her answers."

The disheveled man leaned back in his booth, throwing an arm up on the back of the seat, and took a long sip of the awful coffee, chewing on his words and realizing the company did make it taste better. He was delivering good news, and it was starting to take the bitterness out of it.

"You took a risk with telling her about Vergara. Weren't you concerned that sharing that information would give credence to her conspiracy theories about a *boogey man*?"

"I couldn't leave Nicole's death a mystery; she had to see exactly how it affected her husband and how it tied in with everything else. It fit in perfectly with the guilt story Campbell was selling her."

"And what of Vergara?"

"I killed Vergara," Connelly said with a grin.

So she's not linking Vergara to the man she supposedly met years later? What did you tell them about Merrill Lake? She had the letters…"

"*She* only believed he was the same man because *John* believed he was the same man, and once he was discredited, then everything else fell apart. Letters written by a man lost in his own mind don't hold water, and that's exactly what Campbell told her. Even the journal became invalid, and he's probably tearing down all of those pages from the wall of his study as we speak."

"You didn't confirm that you saw anything at the lake then?"

"Merrill Lake never happened; not the way he told it anyway."

"What about Mrs. Malowski? She's the one who gave her the letters, won't she go back to talk with her or with Dean? Will they be trouble?"

"Mrs. Malowski is no more sane than John was in the end, and she's not a credible source. Dean won't speak to her either because he doesn't want to involve himself with it again. Everyone wants to forget..."

"Everything seems to have fallen into place. I can leave this wretched place then?"

"I don't see why you need to stick around."

"And you're sure that this is over?"

"You mean with *me*?"

"No nagging conscience? No attempts to contact either of them and tell them what you've done?"

"Gwenn was right about me and my loyalties. All I care about right now is what's in this bag, and how I'm going to enjoy spending it. I gave up on heroics and trying to play for the losing team a while ago when I realized that heroes end up dead and forgotten after a while. John was my friend, but as much as I liked the sonovabitch, I also envied him and everything he'd had. He got to leave it all behind, I didn't."

"You resent him for being able to walk away?"

"Not going to lie. I don't feel that it's right that he was able to cut a deal and walk, and not just walk, but come out smelling like roses. He got to marry a beautiful woman, had the nice house, became a career man, and somehow...he became the *good guy*, while I was still some piece of shit in the end."

"That's why I came to you, Mr. Connelly; I knew you were looking for an opportunity to set things right, an opportunity to get what you've been working so hard for all these years. You wanted someone to listen to your story and see that John Chapel wasn't the 'golden boy' everyone thought, and that you were a good man."

"All debts are clear now, things are as they're supposed to be, and John Chapel finally got what was coming to him."

He pushed his plate with the half-eaten toast away and took his last swallow of coffee, then slipped his right hand through the duffel bag, and prepared to head into the parking lot of a hundred lakes. Before he scooted out of the seat, he glanced down at the bag and unzipped it slightly to peer inside.

"You said you trusted me about the money."

"I do...I'm just a bit nervous about duffel bags."

"If I'd wanted you dead, you'd have been dead by now."

"You needed me alive to finish this job for you, and you're letting me walk with a hundred grand just like that, when you could've just paid a tenth of that to some hood to put me down?"

"If I killed you now, in this city, there would be questions. I can't have an already-paranoid girl asking questions. In this line of work, you can't always just go around killing people...because their *lack* of testimony is sometimes enough testimony to get to the truth."

He looked up from the bag with a confused expression. Working with bags of money and stacks of hundreds for as long as he had, he could count it very quickly just with a quick glance and doing the math in his head.

"There's twice what we agree on in here...there's something else?"

"It's the *other* reason I need you alive. Consider it an advance."

"A job? I'm headed out tonight and leaving the states."

"I know where you're going, and you can do this one little thing for me while you're there."

"And what's that?"

"I want you to find Frank Kovacs..."

Chapter 55

The rain is falling quietly...

... against my window now, and I wonder if it is merely catching its breath or saying its goodbyes. Every house on this street is dark, save the few that are illuminated with security, motion or vanity lights, and one home in particular seems quieter and possibly a bit darker than the rest, despite the small lanterns that light up the winding driveway.

For the past several days, this house was alive again and I entertained more guests than I have in many years. Sure, there's always the occasional visitor answering an invitation for a corned beef sandwich or perhaps a glass of brandy to discuss work or business, but those visits are far and few in between - no cause for celebration. The past few days were deserving of the Calvados, and even the good dinnerware.

Now it's quiet once again, and the house feels like a forgotten museum, where few ever visit. It's a place exquisitely decorated with expensive paintings, rugs, and artifacts from all parts of the world, put on display for others to see, in the hopes that they will strike up some interesting conversation. An impressive gallery of far-off places and faces from the past can also be found in this room, discretely displayed on desk corners and end tables of the quiet museum house.

The most impressive still hangs on the western wall and was the latest exhibit to draw in quite a crowd and the most impassioned discussions. The critics raved about the exhibit and their discussions about the pieces were fraught with anger, tears, and fiery words. For a little while, my little museum was the most popular place to visit, and I reveled in that buzz.

I'm not quite ready to tear down my most popular attraction just yet, and I've grown accustomed to the faces I've kept locked away in this room. Besides, they're keeping me company in the absence of the others.

They'd arrived with a knock on my door on a dreary night like this one, and they'd left only a day ago with the slam of that same door. There were no more discussions to be had about my gallery and it finally lost its appeal, so the show was over and those visitors were gone for good. I doubt that my most vocal patron will bother returning to collect a single piece from the exhibit, and so, I will be their curator in this lonely museum, until I decide to take them down.

I will miss her patronage and her presence there the most, despite her defacing the gallery. There is still a gaping hole in the center of the exhibit where 'number 17' had once been, and presently, it is lying on the table in the hall where it awaits restoration. That's where she crumpled and tossed it before she left in haste – my favorite visitor who'd singlehandedly brought my exhibit to an end.

Staring at the empty seat before me, I can still see the auburn-red frame of her beautiful face and the amber-yellow eyes glistening at me as she listens to me prattle on about my proud display. There was an innocence in that face and in that voice of hers that was so soothing to listen to, reminding me of his own Vanessa.

But, just like Vanessa, that innocent girl can never return to me, for I'd lost her in the same fashion; because of my ego and immense pride. I'd even resorted to employing the worst sort of man to help tear down any chance she ever had of retaining her dignity or a shred of that innocence. For less than the cost of the pipe I carry in my jacket pocket, I was able to procure the services of a morally bankrupt man who was willing to do my dirty work. I'm no better than those men he told stories about, exploiting others for profit and ruining lives.

I'd meant well initially in sending for him and trying to get the whole story, so as to eliminate any doubt in my mind (and hers) about John's case. So much more came out that I'd ever anticipated and I wish I'd never made that call. A man's secrets were exposed – secrets that were best left in the grave with their owner – and as a result, his reputation as a good man was forever sullied, and mine with it.

There was no guarantee that the information he'd given us both was even accurate and that, like Gwenn had insisted, it hadn't been corrupted by involving money. Jeremy Connelly was a man motivated by greed, and I wondered if the actual truth could've been purchased for a higher price. Maybe I should've asked to see a list of his fees and what it would've cost for the package that didn't involve completely shattering a woman's faith.

One of the things I'd respected most about Gwenn Chapel was the strength of her convictions and adherence to her faith, even if it wasn't something I believed in. Connelly called her *naïve* and made her feel as if that strength was a character flaw, and something to be ashamed of. The truth was that he condemned her for something that he'd lost long ago, and he might've turned out a different sort of man if he hadn't. Hell, we all might've; John and I included.

Perhaps Connelly had done what I didn't have the heart to do, and did what was 'needed' and not so much what was morally sound. By destroying that faith, and by extension, the things that she clung needlessly to, it might've made it easier for her to let him go and have a life without John Chapel. Who's to say? The whole thing makes my head throb.

I can still hear the voices echo from the fireplace, but they are different sorts than from before. Gwenn's voice still calls from somewhere down the hall, calling after Connelly as he makes his way to the front door. She tried reasoning with him, pleading with him to tell her the truth – whatever truth she thought he knew – and then when that didn't work, she turned to cursing him. He'd only temporarily escaped her wrath because she hesitated at the threshold, still too afraid to go out into that rain after him.

She rushed to the coat closet then and retrieved her own jacket, flustered and frantically trying to go after him. Her last stop was this very room, where snatched up the letters she'd brought with her, and tucked them into John's journal before heading for the front door. I tried to stop her and reason with her again, but utterly failed.

Still she insisted that someone got to Connelly just like they'd gotten to her husband, and said that she could see it in his eyes. I couldn't say that I didn't believe at least part of her story, but I was more concerned for what it was doing to her. At some point you have to let those things go before they destroy you, like it destroyed John.

All I could do was lie to her and tell her that I gave her my best and that I believed that this was at an end. She asked me if I thought I'd done right by him and that if I really thought I'd given her the answers she needed. I couldn't even look her in the eye, because I knew she was right. I knew that I should've looked at the letters, at the very least, and made some sort of effort. But I didn't. I just let her walk away. She told me that I couldn't help her...and she's probably right.

She slammed the door in my face, and she was so angry with me that the rain didn't even faze her. Gwenn believes that there's another enemy out there somewhere, more tangible than the rain, just as difficult to touch, but she isn't going to let that deter her. She doesn't want to hear anymore about the girl in the rain, because she knows there are bigger questions now. I'm just afraid of where those questions will lead her.

At least she's no longer afraid of the rain, and maybe that's some small consolation, and as for me, I no longer feel twenty-six pairs of eyes on me – just one pair. The eyes of the mysterious girl John brought to life on my wall gaze down at me as I pen this page in my personal journal. She was always my favorite because of the expressiveness John captured in those eyes, so full of love and happiness, but now they look so different and they stare at me accusingly. I chalk it up to a very talented hand, and can't help but meet that gaze and wonder if there was something else he was trying to convey there.

She's the one we affectionately called number twenty-six, and though I finally gave her another name for Gwenn's benefit, I'm still just as uncertain of her identity. I saw those eyes in my sleep last night, and this morning there was an epiphany on my lips that gave me a shudder.

Sapientem Custodit Viginti Sex Praestrigiae in Bibliotheca...the wise man keepeth the twenty-six ghosts in his library.

These were certainly ghosts, beings that haunted John Chapel to his last day. No matter their origin, whether created of his own mind, fashioned by guilt or things left unfinished, they were as real as any other thing that haunts a man. He had been right in his word choice, I know that now. They weren't just hallucinations or bad dreams, they were once people with a story, and I'd told John myself once that 'only those who truly lived could leave behind a story'.

I ask her who she is before I turn out the lights in this room every night before bed, and every night she denies me an answer. I will lock her away in this room until she is ready to talk.

~The Journal of James Campbell

Chapter 56

The rain was really coming down again, and had driven away the late afternoon sun. Gwenn had retreated to the safety of her own private nook, however, and hadn't noticed the gloom until she had to squint her eyes to read the pages in her lap. She frowned at the light switch that was only a few feet away, realizing that it would require her to get up from the cozy "nest" she's made for herself on the bed.

There were several pillows heaped behind her back, propping her up at just the right angle for reading and drinking the glass of red wine she had on the table beside her. A quilt that belonged to John's grandmother was draped across her legs to keep out the chill, and a box of crackers and tissues was within reach, to accommodate her other needs. It was a perfectly comfortable spot that she now had to abandon just to reach that small oval knob and raise it a quarter of an inch.

John had installed a dimmer on the light, and took full advantage of the power he had over the luminance in his private place. During the day, when the sun was high, the toggle was low, and as the sun slowly crept behind the horizon, the plastic oval rose to take its place. Dusk was his favorite time of the day, because that's when he had his "mood lighting" which was perfect for reading and was the most relaxing, he'd told her.

In his last days, though, he'd found little joy with his dimmer and would leave it untouched, sitting in almost complete darkness like she was now. He'd scared the hell out of her once when she'd set a laundry basket down just inside the door and his voice called to her from the darkness. She jumped and asked him what he was doing in the dark, and he replied simply, "Sometimes it's nice to sit here and think."

When she later discovered what he was really doing there, it was quite unsettling, and it gave her the shivers whenever she passed that door. That was where he went to talk with "them", and where he spent far too many hours looking for his answers. She'd remembered him being so frustrated and angry when they wouldn't come, and the days when there would be no rain. He would be almost inconsolable, and she'd never understood that longing he had to disconnect from the real world until now.

She was no longer afraid of those faces or that room, and she'd begun to spend most of her free time in that same room as of late waiting for them to appear. She craned her head up at the small window above the day bed, watching the watery patterns play about the glass, and a knowing smile crept upon her face – they would be coming soon.

Turning back to the journal, she decided to struggle in the dim light with a couple more pages, preferring not to disturb her perfect nest just yet. The one helpful thing that Jim had done for her was translating the pages written in Latin and old French (something he still wasn't able to explain with any certainty) so she could discover her own conclusions.

About a third of the way through the journal, she found the place he'd stopped reading, when he decided that it was futile to continue because he considered it a "distorted carbon copy" of the story Connelly was telling.

Sure, John had been far from home, carrying out a gruesome mission for his king, doing unspeakable things to the enemy, but his reasons had been noble: it was the only way he could win back the woman he loved. How could she fault him for that?

They tried redrawing her John as a villain, as a coldblooded murderer, but she knew that he was only doing what had to be done. Who were those men anyway? Murderers themselves, and the worst kind of criminals – Connelly said so himself – and they deserved everything they got.

John believed that the man he'd come face-to-face with in that place was the personification of evil and was so shaken by that encounter that he'd had nightmares about him for the next decade. His guilt over being too late to save the woman he cared about that night eventually caused him to abandon the life he'd built in favor of another one. Campbell had said so himself; said that it was "the burden of guilt" that tormented him. A man can't be burdened by guilt like that if he is without conscience and a noble human soul. Therefore, her husband was a good and decent man, no matter what they say about him.

He didn't deserve to have his name dragged through the mud the way Connelly did, and he was entitled to a better ending than the one those men gave him. It's a good thing they weren't in charge of the epitaph on his headstone, or they would've had a field day with it, she thought to herself as she flipped the pages and read further, trying to find him a better ending.

Finally, in the comfort of the small room that used to be her husband's, she read aloud the final passage. Whether she was reading it for her benefit, to keep the ever present loneliness away, just to make some noise, or in some attempt to summon those faces to her bedside, was something only she knew.

❧❧

With some aid from Andrew de Chauvigney...

...I had tracked Nicolette and Reginald to Orleans. Of course, once my most hated enemy discovered me, I had to fight my way across the bridge spanning the Loire, launching a one-man siege on the Châtelet les Tourelles – the tower protecting the bridge – and left a trail of dead behind me.

The archers rained arrows down on my head, and had they hurled drops of rain, they would have been more effective at slowing my advance. Reginald had been smart in taking refuge across the Loire, in one of the largest and most wealthy cities in France, for it would prove difficult for most to find him there, and almost impossible to reach him across that heavily-fortified bridge.

Most men would have lost their nerve as soon as they set eyes on that fortress from the other bank, but as for me, my resolve had never been stronger.

I was not without fear as I crossed that mighty stone "port", however, as Reginald might have been warned of my coming and either fled further north or done the unthinkable by the time I reached the other side.

If he felt trapped again, there was no telling what he might do in an attempt to escape or barter for his life, just like the last time I'd had him cornered in the tower at Avandale. The fear burned in my stomach like coal in a furnace, causing the flames of my fury to become white-hot, and drive the war machine forward with greater speed. I would not fail her and I would not allow Reginald escape this time.

Finally reaching the end of the stone expanse and the end of bodies willing to stand in my way, I realized that my task would prove more difficult than I'd imagined as I surveyed the colossal city spread before me. The main street split into a dozen smaller avenues, and those, in turn, split into a dozen channels winding through the city like a network of limestone spider webs. It would take me days to canvas those streets, searching every house – some stacked almost on top of each other in some of the more crowded districts – and they would be long gone by the time I'd picked up the trail again.

Tracking them to Orleans wasn't difficult, using my specific skill set I'd used during the war, and coming to know Reginald's proclivities as well as my own. He'd needed to leave Aquitaine, and his allies were on the borders of France.

The nobles of Toulouse seemed an unsteady alliance and a poor choice, and the lure of a wealthy city like Orleans, with water access and its proximity to Paris, seemed like the most likely place he'd run to. I'd found a fisherman at Tours that had no trouble recollecting Reginald for some coin and his beautiful companion free of charge, and from there, I followed the river eastward.

His next, most logical choice would be fleeing to Paris, if flight was his intention, and he was most-likely already packing his fastest steeds for the journey. I stood in the middle of that street, probably looking an awful sight from the carnage I'd just caused, and attempting to make my best guess at which of those spider webs to follow when something peculiar happened. Crossing directly in my field of view, less than an arrow's shot away, was the fugitive and his bride making their way towards the docks.

It was the shock of platinum hair that I initially caught out of the corner of my eye, blowing like a standard in the wind that gave them away. When she saw me barreling through the crowd, hatchet and sword in hand, she let out a squeal to let me know that it was her, and that I was only steps away from liberating her. She was trying to wrench her arm free of his grip, and making her legs go limp so that she had to be dragged, and slowed them both down. Reginald turned and locked eyes with me at that point, and he had liberation plans of his own, deciding that he would never make the docks in time with an unwilling companion.

577

I watched as the nightmare was happening all over again – the one from the tower and the one from the three nights before I'd departed Aquitaine – and I was helpless to prevent the inevitable outcome that I'd seen too many times. He drew his own dagger from his belt and twisted her golden strands in his fingers again, jerking her head back to expose her thin, delicate neck. I'd put my own mark only a few inches away from where he was holding that blade the last time I'd tried to stop him, but this time, my hatchet would not reach either of them.

He was a man without options, a man who'd been as tired of running as I was of giving chase, and the fact that he was willing to resort to this heinous act meant that there were no more places for him to go. Either that or he simply hated me that much, that he would throw away his only remaining possession just to take something away from me. I stopped in my tracks only twenty paces away, not wanting to agitate him any further, but I did not let go of the grip on either weapon. If there was any chance at all that I could reach him in time, I would take that chance, and if not, I would cut out his shriveled heart the moment he took her life.

I'd almost accepted it; that we were never meant to be together, and that my path was going to be much like that of Harold's. Every time I allowed myself to care for someone, they inevitably met a horrible end because I'd failed them in some way. If she died in the streets of Orleans this day, then her sacrifice would not be in vain: I would never love another woman and put them in harm's way.

I looked about the crowd that had gathered, looking for the face of a noble soul, anyone who might intercede on her behalf; anyone who had the courage to do what was right. There was not a single face among them that wasn't stricken with fear, curiosity or both, and it seemed like they were eager to see a little blood spilled for sport. Where were they when I was spilling it in buckets on the bridge?

"This whore's blood is on your hands now, John! No more bartering, no more negotiations, no more playing gentlemen's games for Richard's bemusement! I know it was you that turned the others against me, I know about your little rendezvous with my wife, and I'm not going to the church or to higher powers this time; I'm just going to punish the both of you myself, right here, right now!"

578

"It looks like we are in agreement then; no more pretense and no more involving others! It's just you and me Reginald, so let's settle this like two men who hate one another," John fired back.

"I would just be another corpse at your feet, John, and I'm not foolish enough to face you in single combat. I will die here today, but not before I loose this treacherous bitch's throat, and watch her lies come spilling out on the stone."

"Your death will not be as swift or merciful, Reginald, I promise you that! I will carry you from this place after I've taken out your eyes, and lock you away in a place where I will visit you every day to take my payment in your suffering!"

"You may torture me until your last day if you like; I would rather endure that than the torture and embarrassment I've suffered thus far! I will turn this blade on myself and deprive you of that pleasure when I am finished with her!"

"Then it seems I will see you in hell, and may the devil grant me a small favor in allowing me to be your tormentor until the end of times! Do what you will, Reginald…"

He meant to do exactly what he'd promised, and John watched helplessly as the muscles in his forearm twitched, prepared to deliver the final stroke that would end the terrified woman's life. I stared into those deep blue eyes of hers – as blue as any sea or river I'd crossed to reach her – and would not abandon them until she took her last breath.

I'd hoped she would find some comfort there, see all of the things within them that I'd wanted to say to her at that moment, but could not. I hoped above all things that she saw immeasurable love there and heartrending regret for failing her again. It was some small comfort that I would never fail her again after that day, and she would suffer no longer the misery of this earth.

Because I was focused on those eyes so intently, I did not see the hand of God that day, being swept downward from the heavens to intervene, delivering vengeance to the wicked and reward for the faithful. That hand, more specifically, had bent the yew longbow and sent the hard hickory shaft hurtling through the silent morning sky. It also guided that shaft to hit its mark perfectly, burying itself deep in Reginald's right elbow.

With a scream, as though he'd been struck by the bolt of Zeus itself, his arm went limp and the dagger clattered on the stone. The arrow was buried up to the feathers in his forearm, and the sharp steel tip protruded from his wrist.

I'd almost reached him before he made the desperate plunge into the Loire, but hesitated at the edge to watch him fall into the rushing waters below. It was then that I spotted William Dubois in his perch on the roof of one of the nearby buildings, and I called out to him to take a second shot.

The archer (that had undoubtedly been sent by either Andrew or Richard himself) climbed down from the rooftop and made his way through the crowd towards me. I ordered him to take the shot again, thinking that he hadn't heard me, but he watched Reginald struggle against the current, his bow still hanging loosely in his fingers.

"I was not sent to end his life, John, but to preserve yours," he said to me, solemnly.

"It wasn't my life that was threatened, it was hers, but thank God for your timeliness and your bow, just the same."

He gave me a smile then and said, "What kind of life would you have if you'd lost her?"

To that, I could only offer him a nod of my head and a smile, as I realized the truth in his words: my life would have ended as surely as hers that morning, if things had gone the way I'd foreseen them happening. Instead of clutching her in an embrace, I would have been trying to hold her fast against death's embrace, and she would have turned cold in my arms.

We watched Reginald floundering and trying to swim the breadth of the Loire with one good arm and made a small wager on his chances of success. Like most rats and carrion, he managed not to drown. I watched him clamber up the opposite shore with great effort and asked William about his fate. He told me not to worry about that and to focus only on my own and that of the girl standing at my side.

I could not return to Aquitaine or associate with Richard, because that would have implicated him in the events of the slaughter at Orleans and the subsequent "attempted assassination" of a noble who'd been allied with him previously.

I understood the game, but it would be a difficult thing not seeing my friend again, or being able to enjoy the comforts of a luxurious bed chamber, servants, and the nights of feasting and drinking in the courts of Aquitaine. I would never have traded any of those things for my Nicolette, however, nor would she trade the life we would make together for those things either.

I bade William goodbye, knowing that I would also not likely see him again either, and set off towards Normandy with Nicolette. He'd passed along Richard's parting words of prayer and good fortune as well as my last payment for services before we parted ways, which was a generous sum, and enough to make a moderate living from for many years.

Along the way, we stopped off in a small chapel outside of LeMans and a priest married us there. It wasn't exactly legal, since she was technically still married to Reginald, but it was legitimate enough for our own purposes, and we hoped that God would be understanding and bless our union.

We returned to the place where it all began - literally, the exact spot – and picked up where we left off that summer from years before beside that small lake in the forest. Avandale itself might have been too conspicuous for anyone looking for us, we'd decided, and it was best to make our home in that clearing instead.

I built a small home for us on the site of the old shelter I'd made as a younger man, just big enough for two, and we were provided everything we needed from the lake, the forest, each other, and God. And in the spring of the following year, He had finally approved of our union by blessing us with a child. We would need a bigger house, and our days of carrying on like young lovers beside a lake were drawing to a close.

It wasn't a life of luxury, but it was about as close to perfect as a man could get, even with the hard winters and the roof leaking every time it rained. The rain no longer bothered me, whether dripping on my head or standing out in it by the lake, and in fact, I welcomed it.

There were no more messages hidden within it, no more faces I did not recognize, and no more visions brought to me by the other man. Those ghosts troubled me no more, and I believe I finally understood what they'd been trying to tell me since my first day there by the lake. I was meant to find her and I was meant to spend the rest of my days with that girl I'd first seen in the rain…

~ Journal of John Chapel

Gwenn closed the journal and gave a sigh, wiping the water from her cheeks. She leaned back against the pillows, holding the book close to her like she used to with her bible, arms folded across her chest. The rain was still falling in rivulets on the window, but the faces still had not come, and the voices were still silent. They weren't coming and she just had to accept that like Jim told her and Connelly told her, and hell, even the man in the journal had told her.

She put the journal back on the book shelf with the rest of her husband's eclectic collection and her fingers hesitated on the spine, as if once she'd let go of the book that she was conceding defeat and letting go of it all. She looked once more over her shoulder at the rain-slicked window, checking once more just to be sure they weren't going to show, and then let her fingers drop to her side.

"I hope you found her in that place, John…wherever it is that you've gone," she said, and walked out of the room, turning out the light and closing the door behind her.

Epilogue

Gwenn had returned to her place on the couch, where she'd been staying since the night John left for Merrill Lake, unable to sleep in their old bed. It was a pretty comfortable little setup, complete with an old down comforter, heaps of pillows, and assorted snacks and Kleenex boxes within her reach on the coffee table.

The grandfather clock in the hallway chimed nine o'clock, reminding her that she'd made it another hour without him, and she gave herself a little verbal pat on the back. That's how she'd been able to make it this far, marking the hours mentally and checking off days with a red marker on a calendar in the kitchen.

That, and lots of wine and the big screen television for companionship helped her get by. She sat hard on the couch and flipped the box of a thousand familiar voices and faces on, knowing that the high tech box was always more dependable for delivering them than the rain. There were over three hundred channels in picture-perfect quality and sound, and she visited them all within less than five minutes, dissatisfied with each. She settled for an old black and white movie on the classic movie network, just because it was better background noise for sleeping, and settled back on her heap of pillows.

Within twenty minutes, her eyes fluttered closed and she was beginning to dream about riding around Rome on a scooter with Gregory Peck when she heard a loud noise that interrupted her vacation prematurely. She sat up on the couch and looked around, not certain of where the noise had come from, or if she'd imagined it. It came again, this time from the front door, and a chill ran down the length of her spine, arms and tops of her legs as she sat staring at it. A third rap made her jump and she called out from the safety of her couch-fort before approaching, "Who is it?"

"Mrs. Chapel? It's Henry Marshall…"

She hadn't heard the name in a few days, and the voice in weeks, so she struggled with her tired mind to place both. Swaggering from the couch, not realizing she was exhausted as she was, she leaned on the back of it to support herself as she made her way to the door. As if she hadn't heard him right, or hadn't trusted that she was awake, she asked the voice again to identify itself.

"Doctor Marshall, I talked to you on the phone a couple of weeks ago…about your husband?"

She slid the chain back and peeked through the crack at the man standing on her porch, drenched by the storm that seemed unrelenting. It was Sean Connery's double – that was for certain – and she chuckled to herself each time she saw the man. He was dressed in a similarly-ugly tweed coat and plain slacks, just like his counterpart, and she wondered if they competed in bad fashion as well. On his head was a cap like the ones the newsboys wore in the thirties, and he'd probably had it just as long. The rain was spilling from the thin brim over his face, and if it weren't for his bushy brows, it would be going into his eyes.

"I'm sorry, forgive my manners, come in please," she said, pulling the door open and stepping behind it as if still worried that she needed protection from something unseen.

"It's okay, I didn't plan on staying long and I'm on my way over to Campbell's…I just thought that I should come to see you about this first."

"Oh?" The mention of the purpose of his visit intrigued her, and caused her to come from behind the solid door, to stand on the porch with him, beneath the awning.

She immediately noticed the large manila envelope he was carrying under his arm then, and scrunched up her nose, squinting to get a look at the writing on the front. Gwenn wore glasses for driving and reading usually, but hadn't worn them for days because she had to keep removing them to wipe away the endless stream at the corners of her eyes. The envelope was stamped in two different languages, and she was pretty sure that one of the stamps was printed in French. The return address was partially concealed, but it also was postmarked from France.

"What is it?" She asked, daring to take a step closer.

"As I told you, I sent my team to France some months ago when your husband first brought his…situation to my attention."

Her stomach suddenly twisted and lurched, as if she'd found herself on a roller coaster, and the wine and crackers she'd eaten were doing something wicked inside of her, as she was piecing together what he was trying to tell her. She looked again at the package, the postmark, and remembered the purpose of that team he'd sent there. Marshall had been more receptive and sympathetic to her husband's case than Campbell, and had offered up less conventional explanations which had earned him the scorn of his old colleague.

"I think you just need to see this," he said, opening the envelope and depositing a small, folded cloth into the palm of his large hand. "Go ahead...take it."

He watched her with a smile that was considerably warmer than anything Campbell had ever been able to muster as she fidgeted with the parcel, her hands shaking. Untying a small string cinched around one end and unfolding the maroon cloth, she stared down at the contents, trying to steady her hand so that she wouldn't drop them. In the center of the red cloth were three small cylindrical fragments of what looked like bone or petrified wood about the size in diameter of a BIC pen. A look of confusion crossed her face and she looked up at Marshall expectantly.

From his pocket, he produced a length of leather string about eighteen inches and placed it in her hand in a loop. "These would probably be worn on something very similar to this..."

Turning over the small pieces in her hand, she didn't even need to see the inscription on one of them – *Amor du Lac* – to know what it was that she was looking at now. She read the words quietly anyway as her hands began to shake uncontrollably and her voice began trembling.

"Yes," Marshall echoed. "Love of the lake. They found it on a dig site just a week ago and sent it to me straightaway, along with several photos of the location. They're here in this envelope..."

He attempted to hand the manila envelope to her, but she was lost somewhere else, making her way down the front porch steps into the driveway. Marshall continued to call after her from the stoop, "They found the location from a map your husband had drawn, detailing a place that nobody thought existed. It's quite a remarkable find, really, and I'm headed to Jim's to show him what they've found. They'll have to listen to us now, Gwenn..."

Her hand was shaking so badly that she had to close it around the bone pieces so that they wouldn't be lost in the grass. She just stood for a long time, letting the rain fall upon her head, matting her hair to her face and drowning out his words. Gwenn didn't need to hear what she'd already known to be true; she didn't need to hear confirmation that her husband wasn't crazy, because she'd argued that point until they just wouldn't listen anymore. She didn't need to hear the details or see those photos, because she could see that place in her head, and she'd always believed in it until those others convinced her that it didn't exist.

They'd told her that the faces were just creations of her husband's mind, and their voices weren't real, but she was so certain she'd heard them. She wasn't the only one they'd called out to, however, and the man standing on her porch was proof; they'd sent him to her, she was sure of it. They wouldn't be ignored or stifled, and others would have to listen now to whatever it was they had to say, because she had physical proof in her right fist. They would have to listen to the rain again and stop pretending that they weren't afraid of it.

Marshall returned to his car that he'd left idling in the drive, placing a hand on her shoulder and offering her a ride, which she refused. He nodded, telling her where he could be found when she was ready, and left her standing in the rain as he pulled away.

Her legs could hold her up no longer and she collapsed to the ground beneath the burden of the crushing rain, as the voices there cried out with her against the falling night. The girl in the rain was rooted in place at the end of a drive again. The fear had returned, but with it, her faith in her husband, and that faith would allow her to continue his crusade.

Made in the USA
Middletown, DE
26 February 2015